Hearts & Secrets

Small Town Romance Collection

Alison Reid

Hearts & Secrets - Small Town Romance Collection

by Alison Reid

Introduction to…

Hearts & Secrets

Small Town Romance Collection

Welcome to **Hearts & Secrets**—a collection of small-town romances filled with slow-burning passion, emotional stakes, and secrets that could change everything.

Each novel in this box set is a complete standalone romance, written in the spirit of classic Mills & Boon with a modern edge. You'll meet brooding heroes, determined heroines, and towns where love is never simple. These stories feature second-chance romance, enemies-to-lovers tension, and deeply emotional journeys that prove some loves are worth fighting for, no matter the obstacles.

Inside these pages are tales of forbidden attraction, heartbreak and reconciliation, and love that thrives despite the odds. There is no cheating, and every story delivers a guaranteed happily-ever-after.

Whether you're discovering these characters for the first time or returning to familiar favourites, Hearts & Secrets invites you to immerse yourself in a collection of small-town romances where hearts are tested and love always wins.

Enjoy the journey.

Table of Contents

Branlow

Alison Reid

A complete standalone romance
Previously published individually

Chapter One

North Yorkshire England 1955…

Simone reined in at the crest of the hill, her fingers gliding over Stardust's sleek, satin neck. The filly's velvet-soft ears twitched, her head giving the slightest nod—as if answering a private question. They understood each other in that silent way horse and rider sometimes do, a bond forged not through commands but shared history. Stardust was hers—born and raised under her care—and no one else had ever ridden her. No one ever would.

The wind blew sharply across the moor, rich with the scent of damp earth and distant woodsmoke, curling in under the collar of Simone's waxed jacket. She breathed it in slowly, her lungs filling with air that felt older somehow—as if time moved differently up here. Branlow air. Heavier with memory.

The sky above was the pale, translucent grey of early spring, and the bare-limbed trees stretched like ink strokes against it. Below her, the great estate unfolded in deep, familiar folds—soft hills cloaked in fading winter heather, woods crouched like secrets waiting to be told. It looked the same as always. But she had changed. And she could feel it— some quiet shift inside her. Unease coiling like a shadow she couldn't quite name.

The chimneys of Branlow Hall rose in the near distance, tall and severe against the backdrop of the fells, their old stone streaked with rain and stories. She could just make out the gleam of mullioned windows, catching the weak sunlight like shards of memory. The ivy was thicker than it had been. Someone had trimmed the yews. But otherwise, the house stood untouched—rooted deep into the Dales like something the earth had grown rather than built. Unmoved by time. Unmoved by her absence.

Even after all these years, it still made her chest ache.

The first time she'd seen Branlow, she'd been five years old, clinging to her mother's hand with silent desperation. The drive had seemed endless. The house had loomed suddenly out of the mist, vast and unwelcoming—like a castle that didn't want visitors. She remembered the crunch of gravel under tyres, the way her mother's voice had gone soft and strained, and how Simone had pretended not to notice that she was crying.

And then, five years later, her mother was gone. Just gone. No note. No warning. No reason.

Simone's fingers tightened around the reins, the old pain flaring like a phantom wound. She had tried not to think of that day for years. But something about the wind today— sharp, salt-edged—had brought it rushing back. She'd waited in the woods until dusk that day, refusing to believe what she already knew. Sean had found her. She still remembered the quiet way he'd held her. How his jacket had smelled of horses and rain. How safe she had felt, even as the world broke.

Sean.

She closed her eyes for a moment, blocking out the view. It was foolish to think of him. He belonged to another life. Another Simone. One with scraped knees and skinned pride and impossible dreams.

When she opened her eyes again, Branlow Hall looked almost too perfect—like a painting hung just out of reach. It had always been beautiful, but it had never been hers. Not really. She had lived in its orbit, not its embrace. An outsider with the keys to the kingdom—but never the crown.

She shifted in the saddle, her muscles tightening against the cold. Stardust's hooves stamped restlessly, sensing her tension. Below, the valley curled around the estate like an outstretched hand, protective and ancient. She used to imagine the Dales held Branlow the way Branlow had once held her—fiercely, stubbornly, as though she belonged.

But now?

Now, the house felt like it was watching her. Judging her. Asking what right she had to be here.

Her gaze drifted to the high windows of the east wing—Sean's old room. A flicker of something like heat or panic caught in her throat. He was coming back too. After all this time.

He had been gone four years. And still, the idea of seeing him again made her stomach twist. So much had gone unsaid between them. So many things she didn't want to remember—but couldn't seem to forget.

He'd left without goodbye. Without explanation. Just vanished. And now, just like that, he was home again. The golden boy returning to take his place. His legacy. His inheritance. And maybe—God help her—everything else.

The wind surged again, rattling the trees below. Simone stroked Stardust's neck, steadying herself. She wouldn't let this place undo her. She wouldn't let him undo her. Not this time.

Branlow was beautiful. Powerful. And yes—haunted. But so was she.

She had grown up here. Learned to ride, to work, to hold her tongue. She had learned love and loss here. Learned that family wasn't always about blood. And that leaving didn't always mean being gone.

It was all stitched into her—stone, soil, and sorrow. The Hall. The land. Even Sean.

She just had to remember who she was.

And that, whatever happened next, she'd already survived worse.

For a fleeting, golden moment, Simone felt wholly content. Her gaze swept across the familiar landscape, heart lifting with the quiet majesty of it. Adversities might come and go, sorrows too—small and sharp—but this land remained, unchanging and eternal. The only constant. The only real love of her life: Branlow.

Before them, the earth dipped into a broad, wooded valley before rising again in waves of green and gold. The great sweep of the Dales stretched to the horizon, untamed and beautiful. All of it—everything as far as the eye could see—belonged to Branlow Hall, the Taylor estate since Norman times. Once, the Taylors had owned more. Yet even now, Simone knew she could ride for hours and never cross beyond their borders. It was a quiet, benevolent kingdom—and she was still, in some deep, unspoken way, a favoured subject.

It grounded her. The land. The Hall. The family. It was all stitched into her soul. The tall chimneys, the ivy-clad stone, the gleam of mullioned windows catching sunlight, and the soft rustle of leaves in the parkland beyond—these things weren't just scenery. They were home. Even if she didn't quite belong. Even if she'd always stood just outside the circle. She loved it all fiercely.

Simone narrowed her eyes against the wind, lips tightening slightly. Outwardly, nothing had changed. But underneath, the calm was rippling. Trouble had come—tall, blonde trouble—and it wasn't leaving. Fleur Decker. Simone didn't need confirmation. She knew. Mark was going to marry her.

A new variable had entered perfection, unsettling its quiet rhythm. Tensions, once unthinkable, now hovered in the air—polite unease, soft-spoken discord. Simone longed to fix it, to shake sense into someone, anyone—but she had no right. She was merely the outsider who loved them too much.

Stardust snorted beneath her, and Simone smiled faintly. Coincidence, maybe. But in that moment, it felt like agreement. She stroked the filly's neck again, comforted by their shared intuition.

There had been a time she'd have turned to Sean. They would have talked it through, ridden the hills until the ache eased. But that was another life. She didn't think of Sean now. He had been gone four years. Banished from her life—and she had no intention of letting him back in.

Cleo Taylor rode up the hill and drew her horse alongside Simone's. Neither spoke at first.

Cleo was blonde, too—but not like *her*. Hers was a regal, glacial blonde, like sunlight reflected off snow, cool and distant. Her eyes, unmistakably Taylor blue, held the steel of generations. Beside her, Simone looked like something conjured from fire and autumn—eyes the colour of amber honey, framed with long black lashes; hair a dark, rich red braided down her back, catching glints of gold and mahogany in the pale light.

The contrast between them was striking—Cleo all elegance and reserve, Simone all movement and warmth. Even their sizes added to the effect. Cleo was tall and willowy; Simone, smaller, slighter, but with the vibrant energy of the chestnut mare beneath her. There was a lightness to her—laughter never far, moods swift to change—but not today. Today, her mercurial spirit was tempered by a quiet resolve. She would need to be steady now. Supportive. Silent, when it counted.

Because this was going to last.

Cleo was seething, and Simone could feel it before a word was said. She knew the signs well—they'd been friends all their lives, despite the difference in their stations.

"She's awful," Cleo burst out at last. "Mark must be mad! And that name—Fleur? Honestly. Nobody's called Fleur unless they're in a bad romance novel."

Simone didn't answer at once. Her gaze drifted to the home woods, where the shifting breeze rustled the canopy. One of the oaks was leaning too far—a widow-maker waiting to fall. She'd have to send the men down.

"Mark must love her," she murmured finally, her voice soft. "He came back engaged, didn't he?"

Cleo made a sound of exasperation. "Bah!"

Simone didn't turn her head. "Did you just say bah? Nobody says bah. Except cartoon sheep and people in Dickens. I don't think it's even a real word."

"She's not just Mark's problem," Cleo snapped. "She's a family problem. Mummy's gone all vague. You know what that means."

Simone's mouth twitched with a faint smile, but her eyes remained on the fields. She had noticed the change in Lady Vivian—the way her elegant face had taken on a pinched fragility, her speech slower, mistier. Twice in the last week, their eyes had met across a room, and Simone had seen something raw and vulnerable behind the aristocratic polish. Like a woman holding herself together with sheer hope.

She loved them—all of them. And now there was a viper in their midst. And she could do nothing.

"Simone!" Cleo cried, exasperated. "Will you stop working for five seconds?"

Simone looked over at her at last, calm, and steady. "I am listening. But the facts haven't changed. Your brother's engaged to Miss Decker. Unless we're planning to hire someone to kidnap her and stash her in a barn, this is what it is."

Cleo gave a frustrated sigh, dramatic and drawn-out. "I know. I know. But surely there's something—anything—we can do to stop this disaster?"

"If you think of it, I'm all in," Simone said. "But you'll have to lead the charge."

They nudged their horses forward, trotting toward the ridge.

"That tree needs to come down," Simone murmured, eyes drifting again to the woods.

Cleo groaned and turned to her with theatrical triumph. "I knew you were working! You never stop."

"Managing the estate is my job. And I love it. I wasn't born with a silver spoon in my mouth, remember?"

"You can have mine," Cleo muttered. "Right now, it's choking me."

They rode in silence for a time, winding their way down into the valley before beginning the slow ascent to the high ridge. The late March air was crisp, edged with the last breath of winter, but neither girl seemed to notice.

They had been riding these hills together for years—Taylor land, every inch of it. Cleo had been born at Branlow Hall, in the same nursery her mother had once used. Simone had arrived at five years old, a quiet, sharp-eyed child with flaming red hair and a grip on her mother's hand like she'd never let go. Her father had taken over the Dower House and the running of the estate—and the estate had become Simone's world.

She'd grown up in its rhythms, its demands, its sacred old stones. She knew the land better than anyone, and when her father retired, the mantle would fall to her. It was what she was trained for. What she loved. There was nothing else she wanted.

Cleo broke the silence with sudden, breathless hope. "Sean will think of something!"

Simone flinched, almost imperceptibly, but the cold she'd ignored moments before seeped in like water through a cracked wall.

"Sean?" she repeated, voice carefully neutral.

"He's coming this week," Cleo said, relief flooding her tone. "Why didn't I think of it sooner? He's always fixed things. He'll fix this. Oh, bliss!"

Simone's breath caught. Sean. He couldn't come back. Not now. Not ever. He was gone—exiled from her heart by betrayal and silence. But his face came crashing in uninvited, fierce, and vivid. Masculine angles. Sapphire eyes. Raven-black hair. Sean, the traitor.

She closed her eyes for a beat and forced him away. She wouldn't go back. Not again.

"I didn't know he was coming," she said at last. Her voice when it emerged, was even—cool, even slightly husky. You'd never guess she wanted to scream. To ride hard and fast until everything in her head blurred.

"Daddy only found out yesterday," Cleo replied. "But with all this chaos, I forgot to tell you."

"Why would you?" Simone gave a small, practiced laugh. "It's got nothing to do with me."

"Oh, come on, Simone. You were always Sean's personal project—from the day your father took over the estate. You practically lived at the Hall."

"He spoiled you," Cleo added with fond exasperation. "What did he call you? Sunflower, wasn't it?"

"Among other things," Simone said stiffly. "Mostly bossy ones."

"Sean isn't bossy," Cleo insisted, studying her friend closely. "He's just… in charge. Always has been. One day he'll inherit everything, and he's always known it. It's shaped who he is."

"Has it?" Simone muttered. "Funny, I remember him putting me over his knee once."

Cleo laughed. "Two light smacks on the back of your jeans does not qualify as corporal punishment. You were nine, and a menace. If he hadn't caught you, you'd have driven his new car through the garden wall."

"It was more about the car than me," Simone grumbled.

"He hugged you afterwards," Cleo said pointedly. "You were shaking like a leaf. He was the only one who could ever handle you. The rest of us gave up and let him do it. You were his problem, always."

"Well, I'm twenty-two now," Simone snapped. "Hardly a problem anymore."

Cleo gave her a quick side glance. "You've still got the same temper. And the same red hair. Sean's no better, mind you. He's got a volcanic streak of his own, so just… go easy, will you? We really can't afford another war—not with Fleur Decker already poisoning the well."

Simone's restraint slipped. "I don't see how I could cause more trouble. My name is Symons, not Taylor."

Cleo reeled back, momentarily stunned. Then the Taylor eyes narrowed, flashing blue.

"You wretch! You've always been one of us. Sean had more say in your life than your own father did. He pulled rank to get you into my school. Remember?"

"I never wanted to go to boarding school!" Simone snapped.

"No, because you couldn't bear to be away from Sean." Cleo's voice was lower now, more careful. "I don't know why you turned against him, but I saw it. Don't keep this feud going, Simone. Not now. Not when everything's teetering."

She paused, and the wind played in her hair as if to fill the silence.

"We need all the help we can get," she added. "Especially with Fleur Decker in our midst."

For a moment, they glared at each other—Cleo fiercely loyal, defending her brother without hesitation, and Simone, too full of old memories and buried hurt to back down. Her temper, always close to the surface, sparked in the honey-gold of her eyes, turning them luminous with fury.

But it didn't last.

Their bond was too deep, too weathered by shared history and affection. At the same instant, they both dissolved into laughter.

"I'll try," Simone promised, breathless. "Count on me. But we should head back—I've got jobs waiting."

Cleo lingered, thoughtful. "You know," she said slowly, "I've been thinking. You're really beautiful. Especially when you're mad—those flashing eyes, that hair. If you just…rearranged yourself a bit, we could at least get a bit of fun out of this mess."

Simone reined in sharply and turned a suspicious eye on her friend. "What are you up to?"

Cleo looked faintly indignant. "Fleur thinks she's the bee's knees. All that gloss."

"She's a model," Simone pointed out with a shrug. "Gloss is part of the uniform."

"There's nothing natural about it," Cleo muttered darkly. "Scrape off the paint and you'd find a barn door underneath."

"Not quite," Simone said with a grin. "And what does this have to do with 'rearranging myself'?"

"You're beautiful," Cleo insisted. "Really beautiful. Small, striking, unique. If you made a bit of effort—just a little—you'd make Fleur look like the shallow puddle she is."

"And the point of that would be…?" Simone arched a brow.

"To give me a laugh, for one thing. I honestly can't remember the last time you wore a dress. And that plait—" she gestured with mock horror. "Honestly, Simone."

Simone chuckled. "I'm a working girl."

"And you look it. Fleur actually asked Mummy if you were a stable hand. Or one of the farm workers. I think she thought you'd wandered in from the woods and we were all too polite to tell you to leave."

Simone doubled over with laughter, but Cleo's frown deepened.

"It wasn't that funny. Mummy went icy. She said, 'That is Simone. We are very fond of Simone.' And that was that. But of course, you were blissfully unaware—probably off in your boots and jeans, felling a tree."

Simone was still laughing, but Cleo gave her a sideways glance. "Honestly, what is the matter with you? Once in a while you could swirl in wearing silk. You clean up beautifully. You just… never bother."

"I like me as I am," Simone said simply. "But I'll give it some thought."

She turned Stardust and nudged her into a canter, then a gallop, letting the wind cool the heat in her cheeks and sweep the sting of memory from her mind. But she knew the truth, even if Cleo didn't. There were reasons she kept things simple. Cleo remembered the wild child, the daring rider. She didn't remember the awkward stages—years with braces, Sean's teasing amusement. She had never heard him call her *Simon*, not the way he said Cleo's name. Simone had been the wild one, the scrappy one, the problem.

Cleo didn't know what it was like to be seen as a boyish nuisance. To be patronised, teased, then ignored. She certainly didn't know how many women Sean had loved—and none of them had ever been named Simone.

As they slowed the horses to a walk across the park, the last threads of Simone's temper slipped away. Branlow Hall rose ahead of them, poised on a gentle rise. Its gabled fronts caught the morning sun, gleaming like something out of a childhood dream. Tall windows sparkled between ivy-clad stone, and wide, shallow steps led up to the great carved front door—its weathered wood blackened by time, solid as the centuries it had stood.

The house was framed by sweeping lawns and great copper beeches, by oak and elm. No fussy formal gardens here—just scale and beauty, wild and grand. And Simone loved it with her whole heart. Every path, every window, every ridge of those familiar hills. If she were ever forced to leave, she would never settle anywhere else. This was home. Peace. The only place her soul fit.

They rounded the back toward the stable yard, hooves ringing sharply on cobbles. Two men looked up from their work and smiled in greeting—more Taylors, unmistakable in height and eye colour. But neither bore the startling presence of Sean.

Mark had Cleo's clear blue eyes, but not their brother's sapphire intensity. His hair was merely dark, not raven-black. He was handsome, yes, but lacked Sean's raw, masculine elegance—that sense of effortless command.

Once, perhaps, Sir Michael had been that striking too. But now his white hair and softened expression bore the marks of age. He stood straighter than most men his age, but Simone noticed it—that subtle stoop, the quiet fatigue in his eyes.

One day soon, Sean would carry it all. The weight of this land. The Hall. The title of baronet. He would be Sir Sean. And then everything would change.

It was a thought that had never crossed her mind until today—and when it did, an odd shiver danced over her skin. Sir Sean Taylor. The title suited him in a way that unsettled her—aloof, distant, untouchable. That dazzling white smile, the one that had once lit up her childhood and quietly stolen her teenage heart, rose now in memory like a ghost—mocking rather than comforting. She forced it away. Forced him away. He had left a long time ago—four years, to be exact—and she'd been glad to see him go. She reminded herself of that. Again. Because whatever he had once been, whatever lingering ache still stirred at the thought of him… he was nothing to her now.

"We were just discussing the future of this rare beast," Sir Michael murmured, nodding toward the massive black stallion watching them with sharp, intelligent eyes as the girls dismounted.

"Royal? He's magnificent," Simone said, brushing her hand down Stardust's neck. "So long as I don't have to ride him."

"Terrifying thought," Cleo agreed, eyeing the horse with theatrical wariness. "All he has to do is roll his eyes and I'm gone—even when he's safely boxed. I still don't know why you wanted him, Father."

"Breeding," Sir Michael replied, with a pointed look at Simone. "As she well knows. Though I'll admit he's a handful. Jerry barely manages him."

"That's true enough," said Jerry Barker, approaching from the stables with his usual no-nonsense stride. The veteran head groom gave each girl a nod as he reached for their reins. "I'll take care of these, ladies. The stallion's a fine beast, Sir Michael, but he scares the life out of most folk."

"Sean will be here soon," Mark said casually, brushing dust from his sleeve. "I expect he'll have that brute sorted out in no time. He's been known to tame... other things, too." He shot Simone a sly grin.

Simone didn't return it.

"God knows why he left in the first place," Mark went on. "He could've sent me. I'd have taken Canada over Fleur any day."

"We've always had business outside the estate," Sir Michael said, his voice clipped. "Sean's spent years in Canada and the States. As for why he went—it was his decision, and I trust his reasons. He always has them."

"Naturally," Mark said dryly. "Sean never does anything without a reason. Or without taking command of everyone within a hundred-mile radius."

Sir Michael didn't seem to catch the edge in his son's tone, but Cleo turned her head sharply.

"Mark! What's gotten into you? You've always looked up to him—you still do."

"Of course I do." Mark gave a wry smile. "Maybe I'm just feeling the usual... comparison."

"Rubbish," Sir Michael said firmly, breaking from his reverie. He'd been watching Royal with narrowed eyes, as if measuring the stallion against some long-ago version of himself. "Sean's the best friend you've ever had."

Mark's smile tugged wider, laced with weary humour. "Oh, I agree. He's the best everything."

Simone smiled back at him out of habit, but her thoughts were elsewhere, threading through darker territory. The best everything. The perfect son. The golden boy. Heroic, brilliant—and the greatest traitor of them all.

Chapter Two

She felt a sudden pang of sympathy for Mark. He was kind, open-hearted, and hopelessly overshadowed. Even as children, Sean had stolen every spotlight without even trying. Now Mark was left with a preening fiancée and a lifetime of second place.

And Simone… well, she was watching her place at Branlow Hall dissolve by the hour. Once, she'd been nearly part of the family. Now she was just the estate manager's daughter—and Fleur wasn't going to let her forget it.

It wouldn't take much. One or two more backhanded remarks from Miss Decker and Simone would lose her temper—spectacularly. She knew herself too well. And when that happened, it wouldn't just be awkward. It would be final.

Sean was returning. That much was settled. Which meant everything would change.

From now on, she'd keep her distance—stay in her own home, focus on her work, and remember exactly who she was. Fleur had made it clear, in that polite, honeyed way of hers, that Simone was staff. Nothing more.

Cleo might always see her as family, but it wouldn't last. Before long, their meetings would need to be arranged—deliberate, outside the Hall. Any casual visits now risked crossing paths with either the thorn in everyone's side… or Sean.

And both, as far as Simone was concerned, were best avoided.

"Sean may decide to send you out to Canada, anyway, Mark."

Sir Michael's casual remark snapped Simone back to the present. Sean may decide. The words struck her like a slap. He hadn't taken over yet—not officially. But the implication was there, and it sent a chill up her spine.

That was a bridge she wasn't ready to cross. Not yet. Maybe never.

Because Simone knew—absolutely—that she couldn't work for Sean Taylor.

She turned a sharp glance on Sir Michael, her heartbeat picking up. He looked tired again, distracted. Was he thinking of stepping down? Handing everything over? The idea brought a sudden wave of unease. Surely not. Or—worse—was his mind beginning to wander? That thought brought no comfort either.

She mumbled something about work and made her escape, but not quickly enough.

"There'll be a dinner for Sean when he arrives!" Sir Michael called after her.

The words rang out like a sentence.

Simone didn't dare look back. Her expression must have said it all—because behind her, Mark chuckled, and Cleo's eyes took on a far too speculative gleam. Simone could already see what her friend was plotting: satin, lace, war paint, all for the noble purpose of unsettling Miss Decker.

Oh no, she thought grimly. I have to get out of that dinner.

Naturally, the fatted calf would be served up with ceremony and wine. A proper homecoming for the golden boy. And all she wanted was to disappear. It would be rude not to attend, she knew that—but she'd find a way. Even if it meant desertion under fire.

And yet… there was Lady Vivian to consider. Dear Lady Vivian, whose quiet grace was already stretched thin by Fleur's relentless presence. Simone was fond of her—deeply so—and hated to cause her more strain.

Damn. She bit down on her lower lip as she trudged home, frustrated and unsettled. Why did life always have to get so complicated?

She hadn't seen Sean in four years. Not a single visit. Not a call. Not even a line of polite obligation. He'd vanished without a trace, and now he was simply… returning. Just like that. And there would be no avoiding him this time.

She knew perfectly well how it would look if she refused to attend the dinner. Her father would be disappointed—he was always invited too, after all. And no matter what Miss Decker might believe, Henry Symons was no common labourer. On the Taylor estate, the estate manager stood nearly shoulder to shoulder with the family. And Simone… she was meant to follow in his footsteps.

Not that she believed she ever could. She tried—every day—but her father's shoes were large, his knowledge deep, his presence steady. She could only hope Sir Michael would let her try.

And as for Sean…

She almost laughed. Perhaps, by the time he took over, she'd be a sharp-tongued spinster, dry as dust and too sour to challenge.

For the first time, Simone looked around the estate not with pride—but with dread. The hills, the fields, the wide-open skies—they had always felt eternal. But now the air was shifting. Trouble had arrived in the form of Fleur Decker, and now Sean was returning too.

The storm was gathering. And it was heading straight for her.

By the time she reached the Dower House, her earlier brightness had dulled to a heavy gloom.

It was almost dark when Simone remembered the fencing at Home Farm. She'd noticed the broken section while riding with Cleo earlier but had let it slip her mind completely. Now, with the light fading fast, the oversight felt glaring.

If Jack Gregory didn't get out there and deal with it, there'd be cattle grazing on the front lawn by sunrise.

"Give Jack a ring," her father said as she entered. He was standing in the hall with a stack of papers in one hand. "I need you in the study for an hour or so. Paperwork's piling up."

"I can't just ring him, Dad," she sighed. "It's nearly dark. I had all day to tell him, and I forgot. It's my fault. If I call now, he'll have to drag himself out in the dark. I'll go over and tell him face-to-face."

"He should have spotted it himself."

"Well, he didn't. I'll just nip across."

Henry followed her out, pausing beside her to admire the dusk-wrapped garden. This wasn't Branlow Hall, but it had its own quiet grandeur. The Dower House, though not as ancient, was still stately in its own right—stone-built like the Hall, with clean lines and a quiet dignity.

It sat nestled in a lush acre of gardens, made especially private by tall banks of rhododendrons and thick azaleas that would explode into wild colour in a few weeks' time.

A lovely place. A good life.

And yet, as Simone stepped out into the twilight, she felt the faint stirrings of something else.

Change.

And it was coming whether she was ready or not.

Her father's expression darkened the moment Simone wheeled out her motorbike.

"You're not going on that thing again, are you? One of these days it'll be the death of you!"

"It's the quickest way to get around," she said lightly, swinging her leg over the seat. "And I only ever use it on the estate."

"There are two Land Rovers parked by the gate. That's what they're for. And don't think I didn't see you down in the village the day before yesterday."

"I only went to post a letter to Rhonda," she replied with an innocent smile, trying to sweeten his mood. Her father's rants about the bike were constant—and predictable. The Suzuki 250's high-revving engine drove him mad, no matter how slowly she rode it.

"Why you were there is beside the point. You were there. I don't like that bike."

He gave her a glowering look, but it wavered when she grinned at him, cheeky and unrepentant.

"How is Rhonda, anyway?" he asked, the corners of his mouth twitching.

Simone seized the lifeline. "Still round as a barrel, according to her. Though she insists it's just… strategic plumpness. She says she's grown an inch, so now the weight's better distributed."

Her father laughed and shook his head. "She's a grand girl, Rhonda. Invite her over sometime—after you've gotten rid of that death trap. She's as bad as you."

Simone took that as her cue to leave and kicked the bike into gear, easing out of the yard with a guilty attempt to keep the revs low. As she rolled down the drive, her mind was less on the fencing at Home Farm and more on how to break the news to Jack Gregory without sounding like she was giving orders.

He should have noticed the break himself. But Simone lacked her father's quiet authority—his unshakable, unquestioned command. And perhaps… perhaps she never would possess it. After all, there weren't many female estate managers in England in 1955.

The realisation struck her like a blow to the chest. If she wasn't fit to take over the estate, someone else would. Someone else would live in the Dower House. It would no longer be hers.

And that idea—leaving the land, leaving this life—was unbearable.

No. She would find a way to prove herself. She had to.

She tore down the narrow country lane, trying to leave her dark thoughts behind in the wind. At the bottom, she would cut through the field—it would save time. The sky was already thickening with dusk. Jack would need a lamp, and she briefly considered offering to help.

No. Her father would hit the roof. Sir Michael would too if word got back.

She took the corner too fast, drifting across to the wrong side of the road—just as headlights surged into view.

A sleek, low sports car came barrelling toward her, too fast and too close. She slammed on her brakes. The car braked, too, tyres shrieking—but her bike was already skidding, tilting out of control.

A thousand thoughts exploded in her mind—she had no helmet, she'd never see her father again, never ride across the hills, never see Branlow Hall standing golden in the light…

The bike veered wildly. Simone flew.

Time slowed. She felt herself lifted, weightless, flung like a rag doll through the evening air—light, bright, breakable. She saw sparks fly as her bike hit the road, scraping along the tarmac in a blur of metal. And then came the crash. Not of steel, but of her body, plunging into the grassy ditch beside the road.

The grass gave a little, but not much. The earth beneath was hard. Winded and dazed, she didn't move. Her limbs were sprawled like a marionette with its strings cut, her eyes closed, her face bloodless.

She looked like a crushed wildflower tossed carelessly by fate.

The man who leapt from the car reached her in seconds, his face pale under a deep summer tan. He dropped to his knees beside her, hands moving urgently over her arms and legs, checking for breaks, feeling for breath. His relief was visible when her chest rose, shallow but steady.

A tremor passed over her lips. Her mouth twisted with pain.

Then, slowly, her eyes fluttered open—honey-gold and dazed.

And locked immediately with eyes the colour of lightning struck water—startling, piercing, unmistakable.

Sapphire blue.

Her heart thudded once, violently. She closed her eyes again, hard and fast, like slamming a door.

Too late.

Sean had come home.

"Open your eyes."

The voice was the same—low, commanding, threaded with the authority she remembered too well. And, as always, she obeyed without thinking.

So much for avoiding him.

She blinked up into the face she'd spent four years trying to erase from memory—only to find herself locked in place by the piercing blaze of his eyes. For the briefest moment, all the fury and grief drained from her, leaving only that dazzling blue. A colour that had once filled her whole world.

"Sean…"

"You little fool."

His voice lashed through the air—sharp, scathing, and cutting the fragile moment clean in half.

The warmth in her chest vanished instantly, replaced by instinctive panic. She jerked in his arms, trying to sit up, but he held her fast.

His heart was still thundering.

Seconds ago, she'd been airborne—hair streaming like flame, limbs flung helplessly through the air—and for one gut-wrenching instant, he thought he'd killed her. The woman he had come back to claim. The woman he couldn't stop thinking about, no matter how far or how long he stayed away.

Four years. And still she had that hold on him.

"Lie still," he snapped, his voice rough, his hands already moving to steady her. One at her shoulder, the other braced against her ribs—gentle but unyielding. "You damn near killed yourself."

He didn't mean to sound so angry. But beneath the fury was fear—raw, pulsing fear that refused to ease, even now that she was breathing, blinking, speaking.

Still alive.

Still his.

God help them both.

"I'm perfectly fine." The words came out unconvincingly. When she shut her eyes, the darkness spun and burst with stars. Her voice, usually warm and husky, was faint even to her own ears. He heard it too—his scowl darkened, the lines around his mouth drawn tight with fury.

"I hope we're talking about your body, not your brain," he bit out. "What the hell were you doing on a motorbike? Henry has a lot to answer for."

"I'm twenty-two," she managed, opening her eyes again, forcing strength into her voice.

"Chronologically, maybe. Mentally, you're still twelve." His mouth curled. "Henry never could control you."

She tried to summon a retort, but her head was spinning too fast. He glared down at her like she was a delinquent child—and yet his hands held her with surprising care. Had they not been so gentle, she might have believed he truly wanted to throttle her.

A rough, warm tongue licked her cheek, and she turned her head just enough to see the looming shape of a large, familiar black Great Dane.

"Prince!" she murmured, blinking in disbelief. "The Hound of the Baskervilles lives on. Hello, my sweet. You've aged."

The dog gave her a wide, foolish grin and licked the tip of her nose.

"Back in the car, you idiot," Sean barked, clearly unamused.

"It's not his fault," she muttered.

"Oh, I've never had any doubts about where the fault lies when you're involved."

He leaned over her again. "Let's get you in the car. You don't seem to have broken anything—miraculously."

"My bike!" she protested as he began to lift her.

"It can stay right where it is—in the opposite hedge where you launched it. And if I ever see you on it again, I'll dismantle the whole thing and scatter the pieces from one end of the county to the other."

"You'll do no such thing!"

"It wasn't a suggestion," he growled. "On this estate, you toe the line. Or else."

He didn't say what "or else" meant, but the threat was there—unspoken, formidable—and Simone, for once, wisely kept her mouth shut. She chanced a look at him and was startled by how furious he truly looked. This wasn't teasing. He was shaken, and under the fury, she saw it.

Without another word, he carried her to the car and lowered her gently into the passenger seat. Prince tried to climb in after them, tail thumping, but Sean blocked him with a withering glare.

"Back off, medic," he muttered, slamming the door shut as the dog sulked and licked the window in protest.

Simone sat stiffly in the seat, her breath catching in her throat—not just from the fall, but from the man beside her. The man she had once loved.

The man she had sworn never to see again.

"I was on my way to the Home Farm," Simone managed, her voice small, strained. "There's a fence down. I needed to tell Jack Gregory."

"Tell him tomorrow," Sean snapped, eyes fixed on the road as he started the car.

"The cattle might get out. I saw it earlier, but I was busy and forgot, so it's my fault—"

"The hell it is!" he cut in sharply. "Jack's the one running the farm. That's his job."

"He does run it well," she said, though even she could hear the uncertainty in her voice. "There's no need for all this fury. I'm the one who nearly broke her neck, and I'm quite prepared to take the blame. I was on the wrong side of the road."

He turned to glare at her, his eyes sparking like blue flame. "Believe it or not, it rattles me when I nearly mow down the Estate Manager's daughter. Haven't quite mastered the art of doing it with detachment."

His gaze dropped, scathing, sweeping from the tangled plait down to her mud-splashed trousers and riding boots.

The contempt stung more than it should have.

Simone looked away, biting down hard on the emotion rising in her throat. It was shock, that's all—shock and bruises and exhaustion. Her head slumped against the butter-soft leather of the passenger seat. A Porsche. Of course. Still fast. Still sleek. Still him.

He hadn't changed a bit. Still dark. Still maddening. Still cutting her to pieces without blinking.

"How do you feel?" he asked more quietly, his voice unexpectedly stripped of sarcasm.

She felt the weight of his gaze on her, studying her pale face, the pain she hadn't been able to hide. She shut him out by closing her eyes.

"Wonderful," she murmured. "I'm thinking of going for my evening jog."

There was a pause.

"Still the same idiot, *Simon*?" he said softly.

That did it. She tensed, the movement jarring pain through her ribs.

He was back. And already, he was trying to crush her.

"*Simon's* a boy's name," she said bitterly, not even knowing why it slipped out.

"Oh? Would you prefer something soft and antique? Amelia, perhaps?" His voice dropped into a velvet sneer. "Doesn't suit. I don't know any girls who ride motorbikes."

"You've led a sheltered life," she shot back. "Plenty do."

"But not you, Simone." His voice turned quiet, dangerous. "Never again. I meant what I said. Sell the bike, give it away—or I'll take a sledgehammer to it myself."

"You can't order me around!"

"We'll see," he murmured.

She glared at him, but he didn't return the look—just drove on, calm and unreadable. Her hands clenched in her lap, white-knuckled.

"Now relax," he said, not unkindly. "You're only hurting yourself."

Too late, she thought. No one's ever hurt me the way you have.

And that was the problem. Nothing and no one had the power to wound her like Sean did. It was astonishing how fast he could get under her skin, how fast he could reduce her to this burning, humiliated mess.

She glanced sideways at his profile—so familiar, so exasperatingly composed—and looked away just as quickly. One look at him, and she was back in that emotional quicksand she'd spent four years trying to climb out of.

She shut her eyes again, her body aching, her mind worse.

Well. At least the dreaded reunion was over, though at no small cost to her bones and pride. He'd arrived, and already he was barking orders, slipping back into the role he'd always occupied—in charge. But this time it felt different. Sharper. Final.

A sick little voice whispered inside her: *It's over. All of it. You'll never belong here again.*

Whether it was Fleur's smirks or Sean's return—or both—she couldn't yet tell. But she knew the storm was breaking. And when it did, there'd be no shelter left.

Because Sean Taylor might have been the best of everything.

But he'd never been hers.

Chapter Three

Simone protested weakly as Sean pulled up outside the Dower House and moved to open the door.

"I'm perfectly capable of managing," she insisted, attempting to push herself upright.

"Managing to do what?" he said curtly.

Before she could blink, he'd swept her up into his arms, and even that swift movement sent dizziness crashing over her. She bit down on her lip to stifle the cry of pain that nearly escaped. Sean noticed, of course, but aside from a sharp glance, he ignored it—just as he was clearly trying to ignore her. As far as he was concerned, she was just another reckless nuisance he'd once been foolish enough to tolerate.

"Is that you, Simone?" came her father's voice from the study.

Sean answered for her. "In a manner of speaking."

Henry Symons appeared in the doorway—and went pale.

"My God! Is she badly hurt?"

"I don't think so," Sean said, his voice clipped but fractionally less icy. "But I'd get William Stokes out here just to be sure."

He carried her straight to the settee, laying her down with more gentleness than his tone suggested. Henry was already moving, lifting the receiver, and dialling.

"She won't give up that bike, Mr Sean," he muttered distractedly.

"Why are you calling him Mr Sean?" Simone complained, her voice thick with exhaustion and irritation. "You're just playing into his hands."

Sean didn't seem to hear her—or chose not to. His frosted-blue eyes remained fixed on her, unreadable.

"He's been Sean to you for over sixteen years," she added petulantly. "Next thing, you'll be tugging your forelock."

"He must be all of thirty-one or thirty-two now," Henry said vaguely, still waiting on the line. "One day he'll be Sir Sean."

She bit down on a bitter smile. As if she needed that reminder. Sean didn't need a title to be unreachable. He'd always managed that all on his own.

"Drop it, Henry," Sean interrupted coldly. "I'm starting to think Simone got her insanity from you. And I'm not joking about the bike—she's finished with it."

"Maybe now you're here, she'll listen," Henry replied, with a trace of relief.

"I'm twenty-two," Simone burst out, sitting up abruptly—and immediately wincing. "I'll do as I damn well please."

"Not while you work for Taylor Estates," Sean said, flat as granite.

His gaze locked onto hers, icy and unflinching, until she slumped back down with a soft gasp. Her cheeks were colourless again, lashes trembling against her skin.

Tomorrow, she told herself. Tomorrow she'd fight back. Right now, everything ached too much—inside and out.

"She's pale," Henry murmured, returning from the call. "William's on his way. Sean, don't you want to get back up to the Hall?"

"I'll go when I'm satisfied she's all right," he said. "After all, I'm partly responsible for this."

He dropped into a nearby chair like a man who had no intention of being moved by anyone's opinion—not now, not ever. Simone didn't open her eyes. She didn't need to. Sean had always done exactly what he pleased.

A beat later, her eyes flew open. "The fencing—I forgot to—Jack Gregory needs to know. He'll have to—"

But Sean was already on his feet, striding to the phone.

"Don't bother," he snapped. "I'll handle it."

He dialled the number with a clipped impatience that made Simone wince.

"You've got a fence down," he barked when Jack answered. "We don't want cattle on the front lawn in the morning. Yes, I'm back. And yes, you should've seen it yourself."

He slammed the receiver down, turned—and found Simone watching him, her expression pained, partly from bruises, partly from disappointment.

"Jack's a good man," she said quietly. "That wasn't kind. Or fair."

"I'm not paid to be kind or fair," he said, already reaching for a decanter. Without so much as a glance at her or her father, he poured himself a drink.

Henry glanced between them, uneasy. Sean was back—and the loose rein was gone. Whatever independence Simone had held onto, it was now dangling by a thread.

He looked at his daughter, lying pale and still. She really was a beautiful thing, even more so when quieted like this. Her face had the fragile, luminous look of someone holding pain just beneath the surface. She wasn't as tough as she pretended—not always. Her vivid red hair spilled around her face like flame, too fierce for the girl lying so still.

Henry moved forward, crouched to gently ease off her boots.

Sean watched him grimly, his mouth a thin, angry line.

The silence between them was heavy and awkward, like the opening crack of a thunderstorm.

Simone stayed out of the conversation by keeping her eyes closed. Damn Sean. She was in an impossible fix. She couldn't very well fly at him without causing a stir in the entire household. Besides, he might soon be her employer—hardly ideal to start things off by slapping the boss. But it was obvious he'd returned in precisely the same state of mind. She was still Simone. Still a fool.

How could she ever have idolised a man like that? So much for childhood instincts—and even less for teenage crushes.

When William Stokes arrived, the whole humiliating process began again.

"Can't say I didn't see this coming," he muttered drily, checking her pupils and gently prodding limbs for breaks. "Tearing around on that bike… you're lucky to come off this lightly. Next time—"

"There won't be a next time," Sean said flatly, glaring down at her like she was some unfortunate scientific discovery.

He hadn't even left the room for the examination—not that she was undressed, but still. His silent, looming presence irritated her. That proprietorial lord of the manor attitude had never sat well with her, and it hadn't improved with time. Her father staying made sense. Sean didn't.

She wished William had ordered him out, but even the old doctor—who ought to have had enough seniority to assert some authority—had yielded to Sean's unspoken command. She was beginning to suspect everyone did.

"Well," William said at last, straightening his spine with a crack, "nothing broken. Bit of shock, no doubt. Give her until tomorrow afternoon. If she's still rattled, ring me."

"I'm not rattled now," Simone said irritably, frowning at him.

Sean looked down at her, cool and unimpressed. "Then by all means—spring up and go to bed."

She tried. And promptly crumpled.

He caught her before she hit the floor, sweeping her up as though she weighed nothing.

"Hah," William muttered, peering at her over his spectacles, then sighed and turned toward Henry. "Knows everything, this one. Always did. Red hair. Drink, Henry?"

As Sean carried her from the room, Simone hissed under her breath, "It's time he retired."

Sean chuckled. "Thinking of replacing him with a handsome young doctor?"

"I don't fancy anyone," she snapped. "And for your information, I'm going steady."

A lie. Sort of. She did go out with Jeffery Rogers now and then. He was steady, kind, safe—but she'd never truly considered him seriously. The estate always came first.

"With young Rogers, yes—I've heard," Sean said dryly. "He's twenty-five now, isn't he?"

"He is!" she said defensively, glancing up at him. He was carrying her effortlessly up the stairs as if she were a doll. Unbothered. Unmoved. That rankled more than she wanted to admit.

"I remember him when he was a snivelling boy," Sean mused.

"How condescending. I suppose you remember me as a snivelling boy, too?"

"You never snivelled, Simone."

He was suddenly grinning down at her, the white smile dazzling, his sapphire eyes warm with unexpected amusement. That old, infuriating, heart-melting charm. For a moment, it caught her off guard, drawing up fragments of old feelings—the girl she'd once been, who had adored him.

But there were other memories, too. And she wouldn't forget those.

"You shouldn't be up here," she said abruptly, as he nudged open her bedroom door with his shoulder. "This is my room."

"Relax," he murmured, still smiling. "I promise not to attack without written warning."

She flushed and looked away, unsettled. That teasing white smile made her anxious in all the wrong ways.

"My father should've brought me," she muttered. "You're practically a stranger now."

"Almost." He paused. "Try screaming, see what happens."

"I know exactly what'll happen—he'll shout up the stairs and ask what I've done this time."

Sean laughed and set her gently on the bed. "Can you manage?"

"I'll be fine." She lifted her chin with shaky dignity, ignoring the pain, and he studied her for a long moment before nodding once and turning toward the door.

"Crawl into bed, then. Goodnight."

She watched him walk away, and a strange ache welled up in her chest. So many memories, not all of them bad. He brought it all back—too easily.

"Sean—are you staying?" she asked quietly. "I mean… are you home for long?"

He paused at the threshold, one hand on the doorframe. His eyes locked with hers, clear and unreadable.

"For good, I think. Why?"

She swallowed. "It's a bit tricky. I hate you. It's awkward."

He gave the faintest ghost of a smile. "I know. Trouble is that your father's part of the way of things around here. Until he retires, you're stuck with us."

Her eyes widened. "But… when he does retire—I'll be taking his place."

Sean didn't respond. He simply arched one dark brow and walked out, closing the door softly behind him.

Simone stared at the empty space where he'd been, her heart sinking like a stone. He hadn't said a word—but he didn't need to. She'd understood perfectly. He had no intention of letting her inherit her father's position.

It didn't matter if Sir Michael was still in charge. Sean would have the last word.

She changed into her nightdress in silence, her movements stiff, aching. But it was the hollowness inside that truly hurt.

She lay in bed, restless, her mind refusing to quiet. She'd known this would happen. She'd known Sean's return would ruin everything. But now it felt worse—personal, inescapable. The boy she'd once idolised was now the man standing between her and everything she'd built.

Even her fury couldn't keep the memories at bay. Fragmented images returned— sunlight on the lawns at Branlow Hall, the heat of a summer day, the feel of warm stone beneath bare feet, Sean's raven-black hair catching the light as he rode across the paddocks.

Once, she'd dreamed of living here forever.

Now, she was dreaming of how to survive him.

At eight, Simone had been small and quick, her dark red hair already long, flying loose around her shoulders as she tore across the gardens beside the much taller Cleo. They'd been playing hide-and-seek behind the dense hedges that lined the edge of the rose walk, shrieking and laughing, lost in the freedom of childhood.

The sound of grown-up voices drifting across the lawn had made her freeze—Sean's voice and that of his father. The sound alone was enough to make her uneasy.

"Hello, Cleo. Hiding?"

Sean had appeared suddenly, tall, and confident, his school blazer flapping open as he looked down at his ten-year-old sister. Cleo scowled up at him, hands on hips.

"You've ruined it, Sean! Now she'll find me."

To Simone, the way Cleo spoke to him was nothing short of blasphemy. Even if they were siblings, it was Sean. He was eighteen. Practically an adult. Practically a god.

She stepped out from behind the hedge before he could call her out, her honey-coloured eyes wide and apprehensive, expecting rebuke.

But then—his smile. That flash of white, warm, and sudden, and the gleam of those piercing sapphire eyes that somehow softened when they found her.

Without hesitation, he bent and scooped her up into his arms.

"Hello, Sunflower," he said gently. "We'd better call this one a draw—I think I ruined your game."

"It's not fair," Cleo grumbled as their father and Sean moved off again. "I would've won. Sean's a beast."

"He is not!" Simone had snapped, scandalised. "It was an accident. And Sean is wonderful. When I grow up, I'm going to marry him."

A sudden burst of laughter spun her around. Sean and Sir Michael were still within earshot, clearly having heard every word.

Simone's cheeks flamed as Sean turned and pointed a mock-stern finger at her.

"And that's a promise," he teased. "I'll hold you to it."

She had bolted then, humiliated, but not truly ashamed. He was her hero. He always had been.

Mark, only sixteen at the time, had stood awkward and uncertain at the garden gate, watching her with faint horror before retreating. But not Sean.

Sean had always been something more—her talisman, her saint, her dark-eyed god.

Until, years later, she found him out.

That night, sleep came in restless fragments. Her dreams twisted into fevered images, her body aching, her mind chasing shadows. In the dream, a black panther stalked her— sleek and silent, its sapphire eyes glowing in the dark.

It didn't snarl. It didn't run. It watched her.

And then it followed her—through doorways, across stone floors, through the warmth of the hall and out into the cold, unforgiving world. It hunted her from the inside out, and she woke tangled in the sheets, heart thudding, knowing exactly who it was.

The expected invitation to Sean's "Welcome Home" dinner arrived late that morning, penned in Lady Vivian's elegant hand. Simone, still feeling slightly sore but otherwise fine, considered using her accident as an excuse—until she reached the postscript: If Simone is unwell, we'll simply put it off until tomorrow.

So much for slipping out gracefully. That neatly closed any loophole, and she had no choice but to accept.

Her father had insisted she take the day off, which left her with far too much time to think—never a good thing. And inevitably, her thoughts turned to Sean. Inevitable was the right word. Sean was the storm on the horizon, the gravity in every room. His presence in her life had always felt predestined.

Branlow Hall had been a second home to her since childhood, the great house just beyond the trees, ever present. She had loved it, and she had loved him.

It was Sean who had found her the day her mother left—the day her world caved in. Ten years old, curled up in the long grass at the edge of the woods, trying not to cry, trying not to exist. He'd said nothing at first. Just gathered her into his arms, wiped her tear-streaked face, and held her. Not with fanfare or false promises—just warmth, just safety. Somehow, he had always known what she needed.

She supposed that's when the romantic devotion had begun. He had become the centre of her world: her rescuer, her protector, her silent champion. As she grew, so too did her feelings—though in time the godlike image had cracked.

There had been women. Plenty of them. Sean didn't belong to her, not even close.

Now, as she moved restlessly about her bedroom, Simone tried to shake the memories loose. That schoolgirl crush was long dead. She didn't want to revisit it. What she did need to face was tonight.

Cleo's words lingered in her mind—something about Simone neglecting herself. Was there truth in it? Jeffery never seemed to mind. In fact, he always looked pleased to be seen with her.

After a long shower, she examined her bruises in the mirror. Miraculously few, considering the force of her crash, but a deep ache lingered in her limbs. William Stokes had warned of the aftershock.

Her reflection stared back at her with clear-eyed realism. She wasn't exactly tiny, but she was compact—petite. She had a lovely shape, soft and well-proportioned, her creamy skin a striking contrast to the mass of dark red hair that hung down her back like a velvet curtain. Cleo was right—it needed cutting. Once it had curled softly, but now the weight pulled it straight. Still, there was no time to fix that before dinner. Not that it would make any difference.

She could never outshine Miss Decker. That hope had been Cleo's, not hers.

The phone rang, and she slipped on a silky robe before padding downstairs to answer.

"Simone?" Cleo's voice was bright. "Didn't call earlier in case you were still flat on your back. How are you?"

"Fine, thanks. And how do you know?"

"Sean. He was quite shaken, you know. Said he nearly killed you."

"I was on the wrong side of the road," Simone admitted. She could just imagine Sean describing the incident with that familiar blend of sarcasm and disdain. Miss Decker, no doubt, had been privately delighted. "Prince was first on the scene, anyway. Licked my nose. Very efficient triage."

Cleo burst out laughing. "He's such a fool. It's good to have him back in the house again, barging around after Sean and knocking over side tables. Scared the life out of Fleur."

"Sean did?"

"No, Prince! Fleur gave this little shriek—very graceful, like a soprano in a bad opera. Prince was intrigued. Went right up to her and growled. First time I've ever heard him do that. Quarantine seems to have sharpened his instincts."

"How is your bête noire?" Simone smirked, imagining Fleur jumping in fright. That woman had a stubborn way of trying to look composed on horseback, though she never quite succeeded.

"She's our bête noire, darling. And I expect you to shine tonight."

"Only thing shining will be my bruises. Anyway, it's too late. I can't get into town for a haircut, and I've nothing special to wear."

"I'll come over after lunch," Cleo declared breezily—and hung up before Simone could argue.

Simone stared at the phone with a sigh of resignation. There was no fighting Cleo once she'd made up her mind. She might as well go and inspect her sadly uninspired wardrobe before Cleo began snipping hems and sleeves in the name of fashion.

But first—a strong coffee. If she was going to survive this evening, she would need reinforcements.

When Simone turned from the phone, she nearly jumped out of her skin. Sean was standing silently in the doorway of the drawing room, watching her with that maddening intensity of his.

She hadn't heard him come in. No latch had clicked; no footsteps sounded on the old floorboards. It was one of the quirks of the Dower House—no latches on the doors, just massive old keys, and bolts, most of which were rarely used. They hardly ever locked the place during the day. Often not even at night. This was the Taylor stronghold, after all.

Her sudden pallor didn't go unnoticed.

"Anybody could walk in here," he said coldly, his tone thick with accusation—as if she'd been leaving the place open just to invite disaster. Or him.

"Well, somebody just did," she shot back, recovering her breath. "And gave me the fright of my life."

Sean raised an eyebrow; his gaze fixed on her. "Is that why you've gone so pale?"

"Why else?" she retorted, with more defiance than conviction. "I still feel a bit wobbly, if you must know." She added the last part with quick thinking—maybe she could use it to avoid the dinner after all.

He didn't take the bait. "Sit down. I'll make you a coffee."

The arrogance of it stunned her. As if nothing had happened. As if he hadn't disappeared from her life and left her aching. He was strolling back in like he still owned the place— and her.

"I'll make the coffee," she snapped, glaring at him. "I live here."

"Good. Make one for me too."

Infuriating. And of course he followed her into the kitchen, casually leaning against the table while she moved around him, aware of his presence with every nerve ending. Sean had always had that effect on her—even as a child, she could sense when he was nearby. It was like some invisible current connected them. Unwanted, unshakable.

Chapter Four

She fumbled with the kettle and cups, trying to appear composed. He watched her like a hawk, his expression unreadable, and it made her feel about eight years old again. It was maddening.

"Large or small?" she demanded, turning on him, daring him to make something of it.

His eyes glinted. "Is it a guessing game? Do I get clues?"

"I'm asking what size cup you want," she snapped. "It's not a trick question."

"Large," he said coolly, not even blinking.

She turned away quickly, focusing on the coffee. Her hands were trembling slightly now, and she hated that he noticed.

"You're shaking," he said, a faint note of something—amusement? satisfaction? —in his voice.

"I told you, I'm wobbly," she replied, quick to go on the offensive. "It was a bad fall if you remember. You nearly killed me."

She'd aimed for drama, but all she got in return was a sardonic curve of his lips and those narrowed sapphire eyes.

"Nice try, Simone. But I happen to know you and Cleo conduct most of your lives via the telephone. I doubt she was coaching you through an escape plan. So—what is it this time? Another brilliant scheme brewing? Want to confess now before it blows up in your face?"

"I keep my own counsel," she said crisply. "And I don't do trouble anymore. I think you're confusing me with the teenager you used to patronise."

The moment she said it, she regretted it. Her mouth had always run faster than her sense around Sean. Teenage Simone was the last topic she wanted to open up for analysis.

"Oh, you've changed?" he said smoothly. "Because you look exactly the same to me. And then there's the motorbike. Very 'coming-of-age novel.'"

"I'm sure you're right," she said icily. "But for the record, I'm not involved in any schoolgirl conspiracy tonight. So, you can stop looking for hidden motives and coded signals."

She poured the coffee with a cool elegance that belied the flutter in her chest. Across the room, Sean watched her in silence—still not smiling, still far too close.

She couldn't think why he was here, and his presence was already setting her nerves on edge. He hadn't said why he'd come, and he made no move to collect the coffee she'd made for him. Forced to carry it over herself, she tried to keep her hand steady—but the cup trembled, sloshing hot liquid over her thumb.

She gasped, slammed the cup and saucer onto the table, and shoved her scalded thumb into her mouth.

"Let me see," Sean said sharply.

Before she could object, he caught her hand, inspecting it with a scowl. His blue eyes darkened. "You're not safe to be let out," he muttered, voice taut with frustration.

She snatched her hand away. "I am grown up and in charge of my own life!" she flared, squaring her small shoulders and tossing her head back to meet his gaze.

"So, it would seem," he said, his tone rough. "What's the occasion—waiting for Rogers?"

"What?" His hostility hit her like a slap. What on earth had she done this time?

"Don't play innocent, Simone. It doesn't suit you," he snapped. "Last night you were the same reckless child I've always known—boots, motorbike, a near-death crash. But this morning…" His eyes moved over her, slow and accusing. "You're alone, agitated, obviously expecting someone."

"I've no idea what you're talking about," she said tightly—though the moment he had walked into the room, that had been momentous enough.

His hands shot out and gripped her shoulders, turning her to face him squarely.

"What happened to the plait?"

"I had a shower, the phone rang—"

"And you didn't bother getting dressed again." His voice dipped to a dangerous softness. "All silky-soft like a kitten—and nothing underneath."

Her breath caught. A blush surged up her neck and into her cheeks, and her eyes widened, fierce with shock—and shame. Of course, he mistook it for guilt.

"Let me guess," he bit out. "Rogers called, and now you're waiting for him to drop by. Is that it? And in your own home, no less. Couldn't he take you to the farm? Or does his mother disapprove? While you live on this estate—"

"You arrogant, insulting pig!" she burst out, struggling in his hold. "What gives you the right to storm in here and judge me?"

But his grip only tightened, unyielding. Her red hair tumbled over her shoulders like a warning, and her golden-brown eyes sparked with fury.

"Jeffery isn't like you!" she spat. "He doesn't treat me like some half-formed boy—or a woman who's up for grabs."

"Don't say that," Sean barked, and he gave her a sharp shake.

"Why not?" she panted, on the edge of tears. "You implied it."

God help him, she was beautiful when she was furious.

And utterly, heartbreakingly devastating.

Her words hit like blows—each sharper than the last, slicing through the thin layer of control he still clung to. He hadn't come here to pick a fight. But the moment he saw her—barefoot, flushed, the silk robe clinging to her curves, one freckled shoulder exposed—logic had abandoned him. Along with pride. Along with any sane plan to keep his distance.

All that was left was heat.

And jealousy.

And a gut-deep rage that had nothing to do with her and everything to do with how much he still wanted her.

He was losing it. Losing her.

Because she thought he saw her as casual. Replaceable. A woman "up for grabs."

She didn't know—she couldn't know—that he'd spent the last four years trying to stop himself from coming back and claiming her as his own. Telling himself she was too young. Too close. Too dangerous. Telling himself to wait. Just wait a little longer.

But when his mother had mentioned, so offhandedly, that Simone was seeing Jeffery Rogers "regularly," something inside him had snapped.

She was slipping away.

And suddenly, waiting didn't feel like protection anymore.

It felt like cowardice.

And he hadn't come back to lose her.

"Stop it, Simone," he growled, pulling her against him with more desperation than force. "You had a shock last night. This—" he gestured vaguely between them, breath shallow, heart hammering, "—this isn't helping."

But he didn't let her go.

Not yet.

She let out a short, almost-laugh—bitter, exhausted.

"Astonishing, isn't it? I'm the one who was nearly flattened by a Porsche, and somehow you get to play judge and jury." Her voice wavered. "I was in my own home, minding my own business—and then you show up like a spectre from hell, all fire and fury. And now, this is my fault?"

Sean looked down at her. Something flickered behind the blue—anger, yes, but something else too. Regret?

"I apologise," he said roughly. "It infuriated me to think you were waiting for him. Like that."

"Maybe I was," she said, voice hollow. "Maybe I'm lying."

She turned away, body trembling from more than just rage. He caught her arm again, but as she blinked back tears, his grip slackened. The fire in his eyes cooled to something harder to define.

"Drink your coffee."

"I don't want it now."

"Of course you do." He guided her into a chair, placed the cup in her hands, and sat across from her. "Drink it. Then go back to bed."

"You can't tell me what to do," she muttered, wrapping her hands around the cup.

"I've always told you what to do," he said grimly. "And you always fought me."

It stung more than she wanted to admit. She stared down at the rising steam, cheeks flaming. Was that what she'd always been to him—some tiresome obligation?

"Not for the past four years," she said quietly. "You left, and I grew up. I've got qualifications, responsibilities, direction."

His eyes narrowed, studying her carefully over the rim of his cup.

"Direction?" he echoed. "And what exactly is this laser focus of yours aimed at—work?"

Her chin lifted. "Yes. The estate. My father's work. What else do you think I care about?"

He didn't answer right away, and she hated how his silence made her heart beat faster. Sean had a way of making silence feel like a challenge.

She wasn't sure which unnerved her more: his disapproval—or the fact that a part of her still cared.

His tone had sounded vaguely threatening, and she couldn't forget the look in his eyes the night before. Still, she wasn't about to let him know how much she feared what he could do to her life—how easily he could sweep it all away.

"Working?" she said lightly, lifting her chin. "Not really. I enjoy it, but if I'm honest, I'm far more single-minded about marriage."

His eyes narrowed, sharp and unreadable. "Rogers?"

She hesitated—just long enough to betray her nerves. "Is he the one?" Sean asked coolly. "Or one of many?"

"I'm quite faithful," she breathed, trying to sound dreamy, unbothered. Trying not to show that there was more than one traitor on the estate—and one had just walked into her kitchen.

"Are you?" he said softly.

His gaze burned straight through her, and her heart gave a disloyal flutter. When he reached for her cup and moved it aside, her stomach dropped. His hand slid to her arm, and before she could stop him, he had pulled her to her feet and into his arms.

"Let's test that faithfulness. Kiss me instead of Rogers."

"I—I don't kiss just anyone," she stammered, eyes wide. "I'm not a child anymore."

That only earned her a derisive smile.

"You weren't a child the last time I kissed you," he said smoothly. "And if I recall correctly, you went into a full-blown state of sensual rapture."

She flushed to her hairline. That moment—those few haunting, unforgettable minutes—were the one thing she never allowed herself to remember. Her shame, her humiliation, her undoing.

"Let me go!" she said sharply, going stiff in his arms. But his hand slid down her spine in a slow, lazy stroke, warm even through the silk of her robe. She gasped, her composure cracking.

"Not yet," he murmured. "I'm back, Simone."

"And I'm—what? Fair game?" Her voice broke, and it hurt. God, it hurt. She knew all about his women. He'd always had them. And yet she'd always thought—stupidly, secretly—she might have mattered once.

"Why not?" he said carelessly. "You're conveniently close. And let's not forget—I taught you everything you know. Think of it as a refresher. You can compare it to Jeffery's ardour."

There was no comparison. Not now. Not ever.

He tilted her head, his fingers threading through her hair, and she didn't even resist. His mouth met hers—deep, sure, devastating—and she was lost.

The world fell away. She was spinning, breathless, heart pounding. Her knees gave out and she slumped against him, trembling like a leaf.

"Please, Sean," she whispered when he finally lifted his head, her voice ragged and uncertain.

He looked down at her mockingly, holding her close.

"You said that before, too," he murmured. "But you weren't begging me to stop then."

It was like being slapped with the past. Her shame surged forward, sharp and scorching. She shoved away from him, forcing her unsteady legs to hold.

"I hate you!" she cried, shaking.

"No," he said calmly. "You don't. I'm an addiction, Simone. I always have been. You've grown older, but you're still hooked. Still mine."

"You arrogant, conceited brute! Why are you doing this?"

He raised one infuriating eyebrow. "Because I like knowing you're there when I reach for you."

That did it.

She reached blindly for the coffee, furious enough to throw it at him—but he caught her wrist before she could lift the cup.

"I wouldn't," he warned, voice dangerously low. "You'd miss—and I'd retaliate."

"If you touch me again," she hissed, "I'll tell your mother."

He threw his head back and laughed—laughed at her, openly delighted. "Still a little wild thing. I'm thirty-two, you know. Your father guessed right."

"Old enough to know better! So much for your good breeding. Kindly leave."

He leaned back against the table, sipping his coffee with maddening ease. "Does Rogers never lose his head and kiss you into a trance?"

"Jeffery," she said icily, "is not like you. We have a perfectly civilised relationship."

"Did you say boring?"

"I said leave!" she shouted, pointing furiously to the door.

Sean grinned wide, darkly amused, and finally pushed off from the table.

"If you don't come tonight, Simone," he said over his shoulder, "I'll drive down and fetch you myself."

She stood tall, robe clutched tightly at her throat, jaw firm despite the heat in her cheeks. "I would never let your mother down. I'm very fond of her. And Cleo is my best friend."

"And I'm your worst enemy?" he said, turning just before he stepped out. "Come as you are tonight, Simone. You look wildly feminine. Quite fit to eat."

"Go!"

He went, laughter echoing in his wake as he stepped outside and slammed the car door.

By then, she had collapsed into a chair, trembling with delayed reaction, her legs too weak to hold her any longer.

Sean stepped out into the late morning air, the door thudding shut behind him with a jarring finality. For a moment, he stood motionless, heart hammering like he'd run full tilt.

He touched his lips. Hers still lingered there—warm, familiar, and completely unexpected.

God. He hadn't planned it. Not like that. But the moment he'd seen her in that robe—all softness and shadows, looking nothing like the Simone who wore armour in public—something had cracked. She'd slipped past his defences; past the walls he'd spent four years fortifying.

And she'd kissed him back. Not out of politeness. Not for old times' sake. But like she remembered what they were. What they could be.

Maybe—just maybe—he hadn't lost her after all.

The thought lit something fierce in his chest. Something wild and fragile and dangerously close to hope. He started walking, but the gravel underfoot felt uneven, like the world had shifted ever so slightly on its axis.

Still, he couldn't get ahead of himself. One kiss didn't erase the silence. It didn't undo the hurt. There were years between them—words left unsaid, wounds left open.

And yet…

Her hands had trembled against his chest. She hadn't pulled away.

He let out a long, slow breath. For the first time in what felt like forever, the heaviness inside him eased. Not gone—but lighter.

And for now, that was enough.

Cleo arrived early that afternoon, and Simone was somewhat recovered—her breathing had steadied, at least, as long as she didn't dwell on the turmoil inside. Her dark red hair was tied back in a loose, haphazard bunch when Cleo strode in with purposeful energy.

"That has to go first," Cleo declared with a hint of her brother's familiar forcefulness. "I brought my scissors."

"Are you mad? You're not cutting my hair!" Simone snapped, already bristling at the relentless Taylor pressure.

"Stop that panicky noise," Cleo ordered, settling herself nearby. "I'm only trimming the ends. No topiary work here—I could never manage a peacock, even with hair this thick."

"You're just as bad as Sean," Simone shot back, and Cleo paused, curiosity flickering in her eyes.

"Sean? Has he been by?" Cleo asked casually.

"No," Simone lied, but her cheeks betrayed her, flushing pink. Cleo caught the sign and looked her over sharply in the mirror.

"So, the battle continues?"

"To the death," Simone muttered through gritted teeth.

"I expect you're in love with him," Cleo said easily, as if it were the most natural thing in the world. "I'd like you for a sister-in-law."

"Get rid of Fleur first, and then maybe I'll take a shot at Mark," Simone said, exasperated. The Taylor family's effortless sense of entitlement was infuriating. If it weren't for the fact that she cared for them, they'd have driven her to distraction.

"Sarcasm doesn't become a lady," Cleo said with mock sternness. "Mother says so. Besides, Mark could never control you—he's too sweet."

"Then count me out. And I'm no lady anyway, according to your big brother. I'm just an idiot."

"Well, he's very fond of you," Cleo said, peering at her thoughtfully. "That gives him the right to say what he likes." She brandished the scissors with a grin. "I'd like to cut you a fringe, but I'm not sure I've got the skill."

"You have no skill at all," Simone protested as the scissors flicked dangerously close. Right now, Cleo felt just as insufferable as Sean. Why was she tangled up with the Taylors at all? She ducked her head away.

"Have some faith, will you?" Cleo hissed. "And hold still. Tonight, I'm getting a bit of 'own back.' Fleur's after Sean now."

"What?" Simone froze, eyes wide.

Cleo nodded with satisfaction. "Turns out she knew him in London. She's buttering him up good and proper. If at first, you don't succeed… Meanwhile, Mark's clueless about the undercurrents. Sean's keeping it polite. Mother's anxious, and I'm furious. You, my dear, will restore the balance by turning Fleur green with envy."

"I can't do anything," Simone whispered, stunned.

"We'll see," Cleo said with a sly smile, snipping carefully at the ends of Simone's deep red hair. Simone sat quietly, hoping for the best but too overwhelmed by the news to protest.

Had Fleur been the woman in London? Simone knew Sean had told her once, in that cruel, mocking way he had, that when he left, she was still just a child of eighteen. The thought gnawed at her.

"I don't think I'm coming," she muttered miserably.

"You are. And if you don't, I'll come and fetch you myself." Cleo's tone left no room for argument. Sean had already made his threats, and she knew he was neither slow nor patient.

"But I've nothing to wear."

"Then we'll alter something you have. When you're feeling better, we'll go into town and outfit you properly. You never spend on yourself—you probably have a fortune stashed away somewhere. Time to use it."

Simone gave a wry smile. "It's for my old age."

Cleo caught her hand and studied the palm. "You'll marry a rich man, have a houseful of children with red hair and vivid blue eyes. You'll live in a grand home, with a big black dog."

"And I'll tell Jeffery all this," Simone said with a half-smile, "Though unfortunately, his eyes are brown."

"That lets him off the hook," Cleo said crisply, sweeping into the wardrobe. "Show me what you've got."

Simone hesitated but pulled out a beautiful caftan she'd never worn.

"What's this?" Cleo asked, pouncing on it.

Simone explained, "I bought it on impulse for a dance with Jeffery."

"And?"

"In the end, I chickened out. It was a farmers' do, and I went in the obligatory cotton dress instead. Even that brought disapproval from Mrs. Rogers."

"Jeffery's mother doesn't like cotton dresses?" Cleo giggled.

"Not if they have a scooped back. Too daring, apparently."

Cleo lifted the caftan, its milky coffee colour and autumn-leaf pattern perfect against Simone's red hair.

"You paid a lot for this," Cleo said suspiciously. "Are you serious about Jeffery Rogers?"

"I probably will marry him," Simone snapped, the sting of Sean's taunts fresh in her mind.

"What a mistake. Jeffery's too tame by half." Cleo sighed, unpacking her heated rollers. "Tomorrow you can go to a hairdresser, but tonight, we improvise. And Simone," she warned, voice low and firm, "there's no going back after this. Riding boots are for riding, jeans are for work, and at all other times, you will wear proper clothes. I won't have you turning up inadequately dressed again."

Simone blushed, but Cleo was already busy with the rollers. The morning's events—especially Sean's arms around her—sent a shiver through her skin. She must be mad. Sean was good at everything, including that—just as good as he was at everything else. She knew he'd kissed hundreds of women senseless. It infuriated her, especially remembering how he'd laughed as he left. Did he think he could amuse himself with her while he was here? She was no longer gullible. He'd have to be taught a very severe lesson.

Chapter Five

As Simone dressed for Sean's homecoming dinner, a tight coil of nerves settled in her stomach. She had told herself she could face him calmly, dismissively even. But he had already proven she couldn't. Her hands shook slightly as she fastened her bracelet, and a sick flutter rose in her chest.

She walked to her bedroom window and gazed across the park toward the hall. It gleamed with light, every window ablaze, just as it always had—but tonight the familiar view filled her with more dread than comfort. That house had once meant safety, belonging. Now, it shimmered like a mirage—beautiful and untouchable.

Four years ago, it had looked just like this. Late summer, the gardens sweet with the scent of lilies and roses, warm air full of dusk sounds. Sean had taken her to dinner that night—alone. Not with Cleo or Mark. Just the two of them. And she had been certain it meant something. A shift. A recognition that she wasn't a child anymore.

She'd finished school. She was in college. He no longer visited as he used to, not with little gifts or indulgent grins. In the past, he'd appeared for birthdays, school prize giving's—always the warm, watchful guardian with the dazzling smile. But that night, at eighteen, she had dared to believe he saw her differently.

He had danced with her, his arm strong around her waist, his touch gentle but firm. Once, she'd been sure she felt his lips brush her hair—but when she looked up in soft, astonished hope, he only smiled and asked if she was tired.

She wasn't tired. She was enchanted.

Afterward, he had parked at the hall but walked her home across the lawns and gravel paths, under a sky heavy with stars.

"Oh, look!" she had whispered, stopping by the fence. "The moon's out."

It glowed, low and full, painting silver across the trees. An owl swept past, wide wings carving the night.

"There's a barn owl," she breathed. "At first, I thought it was a bat."

Sean stood close, smiling faintly. "After this glorious hair?" he murmured, brushing a hand down the fall of her curls, letting his eyes follow the motion. Her breath caught. For the first time, she felt truly beautiful.

His fingers lingered. Her body swayed toward his without thought. Her face lifted instinctively, full of longing.

"Simone."

One word. Quiet. Firm. His hands closed on her shoulders, holding her still. She shivered in the warm air, heart crumbling at the sternness in his voice.

"What did I do?" she whispered, wounded. "I'm not a child anymore, Sean. Don't you want to kiss me goodnight?"

Sean's throat worked. He stared at her upturned face—the softness of her mouth, the flicker of fear and longing in her eyes—and knew, with sickening certainty, that if he kissed her again, he wouldn't stop. Not tonight. Not when she looked at him like that, as if the very axis of her world tilted in his direction.

"The way your boyfriends do?" he said roughly. "I'm not one of them."

"I know," she said softly, lowering her eyes. "They don't really kiss me… not properly."

His heart cracked. God help those boys, he thought bitterly. They didn't even know what they'd missed.

"How foolish of them," he said with a tight, mocking smile. "What a missed opportunity."

"I don't let them," she said, still watching the ground. "I don't like it."

He stilled.

Then, voice low: "You expect me to believe that? You just asked me to kiss you."

"That's different." Her voice cracked. "I belong to you, Sean."

"Don't say that."

The words twisted in his gut. Her innocence, her certainty—it undid him. He reached for her face without thinking, brushing a tear from her cheek, but another followed, and another. Her pain was real. So was the truth of what she'd just said.

"It's true," she said brokenly. "It always has been."

He gathered her into his arms, his fingers threading into the softness of her hair, drawing her close with a tenderness he hadn't let himself feel in years.

"Don't cry, Simone," he whispered. "You'll grow out of this. You'll move on."

"I am grown up," she insisted. "And I don't want to move on."

A muscle jumped in his jaw. God, she didn't know. She couldn't know what she was offering, what she was tempting him to become. She was eighteen. Legal. Lovely. So heartbreakingly willing.

But not ready. Not for him. And not for what he wanted to do to her.

For a moment, he looked at her with something like pain—a split-second of struggle in his eyes.

He'd fought it for years. But she'd bloomed under his nose, turned from wild child into something exquisite, something dangerous. And now here she stood, asking for everything he'd denied himself.

He should walk away.

Instead, he kissed her.

His lips claimed hers.

At first, it felt restrained, almost like a warning disguised as tenderness. He told himself he could control it. That he could give her this one perfect moment without losing himself.

But the second she sighed against him—melted into him like she belonged—something snapped.

Desire surged through him, too powerful to suppress. His restraint crumbled. His arms locked around her, pulling her tightly to him, mouth moving over hers with hungry urgency. Her lips parted for him, innocent and eager, and he kissed her like he'd dreamed of doing for years.

He felt her shiver, felt her fingertips slide into his hair, felt the raw need in her body answering the hunger in his. It shook him—this wild, aching truth. He wanted her. Now. Here. Completely.

He could take her.

God help him, she would let him.

But that was exactly why he had to stop.

With a groan torn from his chest, Sean wrenched himself away.

"No," he breathed, voice hoarse. "Enough, Simone."

She blinked, dazed, lips swollen, eyes luminous. "Will you come for me tomorrow?"

"Tomorrow, I leave for London," he said, turning from her before the look in her eyes could break him. "I'm taking over the office there."

"You… you're not coming back?" Her voice was small. Crushed.

He swallowed hard. "Not for some time."

Silence stretched behind him like a wound.

"But—what about us?" she whispered.

He turned sharply. "Us? There is no us, Simone."

The words tasted like ash. But he had to say them. He had to break it. Better her pain now than a ruined life later.

"You're a child," he went on coldly. "I helped raise you. And I think I've borne that burden rather admirably, don't you?"

Her face crumpled.

"You kissed me," she whispered. "You made love to me."

"I kissed you," he said flatly. "On your birthday. After an emotional appeal I should've resisted. It was a mistake. One final lesson. You can now ride, dance, swim—and kiss. That concludes my responsibilities."

She flinched as if he'd struck her.

"There's someone in London," she whispered, her voice unsteady. "Isn't there?"

"A woman," he said—lied—forcing a smile that felt like it might split him open. "Someone real. A grown-up. Not an impulsive girl chasing dreams."

There was no one else. There never had been. There never would be. Simone was the only woman he wanted—but she was too young, too unformed, still dancing on the edge of the world while he already lived inside it.

"I'm eighteen!" she cried. "And I love you."

He clenched his fists, nails biting into his palms. "You're eighteen with your whole life ahead of you. Stop dreaming, Simone. Go out there and live it. One day you'll meet someone who's right for you."

But it won't be me.

Because if I stay—I'll take you. And I'll never be able to let you go.

She stared at him one last time, eyes wide with disbelief, betrayal written in every line of her face. Then she turned—and ran.

He watched her disappear down the lane, fists rigid at his sides, chest heaving like a man who'd just staggered out of a burning house.

And for one blinding second, he almost chased her.

But he didn't.

Because he was already on fire.

That night, she cried until she couldn't breathe. And in the morning, she told herself she hated him.

She buried every memory—except the bitterness.

And now, four years later, he was back. And she was going to his homecoming dinner. But it wasn't the same. She wasn't the same. The foolish girl who had believed in dreams was gone. Now she knew exactly who Sean Taylor was—and she would humiliate him if she could.

She learned more at the homecoming dinner than she'd expected—and she didn't even have to try. The revelations came uninvited, like whispers behind half-closed doors. Branlow Hall was ablaze with light, every downstairs window glowing amber, the grand house exuding warmth and welcome. But Simone stood outside herself, fluttery and anxious. The place she'd once felt so at ease in now seemed unfamiliar, as if the walls had shifted in her absence. Nothing felt the same. But that wasn't the Hall—it was her.

The tension twisting through her had nothing to do with the glowing chandeliers or polished silver. It was inside her, a nervous tangle of memory, pride, and sharp-edged awareness. She had the unsettling sense of being part of a scheme—one that had started as a harmless bid to unsettle Fleur but had somehow shifted focus. Sean was involved now. And making plans around Sean Taylor was like lighting a match near dry grass. Sooner or later, it would burn.

She arrived with her father, who looked resplendent in a well-cut dark suit. He was still striking even with silver in his hair, and she was always proud of him—especially tonight, when she needed his quiet strength to steady her nerves. She clung to his arm as they entered, trying not to show how off-balance she felt. Tonight, she wasn't the girl-next-door or the honorary little sister of the family. No—tonight she was, as Cleo had gleefully declared, dressed to kill. And that, in itself, felt like dangerous territory.

The heated rollers had transformed her thick red hair, coaxing back its natural wave. Instead of the fringe Cleo had threatened, it was parted cleanly down the middle and swept off her face in a cascade that caught the light like polished copper. Her makeup was subtle but masterful—barely there, yet enough to highlight her creamy complexion and draw attention to her honey-brown eyes. They looked almost too large for her delicate face, luminous and uncertain. The caftan was a quiet triumph, drifting over her frame like silk on water, the colour of milky coffee with an autumn-leaf border that moved as she did. Cleo had been right about that too.

Lady Vivian greeted them with delight, clearly relieved by the reinforcements.

"Henry! So lovely to see you. And Simone, my dear—you look beautiful."

It drew every eye in the room. Simone could feel the weight of their glances, none more searing than the one that came from across the room—brilliant blue and unreadable. Sean looked at her. Looked through her. Then, maddeningly, he only smiled and inclined his head politely.

"Look at her! Just look!" Cleo materialised at Simone's elbow and hissed under her breath like an overexcited stage manager. But Simone had already seen what Cleo wanted her to: Fleur, statuesque and composed, standing very much at Sean's side. Wherever he moved, she moved. It was subtle, but Simone saw it for what it was. Possessiveness disguised as elegance.

"She's been stuck to him since he walked in," Cleo growled. "Like she's part of his outfit. I swear, if she could wear him as a scarf, she would. It's disgraceful. Mummy's mortified."

But what Simone wanted to know was: What was Sean doing? Was he accepting Fleur's attention? Encouraging it? Had it been her he went to in London, all those years ago, right after… after that night? If so, what had happened to cool it all down into this curious triangle where Fleur was now engaged to Mark?

Fleur was everything Simone was not—tall, poised, camera-perfect. A society girl turned model, with an effortless way of gliding through a room as though it belonged to her. Her platinum hair, swept up in an elaborate twist, gleamed like moonlight. The black lace dress hugged her slim figure like couture; her beauty the kind that made a room fall silent.

"She's stunning," Simone admitted quietly. "She looks like she belongs in a magazine. I feel like I've come in fancy dress."

"She's a hard-faced, social-climbing nightmare," Cleo snapped. "Just remember—she's your target. You, my love, are the most beautiful woman in this room. You've got youth, charm, and that maddening red hair men lose their minds over. And stop blushing. It's not chic."

"I'll stop blushing when you stop sounding like an overzealous fairy godmother," Simone whispered, flushing deeper. "Just let me pretend things are normal."

"Well," Cleo sighed with exaggerated patience, "they're not."

Simone could only agree—tonight was anything but normal. She caught a glimpse of herself in a gilt-framed mirror as she moved through the room and nearly stopped in her tracks.

For a moment, she didn't recognise herself. The girl in the reflection looked too polished, too composed to be her. Her wide, dark-fringed eyes filled her face—uncertain, a little wild, as though she might bolt at any second. It made her look fragile, on the brink. But sexy? No. She could find nothing remotely seductive in that panicked expression—and to her immense relief, that felt safer somehow.

Then Sean appeared behind her like a shadow, his presence as unmistakable as ever. He handed her a glass, his vivid blue gaze catching hers in the mirror.

"It's champagne, Simone," he said quietly. "Think you can handle it?"

She turned swiftly to face him, her chin lifting. "I can take anything."

His mouth twitched, eyes roaming her face with unsettling precision. "So, it seems. Clearly, Rogers's influence has made a woman of you. What a pity he's not here to witness the transformation. Still—" he leaned in slightly "—you can always count on me."

She gave a short, sharp laugh. "Ha. Counting on you is something I outgrew a long time ago. I've no idea why I ever thought you were trustworthy in the first place. Now that I'm an adult, I can see you clearly—and you don't look particularly dependable."

"This is my homecoming dinner," he said smoothly, voice low with warning. "If you're about to perform one of your little dramas, save it."

"I do not perform," she replied icily. "And as for this dinner, I'll be polite. That's the full extent of my goodwill."

"You'll sit beside me," he told her.

"I'll sit wherever your mother places me."

"She's already taken precautions. She's seated you beside me—because she knows you can't be trusted."

She shot him a glare, eyes narrowed. "Are you suggesting I'll make a scene?"

"Only if I kiss you," he murmured. "And I'd rather not cause a public incident. I wouldn't want the family overhearing your sighs of rapture. You know, Simone—" he leaned in just slightly, his voice still velvet and cruel, "—I've only kissed you twice, and both times you melted like sugar. Makes one wonder how you behave with more regular… company."

There was nothing subtle about that, and she should have known better than to expect restraint. She opened her mouth to retort, but the words died—along with the colour in her cheeks. She blushed furiously, which only seemed to confirm the worst of his assumptions.

Chapter Six

Mercifully, Mark appeared just then with Fleur gliding at his side like a runway model with territorial rights.

"Simone, you look absolutely beautiful. I'm stunned," Mark said, lifting her hand with a theatrical kiss that made her laugh and momentarily forget herself. Mark hadn't disappeared for four years. Mark hadn't crushed her heart. Mark, she could breathe around.

Fleur, however, was not amused.

"Why, of course," she said sweetly. "The little girl from the estate. I didn't recognise you without your plait."

"It's detachable," Simone replied with a bright smile. "I left it hanging in the bathroom."

Mark laughed out loud, and Fleur's expression cooled by several degrees. But before Simone could enjoy her small triumph, the dinner gong rang—and Sean claimed her arm with a grip firm enough to make her stumble slightly.

"Behave yourself," he murmured, steering her away from Mark and Fleur with far too much authority. "I will not be put down."

"Oh, my, my," she muttered, flashing a brilliant smile at Lady Vivian, who looked grateful—and perhaps a touch impressed. "I'll file that one under delusions of grandeur."

"Just behave beautifully," he said, tightening his grip just enough to make her wince. "You look tiny and delectable. It would be a shame to ruin the illusion. Twice in one day, Simone. You've managed to stun me twice."

She leaned in a fraction closer, still smiling for the watching eyes. "I want to tell you something."

"By all means."

"I really don't like you."

"Tell me again," he said under his breath, "when no one's watching."

He paused, raking his eyes down the length of her again, and something in his expression turned serious. Too serious.

"You've definitely... developed possibilities."

Her heart gave a jolt. "W-what do you mean?"

"I mean," he said slowly, "surely this transformation is for my benefit. You've never been very good at subtlety, Simone. I saw Cleo's satisfaction when you walked in. I

saw Mother's surprise when the goose turned out to be a swan. So, I must assume—
this is for me."

He leaned in, voice soft, amused, and maddeningly sure. "Thank you, Simone. I'm
touched."

He handed her courteously to her seat, and Simone sank into it with carefully composed
poise. She was relieved to see Cleo at her left—some small comfort, even if she had
Sean on her right. Directly opposite sat Mark and Fleur, the latter watching her with
coal-black eyes that glittered like polished obsidian. Lady Vivian looked as if she might
leap from her chair at any moment, and down at the far end of the table, her father and
Sir Michael were already deep in conversation about the fifty-acre field, completely
oblivious to the storm gathering at the other end.

Simone should have known Sean would spot the game. Nothing much escaped him.
But what had he meant earlier—developing possibilities? She couldn't stop trembling.
Her hands felt weightless, her throat dry. Had he asked to be seated next to her?

Mark broke the silence, his tone light as they began the first course. "I take it you've
left things in good hands in Canada, Sean?"

"The best," Sean replied smoothly. "Alex Lewis has taken over in London. I stayed
there long enough to get everything running. Now I can finally settle down here."

Simone felt a spark of something—hope? panic? —but it died before it could take shape.

"So that's where you disappeared to? Canada!" Fleur's voice slinked into the space like
perfume. She gave Sean a soft smile, the kind that expected history to answer for itself.
"It's been ages since you and I had dinner together."

A beat of silence fell brittle as glass. Simone noticed the subtle shift in Mark's
expression—his mouth tightened, and something in his eyes dimmed. Saddened to
death, she thought. Cleo nudged her lightly, but Simone kept her eyes on her plate,
finishing her melon and listlessly pushing the cherries through their syrup. So, it had
been Fleur. Whatever had split them up, the damage still lingered.

Mark forced a brittle laugh. "Does this mean I'm second choice?"

Nobody answered. Fleur's silence was oddly damning, and Sean's eyes turned sharp and
glinting.

"Well?" he said coldly. "Does it?"

Even Fleur flushed. "Of course not," she said, too quickly. "What a thing to say. I'm
engaged to Mark, Sean. You disappeared. You missed out."

Her voice tried for playfulness, but there was a coy edge beneath it, and Sean responded
with a shrug—dismissive and chilling. It was unlike him. Too calm, too distant.

"I'm sure I'll survive."

So, he was angry. Had he really expected Fleur to wait for him? Had her engagement
been a shock? Simone's stomach twisted. Mark looked blindsided, and the hush around
the table was thick with tension—unheard of in Branlow Hall's lively dining room.

Two brothers in love with the same woman. Of course, Simone thought bleakly. What else could go wrong?

She couldn't seem to stop pushing her cherries in circles. Her eyes stung and her appetite was gone. Was that Sean's plan now? To distract himself with her? Was she just a convenient amusement?

Then, out of nowhere, Sean reached across and jabbed the cherries with his dessert fork, lifting them clean off her plate and popping them into his mouth.

Simone blinked. Even she was startled.

Fleur gave a strangled little laugh. "What a thing to do!"

"It's common knowledge," Sean said coolly, "that Simone doesn't like cherries in port. She's too polite to say."

That drew more attention than she liked. And worse—he hadn't even bothered with 'Miss Symons'. Not tonight. Just 'Simone', as if she belonged to him in some unspoken, outdated way.

Fleur leaned in, voice like sugared venom. "But to eat them off her plate… I mean!"

Cleo pounced. "Simone's always been Sean's girl," she said, all innocence. "He covers for her every time."

"I see," Fleur replied smoothly. "A family pet."

Cleo didn't miss a beat. "No. Just Sean's pet."

Simone's face flamed, mortified. She hadn't realised Cleo's revenge mission would go this far. But Mark no longer looked stricken, and Lady Vivian was smiling again. Maybe it was worth the embarrassment. Maybe Cleo's little charade was actually working— lessening the sting for Sean or at least shifting the spotlight from Fleur.

"Eat your fish, pet," Sean murmured in her ear, and her whole body went rigid.

She turned her head slightly, voice a hiss. "I will not be your scapegoat, Sean."

He arched a brow, still smiling for the room. "Temper, temper. I thought you were here to dazzle me, not bite."

"If you think I came here for you, then you're even more arrogant than I thought."

"Hmm," he mused quietly, sipping his wine. "Well, you are dazzling. So, who, then? Rogers? Or was it just Cleo's idea of a makeover? She has such fun with her little projects."

"I hope you realise," she said, forcing another brittle smile, "that your wonderful sister thinks you're a complete cad."

He smiled back lazily, as if the insult merely amused him. "Cleo has excellent taste."

The rest of the evening passed more smoothly than expected—at least on the surface. Fleur, though still attached to Sean like a brooch, was just a shade more subdued, and Cleo whispered to Simone with smug satisfaction that it counted as a small but meaningful victory.

Simone wasn't so sure. She had been acutely aware of Sean's sardonic gaze tracking her all night, amused, assessing, unreadable. Of course, he knew exactly what Cleo had orchestrated—how could he not? And though Cleo was determined to pin everything on Fleur, Simone quietly blamed Sean. He took what he wanted—always had. Even if it meant betraying his own brother. If Fleur kept hovering, Simone wouldn't be surprised if Sean simply walked off with her one night without so much as a backward glance.

She sipped her champagne steadily, determined not to care. Eventually, the alcohol caught up to her, a heady warmth rushing through her limbs and making the chandelier above her seem to sway just slightly.

It was Sean who put a stop to it. He appeared beside her without warning, reached for her glass, and downed the rest in one quick gulp.

"That's enough for you," he said dryly. "Your eyes are going crossed."

"I'm not a child," she snapped, reaching to reclaim the glass. Her sleeve slipped back in the movement, revealing a dark bruise already blooming across her forearm.

"Hell." Sean caught her wrist before she could pull the fabric back down, his expression changing in an instant. "How many more of these have you got?"

"Quite a few," she said airily, the haze of champagne softening her sarcasm. "They seem to be multiplying by the hour."

"You should see William Stokes again," he said seriously, his voice lacking its usual mockery. There was concern there—genuine, maybe—and that threw her more than anything else. She swayed slightly, and he steadied her with a firm grip, tucking her into his side.

"Shall I take you home?"

"No fear." She tilted her head up to meet his gaze, her eyes luminous with challenge. If he was about to parade her in front of Fleur like some wounded possession, he had another thing coming. "From now on, I protect myself."

That got the old, lazy smile. "Whoever hurts you, Simone, it won't be me."

"I have bruises that beg to differ," she retorted, lifting her arm just as Fleur approached—too quickly, catching the last part of the conversation.

"Oh, my goodness," Fleur gasped, eyes narrowing. "How did that happen?"

"Sean," Simone said sweetly, her voice lilting with champagne-induced mischief. "He bruises easily. Bit of a beast when roused."

Fleur blanched. Simone realised with sudden clarity that perhaps the beloved bête noire hadn't heard about the accident. A delicious, reckless urge rose in her throat.

She opened her mouth to elaborate, but Sean was faster.

"Cool it," he warned under his breath, his tone like frost.

"I don't recall asking for your opinion," Simone said tartly. She glanced sideways at Fleur.

"Does she always behave like this?" Fleur asked witheringly.

"Rank hath its privileges," Simone replied with a dazzling smile, leaning slightly against Sean. "Being Sean's girl comes with a few perks. He lets me get away with murder."

"You're surely asking for it," he muttered darkly, tightening his grip on her arm. Then, louder: "I'm taking her home, Henry."

Her father looked up from across the room, only half-registering the exchange. "I'll be along soon," he said vaguely.

He had no idea what kind of danger she was in—and ignored all her silent little warnings. Cleo, meanwhile, was grinning like a Cheshire cat, and Mark's gaze bounced warily between everyone, trying to make sense of the undercurrents.

"I hope you feel better tomorrow, dear," Lady Vivian said kindly, pecking Simone on the cheek. "Thank you for coming even when you weren't well. So good of her, wasn't it, Sean?"

"Angelic," he said, his voice perfectly smooth. "She never fails to surprise me."

His mother beamed, oblivious to the ice beneath his words. But Simone wasn't. Right then, all she wanted was to bolt, to vanish into the quiet of her own house and scrub the whole night from memory. But Sean's grip was like iron, and she knew better than to fight him here, with so many watching.

There would be no escape—yet.

In the car, Simone's champagne-fuelled euphoria evaporated as quickly as the night air rushing through the slightly cracked window. Alone with Sean, the silence was thick with tension. There was a storm under his skin—she could feel it—and for all her bravado, she suddenly felt small and wary.

Still, she refused to be afraid of him.

"This is the second time tonight my father's thrown me to the wolves," she muttered icily.

"Wolf," Sean corrected curtly. "Singular. Me. That's how you see me, isn't it, Simone?"

He never used her name unless he was angry. That alone made her glance sharply at his profile, starkly handsome and carved from stone. But she wasn't going to back down now.

"You knew her before," she said, her voice a quiet accusation. "She was your mistress. Mark is shattered."

"So, you've made me the villain again." His voice was cold, bitter. "As if I've always robbed him of everything? The truth, Simone, is that he stole her from me. I had her—and now he's got her."

His open admission shook her. But she wouldn't let it show. Not this time.

"You're better at everything. It's about time Mark got something over you." Her voice wavered. "If he managed to win while you were off playing empire-builder in Canada, then maybe it serves you right." She paused. "Anyway, it's none of my business."

"No," he snapped. "It's not. So, keep out of it. With any luck, I'll have you home in five minutes."

"And you're not coming in," she flung back, her voice sharp.

"I don't waste time on idiots," he bit out.

"Or farmhands," she added, unable to stop herself.

The car screeched to a halt in front of her house, the tyres snarling on gravel. Before she could blink, he turned toward her, eyes blazing.

"Or farmhands," he repeated darkly, "no matter how beautiful. Or how willing."

And then he grabbed her.

She barely had time to gasp before he pulled her into his arms, his fingers tangling roughly in her hair. His mouth crashed down on hers—angry, forceful, possessive. It wasn't a kiss. It was a punishment.

He didn't give her space to breathe, let alone resist. Her head was forced back, her lips bruised beneath his as he devoured her without apology, without restraint. Her heart thundered wildly in her chest, and for a terrifying moment, she couldn't tell fear from excitement.

When his hand slid over her breast, she trembled. He must have felt it—how could he not? But still, he didn't stop. His fingers moved with infuriating expertise, coaxing her body to life even as she tried to push him away.

Then his mouth lifted, but his hand stayed, palm curved around her. "Isn't this what you expected?" he rasped. "The grand finale to your little performance? You and Cleo dressed you up to lure me away from Fleur and protect Mark. Mission accomplished."

She shook her head, mute with shock.

"I'm glad you're not trying to lie out loud," he muttered, voice low and dangerous. "You've always been a terrible liar. Was the plan for me to take you to bed?"

"No!" she choked out at last, but her voice was barely more than a whisper.

"Oh, don't talk like that." Her fingers fluttered to his mouth, but he caught them in a hard grip, pinning her hand.

"I want to take you to bed," he said through clenched teeth. "Do you understand that, Simone? Frustration's a powerful thing. And you… you're a tempting little distraction."

She stared at him, wide-eyed and trembling, her entire body stiff with panic and humiliation.

He threw the door open with a sharp motion and practically shoved her into the cold night.

"Go home, Simone," he snapped. "If you weren't so damn tiny and beautiful, I'd give you a good hiding. Next time you play this game—be ready for what you get."

Her temper flared as she stepped out of the car, spinning to face him.

"For your information," she said, voice clear and cutting, "this dress was bought for a night out with Jeffrey. I just happened to wear it tonight. And yes—he thought I was beautiful, too."

She took a step closer; eyes locked on his.

"But when you think that again—keep your hands to yourself. I'm taken, Sean."

Then she turned on her heel and walked away, not giving him the satisfaction of seeing her shake.

Sean watched her go, her spine straight, chin high, every step radiating fury and pride. The hem of that damned dress swayed against her legs, and he had to grip his steering wheel with both hands to keep from calling her back.

She was fire, defiance, and heartbreak all at once.

Her words still rang in his ears—*keep your hands to yourself… I'm taken.*

She hadn't yelled them. Hadn't sobbed. She'd just said them—cool, sharp, and sure.

And that, somehow, hurt more.

He scrubbed a hand over his face. Christ, what the hell was he doing?

He hadn't meant to touch her. Not like that. But one look at her in that dress, one spark of the old Simone beneath the woman she was becoming, and everything in him had gone to war.

He'd tried to push her away. Protect her. But all he'd done was hurt her. Again.

And now she was walking back into someone else's life. Into someone else's arms.

Still, he didn't stop her.

Because if he did—if he let himself reach for her now—he wouldn't let go.

And he didn't trust himself not to burn them both to the ground.

Inside her room, she stood trembling, horrified by how deeply the moment had affected her. She felt violated, ashamed—and worse, still faintly exhilarated. Her body burned with the imprint of his touch, her breasts tingling under her gown. She sank onto the stool in front of her dressing table and stared into the mirror like she'd never seen herself before.

She looked… undone. Flushed, dishevelled, kissed senseless.

Sean had treated her with open contempt, made her feel cheap, like she was nothing but a substitute for Fleur. And yet—he'd called her beautiful. He'd wanted her.

What a mess.

She undressed quickly, flicked off the light, and crawled into bed with her heart still pounding. When her father came home and tapped on her door, she barely managed to sound sleepy.

"You all right, love?" he asked from the hallway.

"Just tired," she called. "Goodnight."

"That's a relief. I figured you must be fine. Otherwise, Sean would've stayed with you."

She bit her hand to muffle the hysterical laugh that bubbled up. Stayed with her? He'd practically thrown her out of the car. He'd kissed her like he hated her—because he wanted her.

She cried then. Hot, silent tears slipping down her cheeks in the dark.

Even so, as her breath finally slowed and sleep crept in, one truth lingered like an ember in her chest.

He had called her beautiful. Even if it was in anger. Even if it was a lie.

She would make that truth her shield. She would stay neat. Petite. Unshakeable. Fleur might be tall and elegant, the perfect society woman—but Simone had fire. She would learn to control it. Use it.

And next time Sean looked at her, she'd make sure he regretted everything.

Chapter Seven

Cleo had a raging headache the next morning—too much champagne, according to Sir Michael, who sounded vaguely amused as he put Simone through to Cleo's room.

Simone, however, wasn't amused. Her nerves were frayed. She hadn't had the nerve to face the aftermath of last night in person, not with the lingering sense of Sean's fury still haunting her. If Cleo wanted to ride, she'd have to drag herself to the stables like everyone else.

'I can't come,' Cleo groaned. 'My head's splitting in two.'

'You're in the safest place possible,' Simone said, tart and tight. 'If you crawl out of that bed, Sean might finish the job.'

'Was it really that bad? He looked furious when he came back.'

'Not as furious as he was earlier.' Simone's voice had gone cold. 'Count me out of your schemes from now on. He saw through us instantly, and it didn't do the slightest bit of good.'

'None,' Cleo admitted miserably. 'When he got back, he charmed Fleur right off her feet. That's why I drank so much—watching her simper and preen while he smiled like nothing had happened.'

Simone closed her eyes for a second, the image hitting her like a punch to the stomach. Sean smiling at Fleur. Sean forgiving her. Sean possibly… taking her back.

'So, there you are,' Simone snapped, her voice brittle.

'And here I stay,' Cleo muttered. 'He can't reach me here.'

'Don't bank on that,' Simone said darkly. 'If Sean wants something, he gets it—no matter who's in the way.'

That truth tasted bitter on her tongue, and she had no desire to dwell on it. So, she saddled Stardust and rode hard, ignoring the ache in her body, the stiffness in her limbs, the throbbing reminder of last night's humiliations. She needed the rhythm of the ride, the wind on her face, something—anything—to scrub Sean from her thoughts.

But he was everywhere.

In the turn of the lane where he'd once laughed at her hat. In the wood where he'd first taught her to jump. And now, worse than ever, in Fleur's orbit—orbiting back toward him with her painted perfection and model's poise.

Simone was unsaddling Stardust, brushing her down with a little more force than necessary, when Fleur appeared in the yard, dressed head to toe in the sort of pristine riding gear meant to be seen, not used. It was almost comical—like a fashion shoot had wandered onto the farm.

Simone, by contrast, had kept to her neat new image without fuss. White blouse under a navy jumper, breeches that actually fit, and boots that gleamed with polish. She was neat and petite, as Sean had once said, though today the words felt like an old bruise pressing against her ribs.

Fleur barely glanced at her. Her eyes were on Stardust.

'Oh, leave that one saddled. I'll take it out.'

Simone didn't even pause in removing the bridle. 'Sorry. She's mine.'

Fleur blinked. 'Excuse me?'

'This horse,' Simone said quietly, 'is mine. I bought her, reared her, trained her. She's not on offer.'

'Well, I've never heard such cheek,' Fleur huffed. 'Just because you've picked it out for yourself—'

'Her,' Simone corrected again. 'And no—I didn't pick *her*. She's personal property.'

'I'm amazed they let you keep it here. A horse eats a lot.'

'Like a horse,' Simone agreed flatly. 'I'm sure Jerry will help you find something more suitable.'

'I can manage on my own, thank you. I'll take that one.' Fleur pointed at Royal, who promptly bared his teeth in her direction.

Jerry appeared at just the right moment. 'Not that one, miss. He's a stallion and a mean one. Wouldn't trust him with anyone but Mr Sean.'

'Oh, he's good at everything, isn't he?' Fleur said dreamily.

Simone's jaw tightened. Her spine locked. She didn't need to turn around to know that Sean was there—she felt it. The way the atmosphere shifted, the way Fleur preened, the way Jerry suddenly became deferential.

Sean strolled into the yard like he owned it. Maybe he did.

He smiled briefly at Fleur, then looked at Simone—really looked—and something unreadable flickered in his eyes.

'Surely you're not going riding?' he asked.

'I've been,' Simone replied, not meeting his gaze. She went back to unsaddling Stardust, refusing to acknowledge the warmth she still felt for a man who had left her bruised— literally and otherwise.

'Ignoring the bruises?'

'They'll fade,' she said. 'Everything does, eventually.'

He looked like he wanted to say something else, but Fleur was hovering with her sparkling smile and her endless legs, and Jerry was already muttering about the horses again.

Simone watched with narrowed eyes as Sean took the saddle from her hands and carried it into the tack room himself. His hand brushed Stardust's neck gently, intimately.

'She's Simone's, aren't you, my beauty?' he murmured, running his hand down the mare's flank.

The possessive note in his voice made Simone's breath catch. For a second it was as if he was talking about her, not the horse.

Fleur's eyes narrowed. Her smile froze. Simone didn't even bother to return it. She had the message, clear as day: *some things were not hers to take.*

And yet… Simone knew exactly what Sean was doing. The charm, the subtle slights, the theatrics—it was all part of a performance. He was baiting Fleur. Drawing her back in. And Simone? She was a prop.

'Can I ride with you, Sean?' Fleur asked, sugar-sweet.

'I think not,' he replied, eyes on Royal. 'Today's ride is going to be hard work.'

Simone stood rigid as Royal snorted and danced under Sean's hold. The stallion tested him, challenged him, but Sean was immovable. And when he cleared the high fence with a single, breathtaking leap, Simone felt something knot up hard in her chest.

God, he was *magnificent.* And God, she *hated* him.

By the time he returned to the yard and spoke to Fleur in that low, familiar murmur— "Meet me by the end of the Home Woods. I'll show you around the estate…"— Simone had to look away. Fleur's answering smile was smug, almost triumphant, as if she knew she'd won.

Something inside Simone twisted, turned over, and dropped.

It was Mark's job to show his fiancée around—not Sean's.

She fled the yard, every step weighted with a betrayal she had no right to feel. He wasn't hers. He never had been.

But knowing that didn't stop the ache.

Later, in the Land Rover, she tried to distract herself with work. Anything to push away the image of Sean and Fleur, alone in the woods, doing God knew what. But the minute she spotted him riding Royal again, as if nothing had happened, her composure fractured.

'How did you get here?' she snapped when he appeared at the gate.

'I still know all the shortcuts. I saw you watching me.'

'I was admiring Royal,' she lied. 'Your father made a good buy there. When we breed from him—'

'We?' he echoed, all arrogance and ice.

And so, it began again, the push and pull, the insults laced with past intimacy. His barbs cut deep. And when he reminded her—softly, cruelly—that he'd once taken care of her, she could hardly breathe.

'I hate you!' she shouted as he rode off, tears burning hot in her eyes. He never turned. Just raised a hand in farewell, careless and cool.

She cried then—angry, bitter tears that didn't change a thing. He was going to take Fleur. He would get everything, like always. And she'd be left with the memory of a man who had kissed her as if she were the only woman in the world… and discarded her just as easily.

A week later, Simone found herself at the centre of a confrontation so jarring, so utterly unexpected, it felt like the ground beneath her had shifted. There had been no warning, no gradual build-up—just a sudden jolt that would change everything. Whatever lay ahead, there would be no going back.

She was near the edge of the estate, close to the main road where the trees thinned out and the fields gave way to gravel shoulders. The rain had passed but left a dull, grey gloom hanging in the air. It was late in the afternoon, the sort of quiet hour when the world feels strangely hushed. Simone had relaxed her image for once—jeans, a thick green jacket, and hair that was both damp and windswept, clinging in tendrils around her face. She looked less the refined estate worker and more the stubborn country girl who'd once climbed trees and fought boys at school.

After closing the gate behind her, she turned back toward the Land Rover—only to freeze mid-step.

A man stood between her and the vehicle. A complete stranger.

She stopped in her tracks, her breath catching. He didn't appear threatening at first glance—he wasn't especially large—but there was something about him that instantly set her on edge. He was handsome in a polished way—dark brown hair, dark eyes, an expensive coat—but it was the way he watched her that unsettled her. Too focused. Too intent. His smile came too easily.

"Ah, good. A maiden to the rescue," he said smoothly. "I seem to have lost my way."

The way he said it, the smirk playing at the corners of his mouth, made her skin prickle. She didn't smile back.

She glanced around quickly. No sign of a car. No sound of another voice. He appeared to be alone, and on foot. Strange, considering the mud. No one in those immaculate shoes wandered the countryside for fun.

"Where are you trying to get to?" she asked cautiously, squaring her shoulders, trying to look taller than she was.

"The hall, of course," he replied, as if it were obvious.

"The hall?" she echoed, deliberately vague. It could be any hall. Anyone could claim that. Only a few months ago, a girl had been attacked on the far edge of the neighbouring estate. Her nerves went tight.

She shifted slightly, glancing toward a large broken branch half-hidden in the hedgerow. She let her hand drift toward it, brushing her fingers against its rough bark. It was solid. Heavy enough. That would do.

"Branlow Hall," he added when she didn't respond, his voice suddenly too slick. And he stepped closer.

Her grip on the branch tightened.

"Where's your car?" she snapped, trying to inject a note of authority she wasn't sure she felt.

"Just down there," he said, gesturing vaguely toward the bend in the lane. But the hedgerows were too high, and she wasn't about to look away from him to check. Her instincts screamed danger.

He sighed, as if she were being unreasonable. "Look, darling. Try to be a bit more— cooperative."

He moved fast.

Too fast.

Simone reacted on pure adrenaline. She swung the branch with every ounce of force she had. It struck the side of his head with a sickening crack, and he dropped like a stone, sprawling in the mud.

Her heart pounded. Her whole body was shaking. But before she could fully comprehend what had just happened, a roar split the silence.

Sean's Porsche came screeching around the corner, tearing into the lane like a storm on wheels. He saw everything—the stranger crumpled on the ground, Simone standing there, wild-eyed and armed with a tree branch.

She screamed—half in panic, half in release.

Sean was out of the car in an instant, striding toward her with the fury of a man who'd just walked into chaos.

"What the hell do you think you're doing?" he barked, yanking the stick from her hand as though she were a child misbehaving. His grip was firm, shaking her once for good measure before shifting his gaze to the man now groaning in the dirt.

"Are you all right, Alex?"

"God knows," the man muttered, holding the side of his head. He sat up, blinking dazedly, as if unsure what had hit him—literally.

Sean turned back to Simone, his expression thunderous.

"Explain yourself," he demanded, his tone sharp and cutting. He looked more dangerous than the stranger had. And now that the panic was subsiding, Simone could see just how bad this looked. Really bad.

"I—I thought he was going to attack me," she stammered, her voice shaky, her dignity in tatters.

"Thought?" Sean's eyes narrowed dangerously. "So, you got your retaliation in first?"

He gave a short, bitter laugh. "My God, Simone. You always were a lunatic."

He let her go, and she stumbled back against the Land Rover with a soft thud, bracing herself with both hands. Her legs felt like jelly, her chest tight and trembling with leftover panic. The cold from the metal seeped into her through the damp fabric of her jacket, but it was the shame that stung more—shame at panicking, at overreacting, at the way her hands still shook despite the danger being over.

Chapter Eight

Across from her, Sean crossed to Alex and offered a steadying hand, helping the man to stand fully upright. Alex brushed some leaves and mud from his coat, wincing as he touched the side of his head.

"What's the damage, Alex?" Sean asked, his voice a touch more relaxed now, though the edge of concern still lingered.

"Oh, I expect I'll survive," Alex muttered wryly, rubbing his temple. "It wasn't so much the blow, you understand—though she does have quite the swing for someone so dainty—it was the element of surprise. Wet ground, sudden whack, and down I went. I'm glad you know her."

He cast a wary glance at Simone, who stood pale and shaken beside the Land Rover, trying to muster an apologetic smile. But it didn't seem to reassure him at all. He didn't return the smile—in fact, he looked deeply relieved that Sean had arrived.

Sean laughed suddenly, the sound sudden and sharp as the tension broke from his frame. His amusement rang a little too loud in Simone's ears.

"Don't let it put you off that you met the local madwoman first," he said dryly. "Normally, we keep her locked up. Simone, this is Alex Lewis—my right-hand man. Try to remember his face. I don't want you going after him again with a stick, got it?"

His teasing fell flat. Simone was too shaken to appreciate the humour, and she didn't think it was funny anyway. If she had stood still and waited—if she'd been wrong about her instincts—what then? Would Sean still be laughing? It was all very well for him, towering and capable, with a luxury car and years of easy confidence. She wasn't a six-foot-tall force of nature with a rescue squad at her back. She was a woman alone on a lane with a stranger and a gut feeling.

"Where's your car, Alex?" Sean asked, the humour fading slightly from his tone.

"Down the lane," Alex replied pointedly, shooting another reproachful look Simone's way. "Told her that, but she wasn't inclined to believe me."

"She's… trained," Sean murmured with a mocking edge. "To attack strangers. Some kind of rustic survival instinct."

Alex raised an eyebrow but nodded. "I'll be fine now. The shock's wearing off. And that's all she needed to say," he added, addressing Simone with a dry tone. "'Straight down the lane to the hall.' Would've saved us all the theatrics."

"I really am sorry," Simone said hoarsely. "But you were watching me."

She regretted the words the moment they left her mouth. The admission sounded paranoid even to her own ears.

Alex's brows lifted. "I don't usually close my eyes when I see a beautiful girl," he said, not unkindly. "If that's some sort of countryside rule, I'll remember it next time. They don't include those in the London handbook."

He gave Sean a nod and limped off toward his car, leaving Simone feeling somehow even worse than before. Her hands trembling beside her.

Sean turned back to her slowly, the smile gone. His expression sobered.

"And now you," he said, his voice darkening again, every syllable laced with warning. "Miss Symons."

"I know. I'm sorry," she said quickly, stepping away from the Land Rover, still unsteady. "I'll go home. I just need—"

But he was beside her in an instant, steadying her with a hand at her elbow when she swayed.

"You're still shaking," he murmured. "Little idiot."

She didn't argue. She let him hold her—not because it was romantic, not because she wanted him to—but because right now, she was too shaken to resist the comfort. Her body trembled with leftover adrenaline, the aftershock threading through her limbs. Her breath hitched once, sharp, and tight.

"He really scared you, didn't he?"

She gave a small nod; eyes locked on the scuffed toes of her muddy boots.

"He came out of nowhere," she whispered. "And I couldn't see his car. It's so isolated out here. A girl got attacked near here a couple of months ago. I… I didn't know what to do."

"It is isolated," Sean said, his voice harder now. "Too damned isolated for you to be out here alone." He gestured toward the spot where the encounter had happened, frustration bleeding into every movement. "This is exactly what I meant when I said you shouldn't be handling this on your own."

She looked up at him sharply, her breath catching again—but this time, it wasn't fear.

It was something else. Panic, yes—but of a different kind.

"Oh, don't send me away," she said quickly, her voice trembling with something dangerously close to tears. "Please, Sean. Don't."

His expression shifted. "Would it be so very bad?" he asked quietly, watching her face.

She looked up at him helplessly, caught between defiance and vulnerability.

"I don't think I could," she said softly. "Even live, I mean. Everything I am—it's here. It's part of me. This place… it's my life."

Her voice broke on the last word, tears brimming at the corners of her eyes. For a moment he just looked at her, his expression unreadable.

Then he turned her gently away, as if he couldn't bear to see her face crumple further.

"I'll drive you back," Sean said curtly, his jaw tight. "I'll send a couple of the boys down to pick up the Land Rover."

He had already raised the hood of the Porsche, sealing them into its cocoon of warmth. The rain continued to whisper against the glass, a soft percussion that only heightened the tension between them. Inside, the air was warm, the leather seats smelled faintly of musk and pine, and still, Simone gave a little involuntary shiver.

"You know," she said, her voice thin and brittle, "I thought he was going to kiss me."

She was speaking the way she had years ago—back when they'd still understood each other, before Fleur, before ambition and betrayal and growing up had torn everything to shreds. For the span of a heartbeat, she forgot all of it.

"Maybe he was," Sean said quietly. "You've got a wild and beautiful look about you today. It wouldn't be a surprise."

She looked away, not answering. She couldn't handle that—not right now. Not when she was still trembling from adrenaline and fear, not when her heart was already raw.

"Anyway," she added shakily, trying to gather herself, "that's why I hit him."

"Because you don't like being kissed?" His tone curled around the words like a teasing smile. "Surely Jeffery kisses you. I hear you've been stepping out with him nearly every night since I came back."

"That's different… he is allowed to kiss me." She ducked her head, suddenly flushed, as warmth flooded her face. Even now, when she should have been furious, he still had the power to humiliate her.

"Allowed?" Sean echoed. "He kisses your hand, I expect. Read about it in the Boy's Annual, did he?"

He reached for the ignition, and something inside Simone snapped. The sarcasm, the cold amusement, the casual cruelty—she couldn't take it anymore. She lashed out, a flash of emotion overriding all sense. But he caught her hand easily, faster than she could blink, holding it tightly in his own.

"I don't sit still while people hit me, Simone," he said with quiet menace. "I'm not Alex, and I wasn't even thinking of kissing you."

"You're a brute," she spat, the words breaking on a sob. Hot tears spilled over before she could stop them, streaking down her cheeks.

"Why am I a brute?" His grip loosened slightly. "Because I didn't realise you wanted me to kiss you?"

"I don't!" she cried, wrenching her hand away and fumbling for her tears, wiping them with trembling fingers. But he didn't believe her. She could see it in his eyes.

He reached for her again—gently this time—and pulled her across the seat into his arms. She didn't resist. Couldn't. Her whole body was still trembling, and the feel of him, solid and familiar, was too much to fight.

"You do," he murmured, voice low. "You want me to hold you. Kiss you. Love you. Don't you, Simone?"

She shook her head, but her heart betrayed her. Inside, she was screaming yes. Despite everything she knew—his betrayal, Fleur, his supposed plans to push her off the estate— none of it seemed to matter in this moment.

A broken sob escaped her lips, and then his mouth found hers, hard and urgent. This time, she didn't resist at all. Her lips softened under his, opened to him, and the kiss deepened, spiralling out of control. He was Sean. Still her Sean, no matter how much she tried to pretend otherwise.

Desire whipped through her, fierce and unrelenting. Her hands gripped his shoulders as if she might fall through the earth. He cupped her face tenderly, brushed away her tears without breaking the kiss, and then she felt his hand move to the zip of her jacket, tugging it down slowly.

The car seemed to dissolve around them. She could feel nothing but his hands and mouth and the unbearable ache he always left behind. The darkness outside, the rain drumming above, the heat between them—every sensation felt magnified, more vivid than life.

"Let me go," she whispered faintly. But the words rang hollow even to her own ears. She didn't mean it. And he knew that.

"I don't think I can," Sean breathed against her lips. "Not yet."

His hand slid beneath her sweater, brushing against her skin—and then her breast— sending a wild shudder through her. She gasped, curling closer to him, her breath catching in her throat. It was everything she had dreamed at sixteen, at eighteen. The fantasy come to life—Sean's hands, Sean's lips, Sean's voice thick with want.

"Beautiful, wild Simone," he whispered. "Are you even here anymore? Or are you lost in that trance again?"

She was lost, utterly lost, drowning in sensation. Her head tipped back as he deepened the kiss, his mouth consuming her, and her body softened against him, molten and pliant.

Then suddenly—sharply—he stopped. His voice was taut, urgent.

"Stop, Simone."

He pulled back, holding her at arm's length, breathing hard. Her sweater was rumpled, her cheeks flushed, her lips swollen. Her eyes were wide and dazed.

Gently, almost reverently, he straightened her clothes and gave her a soft shake.

"Enough."

The word landed like a slap. Shame surged through her. It was over. Of course it was over. Of course it meant nothing to him. She had been there, convenient. Nothing more.

Tears welled up again.

"Don't," he said roughly, cupping her face. "Don't cry again. If you do, I won't let you go. There's a limit to my self-control, Simone. And when you burn in my arms like that, I burn with you. If this continues… you'll have your first lover right here. And this isn't the time or the place, however much I might want to."

She was too shaken to answer, too bruised by the intensity of her own emotions. Her lips still tingled from his kiss, and she could feel the heat of his hand lingering on her skin.

"I'm sorry," she whispered, barely able to speak. Her hands were trembling. Her whole world had tilted.

"So am I," he said quietly, pulling away and starting the engine. "Because you don't trust me at all anymore, do you? That went out the door with your childhood."

"You still treat me like a child," she choked. "A mad child."

He gave a short, humourless laugh. "Think again, Sunflower. Seconds ago, I was stroking your breast. I know exactly what you are."

He didn't raise his voice. He didn't need to. Every word landed like a stone.

"I acknowledge your womanhood," he added. "But I despise your suspicion."

What did he expect? There was Fleur, looming large like a ghost in the corner of every room. There was Mark, kind and confused. There was the future Sean clearly meant to shape without her. He would take Fleur, the estate, and everything else, and she'd be left with ashes.

No one else would ever touch her again. Not after this. Not after Sean.

He stopped at the Dower House without another word, and she climbed out, shoulders stiff with pride, throat tight with unshed tears. The moment she heard the Porsche drive away; she let go and wept.

Once— not so long ago—he would have followed her inside, taken her in his arms, whispered "Simone" in that low, wrecking voice that always made her melt.

But that man was gone. And he meant to keep walking—right up until she was gone, too.

Gone from Branlow.

Gone from everything she loved.

Gone from him.

And still—wretchedly, helplessly—she loved him.

But maybe it was time.

Time to leave.

She didn't want to. God, she didn't want to. Branlow was her home, her purpose, her heartbeat. But if Sean married Fleur, it would only be a matter of time. Fleur would see to it—Simone could already feel her being edged out. And Sean… Sean would let it happen. He'd send her away. He'd banish her if that's what Fleur asked.

So maybe, just maybe, she needed to stop pretending this place would always be hers.

Maybe it was time to start imagining a future that didn't include Branlow. Or Sean.

Even if she didn't know how to survive without either.

Chapter Nine

There was a long-standing tradition of dinner at the Hall on the last Friday of every month—something Simone had always looked forward to with a quiet sense of belonging. Typically, her father and Sir Michael would vanish into the study with a bottle of something vintage, and Simone would spend the evening exchanging stories with Lady Vivian before slipping away to gossip with Cleo. It was warm, familiar territory. Comforting.

But tonight was different.

She wasn't avoiding Sean—he was making a point of ignoring her. And Fleur had returned, as dazzling and insufferable as ever. Mark, according to Cleo, had grown noticeably aloof, his earlier affection for Fleur now clouded by what Simone suspected was disillusionment. Alex Lewis was back too—excellent news for Cleo, who clearly liked him—but it only reminded Simone of her embarrassing run-in with him. She had flattened him, after all.

Nothing would ever be the same again, she mused as she prepared for the evening. She felt the shift in her bones, like an ache that went deeper than her skin. Her position here, once so secure, now felt impossibly precarious. Any move she made would hurt someone she loved. Her entire life at Branlow had been wrapped in ease and quiet happiness—cherished relationships, unquestioned welcome—but now every step forward felt like walking a tightrope. Her father would never understand, even if she tried to explain. Lady Vivian would be horrified. And Cleo… Cleo didn't know the half of it.

She spun in front of the mirror, assessing herself with a detached eye. These days she looked older. More ethereal, perhaps—leaner, certainly. Mrs. Rogers had taken to calling her "skinny" in that sharp tone that suggested Simone was plotting something. But there was no plan. Only unease. Only a sadness that wouldn't lift.

Still, it gave her a kind of haunting beauty, especially in the sea-green chiffon dress she'd chosen—a recent addition to her expanding wardrobe. Once the shopping had started, she hadn't been able to stop. It was a distraction, something to momentarily fill the emptiness. But the ache always returned.

She clipped on delicate silver earrings and went down to find her father already waiting.

"You grow more beautiful by the week," he said fondly. "A few weeks ago, you were still my tomboy. Now… a woman. One day, Simone, you're going to be swept off your feet."

"I'm planning to be a very determined old maid," she teased lightly, looping her arm through his.

"Planning never stopped a man in love. All it takes is one who's ready to marry and willing to ignore your protests."

"Mrs. Rogers says we're all far too young."

"That woman!" He threw up his hands. "Good Lord, don't tell me you're seriously considering young Rogers?"

"I like Jeffery," Simone said honestly. "He's steady. Kind. He's good to me. He hasn't asked, but I think—maybe—he wants to marry me."

"It all sounds very practical," her father replied, touching her cheek. "But do you want that? A nice, safe marriage?"

Simone looked down. "Jeffery fits into our world."

"Does he?" Her father's voice was gentle but firm. "Your world has always been the Taylors. Don't pretend otherwise."

"It can't stay that way forever," she murmured, walking away restlessly. "When you retire, we'll leave. We're not really a part of their world—not truly."

"They've spent years making sure you were," Henry said quietly. "They've loved you, all of them, since you were small."

"I know." Simone sank onto the arm of a chair, twisting her fingers nervously. "I adore Lady Vivian and Sir Michael. Cleo's always been my best friend. And—Mark…"

Her voice drifted off.

"Aren't we going to mention Sean?" her father prompted gently.

She ducked her head, blushing painfully. "Oh—Sean!" she said with an airy little laugh. "He thinks I'm mad, an idiot."

Henry studied her for a moment, then smiled to himself. "You've always sparked off each other, the two of you. I doubt he even realises you've grown up."

Simone nearly laughed aloud. Grown up? He'd kissed her, touched her, held her like a man long past the point of denial. No, he knew exactly how grown up she was. He just didn't care. Or maybe she was just a useful shield while he rekindled things with Fleur.

"Anyway," Henry added, sensing the undercurrent and backing off, "whoever marries young Rogers better be prepared. That mother of his will live forever, purely out of spite. Mark my words."

They were still laughing as they entered the Hall, and Simone clung to that fleeting moment of warmth. Because as soon as she saw Sean, the smile slipped from her face.

"Is it all right to stare now?" Alex Lewis asked with a teasing grin as he approached, Cleo beaming beside him. Clearly, the story had gotten around—though Cleo insisted Sean hadn't been the one to spread it.

"It's still mortifying," Simone confessed, managing a wry smile.

"You're definitely capable of defending yourself," Alex said, rubbing his temple as if in memory.

"Not according to Sean," Cleo piped up far too loudly. "Sean's been looking after her since she was knee-high. Given half a chance, he'd still do it."

Simone shot her a mortified glare—and turned pale as Sean appeared, tall and unreadable.

He didn't look at her. Not even a glance.

"Ready, Henry?" Sean asked briskly. "Let's get half an hour in before dinner. You'd better come too, Alex. That's what you're here for—even if Cleo thinks you're here to entertain her."

He turned on his heel without waiting. The men followed, Mark caught up in their wake. So that was it. Sean was taking over. The quiet, meandering days of the past were over. Sir Michael might have looked relieved, but to Simone, it felt like a funeral bell tolling in her chest.

"I take it you and Sean aren't speaking?" Cleo said, still pink from Sean's remark, clearly regretting her earlier quip.

"We have nothing to say to each other," Simone snapped.

"Don't take it out on me," Cleo murmured. "I just don't get it. I always thought he adored you. And now look at you—an absolute dream, just waiting to be swept off your feet."

"I'm grown up now, Cleo. I don't need Sean to protect me. That was a long time ago. Let it go. Please."

Cleo must have seen something in her face—some deep fracture—because she fell silent and steered Simone away, turning them discreetly as Fleur emerged.

But Fleur couldn't be avoided forever. At dinner, Simone found herself seated directly opposite Sean, and what little appetite she had left vanished completely. She was grateful for Alex's cheerful chatter, and even more so for Cleo, who leaned over repeatedly to draw her into conversation, shielding her as best she could.

"Isn't this just a wonderful old place?" Fleur gushed, sweeping her gaze around the grand dining room like it already belonged to her. "Did you know the Taylors came over with the Norman Conquest?" she asked Alex.

"Er—yes," he replied quickly, but it didn't help.

"Sir John Taylor was the first with a proper English name. He had three sons, but two died—"

"One was hanged for murder," Mark interrupted, his voice cold. "Can we skip the history lesson, Fleur?"

"Well, I'm proud of doing the research," she pouted. "Maybe the farm bailiff and his daughter didn't know."

A silence followed, sharp as a slap.

"Henry knows more about this estate than any of us," Sir Michael said, voice suddenly hard. "He's not just the manager—he oversees more than one estate. Simone is just as qualified."

Simone had never heard Sir Michael sound so clipped. It startled her more than Fleur's insult. But none of it mattered, not really. Her qualifications weren't going to save her. Sean was going to get rid of her anyway.

"Oh, I'm sorry," Fleur cooed insincerely, her wide eyes pretending innocence. "I didn't mean to offend anyone."

Alex looked faintly horrified. Cleo was openly scowling.

"My family came over with the Normans, too," Fleur added with a self-satisfied smile.

"The French probably couldn't off-load them fast enough," Cleo muttered, abandoning all pretence of civility.

"That will do, Cleo!" Sean's voice cracked like a whip, sharp enough to silence the entire room.

Cleo stared back at him, defiant—until her nerve broke and she looked away.

There had never been a dinner like this at Branlow Hall. All the gentle harmony of the place had been shattered. After the meal, the men left again, but this time Alex and Mark stayed behind. Cleo made it clear she was delighted by Alex's company, and Fleur, unable to draw Sean's attention, was forced to settle for Mark—who didn't look like he intended to be charmed tonight.

Simone sat back quietly, watching the tangled drama unfold. Everything that had once been safe was changing, slipping through her fingers like water.

And Sean hadn't even looked at her. Not once.

Simone wandered out onto the terrace, wrapping her arms around herself as the cool night air brushed against her bare skin. The evening was unusually cold for the season; the kind of chill that made everything feel more fragile. But she needed the solitude. The soft glow of moonlight spilled over the estate, bathing the familiar landscape in silver and shadow. She gazed out at it all—every hedgerow, every tree line—trying to imprint the view in her memory. She loved this place with a quiet, desperate ache. And now, more than ever, she feared she was going to lose it.

It hadn't escaped her notice that when Cleo had made that sharp comment about Fleur, it had been Sir Michael—not Sean—who'd spoken up in her and her father's defence. Sean had stayed silent, his mouth tight, his gaze unreadable. That told Simone everything. He might once have leapt to shield her, but not anymore. Now it seemed he only had eyes for Fleur—and a future in which Simone no longer belonged.

The pain of that tightened inside her chest, low and hard.

Footsteps sounded behind her, and she knew who it was before she turned. She stiffened, the muscles in her shoulders drawing tight. Her heart gave a small, traitorous leap even as her mind flooded with fresh resentment.

Sean.

His presence filled the air around her—powerful, quiet, unmistakable. And unwelcome.

"You're freezing," he said, his voice low.

"Only a little," she replied, not looking at him. "I'm just… taking a final look. I doubt I'll be here for another dinner. And now that you've taken over the reins, I suppose it's only a matter of time before I'm off the estate entirely."

"Simone—" He stepped closer, but she backed away quickly, her eyes flashing with fury and something dangerously close to heartbreak.

"Don't," she snapped. "Don't say my name like that. Don't come out here pretending to care. I'm not some naïve village girl who doesn't know what you are. Go on—go back inside and soak up Fleur's adoration. She worships you enough to make up for the rest of us."

The words landed between them like shards of broken glass, and for a moment, Sean simply stared at her. The moonlight caught the sharp lines of his face, and his expression turned cold—glacial.

"Fleur is engaged to my brother," he said, every syllable clipped.

"So?" Simone shot back. "I'm almost engaged to Jeffery, and it didn't stop you from kissing me. I doubt it's stopping you with her either—not when she throws herself at you every time, you're in the room."

She was trembling now, not from the cold but from the storm surging inside her. The ache, the betrayal, the longing—she couldn't hold any of it back.

"Tell me," she went on bitterly, "did Fleur turn to Mark because you weren't faithful? Or did she just miscalculate and think he was the one who'd inherit the Hall? She obvious she has a nose for power."

Sean went very still.

Even in the silvery darkness, she could see his face go white, his jaw tightening like stone. She had gone too far, and she knew it. Still, the words kept echoing between them, her anguish spilling out in raw, unforgivable truths.

His body shifted slightly, a subtle, dangerous movement—and something in his eyes made her breath catch. There was something feral there. Something wounded.

And then she ran.

Like a startled doe, she fled down the terrace steps, her sea-green dress billowing behind her, catching the moonlight in trembling waves. She darted across the lawn, the long grass brushing her ankles, breath tearing in and out of her chest. Panic made her heart pound wildly. He would catch her. He always did.

Was he furious? Humiliated? Ready to strike back in the only way he knew how?

There had always been something barely contained in Sean, a simmering violence beneath the polished surface. She had never feared it before. But now, with her nerves frayed and her emotions raw, she wasn't sure what he might do.

She didn't make it to the trees.

He caught her from behind, strong arms lifting her off her feet as if she weighed nothing at all. She shrieked once in surprise, but the sound died as he strode across the lawn toward the summerhouse.

"Put me down!" she cried, pounding against his chest, but he didn't respond—not with words.

The door slammed open, then shut again with a solid thud behind them. He let her go at last—let her drop to her feet like a bundle of nerves and indignation—and she stumbled slightly, breathless, flushed, and wide-eyed.

Her hair was tumbling around her shoulders, her chest rising and falling with each gasping breath. The summerhouse smelled faintly of old roses and woodsmoke, a memory of gentler times. But nothing about this was gentle.

Sean stood in front of the door, unmoving, blocking her path.

And in the moonlight streaming through the windows, they stared at each other—two storms colliding.

How she stayed upright, Simone couldn't say. Her legs felt like reeds, swaying under the pressure of adrenaline and dread. She edged away from him instinctively, her fingers brushing the rough stone wall of the summerhouse, grateful for the moonlight that filtered through the tall windows. It poured in, silver and cold, outlining Sean in stark silhouette. It helped her see him—but offered no protection.

Sean in a rage was something else entirely, a force she hadn't faced like this before. And the worst part was knowing she'd provoked it. She'd pushed every button she could find, flung her hurt at him like knives, and now there was no backing down.

There would be no mercy here. No rescue. She could already imagine the headline: Death in the Summerhouse. Simone Symons, twenty-two, cut down by a man she couldn't stop loving and couldn't stop provoking.

"So, I'm the worst kind of villain," he said, his voice icy. "I steal my brother's fiancée—after discarding her, naturally—and I throw poor, helpless young women out into the cruel world. That about sum it up?"

"I'm not helpless," she whispered, lips trembling.

"No," he bit out. "No, you're not. You've got a tongue like a blade and no real sense of what it does when you swing it. Honestly, I think I'd rather deal with a stick like Alex's than another one of your verbal assaults."

She flinched but forced herself to meet his gaze. "Why do you have to be like this?" The question slipped out in a choked cry. "Why did you have to change? You used to be—God, you used to be mine."

His breath caught, just slightly. Then he stepped closer, and the temperature in the room dropped.

"How am I, Simone?" he asked softly, dangerously. "Tell me. Because from where I'm standing, I'm your sworn enemy now. But once—I was more. A lot more."

"I didn't know then how treacherous you could be."

His eyes darkened. "Treacherous?"

She nodded, chest heaving. "Yes. Every day I find out something new. Something I wish I didn't know."

He advanced suddenly, expression fierce, and she didn't have time to move before he caught her by the waist and pulled her hard against him.

"I used to think you were sweet," he growled. "A little wild, sure. But sweet. Normal. Now? Now I think you're mad, Simone. Completely mad."

He crushed her in his arms before she could respond, his mouth finding hers with a fury that made her gasp. She struggled against the kiss, but he held her easily, bending her over his arm until her balance threatened to give.

"Don't bother pleading," he rasped. "You ran out into the night like some lost thing—and I came after you. Do you really think they'll come looking for you yet? There's plenty of time, Simone. Plenty."

She whimpered, her body trembling violently now—not from fear alone, but from the emotional onslaught. His mouth ravaged hers, hot and demanding, and she could feel her own betrayal in the way her arms clung to him, her lips giving way to his.

Then—just as suddenly—his grip changed.

The steel of his anger softened, his mouth lifting from hers only to rain scattered, fevered kisses across her face. His arms became a fierce shelter, no less possessive but no longer cruel.

"You crazy little wildcat," he murmured. "You're jealous."

"I'm not," she breathed, but the protest was hollow.

"Of course you are. You always were. You think I didn't notice the way you watched me? You wanted me when you were sixteen. You want me now."

"You're wicked," she whispered. "I never really knew you. Not the real you."

His lips brushed her temple, his voice lowering to a tender, unbearable murmur. "You will, Sunflower. Completely."

And then there were no more words.

She stopped thinking—stopped resisting. Her whole world narrowed to the feel of his hands, the burn of his mouth, the way he murmured her name like a secret. She let him hold her, kiss her, stroke her spine through the delicate fabric of her gown. She let herself want him. Because she did. That was the hard truth.

But he must never know.

Even if she let him have everything—her body, her soul—she would never say the words. She would never give him that last piece. That was her only weapon. Her only safety.

"Simone…" he whispered against her throat, his breath ragged. His hands gripped her hips, possessive and sure, and she knew it wouldn't be long before his self-control snapped altogether.

They were alone here. More alone than they had ever been. She clung to him, heart hammering, drowning in the fire between them—

"Sean!"

The voice cut through the haze like a blade. High, delicate, unmistakably hers.

Fleur.

Chapter Ten

Simone froze. Sean did too, his entire body going rigid. Outside, Fleur's voice floated again across the lawn, sweet and poised and perfectly pitched.

"Sean! Are you out there?"

Just like that, the spell shattered.

Even as he held her, Fleur was calling for him—claiming him—and Simone could feel the walls of her soul come crashing down.

She wrenched away, shaking, stumbling back from his arms. "Better go before she bursts into tears or screams the place down," she said bitterly. "I'll just wait here in the dark, like your dirty little secret."

His jaw clenched. He took a step toward her again, but she raised a hand. "Don't. Just don't."

For a moment, he said nothing. Then he smiled—a cold, humourless smile that chilled her more than his fury ever had.

"So, it's war, then?"

She didn't hesitate. "Yes. And I'll win it."

"That's bold of you." His voice was like velvet over broken glass. "But all right, Simone. I accept your challenge. Let me know when you're ready to lower the flag."

"Never," she hissed.

"Never," he repeated softly. "That's a long time. And just remember—I'm home for good."

"For bad," she snapped. "Really, truly bad." Her hands curled into fists. "You'll break Mark's heart between you, you and her."

"I plan to break yours first," he said but his eyes told a different story. "Then I'll deal with the rest. And don't forget—I have every advantage. You want me. And I intend to take you."

Then he turned and walked out.

Simone stumbled to the window and watched as he crossed the lawn to Fleur, who linked her arm through his like it belonged there. Together, they strolled back toward the house, perfectly framed in moonlight like a couple in some romantic painting.

Simone's fists clenched. Rage surged hot through her chest, banishing the last dreamy residue of his kisses. He thought he could have everything—her, Fleur, the estate, the legacy. That he could reach for her when it suited him, like a man choosing fruit from a tree.

Well, she had news for him.

She had declared war—and she wasn't going down quietly.

As a matter of quiet rebellion, Simone had her motorbike repaired. She didn't ask for permission. She didn't even mention it to Sean. Since the accident, he hadn't spoken of it—not once. He was used to obedience, she supposed. Used to people falling in line with his orders without question.

Well, that time had passed.

Defiance had taken root—firm, wild, and unshakable. Whatever he said now would be measured, challenged, and most likely scorned. What could he do to her that he hadn't already done? He was going to get rid of her. Push her out of the estate. Out of Branlow. Out of everything she loved.

There was nothing left to lose.

Still, she was glad the bike was tucked away in the old shed, out of sight, when he strode into the Dower House a week later without so much as a knock.

His presence hit the air like a thunderclap—clipped, tense, and entirely unwelcome.

"Where's Henry?" he barked, without preamble. No greeting. No eye contact. His voice was hard enough to chip stone.

Simone looked up from her desk, composed and cool. "He's over at Little Ripton," she said smoothly. "Can I help?"

If he was going to play the autocratic master, she could certainly play the obedient serf. It amused her, in a bitter sort of way.

He didn't crack a smile. "These reports are wrong." He tossed a sheaf of papers onto the table with barely disguised irritation. "Let him know when he comes back."

She glanced down at the papers. Her expression shifted immediately, her composure cracking like thin ice.

"I did these," she said sharply, lifting her head with a sudden flush of anger. "They're not wrong."

"Then you'll have no trouble finding the mistakes." He folded his arms across his chest, eyes glinting like cut glass. "The totals don't add up. Thank heavens it wasn't Henry— I thought for a moment he must be slipping."

"Oh, I'll never be able to fill his shoes," she snapped, cool deference long forgotten. "No danger of that. I've been reminded often enough."

"And you won't get the chance," he said flatly. "I think we've established that."

The words hit her like a slap. Her chest burned, and she blinked hard against the sting of tears. She snatched the reports up, gripping the pages so tightly her knuckles went white.

"I'm sure you'll spot the mistake," he added, turning as if already finished with her. "A couple of hours should do it. And while we're on the subject of work—there are two broken gates at the road end of the estate. See to it."

She stared at his retreating back, fury climbing up her throat like bile.

"I can't be everywhere at once!" she shouted after him.

He paused with maddening calm, half-turned. "You ride with Cleo every morning. That appears to be pleasure. Work, as far as I can tell, begins at ten for you. Everyone else on this estate starts at eight."

"So now I'm just a worker?" she said, seething. "Do I get a punch card and a whistle too? Or will you be conducting a full time-and-motion study?"

"It won't be necessary." His voice was quiet now, lethal in its steadiness. "Put in the time and I'm sure the motion will take care of itself. And yes—you've reminded me often enough that you're nothing more than a worker. So, work. Fix the gates."

Then he left, slamming the door behind him.

Simone stood frozen for a moment, breath shallow, heart thudding, her fists clenched at her sides. Then, in a fit of furious energy, she swept her untouched lunch off the table and stormed out of the house.

The estate joiner was in the middle of his own meal when she arrived. But as soon as she mentioned Sean's name—and his displeasure—the poor man abandoned his sandwich and followed her without question.

The two of them spent the next several hours scouring the estate. Simone was relentless, her eyes sharp, her tone clipped, her boots caked with mud by the end of it. She refused to let Sean find a single thing out of place. Not one.

When Jeffery called that night, hoping for a gentle chat, she all but bit his head off. Then had to call back to apologise. Then spent two full hours poring over the damn reports until she found it—a single, stupid miscalculation buried in the totals. Something Sean could've pointed out in five seconds.

But of course, he hadn't.

Because humiliating her had been the point.

When she finally climbed into bed, her fury still hadn't cooled. It simmered beneath her skin like a fever, every muscle in her body tense with exhaustion and resentment.

If Sean thought he could reduce her to a clipboard and a punch clock, he was going to find out just how wrong he was.

And if he planned to force her out—he'd have to fight her for every inch.

She was out by half-past seven the next morning, bundled in a jacket against the chill, her breath fogging in the crisp air. The sun was only just creeping over the trees, gilding the frost-laced paddocks with gold. Simone made her way to the stables, jaw clenched with resolve. She saddled Stardust with quick, efficient movements and led the mare into the yard.

The moment was shattered by the crunch of boots on gravel.

Sean.

He strode into view like something out of a romantic novel—broad-shouldered, infuriatingly self-assured in a white polo-neck and worn jeans, every inch the arrogant country lord. But she was in no mood to be impressed. Her face, taut with fury, could have cut glass.

"Riding?" he asked, his tone sharp with challenge. Clearly, he'd expected her defiance. He was growing accustomed to it.

"No." She glanced at her watch, raising her brows. "It's seven-forty, Mr. Sean. At the moment, I'm still on my own time. I'll be out with a pitchfork alongside the other lads at eight sharp."

His mouth tightened. "Listen, you pint-sized witch—"

He took a threatening step toward her, but she met his blazing gaze with serene, honey-eyed innocence.

"I'm only following orders, sir," she said sweetly.

For one terrifying moment she thought he might explode. She could practically hear the grind of his teeth. But fate intervened in the form of Cleo, breezing into the yard with her usual early-morning cheer.

"What's going on here?" she asked, eyes flicking between them. "Riding without me, Simone? That's low. I thought we were a team."

Simone turned to her calmly. "I won't be riding with you anymore. I'm moving Stardust to different quarters."

"What?" Cleo frowned. "Why on earth would you do that? Stardust belongs here. This is her home."

"There's a small loose box behind the Dower House. She'll be fine there. These stables are for the family, Cleo. I'm ashamed it took me so long to realise I was overstepping."

Her voice was calm, but the quiet dignity in it seemed to shake Cleo. Even she couldn't pretend not to hear the deeper meaning. Sean certainly heard it—and bristled visibly, his hands clenched at his sides.

"What have you said to her?" Cleo demanded, rounding on her brother with real fire in her voice—for the first time ever, perhaps.

"Keep out of it," Sean growled through gritted teeth.

"I will not. Simone is my friend."

"Then heaven help you," he bit out. "I hope you can manage her."

He turned sharply and strode away without another word; whatever purpose had brought him there abandoned. Cleo watched him go, her brow furrowed.

"What's gotten into him?" she muttered. "He's being… well, nasty."

"Hah!" Simone let out a tight little laugh of satisfaction, leading Stardust out of the yard. "Now you're beginning to see it. And for the record, I'm not allowed to ride with you anymore. Orders."

"I don't understand any of this," Cleo said helplessly, trotting beside her. "Honestly, I thought he—he loved you."

"Loved me?" Simone scoffed. "Don't be ridiculous. Remember that palm-reading of yours? The dark man, the big black dog, the heartbreak? You weren't wrong. You just didn't realise he was already standing in the room."

The big black dog appeared as if on cue.

Prince bounded around the corner, tongue lolling, tail wagging with all the good-natured charm of his breed. He trotted straight up to her, but Stardust shied away with a nervous snort, tossing her head.

Simone's temper flared.

"Get lost!" she snapped, and Prince immediately stopped, startled. He lowered his body to the ground, eyes wide and mournful, his tail swishing uncertainly.

The sight undid her. With a sigh, she reached down and scratched behind his ears. "Oh, I'm sorry. It's not your fault, is it? You're just the innocent party in all this. You don't know what it's like to live under the same roof as a tyrant."

She lifted her head—and froze.

Sean was standing on the front steps of the house, arms folded, watching the whole scene in brooding silence. His expression was unreadable, but the black frown etched into his face told her everything she needed to know.

She stared right through him. Then, head high, she turned and walked away, leading Stardust down the drive toward the Dower House.

She hoped every single person in the family was watching. She hoped they all saw what he'd driven her to—banished from the stables, reduced to riding alone, pushed into shabby outbuildings like a stranger.

Of course, Cleo didn't tell tales, even if she might've wanted to. Loyalty to her beloved brother ran deep, and perhaps Simone should've been grateful. But no one else seemed to notice the change—no one, except her father.

He said nothing outright, but when she came in from her early ride the next morning, hair windswept, cheeks flushed, his gaze lingered.

"Oh, battling with Sean again, are you?" he murmured, as if it were the most natural thing in the world.

She gave a weary half-smile but didn't answer.

Was she battling? Or just trying to survive?

Life had been blissful before Sean returned. Now every day felt like a siege. Grim. Bitter. Exhausting.

But she wouldn't give in.

Not now. Not ever.

And in time, they'd all see him for what he was—every last one of them.

Cleo already was. The rest would follow.

Sean watched her walk away with Stardust, tension coiling tight in his gut. This was getting out of hand.

He'd come back to claim her—not in some possessive, brutish way, but in the only way he knew how. To hold her. To fight for her. To finally make things right.

But it was clear now—painfully clear—that he'd hurt her more deeply than he'd ever allowed himself to believe. When he walked away and called her a child, he hadn't just broken things between them—he'd broken her.

And he didn't know how to take that back.

Every time they were together, the distance seemed to stretch wider. Like something unseen was shifting beneath them, tilting the ground, undoing any hope of solid footing.

Words came out wrong.

Silences cut deeper than anything either of them dared say.

And still, he couldn't let go.

He wanted her to be his again. Wanted the past to loosen its grip, to rewind to the days when she looked at him like he was the sun.

But this—this wasn't that.

And if he didn't stop pushing, he'd lose her completely.

Not just from Branlow.

From everything.

And that thought chilled him more than any winter wind ever could.

She continued to go out with Jeffery as a matter of self-preservation—although Mrs. Rogers, with her constant supervision and thinly veiled condescension, often drove Simone dangerously close to homicide.

"You know there's no way I can get married yet, Simone," Jeffery said quietly one evening as he drove her home from a dance. "Mother's not quite ready to face having another woman in the house."

Simone turned to stare at him, stunned. A strange, fluttering panic stirred in her chest. Marriage. That word. She hadn't truly thought about it—at least not with Jeffery. It had always been safe, theoretical. A comfortable arrangement in some distant future. And now here it was, dropped into the conversation like a stone into a still pond.

"I didn't know you even… contemplated it," she managed, struggling to keep her voice light. "I thought your mother thought you were far too young."

"She does," he agreed with a small laugh, tightening his hold on her hand. "But it's not just that. I think you intimidate her a little. You've got all this fire, this independent streak, and she's not sure how you'd take to the—well—the discipline of the farm."

"Me?" Simone's voice cracked, incredulous. "Discipline?"

It was one thing to be flippant with her father, quite another to be faced with this oddly pragmatic proposal—if that's what it was. Jeffery's voice was so calm, so matter of fact. As if he were talking about acquiring a heifer, not a wife.

"You know I mean to marry you, Simone," he said, entirely serious now. "You've always known. I'm not flashy or emotional, but I care about you deeply."

She looked away, her throat tightening. "I… I know you do. You're a really good friend."

"Well, then. That's what a marriage should be, don't you think? Two people who get on. Partners. Friends for life." He hesitated. "But you'd have to… moderate certain things. Learn to be more patient. Less quick with your tongue. That worries Mother, I won't lie."

Simone gave a strangled little laugh. "How kind of her to be concerned. I didn't realise she spent so much time thinking about how I'll turn out."

The hysteria started to rise—hot and choking. A lovely, safe marriage. Lifelong friendship. And Mrs. Rogers standing sentinel, arms folded, waiting for her to misstep. They were dissecting her—measuring her strengths, flagging her flaws, as though she were a prize cow at the county fair.

"Honestly, I think I've already turned out," she said, her tone dry. "You don't change people at my age, Jeffery."

"You're so dramatic sometimes," he chuckled indulgently. "You're still just a girl. We're both years away from anything official, and Mother agrees. No rush."

"Of course," she said, forcing a smile. "Still… I don't feel very much like a girl anymore."

She paused, then added flippantly, "I've had several passionate affairs."

The words flew out before she could stop them—just to shock him, to puncture his complacency. But the moment they left her lips, she regretted them. Because all it did was conjure Sean's face. The only passionate affair she'd ever had had been entirely in her mind—and always, irrevocably, with Sean.

Jeffery recoiled slightly, then surprised her by grabbing her arms. "If I didn't know you love to say wicked things, I'd be furious," he snapped. "You never know when to stop, do you?"

No, she didn't. Her tongue was always getting her into trouble—and unlike Jeffery, Sean never found it charming anymore.

"It's all talk," she said softly. "I don't know why I say things like that."

"Then try to control yourself," Jeffery said sternly. "This is why I think you're not ready. You need to grow up, Simone. One day you'll realise that."

He softened a little, giving her a lopsided smile as he pulled her into a loose embrace. "Don't worry. I'll take care of you."

She stiffened. She didn't need anyone to take care of her. She almost told him so. But Sean's voice echoed in her head instead.

"I took care of you."

Not anymore. That time had passed. Now she was fighting him with every breath.

Simone threw herself into work like a woman possessed. She rose at six and didn't collapse into bed until long after eleven. She was determined to give Sean no ammunition, no opportunity to criticise her. And though he said nothing, she could feel him watching—always watching. His silence was heavier than words.

Her father noticed, of course.

"Well, there's never been much of you," he muttered one morning as she passed him in the hall, "but what there is, is disappearing. You're fading away, love. I don't know what's driving you, but I know something is. You're up before the crows and still on your feet after supper. Every time I look around, you've already done what I was going to do."

She couldn't tell him. He still saw Sean as faultless—the charming prodigal son returned. If he knew Simone had been scolded, worked harder than ever, he'd march straight up to the Hall and confront Sean himself—and that would only make things worse.

So, she smiled and shrugged it off. "Just trying to stay ahead of the season," she said vaguely.

Losing her morning rides and gossip sessions with Cleo had left a hole in her day, but Cleo, ever loyal, had started coming down to the Dower House more often. Through her, Simone kept up with the goings-on at the Hall, even though she never set foot inside anymore.

Lady Vivian had complained gently—once or twice—but Simone fended her off with excuses about the new planting schedule and livestock rotation.

The truth, though, was a weight pressing on her chest.

She missed them.

Missed the warmth of the Hall, the long family dinners, the laughter. She missed Lady Vivian's gentle fussing, Sir Michael's dry humour, and Cleo's endless chatter. Most of all, she missed the version of herself who had once belonged there.

But now… she was a liar.

A liar who pretended not to care, who worked herself into exhaustion just to avoid facing Sean, who masked her aching heart with biting wit.

He had turned her into this. And no one even saw it.

Not yet.

But one day, they would.

She'd already started applying for jobs—quietly, without telling anyone. Because deep down, she knew she couldn't keep living like this. Not in the shadow of a life that was never really hers to begin with.

Something had to change. And this time, it would be her.

Chapter Eleven

A few days later, Jeffery surprised Simone by showing up on the estate.

She had left the Land Rover parked by the lower gate and walked down through the dew-drenched grass to check on the thinning work in the woods. The men had done a fair job, but for reasons best known to themselves had left a massive fallen tree right on the boundary—its thick trunk sprawled across the edge, halfway into the adjoining field. Unless there was a good explanation, she'd have them back this afternoon to deal with it properly.

She stood with her arms crossed, brow furrowed, debating logistics, when she heard her name echoing across the hill. Turning, she spotted Jeffery waving as he made his way toward her, having parked some distance up the lane.

She met him halfway; her hands shoved deep in the pockets of her jeans. With her red hair catching the sunlight and her green sweater hugging her petite frame, she looked like a wild thing conjured out of the forest itself. She hadn't bothered with a jacket—it had seemed warm enough earlier, but now the breeze bit through the knit and raised goosebumps along her arms. Hopefully, he wasn't planning to linger.

Still, she was pleased to see him. Her loneliness had grown thick lately, curling around her like ivy. Even Jeffery, with his predictability and solemn charm, was a welcome reprieve.

"What brings you out here?" she asked, smiling despite herself.

"Good neighbourliness," he replied with his usual gravity. "Did you know the river's rising? Quite fast, actually."

Her smile vanished. "No, I haven't had a chance to get over that way. Is it serious?"

"Could be," he said. "Looks like there's been a fair bit of rain in the hills. Thought I'd warn you—it might be worth alerting the lower farms."

"Thanks, Jeffery." She looked away, already calculating the route she'd take for a check-in run. Flooding wasn't uncommon this time of year, but it could get dangerous quickly.

"I was hoping," he added, more hesitantly now, "that you might come with me to the Carley dance tomorrow night. It's been a while."

Excuses flared to life instantly. She was bone-tired by evening, and the thought of dressing up and smiling through small talk was almost painful. Worse, the evening would likely end with another encounter with Mrs. Rogers, whose vigilance and veiled criticisms had become almost comedic—if they weren't so exhausting.

Her father had once joked that anyone foolish enough to cross Jeffery's mother wouldn't survive the day. "If she didn't kill them outright," he'd said, chuckling over his newspaper, "she'd lecture them into the grave."

And she would lecture Simone, no doubt. She always did.

"I'm not sure if I can," Simone said carefully. "There's still a lot to do—fencing, and the lower pasture's a mess. And now the river…"

"I don't see why you have to do it all yourself," he said, his voice sharper than she expected. "You're not a farmhand. We get by just fine without all the manpower the Taylors throw around."

She blinked, surprised by the edge in his tone. Was that jealousy? She'd never imagined Jeffery, of all people, resenting the Taylors. His own farm was prosperous—larger than most in the district—and well-managed. He'd never seemed the type to compare.

"You don't have two estates here and one in Scotland to run," she reminded him calmly. "There are fifteen properties across the holdings, and three farms just on this estate. It's a business—and I help run it."

"We all know about the Taylor estates," he grumbled. "I bet they've got their eye on our land, too."

"Don't be ridiculous!" she snapped. "They don't go around snatching farms. This isn't some Victorian melodrama."

"They've already got everything else," he muttered.

"Because they work for it," she flared. "Everybody does. You think Sean and Cleo sit around eating cream buns all day? You've no idea how hard it is to keep everything running."

"Cleo?" he scoffed. "From what I hear, she does a lot more gadding about than grafting."

That did it. Simone's temper ignited.

"For your information, Cleo is a trained secretary. She works in the estate office six days a week and handles more paperwork in a morning than most people do in a week. And she's my friend, Jeffery. I won't have you sneering at her."

"Well," he said stiffly, "she won't want much to do with you once you marry a farmer. That's what Mother says—she saw you two shopping the other day. She reckons Cleo will drop you the minute you're hitched to an ordinary man."

"If I do marry a farmer," Simone snapped, unable to keep the fury out of her voice. "What is this—some gossip circle over tea and biscuits, planning out my future like I'm not even involved?"

She was seeing a side of Jeffery that unnerved her—quietly possessive, casually dismissive, and oddly entitled.

"You know we'll marry, Simone," he said, in a voice that sounded like fact, not hope. "Even if we don't talk about it."

"Maybe the reason we don't talk about it," she said coldly, "is because you've already decided for both of us."

She folded her arms tightly across her chest. He sounded so certain. So fixed. Like Sean—but with less fire and more quiet control.

"It's not necessary to discuss it," Jeffery muttered. "We've been going steady for four years. Everyone expects it."

Was that really the only reason he wanted to marry her—because everyone expected it?

The thought hit Simone like a fist. For one dizzy second, she pictured Sean proposing. No—telling her. In the vision he simply seized her hand, dragged her off beneath a thundercloud sky, and that would be that. A shiver slid over her skin. When Sean kissed her, she was utterly lost; loving him felt like a life-sentence with no parole. Perhaps she was doomed to be alone, craving something normal men like Jeffery could never ignite.

Jeffery, meanwhile, kept driving, missing the way her expression had clouded. "I didn't mean to upset you," he coaxed. "It's just—you're so involved with the Taylors. Mother thinks that spoils a girl for settling down to an ordinary farmer's life."

"Does she?" Simone murmured, panic fluttering. Marriage had never sounded so final, so claustrophobic. "How do you even know you want to marry me, Jeffery? You hardly ever kiss me properly. We might not be suited."

"There's more to marriage than that." His tone suggested she was being childish. "Romance is fine in its place, but compatibility matters. Shared goals, discipline—"

"Discipline?" She nearly laughed. But he pressed on, oblivious.

"When we're married—"

"Kiss me," she blurted, startling even herself.

Arms folded across her chest, chin lifted in defiance, she added, "Right now."

"Simone!" Jeffery looked around, flustered. "This is neither the time nor the place—"

Exactly what Sean had said the night he'd stolen her breath with one low, possessive line. This isn't the time or the place.

Sean's voice echoed through her mind, sharp and unwelcome.

"I'm waiting," she said, fiercer now.

Jeffery hesitated, then gently gathered her into his arms, and pressed a soft kiss to her lips.

She didn't let him retreat.

Her arms looped around his neck, pulling him closer as she crushed her mouth to his, lips parting in reckless invitation.

For a moment, he froze. Then—surprised but clearly intrigued—he responded, his kiss deepening with unfamiliar urgency as he drew her close.

Heat flared. But not the right kind.

It was awkward. Off. Like a scene from a costume drama where both leads had been miscast.

She broke away just as he tried to pull her closer, her heart pounding—not with pleasure, but with dread.

Jeffery stepped back, flushed, and breathless, smoothing his hair with a trembling hand.

"No," he said, voice tight. "I'm not kissing you like that again. One thing leads to another, and I respect you too much. We'll wait until we're formally engaged."

Embarrassment—and an odd relief—washed through her. She'd proved what she'd feared: no lightning bolt, no molten wings, no soul-shaking surrender. Only Sean could do that. And that, too, was a sort of prison.

"I'm sorry, Jeffery," she mumbled. "I don't know what came over me."

He brightened, misreading her contrition. "Mother thinks you're a tomboy, of course, but she likes you. And don't worry about being… enthusiastic." He cleared his throat. "You're safe with me."

Too safe, she thought bleakly. She'd never tell him the kiss had been an experiment—and a failure.

"Will she ever let you marry, do you think?" She tried for lightness and heard the wobble in her voice. "You said she isn't ready for another woman in the house."

"Heavens, what a question! I'm only twenty-five. We have years yet. Lots of living to do first."

"You and your mother?" The quip slipped out before she could stop it.

"Don't be a tease, Simone." His brows pinched in a familiar frown—half scold, half sermon. He had inherited that look from Mrs Rogers along with the sense of duty.

Before she could soften the moment, the car crested the rise near the Sow Hedge—and there, idling beneath an oak, was Sean's gun-metal Porsche, top down, sunlight glinting off the windscreen. He lounged behind the wheel, one arm resting on the door, blue eyes inscrutable behind dark lashes. Had he been sitting there the whole time? Had he witnessed her ill-advised experiment? Her stomach knotted.

Jeffery slowed. "Morning, Sean. Everything all right?" he called politely.

"Any problems?" Sean's tone was casual, but his gaze grazed Simone with an intensity that made her skin prickle.

"No. Just giving Simone a heads-up. River's rising. Neighbourly duty," Jeffery replied. He threw Simone a look—part warning, part possessive—before reversing and continuing down the lane.

Sean lifted a hand in lazy farewell, then watched the truck disappear. Only then did he turn that piercing gaze back on Simone. She felt pinned, inspected, as if every secret were suddenly visible. Flight seemed wise. She willed her legs to move but instead managed a stiff little wave at Jeffery's retreating vehicle—a gesture more for Sean's benefit than anyone else's.

Simone never got the chance to flee.

Sean lounged in the driver's seat, one arm draped casually over the door, his body relaxed but his eyes anything but. They lifted to meet hers—sharp, amused, and gleaming with something that danced dangerously close to mockery.

"I saw your little love scene," he drawled. His voice was low, teasing—but it carried an edge that cut.

Heat surged to Simone's cheeks. Her eyes flashed. "You have no business spying on us!"

"Spying?" His smile was cool and razor-sharp. "My dear Simone, you were right there in the open. Practically kissing him to death. I could see you from a mile off."

The sarcasm landed like a slap. And worse—he'd called her Simone again. Not darling girl, not sweetheart. Just her name. Crisp. Distant. Detached.

Her stomach twisted. He was angry, yes—but now he was calm. Toying with her. Giving himself space to wound.

Her pride flared. She held her ground, even as embarrassment darkened her eyes.

"Were you making a comparison?" He asked, voice low, laced with challenge.

God help her, she had. And it had been a reckless, disastrous mistake.

"How could Jeffery possibly compare to you?" she spat. "He's quiet. Kind. Not a lecherous—"

She didn't get to finish.

Sean moved fast—so fast she barely registered it. He sprang from the car like a whip crack, fierce and fluid, and in two strides he was on her.

Before she could blink, let alone stand her ground, she turned and ran—heart pounding, breath ragged—as she tore down the hill, feet slipping on the damp grass. The woods loomed ahead like a haven.

But he caught her just at the edge.

His hand locked around her arm, unyielding as iron. He spun her to face him, fury burning in his eyes.

"There are some names I don't take from anyone," he ground out, voice low and dangerous, "not even a red-haired vixen like you."

She ripped her arm from his grasp, shoulders squaring, rage blazing in her chest. "You don't have to take anything from me, Mr. Taylor. I've made up my mind. I'm leaving."

He stared at her.

"I'll send my resignation. I'll find another job—any job—until Jeffery and I get married."

His hands closed over her arms again, harder this time, cutting off blood and breath and thought.

"So that's what this is?" he said, voice guttural. "He proposed to you?"

Her throat tightened. She tried to speak, but the truth clung like ash to her tongue. Shame, loss, and foolishness swelled in her chest. She tugged at his grip, struggling to pull free—but he shook her once, hard, and the last of her resolve shattered.

The tears came, hot and fast, pouring down her cheeks in a storm she couldn't hold back.

Sean froze. Then, slowly, he let her go.

She crumpled to the grass, head bowed, shoulders shaking. The weight of everything—of him—pressed down on her like stone. Life without him stretched ahead, long, and joyless and empty.

It took him a moment to recover. Then he knelt beside her, cupping her face in his hands. His touch had gentled, but his eyes were still raw with feeling.

"I've hurt you," he said softly. "Don't cry, Simone. Please. I'm sorry—truly sorry, sweetheart."

"You're not!" she sobbed fiercely. "You love hurting me. You always have—and you always will. And don't call me that!"

"I've always called you that," he said softly.

"When I was a child, it was okay. It's not okay now."

He lowered himself beside her on the grass, his arms wrapping around her as he gazed down at her desperate, beautiful face.

"You've finally driven me away," she cried between ragged sobs. "You know how it will hurt my father. He hates Mrs Rogers—he'll never come to see me. I'll have to meet him in secret."

"Are they trying to make a slave of you, Simone?" His hand cradled her head, but she didn't notice. Nor did she see the flicker of amusement in his eyes.

"I'm supposed to have more self-discipline," she choked out, crushed by misery.

"The *hell* you are," he growled. "Nobody disciplines the Taylors."

"I'm not one," she whispered brokenly.

"By mutual agreement, you probably are." His fingers tangled in her wild red hair. "My mother loves you like her own."

It was a small comfort, but it settled something fragile inside her. Her sobs softened, the storm within her quieting beneath his touch.

"Besides," she admitted, "I don't think I'm going to marry Jeffery. And if you say his mother wouldn't let him—"

"I wasn't going to," he said with a dark grin. "I think we've had enough mileage out of Jeffery."

He swept her fully into his arms, lifting her off the ground. She went limp, a small captive caught by fascination, her luminous eyes searching his face, her flushed cheeks paling.

"Why aren't you marrying Jeffery?" His voice was low, urgent.

"I don't think he wants me. Not really."

"That's just as well. He can't have you."

His gaze dropped to her trembling lips and the world narrowed to that one still, sacred moment. Her heart slowed.

"Why do you say things like that?" she whispered.

"You know why." His voice dropped to a husky whisper. "For the same reason you smothered that poor boy with kisses. It's frustration—because this is what you want. What we both want."

His dark head lowered, eyes locked on hers until she closed them, surrendering. She floated higher into his arms as his lips claimed hers.

Her response was instant, igniting his desire like wildfire. From anger and tears to enchantment, she was spellbound—ready for his touch as if he had willed it into being. Her light body trembled in his embrace, every curve pressed close, as if made for him alone. His arms tightened convulsively, one hand tangling fiercely in her thick hair, drawing her mouth closer.

She had always been tempestuous—golden-eyed, flaming red hair, a radiant creature almost part of the wind and sky. He had wanted her for years, his recent fury sharpening his hunger until it burned dangerously bright.

"Open your mouth," he commanded against her lips.

Strangely, she had kept them closed, haunted by Jeffery's words that made her feel cheap. She pulled back, searching his face.

"Why?" Her voice was breathless, wary. "Why must I open my mouth?"

His fingers brushed her cheek, thumb tracing the soft curve of her lips, his gaze fixed on their sweet promise.

"Because when you open your mouth, you're saying yes to me," he murmured. "Say yes, Simone."

Her lips parted willingly, soft, and warm against his strength. He took them fiercely, draining her sweetness, losing almost all control. She quivered, a shudder of electric delight rippling through her as he lowered her to the grass, his body pressing over hers.

There was no way she'd be this close otherwise—naked beneath his touch, their skins igniting. Desire flamed white-hot.

Her slender arms curled around his neck, fingers threading through his glossy black hair. She felt the tension coiling inside him, holding back the raw drive to claim her utterly.

She thought only of the moment—of being crushed to Sean, tasting him, surrendering to every dream she'd ever had.

She murmured his name—Sean, Sean—over and over, caught in a deep, consuming ecstasy as his lips traced fire across her skin. His mouth moved back to hers, hungry and tender, hands trembling as they mapped the curves of her body with slow, fierce strokes.

His mouth worshipped her breasts, then travelled down to the taut tension of her stomach. She moved against him, wild and breathless, little cries spilling out until he stilled her with his lips.

The anger, the tears, the desperate need—they had driven them both into a sensual madness, obliterating all else but the taste and feel of each other.

She had waited her whole life for this—the powerful, sleek body covering hers, the urgent hands, the relentless hunger.

Sexual rapture swept her away on clouded wings.

"Sean! Sean!" she whispered, lost in the heat of him.

He answered by capturing her mouth again, more tender now, lips fused with hers in a sweet, endless compulsion. His hands trembled as they stroked her body slowly, reverently.

Her jeans' zipper slipped down, and joy burst through her with no trace of fear—not with Sean. She had never wanted anyone else and never would.

Her hips lifted of their own accord, moulding to him, and he sighed, a deep, shuddering sound, knowing they were poised on the edge of belonging—ready to leap together into forever.

"Oh God, this is madness!" He buried his face between her breasts.

She cried out, a broken plea.

"Don't stop, Sean. Don't leave me."

Chapter Twelve

They were words from long ago—echoes from her eighteenth birthday, when his kiss had ignited her into a blaze of longing. They rang in her head now, stirring memory, stirring pain, returning not just reason but a sweeping, hollow desolation.

"Don't," he said sharply, his voice tight, his body still taut above hers. He was attuned to every flicker of her expression, every change in her breathing, and he saw it—the moment her eyes opened wide and accusing.

"Don't throw us back into that."

But she had already shut him out. Her eyes closed again, tightly this time—not with surrender, but rejection. Her body stiffened, turning cold beneath his. The heat between them faded into something brittle and unyielding.

She lay still for a long moment, breathing hard, not looking at him, and then her volatile spirit snapped. With a cry of fury, she launched into him, her small fists pounding his chest, striking at his shoulders, even angling toward his face.

"Did you have nothing better to do today?" she cried. "Isn't there anyone else available but the hired help?" Tears rushed into her honey-gold eyes, blinding her. "It's not far to London if you start now!"

He caught her hands mid-swing, trapping them above her head in one swift, brutal movement. His grip was tight, just shy of painful, and his face was thunder.

"Stop it," he ground out. "I've had enough. You think you're the only one burning inside?" His voice was low and furious. "You wanted this. You wanted me. What did you expect? A polite proposal under the orchard trees while the merry country-folk applauded?"

"I saw you and Jeffery from a mile away. You really think we're invisible because we want each other?"

"Oh!" she cried, helpless in his grip, her whole body trembling. "Must the droit de seigneur be claimed at the castle?"

"I told you to stop!" he said, the warning in his voice edged with something darker.

But she didn't fight him anymore. She couldn't. The strength had left her limbs. She lay quiet, defeated, and he let her go slowly, watching her warily.

To his surprise, she didn't spring up and dash away like before. She just stayed there, limp as a rag doll, her breathing uneven, her eyes full of something lost and bewildered. The defiance had drained out of her, and all that was left was confusion.

He knelt beside her, straightening her sweater with rough gentleness, then helped her to her feet, steadying her when she swayed.

"You're a cruel brute," she murmured, her voice trembling. "A pig, even."

"That's right," he said grimly. "But don't push your luck. You've just learned where that gets you."

"I don't care." Still breathless, she fell back into defiance like it was the only shield she had left. "We've just proven that. Come on then."

He got his arm around her, not roughly, and began leading her back to the road. As they climbed the incline together, common sense returned. The slope gave them a clear view in every direction—they could have been seen by anyone.

She winced. He'd been right.

"I'm sorry," she muttered, her head low.

"Again," he replied dryly. "Repeat after me: I am not fit to be let out."

"I am not fit to be let out," she echoed solemnly, earning a sideways glance.

He marched her to his car and pushed the door open.

"What about the Land Rover? And the tree? And I still haven't—"

"Shut up!" Sean snapped. "You're going to drive me insane. The Land Rover stays where it is until I deal with it. Like everything else—it's mine."

"That's right," she said coolly. "You're the boss now."

"Sir, if you please. You forgot to say sir. Isn't that what I am these days?"

Despite everything that had just passed between them, he still looked a little grim—and she decided now was not the time to push further.

"Where are we going?" she asked at last, once it became clear they were heading off the estate.

"I'm going to the village. You're coming with me."

"I look a mess."

"Kissed to pieces," he said, eyes flicking over her, "but not a mess. It's your new image. Stunning."

"Is that why you kissed me?"

"Careful," he warned in a velvet tone. "You're alone with a cruel, untrustworthy brute—miles from anywhere."

A shiver ran through her. To shake it off, she changed course abruptly. "Where's Prince?"

"The treacherous dog of a treacherous master?" His mouth twisted again, and she turned to him with unexpected pleading in her gaze.

"I thought this was a truce?" she asked softly. "How can we call it that if you keep saying things like that?"

"It won't last," he said honestly. "You don't trust me—not really. Not when that peculiar little brain of yours starts ticking. But let's try."

"Fine. Then where is Prince?" she pressed, unwilling to let go of the small olive branch.

"I don't bring him every time. He wants too much. He's convinced he should drive. I threaten him."

That made her laugh, a soft, surprised sound that lightened something in both of them. She turned to him, all resistance gone for a moment, and let her heart speak.

"Sometimes… sometimes I adore you," she said gently.

"But mostly you don't trust me." He gave her a sidelong look. "Here we are."

They rolled into the village, Sean acknowledging greetings with casual waves. Simone bit her lip. She didn't want to be anywhere else. Just being near him again—no walls, no barriers—was like sunlight after a long storm. Fleur felt distant now, irrelevant. She could still taste Sean's kiss on her lips.

He led her into the tearoom with quiet insistence and ordered her a cup of tea. At first, she was nervous, jittery from the emotional whiplash of the day—but when Sean set his mind to charming her, he was utterly disarming. He could make her feel like she was the only woman in the world.

She relaxed, slowly, drawn into his quiet magnetism.

He made her laugh. He made her feel seen.

And though she wouldn't say it aloud, not yet, she had loved him all her life. Just sitting there across from him, lost in his voice and the way his mouth curved when he teased her—it was magic.

It always had been.

Later, Simone sat quietly in Sean's car, the warmth of the tea still in her hands, the turmoil in her heart louder than anything outside. He'd gone into the post office, leaving her with only the sound of ticking minutes and her own racing thoughts.

And that was when Jeffery pulled up.

She saw the moment he spotted her—his car hesitated, then braked hard. The gears ground in protest as he reversed, and within seconds he was out, towering over the car, his face dark with something between confusion and fury.

"What are you doing here? In his car?" he demanded.

Simone sat a little straighter, the sting of his tone igniting her pride. "I'm with Sean. We came in for a cup of tea."

She tried not to sound defiant, but she wasn't going to feel guilty—not when Jeffery was glaring at her like she belonged to him, as if he had every right to question her movements.

"I don't like it," he said flatly. "Even if you do work for him. You're my girl, and I'll feel an utter fool if people see you out with Sean Taylor."

"I'm sorry, Jeffery, but…" She braced herself to say it—to tell him the truth, to end whatever fragile illusion he was clinging to—but the chance was gone in a heartbeat.

Sean had returned.

He walked up slowly, his eyes glinting like frosted steel as he took in Simone's flushed cheeks and Jeffery's confrontational stance. Without a word, he opened the driver's door and got in, starting the engine.

His mouth was a straight, unreadable line. Simone could feel the tension vibrating off him.

"I'll talk to you at the dance tomorrow," Jeffery said tightly.

"I'm afraid not," Sean said coolly. "Simone's going out with me."

Then they were moving, the car gliding away from the kerb, leaving Jeffery behind, fists clenched, scowling at their retreating taillights.

Simone turned toward Sean, wide-eyed. "Why did you say that? Why? It'll be all over the village by morning. Jeffery tells his mother everything."

"Good," Sean said without an ounce of apology. "Let her chew on that for a while. We've seen enough of young Rogers."

"Would you stop that? He's twenty-five!"

"A twenty-five-year-old boy," Sean replied dryly. "You can do better. And you will."

"You can't just decide that!"

"Strange," he murmured, "I thought I just had."

She gaped at him, trying to make sense of the high-handedness, the casual arrogance.

"I have my reasons," he continued. "First—because I raised you to have some standards. Jeffery and his formidable mother don't qualify. My mother and Cleo would never step foot in a house run by Mrs Rogers. And neither, as you know, would Henry. You'd be alone out there. And you—disciplined?" He shot her a glance. "Can you imagine it?"

She opened her mouth to argue but he cut her off.

"Second, you don't belong at a farmer's dance. Your new image deserves better. You belong in places that challenge your wit, match your spirit. That's what I've prepared you for, whether you like it or not."

"I think I have a virus," Simone said, stunned. "I'm hearing words, but they're not making any sense. You can't mean this."

"I mean every word. From now on, you're going out with me. Regularly. Until Rogers is nothing more than a footnote."

"I refuse," she snapped, her heart thundering, trying to drown out the sudden hope and terror that surged in her chest. "This is outrageous. It's ridiculous. It's snobbish."

"I'm not a snob," he said calmly. "I simply know what's right for you. I always have."

She folded her arms across her chest, fuming. "That's not a reason. That's control."

"There is another reason. The real one."

She turned her head sharply, waiting.

"I want you," he said simply. "Not out there in a field, in a moment of madness. Properly. Completely."

The words silenced her. Her mind emptied. She could barely breathe. Was this Sean— her childhood idol, the untouchable one—declaring war on her independence, her heart?

He glanced sideways at her, noting the pale sweep of her cheek, the tension in her jaw, the fingers curled tightly in her lap.

"There's no need to be nervous," he said more gently. "I'll make you happy. You'll wake up in my arms."

"Stop," she whispered. "Sean, please don't talk like that. I—I feel strange."

"You wanted me to stop earlier, but you didn't mean it. And you know it."

"I didn't!" Her voice cracked. "I didn't mean… this. You haven't wanted me—if you had, you would have—"

"I've wanted you for years," he said, his voice low and rough. "I knew it when you were sixteen and looking at me with those wide eyes like I hung the moon. That's why I packed you off with Cleo—to keep you safe. You were too young, Simone. Even at eighteen, still a wild flame. But now you're a woman. The most passionate, dangerous woman I've ever known. And I'm done waiting."

She trembled. "Are you saying—are you proposing to me?"

He laughed softly, but not kindly. "Proposing? No. Not yet. Marriage isn't what I'm thinking of at the moment."

She looked up at the blue sky through the windscreen, trying to steady herself against the motion of the car. The trees flew past in a blur of green and sunlight. Her heart plummeted.

She had thought… hoped… he was offering love. A future. But no. He was offering possession. And only locally.

She couldn't speak. Not when her mind was racing through every heartbreak she'd endured because of him.

"Don't be frightened," he murmured, taking her cold hand in his and brushing it with his lips. "Haven't I always taken care of you?"

She didn't answer. She was too afraid of what would come out if she opened her mouth.

Because what she wanted wasn't safety. It was Sean. Completely.

And that was the one thing he didn't seem ready to give.

And terribly, irrevocably, Simone knew he would—if she gave in.

She hadn't spoken a word on the drive back. Silence wrapped around her like a shroud, and she couldn't look at Sean. She doubted she'd ever be able to again.

As the car pulled up outside the Dower House, a hollow dread settled in her chest. She didn't belong here anymore—not at Branlow Hall, not in this skin that felt suddenly foreign. The impulse to flee struck her so violently she almost reached for the door handle before the car stopped. She wanted to run. Far, fast, and blindly.

But instead, she sat frozen, brittle with disbelief. This wasn't some sly, whispered seduction. It was all out in the open now, the rules laid bare and non-negotiable. Sean had drawn the lines—and she was expected to step neatly inside them.

He was calm. Controlled. Impeccably normal.

He got out and came around to open the door for her, helping her out with the kind of smooth courtesy that made her stomach twist. Of course he would. She was his new mistress, after all. The local madwoman had finally been tamed.

He didn't step aside immediately, and her eyes dropped instinctively to his sweater, to the breadth of his chest. She couldn't raise her gaze any higher. Not now. Maybe not ever.

"No more work today," he said gently, his voice brushing against her like velvet over steel. "I'll deal with the Land Rover and let the tenants know about the river."

She said nothing.

He reached out, tilting her face toward him, and her eyes—wide, startled, lost—met his.

"I'll call for you at eight. We're going to dinner. Then a nightclub. I like the green dress."

"Yes, Sean."

The words came automatically, void of defiance. She could have shouted. Could have thrown it all back in his face. But she didn't want to. That was the truly frightening thing. She felt like a vessel he'd emptied and now claimed as his own—pliable, waiting to be filled again, remade in his image.

His soft laugh slid through her like a current. And then his hand moved from her chin to her cheek, stroking her face like a promise or a warning.

"You'll get used to it," he said, almost kindly. "Sometimes we'll even fight. But I'm not going to rush you."

He bent and kissed her, slow and unhurried, his lips brushing hers with a proprietary finality.

"Eight o'clock," he said, and walked back to his car. Moments later, he was gone.

Simone stood there a moment longer, not moving, not breathing. Then she turned and walked inside like a sleepwalker.

I'm a shadow, she thought numbly. I don't really exist.

Everything felt unreal, like the slow spin of a dream after waking. The house was quiet—her father out, the staff elsewhere—and for that she was grateful. No one to see her like this. Not that they'd see anything at all. She wasn't real. She didn't cast a shadow. If she looked into a mirror, she was certain nothing would be there.

She avoided the mirror anyway.

In the kitchen, she tried to pour herself a cup of tea. The saucer rattled beneath her shaking hand, and she stared at it, startled by the sound. Even that slight clatter felt too loud, too alive.

The tea didn't help. It tasted distant, like something meant for someone else.

She sat, hands wrapped around the cup, but no warmth seeped into her fingers. She couldn't think—not until Sean allowed it. Until then, she would drift, a body without a will, a spirit without direction.

A ghost in her own skin.

Sean drove away from the Dower House, jaw tight, hands clenched on the wheel.

He couldn't stop seeing it—that moment burned behind his eyes like a brand. Simone in Jeffery's arms. Jeffery kissing her like she belonged to him. Like he had the right.

Sean had wanted to kill him.

No—not in the vague, jealous way a man sometimes does. He'd wanted to walk right up to him and tear him limb from limb. Rip his head off. Drag Simone away and tell her she was his—*still*, always.

The fury had been so sudden, so consuming, he'd barely trusted himself not to act on it.

And worse than the rage… was the ache. The hollow, bone-deep ache of knowing it was his own damned fault.

He'd left her. Pushed her away. Told her she was a child when all she'd ever done was idolise him.

And then, today—he'd done it again. Let his temper flare, let his jealousy take the wheel, and when it landed on her, it broke something in her eyes.

She'd cried.

Not scream, not fought—just broke.

And when she said, *"You love hurting me. You always have,"* something inside him shattered.

Is that what she *really* thought?

God.

He never meant to hurt her. That had never been the plan. He'd meant to protect her—from him, from the world, from the future he didn't know how to promise. But somewhere along the way, protection had started to look a lot like punishment.

And the worst part?

When she looked up at him, all flushed and furious, standing her ground like the wild thing she was… he'd wanted her.

Desperately.

He wanted to take her up on that hill and lose himself in her completely. And she would've let him—he knew that. Felt it in the way she trembled under his hands.

But he hadn't.

Because she deserved more than that.

Not taken in anger, not as a salve for jealousy or a reckless answer to pain. Not when she was trembling and furious, her heart already bruised and breaking.

She wasn't his to claim like that. Not when she was still half in tears, still raw from words he hadn't meant but had thrown anyway.

She deserved to be wanted for the right reasons.

And he wanted to be the man who gave her that—who chose her, not in a moment of weakness or want, but with clarity, with intention.

Not just the man who took.

He'd already taken too much.

It was time he started showing her how she truly deserved to be treated—with care, with respect. No more sharp words. No more pushing her away just to pull her back again.

No more hurt.

Not from him.

Chapter Thirteen

Even as Simone dressed, reality felt elusive. Fleeting. Unreal.

She remembered one thing clearly: Sean wanted the green dress.

That much had stayed with her, echoing through the haze in her mind like a directive she didn't dare question.

She hadn't spoken properly to her father all day. When he came home, she'd called down vaguely from the landing, grateful when her voice carried—thin but audible—as if that brief thread of normality could anchor her. It gave her just enough courage to glance in the mirror.

But she couldn't hold her own gaze.

Her eyes looked too wide, too dark in her pale face, like someone else's had been painted onto hers. Her hair, glowing copper, and fire was the only thing that still felt familiar, the only part of her that hadn't been rearranged by Sean's hands or his words.

She drifted downstairs like a ghost made of silk and nerves. Her father glanced up from the sideboard where he was pouring a drink—and froze.

"Heavens, love. Are you alright?"

"Perfectly." She mustered a bright smile that felt absurdly fake, certain she looked like a scarecrow in lipstick and silk.

"I've never seen you look so lovely—but you're pale. Too pale." He stared at her, then added gently, "Tell that young Rogers to get you home early. Wherever is he taking you, dressed like that?"

"I—I'm going out with Sean." The name caught in her throat, the syllables barely a whisper.

Her father's face changed. Softened.

"Ah. That explains it."

She didn't know what it explained, but he said it with such kindness it almost undid her. When the sound of Sean's car rolled up the drive, she had to stop herself from blurting, Come with me, Dad. Just come along. Please don't let me go alone.

There was nothing secretive about Sean. He strode into the house like he always had, as if he still belonged in every room.

"I suppose you've heard about the river, Henry?" he said casually, greeting her father like nothing in the world had shifted. "I've passed the word around. If anyone gets their stock trapped now, they've only themselves to blame."

"Even the beck's rising," her father said with a grim nod. "Could be bad this year."

They sounded so normal, both of them. She wanted to scream. Instead, she stood in silence, feeling her throat constrict, her heart hammering wildly as one mad thought bloomed: *Daddy, I'm going to be Sean's mistress. I'd like you to be the first to know.*

Sean turned to her, smiling. His eyes softened and he reached out a hand.

"Come on, Sunflower. I've booked the table."

And that was it. She slipped her hand into his, let him lead her out into the moonlit evening.

She didn't feel the cold. Didn't feel anything.

At the car, Sean paused and looked down at her. His gaze traced her face, her hair, her trembling mouth.

"Full beautiful—a fairy's child," he murmured, quoting softly, and kissed her cheek like a benediction. "I really think you need a strong drink."

The brandy came first. It was the only thing she could stomach as they waited for their table. It brought a trace of colour back to her face, enough for Sean to smile approvingly.

People were looking at her—she was sure of it—and every glance felt magnified, like heat on glass.

Sean noticed. He always noticed.

"They're only admiring you," he said with a quiet smirk, drawing her in closer. "Don't look around for a stick."

But she wasn't that girl anymore. The girl who would've snapped back with something clever, ridiculous, or defiant. That Simone had vanished into the fog somewhere between his kiss and his command.

Over dinner, Sean was charm itself—amused, attentive, never letting her retreat too far into herself. He directed her gently back to her food when she forgot to eat, his voice coaxing, his eyes dancing with light.

Afterward came the floor show—then the surprise: the casino.

She'd never been to one. Not even close. But the lights, the glittering sound of chips and laughter, the charged energy of the place—it pulled her in like a tide.

Sean stood behind her at the roulette table, guiding her gently, murmuring advice into her ear, his hand resting lightly on her chair.

At first, she was nervous, stiff, overwhelmed. But then came a win—then another— and she turned, wide-eyed, to see his reaction.

"I won!" she gasped, colour rising to her cheeks for the first time all day.

"I know. Don't get hooked," he said with a smile. But his eyes told her something else.

Oh, she was hooked. But not on the thrill of the wheel. Not on the chips in her hand or the buzz in the air.

She was hooked on him. And he knew it.

Flustered, she turned back to the table, going in for one more round. Her fingers trembled now—not with nerves, but anticipation.

And then she felt it.

Sean's hands, warm and steady, came to rest on her shoulders. He didn't move them, just let them settle there—possessive, protective, terrifying.

Then, gently, he began to caress the nape of her neck, his thumbs moving in slow, imperceptible circles beneath the fall of her hair.

She melted. Her bones dissolved.

She wanted to tip back her head and close her eyes and let the world vanish. She wanted him to lift her from the chair, take her away, and never put her down again.

She didn't even know what game she was playing anymore.

All she knew was the touch of his hands and the heat blooming inside her—and that she was already losing, completely, to Sean Taylor.

Sean drove her home well after midnight—long past the hour Jeffery would've been tucked into bed, safe and proper under Mrs. Rogers' ever-watchful eye.

Simone, by contrast, felt like something out of a novel—a wicked lady, glamorous, elusive, pursued and deeply desired.

For most of the drive, Sean kept up a light, teasing commentary, coaxing laughter from her until—for brief, blessed stretches—she forgot the knot of tension at the base of her spine, forgot what it meant to belong to Sean Taylor, even temporarily.

When they reached the Dower House, the hush of night had settled in completely. Her father's car was parked neatly in its usual place, the house dark except for the warm, golden light glowing in the front hall.

Sean eased the car to a stop with quiet precision, then turned to her.

And the trembling started all over again.

He leaned across the car, his fingers gentle as they tilted her face toward him, brushing her cheek with the backs of his knuckles.

"Kiss your date goodnight," he said softly, almost teasing—but his voice had a depth that pulled at something inside her.

Then his lips met hers. A feather-light touch, just a brush—but her lips parted before she could stop them, a tremor catching in her breath.

His mouth lingered, just barely there, as he murmured against her lips, "Want me?"

She couldn't move, couldn't speak. Her answer was in the way she trembled beneath his touch, in the wild pulse fluttering at her throat.

Sean drew back a fraction, just enough to study her face. One hand slid gently around her neck, his thumb resting in the hollow just below her jaw. The possessive warmth of his palm only deepened her confusion.

"Don't be frightened," he said, his voice low and steady. "I'll never hurt you."

She stared at him, spellbound, caught in the way his eyes devoured her face, smiling with something softer now.

"Did you enjoy tonight?"

"Yes… thank you, Sean." It came out as a whisper, barely audible.

His smile deepened.

"You're afraid of yourself," he said gently. "But when I take you, I want it to be a joy, not a terror. You're beautiful, Simone. Goodnight."

He kissed her again—quickly this time—then got out of the car to open the door for her like the gentleman he could so effortlessly pretend to be.

"Lock the house," he said with a sudden crooked grin, "just in case someone tries to steal Henry."

She smiled despite herself and stepped out, the gravel crunching softly under her heels.

When she reached the door, he called her name.

"Simone."

She turned, her hand on the doorknob. He stood outlined in moonlight, tall and magnetic, impossibly handsome in the half-light, his expression unreadable but intensely focused on her.

"Tomorrow morning," he said quietly. "Bring Stardust back to the stables. I want to ride with you." Then he added with a faint smile, "Although I suppose that's usually Cleo's pleasure."

Simone hesitated. "Stardust seems to have settled here."

"She knows where she belongs," he replied evenly. "So do you." His gaze flickered once more over her face. "I'll ring you."

Then he was gone, his taillights vanishing down the lane like something out of a dream.

Simone stood in the hall for a long time afterward, still wrapped in moonlight and sensation, feeling dazed and barely real—but alive again. Sparked.

He had been wonderful to her. Attentive. Gentle. Possessive. She touched her lips, still warm from his kiss, her pulse still erratic.

He would take her. She knew it. And she wouldn't stop him.

That night she slept deeply, dreamlessly—except for one recurring truth woven through the dark:

Every dream she'd ever had had always been of Sean.

"Simone! You're back!"

Cleo leaned across the saddle to hug her as Simone galloped up, breathless.

"I didn't wait—I thought our rides were done for good. Has Sean relented?"

"Yes," Simone said shortly, drawing her horse in beside Cleo's. The fresh morning air, the rhythmic thud of hooves—none of it seemed to clear the tangle in her chest. At this moment, she wanted peace, not questions. But this was Cleo—discretion wasn't exactly part of her repertoire.

Cleo glanced over, her eyes narrowing. "You've got little purple shadows under your eyes. I've never seen that before. Did Jeffery keep you out late? I called at ten and your father said you were still out. But Jeffery's usually tucked up by then, reading the Farmer's Almanac with his mum, isn't he?"

"I wasn't out with Jeffery," Simone said, trying to sound breezy.

Please, don't push. Just leave it, Cleo. Don't find out until you have to.

But Cleo was in full sparkle mode, all eyes and mischief, turning to Simone with a delighted gasp. "You've found someone else! Thank the saints above—I thought I was going to have to stage an intervention. I cannot stand Jeffery."

"He's not too keen on you either," Simone retorted, hoping the jab might redirect her. It only worked for a second.

"He said so. The nerve! Well, I suppose he doesn't like that I object to him turning you into a decorative paperweight. I was dreading being forced into sister-in-law status with the Rogers family. So come on, who is it? Spill!"

Cornered, Simone knew she had no choice. Sean hadn't exactly made it a covert mission—he'd picked her up at her own house and chatted away with her father like they were old chums.

"I went out with Sean," she said, trying to keep it neutral. "We had dinner. And… went to the casino."

Cleo reined in hard, staring at her like she'd grown a second head. Then, a slow grin crept over her face.

"Oh! Oh, oh!" she crowed, her voice dancing with glee. "He was whistling this morning. Whistling, Simone. Like a man who'd just won the lottery. The glares are gone, and I saw a handsome stranger with a big black dog looking suspiciously smug!"

"I see a raving lunatic with a big black eye if you don't stop," Simone snapped, her cheeks flushed. "This is a truce. Temporary."

What else could she say? If Cleo ever got wind of Sean's intentions—if she even suspected the kind of proposition he'd made—she'd have a full-blown fit. And Lady Vivian? She'd dissolve into lace and scandal.

"Well, you're riding again, aren't you? That tells me Stardust will be back in her rightful stall before sundown."

"She will not," Simone said firmly, turning her horse to follow Cleo up the hill. "I decide where my horse lives. This truce may end at any second, and I'm not going through that drama again."

Right then and there, she decided to defy Sean. If she gave him an inch, he'd take the whole estate. No, she'd keep Stardust tucked away down at the Dower House, sneakily if necessary. Sean didn't check the stables every day—surely, he wouldn't notice a single missing mare.

"Sean looks happy, though," Cleo commented, her tone thoughtful as they crested the rise. "And that's saying something. He's been a bear with a sore head for months. Fleur is absolutely fuming—I don't know why she's still hanging about, being snide to us in our house. Mark looks like he's preparing for war but hasn't figured out how to declare it. And Sean is… well, Sean is acting oddly civilised. Which means…"

She shot Simone a knowing glance. "Something's brewing. The vat is definitely starting to boil."

A ripple of cold crept across Simone's skin. It wasn't the breeze—it was the thought. Sean could out-plan anyone, charm or bulldoze his way through any obstacle. Was she tangled in one of his schemes? Was this all part of some slow-burning strategy involving Fleur?

"Is Alex coming up this weekend?" she asked suddenly, eager to reroute the conversation. She had the quiet satisfaction of seeing Cleo blush, pink blooming high on her cheeks.

"I don't think so. He's very busy, you know. He rang last night and said he might come up next weekend."

"I see a dark stranger with a respectable job in London," Simone said slyly, arching an eyebrow.

Cleo burst into laughter. "I like him, Simone. He's such fun. I think he likes me too." Then she added, mock-serious, "And don't hit him again. I'd resent it."

It startled Simone to remember how fiery she'd been not so long ago. Back when she was filled with certainties, instincts, righteous fury. Now? She was full of doubt and foreboding—longing to see Sean, terrified of what would happen when she did.

"Alex will definitely be here for the Easter ball," Cleo added.

Simone's stomach dropped.

The Easter ball. How had she forgotten that?

Every year it was the same: a grand charity event at Branlow Hall, the whole family working together, the entire county turning out in their best. She'd always been a part of it—ever since she was old enough to tie ribbons and polish glassware. But this year, everything had changed. She had changed.

By then, Sean might be her lover.

The thought made her tremble. If anyone else had told her that a man like Sean could unmoor her this way, she'd have either collapsed in laughter or launched a solid punch at their jaw. But with Sean, it was different. Dangerous.

If he kept on as he had last night—with that gentleness, that wicked humour, those maddening, melting kisses—then she was already lost.

Chapter Fourteen

This morning, she had floated through the hours, remembering how tender he'd been. Now she felt like two women in one body—a scandalous siren in a green dress and a confused girl still aching for direction.

And Fleur was still there. Still hanging around Branlow Hall like a shadow in silk.

Nothing was going to sort itself out. Not in this lifetime.

"Race you!" Cleo cried, abruptly yanking Simone out of her thoughts. She dug in her heels and took off toward the edge of the woods, her laughter trailing behind her like a ribbon.

For once, she won. She reined in hard at the clearing and turned in her saddle, flushed with victory and a bright glint in her eye. "I've got a plan!"

Simone groaned. "Count me out. I was the victim of your last plan. Remember the raspberry cordial incident? Or the fencing instructor with the wandering hands?"

Cleo waved away her objections, gleeful. "This one's different. It's about Mark. And the Easter ball."

Simone arched a brow. "Mark? What about him?"

"Invite Rhonda! He adores her. She tickles him to death—always has. Maybe if we set them up properly this time, he'll finally fall."

"And what does he do with Fleur in the meantime? Drop her off at the train station and hope she boards the next express?"

"Things have a habit of working out," Cleo said serenely, the confidence of someone whose own love life was firmly in bloom.

Simone laughed—dryly, without humour. "Things," in her world, had a habit of biting back. She didn't even know if Mark had the spine to go up against Fleur, and if he did manage to get rid of her, that would clear the field for Sean.

And that—more than anything—was what frightened her.

"Invite her and see," Cleo pleaded, clearly sensing victory.

"No!" The word burst out of Simone before she could soften it. This wasn't about Mark. It wasn't even about Rhonda. It was her. She didn't want to lose Sean. And the moment Fleur was out of the way; she might have to face the full weight of what Sean wanted—and what she might give in to.

"I'll keep on at you," Cleo warned smugly, turning her horse with the assurance of someone who always got her way eventually.

Another plan. Another scheme. Cleo had always been a great one for planning, even when they were girls—but more often than not, it had been Simone who'd suffered when the plans went wrong.

And something told her this plan, like all the rest, might lead to heartache.

As they neared the hall, Prince came bounding out from around the corner, his black coat gleaming in the sun. Simone's heart thudded hard. Prince was never far from Sean unless ordered back—his sudden appearance could mean only one thing.

Sean was close.

Sure enough, when they rode into the stable-yard, there he was—leaning casually against the fence, deep in conversation with Jerry. He turned as they approached, his blue eyes instantly locking onto Simone.

He crossed the yard in three easy strides, hand coming up to stroke Stardust's silky mane with familiar ease.

"Have a nice ride?" he asked, gaze steady and amused.

Simone nodded like a fool, her heart in her throat, her voice nowhere to be found.

His smile curled slowly, the kind that warmed and unnerved her in equal measure. He held up his arms. "Going to get down, then?"

What choice did she have? With Cleo already watching like a cat at a cream bowl, Simone slid down into his arms. For a moment—just a breath—he held her there. Not casually. Not indifferently. And certainly not as a brother figure.

She could feel Cleo's bubbling glee behind her, but there was nothing she could do about it.

Sean released her slowly, his hands trailing away with reluctant precision, and Simone blushed furiously.

Cleo tossed her reins to Jerry with a grin. "Unsaddle for me, Jerry, and I won't tell anyone you dye your hair."

"Cheeky madam!" Jerry chuckled, taking the reins. "That Miss Cleo's a real card," he added, shaking his head as he disappeared into the stables.

Simone gave her friend a helpless look as Cleo sauntered off—very obviously giving them space. That left her standing awkwardly in front of Sean, the horses, the truth… all of it.

"I had to tell her we went out last night," she murmured, eyes fixed on her boots.

Sean tilted her chin up with one commanding finger, forcing her to meet his gaze. "Had to tell her?" His voice was low, firm. "It's no secret, is it? Pretty soon it'll be clear to everyone that you're going out with me—and not with Jeffery."

"I… I didn't know if you wanted anyone to know. I thought—"

"Didn't I call for you at home last night?" he asked pointedly. "I'll be calling again tonight."

Her eyes flew to his face. "Are we going out?"

The question slipped out before she could stop it, and her pleasure was so immediate, so unguarded, that Sean's arms moved easily around her, forming a loose, protective circle behind her back.

"We are," he said with a smile. "But this time I'll have you in earlier. You've got little shadows under your eyes, and no heroic deeds today, alright?"

Before she could answer, a high laugh sliced through the moment like a blade across silk.

Fleur.

She swept into the yard with that theatrical tilt of her head and bright, mocking eyes. "Oh, Sean! Whatever is this? Playing the wicked squire with the local help?"

The words landed like a slap, and Simone went rigid, the glow inside her instantly extinguished. She stiffened beneath Sean's arm, shame and defensiveness rising like twin flames.

But Sean's arm didn't fall away. In fact, he pulled her closer.

His jaw was tight. "Didn't you get the message?" he said coldly. "I thought you knew Simone was my girl."

Fleur's brows lifted in open disbelief. "Since when?" She laughed again, still convinced this was some kind of elaborate tease.

Sean looked down at Simone with a softness that made her breath catch. "How long have I known you?"

"About… seventeen years," she answered, her voice shaky, the words catching in her throat.

"There you go," he said simply. "Since then."

Fleur opened her mouth and closed it again. For once, she was speechless.

Sean leaned down and brushed the tip of Simone's nose with a kiss. "In case I don't see you before," he murmured, "I'll pick you up at seven. If we head out early, you can be tucked in before midnight. I don't want you tired."

He said it so casually, but his meaning curled through her like a touch on bare skin.

Simone barely managed a nod before she turned and walked away—escaped was more like it. Her knees threatened to give out and her thoughts were tangled beyond saving. Sean was angry with Fleur. That much had been clear. But she wasn't sure he even noticed she'd taken Stardust with her.

That public display, that kiss in front of Fleur—was it for her? Or for Fleur?

He was staking his claim, yes. Openly, deliberately. And in some secret, aching corner of her heart, it thrilled her. But she knew what no one else did—what he had said.

He didn't want marriage. He wanted her as a mistress. A possession. A pleasure.

It was exhilarating. And humiliating. And heartbreakingly tragic—all at once.

And maybe—just maybe—that was a lie too. Cleo had said he was behaving strangely. And hadn't that little scene in the stable yard been entirely out of character for Sean? Public affection? Soft declarations? Protectiveness?

Fleur had been rattled. Furious. Shaken.

Maybe that had been the point. Maybe Simone was the message, wrapped in silk and kissed in daylight, meant for Fleur's eyes.

And maybe… just maybe… she didn't care.

By the end of the week, Simone was more bewildered than ever. Sean had taken her out nearly every evening, each time sweeping her into his world with such casual charm and quiet attentiveness that she barely recognised herself anymore. He entertained her, looked after her, kissed her goodnight with an affection that was both restrained and promising—and never once stepped beyond that invisible line.

It left her walking on air and tied in emotional knots.

She stopped trying to understand what it all meant. Every time she tried to pin it down, it slipped away like mist in sunlight. So, she took refuge in living one day at a time—one look, one laugh, one kiss at a time.

And if, at the back of her mind, she knew Fleur must have noticed Sean's near-nightly disappearances, she refused to let it fester. It would ruin everything. Sean was with her, not Fleur. That had to be enough.

Maybe, she told herself, it would have to be enough forever.

But then, at the end of the week, Sean went down to London—and the illusion fractured.

She missed him more than she thought possible. It ached—sharp and real. The idea of Fleur waiting there for him was like a physical blow, knocking the breath out of her. She couldn't ask, couldn't accuse, couldn't claim anything.

So, she worked. She filled her days with chores and plans, anything to keep herself from thinking too much. On Saturday evening, Cleo came down to have dinner with her, looking just as distracted.

Alex couldn't get away for the weekend either and she was missing him miserably.

"Fleur's running riot, you know," Cleo said as they curled up with coffee before the fire in the drawing room. The logs crackled cheerfully, but neither of them was smiling. "Mark's more or less ignoring her. It's extraordinary—some days he looks right through her. And Fleur's been watching Sean all week like he might grow horns and a tail at any minute."

Simone stirred her coffee slowly. "She knows I've been going out with him," she said quietly.

Cleo turned her head sharply, her expression softening. She reached over and patted Simone's hand. "Are you really? Is it official then?" Her eyes sparkled a little. "I've always known how you felt about Sean. All that sparring—it was camouflage. Poor Jeffery never stood a chance."

Simone gave a thin, wry smile. "Cleo—"

"How beautifully things are working out!" Cleo sighed, leaning back against the cushions like a cat settling into cream. "You and Sean, Alex, and me… All we have to do is get rid of Fleur. I was really rather banking on Rhonda."

"Oh, don't," Simone groaned. "No more plans. Please."

"But darling, I have to see to Mark. He is my brother. We'll all be so happy—you married to Sean, Alex and me living blissfully ever after—"

She broke off mid-sentence, her eyes darting to Simone's stricken expression.

"…Anyway," she added hastily, "we've got a bit of peace coming. Fleur's going back to London tomorrow. Some new job, apparently."

Simone nearly dropped her coffee.

Fleur was going to London.

Sean was in London.

She gripped the cup tighter, swallowing hard past the lump in her throat. It was so blindingly obvious. Surely Cleo could see it? But her friend's cheerfulness had a dreamy, self-satisfied edge. Cleo saw only what she wanted to see.

Simone felt ancient in that moment. Older than Cleo. Older than herself. She wasn't the impulsive, spirited girl she'd been weeks ago. Something inside her had shifted. Solidified. Hardened with quiet dread.

Before the summer was over, this would all be settled—and in her heart, she feared the ending. Sean would choose the woman he truly wanted. And desperately, painfully, she knew that woman would not be her.

The rain came down heavily on Sunday, fat drops rattling the windows like impatient fingers. The river swelled with alarming speed, rising high enough to spill over in several places.

They'd been forewarned, thank goodness, and most of the stock had already been moved to higher ground. But the weather put her father in a foul mood.

"I've never known it to be fine for the show," he grumbled, standing in his boots by the back door, dripping and cross. "All that work, and it pours at least two days out of four. Every year!"

He was referring to the annual agricultural show held in the neighbouring town—a four-day event that drew breeders and buyers from across the country. Part fair, part marketplace, it was a highlight of the calendar. Children came for the stalls and games, families for the food and spectacle, and farmers for the serious business of judging and purchasing livestock.

Her father and Sir Michael went every day without fail—they were both stewards and took great pride in the event.

Simone usually attended for one day, slipping in to watch the horse-jumping and chat with old friends.

This year, she wasn't sure she could bear it.

Everything was changing. The show would be the same—muddy, noisy, bursting with life. But she wasn't the same. Not anymore.

Chapter Fifteen

On Monday morning, the phone rang—and just the sound of Sean's voice made Simone's knees give way. She had to sit down before she dropped the receiver.

"I can't get back until tomorrow," he told her. "Alex and I have a few things to iron out here. Something unexpected came up."

The words were simple enough, but Simone could barely hear them past the roaring in her ears. Something unexpected. She didn't need to guess what that something was. Fleur. Fleur had gone down to London—gone to him. And he hadn't come back.

She couldn't summon a breezy reply. There was no lightness in her voice, no pretend ease. Only the truth, sitting like stone in her chest.

There was a pause. "Simone? Are you still there?" His voice sharpened with concern.

She forced her thoughts back under control, blinking hard. "Yes. I'm here. I'll see you tomorrow, then?"

"Of course you will," he said softly.

And the sound of it—the warmth in his voice, the gentle possession—made tears prick at the back of her eyes. Even now, even knowing, she couldn't help melting under it. He had this way of speaking that undid her entirely. She had no doubt he wanted her. But how many other women had he wanted, and said the same things to?

Her throat tightened. "It's been raining here. Has it rained in London?"

It was a stupid question, but she couldn't think of anything else. Keep it light, she told herself. Keep it normal.

Sean chuckled, a low, intimate sound that sent a tremor down her spine. "Are we falling back on that good old standby—the weather?"

"I thought you might want to know," she murmured. "The river's spilled a bit more."

"I appreciate the update," he said, amused. "But that's not what I wanted to hear. Are you missing me?"

His voice dropped, smooth and seductive, and she gripped the receiver tighter, white-knuckled. The ache inside her deepened. Yes. God, yes. She was missing him in ways she didn't know how to name.

She didn't answer.

"Simone?"

"Yes," she whispered. "I'm missing you."

There was a pause, barely a breath, and then his voice returned, quiet and warm.

"I'll be back tomorrow, sweetheart. As soon as I can. It might be late, but we'll drive straight out, just us. A little country pub—no dressing up. Just you and me."

When he said goodbye, the line clicked silent—but she didn't move. She just sat there, staring at the ceiling, her chest rising and falling like she'd run a race. She loved him. Helplessly, completely. He was her past, her present—and she feared, her undoing.

When he finally reached for her—truly reached—she would melt into him without resistance. There had only ever been Sean. Her battles with him had always been a smokescreen for the one she was fighting with herself.

The phone rang again, startling her. Cleo's cheerful voice rang down the line.

"You sound like you've been crying," she said briskly. "That's it. On with the plastic mac. We're going to the show."

"I've got things to do," Simone said half-heartedly, rubbing a hand over her face.

"Leave them. Who's going to complain? Sean's in charge now—and he adores you."

Temporarily, Simone thought, the word curling bitterly in her chest. Temporarily. And he didn't adore her. He desired her. There was a difference—and one that could destroy her if she wasn't careful.

Any sensible woman would walk away, put oceans between herself and this place, this love. But she wasn't sensible. She was bound to him by something older than logic. A feeling that had taken root in childhood and grown, quietly and insistently, through every season of her life.

By the time they arrived at the show ground, the rain had stopped. A watery sun broke through the clouds, lighting up the puddles and the soft mist still curling over the hills. The grass underfoot squelched a little, but no one seemed to mind. Wellington boots and waxed jackets ruled the day.

Simone leaned against the rail beside Cleo, watching the horse-jumping with eyes that didn't quite see. She smiled at the familiar faces, laughed in the right places, but she felt… removed. As though she were watching herself from a great distance, as though the version of her that had once belonged here had drifted far out to sea.

Cleo chatted happily beside her, drawing smiles and waves from neighbours they'd known all their lives. Simone felt like she was standing in the middle of a warm, familiar crowd—and yet utterly alone.

When someone called Cleo over to admire a pony, Simone stood awkwardly by the fence, her hands curled in her sleeves, trying to pretend she didn't feel like clinging to her friend's arm. She had come to this—a girl who once roared with fire now left adrift by a man's absence.

That was when Jeffery appeared—stalking towards her with stiff shoulders and a face like thunder. He halted in front of Simone, his eyes hard and glittering.

"I've been waiting for her to go," he announced grimly, nodding in the direction Cleo had vanished. "I've been watching you for the past half hour. I want to talk to you."

Simone straightened, heart suddenly heavy in her chest—but she forced a smile and tried to keep things light.

"Well, here I am," she said, her tone almost gaily flippant. "The weather's brightened, I see."

"It can do as it likes," he snapped. "I'm not interested in the damned weather. Your conduct is my problem. You've been seen out with Taylor every night."

Simone looked at him calmly, her voice cooling to match his. So, this was how it was going to be—an interrogation, a scolding. From Jeffery, of all people. He stood before her like a wronged husband rather than someone she'd gone out with a few times. Clearly, he saw himself as judge and jury.

"Yes," she said evenly. "I have been. I can't think what's so shocking about that. We're not engaged, Jeffery."

"I've put a lot of time into you," he grated. "I didn't do that just so you could go parading around with Sean Taylor like some—some…"

"Some what?" she asked, her eyes narrowing. "Be careful."

His lips curled, but he didn't take the warning. "That's not the image I want in a wife. Flashy clothes. Late nights. Hanging on the arm of a man like him—he's always had women buzzing around him, but you're not going to be one of them. This stops now. You're my girl."

She blinked at him. My girl? His voice held a tone she'd never heard before—something rough, possessive, even contemptuous. She didn't know this Jeffery. She wasn't sure she ever had.

"I wasn't aware I belonged to anyone," she replied, her voice soft but firm. "And I don't remember showing off my gowns for your approval. Do you have a telescope set up across the fields?"

"Don't think you can talk your way out of this," he snapped. "I won't stand by and watch you make a fool of yourself. Not with him. People are talking."

"I imagine they are," she said calmly. "That's usually what people do. But unless you've been promoted to village chaperone, Jeffery, I suggest you mind your own business."

His face darkened. "You're not going to twist this into something clever, Simone. He's not serious. You're just a bit of fun to him. And I won't have my girl caught up in it."

She took a step back, her eyes cold now. "Let's get something straight. I am not your anything."

But before Jeffery could explode again, a cool voice cut in like a blade through velvet.

"Simone is Sean's girl. Always was, always will be."

Cleo had returned silently, and now she took Simone's arm with quiet authority, her chin lifted and her eyes gleaming with disdain.

Jeffery turned on her, face flushed. "You stay out of this, Miss Uppity Taylor!"

"Oh, how crude," Cleo drawled, lifting one aristocratic brow as though he'd just tracked mud into her drawing room. "You're doing your family's reputation no favours, I assure you."

She turned to Simone, her voice brisk. "Come along. Daddy's offering us tea in the members' stand."

"Pah!" Jeffery scoffed behind them; arms folded tightly across his chest.

Simone raised a brow of her own. "Isn't that what goats say?"

Cleo grinned as they walked away. "Extraordinary. Come along before he starts quoting scripture."

Simone followed, her laughter rising, light and surprising. The tension in her chest began to ease. Somehow, she hadn't lost her temper—hadn't turned and lashed out. That was new. She felt curiously proud of herself, and even a little amused. What a scene. What a ridiculous little drama her life had become.

They rounded the corner of the grandstand and stopped, looking at each other—and promptly fell into each other's arms, shaking with laughter.

"How cruel we are," Simone said, wiping her eyes. "Honestly, it's not very nice."

"Jeffery had it coming," Cleo replied. "If Sean had caught him speaking to you like that, we'd be scraping what's left of him off the stable walls. You were surprisingly calm, though," she added, studying her friend with interest. "Actually, I stepped in just in time. I think if I'd waited a second longer, you would have clocked him."

Simone sighed. "I don't do things like that anymore." She touched her hair absently. "Sean has tamed me."

"God help us all," Cleo muttered, but affection softened her sarcasm.

"I should never have gone out with Jeffery," Simone said, more to herself than to Cleo. "I suppose I led him on a bit. Now he's hurt."

Cleo snorted. "Oh, please. He'll go running back to Mummy, and the two of them will dine out on your 'betrayal' for months. Don't waste a second of guilt on it. Let's go get that tea while it's still warm—and before Jeffery decides to challenge Sean to pistols at dawn."

She was in the village when Sean came home. She didn't see him arrive, and he didn't send word.

All day she'd been in a kind of daze—her limbs moving, her voice answering people automatically, but her thoughts elsewhere entirely. By lunchtime she had abandoned any attempt at productivity, changed into her new jeans and a green sweater that had cost more than she dared admit, and begun getting ready far too early. Sean liked her in green. She remembered that. And just remembering it made her heart beat faster.

She ignored the quiet warning in her chest—that frantic hope only ever led to heartbreak—and curled her hair more carefully than usual. Nothing else mattered. She had only to see him. To be with him.

When she got back home, it was almost the time he'd said he might arrive. Her nerves were stretched so tightly that every passing car made her breath hitch, and when the phone rang, she nearly dropped it.

It was Cleo.

"I just wanted to remind you it's the ball this weekend," she said breezily. "We've got to get everything organised. Mummy wants to know if you're in for your usual stint?"

"Of course I am," Simone replied, distracted. "I'll come up in the morning for the planning. I am waiting for Sean to get back. We are going out tonight, so I—"

"Oh. I thought you knew." There was a slight pause. "He's here already."

Simone went still. Her grip on the phone tightened.

"Here?"

"Yes—he's been back for a couple of hours now. I saw Prince in the yard, and then Sean came in and commandeered the phone."

Something inside Simone went cold, as if a window had been flung open in her heart and let in a freezing wind.

He was home. And he hadn't come. He hadn't even called. After all those gentle words, after that longing in her voice—after London—he'd changed his mind. She could feel it. Her instincts were never wrong.

Then she heard it—his voice in the background, clipped and unmistakably cool.

"Put her on."

Cleo didn't even say goodbye. There was a faint click, and then Sean's voice filled her ear.

"What could be wrong? I'm back," he said, but it wasn't warm. It was sardonic, that particular tone he used when something had displeased him, and he didn't want to admit it.

"I didn't expect you until now," she murmured, trying to keep her voice steady, even as her body began to tremble.

"I managed to get away early. If you're ready, I'll be down in fifteen minutes."

And then he hung up.

No teasing murmur. No, "I missed you." No sign that the voice on the other end belonged to the man who had whispered into her soul just days ago.

Simone stared at the receiver, the silence in the room louder than her thoughts.

She rushed to the mirror, touching her hair even though she'd already styled it, smoothing her sweater, pinching colour into her cheeks. She had done everything right. She looked her best without looking obvious—he'd told her not to dress up, and she'd obeyed. She looked… nice. Casual. Attractive.

But something was wrong.

He hadn't even wanted to speak to her first. Not really. It felt like duty now. And she knew—she knew—he was going to end things tonight. He'd had time to think. To compare. Perhaps Fleur had followed him down to London. Perhaps he'd come back early to speak to Mark. Perhaps—

She pressed a hand to her stomach.

He's going to tell me he's marrying her. That's why he's cold. It's done.

The trembling began in earnest now, low in her spine and threading out through her limbs like ice.

She didn't know what else to do. Whenever she was agitated, there was only one place that ever calmed her. Stardust.

Without even pausing to grab a coat, she went out into the fading light and all but ran to the loose box, as if the mare could somehow shield her from what was coming. Just a few minutes of calm. Just a breath of the past before the future arrived like a wrecking ball.

She flung the stable doors open—and froze.

The loose box was empty.

For a second she couldn't move, couldn't even breathe. The space where Stardust should have been yawned back at her like a hollow wound. Then, with her heart crashing against her ribs, Simone turned and bolted back around the side of the house, panic clawing at her chest.

Gone. Stardust is gone. Someone's taken her.

She didn't even think—just sprinted toward the front door, her only thought to ring the police. It wasn't that Stardust was irreplaceable in value, though she was well-bred and spirited. But if someone was stealing horses, why bypass the stables at Branlow Hall? Royal alone was worth a small fortune. Why take Stardust? How had they even got onto the estate without being seen?

As she tore around the bend into the drive, a sleek car purred in—Sean's car.

It looked menacing in the fading light. So did he.

He stepped out of the driver's seat slowly, almost too calmly, unfolding his tall frame like a panther that had just cornered its prey. He didn't come running. Didn't ask what was wrong. He simply stood there, watching her, cold and unreadable.

Simone stopped dead, breathless from running, but too upset to be cautious. She rushed straight to him, practically vibrating with anxiety.

"Stardust is missing!" she cried. "She's gone, Sean—I went to check her, and the box is empty—someone's taken her!"

Still, he didn't react. No alarm. No rush of concern. He simply walked around the car and opened the passenger door.

"Get in," he said flatly.

She stared at him. "Didn't you hear me? I said she's missing! It's getting dark, Sean—I have to call someone. We have to look for her!"

"Stardust is not missing," he replied, voice clipped and cool. "She's back where she belongs. At the Hall."

He nudged her into the car before she could form another protest and slammed the door behind her, then circled back to the driver's side.

"What do you mean she's back there?" she demanded, heart still hammering. "She couldn't have gone back on her own—"

"I came home early," he cut in, steering the car down the long drive. "You were out, so I walked round. And what do I find? Your horse locked away in that ridiculous little box like some forgotten garden ornament. Not where she's supposed to be."

"I decided to keep her here," Simone said defensively, trying to tamp down the storm of nerves inside her. "It's not illegal. She's my horse."

"And yet not a word to me. Not one little whisper, Simone. Not in all the days we've spent together." His jaw flexed, the muscle there tight with restraint. "You don't change, do you? Always defiant. Always ready to push back."

"I'm not defiant! I just didn't think it mattered that much. Anyone else would've found it funny—"

"But I'm not anyone else," he snapped. "And I don't find it funny when someone I care about lies to me."

"I didn't lie! I simply didn't tell you—"

"That's not the part that bothers me." His tone dropped to a grim register. "The part that bothers me, Simone, is what else I saw while I was retrieving your precious horse."

He shot her a look that sent a shiver up her spine.

"There was a second door open," he continued, voice like steel. "Inside was a motorbike. Gleaming. Recently repaired. Care to explain?"

She froze. He saw it. Her breath caught.

"I haven't ridden it!" she snapped, more from instinct than logic. "Not that it's your business. It's mine, Sean."

"Not anymore," he said icily. "I've removed it."

"You—what?" Her fury ignited like a struck match. "You had no right! That bike is mine, and you don't get to just take my things!"

"I have every right when you act like you're trying to kill yourself," he growled, turning to glare at her with blistering intensity. "Do you think I'm going to stand by and watch you destroy yourself because you're too proud to admit you need help?"

"If I want to ride a motorbike, I will! If I want to keep my horse here, I will! I don't need your permission!"

"And if I want to protect you from yourself, I damn well will," he shot back. "Because you're mine."

"Not yet, I'm not!" she shouted, voice cracking under the weight of her fury and confusion. "You think you can just take over? Do whatever you like with my life? After you went to London? After you spent days with Fleur—?"

"That's enough."

But she wasn't finished.

"I'm not a child. I'm not your project. And I'm not your mistress to be tucked away when you're bored or need a distraction. After this, I can even see Jeffery's good points—at least he didn't—"

"Don't ever compare me to that man again," Sean snapped, his voice like a whip crack.

Simone's breath came fast. Her chest rose and fell with the force of her fury, her cheeks flushed, her fists trembling in her lap. She stared at him, heart thudding painfully in her chest.

"I'm leaving Branlow," she said suddenly, her voice low and sharp with finality.

Silence.

"I mean it, Sean. Let me out. I'll walk back."

He didn't move. Didn't flinch.

His jaw was clenched so tight the muscle beneath his cheekbone twitched with barely contained restraint. His eyes stayed fixed ahead, dark, and unreadable, and his grip on the steering wheel had gone bone-white.

He wasn't going to lose her.

She was his.

Then, finally—quietly, too quietly—he said,

"You're not going anywhere."

Chapter Sixteen

Simone made a grab for the door handle, heart pounding, her anger overriding all reason. She wasn't thinking—she only knew she had to get out, away from him, away from this suffocating heat of confusion and want and helplessness.

Sean's hand shot out and caught her arm.

"Stop that!"

It was all he had time to say.

Simone reacted without thinking, her body a live wire. She lashed out instinctively, her arm knocking his hand away—and in the same motion, she clipped the steering wheel.

The car veered.

Sean tried to regain control, but it was too late. The wheel spun violently in his grip, and the car swerved off the narrow country lane, tyres screeching as it ploughed towards the ditch.

There was a split second of suspended horror.

Then the car pitched forward—hard and fast—and dove nose-first into the deep gully beside the road.

Sean flung himself across her, instinct taking over. His arm curled around her body in one sweeping motion, shielding her as the car crashed.

The noise was deafening. Metal crumpling. Glass shattering. The sickening thud of impact.

And then silence—an eerie, ringing silence.

Sean groaned low in his throat and slumped heavily against her. His head had struck the windscreen, and blood was already pouring down the side of his face, dark and slick, sliding along the sharp line of his jaw.

"Sean! Sean! Oh, Sean!"

She clutched his hand like a lifeline, her voice a cracked whisper of anguish as she stared down at him, her entire body trembling. He was slumped against the passenger-side door, blood trailing down the side of his face, his eyes closed, his body terrifyingly still. Panic rose like a tide, choking her.

Why didn't people come when you needed them? They were always around when you didn't want them—interrupting, interfering, but now? Now there was nothing but the wind and the rain and the terrible silence.

She moaned his name over and over, like a prayer, a lament, a plea.

Then—he stirred.

His eyes opened slowly, hazy, and unfocused, and he blinked up at her with dazed confusion. The powerful lines of his body looked broken in the awkward slant of the wrecked car.

"I'll live, Simone," he muttered, his voice rough and hoarse, every word sounding as if it cost him. "Just… help me out of this damned car and up to the hall."

"Our house is closer," she said urgently, brushing damp hair from his forehead with shaking fingers. Her hands fluttered against his face in helpless desperation. "I'll call the doctor. I'll call your mother. I'll—"

"Just move back and let me out," he said with a ghost of his usual dry humour, wiping at the blood on his temple with the back of his hand. "We'll decide which panic-stricken action to take once we're not upside down."

"You're bleeding," she cried, her voice catching. "Oh God, I almost killed you!"

He gave a faint smile, even as his eyes glazed over again. "Nothing in this world is ever truly new. You've been killing me slowly for years. Now let's get out of here before you finish the job."

She crawled out first, scrambling through the angled wreck, her door now tilted toward the sky. Rain had started to fall again, cold needles pelting down as the countryside around them sank deeper into grey.

Sean followed, groaning under his breath as he braced himself and dragged his tall frame free. He looked awful—ashen, unsteady, but still somehow standing.

Simone rushed to his side, her arm slipping around his waist instinctively. He staggered a bit, then looked down at her, the corners of his mouth twitching.

"If I lean on you," he said dryly, "we'll both be on the ground. Just hold my hand, Simone. We'll get out of this damned rain."

He called her Simone. And somehow, that alone made her want to cry. She had thought—just for a dreadful, hollow moment—that she'd never hear his voice again. He could've called her anything, and it would have made her weep with relief.

They made it to the Dower House slowly, step by soaked step. Once inside, she guided him into the drawing-room. The fire was still glowing in the grate, and the warmth felt surreal after the cold chaos outside. He sank down onto the settee like a man who'd just walked through a battlefield, his long frame sagging, his face pale and bloodied.

Simone bit her lip as she hovered near him, helpless again for a moment, then dashed out and returned with a towel. Kneeling beside him, she dabbed gently at the drying blood on his forehead, her hands steadying with the familiarity of caring for someone.

"I'll just clean you up first, and then I'll phone the doctor," she murmured, her brows drawn together in concentration. The room was quiet but for the soft crackle of the fire and the whisper of the wind outside. Her father and Sir Michael would still be at the agricultural show. No one was home. And Lady Vivian—this would devastate her. She adored Sean. Everyone did. But no one loved him like she did.

Sean reached out and caught her wrist gently, his fingers cool and firm.

"Just make me some tea," he said, his voice softer now, touched with wry affection. "I'm slowly coming back to life. No need to ring anyone."

"You made me call the doctor when I skidded," she argued, blinking down at him, alarm still buzzing under her skin. "You look—awful."

"It's just a bump," he said with a tired smile. "Nothing to worry about."

"But you're so pale!" she whispered, not bothering to hide the tears in her voice now.

Sean reached up with effort and brushed a knuckle against her cheek. "I've had worse. I'm not going anywhere, Simone."

She sat back on her heels, clutching the towel tightly. He wasn't going anywhere—for now. But what about tomorrow? Or next week? Or whenever Fleur decided to make her move?

The moment felt so fragile, hanging in the warmth of the firelight like a soap bubble ready to burst.

"Just make me some tea, Simone. I'm slowly recovering. No need for the doctor."

"You made me see one when I skidded," she said, her voice tight with emotion. "And you look awful."

"It's just a bump. Nothing serious."

"But you're so pale!"

She dropped to her knees in front of him, suddenly overwhelmed. The fear that had clutched at her during the crash still hadn't let go. What if he hadn't woken up? What if that blood, that silence, had meant the end? Her heart ached just remembering it.

Her fingers trembled as she brushed back the thick black hair from his brow. The bruise was larger than she'd expected, already turning a sickly shade of purple, with a crust of blood at its edge. She gasped softly, and her eyes welled again.

"Oh, Sean…"

Without thinking, she leaned forward and wrapped her arms around him. She wanted to rock him, hold him, shield him. He wouldn't have been hurt if he hadn't thrown himself over her. He'd taken the blow that should have been hers. The thought undid her.

"Sean," she sobbed into his shoulder, cradling his body, clinging to him as though she could protect him now, after the damage was done.

They toppled together—slowly, almost gently. His strength wasn't there to stop the fall, and her desperate embrace only dragged them down. She landed on the rug beneath him, Sean's weight half draped across her, his head against her shoulder, his breath hot on her throat.

He lifted his head slightly, looking down at her with faint amusement despite his pallor. "I'm no match for your fiery strength at the moment," he murmured. "We seem to be back where we started—in a state of collapse."

"Don't joke," she said, her voice cracking. "Please, Sean. You're too ill."

"Honestly," he said, softer now, "I'm not."

She searched his face desperately. He looked better lying down—less colourless, more himself. He shifted, propping himself up on one elbow to meet her anxious gaze.

"I'm all right," he promised gently. "I'm not going to end up a body on the rug."

"Don't say that," she whispered. "Don't even joke. It was my fault. I lost control. My temper, my stupid, selfish ways—I nearly got you killed."

He reached out and touched her face, wiping away her tears with the back of his fingers.

"Not a stupid temper," he said. "Just passionate. And you didn't hurt me. Not really."

She stared at him, her chest tightening. Why had she believed he'd betrayed her? What had he really done except leave—for reasons that had always been more about duty than desire? He'd gone to Canada, then London… and why not? She hadn't been a woman then, just a girl with a crush. And she hadn't forgiven him for growing up, for stepping away, for not reading her mind.

Who had been treacherous? Him—or her?

More tears filled her eyes, hot and sudden. She turned her face away, blinking quickly, but his hand turned her chin gently back toward him.

"You're crying again," he said, his voice low. "What's hurting you, Simone?"

"Nothing," she lied softly. "I just didn't want you to die."

"I'm not dead," he murmured, and bent his head to kiss the tears from her cheeks. His lips lingered, brushing along the line of her jaw, her temple, the corner of her mouth.

And then his mouth claimed hers.

There was no rush, no hesitation. Only that deep, familiar warmth that swept through her as she sank into the kiss, trembling beneath him. She should have called for help—should have insisted on the doctor—but she couldn't move. Not when he kissed her like that.

"Don't move," he whispered against her lips. "Don't move away from me. I need you here."

Almost instinctively, her arms circled his neck, drawing him closer. She felt his body stir—heat and strength returning—and his hand slid beneath her sweater, slow and certain.

"I dream of this," he murmured. "Looking down and seeing you like this, feeling you beneath me."

Her breath hitched. His weight pressed her into the soft rug, firm, and possessive. She felt the heat of him, the sharp edge of longing, and it thrilled her even as it made her ache.

"Do you want me?" he asked, his voice low and rough.

Her answer was in her eyes, in her parted lips, in the way her body arched toward his.

"Do you?" he asked again, almost desperate now.

"Yes… Oh God, yes."

"Then come to me, Simone. I've waited too long. I ache for you."

She surged against him, clutching at his back, needing to feel all of him. His hands moved urgently now, stripping away the sweater, baring her to his touch. He stared down at her as if in awe, his eyes dark with hunger.

"What I've dreamed of," he said, reverently. "What I never stopped wanting."

He bent to take her breast in his mouth, and she cried out softly, her body shivering with need. His touch was fire—his kisses a brand. She arched into him, gasping, whispering his name as his mouth and hands claimed her.

"Do you love me?" he demanded suddenly, fiercely. "Do you love me, Simone?"

"Yes!" she sobbed. "I've always loved you. I can't live without you. I don't want to."

Her words seemed to unhinge something in him. He crushed her against him, his mouth roaming over her skin, his hands trembling slightly. And then—something changed.

His body, so vibrant and urgent a moment before, went oddly still. He sagged over her, his mouth slack, his hands sliding away.

"Sean?" she whispered, her heart stuttering.

He didn't answer.

His weight was heavier now, limp. Too limp.

"Sean!" She pushed at him, panic flaring. "Sean!"

No response.

She rolled him with effort, saw the pallor of his skin, the way his eyes fluttered closed, and her breath caught in her throat. His head lolled slightly. He had passed out. Again.

And this time—he wasn't waking up.

In a wild panic, Simone opened her eyes—and froze.

Sean had rolled away from her, his tall frame slumped on the rug, eyes closed, his skin chalk-white beneath the faint remnants of his tan. For one terrifying moment, he looked lifeless.

"Sean…" His name tore from her in a whisper, raw with disbelief.

He stirred faintly at the sound—barely a murmur—but then fell still again, motionless.

Unconscious.

Her breath seized in her throat. She wanted to scream, to cry out until someone came running, but no sound escaped. Instead, she scrambled forward, kneeling beside him with shaking hands. She grabbed one of his hands in both of hers and began rubbing it frantically, trying to stir him, to warm him—to do something.

"Sean, please…"

Nothing. Her fear tipped into desperation. She pressed her ear to his chest, struggling to hear past the erratic thud of her own heart. There—faint but steady—a heartbeat. Strong and real.

Relief almost floored her.

He was alive. But she needed help.

Now.

She stumbled to her feet, rushing to the phone, not even bothering to throw on the sweater he had peeled from her minutes earlier. Her fingers fumbled the buttons, eyes wet and unfocused.

It was Sean's father who answered.

"Simone? What is it?"

"Come—oh, please come quickly! Get the doctor. Sean's hurt!"

"Simone, calm down," Sir Michael said sharply. "Tell me slowly. What happened?"

His voice grounded her. She gulped in air, forced herself to speak clearly, though her voice trembled with every word. She told him about the accident, about Sean collapsing. Her hands wouldn't stop shaking.

"We'll be there in two minutes," he said without hesitation. "William Stokes is here now—he came back with your father and me. Hold on. We're on our way."

When they arrived at the Dower House, Simone was properly dressed, though her face was the colour of ashes. She knelt by Sean, wiping gently at the dried blood near his temple, trying to seem calm. But her eyes told the truth: she was terrified.

"I managed to get him back here," she said quietly, her voice flat. "He said he was fine. I was going to make him some tea, and then… then he just collapsed."

The guilt was written all over her. Every shadow beneath her eyes, every tremble of her lips, shouted: It's my fault.

They moved quickly. William checked him over, then made the call to transfer him to hospital. The X-rays ruled out anything serious—no skull fracture, no internal bleeding—but the concussion was confirmed.

"He's groggy and needs monitoring," William said, emerging from the room into the waiting area. "We'll keep him overnight, just to be safe."

"Can I go in?" Simone asked immediately.

William shook his head. "No. You've had a terrible shock yourself. He's sedated and resting. I've already told you—he'll be fine. It's time you went home and got some rest too."

"I'm all right. Really—"

"Bed, Simone," her father said, stepping up beside her. "Now. Let's go."

She couldn't argue—not against the united front of the three men. And besides, she wasn't anything official in Sean's life. Not his fiancée. Not his wife. What had happened between them tonight was still wrapped in shadows and secrecy—something beautiful, yes, but something no one else could know.

She went with her father, silent, withdrawn.

In the ambulance, before they'd reached the hospital, Sean had opened his eyes. She'd been clutching his hand, her heart in her throat.

"Hello, Sunflower," he'd murmured, his voice slightly slurred, eyes unfocused. "What are you doing here?"

The nickname pierced her like a blade. He hadn't called her that since they were teenagers.

"You had an accident," she'd whispered urgently. "You hit your head. You don't remember?"

"Oh… yes," he said softly, his brow furrowing. "You lost your temper again."

And then he'd closed his eyes, his hand patting hers once before going limp again.

Didn't he remember what happened before that?

The kisses, the heat, the way they'd clung to each other.

The thought gnawed at her all the way home.

That night, she didn't argue when her father insisted she take the sleeping pills. Everything felt surreal—like a dream slipping through her fingers.

Sean was allowed home the next afternoon, to his immense irritation. He was delivered back to Branlow by ambulance and, to his dismay, immediately sedated again by William Stokes, who seemed almost pleased to have bested him.

"You can't ignore a head injury," William told Sir Michael firmly. "Let him rest another two days. No arguments."

Chapter Seventeen

Simone had gone up to the Hall earlier to help with preparations for the Easter Ball. By the time she arrived, Sean was already back, asleep. She wanted to ask to see him—but didn't dare. What if they guessed?

Perhaps she could sneak up to his room. But if someone saw… What would they think?

She kept her head down, pretending focus, helping Cleo and Lady Vivian with arrangements. Fleur, meanwhile, floated around like she was Sean's fiancée, giving orders and speaking in whispers, as if the house were a monastery.

"She's insufferable," Cleo muttered when they finally sat down for tea. "She even went in to speak to Cook! Mummy had to spend ten minutes smoothing that one over. You'd think Fleur was planning the wedding and the coronation."

Simone forced a faint smile, her heart not in it.

"Thank goodness the day's over," Cleo sighed as they walked together down the drive. "I'll walk part of the way with you. I need fresh air."

"Nothing's going right," Cleo grumbled. "We've done this ball every year—we know it by heart—but Fleur's getting in the way just enough to make everything harder. Mummy keeps giving her these little jobs to make her feel useful. Useful!" She groaned. "Honestly, it's like threading a needle in the dark."

"And then there's Sean," Simone said softly, her voice catching.

Cleo looked at her with concern.

"It was all my fault," Simone whispered. "We were arguing. I—I knocked the wheel. He threw himself across me to protect me, and now…"

Tears pricked her eyes again. She stopped walking, wiping her face with her sleeve.

"You love him," Cleo said simply, squeezing her arm. "He'll be all right."

But Simone wasn't crying for Sean's condition—not entirely. He would recover. He was strong, sharp, impossible to keep down.

She was crying because she knew now how little she belonged. The line between being part of the Taylors' world and merely orbiting around it had never felt clearer. No matter what she and Sean shared—no matter the whispered confessions or hungry kisses—she was still the outsider. A girl with a childhood crush. A shadow, not a partner.

Even if her dreams came true… even if he married her…

Would she ever truly belong?

The next day, Simone arrived at the Hall to find Lady Vivian uncharacteristically flustered, hovering near the library with a look of restrained exasperation. For the first time in Simone's life, she appeared dangerously close to losing her temper.

"I want you to go up to Sean and talk him to pieces," she declared the moment she saw her.

Simone blinked. "You—you want me to go to his room?"

"I most certainly do." Lady Vivian's brooch glinted with every agitated movement. "He's being impossible. He insists on getting up after lunch, and nothing I say makes a dent. I've had to intercept every telephone call and keep London at bay. If he hears even one word from the office, he'll be up and gone. And he's not well enough."

Simone nodded slowly, her heart thudding. "You want me to… distract him?"

"Exactly. Keep him entertained. Pacified. Occupied. Talk his ears off if you must. The last room on the corridor overlooking the park—you know it."

Simone did. She had wandered those corridors as a girl, but she had never once stepped into Sean's bedroom. The thought sent her pulse racing. It felt strange, like being invited through a door she'd never had the right to touch. And yesterday—when she'd wanted nothing more than to see him—she hadn't dared to ask. Now, Lady Vivian was practically pushing her up the stairs.

But the truth was, she was scared—scared of what she'd find. Would he be cold? Angry? Had he remembered anything from the night before? The way she'd whispered that she loved him, held him, touched him… Would he mock her? Pretend it never happened?

Her hand trembled slightly as she tapped on the door.

"Come in!" he barked. His voice was clipped, irritable—not the warm welcome she'd secretly hoped for.

She stepped inside cautiously and paused in the doorway, unsure.

Sean was sitting up in bed, propped against a mountain of pillows, his dark silk pyjamas a striking contrast to the crisp white bedding. He looked every inch the fallen hero: bruised temple, strong jaw shadowed with stubble, blue eyes flashing with restless frustration.

But when he saw her, his scowl vanished. He said nothing at first—just stared.

The sunlight spilled through the tall window behind her, catching her hair and turning it to copper fire. She wore a dark blue dress, simple and soft, but she felt suddenly overexposed under his gaze, her nerves taut.

"I—I was sent to talk you into submission," she said quickly, clasping her hands together. "Your mother's orders."

He arched an eyebrow, a flicker of amusement replacing irritation. "Ah. She played her trump card. Clever woman. So, you're the warden, and I'm the unruly prisoner?"

"I'm here to talk you to pieces," Simone said, trying for seriousness. "That's the mission."

He chuckled, the low sound curling around her like smoke. "Come and do it, then. I'm bored to death."

He patted the bed beside him invitingly. She hesitated, hovering like a nervous guest.

"You can sit," he added, wryly. "I promise to suppress the primal urge to drag you under the covers."

Her cheeks flamed. In a rush, she fetched the nearest chair and planted it beside the bed, sitting stiffly with her hands folded in her lap as if she were visiting a distant cousin in hospital.

"You've got a bad bruise," she said after a pause, studying his temple instead of his mocking eyes.

"Mm," he murmured, tilting his head. "So, step one in the operation is to list my ailments?"

"It was conversation," she said, rallying. "You don't look terrible. Just… tired."

"Well done. What's step two?"

"If you're going to be like this, I'll leave," she snapped, pushing the chair back and standing abruptly.

His hand shot out and caught her wrist in a firm grip. "If you do, I'll get up and go saddle Royal."

"You wouldn't!"

"I would." His expression didn't waver. "Sit closer. I want to hold your hand."

Before she could argue, he tugged gently and she found herself sitting on the edge of the bed, her hand in his, her heart hammering like mad.

"Now talk," he murmured.

"I—I don't know what to say anymore," she admitted.

"Bedrooms frighten you?" he asked softly, watching her with disconcerting tenderness. When she didn't answer, he sobered. "Are you alright? You weren't hurt in the crash?"

"No. Just shaken. I—I thought I'd killed you."

"You didn't," he said seriously. "Don't go blaming yourself. I was the fool who tried to drive while arguing with a redhead."

She gave a watery smile, but her voice was quiet. "You said you didn't need a doctor, but then you collapsed."

He frowned. "You got me back to the house?"

"The Dower House," she clarified. "I helped you in. You were so pale."

He stared at her, brows drawing together. "Strange… I don't remember that."

Her heart sank.

"You don't remember anything?"

"I remember the crash. I remember the ditch and hitting my head." He rubbed the spot ruefully. "Then it gets a little… hazy."

She looked down. So, he didn't remember. The passion, the confessions, the way her heart had split open for him—it was lost.

"Are you sure you're not making up this whole 'rescue' story to convince me to stay in bed?" he teased, but his voice was softer now.

"No," she said firmly. "It all happened."

He studied her for a long moment. "Have I forgotten anything else? You didn't suddenly fall madly in love with me while I was unconscious, did you?"

Her face turned crimson, and she dropped her gaze again.

He tilted her chin up gently. "Simone," he said, voice low. "Are we together now? Or did I dream that part too?"

"No… I mean, I don't know," she whispered.

"Then let's make it real," he said, and before she could protest, he cupped her face and kissed her—hungrily, insistently.

When he pulled back, his voice was raw. "I needed that. And I need you. Just as soon as I get out of this bloody bed."

Simone sat frozen, her lips tingling. She didn't know what to say. He was different from the night before—casual, teasing, as if none of it had mattered. No mention of Stardust. No anger about the motorbike. Just charm and desire and a relentless sense of possession.

She was still trying to process it when a knock came at the door. Sean cursed under his breath.

"Clearly we need a private island," he muttered. "Come in!"

The door opened—and there stood Fleur.

When she saw Simone sitting on the bed, her face twisted with fury.

"Isn't this a bit much, Sean?" she snapped. "Now that girl is in your room?"

Simone stood up like a lit match. "That girl?" she echoed, eyes blazing. "Which girl exactly are you referring to?"

Sean reached out and caught her flailing hands, pulling her gently back, but his voice turned to ice as he addressed Fleur.

"Here I was, worrying about a little lost memory," he said coldly. "Yours seems to be malfunctioning too. You're engaged to Mark, Fleur. This is my room. And as for Simone—didn't we make our relationship quite clear last time?"

Fleur paled, then flushed crimson.

"Funny," she said bitterly. "You never mentioned her when we were in London."

"You were so devoted," Sean said dryly. "You loved me so deeply you agreed to marry my brother. Touching."

With a huff and a swirl of designer fabric, Fleur turned and stormed out.

Simone sat back down, shaken.

"Don't let her upset you, Simone," Sean said quietly. "She's not our problem."

"No," she murmured, her voice barely audible. "She's Mark's problem. She's going to marry him... but it's you she wants."

He reached out, but she was already on her feet, slipping free from his grasp.

He didn't stop her.

What was the point?

She had just been witness to the tail end of a lovers' quarrel—an argument between two people who clearly had history, unresolved feelings, and a kind of entitlement to one another Simone could never lay claim to.

She closed the door behind her softly and stood in the corridor, frozen. The stillness pressed in on her like a vice. The dam broke without sound—tears slipping from beneath her tightly shut lashes, tracing down her cheeks in quiet surrender.

She didn't sob. She didn't make a sound.

She just stood there, the sting of Fleur's venom still echoing, the weight of Sean's silence heavier than any denial.

A moment later, she turned and moved quickly, not wanting to be seen. She knew this house like her own—every staircase, every shortcut, every hidden door. The back stairs welcomed her like a familiar escape route, and she descended them swiftly, boots soundless on the old wooden treads.

Outside in the courtyard, she finally let out a shaky breath, the air cold and sharp in her lungs.

It would never feel like home again.

Not after this.

She had doubted, but now she knew. From Sean's own lips, without meaning to—he had confirmed her fears. Fleur still held a piece of him. Maybe more than a piece. Maybe enough to make what happened between them in the Dower House... a mistake.

Simone squared her shoulders and walked on, blinking back the tears she didn't have time for. Whatever fantasies she'd let herself believe—they didn't belong here.

Not anymore.

When Cleo rang the next morning, her voice was strained with frustration.

"Sean got up and went to London," she said flatly. "Bruise, stitches, concussion—and he still left. Nothing could stop him."

Simone sat in silence, the phone pressed to her ear, unable to speak. Of course he had gone. There was only one reason left, and all she could do now was wait for Fleur to join him.

She hung up and sat down slowly, as if her body had suddenly forgotten how to move. It felt like all the air had been drained from her lungs, like she was nothing more than a shell, echoing with absence. There wasn't a single scrap of life left in her. Until the bright jolt of tyres on gravel pulled her from the fog.

A little sports car—orange, ridiculous, and completely out of place—screeched to a stop in front of the Dower House. The door flung open, and Rhonda emerged in a blur of curly brown hair, pink cheeks, and wide-eyed excitement.

"Simone!" she shouted, practically barrelling across the gravel. "I'm here! Lead me to the Easter Ball!"

Simone barely had time to react before she was swept into an exuberant hug, nearly lifted off the ground.

"I—I don't understand—" she stammered.

"Cleo invited me," Rhonda said, grinning wickedly. "I was under strict orders not to tell. She wanted it to be a surprise."

Cleo didn't do surprises. She did ambushes. But for once, Simone didn't care. She had never been so glad to see anyone in her life.

Rhonda: the one shining thing to come out of boarding school. The nut-brown maiden with a crooked smile and a laugh like sunlight. Simone had arrived at school devastated, certain she'd been exiled from Branlow and Sean forever. But Rhonda had arrived the same day—wild, rebellious, and ready to take on the world. They'd bonded instantly, and somehow, miraculously, she was here again now. Just when Simone needed her most.

"I've got the most fabulous dress for the ball," Rhonda announced later as she spun into the front hall, tossing her bag onto the stairs. "It's orange!"

Simone didn't know whether to laugh or cry. But one thing she did know: Rhonda wouldn't let her wallow for long. She never stopped talking, never stopped doing. Already, the air felt lighter.

That evening, she kept both Simone and her father thoroughly entertained, pulling stories out of thin air and making them laugh until their sides ached. But it wasn't until bedtime, when Rhonda flopped onto Simone's bed and kicked off her shoes, that the mood changed.

"So," she said, chin propped on her hand, "how's the fabulous Sean?"

Simone froze; her brush stilled in her hand. "He's in London," she said softly.

Rhonda tilted her head, watching her. She had spent night after night at school listening to Simone pine and dream, pouring every aching heartbeat into words. This wasn't a schoolgirl crush anymore, though. It hadn't been for years.

She came to kneel beside Simone and looked up at her with those warm, steady brown eyes.

"You've never changed, have you? It's still him."

Simone's shoulders sagged. "There's someone else," she whispered. "I think… I think he's going to marry her."

She didn't mean to cry. But the words cracked something open and suddenly she was shaking, the brush falling from her fingers as she buried her face in her hands. Rhonda was on her feet in an instant, wrapping her in a tight hug.

"Oh, Simone. I'm so sorry. What can I do?"

"Just back me up," Simone managed through her tears. "Get me out of there if I need to go. Don't let me make a fool of myself."

"As if you could," Rhonda said gently.

"Oh, I would," Simone insisted. Her voice was raw. "If Sean marries, I'll have to leave Branlow. Maybe even before that. I couldn't bear to stay if—"

She broke off, unable to finish. She couldn't tell Rhonda. Couldn't say that Sean had only wanted her for a little while. That he'd wanted her, even as Fleur waited in the wings. It would make Sean the villain—and she couldn't do that. Not even now.

She had practically begged for his attention all her life. She'd clung to every scrap of it. Could she really blame him for finally responding?

She found herself talking, telling Rhonda everything else—the motorbike, the quarrel, the crash, Jeffery's mother, all of it. Everything except what had nearly happened between her and Sean that afternoon by the fire.

Rhonda listened in silence, hands resting lightly in her lap.

"Are you sure there's a woman in London?" she asked at last. "Because it sounds like he barely lets you out of his sight."

"I don't want guarding!" Simone snapped. "I want him to love me. And you can't make that happen."

She sighed, brushing tears from her cheeks. "Anyway… he left for her when I was eighteen. I never knew who she was. But now… I'm sure."

She didn't name Fleur. She couldn't bring herself to say it aloud. Instead, she looked up and added, almost absently, "Mark's engaged."

"Really?" Rhonda said, raising a brow. "That's a shame. I always thought Mark was lovely. So much gentler than Sean."

Sean could be gentle. He could cradle her in arms of iron and make her feel like glass. He could kiss her until the world disappeared. But that softness was never without intensity. He lived in extremes. And he had never belonged to her.

"Sean can't afford to be gentle," she said fiercely. "He's the heir. One day it will all be his. He's been trained to carry it all—Branlow, the family, the legacy."

Rhonda gave her a long, searching look. "I'm glad I'm not in love like that."

"So am I," Simone said. But her voice was flat. It was a lie, and they both knew it.

Then she added, "Stay out of Mark's path, Rhonda. Please. Don't give Fleur a reason to lash out. You don't want to be on the receiving end of her spite."

"Fleur?" Rhonda repeated. "That's actually her name? Oh, come on. Nobody is really called that."

Simone let out a weak laugh—too tired to fight. Too tired for anything, really.

The girls sat in silence for a moment, the night wrapped around them like a thick, invisible shawl. Simone stared at her reflection in the mirror—older, wearier. Watching herself like a stranger.

Where had the old Simone gone?

Once, she would've fought for what she wanted. Kicked and screamed. Thrown fits and ultimatums. Now she just watched, waited, and tried not to cry.

She wasn't the firebrand anymore.

She was Miss Simone Symons. The voice of reason. The girl who kept everyone else out of mischief.

And it broke her heart.

Chapter Eighteen

Simone's hands trembled as she dressed for the ball. She could barely hold her mascara wand, let alone steady her thoughts. Sean would be there.

And no one—no one—must know how much it was costing her to walk into that room tonight. Not a glance, not a flicker of expression could give her away.

In front of the mirror, she layered soft plum shadow over her eyelids, deepened her lashes with mascara, and studied herself critically. Her skin looked almost translucent. Pale. Fragile. Her lips were full but colourless, and she left them bare, adding only a hint of gloss. The only part of her that looked alive was her hair—dark and gleaming, swept up and pinned with quiet elegance, the ends falling in soft waves to brush her bare shoulders.

She stepped into her dress—not green. Never green. Not for Sean. Not tonight.

Instead, she'd chosen lilac. A pale, drifting chiffon that floated over a satin slip of the same hue. It clung to her subtly, the neckline dipping low and leaving her creamy shoulders bare. It was romantic. Distant. Untouchable.

Exactly how she needed to feel.

She fastened her necklace with trembling fingers. The clasp kept slipping, her hands so unsteady she nearly dropped it twice. She was just reaching for her perfume when Rhonda entered the room.

For once, the whirlwind stilled.

Rhonda took one look at her and exhaled softly. "Oh, Simone. You're beautiful. Like a dream."

Then she did something unexpected. She crossed the room and kissed Simone gently on the cheek.

"Why don't you just back out of this?" she asked quietly. "You look like it's torture."

"Do I really look that bad?" Simone asked with a faint, brittle smile.

"You look flawless," Rhonda said honestly. "But I know you. And I can see what this is costing you."

Simone turned back to the mirror, adjusting a strand of hair that didn't need adjusting.

"I can't back out," she said calmly. "I've never run away from anything in my life."

"Then I'll be right beside you," Rhonda vowed. She twirled once on the spot. "Thoughts on the orange dress?"

Simone turned, grateful for the distraction. Rhonda's dress shimmered with every movement—a dreamy blend of warm amber and soft bronze that shifted colour like sunlight through honey. It hugged her figure in all the right places, strapless and daring without being vulgar.

It suited her perfectly: glowing, confident, and just a little mischievous.

"It's not orange," Simone said, smiling genuinely for the first time all evening. "It's… astonishing."

Rhonda grinned. "Good. I intend to knock them all sideways."

Simone's stomach twisted. Who did she mean? Mark? The entire family?

The momentary calm vanished. Her insides quaked again.

Her father, arriving downstairs with a broad smile, took one look at them and beamed.

"My word, you two look like film stars. Absolute knockouts."

Simone clung to his arm as they walked to the hall, as if she could draw strength from the solid, familiar weight of him beside her. She had never needed him more.

He glanced down at her, concern flickering in his eyes. "What is it, love? You're not ill, are you?"

"I'm fine," she lied, the smile returning to her lips by sheer force of will.

Rhonda caught her other arm and gave it a reassuring squeeze just as Sir Michael and Lady Vivian stepped out to greet them.

"I'll keep an eye on her," she whispered to Henry.

"No need," he murmured back with a smile. "Sean's back."

Simone had already noticed. Sean wasn't anywhere in the hall, but right at the top of the grand staircase, the great black dog sat like a statue, surveying the arriving guests with steady interest. Prince. Perfectly still, alert but unmoving, as though under strict orders.

And who else could give a command like that and be instantly obeyed?

Only Sean.

Moments later, her father was swept up in the tide of guests—old friends, distant relations, patrons of the estate's charities—streaming through the doors with laughter and bright greetings. The Easter ball, as always, promised to be a glittering success.

Mark appeared with Fleur on his arm. Fleur was stunning, in a severe way— immaculately groomed, detached, and wearing just enough of a smile to appear civil. The cool aloofness might have suited an art gallery, but it didn't belong at a warm- hearted charity event. Her displeasure was thinly veiled when Mark paused to compliment Simone and Rhonda.

"So many beauties tonight," he said, flashing a grin. "One could easily become addicted."

To Simone, he was like a brother. But to Rhonda, the comment sent a soft blush blooming across her cheeks. Fleur didn't miss it. She swept forward as if claiming her rightful place at the top of the social order, inserting herself among Lady Vivian and Sir Michael, as though she were mistress of the house.

Mark leaned closer to Simone, speaking under his breath. "There are drinks—if you know where to look."

And then, almost offhand: "Sean will be down any minute."

Which, Simone thought wryly, likely meant she was to stay exactly where she was—while Mark slipped away with Rhonda. He had been dancing around her since the moment she'd arrived. Bold, perhaps foolishly so. But as it hadn't been Rhonda doing the chasing, Simone didn't feel obliged to interfere.

Not that she was standing there waiting for Sean.

She just—couldn't move.

All around her, laughter echoed beneath the high ceiling, and the string quartet in the old ballroom was already tuning up. Guests milled about in jewel-toned gowns and fine tuxedos, sipping champagne and greeting one another with affection and flair.

And yet Simone stood alone, like a lone figure under glass. The chandelier above cast fractured light across her bare shoulders and pale lilac gown, but her pulse beat loud and unsteady in her ears.

Then he came.

She didn't hear his footsteps. She simply looked up—and there he was.

Sean stood at the head of the staircase, tall and utterly still, his dinner jacket black as night, his presence magnetic and unsettling. At his side, Prince rose with a low huff of excitement. But Sean snapped his fingers once and pointed. Prince sank obediently back to the floor.

So did Simone's breath.

He started down the stairs, but when he reached the halfway point, his eyes found hers—and he stopped.

His entire expression changed.

Just a heartbeat before, his mouth had held the hint of a smile, his body loose and graceful. But now, his gaze pinned her in place. He didn't move. Didn't blink. His face grew unreadable, and for a moment Simone felt as if the entire hall had faded around them.

Sean stopped, frozen halfway down the staircase as his eyes locked on hers.

In that moment, there was no one else. No movement. No sound. Just Simone.

She stood at the bottom of the stairs, framed by the soft flicker of candlelight, her posture regal, composed—utterly breathtaking. The lilac gown skimmed her curves with effortless grace, catching the light in delicate whispers of silk. Her red hair was swept into a loose updo, a few rebellious tendrils curling at her temples. Her bare shoulders glowed pale and smooth against the elegant fall of fabric.

She stole the breath from his lungs.

She was the most beautiful thing he had ever seen.

But then—his chest tightened.

There was something in her face. A hesitation. A flicker of doubt behind her eyes, the kind she couldn't quite mask. Her smile was there, but it didn't reach all the way.

Had she changed her mind?

God. Had she stopped loving him?

His jaw clenched. He didn't let it show—not to anyone watching—but inside, something reeled. His heart gave one heavy, uncertain thud, as if bracing for impact.

His hair gleamed as dark as ink, his jaw clean-shaven, and those piercing sapphire eyes locked on her like a force of nature.

And she knew.

She didn't need words.

Whatever decision he had made—he had made it already. Perhaps he hadn't said the words aloud, hadn't made any formal arrangement... but the truth was written on his face, in the stillness of his body, in the taut lines around his mouth.

He was going to tell her.

That's why Mark was off charming Rhonda without a second thought. That's why Fleur had taken her place among the family as if it were already hers. Somewhere, somehow, decisions had been made. Peace had been brokered.

And Simone—Simone had been left standing in the chandelier's glow, utterly alone.

Simone was trembling again. She couldn't help it. No amount of steady breathing or mental bracing could stop the fine tremors that crept through her limbs. And then Sean moved—descended the last few stairs without taking his eyes off her. His face was unreadable, his mouth unsmiling, but his focus was absolute.

He came to a halt in front of her, tall and commanding, and for a moment all she could do was stare up at him, her throat dry, her pulse out of sync with the music drifting in from the ballroom.

"In the first place," he said, his voice low and deliberate, "you get more beautiful. In the second—" his eyes searched her face "—I think you'd better tell me what's wrong."

"Nothing," she managed, barely keeping her voice level. Her throat ached from holding back the emotion rising inside her, the tears that burned at the corners of her eyes. But he was studying her too closely. He could always see right through her.

"Nothing?" he repeated and took both her hands in his. She barely noticed the people calling his name across the hall, vying for his attention. He ignored them all.

"You're like some illusion," he murmured, his hands warm and steady around hers. "Some celestial being I conjured up out of my imagination… too perfect to be real."

His grip tightened slightly, anchoring her as his narrowed blue eyes flicked over her face with unsettling precision. "But there's something else. What is it, Simone? You're either ill, or you're carrying some great weight inside that you won't let out."

"I'm perfectly alright," she said, fighting the tremor in her voice, her chin lifting with determination.

"Perfect?" he echoed dryly. "Perhaps. But alright?" He shook his head. "Not even close."

She forced a smile—brilliant, brittle, too bright. It didn't fool him.

Sean stared at her for a long, breathless second. Then his jaw tightened, and he turned slightly, still holding one of her hands. "Very well," he said curtly. "I'll play along. For now."

His tone was cold, clipped—and that stung far more than it should have. She tried to pull her hand free, but his grip only shifted, firm and unrelenting.

"Be still," he said under his breath, the words not loud, but sharp. "Until I know what this is, you're not slipping away from me again."

"I can't," she whispered. "Rhonda's here. I need to look after her—"

Sean's brows lifted. "Rhonda?" he repeated, as if she'd said something ridiculous. "Since when has Rhonda needed looking after?"

He gave her a pointed look. "I know she's here. I was told—quite enthusiastically—on arrival."

That gave Simone pause. Cleo. What had she said?

"I suppose Cleo told you?" she asked carefully.

His smile turned dry. "Cleo? Of course not." He glanced toward the ballroom. "Mark told me. Very freely, I might add."

Simone's heart sank. That could mean anything. Especially with Cleo involved.

He leaned slightly closer; voice dipped in something darker. "Isn't it odd that, after years away, your school friend just happens to appear at this particular Easter ball?"

"She came to see me," Simone replied firmly, lifting her chin again.

"And yet," he said, eyes glinting, "she seems to be spending all her time with Mark."

He released her wrist then—but not before trailing his fingers down her arm in a way that sent heat flaring under her skin.

"We didn't order fireworks for tonight," he added, glancing toward the ballroom doors. "But who knows… we may get some."

She had the sinking feeling that Sean was counting this as just another plot—Rhonda's arrival, her pale complexion, the way her hands trembled. Maybe he thought it was all connected. Maybe he believed she was trembling from nerves over some scheme, not heartbreak. Good. Let him. If that was the story he told himself, it would keep him off the scent of the real reason. At least he hadn't told her that Fleur was going back to him. He must be waiting—biding his time until the ball was over.

The band struck up as they stepped into the ballroom. A hush of awe still stole over her, just as it always had. The room was nothing short of a dream—used only on rare, grand occasions. High and vast and rich with history, it glittered tonight beneath four enormous chandeliers, each one shimmering like a galaxy of stars. At the far end, the old minstrels' gallery had been strung with balloons and ribbons, incongruous and festive, echoing with the music rising from the band below. Couples were already dancing, their laughter mingling with the swell of the orchestra.

"This place is more suited to the minuet than the modern dance," Sean murmured beside her, his voice low, almost wistful.

"I know." Her eyes scanned the floor, memory tugging at her. As a child, she had spent hours here, dancing across the parquet alone in borrowed shoes and dreams far too large for her young heart. Even then, her hero had already begun to take shape in her mind— dark-haired, elusive, and always just out of reach.

She glanced up at Sean—and found him watching her.

"Are you going to tell me what's wrong?" he asked quietly.

She gave him a bright smile. Too bright. "Why, nothing."

His lips twitched in wry amusement. "All right, Simone. Have it your way. If you collapse, I'll just pick you up. If you try to sneak off, I'll follow. Either way, you'll tell me—sooner or later. Might as well dance."

Without waiting for her answer, his arms came around her, and he swept her into motion. The floor blurred. The music carried them. And for the briefest while, the cold ache inside her began to melt, just a little. Her colour returned, faintly. She wasn't going to have to face anything tonight—not yet. She could keep the pain buried, where it belonged. Later, she'd go away. She had already written for an interview. She hadn't told her father yet. She hadn't found the courage.

Even the thought of leaving—of never seeing Sean again—made her stomach knot and her throat tighten. He must have felt it. He pulled her closer, his dark head bending toward her.

"Tell me, Simone," he murmured, lips brushing her temple. "What is it?"

"There's nothing." Her heart thundered against her ribs, surely loud enough for him to feel.

But he didn't back off. His thumb grazed her palm—deliberately slow, erotically sure.

"There are a dozen places in this house I could take you right now," he whispered against her ear. "No one would find us. With this crowd, no one would even look."

A shiver ran through her. Her legs brushed his. He moved with her, pressed against her, closer than was proper. His lips grazed the curve of her neck.

"I want you, Simone. I want you in my arms when I wake up. This can't go on. Not like this. Neither of us can take it."

She didn't answer. She couldn't. Her breath caught, and when she finally met his eyes, she shook her head, looking away quickly.

"I can't," she whispered. "I know about you and Fleur. There's no point pretending anymore. If you want a mistress, I think you already have one." Her voice faltered, but she pushed through. "And even if you didn't… I've realised that I—I just can't."

His hands clenched. A muscle ticked in his jaw. He was about to say something— something she might not survive—but then his gaze shifted. A flicker of movement at the entrance caught his eye, and his entire body went rigid.

"I'll be damned," he muttered, low and furious. "I can't believe this."

Simone turned—and froze.

Jeffery.

And his mother.

They stood just inside the doorway, chatting with someone they clearly knew, Mrs. Rogers animated and smiling, Jeffery scanning the crowd. Simone knew—without the smallest doubt—that he was looking for her.

Sean was seething. She could feel the rage radiating off him in waves, his body tight and braced with fury. But this was a charity ball, not a family dispute. He was the host. There was nothing he could do but endure it with gritted teeth.

"This is why, isn't it?" he ground out, his voice barely a whisper. "This is what you're hiding. This is why you've been floating around like a ghost."

"Don't be ridiculous, Sean," she said quickly. "Everyone comes to these things. You've probably just never noticed them before—"

"Oh, I notice everything," he said, his voice flat and clipped. "And trust me, they don't come. Never. Not once. Until tonight."

She hesitated, her pulse thundering again.

"And we both know," he continued, eyes narrowing, "exactly who Jeffery Rogers is looking for."

She opened her mouth, but nothing came out.

His gaze turned accusing. "Is this what's been tearing you apart? Was it so hard to tell me? You couldn't just say it? That it is Rogers you want?"

She couldn't stand there shouting at him. Not in the middle of the ballroom. People were already glancing over curiously, and Jeffery—of all people—was trying to catch her eye, as though they shared some private connection. The nerve of men. Sean was looking at her as if she were the one who'd broken trust, as if she'd been sneaking around behind his back. And all the while, he'd been with Fleur—every opportunity, every chance he got.

And Jeffery's cool, calculated cheek took her breath away. At the show, he'd been downright insulting—rude to her, dismissive to Cleo—and now he turned up at the ball with that smug look on his face, like he belonged. She didn't know why she bothered. With any of them.

Chapter Nineteen

Without another word, Simone pulled free of Sean's grip and stormed out of the ballroom, cutting directly past Jeffery and ignoring him completely. Fury bubbled in her chest, her hands clenched into fists, her heels striking the floor like gunfire. She muttered to herself as she reached the entrance hall, every footstep building her outrage.

She didn't hear Sean until he was behind her—until he caught her firmly by the arm and all but propelled her into the library, slamming the door behind them.

"Now you'll tell me!" he rasped, eyes blazing. "If it's Rogers you want after all, you can damn well stand there, look me in the face, and say it."

"I wouldn't have Jeffery if he came gift-wrapped in gold and tied with a bow!" Simone snapped, spinning toward him. "And just because you're standing in your baronial hall doesn't mean you get to throw your weight around with me!"

"Then why is he here?" Sean shot back, his voice low and deadly.

"He bought a ticket like everyone else. You think Mrs. Rogers would waste ten pounds a head unless it was planned weeks ago. Now let me out. I'm going home. The Easter ball can take care of itself!"

She turned, trembling, and then swung back with glittering defiance. "And while we're on the subject, I've already applied for another job. I'm resigning. Monday."

Sean went still. Too still. "Oh, are you?" he said, voice quiet and dangerous. "And what exactly are you resigning from? Does that include me? Us?"

"We don't have an 'us,'" Simone said stiffly, willing her voice to stop shaking. "A few kisses? That's not a relationship. Plenty of people have kissed me. I'd hardly call it serious."

Her throat tightened. She could barely say the next part. "Don't forget I know all about Fleur. And your plans. Anyway, I was—" she faltered, "I was playing you along."

Sean's eyes widened, the blue of them darkening like a storm. For a second, she thought he might actually laugh—but what came out was worse. A cold, dangerous smile.

"Were you?" he purred, voice low and lethal. "Well then, I must congratulate you. You're quite the actress. I had no idea." He moved to the door, yanked it open, and stood aside with mockery curling his lip. "Let's go back to the ball, shall we? Just a pair of old friends, catching up."

Simone's heart pounded. She knew Sean. Knew him too well. He never took things like this. Not quietly. Not calmly. She tried to muster some dignity.

"Fine," she said tightly. "We'll go back. But then I'm leaving. This has been... upsetting."

She stepped forward, trying to pass, but the moment she reached him his hand closed gently—yet with unshakable firmness—around her wrist.

"Come back to the ballroom first," he said, his voice now coaxing, smooth. "People saw us leave. We weren't exactly laughing. No point upsetting the family."

She hesitated. Rhonda was there. Her father. Cleo. It was true. She nodded slowly.

"Alright."

He didn't release her wrist. His hand simply slid down until their fingers were intertwined. As they walked back through the entrance hall, she stiffened slightly at the contact—but he just tightened his grip gently and looked down at her with a half-smile.

"Surely we can manage a united front," he said quietly. "Unless you'd rather have everyone believe we've had a lover's quarrel?"

She didn't want that. She loved everyone too much to cause a scene, to become the centre of speculation and gossip.

"No," she said softly.

Her fingers relaxed in his, and for a heartbeat he held her hand tighter—almost protectively.

"That's my girl," he murmured.

The words sliced through her.

If only she were. If only she truly were his girl. But it would never be enough—not halfway, not for a little while. She couldn't survive that. She couldn't share him with Fleur or anyone else. She had known it for days. She knew it now with painful, perfect clarity.

She loved Sean.

Too much.

And if she couldn't have forever with him… she couldn't have anything at all.

By the time they returned to the ballroom, the entire family had gathered to play host, doing their part with smiles and charm. Sean threaded through the crowd with purpose, weaving her beside him as if they were one unit. He looked completely composed— too composed, Simone thought uneasily. Not a flicker of the towering rage she'd seen in the library showed on his face.

His hand was warm and unyielding around hers, holding her with quiet command. He nodded and smiled to those who greeted him but didn't pause for conversation. His charm was automatic, his focus razor-sharp. There was a quiet intensity about him now that made her stomach clench. Sean wasn't letting this go. He never backed down. And this… this was far too calm. Far too quiet.

She tried to distract herself, tried to look anywhere else. The family, at least, looked resplendent. She found herself unconsciously including Alex among them—he fit so naturally. Only Fleur seemed like an outsider now, an exquisite ornament too sharp for the setting.

Sean leaned across and said something low to Mark, who raised an eyebrow, then slipped through the crowd with a purposeful air. Simone tried to move toward Rhonda—who was in deep, animated conversation with Lady Vivian—but before she could take a step, Sean's grip tightened on her hand, snapping her back to his side.

It was like being yanked by Prince's leash. His hold was nearly painful now, but he didn't look at her—just kept walking. She dared not resist. Too many eyes were turning toward them.

And then the music stopped.

The silence fell like a dropped curtain. Simone's breath caught. The crowd turned, puzzled, and she could feel every heartbeat echo in her chest like a drum. Mark was reappearing, weaving through guests, a slight frown creasing his brow.

Her heart kicked hard. Sean had ordered the band to stop. But why?

Cleo liked to scheme and plot—but Sean? He acted. Decisively. Instantly. She had no idea what he was planning, but instinct screamed that she should run.

Except she couldn't. His grip on her was iron. And she knew—there would be no escape.

Then, he spoke.

"I'm sorry to interrupt the dancing," he said, projecting his voice just enough to carry across the room. "But this seemed too good a moment to waste."

People turned toward them with interest, the music's absence sharpening their curiosity. Simone felt faint.

"This is the one time of year when everyone who knows us is gathered together in one place," he continued, flashing that dazzling, deceptive smile. "And I'm not above a bit of theatre when the occasion calls for it."

He reached into his pocket with maddening calm, turned to her—and suddenly the world narrowed to just them.

"The Easter Ball seemed like the perfect moment," he said, "for Simone and I to tell you that we are officially engaged."

She didn't even have time to breathe. The ring was on her finger before the meaning of his words had fully landed—a ruby, rich and blood-deep, surrounded by a constellation of diamonds. It gleamed under the chandeliers, exquisite, unmistakably custom-made. And expensive. Very expensive.

For one long, dazed moment, Simone just stared at it.

Then the room erupted.

Cleo and Rhonda shrieked in tandem, voices bright with glee. The guests clapped, laughed, gasped, rushed toward them with congratulations. The band struck up again, this time a soft, romantic waltz. The crowd closed in around them, effusive and delighted, and Simone stood in the centre of it, stunned—like a statue that had forgotten how to move.

"You sly dog," Mark laughed, clapping Sean on the shoulder. "No wonder you had me cut the music. Simone looks like she's been hit by a thunderbolt!"

"She's swept off her feet," Sean murmured smoothly, his arm sliding around her waist. "Aren't you, sweetheart?" He pulled her closer, and there was something in his tone— something dark, tight, controlled—that made her shiver.

To everyone else, he looked the picture of romance.

To Simone, it felt like a warning.

People were kissing her cheeks, laughing, wishing her joy. She tried to smile, tried to nod, but inside her mind was a thunderstorm. She couldn't think. She couldn't breathe. Nothing made sense.

Why had he done this?

Why now?

There had to be a reason—something beyond what he'd said, something calculated and dangerous. But she couldn't piece it together. Not with her heart racing and the weight of the ruby burning on her finger.

She was trapped in the middle of a fairytale… and she couldn't wake up.

Sir Michael kissed Simone's cheek with such enthusiasm she nearly stumbled. There was no mistaking his delight.

"Well," he declared, beaming, "it's been a long time coming, but it had to happen, of course."

He looked over at Sean with a father's pride and a conspirator's grin. "We've had some tricky times along the way."

Before she could respond, Cleo swooped in, tugging her right out of Sean's arm with a breath-stealing hug.

"What did I tell you?" she whispered with wicked glee. "Two down, one to go."

Simone gave a smile that barely masked the frantic scream inside her chest. Around them, everyone was all joy and congratulations, but only Rhonda—steady, perceptive Rhonda—caught the wild panic in Simone's eyes. She gave her a sharp, knowing glance, but there was nothing to say. Nothing she could say. Not here. Not now.

Simone was engaged to Sean Taylor—and no one had the faintest idea what was seething beneath the surface.

Sean turned to her father with a casual grin. "I never quite asked your permission, Henry."

"That would've been old-fashioned nonsense," her father replied cheerfully, hugging Simone again. "Besides, if I'm honest—and heaven help me for saying so—I probably handed her over to you years ago."

Simone managed a shaky laugh, but her voice wavered as she turned to Lady Vivian, who had just reached them.

"I—I'm sorry you couldn't know first," she said quietly, awkward in a way she never usually was with Sean's mother.

"My dear," Lady Vivian said warmly, taking both of Simone's hands, "it was a delightful way of doing things. And very like Sean. He's always had a flair for the unexpected." She smiled with gentle pride. "In any case, it wasn't really a shock. It was just a matter of time. You do know how fond we are of you, don't you?"

Yes. She did. That was the cruellest part. They had always felt like her family—long before Sean had ever kissed her. But how would they feel if they knew the truth? The full, black, shameful truth?

"Come on," Sean said smoothly, drawing her back into his arms. "We'll have champagne when the crowd clears. Right now, I'm going to dance you away on those trembling legs of yours."

Trembling? Oh yes. But not for the reasons he thought.

Around them, people continued to dance and toast, couples swirling past with cheers and fond remarks. If Simone hadn't been locked inside her own private nightmare, she might have laughed at the look on Mrs Rogers' face. The woman looked personally insulted by the news—an unexpected engagement where she'd never wanted one. Her disapproval hung in the air like stale perfume.

Jeffery himself kept well away, his expression thunderous. Serves him right, she thought grimly. He had no right to come at all.

But it was Fleur who drew Simone's eye—and chilled her blood.

She stood off to one side, utterly silent, not offering a single word of congratulations. Cloaked in elegance, icy and unreadable, she seemed carved from marble. Not a single flicker of emotion crossed her face.

Simone's stomach twisted.

Sean knew.

She could feel it in the tension of his grip, in the cool calm of his movements. He hadn't exploded—but that didn't mean he didn't know. That was the worst part. She couldn't tell what he was thinking. It was impossible to read him. He gave nothing away.

And yet the closer she was to him, the more her instincts screamed.

It took every ounce of courage to tilt her head slightly and whisper beneath the swell of music, "Why did you do it?"

She didn't think he would answer. But he did.

His tone was flat, deliberate.

"I want you, Simone. This makes it official. Isn't that what you expected to hear?"

Her throat closed. "I—I told you that—"

"That you couldn't. Wouldn't. Didn't want to?" he murmured with a flicker of cold amusement. "You've never been very good at lying. If I picked you up right now and took you upstairs, you'd be mine. Willingly."

Her heart slammed against her ribs.

"Then if you're so sure of yourself," she whispered, "why the engagement?"

He didn't even blink. "I have a family, sweetheart. Surely, you've noticed. They expect things done properly. Appearances are everything."

He sounded detached, as if discussing weather or wine—not a woman's life.

A sob caught in her throat, and she turned her face away. But Sean leaned closer and whispered, almost lazily, "Don't cry."

There was steel under the softness.

"If you do," he continued quietly, "we'll be out of this ballroom in under sixty seconds. And I'm making no promises about where we'll end up."

It silenced her completely.

Gradually, his arms loosened. The rigid hold softened into something more bearable, and the tension between them dissolved just enough to keep the illusion alive.

"One day," Sean murmured, his voice brushing her ear, "when you're not quite such an idiot, I'll explain myself properly. In the meantime… congratulations, Miss Symons. You're an engaged lady. And Jeffery Rogers is off our backs."

She lifted her eyes to his, desperate to find something—truth, deception, regret, anything. But his face told her nothing. He just looked back at her with those dazzling blue eyes, satisfied, unreadable.

Everyone else might be celebrating.

But Simone knew what they didn't.

Fleur had never offered a single word of good wish. Mark didn't seem to care who Fleur ended up with—he was dancing with Rhonda and laughing like he hadn't a single worry in the world.

Simone, however, was drowning in questions.

And one terrifying certainty remained: Sean had a plan.

She just didn't know what it was.

If appearances were to be believed, Sean had planned nothing at all. He'd simply announced their engagement like a man swept away by love—calm, assured, affectionate. He acted as though this were the most natural next step in the world, and that made it harder to breathe.

Chapter Twenty

When the ball finally ended and the family gathered in the drawing room for a light supper and champagne toasts, Sean gave every impression of being completely, incandescently happy. If he wasn't resting an arm around Simone, he was lacing his fingers through hers. There was never a moment he didn't have some part of her under quiet control.

Simone, on the other hand, was wound so tightly she felt she might shatter if anyone touched her the wrong way. Her head throbbed with unspoken questions and half-formed fears. She didn't dare voice a single one. Sean dominated every inch of her space. His presence was a quiet, constant pressure—subtle but unrelenting—and each time she looked up, those brilliant eyes pinned her in place, stripping away whatever composure she clung to.

The others were radiant with joy. This was exactly what they'd hoped for—what they'd expected. Alex, still glowing from Cleo's side, looked every bit the romantic, smiling at Simone with brotherly warmth. Her father was over the moon. And while Rhonda's sharp, intelligent gaze occasionally flickered to her with concern, even she eventually gave up trying to interpret the truth behind Simone's smile.

Especially when Sean sat on the settee and casually pulled Simone into the curve of his shoulder, as if she had belonged there forever.

"I bet there are secret passages in this house," Rhonda said with sudden enthusiasm, leaning forward on the edge of her seat.

"Several," Sean replied, a small smile playing at his lips. "There's a priest hole on the main corridor upstairs, and somewhere out there in the woods, there's a tunnel for escaping in times of trouble. We used to use it for dares."

"Gosh!" Rhonda's eyes sparkled like a girl at Christmas. "A real escape route? That's brilliant!"

Mark chuckled. "Come here," he said with a wink. "If you can keep a secret, I'll show you something."

Rhonda leapt to her feet instantly, light on her toes. She stood beside Mark as he pressed a small, almost invisible panel on the old carved wall. A door slid open silently, revealing a narrow passage beyond.

Rhonda gasped. "No way."

Mark stepped inside and turned with a grin. "What's the matter? Lost your nerve?"

"Not likely." Rhonda flashed a grin. "I'm game for anything."

With that, she stepped into the shadowy opening—and the panel slid shut behind them. A soft squeal followed, along with Mark's laugh, and for a moment Simone felt the tension lift, if only slightly.

"I didn't know about that!" she complained to Sean, half intrigued, half exasperated.

"We didn't tell you," Sean said, watching the passage. "You were always too curious—and small enough to disappear in a crawl space for hours. We'd have had to demolish the place just to find you again. And this is a listed property, after all."

His eyes glinted, and he bent his head to kiss her—right there, in front of everyone.

To the others, it was charming, romantic. To Simone, it was another reminder: she was no longer her own.

"Well," Lady Vivian said with a bemused laugh, "I hope Mark hasn't forgotten the exit. We may have to send in a search party."

"They're taking their time," Cleo said dryly, her eyes flicking—almost pointedly—to Fleur, who sat rigidly upright and hadn't smiled once.

Simone noticed the change instantly. Fleur's expression was a mask of ice, her eyes brittle with fury. Her lips, painted a perfect crimson, were pressed tightly together. The fireworks, it seemed, were primed.

But the wall slid open again, and Rhonda emerged laughing, her cheeks flushed a glowing apricot. Mark followed her, looking thoroughly pleased with himself.

"I would absolutely hate to go crawling through some filthy tunnel," Fleur said archly, her voice cutting into the joy like glass.

"Oh, it wasn't filthy," Rhonda countered breezily. "Just a few cobwebs. And it's got a light switch, though someone took their time turning it on."

Mark grinned. "I wanted to see if her nerve would crack. It almost did."

"But not quite," Rhonda tossed back playfully, and Simone could almost hear the clash of swords.

Fleur's laugh was thin. "Seems rather pointless to have a passage that goes nowhere."

"It doesn't go nowhere," Cleo said sweetly, all innocence. "Doesn't one of them come out in your room, Mark?"

"And in the kitchen," Lady Vivian added quickly, looking flustered. "And the study, I believe."

It was too late. Cleo's barb had hit its target. Rhonda's blush deepened, while Fleur bristled visibly, her elegant frame stiff with restrained outrage.

Simone felt Sean's hand move up to cradle the back of her neck, the pressure warm and unmistakably possessive.

"Just in case the rockets go off," he murmured under his breath, "did you have a hand in this?"

He turned her chin toward him and searched her face.

"No, Sean. Honestly," she said quickly, unsure whether she was lying or not. Cleo's plans had a way of sucking everyone in, and Rhonda was staying with her.

"Lucky for you," he warned, eyes narrowing. "Otherwise, I might be forced to take drastic measures. One of those exits happens to open into my room."

His tone was teasing, but there was steel beneath the velvet. His fingers brushed the nape of her neck, and she shivered, pulse quickening. The sensuality in his gaze was unmistakable, and her body reacted even as her mind screamed for caution.

"Please, Sean," she whispered, terrified someone might see her unravelling right in front of them.

"Oh, you'll say that," he said with quiet certainty, his voice low and electric. "You'll be begging soon enough. I promise."

Simone didn't know how the family managed it, but somehow, without a word, they diffused the storm. As if by silent agreement, they moved with the smooth grace of breeding and diplomacy, restoring calm with practised poise. No one addressed the drama directly, but the atmosphere shifted—elegance suppressing tension like silk laid over fire.

Only Cleo remained defiantly unrepentant. Simone caught Lady Vivian's eyes flashing with rare, reproachful anger as they rested on her fair and unapologetic daughter. Rhonda, by contrast, had grown quiet and subdued, and from the tight line of Mark's jaw, Simone suspected he wasn't just annoyed with Cleo—he was furious that Rhonda had been humiliated.

Simone gave a small, shaken sigh of relief when it seemed the worst had passed. Crisis averted. For now.

Sean's low chuckle tickled her ear, smooth and knowing. "I do believe you've grown up, Simone," he murmured. "That little scene actually worried you. Those golden eyes of yours aren't looking for a fight anymore. You're starting to behave like an engaged lady."

"When Cleo stirs things up, I feel more like a spinster aunt at a church fête," she muttered.

"I promise you," he murmured, voice velvet-dark, "that feeling won't last long."

By the time they returned to the Dower House, it was nearly half-past two in the morning. Her father offered to drive both girls back, but when he reached for Simone, Sean stepped in smoothly.

"Surely I'm allowed to walk my fiancée home, Henry?" he said with a wide, genial smile.

"I'd be disappointed if you didn't," her father replied with a laugh. "I'd start worrying about what's become of young love."

If only he knew. What had young love become? Schemes. Secrets. Mistresses and fiancées in the same breath. But Simone couldn't run sobbing to her father. Even if she did, he'd probably just laugh and hand her back to Sean with a quip and a wink.

No one knew she was drowning in confusion, hurt, and disbelief.

Except Sean.

They walked in silence under the cold April moon, the shadows crisp and silver edged. The other two had already arrived back, leaving only the hush of night and the crunch of gravel underfoot. Simone drew her wrap tighter around her, as if it might shield her from the man beside her.

When they reached the rhododendron hedge, far from the glow of the house, Sean stopped and turned her toward him. His arms closed around her slowly, and for a moment he simply stared at her, his sapphire gaze searching her face with unsettling intensity.

Tears prickled behind her eyes. She hated that he could do this—see through her with such ease.

"What do I have to do to make you trust me?" he asked at last, his voice low and rough, as though even he was exhausted by her resistance.

"We didn't have to get engaged," she choked. "You didn't give me a choice."

He cupped her cheek gently, angling her face back to his. "You don't want a choice," he said softly. "You made yours when you were ten years old. It's always been me. Rogers was just another one of your madcap attempts to escape what you already felt."

"You can say that," she cried, "but you don't know whether it's true or not. You've always been this force in my life. Maybe I just want to be free of it. Maybe I need to."

"Ah. So, you're going to run?" He arched a brow, amusement and disbelief mingling on his face.

Her temper flared. He always assumed she'd be there, waiting—faithful, unchanging, undemanding. Well, maybe that Simone was gone.

"I don't have to run," she snapped. "The first step is already done. I'm getting a new job."

"There's nowhere on this earth I wouldn't find you." His tone was quiet. Implacable.

She broke then, rage and heartbreak bursting out of her in a rush. "Why? Why? WHY?!" she shouted, fists striking his chest. "You don't get to claim me just because you want to. You left me, Sean. You left and lived your life while I stood still!"

He caught her wrists in one strong hand, eyes blazing. "Because you're mine," he said with calm finality. "You've been mine for as long as I can remember. And now I want more than your memories. I want your nights. I want your mornings. I want to wake up with you next to me, skin to skin. I want to own you, Simone—mind, body, and soul."

His voice was low and deadly serious, and his mouth crashed down on hers with no tenderness—only a fierce, angry hunger. He pulled her against him, taut and trembling, and she didn't resist. Her body folded into his, lost as always, helpless in his arms.

The kiss changed. The edge softened. His hands grew reverent, tracing the curve of her neck, branding her with heat, making her shiver.

"Sean… Sean…" It was barely a whisper—part plea, part surrender.

His hand slid beneath the chiffon of her dress, finding her breast with slow, aching possession, and she gasped at the contact, all thoughts of resistance vanishing.

"I don't know which one of us is mad," he murmured thickly. "You, for fighting this, or me, for not claiming you years ago."

He kissed her again, deeper this time, until her knees buckled and she clung to him to stay upright. When he finally pulled back, they were both breathless.

"I'm not sure about the aunt bit," he said, voice low and rough. "But I can promise you—the days of being a maiden are just about over."

Then, softly but firmly, he eased her away from him. "Go home, Simone. While I can still let you."

Somehow, she made it to the house, though it felt more like drifting than walking. She was weightless, untethered, as if reality had loosened its grip. He had that power—Sean could empty her of every coherent thought, leave her utterly blank except for the fierce ache of him.

She was desperately, irrevocably in love with him—and she had no idea what he truly meant to do with that knowledge.

He made her feel wicked, undone, enslaved to her own desire. She didn't need to look back; he was already inside her, seared into her mind. She could still taste the kiss on her lips, still feel the lingering heat of his hands against her skin, the press of his mouth, the weight of his body.

She stepped into the house without knowing how she got there and crossed the hall in a daze. At the base of the staircase, she sank down onto the bottom step like a woman under a spell—barely breathing, barely aware of anything but the echo of him inside her.

Too stunned to cry. Too overwhelmed to think. Just trembling, bewitchingly still, lost.

In the morning, Simone received a most astonishing phone call. Cleo rang straight after breakfast, her voice breathless with excitement.

"Listen! I can't stay on the phone long—if Sean catches me, he'll kill me. Actually, I'm not sure if he's going to strangle me or kiss me when he gets back. You never can tell with Sean."

Simone's stomach dropped. "Cleo, what have you done?"

"Me?" Cleo sounded scandalised. "Nothing at all! What would I do?" Her voice was all innocence, but Simone knew better—and the warning signs were deafening.

"If you've got news, tell me now," Simone said firmly, though her knees felt weak.

"That's what I'm trying to do! Though I expect Sean will tell you himself. I just wanted to be first."

Of course she did. With Cleo, delivering scandal was practically a competitive sport. Simone braced herself. Whatever plot had been hatched, it had worked. Or detonated.

"It's Fleur," Cleo whispered dramatically. "This house has never seen such a scene. She screamed at Mark and threw his ring at him."

"What?" Simone's mind stalled. Fleur? The icily controlled Fleur making a spectacle? That was hard to imagine.

"I swear it's true! A full-on meltdown over breakfast. Mummy was absolutely aghast. I mean, Fleur's always had a certain air, but today she went full fishwife. She hurled the ring across the room just as we walked in. Said she wasn't engaged to Mark anymore and didn't care who heard it."

"Oh dear," Simone murmured, adopting the dry tone of an elderly aunt. "Was Mark upset?"

"Not that you'd notice. He looked thunderous, but then he marched over and chucked the ring into the fire. A diamond ring, Simone! I think he thought Fleur might try to get it back." Cleo paused, then dissolved into giggles. "Well, that did it. Fleur went off like a rocket and Sean had to intervene. I thought Mummy was going to faint."

Simone closed her eyes. "Where is Fleur now?"

"Gone. Packed off with her luggage. Sean drove her to the station personally. Mark's stomping about the woods. Daddy's pretending nothing happened—he's buried in the Financial Times. Mummy took to her bed with a cold compress. You should have come for breakfast."

"Thank you, but there are some things I can happily miss," Simone replied dryly.

"I'll give you all the juicy details later. Must dash—Sean could walk in any minute and I'm not in the mood to be vaporised. Honestly, he looked at all of us like we were schoolchildren in disgrace. He hates scenes."

Cleo rang off, leaving Simone blinking at the receiver.

So, Fleur and Mark were finished. Just like that. Had that been the plan all along? Cleo liked to think she was the mastermind, but Sean had always been the real strategist. Had he engineered the whole thing to clear the way for Fleur?

No. That didn't track.

Sean was a master of many things—but manipulating the family into embracing Fleur as his bride? Impossible. Not after this morning's debacle. No one would forget the chaos Fleur had stirred up. And knowing Sean, he wouldn't want that kind of wedge between himself and the people he genuinely loved.

So, what had his reaction really meant?

Cleo had said he hated the drama. Fair enough. But Sean had weathered plenty of passionate flare-ups before—with her. They'd had rows that shook the walls and kisses that followed like lightning after thunder. So why had this one rattled him?

Unless…

Unless it wasn't meant to be a marriage at all.

Unless Fleur was only ever meant to be a lover.

His mistress.

The thought struck cold and fast. Was that the plan? Keep Fleur on the side while marrying Simone for the estate, for duty, for peace?

She couldn't live like that. Wouldn't.

She'd rather walk away forever.

Later, when she finally told Rhonda, her friend's face went pale.

"I think I'd better go home, Simone," Rhonda said softly. "I feel like I've caused all this."

"How could it be your fault?"

"Mark was… kind to me. I didn't push him away. I knew Fleur noticed, and part of me thought she deserved it. But I never meant to interfere in someone else's engagement."

Simone gave her a long look, heart aching a little for Rhonda's quiet honesty. "You're a good person."

Rhonda gave a wry smile. "Fat lot of good it's done me—no, scratch that. Never say fat."

She turned back to her packing and Simone stood there, watching for a moment. Then something inside her settled into decision.

"I'm coming with you."

"What?" Rhonda spun around, horrified. "Simone, no! Sean will kill me."

"He can't kill all of us. Right now, Cleo's probably first in line. I need to get away. Help me, please."

"You know I'd help you," Rhonda said. "But Simone… you're engaged."

Simone looked down at the sparkling ruby on her finger, then met Rhonda's gaze.

"Exactly."

Simone looked back down at the ring, its fire catching the morning light. Slowly, she slipped it off and curled her fingers around it.

"I can't marry a man who doesn't love me," she whispered. "I can't marry a man who has a mistress."

Rhonda stared at her, aghast. "Are you sure he does?"

Simone gave a small, hollow laugh. "I told him I knew about her. I said it straight out." Her voice dropped. "And he didn't deny it."

"Oh, Simone," Rhonda breathed. "I'm so sorry. And I thought Sean did love you."

Simone crossed to the desk and scribbled a short note with trembling fingers:

Sean, I'm sorry. I can't marry a man who doesn't love me.

She folded it once and placed the ring on top of it.

Rhonda took a deep breath and gave a tight smile. "Well, pack your bag. He may not kill me outright. And let's be honest—I was born to be a martyr. I've always known it."

Her father wasn't quite so resigned.

"Talk to Sean before you go," he said gently, watching her with worried eyes. "Just talk to him."

Simone shook her head, her throat too tight to speak for a moment. When she finally found her voice, it came out small and broken. "I can't, Dad. He doesn't love me."

He looked at her, something unreadable flickering in his eyes. "Sean loves you."

"No," she said, shaking her head, pain flashing across her face. "He's never said it. Not once. He didn't even ask me to marry him. He just… announced it. I think he did it to make his family happy. To shut everyone up."

He sighed and ruffled a hand through his hair. "You and Sean…" His voice was laced with affection and frustration in equal parts. "It's time you two got married—all this drama is aging your poor father."

He leaned in and kissed her on the cheek. "Go on, then. But don't be surprised if, when you come back, I've taken up drinking again and have a black eye to show for it."

Simone gave a watery smile. "I'm sorry, Dad. But I deserve to be loved by the man I marry. Please give Sean his ring back. I left a note with it."

Her father exhaled slowly and didn't argue. What could he say? Simone was already walking out the door.

"For God's sake, go—before Sean gets down here!"

Chapter Twenty-One

Simone didn't need the warning. Her heart was already pounding as she slipped out the door beside Rhonda. Thanks to Cleo, they knew Sean was still occupied at home—for now. But that window would close fast.

Rhonda didn't waste time. She backed the car out quickly, her jaw set, and they made a wide detour to avoid the station in case Sean had already set off. It wasn't until they were miles down the motorway, the countryside slipping past in a blur, that either of them began to breathe properly.

Sean drove a Porsche. They both knew it. Neither said the words hot pursuit, but the thought lingered, silent and real.

"I feel like I'm smuggling Marie Antoinette away from the mob," Rhonda muttered, eyes fixed on the road. "At great personal risk. How long do you think it'll take before he catches up? I might need to start praying."

Simone gave a faint, joyless smile. "He probably won't even bother." Her voice was flat. "I'm making it easy for him. He'll go straight to Fleur in London. Stay with her. He won't need to look for me."

Rhonda's fingers tightened on the wheel, her expression darkening, but Simone placed a hand gently on her arm.

"Drop me off in London," she said quietly. "Please. I don't want you dragged into this. If you don't know where I'm staying, he can't harass you."

When they finally got to London, Rhonda pulled the car to the side of the road, glancing over with concern. "Are you sure, Simone? You can come stay with me."

"Yes, I'm sure. Your place is the first place he will look," she said with a sad but steady nod. "I can't settle for someone who doesn't respect me. Or love me. I know that much."

Rhonda leaned across and hugged her tightly. "You're braver than I'd be."

Simone kissed her cheek. "Thank you, Rhonda. For everything."

She grabbed her bag, then she stepped out into the streets of London, the spring air brushing her face like a reminder she was free—but not unscathed.

Later, she found a quiet guesthouse tucked between shops and cafes. The room was small and clean, the bed a narrow little island she collapsed onto fully clothed. She lay there for a moment, staring at the ceiling… then the tears came, hot and fast, the sobs shaking her until she had no more strength to keep them in.

She had left Sean. Walked away from the illusion, torn it down with her own trembling hands.

But it didn't feel like freedom.

It felt like grief.

Bone-deep. Soul-crushing. The kind that hollowed her out from the inside and left nothing but silence in its wake.

As soon as Sean dropped Fleur off at the train station, he didn't even wait for her train to pull away. He spun the car around and headed home.

Not to gloat, not to breathe easier now that Fleur was out of the house—though that helped—but to check on Mark. The scene that morning had been brutal, and even if Mark had played it cool, Sean knew better. His brother could be cold as ice on the outside, but inside, there was a temper—and a heart—that didn't always show.

He found Mark in the study, lounging in a deep leather armchair with a drink in his hand and a brooding expression that looked more thoughtful than angry.

"You alright?" Sean asked, leaning against the doorway.

Mark glanced up. "Am I supposed to be?"

Sean crossed the room and dropped into the chair opposite. "Just checking."

Mark shrugged. "Fleur was never it. She knew it. I knew it. Honestly, I'm more annoyed I tossed a diamond ring into the fire. That thing cost a fortune."

Sean gave a low chuckle, but there was a thread of unease in it. He was just about to press further when a knock sounded at the door.

It opened before either of them could answer.

Lady Vivian looked up from her embroidery in the adjacent drawing room, her needle pausing mid-stitch. The moment she saw Henry's face through the open doorway, she set the hoop aside and rose gracefully, the rustle of silk echoing softly in the quiet.

"Ah, Henry," she said, her voice warm but immediately alert. "Is everything quite alright? You look worried."

Sean stood as soon as he saw Simone's father step into the room. "What's happened?" His tone was clipped, already bracing.

Mark, who had been seated near the hearth, rose too, brows drawn in concern. "Is Simone alright?"

Henry raised a hand before anyone could say more. His expression was drawn, as if he'd aged ten years in a single morning. "I needed to see you. I saw your car had returned."

Sean stepped forward, heart beginning to pound. "What is it?"

Without a word, Henry reached into the pocket of his coat and pulled out two things: a small, folded piece of stationery—and Simone's engagement ring. He held them out to Sean, his hand steady despite the heaviness in his voice. "Simone left this. Early this morning."

The room stilled.

Sean stared at the items for a beat before taking them in silence.

He looked at the ring first. Its familiar weight sat in his palm like a cruel joke. The ruby caught the light, bold and beautiful—defiant, abandoned.

His fingers were steady.

His pulse was not.

Then he unfolded the note. It wasn't long. Just one line written in Simone's unmistakable hand.

Sean, I'm sorry, but I can't marry a man who doesn't love me. —S

Thirteen words.

Each one landing like a punch to the gut.

He read it once. Then again. As if repetition might soften the blow. But the words didn't change. Her voice was there—quiet, resolute. A farewell dressed in grace.

"I tried to stop her," Henry said gently, his voice rough with regret as he looked at Sean. "She wouldn't listen. Said she deserved a husband who loves her—and that she wouldn't settle for anything less."

Lady Vivian pressed a hand to her chest, her breath catching. "Oh, my poor girl…" Her gaze shifted to Sean, sharp and searching now, her tone no longer gentle. "Why does she think you don't love her?"

Sean didn't answer. His jaw tightened, his eyes shadowed with something raw and unguarded. The ring still sat in his palm like an accusation. The note burned quietly in his hand.

Because I never said it.

Because I let pride speak where love should have.

Because I made her doubt what was never in doubt for me.

But none of that came out.

Instead, he stood there, mute beneath the weight of what he hadn't done—of everything he hadn't said.

Lady Vivian's voice softened, but the steel beneath it remained. "She's not the kind of girl who runs, Sean. If she left—it's because she truly believes you don't have feelings for her."

Sean folded the note slowly; with the kind of care, one gave to something precious—and ruined. He slipped it into his jacket pocket alongside the ring, like he was putting away the last fragile piece of her.

"Did she say where she was going?"

"Just… London." Henry gave a tired sigh. "Rhonda took her. She said she needed a clean break."

Lady Vivian sank back into a chair, visibly shaken. "She did look a bit pale last night. Even after your announcement. I thought she was just a little overwhelmed."

"I should have said something," Mark muttered. "Rhonda said that there was something off with Simone. I thought maybe it was nerves…"

Of course it wasn't.

Sean clenched his jaw, everything inside him buckling under the weight of what he'd lost. Rhonda. Cleo. Even Mark. They had all sensed it unravelling. And he—arrogant, blind—had believed a grand, public announcement would fix it. That if he declared his claim boldly enough, if he kissed her in front of everyone and slipped that ring on her finger, she'd stay.

That she'd stop fighting him.

That she'd surrender to the path he'd chosen—for both of them.

That she'd simply accept her fate because he had decided it.

But she hadn't.

She was gone now.

Without a fight. Without slamming a door. Without even demanding that he explain himself.

Because she'd already stopped believing he would.

He had felt it last night—in the tremble of her hands, in the way she didn't lean into him like she used to. In the way she had asked *why*. In her quiet. Not the soft quiet of trust, but the heavy silence of someone retreating into herself. Of someone already grieving what was still right in front of her.

He had told her he wanted her.

Made her feel it—in every kiss, every bruising touch.

But he hadn't said the words she needed most.

I love you.

And now, she was gone.

Sean turned sharply and strode out of the room, fury and fear tightening around his chest like steel bands. He took the stairs two at a time, heading straight for his keys, his thoughts already outpacing him.

There was no point calling Rhonda. He needed to see her in person.

Rhonda was soft in all the ways that mattered—honest, kind, quietly steadfast. She listened. She cared. And if he could just sit across from her, look her in the eye, maybe she'd understand. Maybe he could make her see that he wasn't the man Simone thought he was. Not entirely.

He didn't want to threaten, didn't want to storm in like some entitled brute demanding access. That wasn't the way.

Not this time.

He just needed a chance—to explain, to ask, to try.

But if Simone thought she could vanish without hearing the truth—not in a note, not in a whisper behind closed doors, but from him—then she didn't know him at all.

He loved her.

Had loved her since she was fifteen and he'd walked into the Dower House to find her curled up in the library window seat—barefoot, covered in ink, defying him with that maddening gold stare and far too many questions.

He loved her in a way that scared the hell out of him. That made him hard when he should've been gentle. Silent when he should've spoken. Possessive when all she wanted was reassurance.

And he'd never told her. Not once.

Because he'd thought she just knew.

But obviously she didn't.

Maybe he'd made her doubt everything.

And now, maybe he'd lost her.

No. He wasn't giving up that easily.

London was massive, but so was his reach. If she'd checked in anywhere under her name, he'd find her. It wouldn't take long. It never did.

But this wasn't about tracking her down just to prove he could.

This was about standing in front of her, cupping that proud, wounded face in his hands, and finally saying the thing she had waited too long to hear:

I love you. I always have. And I'm sorry.

Even if she walked away again.

Even if she never looked back.

She needed to hear it.

And he—finally—was ready to say it.

Rhonda was sipping her tea in the kitchen when the doorbell rang with sharp insistence. Rhonda looked up from her cup of tea, her stomach sinking before she even opened the door. She didn't need to check the peephole. She already knew.

She pulled the door open.

"Sean."

He was tense, controlled—but only just. His jaw was tight, his eyes fierce with some mixture of fury and desperation.

"Where is she?"

Rhonda blinked. "Hello to you too."

Sean's nostrils flared. "Please, Rhonda. I know she was with you. Her father told me you left together. Tell me where she is."

"She made me drop her off," Rhonda said calmly, stepping aside so he could come in. "On purpose. So, I wouldn't know where she was staying."

Sean halted in the middle of the living room, running a hand through his hair with a rough exhale. "Damn it. Of course she did. She knew I'd come straight to you."

Rhonda crossed her arms. "Yes. She did."

Sean turned to her, something wounded and raw flashing through his features. "You don't understand. I have to find her."

"Then let me ask you something first." Rhonda's voice had steel in it now. "Are you still keeping the mistress?"

That stopped him cold.

"What?"

"Don't go after her," Rhonda said evenly, "if you're still stringing someone else along. Simone could probably live with you not loving her—not easily, but maybe. But she won't live with being disrespected. You break her heart, she'll survive. But if you treat her like she's second to anyone—you'll destroy her."

Sean looked like he'd taken a punch to the chest. He stared at Rhonda. "She thinks I have a mistress?"

Rhonda's silence was answer enough.

"She told me she knew," she said quietly. "She said that she told you she knew, and you didn't deny it."

"Bloody hell," Sean breathed, backing a step toward the wall as if steadying himself. "I thought she was just being jealous—lashing out. I didn't think she actually believed it."

Rhonda's eyes narrowed. "So, it's not true?"

"No!" His answer came instantly, fiercely. "There's no mistress. There never was. Fleur… God, Rhonda, Fleur was never mine. That was Mark's disaster, not mine. I hated every second of her being in that house. I didn't even realise Simone really thought—" He cut himself off, his voice breaking with disbelief. "She thinks I've been lying to her."

"She thinks," Rhonda said gently, "that you've been holding her in one hand and Fleur in the other. And you never told her she was the one who mattered."

Sean dragged a hand down his face. "Because I thought she knew. I thought I'd made it clear in every way but words. I've loved that girl since she was fifteen and ran barefoot through my mother's rose garden like she owned the world. I just—God, I never said it."

"Then find her," Rhonda said softly. "And say it."

Sean looked up, something shifting in his gaze. The fury remained—but now it was focused, clean, burning with intent.

"Thank you," he said, already turning for the door.

"And Sean?"

He paused.

Rhonda met his eyes, unflinching. "I don't care how powerful people think you are. If you hurt her again… I'll make damn sure your next mistress is a ghost. And not the kind that leaves quietly."

A flicker passed through Sean's eyes—something like remorse, maybe even shame. He gave a tight, humourless smile. "There won't be a next. Simone is it. Always has been."

And then he was gone.

He slid into the driver's seat and just sat there, hands resting uselessly on the wheel, his breath fogging the glass. The quiet was oppressive, pressing in around him like punishment. His mind wouldn't stop replaying last night—her voice still fresh, still aching.

"I can't," she had whispered. "I know about you and Fleur. There's no point pretending anymore. If you want a mistress, I think you already have one."

He hadn't said a word in his defence. Just stood there—furious, bristling with indignation over Jeffery's smug presence at the ball, too incensed to hear her. Too arrogant to see the wound in her eyes.

He hadn't told her there was no other woman. That Fleur had never been anything at all ever. That since Simone, no one else had ever come close.

And now, because of his silence, she thought he'd kept a mistress. That he'd claimed her in front of his family while still tangled up with someone else.

He'd been angry.

But now?

Now he was sick with the weight of it.

What kind of man didn't even listen when the woman he loved begged for honesty?

A damned arrogant bastard. That's who.

And if he didn't find her soon, if she slipped too far out of reach… he might lose her forever.

Simone sat in the cramped guest house room and stared blankly at the faded wallpaper, as if the pale, curling pattern might somehow offer answers. It didn't. Nothing did.

It had been two days—two long, aching days of silence and solitude.

No contact with anyone. She had stayed in the room, not wanting to be seen by anyone.

She should've felt safe. Free. But all she felt was hollow.

The ruby ring was gone from her finger, yet its weight still clung to her skin like a bruise. She could feel the cool press of the band as though it hadn't left at all—only now, it marked a promise that had never truly been hers. A dream she'd worn too long. A future built on illusion.

Because he didn't love her.

Not really.

Not in the way she needed.

Maybe he wanted her—her body, her presence, her loyalty—but love? That quiet, unwavering, soul-baring love?

He hadn't said the words. Not once. Not when it mattered.

And that silence had said everything.

She pulled her knees to her chest, curling in on herself on the narrow bed, her cheek resting on the crook of her arm. Outside, the city moved on—cars, voices, distant footsteps—but in here, time had thickened into something sluggish and airless. Every second stretched, heavy and sharp with all the things she didn't say before she left.

Maybe she should've stayed. Fought. Demanded answers.

But she hadn't had the strength.

Not when she'd looked at Sean and seen possession in his eyes instead of tenderness.

Not when his kiss had left her trembling—not from passion, but from the terrifying knowledge of how easily he could take everything from her... and still keep his own heart locked away.

He hadn't even asked her to marry him.

No quiet moment. No question. No choice.

Just a bold, public declaration—as if her life, her future, her consent was his to command.

That wasn't love.

And it sure as hell wasn't how she wanted her marriage to begin... or to go on.

She wanted more than heat and history and the weight of expectation.

She wanted to be chosen—not claimed.

And besides... he had Fleur now.

That thought sat bitterly in her chest. Fleur, with her icy poise and clipped smile. Fleur, who had been part of Sean's world in ways Simone could never quite touch.

He might've ended things with her, but Simone knew how these things went. Breakups could be undone. Feelings didn't just vanish.

No matter what Cleo said.

No matter how tightly Rhonda hugged her goodbye.

Sean and Fleur made sense—at least on paper.

She and Sean? They made chaos.

And Simone was tired of chaos.

So, she'd walked away.

And now, in this borrowed room in a too-quiet part of London, she waited for her heart to stop hoping.

She couldn't be a convenience, a claim, a performance for his polished family and their glittering friends. Not when every kiss from him made her soul ache. Not when she knew there was someone else—Fleur—still tangled in the margins of his life.

She curled her knees up to her chest on the narrow bed, trying not to cry again. She'd done enough of that. The pillow was already damp from earlier, her suitcase still half-unpacked on the floor. She wasn't even sure why she'd come here. London was loud, crowded, a blur of strangers. But she'd needed to vanish. To breathe. To be somewhere that wasn't filled with memories of Sean—his voice, his scent, his hands.

And yet he was everywhere.

In her mind. Beneath her skin.

She wrapped her arms tighter around herself.

"Stupid," she whispered. "You're so stupid, Simone."

But hadn't she always been? From the moment she'd first met him, too tall and too clever and too arrogant for words—and somehow already under her skin. He was older, already aloof, already watching her with those cool sapphire eyes. He'd teased her, challenged her, infuriated her.

And she'd fallen in love with him anyway.

She loved him still. God help her, she loved him more than ever.

But what good was that if he couldn't even say the words?

Chapter Twenty-Two

Simone hadn't eaten in over two days. Not properly. Not since she'd left the Dower House with nothing but a suitcase and a breaking heart. At first, the emptiness in her stomach had matched the one in her chest. Food had felt pointless. Heavy. Like forcing sweetness into a mouth that only tasted bitterness.

But now—now her hands trembled slightly as she tied back her hair. Her head felt light, her vision a little too soft around the edges. Her body was reminding her that even grief had its limits. Even sorrow needed sustenance.

She stood, slowly, slipping on her coat and clutching her handbag like it might anchor her. Outside, the London morning was grey and indifferent, the kind that didn't care if your world was ending. She walked a few quiet streets, eyes lowered, until she spotted a small café tucked between a bookstore and a florist.

It smelled of coffee and warm bread.

She stepped inside and slid into a window seat at the back, grateful for the hush. No one looked at her twice.

A waitress appeared with a tired smile and handed her a menu. Simone ordered a grilled cheese toastie and tomato soup—simple, comforting, something her mum might have made when she was little and feverish. A safe choice. Warmth and salt and familiarity.

When the food arrived, she surprised herself by eating almost all of it. Slowly. Mechanically. But it was something.

She sipped her tea and stared out the window at the rain streaking faint lines down the glass.

She still felt hollow. Still bruised from the inside out. But at least now she was steady.

She had done the right thing.

Even if her heart still clung to Sean's shadow. Even if she could still taste his kiss in the back of her memory. Even if it killed her.

She'd meant what she'd written.

She couldn't marry a man who didn't love her. She couldn't build a life with someone who only knew how to possess, not protect. And Sean—beautiful, complicated, brilliant Sean—just wasn't that man. He didn't see her pain. Didn't hear her voice. He hadn't even denied it when she told him she knew about Fleur.

He'd just ignored what she admitted.

Her throat tightened.

Maybe one day it wouldn't hurt so much. Maybe one day she'd meet someone who saw her clearly—who listened, who stayed, who didn't need a dramatic announcement or a public claim to know she was worth fighting for.

Until then, she had herself.

And that would have to be enough.

Simone finished her meal slowly, letting the warmth of the soup settle in her stomach and the melted cheese dull the edge of her emptiness. It hadn't fixed anything, but at least she no longer felt like she might faint on the pavement.

Outside, the air was cool and damp, the faintest drizzle misting the streets. She didn't rush. She kept her head down, hands tucked into the pockets of her coat, walking at a pace that let her breathe in the quiet. She'd always liked grey days—there was something honest about them. No pretending. No need to smile when the sky didn't bother either.

By the time she reached the guest house, her hair was damp and her shoes slightly scuffed. The familiar creak of the old steps greeted her as she pushed open the door and climbed back up to her room. She didn't turn on the light. She didn't need it.

For a moment, the silence wrapped around her like a shroud. The guest house room was sparse but clean—faded wallpaper, mismatched curtains, a soft ticking clock on the wall. It had no history, no memories.

No Sean.

She picked up a book from her bag and opened it, trying to read. The words blurred together. Her eyes moved across the page but absorbed nothing.

She couldn't concentrate.

She couldn't think about what tomorrow would bring, or where she was supposed to go next. Her job. Her life. Her future—it all sat just outside the door, waiting for her to gather the strength to face it.

But not yet.

Right now, she could only sit in the quiet, curled up with the ache of a love that had never been hers to begin with.

She wasn't ready to think about the future.

Especially not a future without Sean.

Sean hadn't slept properly in two nights. His London flat was a wreck—half-drunk coffee cups littered the counter, clothes draped where they fell, unopened newspapers stacked like unanswered questions.

But none of it mattered.

There was no Simone.

Not in his apartment. Not in his arms. Not even in reach.

And she wouldn't be, not when she was this hurt. Not when she'd walked away with tears in her eyes and a quiet, devastating finality in her step.

He knew her too well. Knew that once Simone decided to retreat, she didn't leave breadcrumbs. Her pride wouldn't allow it. Her strength—so soft and stubborn—would carry her far from anything that hurt.

And right now, that meant him.

She wouldn't come home. Not until she believed he deserved to be heard.

And right now, he didn't.

He'd scoured half the city already. Called in favours. Visited hotels. Questioned old friends. Even dropped by the tucked-away bookshops she loved, hoping to catch a glimpse of that unmistakable red hair.

Nothing.

It was as if she'd melted into the city and taken all the light with her.

The ache in his chest had settled into something colder now—sharp-edged regret, grinding exhaustion, and a helpless fury that no amount of pacing or planning could burn off.

Still, he couldn't stop moving.

He grabbed his jacket—no plan, no destination, just the gnawing need to move, to do something before the walls closed in.

He was halfway to locking the apartment door when the phone rang.

The sound sliced through the silence. He froze—then lunged.

Snatching it off the table, he answered on the first ring.

"Hello?"

No greeting. No hesitation. Just four clipped, breathless words.

"I just saw Simone."

Sean's grip on the receiver tightened, his knuckles turning white. "Tell me exactly where?"

Alex's voice crackled over the line, clipped and urgent. "A guest house off Rosemead Street—Number Six. She walked there from a café nearby. Looked like she hadn't slept in days."

Sean grabbed a pen from the hall table, scribbled the address on the back of an envelope. He was already reaching for his coat.

"I wasn't looking for her," Alex said. "Just passing through. It was pure luck."

"Thank you," Sean said, already halfway to the door.

He hung up the receiver with a sharp click, the sound ringing through the silence like a starting gun.

His hands were shaking.

He didn't stop to think. Didn't pause to plan. Just the address burned into his palm and one thought running like fire through his veins:

He had to see her. Before it was too late.

He slammed the door behind him and took the stairs two at a time instead of waiting for the lift, heart hammering against his ribs. Three days. Three days of silence; of knowing he'd driven her away. Not just with his arrogance. Not just with that stupid public announcement.

But with his silence.

He should've told her.

Should've fought for her.

But now—*now* he had a second chance.

And God help anyone who got in his way.

The knock came just before midday.

Simone froze.

She sat motionless on the bed, the dog-eared novel limp in her lap, her heart thudding once—twice—hard and high in her chest.

Another knock. Firmer this time.

She stood slowly, her limbs heavy with dread. A part of her knew. She didn't want to know, but she did.

She crossed the room, ignoring the breathlessness rising in her throat, and looked through the peephole.

Sean.

Of course.

She didn't open the door.

"Simone," came his voice, low but unmistakably him. "I know you're in there."

She stayed quiet. Let the silence speak.

"I'm not here to make a scene," he continued. "I just want to talk."

She swallowed hard, throat tight. Her fingers hovered near the latch but didn't move.

"There's no point?" she said through the door, keeping her voice even, cold. "You don't talk. You command. You call me names like idiot and little wretch and act like I'm a problem to be handled, not a person with a heart."

He didn't answer right away. The pause stretched.

"Simone," he said again, softer now. "I know I've said things I shouldn't have. And I didn't listen when it mattered. But I'm here now. Please."

She hated how her body reacted to that voice, how it twisted something deep inside her. But the ache was still too fresh, too sharp. She wasn't going to open the door just because he'd finally shown up.

She leaned her forehead against the door, the wood cool beneath her skin, and closed her eyes.

"You can't just show up and expect me to go back," she whispered. "You didn't even ask me to marry you, Sean. You just… declared it. Like I was something you could claim. I can't live like that."

"I know," he said, his voice low, stripped of its usual edge. Regret seeped through the cracks, soft and unmistakable. "That's why I'm here. I need to tell you the truth. I should've done it before. You deserved that—deserved more than a public scene and a ring you never asked for."

Her fingers curled tighter around the doorknob, her knuckles pale. She wasn't ready. Her heart was too raw, too full of questions and silences and aching memories. Too battered by everything he hadn't said—and the one thing he'd never managed to.

"Please, Sean," she murmured. "Just go. Let me try to forget you."

There was a long pause.

And then, softer than she'd ever heard him—barely more than breath:

"Please, Simone."

No arrogance. No bravado. Just a quiet, aching plea. And it undid her.

Her breath hitched as she reached for the lock, the sound of it clicking echoing like thunder in the stillness. She opened the door a few inches. The chain remained.

But it was a beginning.

She didn't say anything at first. She just looked at him—really looked—to see if he was hiding that familiar anger behind his eyes, if the fury she'd known so well was lurking, waiting to explode.

But it wasn't there.

Sean stood just beyond the threshold, the hall light catching on the hollow planes of his face. His clothes were rumpled, the collar of his shirt askew like he'd slept in it—or hadn't slept at all. His jaw was shadowed with stubble, his coat hanging open as though he'd thrown it on without thinking. He looked nothing like the confident man who always had a plan. He looked like a man unravelling.

Not furious.

Not smug.

Just… raw.

Simone's voice barely rose above a whisper, hoarse from too many sleepless nights. "What do you want, Sean?"

He exhaled slowly, like it hurt. "To talk," he said. "That's all. Just talk."

Her fingers hovered at the chain. "If you start barking orders again or calling me names like I'm some foolish girl—I want you to leave. For good."

Sean didn't argue. Didn't try to charm his way through it.

"Okay," he said quietly. "I promise."

She watched him, really watched him—for the first time since she'd walked away.

Gone was the man who always had the upper hand. The one who never flinched, who could silence a room with a glance or win a battle with a smile. He wasn't standing here.

All that remained was the man underneath.

Worn down. Frayed at the edges. Stripped of all pretence.

And—for the first time in years—maybe worth listening to.

In that stillness, something old stirred in her memory.

She saw the boy who once helped her untangle a hedgehog from the rose bushes at the Dower House, who scraped up his hands and didn't complain. The one who used to argue with her about books he hadn't even read, just to keep her talking. The boy who used to look at her like she mattered more than anything—before pride, pain, and promises had pulled them in opposite directions.

Something in her chest shifted.

She hesitated a moment longer.

Then—quietly, reluctantly—she slid the chain free and opened the door.

Just enough for him to enter.

Sean let out the breath he'd been holding and stepped inside.

For a long moment, he didn't speak. He just looked at her.

She stood still, pale, and wary, arms wrapped tightly around her torso like a makeshift shield. Her red hair was tousled, her eyes rimmed with exhaustion. And yet—she'd let him in. She hadn't slammed the door. Hadn't walked away.

That small act of grace eased something sharp in his chest.

But it didn't soften the stakes. He knew this was it—his one chance to make things right. If he didn't tell her the truth now, if he let pride or fear twist his tongue, she'd be gone for good. And he wouldn't deserve another shot.

"There's nobody else," he said at last, his voice low and steady. "There hasn't been anyone else since you were eighteen."

She blinked. Her breath caught, disbelief flickering in her eyes.

"It's been four years," she whispered. "Four years, Sean."

He gave a faint, self-deprecating smile. "I have enormous reserves of discipline," he said. "Except when it comes to you."

He raked a hand through his hair, frustration and regret crackling off him like static.

"Fleur and I were never a thing," he said. "She wanted to be—desperately. But I wasn't interested. Not once. I think she just… lingered. Long enough, and loud enough, to make it look like there was something going on. Maybe she thought if she waited me out, I'd eventually give in."

He looked her square in the eye, his voice firm. "That was never going to happen."

Simone didn't respond right away. She stood there, watching him, her expression unreadable. Silent. Cautious.

But something had shifted. The raw, blazing anger was gone. In its place was a quieter storm—uncertainty, ache, the kind of pain that hadn't been fed in days but still lingered like a bruise. Not bleeding anymore. Just tender. Guarded.

Sean took a step forward, then checked himself.

"I should've told you everything that night," he said quietly. "The moment you said you knew. God, Simone… I was so wound up, so jealous of Jeffery, I couldn't think straight. I thought I was about to lose you, and I panicked. I was so focused on locking it all down—securing your hand, making it official—I didn't stop to listen."

Her brow drew tight, her voice faint. "You were jealous?"

"Of course I was," he said, no hesitation. "I was furious. And terrified. Because I love you."

She blinked, as if trying to absorb the words. Then she took a shaky step back and lowered herself onto the edge of the bed, eyes wide and stunned.

"You do?" she whispered.

The words she had once begged for in silence. Words she'd imagined in a hundred different ways—but hearing them now, raw, and unadorned, she didn't know what to believe.

Did she dare?

He knelt in front of her and took her hands gently in his. "I love you," he said again, softer this time—like a confession wrenched from somewhere raw and buried. "My beautiful, maddening girl… I love you, and I want you. I've loved you since you were absurdly young. If I'd followed my instincts, we'd have been married the day you turned eighteen. You were always—so clearly, so wonderfully—mine."

He lifted her fingers to his lips and pressed a kiss to each knuckle. She didn't pull away.

"You love me," she echoed, her voice a breath of disbelief. "Really?"

"Yes. More than anything." His eyes dropped to their joined hands. "Is it so hard to believe?"

"You always said you wanted me," she whispered. "But you never said…"

"I want you because I love you," he said, lifting his gaze to hers, steady and sure.

Then, slowly, he stood—bringing her with him—and wrapped his arms around her. She didn't resist.

He didn't speak again. Instead, he kissed her. A brush at first, light as a vow. Then deeper, fuller, like he meant to pour every unsaid word into her skin, every lost moment into her mouth. He kissed her like it was the only language he trusted—and she understood it.

"No more games," he murmured against her lips. "No more half-truths. No more hiding, sweetheart. We've wasted too much time already."

Her body softened into his, the angles and curves of her sliding into place like a memory long denied. The ache between them, always just beneath the surface, surged forward now with wild urgency.

"The night of the accident," he said softly, still holding her, "I didn't forget anything. I remembered every word you said—that you loved me."

Her eyes flew to his, startled. "But you told me you didn't remember."

"You were so upset. So unsure. You crept into my room like a frightened little faun, trying to protect me. Trying to give me something I didn't deserve. I couldn't take advantage of that—not without you knowing I remembered everything."

His voice dropped, rough and tender. "And God, I wanted you. That night. More than I can say. Just like I want you now."

Her breath hitched. Her heart thundered in her chest. The look in his eyes—the ache and reverence in it—was undoing her completely.

"Then why did you leave for London the next morning?" she asked, the question trembling out of her. "I can't pretend that didn't hurt, Sean."

He drew back just enough to see her clearly. His expression softened, reverent.

"I went to get your ring," he said. "I'd already commissioned it the week I got back to Branlow. I didn't want to wait another day. I came back to Branlow... *for you.*"

Her lips parted, stunned. Emotion welled in her eyes.

"You said you loved me after the accident," he went on, his voice barely above a whisper. "I believed you. And I thought—for the first time—that maybe the fight was finally over. That we could stop pretending and start living. Together."

He looked down at her then, his gaze heavy and full of heat, the blue of his irises swallowed by dark pupils. She could barely breathe as she lifted her arms and slowly encircled his neck.

"Sean..." she whispered, dazed, breathless.

His forehead dropped to hers. "Do you forgive me, sweetheart? Tell me I haven't lost you."

Her eyes brimmed with tears, but her voice was steady.

"I love you, Sean. I always have. I could never love anyone else."

A shaky breath left his chest—half relief, half wonder—as he held her tighter. And this time, he knew. He wasn't holding onto hope, guilt, or fear.

He was holding her. And she was holding him right back.

He kissed her—slow at first, reverent, as if trying to make up for every lost moment. But then the dam broke. His hands framed her face, his mouth claiming hers with a hunger that sent shivers racing down her spine. It was all heat and tenderness, apology and promise, every emotion he'd kept buried pouring into the space between them.

Her fingers tangled in his hair, her body arching instinctively toward him, drawn by the pull that had always existed between them—inevitable, magnetic, undeniable.

But then—he pulled back just slightly, his breath catching as he looked at her. Her lips were still parted, her eyes shimmering with emotion. His chest rose and fell in shallow waves, the air between them thick with everything unsaid.

"Can we go to my apartment?" he whispered. "Get out of here?"

His gaze swept the modest guest room—the plain walls, the narrow bed, the tired curtains that barely held back the city light. This wasn't where she belonged. She deserved more than this. She deserved everything.

"Yes," she said softly.

He cupped her cheek, brushing his thumb across her skin with aching tenderness. "I love you, Simone," he murmured, voice like velvet and truth. "And just so we're clear, my sweet—I want you because I love you. Always."

Emotion gathered in her throat, thick and overwhelming. "I love you too, Sean," she whispered. "I want to be with you. I always have."

They moved together then—quietly, deliberately—as if neither of them wanted to break the fragile spell forming around them. He helped her pack her things, folding each item with care, kissing her between sweaters and stockings, his lips brushing hers like a benediction. As if he needed to keep touching her, just to believe this was real. That she was really his again.

At the front desk, Simone returned the brass key with a murmured thank you, her fingers brushing the counter. Sean stood beside her the entire time, his hand firmly wrapped around hers—grounding her, anchoring himself.

And he didn't let go. Not once.

Outside, the chill wrapped around them like a shawl of winter mist, but Simone barely felt it. Her focus was on him—on the strange, surreal magic of being at his side again.

Sean stopped beside a sleek black Porsche, the metal gleaming beneath the afternoon light.

She blinked. "This isn't your car."

"I couldn't wait for mine to be repaired." He opened the door for her, his voice quiet but resolute. "So, I bought one."

Before she could respond, he helped her in with the same care he always had. Then he leaned down and brushed a kiss across her lips—tender, certain, full of promise.

By the time he slid into the driver's seat and turned to look at her, the tension that had gripped them both for days had begun to ease. The silence between them wasn't heavy anymore. It was warm. Full of beginning.

Chapter Twenty-Three

The Porsche purred softly through the afternoon traffic, gliding between the city's bustle like it had a purpose all its own. Simone sat angled slightly toward the window, her fingers curled loosely in Sean's where their hands rested on the centre console. Neither of them spoke much. But the silence between them wasn't empty—it was content. Heavy with understanding. With forgiveness. With everything they'd said… and everything they no longer needed to.

When Sean finally pulled into the underground garage beneath his building, the low rumble of the engine faded to stillness. Simone turned to him, her expression tender, uncertain—like she was still finding her footing on new ground.

He looked at her and gave her hand the smallest squeeze.

"You're finally home," he said softly.

They rode the lift in silence, side by side. She could feel the tension radiating off him—not the old kind, not the angry edge that once kept her on guard—but a deep, aching restraint. Like he was holding back an ocean.

The penthouse was warm, softly lit, and—like him—striking in its simplicity. Dark wood floors stretched beneath clean lines and elegant furnishings, while floor-to-ceiling windows framed the sweep of the city skyline. But it was the quieter details that caught her breath: the books scattered across the shelves, the half-folded jumper tossed over the arm of the couch, the faint scent of cedar and something unmistakably Sean lingering in the air.

She turned slowly in a circle, taking it all in. "This place is beautiful," she said, her voice light. Then, with a faint smirk, "Well… it would be, if you ever cleaned it."

Sean rubbed the back of his neck sheepishly, following her gaze across the cluttered coffee table and the jacket draped over a dining chair. "Yeah… I wasn't exactly expecting company," he said. "I was kind of… preoccupied."

Her smile softened, the joke giving way to something quieter beneath. She knew exactly what—or rather, who—had occupied his mind.

"You were looking for me," she murmured, more a realisation than a question.

His eyes met hers, steady and unflinching. "Every minute."

She looked away, blinking once, her fingers drifting along the spine of a book on his shelf. A moment passed. Then she turned back to him—her gaze softer now, the fury gone, replaced by something far more disarming: uncertainty.

"Well," she said quietly, stepping further into the room, "you found me."

Sean's throat tightened. He closed the distance and pulled her gently into his arms, like he was afraid she might vanish if he moved too fast.

"This thing between us," he murmured against her hair, "it's always been too intense to ignore."

"I know," she whispered.

He kissed her then—slow, reverent. A kiss that held restraint, though every line of his body ached for more.

When he pulled back, he tucked a strand of hair behind her ear. "I want you to rest. Later, we're going out to dinner."

Her brows lifted slightly. "We are?"

"Yes." A small smile touched his lips as he turned toward the hallway. "Come. I'll show you to a room."

She followed, then stopped just short of the threshold, confusion flickering across her features. "Sean... I want to be with you."

His eyes met hers—warm, certain, full of feeling. "I want that too. More than anything. But there are a few things that need to be done first. Properly."

"Like what?"

He leaned in and pressed a soft kiss to the tip of her nose. "Trust me."

Then he guided her into the spare bedroom—quiet, sunlit, and freshly prepared—and lingered a moment at the door.

"Sleep," he said gently. "Then dress for dinner. We leave at seven."

And with a soft click, he closed the door behind him.

Simone had fallen asleep almost the moment her head touched the pillow. The exhaustion of a sleepless night—and the emotional weight of everything—had finally caught up to her.

When she woke, the room was bathed in soft golden light. She slipped into the bathroom, showered, and dressed slowly, carefully. The green gown she chose shimmered faintly in the mirror's reflection. She'd packed it without thinking, simply because Sean had once told her it brought out her eyes.

Now she was glad she had.

When she stepped out of the bedroom, refreshed and radiant, her hair swept into an elegant twist, a touch of colour on her lips, Sean rose slowly from the armchair. His gaze swept over her, and he stilled—utterly quiet, completely captivated.

"You look stunning," he said at last, his voice low, almost reverent.

She stepped toward him and reached up to smooth a wrinkle from the lapel of his jacket. "You don't look so bad yourself."

His mouth curved slightly. "Did you sleep?"

"Yes, thank you. I feel human again."

"Good," he said, his expression turning a shade more serious. "Because I need you wide awake for this."

She tilted her head, curiosity sparking in her eyes. "For what?"

But he only smiled and offered her his arm. "Come. You'll see."

He took her to a high-end restaurant tucked away in Mayfair—romantic, candlelit, full of quiet corners and polished service. Over champagne and seafood, they talked. Laughed. Stole glances. Stole touches. And when dessert was cleared, Sean reached across the table and took her hand.

"Simone," he said softly, his thumb brushing over her knuckles, "you must know by now… you are the love of my life."

Her breath caught.

"I love you more than I can put into words. More than I have the right to. I can't undo the past, but I can be better."

He reached into his jacket pocket and took out a small velvet box.

Her heart stopped.

He opened it.

Nestled inside, glittering in the low candlelight, was the ruby ring she'd worn briefly that night at the Easter Ball—before everything had fallen apart.

Simone's hand trembled as she looked down at it.

"I should've done this properly the first time," Sean said. "No public spectacle. No pressure. Just you and me." He paused, then added with quiet gravity, "Will you do me the honour of being my wife? My partner. My home. My lover. My everything."

Simone looked up, tears shimmering on her lashes—and this time, they were full of light, not sorrow. Her lips parted on a trembling breath, and then she nodded.

"Yes," she whispered. "Yes, Sean."

Relief, fierce and unfiltered, swept across his face. With careful hands, he slipped the ruby ring onto her finger—where it belonged.

Then he stood, came around the table, and pulled her to her feet.

Without a word, he gathered her into his arms and kissed her—slowly, deeply, as if he was sealing a promise into her soul. It wasn't just passion. It was reverence. Devotion. The kind of kiss that said: *You're mine, and I'll never let you go again.*

When they finally parted, her forehead rested against his, and for a long, suspended moment, the world outside them simply ceased to exist.

Later, after the quiet luxury of the restaurant had faded behind them, they returned to Sean's apartment. The air between them thrummed with tension—soft and simmering, like a storm building on the horizon.

The door had barely closed before he reached for her, drawing her into his arms with a tenderness that stole her breath. For a heartbeat, he just held her—one hand at her waist, the other cradling her cheek—like he needed to be sure she was real.

Then he kissed her.

Slowly. Deliberately. Achingly gentle at first, his lips brushed over hers with a reverence that made her heart twist. He didn't demand—he invited. Coaxed. And when she gave in—when her fingers curled into his shirt and her body leaned into his—the kiss deepened.

His mouth claimed hers with a hunger too long restrained. His tongue swept against hers, slow and sure, a sensual stroke that sent shivers racing down her spine. He tasted like wine and heat and everything she remembered—everything she'd missed.

She clung to him, lost in the moment, the rest of the world forgotten once more.

She swayed against him, and he pulled her closer, his hands strong on her hips, letting her feel the full, aching desire he'd kept restrained for too long.

"With you," he said thickly, voice rough, "there are no half-measures. I see you and I want you. And nothing else matters except making you mine."

"Sean," she breathed. "Please…"

He swept her into his arms and carried her to the bedroom, setting her gently on her feet beside the bed. She touched his cheek, her hand trembling slightly against the rasp of stubble. He drew her into his body, hard against soft, and held her like a man on the edge.

"If you tell me to stop, I will," he groaned.

She looked up at him, her voice breaking. "No, Sean. Please don't stop. I love you."

That was all he needed to hear. His hands shook as he undressed her, reverently, slowly, and then himself—baring not just skin but everything he'd ever held back. When they were both naked, he lifted her again, cradling her in his arms and laying her gently on the bed.

"I've wanted you for so long," he whispered against her skin. "My wild, brilliant girl… You've always been the one."

"I would've come to you at any time," she said brokenly. "I never forgave you for leaving me."

"I didn't leave you. I went away, yes—but you were with me the whole time. Even at eighteen, you were still too young. I had to wait. You were safe, but I loved you so much, Simone… so fiercely."

Tears welled in her eyes, and he kissed them away.

His mouth traced a trail from her throat to her breasts, his hands coaxing soft moans from her lips, the sound making his eyes darken with hunger. She arched into him, whispering his name.

"Tell me you want me," he said, voice hoarse and desperate.

"I want you, Sean," she gasped.

"Tell me you love me."

"I love you. I love you."

Her voice cracked, trembling under the weight of everything she felt, and then his hand slid between her thighs. His fingers found her with practiced ease, moving through her slick warmth with slow, devastating precision.

She cried out, her back arching, hips lifting to meet him, helpless against the pleasure he coaxed from her.

"That's it, sweetheart," he murmured, his voice rough with restraint. "Let go."

And she did.

Her body shattered around his touch—wave after wave of release crashing through her as her breath caught and her fingers gripped his shoulders. But he didn't stop. He stayed with her, steady and sure, until the last tremor passed.

Then he moved over her, covering her fully, his body settling between her thighs as though it was the only place he belonged.

And in that moment—nothing else existed.

"I need you," he said raggedly. "God, Simone… you're so beautiful."

Then, with a reverence that made her breath hitch, he guided himself into her.

He moved slowly, carefully, every inch a promise. Her gasp broke the silence, her fingers digging into his back. He stilled, watching her face as it flickered with tension, waiting—just breathing with her—until she softened beneath him.

Then he began to move.

"You're mine now," he murmured.

"Yes, Sean," she whispered, tears in her eyes. "I'm yours. Always. I love you."

"I love you too," he breathed, his voice wrecked. "You feel… God, you feel better than anything I ever imagined."

Their rhythm built, wild and unrestrained, years of longing igniting between every breath. Her cries rose, unguarded and raw, as she splintered beneath him. He followed, a broken sound tearing from his throat as he gave her everything he had.

"I'm here," he panted, his forehead resting against hers. "I'm right here, sweetheart."

She was crying softly now, arms wrapped tightly around him, and he didn't move. He just held her—anchored her—as though letting go might mean losing her all over again.

"To say I love you doesn't even come close," he whispered, his voice thick with emotion. "There's no word strong enough for what I feel. Maybe we knew each other in another life. Maybe we've always belonged."

"Don't say that," she whispered back. "What if we'd never found each other?"

"I would've," he said without hesitation, brushing her hair from her face. "Even if I had to search across time itself—I would've found you."

He wiped her tears with the gentlest touch, his fingertips barely skimming the curve of her cheek. She lay still beneath him, breath catching, heart pounding, dazed and overwhelmed by the storm of emotion that had passed between them. Love. Need. Relief. It wrapped around them like a blanket—warm, fierce, and unbreakable.

She shifted slightly, as if to rise, but his hand slid to her waist, halting her with a quiet strength.

"No," he whispered, pressing a kiss to her temple, his lips lingering there. "Don't go. Not yet."

His voice was low, threaded with longing and something rawer—something unspoken for far too long.

"Forgive me, my love… but I can't let you go. Not when I've only just found you again."

There was so much tenderness in his voice, so much need, that she closed her eyes and wrapped her arms around him again, surrendering to the safety of it, the fire, the belonging.

And as he took her again—slow and deep—she knew there was no going back.

She was his.

And he was finally, truly… hers.

They made love again before drifting into sleep, tangled together beneath the soft weight of his duvet. And then once more—when the moon was high and their bodies, still aching and attuned, found each other in the dark with a hunger that had nothing to do with lust and everything to do with love denied too long.

By morning, they woke in a slow blur of warm limbs and silent promises. Sean took her hand and pulled her into the shower with him. Steam curled around them, the water cascading over their bodies as if to cleanse what had come before. There was laughter between the kisses this time, teasing touches and whispered endearments, and when he pressed her back against the cool tile and entered her again, it was with the kind of gentleness that broke her wide open.

Afterward, he dried her slowly, reverently, like he was memorising every inch of her all over again.

Then he wrapped her in one of his bathrobes.

It was far too big—swallowing her frame entirely—but the sight of her in it made something soft and fierce rise in his chest.

"You look cute," he said, tugging the collar gently around her throat and brushing a kiss there.

She rolled her eyes, smiling. "I look like I've raided your closet and gotten lost in it."

"You look like you belong in it," he murmured. "Like you belong here."

Simone went quiet, her fingers gripping the lapels of the robe. And for a moment, neither of them spoke. The past still lingered around the edges, full of mistakes and pain and years lost. But right now—wrapped in warmth, his scent on her skin, his hands still cradling her hips—she let herself believe in the beginning of something new.

Later that morning, while Simone sat wrapped in his robe and curled up on the couch, Sean moved through the kitchen with surprising ease, barefoot and shirtless, preparing breakfast. The scent of strong coffee, warm sourdough, and softly scrambled eggs filled the penthouse.

He set the plate in front of her and kissed the top of her head. "Eat all of it," he said gruffly. "You've barely eaten in days."

She smiled faintly, touched by the way he fussed without making a fuss. And when she finished, he handed her a cup of tea just the way she liked it.

Then he leaned against the counter, that boyish grin tugging at his lips—mischief and heat simmering in his gaze as it swept over her slowly, deliberately, like he was memorising her all over again. A look that made her stomach dip and her pulse trip over itself.

"We need to go to Branlow," he said, his voice low and rough. "So, everyone knows I finally woke the hell up. That you're mine—and I'm yours."

He pushed off the counter and crossed the space between them in two strides, his hand finding her waist, his fingers grazing her hip in a way that made her breath catch. "Let's go home, sweetheart. But I'll warn you now—I don't think I'll be able to keep my hands off you once we get there."

She tilted her face up to his, her heart thudding, heat blooming under her skin. "Then we need to get married quickly."

His eyes darkened with something fierce and aching. "I hope you know—everywhere I go, you go. I can't think straight when you're not beside me. I don't even want to."

And then he kissed her—slow and claiming, his mouth slanting over hers with deep, lingering hunger. It wasn't just desire. It was a promise. A vow. A homecoming wrapped in heat and longing.

They were going home—but not just yet.

First, he swept her into his arms and carried her to the bedroom.

And it wasn't for sleep.

Epilogue

There was a knock at the door.

"I'll get it," Simone said, already moving.

She opened it just a crack at first—old habits—but relaxed when she saw him.

Sean stood there, hands in his pockets, his usual effortless confidence softened by affection. "Hey," he said. "Just checking everything's okay up here."

"All good," Simone replied, smiling. "Cleo's sending poor Rhonda around the bend with last-minute tweaks, but other than that, things are under control. Rhonda looks gorgeous. Mark's going to be floored."

Sean reached for her hand where it rested on the edge of the doorframe, lifting it to his lips and pressing a kiss to her knuckles. "Well, if she's even half as beautiful as you were on our wedding day, he's a lucky man."

A flush rose to Simone's cheeks, but her eyes sparkled. She leaned into him, rose onto her toes, and kissed her husband—her husband of six months—with a tenderness that hadn't faded one bit since their vows.

"I'll see you down there," she murmured against his lips.

He gave her that slow, heart-stealing smile. "Not soon enough."

Soon, Rhonda's father appeared to escort his daughter down the aisle, his face full of pride and quiet emotion. But before that moment, it was Simone's turn.

As bridesmaid, she stepped out first, the soft rustle of her gown brushing against the path. The estate had been transformed once again into a wonderland—just as it had been on her own wedding day. Twinkling candle lights draped the trees, roses bloomed in carefully arranged clusters, and the air was rich with the scent of summer and celebration.

Simone walked slowly, her gaze briefly flicking ahead to the altar—where Sean stood beside the groom, Mark, as best man.

And he was watching her.

That look—the one that had melted her heart on their wedding day—was still there, undimmed by time. If anything, it had deepened. His love for her no longer carried the sharp edges of uncertainty and longing. It was solid now. Certain. Fierce in its quiet strength.

Yes, they'd had arguments—what couple didn't? But the making up afterward... that was always the best part. Passionate, intense, and laced with laughter. He never let her go to bed angry. And somehow, every disagreement only seemed to bring them closer.

As Simone reached the front and took her place, Sean's gaze didn't waver. He gave her the smallest, most devastating smile—one only she would see. One that said: *I see you. I love you. Always.*

And as the music shifted and Rhonda appeared on her father's arm, Simone felt her heart swell.

Love like this—true love—was worth waiting for.

And it was absolutely worth fighting for.

The ceremony had gone off without a hitch. Rhonda and Mark had looked radiant, every bit as deeply in love as Sean and Simone had been on their own wedding day.

As the music shifted and the dance floor in the ballroom began to empty, Sean led Simone away, his hand warm at the small of her back. Before they could make it far, Cleo appeared—her arm looped through Alex's, both of them glowing with newlywed joy, having tied the knot just three months earlier.

"It's nearly time for Rhonda to get changed for the honeymoon," Cleo said with a meaningful glance at Simone.

Sean groaned playfully and tightened his hold. "Do I really have to let you go? I'm sure Mark wouldn't mind helping her out of that gown."

Alex chuckled while Cleo rolled her eyes in mock disapproval.

"Really?" Cleo said, arching a brow. "No class, these men."

Simone tried to stifle a laugh, failing completely. "Honestly. You give them one glass of champagne and suddenly they're twelve again."

Sean leaned in, brushing his lips against her temple. "I'll behave… eventually. But I make no promises when we get home."

"We are home," Simone reminded him with a smile. She had moved into the main house with Sean the day they were married, and it had felt right from the moment she stepped through the door.

She gave him a look—half exasperated, half utterly in love. "You never behave".

He grinned, unabashed. "And you love it."

She didn't deny it. Instead, she leaned in and pressed a soft kiss to his cheek before slipping from his arms to help Rhonda.

But even as she stepped away, she felt Sean's gaze on her—steady, warm, and unmistakably hers.

Outside, the night air was cool, the moon hanging bright and full above the estate, casting everything in a soft golden light. Beneath it, Rhonda and Mark stood hand in hand, ready to leave for their honeymoon in France—tracing the same path Simone and Sean had taken on their own magical escape through Italy and France just months before.

Simone stood with Sean behind her, his arms wrapped snugly around her waist, her back leaning gently against his chest. Together, they waved the newlyweds off as laughter, music, and the rustle of dresses filled the early evening air.

There was joy in the air—pure, unfiltered—and yet something quieter bloomed in Simone's chest. A hum of certainty. A whisper of something more.

As the other guests drifted back into the ballroom, Simone didn't move she just reached for Sean's hands and gently slid them lower, resting them over her still-flat stomach. She kept her hands atop his, holding them in place. Anchoring them there.

He kissed her neck softly. "You okay, sweetheart?"

She turned her head to meet his eyes, a smile playing at her lips—nervous and radiant all at once.

"You know I love you, don't you?"

"Of course," he said with a smile, brushing his nose against hers. "And I love you."

She hesitated, just a beat. Then said, quietly, "Well… there's going to be more of me to love soon."

Sean blinked, his eyes dropping to their joined hands on her belly. For a moment, the world around them seemed to still.

Then—slowly, wonderingly—he looked back up at her, emotion catching in his throat.

"You're…?"

Simone nodded, her eyes already brimming. "Yes."

His breath hitched, and then his arms tightened around her as if he could shield her from the world, as if holding her close would somehow make it all real faster. His breath was shaky against her neck, warm and uneven.

"I didn't think I could love you more," he whispered again, pressing a kiss just below her ear, "but I do. I do, Simone. God, I do."

She laughed softly through her tears, turning in his arms so they were face to face. His eyes were glassy, his expression raw with emotion. She touched his cheek, thumb brushing over the stubble along his jawline.

"I was going to wait to tell you," she said, voice trembling. "But this… this moment— it felt right."

He framed her face gently in his hands, his thumbs sweeping over her cheeks like she was something delicate and rare. "How long have you known?"

"A few days," she admitted. "I suspected it right before Rhonda arrived. I didn't want to say anything until I was sure."

Sean let out a breath, half-laugh, half-sob. "You're sure now?"

She nodded. "The doctor confirmed it yesterday. I wanted to tell you this morning, but then everything was so beautiful, the wedding—"

He kissed her. A kiss filled with wonder, with reverence, with a thousand unspoken promises. When he pulled back, his voice was husky. "You've given me everything I've ever wanted. A life with you. And now this."

Her hand went back to his, resting again over her stomach. "You're going to be the most ridiculous, overprotective father," she said, smiling through happy tears.

"And you," he said, his forehead against hers, "are going to be the most beautiful, brilliant mother."

They stood like that a while longer, the music drifting softly through the warm evening air, laughter and clinking glasses echoing behind them. But for that moment, there was only the two of them—wrapped in something deeper than joy, quieter than excitement.

Simone leaned back to look in his eyes, her heart full. "Do you think we should tell the family? Or wait until Mark and Rhonda get back from their honeymoon?"

He shook his head gently. "Let's keep it our secret for a little while longer. Just you and me."

Simone grinned, her eyes dancing. "I'm glad you said that."

He kissed her again—slowly, tenderly—his hands still cradling the place where their future had just begun to grow. "Come on," he said, his voice low, playful. "Let's go celebrate."

Then he wiggled his eyebrows. "Our way."

She swatted his chest with a laugh. "You're wicked."

"Utterly," he agreed, smug and unrepentant.

And together, hand in hand, they stepped back toward the celebration—toward music, family, laughter.

Toward their next chapter.

The End

Beneath the Lies

Alison Reid

A complete standalone romance

Previously published individually

Chapter One

Lily closed the car door and tightened her grip on the stroller handle, her knuckles whitening as if anchoring herself in place. The metal felt cold beneath her palms, solid and real—something she could hold onto while everything else threatened to tilt. She'd just driven over six long hours from Asheville—the city that had become her refuge, her shelter, her home for the last three years. Her pulse fluttered, too fast and too loud, like her body couldn't quite accept that she was here.

Back.

Standing on familiar ground she'd once sworn she'd never see again.

Three years had passed since she'd last set foot in Willow Creek.

The town unfolded before her exactly as she remembered it—small, postcard-perfect, and deceptively charming, tucked deep into the folds of the Blue Ridge Mountains. It was the kind of place featured on calendars and tourism brochures, all soft light and quaint promises. Time had barely touched it. Or maybe it had, and Willow Creek had simply refused to show the wear, clinging stubbornly to its image of permanence and peace.

Brightly painted storefronts lined the narrow main street, their façades cheerful and quaint, as if daring anyone to believe that nothing ugly had ever happened here. Flower boxes overflowed with petunias and trailing ivy, softening the hard edges of old brick and weathered wood. Hand-painted signs creaked lazily in the mountain breeze, their familiar names tugging at her chest with quiet, insistent force—reminders of places she'd once belonged.

The air was thick with scent and memory—warm cinnamon sugar drifting from Marigold's Café, mingling with the clean, sharp tang of pine rolling down from the ridge above town. It was the smell of her childhood. Of Sunday mornings and summer evenings. Of laughter, routine, and a life she'd once believed was unbreakable.

The town's single stoplight blinked steadily over the worn brick crosswalk, unchanged and patient, as if it had been waiting for her return. Conversation hummed softly around her—shopkeepers leaning in their doorways, voices low and intimate, exchanging news about the weather, illnesses, weddings, and breakups. About who'd left. Who'd stayed. Who'd come back.

And now… her.

Lily felt the weight of it almost immediately—the subtle shift in the air, the prickle between her shoulder blades. Eyes lifted. Heads tilted. Curiosity sharpened into recognition. She could practically hear the questions forming, the stories already being stitched together.

She knew that look.

Willow Creek might have been beautiful, but it was also small. A place where everyone knew everyone else's business—and if they didn't, they filled in the gaps themselves. A place where secrets didn't stay buried. They were dug up, examined, reshaped, and passed from mouth to mouth until they hardly resembled the truth at all.

Lily swallowed and glanced down at the stroller, at Mandy sleeping peacefully, blissfully unaware of the town that had already begun to notice her. The tight knot in Lily's chest loosened just a little. She softened instantly, her grip easing as she brushed her fingers over Mandy's blanket, smoothing an imaginary crease.

"I've got you," she murmured under her breath, the words more vow than reassurance. "No matter what."

She drew in a steadying breath, squared her shoulders, and took her first step down Willow Creek's main street—back into the town that had once broken her, and the life she wasn't sure she was strong enough to face again.

Everything looked smaller than she remembered—cosier, almost—but also achingly unchanged, frozen in time while her own life had been torn apart and remade. Every painted storefront and cobblestone corner whispered memories she'd tried desperately to outrun. Memories of a life she'd been forced to leave behind. A life she wished, with every bruised piece of her heart, she'd never had to abandon.

Her daughter, Mandy, slept soundly in the stroller, her tiny chest rising and falling in soft, even breaths. She didn't stir when Lily lifted her from the car, not even when the wheels bumped gently over the uneven cobblestones of Main Street. Mandy slept the way only toddlers could—utterly trusting that the world around her was safe.

Lily paused to look at her.

Her whole world. Her reason for coming back. Her reason for surviving.

Just over two years old, Mandy had a head of silky blonde curls that refused to stay tamed, even after a nap, and eyes the brightest, clearest blue Lily had ever seen—eyes that could melt her heart with a single blink. Her cheeks were round and rosy, lips soft and pink, and she had the sweetest little button nose Lily kissed every chance she got.

She was the most precious thing Lily had ever laid eyes on—a tiny miracle wrapped in softness and possibility, sleeping peacefully in her stroller. And even though Mandy wasn't her flesh and blood, she was hers in every way that mattered. Her daughter. Her responsibility. Her heart.

The sight of her like this—safe, warm, whole—pulled Lily under without warning, her thoughts dissolving as memory began to take hold.

Miranda—Lily's stepsister by another mother—had been pregnant when Lily arrived on her doorstep three years ago, exhausted and searching for somewhere safe to land. Miranda had only found out she was expecting that very week. The news was still raw, barely settled, when she told her boyfriend. He'd listened in silence… and then vanished. He ran without a word, leaving nothing behind but unanswered questions and an empty space where he should have been.

Miranda hadn't cried over him. Not once. Instead, she'd lifted her chin, placed a steady hand over her still-flat stomach, and said with quiet resolve, *"This little one is better off without him."*

Lily had never learned the man's name. She'd never wanted to. He didn't matter. He never would.

The pregnancy itself had seemed almost charmed, as though fate were trying to soften what had already been taken. There was no morning sickness, no bone-deep exhaustion, none of the complications Lily had feared. Miranda glowed in a quiet, effortless way—her skin luminous, her smile easy. She laughed often, teased Lily for worrying too much, brushed off every anxious question with gentle amusement.

Every doctor's appointment brought good news. *Everything looks perfect. She's developing beautifully. There's nothing to worry about.* Lily had believed them. She'd let herself believe this story was heading toward a happy ending.

When Miranda went into labour, Lily never left her side. She counted breaths when Miranda lost track of them, wiped sweat from her brow, whispered encouragement through every contraction. She held her hand and anchored her when the pain surged too strong, murmuring that she was doing great, that she was almost there.

Four hours later, a tiny cry filled the room—a sharp, indignant sound that cut through the exhaustion like light. A little girl, red-faced and furious at the world, perfect in every way.

Miranda smiled through her weariness and whispered her name.

"Mandy."

A miracle.

And then—everything went wrong.

Lily remembered the words the doctors used: *postpartum haemorrhage.* She'd learned later what it meant, how even now—despite modern medicine, despite all the knowledge and technology—women still died in childbirth. At the time, the phrase had sounded clinical. Distant. Almost harmless.

Until it wasn't.

Until there was blood.

Until the room shifted, urgency snapping into place like a trap.

Until Lily saw the fear flicker in the nurses' eyes before they masked it and began to move faster, voices sharper, movements more precise.

They spoke to Miranda quietly at first. Carefully.

Then more firmly.

They couldn't stop the bleeding.

They had tried everything.

Miranda knew before anyone said it aloud. Lily saw it in her eyes—the calm acceptance settling in, heavy and final. She turned her head and looked at Lily—really looked at her—as if memorising her. Her skin had gone pale, almost translucent, her breaths shallow and uneven, her strength slipping away with each one.

Lily clutched her hand so tightly her fingers ached, as though sheer will might tether her sister to the world.

Miranda squeezed back—weak, but deliberate.

"Lily…" Her voice was barely more than air.

"I'm here," Lily whispered, leaning closer, tears blurring everything. "I'm right here."

Miranda's eyes shone, fixed on her. "Tell Mandy I loved her," she said softly. "Tell her I loved her from the moment I knew she existed."

Lily pressed her forehead to her sister's hand, her heart cracking open. "I will," she whispered. "I promise. I'll tell her every day."

"And tell her…" Miranda swallowed, gathering what little strength remained. "Tell her I didn't want to leave her."

Lily nodded frantically, unable to speak past the ache lodged in her throat.

Miranda's grip tightened just slightly. "You have to be her mother now," she said, fragile and fierce all at once. "Promise me, Lily. Promise me you'll love her as if she's your own."

Lily didn't hesitate. Not for a heartbeat.

"Yes," she said immediately, her voice breaking. "Of course. I promise."

Miranda's lips curved into the faintest smile, relief softening her features. Her grip loosened. Her eyes fluttered. And then—gently, quietly—she slipped away.

Lily had kept that promise.

Every single day since.

Everything Lily had endured—every sacrifice, every lonely night filled with fear and doubt, every moment she'd forced herself forward when she thought she had nothing left—had been worth it for the little girl sleeping peacefully before her now. Mandy had healed parts of Lily she hadn't even known were broken.

She was her miracle. Her purpose. The one beautiful thing born from so much loss.

Mandy was her life now—her anchor, her hope—and the only part of Lily's world Lily faced without fear.

She leaned down and gently tucked the thin blanket more securely around Mandy's tiny body, smoothing the soft fabric over her curled fists. A faint, involuntary smile brushed Lily's lips as Mandy sighed in her sleep, lashes fluttering like butterfly wings, her breathing slow and even—utterly unaware of the world waiting for her.

Straightening, Lily drew in a steadying breath and turned toward Marigold's Café.

The familiar bell above the door would chime the moment she stepped inside. And then the whispers would begin. They always did. Willow Creek's gossips could sniff out a story from a mile away, and her return—especially with a child in tow—was practically a holiday gift wrapped in scandal.

But Lily lifted her chin.

Let them look.

Let them whisper.

Let them assume whatever they wanted.

She had survived worse than gossip. Far worse.

And she knew, without question, that she had nothing to be ashamed of.

She was home for one reason only: her father needed her. He was dying—diagnosed with late-stage prostate cancer—and Lily and Mandy were all the family he had left. That truth settled in her chest, heavy but resolute, strengthening her spine as she reached for the café door.

The bell above it gave a bright, almost too-cheerful ring as she stepped inside, slicing through the low hum of conversation.

Two women she recognised from high school looked up sharply. Their eyes widened in identical surprise before one leaned toward the other, whispering behind her hand. Lily didn't flinch. She'd expected this. She'd prepared herself for it.

From behind the counter, Beryl—the owner of Marigold's Café for as long as Lily could remember—wiped her hands on her apron and let out a low, knowing whistle.

"Well," she said, eyebrows lifting, "look who it is."

Beryl's eyes softened almost immediately, the familiar warmth shining through—the same warmth that had always made the café feel like a second home. "Lily Hart," she said, shaking her head with a mix of disbelief and fond amusement. "Back in Willow Creek, and with a little one no less. You've been missed… though I'll admit, we never thought we'd see you walking through that door again."

Lily managed a small, careful smile. "It's been a long time, Beryl. I just… I need a cup of coffee. Black, please."

Beryl nodded, already moving toward the espresso machine with practiced ease. "You got it." She glanced down at Mandy nestled in the stroller and added with a grin, "And don't you worry, sweet pea—we'll make sure she gets plenty of sugar-free cookies."

Near the window, a woman Lily recognised from high school leaned forward, her voice carrying just enough. "Is… is that the baby?"

Lily didn't flinch. They didn't need to know the truth. Mandy wasn't hers by birth—but she was hers by choice, by promise, by love.

The woman blinked, startled, then leaned back, muttering to her friend. Lily caught only fragments— *"Is that why she broke up with Dr. Cahill?" "Did Nate know she was pregnant?"*—before the conversation drifted. She shut it all out.

Beryl returned with a steaming cup and set it carefully on the counter. "Here you go, hon. One black coffee." She winked. "On the house… for old times' sake."

Lily nodded in gratitude and took a slow sip, letting the warmth and bitterness ground her. She could feel every pair of eyes on her, every whispered assumption—but Mandy's peaceful face reminded her why she was here, and why nothing in Willow Creek could truly scare her anymore.

Beryl leaned closer, lowering her voice to a quiet, sympathetic murmur. "I'm sorry about your father, Lily. Is that why you're back?"

Lily's fingers tightened instinctively around the stroller handle, grounding herself. "Yes," she said softly, her voice steady but carrying a tremor she didn't bother hiding. "I'll be staying for as long as he needs me."

She paused, glancing around the café—at the worn wooden tables, the faded photographs lining the walls, memories of afternoons spent laughing with her father over coffee and pie. A bittersweet smile touched her lips. "Could I… could I get one of your apple pies? The one Dad likes?"

Beryl's eyes softened further, a flicker of recognition and sadness crossing her face. "Of course, hon. That pie's been waiting for you… just like he has." She turned back toward the counter. "And I'll make it a warm one—just like old times."

Mandy stirred in her stroller, waking from her nap. Little fingers curled and uncurled as she blinked up at Lily. "Mummy…" she murmured sleepily.

Lily's heart softened instantly. She bent and lifted her into her arms, pressing a gentle kiss to her hair. Mandy tucked her tiny face into Lily's shoulder, clutching her jacket with both hands. Lily hugged her closer, feeling the familiar, grounding weight of the child she had promised to protect.

For the first time since pulling into town, she let herself breathe—not fully, not freely—but enough to know she was exactly where she needed to be.

Moments later, Beryl returned carrying the warm apple pie, its sweet aroma filling the café. She crouched slightly, smiling at Mandy. "And what's this little one's name?"

"Mandy," Lily said softly, brushing a curl from her forehead. "Say hello, sweetheart."

Mandy's eyes widened, and she gave a shy little wave.

Beryl chuckled. "Well, isn't she just perfect. She'll cheer your dad up good and proper, I'm sure of it."

"I hope so," Lily replied quietly.

She carefully placed Mandy back in the stroller, paid for the pie, and turned toward the door. The murmurs started again, but Lily ignored them, refusing to give anyone the satisfaction of a reaction.

Beryl shot a sharp glance toward the women by the window. "Ignore them, Lily. They're not worth it."

Lily nodded, a small smile forming. "Thanks, Beryl. I will. I haven't done anything to be ashamed of."

She adjusted Mandy one last time, drew in a steadying breath, and reached for the door.

Just as her fingers brushed the handle, the bell above it tinkled again.

Two men stepped inside.

Both froze.

So did Lily.

Her fingers tightened on the stroller handle, her pulse thudding in her ears—loud, relentless. She knew that stance. That presence. The memory struck like a blow to the chest, knocking the air from her lungs.

One of the men's eyes locked on hers—dark, familiar, unmistakable—and Lily's breath caught.

Time slowed. The café faded into a dull hum.

She had imagined this moment for years. Dreaded it. Rehearsed it.

Nothing had prepared her for the reality of him standing there.

Chapter Two

Dr. Nathaniel Cahill's day had begun like so many others—long, exhausting, and demanding every ounce of his concentration from the moment he stepped through the hospital doors. The corridors smelled of antiseptic layered with faint perfume and brewed coffee, the sterile tang clinging to everything. Fluorescent lights hummed overhead, their steady glow blending with the soft beeps of monitors and the occasional, fragile cry of a newborn beginning life under less-than-ideal circumstances.

He moved through it all with practiced ease, his steps confident, purposeful. Someone watching him would have seen calm efficiency, the assurance of a man who had done this a thousand times before. But beneath that control was weight. Pressure. Being an obstetrician wasn't just a job—it was a responsibility that never truly left him. Lives depended on his decisions. Seconds mattered. Mistakes were unforgivable.

And yet, despite his discipline, his focus slipped.

As he leaned over a bassinet to adjust the oxygen line for a premature infant, his hands steady and precise, his thoughts drifted—sliding past white walls and medical charts to places he didn't want them to go. Places he'd spent nearly three years trying to lock away.

Nate was tall and athletic, his dark hair slightly mussed from too little sleep and far too many hours on call. His hazel eyes—sharp, observant, unsettlingly perceptive—could read a room in seconds, could spot danger or distress before anyone else noticed. But they revealed very little of what lived beneath the surface. Control had always been his currency—restraint, precision, reliability. It was how he survived. How he functioned.

Trust, though?

Trust had become fragile. Brittle. Something easily shattered.

A betrayal had done that. One that had left scars far deeper than anyone realised.

Lately—no, always—his thoughts circled back to the past. To mistakes. To a woman he had loved so completely it still startled him how much power she held over him, even now.

Lily Hart.

The name surfaced like a bruise pressed too hard.

He straightened slowly, scrubbing a hand over his jaw, feeling the tension lodged there. Trust hadn't come easily to him even before Lily. But what she'd done—what he believed she'd done—had broken something fundamental inside him. He had loved her more than life itself. Had built a future around her without hesitation, without doubt.

And then, in a single, devastating moment, that future had collapsed into ash.

The soft murmur of nurses, the distant laughter of families in the waiting room—none of it registered as he made his way to the break room. He poured himself a cup of coffee, black, strong, and bitter—the only way he ever drank it—and stared out the window overlooking the parking lot.

Sunlight glinted harmlessly off car windshields, familiar and mundane, but today it felt heavy. Accusatory. Like it knew things he wished he could forget.

For years, he had buried himself in work, convincing himself it was the only way to heal. The only way to dull the hollow ache Lily had left behind. But even here—surrounded by order, logic, and medicine—emotion refused to stay contained. A knot of unresolved longing twisted stubbornly in his chest.

"There you are, Nate."

The voice was smooth. Deliberate. Far too familiar.

He glanced up to see Nurse Cassandra Monroe leaning casually against the doorway, a sly, knowing smile curving her lips as if she belonged there. As if she belonged anywhere near him.

Cassie.

His college girlfriend. His first real love—if he could even call it that now. Compared to what he'd felt for Lily, what he still felt, his emotions for Cassie barely registered. They seemed shallow in hindsight, insignificant, eclipsed entirely by the woman who had broken him.

And yet, here Cassie was. Back in his orbit. Confident. Persistent. Radiating the kind of charm she'd always relied on.

Either oblivious to his lack of interest—or simply choosing to ignore it.

Nate took a measured sip of his coffee, letting the bitterness ground him. "Is there a problem, Nurse Monroe?" His tone was polite, professional—and edged with steel.

Cassie chuckled softly, pushing herself off the doorframe and stepping closer, hands resting on the counter as if she owned the space. "Nate… Nurse Monroe? Seriously? You can call me Cassie."

His eyes narrowed slightly, impatience flickering through his controlled exterior. "I think I'll stick to Nurse Monroe while I'm at the hospital," he replied evenly. Every word was deliberate. Precise. Controlled—the way he had trained himself to be.

She tilted her head, teasing. "How about you take me out to dinner this weekend?"

"I don't think so." He tossed his empty cup into the bin. "I've told you before—it's not going to happen, Nurse Monroe."

Her smile faltered, sharpening into something less pleasant. "When are you going to get over that cheating—bitch, Nate? It's been nearly three years. You haven't dated anyone since."

His jaw tightened instantly. Every muscle went rigid.

"That," he said quietly, his voice low and cold, "is none of your business."

Cassie hesitated, sensing the shift—but she didn't retreat. "Still not over Lily, huh?"

The name hit him like a blow.

Nate's gaze darkened, taut with restraint, his control stretched thin. "She's not part of this conversation," he said sharply, turning back to the window.

Outside, the sunlight still glinted off the cars, bright and ordinary.

Inside, a memory stirred—vivid, dangerous, and very much alive.

He saw them again on the old wooden bridge near the creek, frozen in time the way memories always were—brighter, sharper, more alive than reality ever managed to be. The water had glinted below them, sunlight dancing across its surface, while the world beyond the bridge faded into nothing at all. It had been just the two of them, arms entwined, laughter spilling freely, unguarded and full of promise.

Lily's hair had caught the sunlight that day, a wild tumble of gold lifting in the breeze as she leaned into him, her eyes sparkling with mischief and unshakable trust. He had held her hand as if it were the most natural thing in the world, as if letting go was something he would never have to consider. He'd spoken of forever so easily then, without understanding how fragile the word could be, how easily it could shatter.

Her laughter echoed now in the quiet of his mind, a sound that carried warmth and ache in equal measure.

It had been the first time they kissed.

She'd been only nineteen—so young, so earnest, still discovering the edges of herself and the world. He had been twenty-seven, older, steadier, already marked by responsibility and restraint. He'd known he should step back. Should protect her innocence. But when she'd looked up at him that day, lips curved in a teasing smile that made his chest tighten, resistance had been impossible.

He'd pulled her gently into his arms, careful, reverent, lowering his head as if the moment were something sacred. And the instant their lips met—soft, tentative, perfect—everything inside him had shifted. The world had tilted on its axis. He had known, with bone-deep certainty, that Lily Hart was the only woman he would ever love.

The sharp click of the break room door shattered the memory.

Dr. Caleb Winters strode inside, his expression hardening the instant his gaze landed on Cassie. He didn't bother with pleasantries. "Nothing to do, Nurse Monroe?" he asked evenly, though there was nothing casual about the way his eyes pinned her in place.

Cassie's smirk faltered beneath Caleb's weighty stare. Nate noticed, not for the first time, how little patience his best friend had ever had for her—even back when Nate had been dating her. Caleb had never pretended otherwise.

Without another word, Cassie spun on her heel, shooting Caleb a sharp, venomous look over her shoulder before stalking out of the room.

Caleb snorted, crossing to the counter to pour himself a cup of coffee. "When are you going to get rid of that witch?"

"I've tried," Nate admitted, shaking his head. "She doesn't take a hint."

"Well, I'm grateful you're not considering dating her again," Caleb said, eyeing him closely. "You're not... are you?"

Nate let out a short, humourless chuckle. "No, Caleb. Definitely not."

"Good." Caleb nodded, then took a sip of his coffee before grimacing and dumping the rest down the sink. He tossed the cup in the bin. "You finished for the day?"

"Yeah," Nate replied, stretching his arms overhead. Some of the tension eased from his shoulders.

Caleb grinned. "Perfect. I could use a real coffee. Let's hit Marigold's before you head home. None of that hospital sludge—real cups, real people."

"Sounds good," Nate said, a faint smirk tugging at his mouth.

For a moment, the weight of the hospital, Cassie, and memories he kept carefully buried loosened their grip. With Caleb beside him, it was easier to breathe. Easier to pretend the world beyond the hospital walls wasn't so heavy.

They parked along the familiar cobblestone street and walked toward Marigold's Café. Late afternoon sunlight stretched long shadows across quaint storefronts, bathing the town in a soft, golden glow. Nate realised he'd spent years refusing to see the charm of Willow Creek, afraid it might remind him of too much.

Caleb's voice broke through his thoughts, low and serious. "Edward Hart won't last much longer. He's refusing further treatment. Not that it would do any good at this point."

Nate's steps slowed. "That's... damn. I liked Edward. He was a good man. A great sheriff."

Caleb nodded. "He told me yesterday Lily's coming home."

The name struck like a jolt to the chest.

"Lily..." Nate murmured, the sound escaping before he could stop it.

"She needs to be here for him," Caleb added gently.

"She hasn't bothered in three years," Nate said, bitterness slipping into his voice.

"He went to her," Caleb countered. "Visited when he could. He can't travel now. She's the only family he has left."

Nate exhaled slowly, focusing on the pavement. "As long as she stays away from me," he muttered, old resentment stirring.

Caleb frowned. "Nate... I don't believe she betrayed you. She was too loyal. Too damn good."

"You're biased," Nate said dryly.

"Yeah," Caleb admitted with a grin. "And she knew it. Told me flat-out she'd never hurt you. You really think Derek Monroe could've talked her into cheating? No chance." He shook his head; laughter edged with disbelief.

Nate managed a tight smile—the first real crack in his armour.

They reached Marigold's Café. Caleb pushed open the door.

The bell chimed.

Nate froze.

Something in the air shifted—sharp, electric, undeniable.

And then he saw her.

Lily.

Standing there.

With a child in a stroller.

The world blurred. Sound dulled to a distant roar. His chest constricted, heart slamming painfully against his ribs as years of anger, longing, and heartbreak collided all at once.

Time slowed.

The sight hit him like a physical blow.

Lily's eyes lifted—those same soft, familiar eyes he'd once known better than his own reflection—and locked onto his. Shock flared. Disbelief. And beneath it all, a flicker of hope so dangerous he refused to name it.

She looked different. Thinner. Paler. Shadows beneath her eyes told stories of sleepless nights and quiet struggles. But she was still Lily. His beautiful, radiant Lily.

And yet, she stood there with a child—proof of a life he had been painfully, irrevocably absent from.

They held each other's gaze for what felt like an eternity—two people locked in a silent standoff, a battlefield of unspoken words, unhealed wounds, and longing that had never truly been buried. The café around them faded into a blur of sound and movement, as though the world itself had paused, waiting to see who would break first.

Caleb, blissfully unaware of the storm raging between them, stepped forward. "Lily!" he said warmly, his voice cutting cleanly through the tension. He crossed the space between them and pulled her into a brief, genuine hug. "It's so good to see you."

The spell shattered.

Lily blinked, breath catching before she exhaled slowly and returned the embrace. "Thanks," she said softly. "It's good to see you too." She managed a small, brittle smile—one that didn't quite reach her tired eyes.

Caleb had always been kind to her. Steady. Gentle. Impossible not to like. She had known about his crush for years, though he'd never acted on it, never crossed a line. Three years ago, though, her heart had belonged to only one man—and even now, despite everything, it still felt tethered there.

She stepped back, brushing a loose strand of hair behind her ear in a nervous, familiar gesture. "Thank you for looking after Dad so well," she said quietly. "I… I know he's in the best hands."

Caleb's expression softened, sympathy clouding his eyes. "I wish there was more I could do," he said gently.

But Nate still hadn't spoken.

He wasn't even looking at her anymore.

His gaze had shifted—fixed, unblinking—on the child in the stroller beside her. A little girl with soft curls and wide, curious eyes. A little girl who stared back at him with something he couldn't quite name… something achingly familiar that lodged beneath his ribs and stole his breath.

Caleb noticed the sudden stillness and followed Nate's line of sight.

Lily felt it instantly. Her hands tightened around the stroller handle, fingers curling as though bracing for impact.

And Nate—Nate felt the ground tilt beneath him as a single, brutal thought slammed into him with devastating force.

A child.

Her child.

Caleb crouched beside the stroller, his expression melting into warmth. He brushed a gentle finger along the little girl's cheek. "And who is this gorgeous girl?" he asked softly.

Lily glanced down, throat tight, then straightened as if drawing strength from somewhere deep inside. "This is Mandy," she said quietly. "My daughter."

Nate's eyes snapped to hers.

Sharp. Searching. Devastated.

For a heartbeat, he couldn't breathe.

A hollow punch landed deep in his chest—cold and brutal, stealing the air from his lungs. He had never admitted it to anyone, not even Caleb, but a small, foolish sliver of hope had lingered in him. Maybe Lily hadn't betrayed him. Maybe the rumours had been lies. Maybe Derek Monroe had twisted the truth.

But this—

This child.

She was the perfect age.

The truth sat there in a stroller, tiny and innocent, stripping away the last thread of denial he had clung to.

Mandy blinked up at Caleb, her smile shy but sweet. "Hello," she said in a soft, melodic voice.

Caleb's face lit up. "Well, hello there, sweetheart," he murmured. "Aren't you just beautiful?"

Nate heard none of it.

All he could hear was the roar of blood in his ears. All he could see was Lily—standing there with a child she had never told him about. A life she had built without him.

And for the first time in years, the betrayal didn't just hurt.

It broke him all over again.

Without a single word to Lily—without even looking at her—Nate turned to Caleb, his voice clipped, controlled, and dangerously brittle. "I'll see you at work tomorrow."

Before Caleb could respond, Nate pivoted and walked out, his stride stiff, almost jarring in its urgency.

"Nate?" Caleb called, straightening sharply.

But Nate didn't slow. Didn't turn. Didn't breathe. By the time Caleb reached the door, Nate was already halfway across the street, shoulders rigid, fists clenched, moving as though the ground beneath him might shatter if he stayed a second longer.

Lily released a slow, weary sigh, her grip tightening on the stroller. "I see he still doesn't believe me," she murmured, bitterness threading through her voice despite her effort to contain it.

Caleb winced. "Lily… I'm sorry. He just—"

"I know," she said gently, though her voice wavered.

She forced a brittle smile, but inside her thoughts spiralled painfully. *He believes I betrayed him.*

Her gaze flicked to the door Nate had stormed through, her chest aching. *But what about his betrayal?* she thought bitterly. *That never seemed to matter, did it? He was allowed to cheat… and I wasn't.*

She swallowed hard, blinking back the sting. *Not that I ever did.*

The truth pressed down on her, sharp and heavy, unspoken but undeniable. *I am still a virgin, for God's sake.*

Around them, murmured whispers rose—soft but sharp, cutting little jabs of judgment. *Poor Dr. Cahill… to rub that child in his face.*

Lily ignored them, lifting her chin and turning her attention back to Caleb. "I'd better go," she said quietly. "I just arrived in town. I'm heading to Dad's."

"Do you mind if I come too?" Caleb asked.

"No. Not at all."

He held the café door open for her, walked her to her car, helped with the stroller and Mandy. "I'll see you there," he said warmly.

Lily nodded, settling Mandy securely, her heart heavy but resolute.

The storm had finally broken.

And nothing—nothing—would ever be the same again.

Chapter Three

Lily slid into the driver's seat and reached back to secure Mandy in her car seat, double-checking the straps with careful, practiced hands. Only when she was certain her daughter was safe did she allow herself to relax, even a fraction. She rolled down the window and looked back at Caleb.

"Thanks for everything, Caleb. Really," she said softly. "I'll see you soon."

He smiled, warm and reassuring. "Anytime, Lily."

As she pulled away from the curb, a flicker of relief eased through her chest. For the first time since returning to Willow Creek, she felt a tenuous tether to normalcy—someone steady beside her in the storm, someone who didn't look at her with suspicion or judgment.

But relief never lasted long.

As the familiar streets blurred past her windshield, Lily's thoughts drifted backward, unbidden, pulled once more to the night her world had first begun to unravel.

Cassandra Monroe.

Nate's ex-girlfriend from college.

At first, Lily had been wary—how could she not be? There was history there, a shared past she would never fully understand, and an undercurrent of tension she'd felt from the very beginning. But Nate had reassured her, again and again. Cassie was part of his past, nothing more. Over time, Cassie had been polite. Pleasant. Even kind. Slowly, cautiously, Lily had begun to believe they might coexist peacefully. Maybe, eventually, even become friends.

She had been wrong.

That night, everything shifted.

Lily had been walking toward Nate's apartment when she saw Cassie coming from the same direction. Tears streaked Cassie's face, cutting through the careful composure she always wore like armour. Her shoulders were shaking, her steps uneven, as if she were barely holding herself together.

Alarmed, Lily had quickened her pace. "Cassie?" she'd called softly. "Are you… are you okay?"

Cassie stopped abruptly, turning toward her. Her shoulders trembled, and when she spoke, her voice was broken and raw. "I'm so sorry, Lily," she whispered. "I swear, I didn't mean for it to happen."

Confusion had twisted sharply in Lily's stomach. "What… what are you talking about?" she asked gently, even as her heart began to hammer painfully against her ribs.

Cassie hesitated, biting her lip, eyes darting away before finally blurting it out in a rush of panic and shame. She grabbed Lily's hands, her fingers digging in as though clinging to the last thread of forgiveness available to her. "I didn't mean to," she sobbed. "I didn't mean to sleep with him."

The world tilted.

"Who…?" Lily whispered, the word barely audible, her throat closing around it.

"Nate," Cassie said, the name tumbling from her lips like a confession she could no longer contain.

Everything Lily believed about love, trust, and the life she was building shattered in that instant.

She had gone to Nate immediately, desperate for clarity, for reassurance, for the truth. She needed him to deny it. Needed him to tell her Cassie was lying.

Instead, he had looked at her with suspicion and pain—and turned the accusation on her.

"You slept with Derek Monroe," he had said, his voice tight with hurt and anger. "Don't lie to me, Lily."

The words had stunned her.

It was a lie. A cruel, impossible lie. Lily had been saving herself for Nate—for their future, for the life they had planned together. Just a week earlier, he had asked her to marry him, and she had said yes without hesitation, offering him her heart, her trust, her entire future.

And yet, in that moment, all of it had meant nothing.

The pain of being falsely accused had cut deeper than anything she had known. Deeper even than Cassie's confession. Her honesty, her devotion, had been met with doubt and condemnation.

She had left that night with tears streaming down her face, her heart in pieces, the sound of his anger echoing in her ears.

She had gone home and told her father she was leaving.

Edward Hart had tried to stop her. He had begged her to stay, to talk to Nate, to give him time to explain, to fight for what they had once shared. But Lily had been too shattered. Too raw. The weight of betrayal—real and imagined—pressed so heavily on her chest she could barely breathe.

So, in the early hours of the morning, before Willow Creek had even stirred awake, she packed what little she owned into her car. She didn't look back as the town disappeared in her rearview mirror, the familiar streets and the rolling Blue Ridge Mountains fading into the distance.

She drove toward Asheville—toward Miranda's home—more than six hours away. Toward a place where she could breathe. Where she could grieve. Where she could try to stitch her broken heart back together.

But even as the miles stretched behind her, the ache remained—hollow and unrelenting. The echo of a love lost. A trust shattered. And the quiet, devastating knowledge that some wounds, no matter how much time passed, were never meant to fully heal.

The engine hummed beneath Nate, steady and indifferent, but his hands gripped the steering wheel as if it were the only thing keeping him upright. Willow Creek's streets blurred past his windshield—familiar roads that suddenly felt foreign, distorted, as though he were driving through a version of his hometown that no longer belonged to him.

He couldn't stop seeing her.

Lily.

Standing there so calmly. So composed. With a child.

The realisation slammed into him like a punch to the chest, knocking the breath from his lungs.

She cheated on me. With Derek Monroe.

His stomach twisted, bitter and tight, as though something corrosive had lodged there and refused to dissolve. He had trusted her. Loved her beyond reason, beyond logic. He had built a future around her, imagined a lifetime that began and ended with her smile. And she had given herself to someone else.

Derek had confessed—cocky, unrepentant, almost proud of his so-called achievement. He'd insisted it hadn't been planned, that it had "just happened," as if that made the betrayal any easier to swallow. He told Nate that Lily had no intention of marrying him. That she had chosen Derek instead. That they were planning a life together.

Each word had landed like a blow.

The child—tiny, innocent, perfect—was proof of his worst nightmare made flesh.

His jaw clenched, fingers whitening around the wheel until his knuckles ached. She betrayed me. She betrayed us. How could she do that to me? To what we had?

Every turn, every stoplight, every familiar storefront only dragged the image back into focus: Lily's composed expression, the quiet confidence in her posture, the gentle, instinctive way she'd looked down at the little girl. The tenderness in her eyes.

His chest burned with a raw, hollow fury tangled tightly with heartbreak. He wanted to scream. To hit something. To make the world hurt the way he did inside.

And yet—infuriatingly—beneath the anger, beneath the betrayal, something else throbbed.

Love.

A stubborn, unrelenting ache he had never truly managed to kill.

He had never stopped loving her. Not for a single day. Not even when he told himself he had. That love now twisted painfully with grief and disbelief, leaving him hollowed out, as though the best part of him had been carved away and taken with her.

By the time he pulled into his driveway, Nate was utterly drained—not from the drive, not from the day, but from the tidal wave of emotion battering him from the inside out. He shut off the engine but didn't move, his hands still wrapped around the steering wheel as he stared at the darkened house in front of him, as if it might offer answers. Or absolution. Or mercy.

The truth loomed heavy and unavoidable.

Lily had moved on without him.

And she had done it in the cruelest, most undeniable way possible.

He exhaled slowly and leaned forward, pressing his forehead against the steering wheel, eyes closing as he tried—futilely—to quiet the surge of grief, fury, and longing battling inside his chest. But he knew, deep down, that nothing could undo what he had seen.

Not time.

Not distance.

Not denial.

His mind drifted back, unbidden, dragged into the past like a wound ripped open anew.

That night.

The last night he had seen Lily.

The memory struck with the sharpness of glass, every detail painfully vivid.

She had shown up at his apartment with red, swollen eyes, her face streaked with tears. At first, he had assumed it was guilt—the aftermath of what she'd done with Derek Monroe. He hadn't wanted to believe it. Not his Lily. Not the woman he knew to be sweet, honest, innocent to her core.

She had looked at him desperately and whispered, "Please… tell me it's not true. Tell me you didn't sleep with Cassie."

The words had stunned him.

In that moment, he had thought she was deflecting—trying to twist the blame away from herself, trying to ease her own guilt by accusing him instead.

"Are you kidding me?" he'd demanded, his voice tight, jaw clenched, hurt boiling violently to the surface. "You're trying to turn this on me? How could you, Lily?"

She had stared at him, bewildered, tears spilling freely now. "What are you talking about, Nate? I didn't—"

"You think I don't know?" he'd snapped, pacing the small living room like a caged animal. "I know, Lily. I know you slept with Derek. How could you do that to me?"

She had flinched as though struck. "No! Nate—no! That didn't happen!"

But he hadn't listened. He hadn't stopped. Pride and pain had fused together, blinding him.

"And what about you?" she'd fired back, her voice shaking with disbelief and hurt. "I know you slept with Cassie Monroe! Don't you dare stand there and act like I'm the one who's done something wrong!"

The accusation had stunned him into silence.

He'd opened his mouth to deny it—to swear she was wrong—but the words had lodged in his throat. Not because it was true—he hadn't slept with Cassie—but because the accusation had shaken him. She wasn't confessing. She wasn't apologising.

She was accusing him.

And he couldn't see past that.

The argument had spiralled out of control—voices raised, hearts raw, words thrown like knives. Misunderstanding had shredded the bond they had built over years of shared laughter, quiet moments, and whispered dreams. Every accusation carved deeper wounds, leaving them both bleeding in opposite corners of the same room.

In the end, Lily had stormed out, tears streaming down her face, her small figure swallowed by the night as though darkness itself might absorb her pain. Nate hadn't followed. Pride, shock, and the awful certainty that something irreparable had just fractured between them had frozen him in place.

The door had barely finished closing when he noticed the ring.

It sat on the kitchen counter, catching the light from the overhead fixture—too bright, too perfect. The diamond he'd chosen with such care, imagining it on her hand for the rest of their lives, lay abandoned, cold and accusing.

She had taken it off.

Not thrown it.

Not hidden it.

Left it where he couldn't miss it.

Nate stood there for a long time, breathing in the apartment that still smelled like her shampoo, still held the warmth of her body, still remembered the sound of her laughter. Every memory turned sharp, slicing instead of comforting.

When he finally picked up the ring, it cut into his palm, the weight of it unbearable. Final.

The next morning, she was gone.

He hadn't even heard it from her.

The town gossip had told him first.

Caleb had confirmed it later—quietly, carefully. Lily had left town completely shattered.

"Go after her," Caleb had said.

Nate had stared at him like he'd lost his mind. "She cheated on me, Caleb!" he'd yelled, anger and heartbreak bleeding into one. He'd dismissed Caleb's defence as bias—Caleb had always liked Lily, and Nate had convinced himself his friend's judgment was compromised.

"There is no way in hell that girl cheated on you," Caleb had shot back, furious. "And if you really believe she could do something like that? You don't deserve her."

Caleb had stormed out.

They hadn't spoken for a month.

Nate had been left with nothing but silence. Absence. And the gnawing ache of betrayal—both real and imagined.

And now, years later, seeing Lily standing in that café with a child, all of it came crashing back—the heartbreak, the misunderstanding, the words they could never take back.

His chest tightened.

His hands trembled slightly on the steering wheel.

And for the first time since that night, a terrible, creeping doubt whispered through the cracks in his certainty.

What if I was wrong?

He had thought—no, he had *known*—that he was going to marry Lily.

Not even a week before his world had shattered, he had asked her to be his wife. The memory still felt unreal, like something borrowed from another lifetime, belonging to a version of himself who had believed too easily in forever.

He had spent days planning it, obsessing over every detail, wanting the moment to be perfect in a way only someone hopelessly in love could understand. He hadn't wanted a restaurant or an audience or anything loud or showy. He wanted *them*. He wanted a place that belonged to their history, their quiet escapes from the world.

So, he'd taken her hiking in the Blue Ridge Mountains—one of their favourite places, a sanctuary where the world slowed and nothing existed beyond the two of them.

The sun had been warm on their backs, filtering through the canopy of leaves above, casting soft, dappled patterns across the narrow trail. Birds chirped overhead, unbothered and free, while the faint scent of wildflowers mingled with the crisp, clean mountain air. It had been peaceful in a way that made him believe, foolishly, that peace could last forever.

They'd stopped for lunch on a flat stretch of rock overlooking a valley that rolled out in endless green waves, layered and alive beneath the open sky. Lily had laughed as she unpacked their modest picnic basket, teasing him the way she always did—about how he had a talent for turning even the simplest moments into grand adventures.

He had watched her then, memorising her without knowing he was doing it. The way the sunlight caught in her hair. The ease of her smile. The sound of her laughter echoing off the rocks like something sacred.

After they'd eaten, he'd helped her pack everything away, his fingers brushing stray strands of hair from her face. His heart had been hammering so loudly he'd been certain she could hear it. The moment felt suspended in time, fragile and perfect.

And then he'd dropped to one knee.

The cool stone had pressed into his leg, grounding him, though he barely noticed the sensation. All he'd been aware of was her—Lily, standing in front of him, looking at him with that familiar blend of curiosity and affection.

He reached into his pocket and drew out the small velvet box, his hands steady despite the storm tearing through his chest. When he opened it, the diamond solitaire caught the light—a single, flawless stone, simple and timeless, chosen because it reminded him of her. Clear. Honest. Unbreakable.

"Lily," he said, his voice low but sure, every word carved from truth. "You are the only woman I have ever loved. I can't imagine a life that doesn't begin and end with you. I don't want a future unless you're in it." His throat tightened. "Will you marry me?"

Her breath hitched. Her eyes widened, filling instantly—shock giving way to something deeper. Trust. Devotion. A love so open it nearly undid him. She lifted one trembling hand to cover her mouth, the other reaching out to touch his cheek, as if she needed to reassure herself he was real, that this moment wasn't a dream.

"Yes," she whispered, the word fragile and sacred.

Just one word—but it had felt like a promise sealed into his bones.

He'd pulled her into his arms, kissing her with everything he was—every hope, every dream, every future he'd already begun to imagine. In that moment, he'd felt invincible. Certain. Untouchable.

And in that instant—the diamond gleaming on her finger—Nate believed with absolute certainty that nothing in the world could ever tear them apart.

But only days later, that love had been shattered.

Not cracked. Not damaged.

Obliterated.

It lay in ruins, buried beneath betrayal, accusations, and the cruel twist of fate that had stolen everything he'd thought was his. Every dream. Every plan. Every quiet moment he'd imagined sharing with her had vanished in an instant, leaving behind only a hollow ache that pulsed with each heartbeat.

He forced himself out of the car, legs stiff and unsteady, fumbling with the keys before finally pushing open the front door. The familiar creak of the hinges and the clean scent of fresh paint and polished wood should have been comforting. Instead, it felt like a cruel reminder of everything he'd lost.

He'd put a deposit on this house just before proposing—a place he'd chosen carefully, deliberately. A home he'd imagined filling with laughter, with voices echoing off the walls, with the soft chaos of family life. He had pictured Lily in the kitchen, sunlight spilling across the counters. Sunday mornings with coffee and shared glances. Anniversaries. Birthdays. Children's toys scattered across the floor.

Their children.

Now the house stood empty, silent, holding only the ghosts of a future that would never come.

Nate stepped inside, the floorboards groaning beneath his weight, and felt the emptiness settle over him like a shroud. The dreams he'd carried so vividly, so tangibly, now felt cruel in their absence—mocking him with what could have been.

He sank into the living room chair, dragging a hand over his face as the sting of loss tightened around his chest like a vice. Outside, life carried on—cars passed, people laughed, the ordinary hum of the world continued, oblivious to the devastation unfolding inside him.

But for Nate, time had frozen.

All that remained were echoes—her laughter, the curve of her smile, the ghost of her presence—and the unbearable truth that Lily, *his* Lily, was gone from his life in every way that mattered.

He couldn't stay here like this.

He needed to stop spiralling. To reclaim some semblance of control.

With a harsh exhale, he forced himself to the bedroom, stripped off his clothes, and stepped into the shower. Hot water slammed against his skin, relentless and unforgiving, a stark reminder that he was still alive. Still breathing. Still standing.

His mind churned even as the water streamed over him. Lily was back in Willow Creek. That truth was inescapable. She wasn't going to disappear again, and neither were the places they shared, the memories they'd built.

He couldn't afford to fall apart every time he saw her.

Not again.

Not like today—fleeing, unravelling, losing all the control he'd fought so hard to rebuild.

He had to hold himself together. Had to armour himself against the flood of old emotions—the memories, the anger, the ache that threatened to drag him under.

He clenched his fists beneath the running water, letting the heat burn into his muscles, as though it could sear away the raw edges of grief and betrayal.

When he finally stepped out, water dripping from his hair, a cold clarity settled over him.

He couldn't change the past.

He couldn't undo the pain.

But he could control himself.

And if Lily was going to be part of his world again, he would meet her on his own terms—not as the man shattered by heartbreak, but as the man who refused to let it break him twice.

Chapter Four

Lily pulled into the familiar driveway of her father's home, the late-afternoon sun spilling warm, amber light across the yard in long, slanting bands. The sight of it made her chest tighten—not from fear, but from the sheer weight of memory. Her heart was still clenched from the encounter at the café—tight from Nate, from the past, from everything she had tried so hard to outrun—but she drew a deep, steadying breath and let the house anchor her.

It looked just as it always had.

Sturdy.

Welcoming.

A refuge.

The white weatherboards bore the same faint chips along the edges, the porch rail still leaned just slightly to the left, and the old oak near the fence cast its familiar, protective shadow across the lawn. Time had touched it gently, if at all. And for a moment, Lily allowed herself to believe that maybe some things truly could remain unchanged—safe, dependable—even when everything else felt fragile.

She parked the car and stepped out, the gravel crunching softly beneath her shoes. Moving around to the back seat, she carefully unbuckled Mandy from her car seat. The little girl wriggled immediately, letting out a soft, impatient coo as Lily lifted her into her arms.

Mandy's small, solid warmth pressed against her chest, grounding her in a way nothing else could. This child—this miracle born of love and loss—was hers. Entirely. And yet, even as she held her close, some shadow of the past tugged faintly at the edges of Lily's thoughts, whispering of things unresolved.

"Okay, sweet girl," she murmured, brushing a gentle kiss to Mandy's forehead, breathing in the clean, familiar scent of her. "Let's get you inside."

"Need a hand?"

Lily turned, to see Caleb walking up the driveway. His presence was welcome, his easy smile and unhurried stride softening something tight and knotted inside her chest.

"I can help with her," he said, nodding toward Mandy, his tone warm and practical.

"Would you?" Lily asked, relief threading through her voice. She hesitated only a heartbeat before gently handing Mandy over, trusting instinct and familiarity.

The moment Caleb cradled her, Mandy lit up.

Her little face broke into a wide, radiant grin, blue eyes sparkling as she giggled and reached for him with soft, eager hands. It was as though she sensed his calm, responding to it instinctively.

Caleb laughed quietly, the sound low and genuine. "Well, hello there, Mandy," he said warmly. "Aren't you just the happiest little thing?"

He bounced her lightly, earning another delighted squeal that echoed across the quiet yard.

Lily felt her lips curve despite the heaviness pressing on her chest. For a fleeting moment, her world narrowed to this—the sound of her daughter's laughter, the warmth of the sun on her back, and the sight of Caleb's steady hands holding Mandy securely.

"She's perfect," Caleb murmured, giving Mandy a playful little spin that made her laugh again.

"Yes," Lily whispered, emotion catching in her throat. "She really is."

The smile lingered… then slowly faded.

"Actually," she said after a moment, her voice softening, turning serious, "before we go in… could you give me a rundown of what to expect? I've been reading about prostate cancer, but I need to know how to help Dad. What he'll need. What I should watch for."

Caleb nodded, continuing to bounce Mandy gently as she babbled happily against his chest. "He tires quickly," he said calmly. "The medication makes him drowsy, so he may fall asleep without warning. If he's holding Mandy, just make sure you're right there beside him—just in case."

His eyes softened with quiet honesty. "And his immune system is weak. Be extra careful with germs, especially with her around."

Lily swallowed hard. "Will he be okay to hold her?" she asked, worry threading through her voice. "I don't want to risk—"

"He'll want to," Caleb interrupted gently. "And honestly? She'll lift his spirits more than anything else could. Just keep her hands clean and make sure she's healthy. That's enough."

Then his voice lowered, the truth slipping through. "To be honest… he hasn't got long. He'll act strong—he always does—but he's declining. Eventually, he'll need respite care. More support than one person can manage alone."

The words landed heavily, even though Lily had expected them. Knowing was one thing. Hearing it aloud was another entirely.

She blinked hard and looked at Mandy, nestled contentedly against Caleb's chest, her tiny fingers gripping his shirt. The road ahead suddenly felt sharper. Steeper. But in that fragile moment, Lily allowed herself a small, grateful smile.

Her daughter's laughter.

Caleb's steady presence.

The familiarity of her father's home waiting just beyond the front door.

It wasn't much—but it was enough.

She reached back into the car, grabbing her bag and the apple pie from the café. "Are you okay with her for a minute?" she asked quietly.

"Absolutely," Caleb said with a grin. "She's a cutie—and I think she likes me."

Mandy squealed again, as if agreeing.

They walked together toward the porch, the soft golden light of late afternoon spilling across the old timber steps and bathing everything in a gentle, almost forgiving glow. The house, weathered and familiar, seemed to breathe around them, warmer and more inviting than it had in years. For the first time that afternoon, Lily felt a flicker of something she hadn't allowed herself in a long time: peace.

Caleb carried Mandy carefully up the steps, her small body pressing snugly against his chest, while Lily followed closely behind, bag slung over her shoulder. The little girl wriggled with quiet excitement, letting out soft coos that blended with the distant chirping of birds settling in for the evening. Lily's pulse slowed just slightly as she watched her daughter's small, trusting face illuminated by the golden light.

The front door swung open, and Edward Hart appeared, his frail frame catching the sun, eyes brightening despite the shadows of illness lining his features. "Lily!" he exclaimed, voice carrying both relief and joy. "Finally, you're home."

Lily set her bag down and stepped forward, enveloped in his arms. His hug was warm, familiar, but thinner than she remembered, the tremor of weakness beneath his strength a reminder of how much time and illness had taken from him. She pressed her cheek to his shoulder, breathing in the scent of him—aftershave and soap, faintly familiar, grounding—and felt the tight knot in her chest loosen a fraction.

When he pulled back, Edward's eyes immediately moved to Mandy in Caleb's arms. His face softened into awe and wonder. "And my beautiful granddaughter," he whispered, voice catching slightly. "Finally, here."

"Mandy's been looking forward to it too," Lily said, her voice wavering faintly, betraying the surge of emotion she held back.

"She's beautiful," Edward murmured again. Mandy giggled, waving her tiny hands toward him, and the sound drew a genuine, relieved smile from Lily, one that reached her eyes and softened the lingering tension in her shoulders.

"I brought an apple pie from the café," Lily said, moving toward the kitchen. "How about I make some coffee, and we can all have a slice?" She glanced at Caleb. "You'll join us, won't you?"

"I'd love to," Caleb replied warmly, still cradling Mandy with practiced ease. He looked at Lily with gentle curiosity. "Maybe you can tell me what you've been up to. Everything I've missed while you were away."

"I'd like that," she said softly, a small smile tugging at her lips.

"Off to a good start, then," he teased, bouncing Mandy lightly in his arms. The little girl squealed in delight, the sound a ripple of pure joy that made Lily's chest ache with a mixture of happiness and longing.

For the first time in hours—maybe days—Lily felt the smallest spark of hope, fragile but undeniable.

She moved around the kitchen, brewing coffee and slicing the warm apple pie. The rich, roasted aroma of the beans mingled with the sweet, spicy scent of apples and cinnamon, wrapping the room in a comforting, familiar warmth. It softened the sharp edges of the day, the weight of the past, and the tension that had tightened in her chest since leaving the café.

Caleb and Edward fussed gently over Mandy, her high-pitched squeals and delighted babbles filling the room with life. For Lily, it was a quiet relief—having help, having someone steady nearby. Raising a child alone had been both the greatest joy and the hardest climb. With Caleb here, the weight didn't feel quite so crushing.

They sat together at the small kitchen table, savouring the pie and the rare, gentle quiet. Edward held Mandy for a time, his frail hands surprisingly steady as she cooed and wriggled happily in his lap. But Lily noticed the signs: the drooping eyelids, the slack shoulders. Caleb leaned in smoothly, helping ease Edward into a nearby armchair. The older man settled with surprising ease and drifted off almost instantly, letting sleep claim him.

Lily laid toys across the floor, guiding Mandy as she crawled happily through toward them. Caleb settled opposite Lily, watching with a soft, reassuring smile.

"So," he said lightly, a warmth threading his tone, "what have you been up to? Where are you living now? What do you do for work these days?"

Lily laughed softly, the sound mingling with the hum of the house and the distant cooing of Mandy. "One question at a time, Caleb," she said, raising a playful brow.

He grinned. "Fair enough."

"I just sold my stepsister's home in Asheville," she said quietly, the words carrying a soft weight. "She left it to me in her will."

Caleb's expression softened, his eyes reflecting both sympathy and quiet respect. "I was sorry to hear about her passing. My condolences, Lily."

"Thanks." Her voice lowered, drifting into thought as her gaze followed Mandy, playing happily among the toys.

Miranda.

Her stepsister.

Her best friend.

Gone too soon.

When Lily had left Willow Creek nearly three years ago, she'd stayed with Miranda, her stepsister and closest friend. Lily had been there for every moment of her pregnancy—every doctor's appointment, every birthing class, every sleepless night filled with a mixture of worry and excitement. She had paced hospital corridors, whispered encouragements, and held Miranda's hand through contractions that tested both their strength and patience. And when Miranda's untimely death stole her from the world too soon, Lily hadn't hesitated for a single heartbeat. The moment she could, she had adopted Mandy, claiming her not by blood, but by love, with a promise to protect her forever.

Everyone assumed Mandy was her biological daughter. Lily never corrected them. It wasn't their business, and it never would be. The only other person who knew the truth was her father, Edward Hart. And now, looking down at Mandy gurgling happily on the floor, toys scattered around her in chaotic delight, while Edward slept peacefully nearby, the weight of everything—the past, the loss, the return—settled over Lily softly, almost like a quiet benediction.

And for the first time in a long while… she didn't feel entirely alone.

Watching Mandy play now, small hands banging together tiny wooden animals with uncoordinated delight, Lily felt a protective, aching swell of love in her chest. Every giggle, every bright glance toward Caleb as he made silly faces or tapped her tiny nose, eased the tight knot of tension in Lily's shoulders and chest. She had her daughter. She had her father, even if only for borrowed time. And here was Caleb—steady, gentle, and kind—making the impossible just a little more bearable.

"So," she said, drawing in a quiet, grounding breath, "as for where I live… here, for the moment. I'll stay with Dad as long as he needs me." Her gaze drifted to Edward, slumped peacefully in his armchair, his breaths shallow but even, his frailty softened by rest. Her expression softened with unmistakable affection, tinged with the ache of knowing how short their time together might be.

"Well, I hope you stay for good," Caleb said gently, his tone light yet sincere, carrying the kind of warmth that could almost chase away the ghosts of doubt.

Lily's brows lifted, skepticism flickering across her face. "I don't know, Caleb. I don't exactly feel… welcome in this town anymore," she admitted, her voice quiet, laced with the remnants of the morning's tension. "Especially after how Nate acted today."

"He—" Caleb began, instinctively moving to defend his friend, but Lily raised a hand, stopping him with a small, tired shake of her head.

"It's okay, Caleb. Really. I know how close you and Nate are. I don't want that coming between us or turning every conversation into a battlefield. So… let's just leave that subject alone. The last thing I want is to cause trouble for either of you."

Caleb nodded slowly, appreciation flickering in his warm brown eyes. "Fair enough," he said, sincerity settling into his voice. He respected her more for it—her restraint, her grace, her ability to protect the fragile peace around her even after everything she'd endured.

Mandy squealed at that moment, a bright, unexpected punctuation to the quiet, and both Lily and Caleb glanced down at her, grateful for the distraction from the weight of their conversation.

"What do you do for a living?" Caleb asked again, this time with a smile so open, so genuinely curious, that Lily felt herself relax further.

"I write and illustrate children's books," she replied, a touch of pride threading through her voice.

Caleb's eyebrows shot up in genuine interest. "Really? That's amazing. Do you have any I could see?" The eagerness in his tone wasn't merely polite—it was real, invested, and warm.

Lily reached for her bag, digging past a tangle of Mandy's spare socks, a half-eaten biscuit, and a rattling toy before finally pulling out a thin hardcover. "This is my latest one," she said quietly, holding it out.

Caleb took it carefully, as if it were something precious rather than a sticky-finger-proof board book. He flipped through the pages slowly, studying each illustration with surprising seriousness. After a moment, he let out a low whistle. "Wow… Lily, this is really good. You've got a gift. You must be proud."

"I am," she admitted, cheeks warming at the compliment. "I'm lucky—I love what I do, and it pays the bills."

What she didn't say was that her books had done far more than pay bills. They had given her independence, security, and a quiet sense of accomplishment she rarely allowed herself to acknowledge. For now, though, it was enough to simply be grateful.

Caleb closed the book and handed it back with a smile. "Well, if this is what you've been doing with your time away… I'd say you've been making something beautiful."

Lily's chest squeezed unexpectedly at his words. "Thank you, Caleb. That means more than you know," she murmured.

"What about yourself?" Lily asked, shifting slightly to face him. "I heard you're head of the oncology department now."

Caleb's expression softened, pride quietly shining through. "I am. I've been fortunate," he said modestly.

"Don't be so modest," she teased gently. "I know you're brilliant."

A faint blush crept across his cheeks, but before he could respond, Lily drew in a steadying breath and asked, more tentative now, "How is Nate?"

Caleb's posture changed subtly, his shoulders stiffening for the briefest moment as he chose his words with care. "He runs the paediatric department now," he said slowly.

Lily's lips curved into a small, genuine smile. "That's good. I'm happy for him," she said, soft and honest.

Caleb studied her for a long moment, as if weighing her sincerity. "You... really mean that, don't you?"

She blinked, surprised by the question. "Yes, I do. We didn't work out, but that doesn't mean I want him miserable. I honestly hope he's doing well."

Caleb nodded, thoughtful. Then his voice softened, careful, gentle. "What about you, though, Lily? How are you really doing?"

"I'm fine," she said quickly. Too quickly. "I have my work, and Mandy keeps me busy."

He hesitated, then asked gently, "No husband? Boyfriend?"

Lily laughed, a light, self-deprecating sound that she hadn't allowed herself in some time. "No. To be honest... I haven't been on a date since Nate."

Caleb's brows shot up in surprise. "What? Why?"

She shrugged, eyes drifting down to her hands. "Just... not interested."

When she lifted her gaze again, her eyes shimmered faintly—just long enough for Caleb to notice. "Still not ready, I suppose," she added softly, her voice thin at the edges.

Caleb didn't press. He simply nodded, understanding written plainly on his face. And for the first time in years, Lily didn't feel judged for where she was—or wasn't—yet.

They talked a little longer, the room warm around them, filled with sunlight, the faint scent of coffee, and the soft hum of domestic life. Then a gentle thump-thump on the floor drew their attention. Mandy had abandoned her toys and crawled straight to Lily, tiny hands reaching up in the unmistakable pick-me-up plea.

Lily scooped her daughter into her arms, brushing a soft kiss to her cheek. "You're tired, aren't you, sweetheart?" she murmured, tickling her belly just enough to earn a drowsy, delighted giggle.

She turned to Caleb with a grateful smile. "I'd better let you go so I can get this little one to bed."

Caleb rose with her, slipping his hands casually into his pockets. "Of course. You've had a big day."

"Thanks, Caleb," Lily said softly. "I really appreciate you making me feel welcome. I wasn't sure how I was going to cope if I had to face just the whispers and gossip."

His expression tightened with a flash of frustration for her sake. "Ignore them, Lily. You have nothing to be ashamed of."

"I know," she replied, offering a tired half-smile. "But that doesn't stop people from gossiping."

She didn't voice the rest—the words that echoed silently in her chest anyway. It hurts... especially when I've done nothing wrong.

Caleb seemed to sense it, even unspoken. His voice softened further. "If anyone gives you trouble, you let me know. You're not alone here, okay?"

Lily's chest swelled, equal parts relief and gratitude. "Okay," she whispered.

And for the first time since driving back into Willow Creek, she allowed herself to truly believe it.

Chapter Five

Nate sat on his front porch, the wooden slats still warm from the lingering kiss of the late-afternoon sun. The beer in his hand had gone untouched for the last ten minutes, condensation sliding cold and wet across his palm. He wasn't even sure why he'd grabbed it—habit, maybe. Something to hold onto while the world inside him threatened to unravel, fragment by fragment.

The crunch of gravel reached him before the car came into view. Caleb's SUV rolled into the driveway, steady, familiar, inevitable. Nate's jaw tightened. He didn't need to guess why his friend was here; he'd known this conversation was coming the moment he had stormed out of that café, fleeing like a man desperate to escape a fire that was only burning inside.

Caleb climbed out of the SUV and closed the door with a soft, deliberate thud. He didn't speak as he walked up the porch steps, his presence quiet but firm, the kind that demanded attention without needing words. When he lowered himself into the chair beside Nate, there was a heaviness in his sigh—like a man carrying a burden he'd been forced to shoulder.

For a long moment, they sat in silence. Crickets hummed softly in the grass, and a warm breeze rustled through the trees, carrying the faint scent of pine and earth. Nate stared straight ahead, pretending he wasn't bracing for impact, pretending that his chest wasn't still pounding from the sight of Lily and her child.

Finally, Caleb exhaled, a low, deliberate sound that broke the tension. "You okay?"

Nate lifted the bottle, taking a sip—though it tasted like nothing—and let it linger. "Yeah," he said, voice casual, eyes fixed on the yard. "Why?"

Caleb let out a humourless chuckle, one that carried no mirth, only understanding—and maybe a hint of exasperation. "Come on, Nate."

Nate's shoulders stiffened, his fingers tightening around the bottle.

"You know why I'm asking," Caleb said, low but firm, a steady weight behind every word. "What you did at the café… that was harsh."

Nate flinched inwardly, but his face remained a mask. "I didn't do anything," he muttered, tone flat.

"You walked out, Nate. The second you saw her."

The memory hit him like a fist to the ribs. Lily—standing there—eyes wide, a flicker of hope and fear, of something he'd never noticed before. He had barely been able to breathe.

"I didn't walk out," he murmured, trying to control the tremor in his voice. "I just… didn't want to cause a scene."

Caleb arched a brow, calm but insistent. "Looked more like you were running."

Nate's grip on the bottle tightened, knuckles whitening. "What was I supposed to do, Caleb? Pretend everything's fine? Pretend she didn't…" He stopped, the rest of the words caught somewhere deep in his chest, too heavy to release.

Caleb watched him quietly, gaze steady, unwavering. "It's been three years, Nate."

"Three years doesn't erase what she did," Nate said, voice raw, rougher than intended. He stared down at the beer label, picking at it with his thumb, as if he could tear apart the paper and make the pain less real. "Or how I feel," he added bitterly.

Caleb nodded slowly, letting the words hang, letting Nate feel their weight. "And seeing her again?" he prompted softly, careful now.

Nate swallowed hard, throat tight, muscles taut. "It just… blindsided me. She blindsided me. The baby blindsided me." His voice wavered, but he didn't let it break entirely.

Caleb leaned back in his chair, eyes sharp but gentle, the kind that could cut through the chaos of Nate's mind with quiet precision. "Yeah, I figured. But Nate… she didn't deserve to be treated like that."

Nate's jaw clenched, teeth grinding against the familiar ache in his chest. His heart pounded, thoughts spinning in a tangled storm of anger, disbelief, and longing he couldn't name. And yet—for the first time all day—he didn't snap, didn't lash out, didn't fight. He just breathed. Raggedly, unevenly. Because Caleb was right. And that truth—simple, undeniable—stung deeper than any betrayal Lily had ever inflicted.

After a long, stretching silence, Caleb finally exhaled. "I just left her place."

Nate's head snapped toward him. "Wait—you were at her house?" His voice sharpened instantly. "Why?"

Caleb ran a hand down his face, fatigue lining his features. "I wanted to catch up with her." He hesitated, then added quietly, "I like Lily. Always have."

Nate stared at him, stunned, rubbing the back of his neck as if the motion might shake the words loose. The air felt suddenly too thick, too tight.

Caleb's voice softened, steady and deliberate. "Nate, I told you three years ago I didn't believe she betrayed you. I still don't."

Nate's head whipped toward him, pain flashing bare and unguarded in his eyes. "How can you say that?" His voice cracked once, betraying everything he'd tried to lock away. "You saw the baby. She's the right age."

Caleb blinked, genuinely incredulous. "So, you honestly think that little girl—who looks like an angel—belongs to Derek Monroe?" He shook his head slowly. "Are you serious?"

"I…" Nate faltered, shoulders sagging, the fight draining out of him. "I don't know."

Caleb leaned forward, elbows braced on his knees, voice low and unwavering. "Nate. It's not. There's no way it is."

The certainty hit him like a blow—solid, unyielding. More conviction than Nate had allowed himself to feel in years.

If Mandy wasn't Derek's… then Nate could have it all wrong. Painfully. Catastrophically wrong. And that possibility hurt more than the betrayal he'd spent three years nursing like an open wound.

"She asked me about you," Caleb said quietly.

Nate stiffened. "Why?"

"She said she knows it didn't work out," Caleb replied, choosing his words carefully. "But she wants you to be happy."

"Ha." Nate scoffed, the sound hollow and brittle. "Seriously, Caleb? You believe that?"

"Yes," Caleb said without hesitation. "I saw it in her face." His gaze sharpened. "And there's something else. She's still hurting, Nate. Badly."

Nate shook his head, a reflex more than a decision. "No. I don't believe that."

"Believe it," Caleb pressed. "I looked her in the eye when she told me she hasn't dated anyone since you."

Nate let out a bitter, disbelieving laugh. "Well, that can't be true. She has a daughter."

Caleb held his gaze, steady and unflinching. "I'm telling you, Nate—she was telling the truth. I don't know how I know, but I know." His voice lowered. "She wasn't lying. I'd bet my life on it."

Nate stared at the ground, the words lodging painfully in his throat, impossible to swallow, impossible to ignore.

After a brief pause, Caleb's tone shifted, a teasing edge creeping in. "Well… if you aren't interested, I am."

Nate looked up sharply, confusion and disbelief etched across his face. "…You?"

Caleb's grin came easy, confident, threaded with both mischief and sincerity. "Yep. I'm interested. And I've been waiting a long time, so I don't plan on letting her slip away."

Nate blinked at him, dumbfounded, the tight coil in his chest twisting even tighter. Caleb's words didn't just surprise him—they rattled the walls Nate had painstakingly built around his heart, shaking loose doubts he'd buried beneath anger and pride.

"I made it clear to you a long time ago," Caleb continued, his voice softening, earnest now, "that Lily was a catch. That hasn't changed. And that's why I know she never betrayed you." He met Nate's eyes squarely. "Even when I joked about my crush on her, she made it absolutely clear—no hesitation, no ambiguity—that she would never, ever do anything to hurt you."

Nate's throat tightened. He swallowed hard, the bitter residue of years of misunderstanding and resentment mixing with a dawning, painful awareness. Caleb wasn't just defending Lily—he was holding up a mirror to Nate's doubts, the ones he'd never wanted to face.

Caleb stretched casually, but there was a subtle firmness in his movements, an unmistakable resolve beneath the ease. "I'll be seeing a lot of Lily because of Edward," he said, glancing over with a half-smile. "And I'll be trying to convince her to go out with me."

He paused, then added, carefully but honestly, "Will you… be okay with that?"

Nate's hands tightened around the beer bottle, knuckles whitening as though gripping harder could anchor him against the storm of feelings raging inside. Yet he didn't rise from the porch chair. He wanted to argue, to stake his claim, to remind Caleb that Lily had been his once, that a part of her still belonged to him. But the words lodged in his throat, choked by a mix of anger, jealousy, and something deeper, something he refused to name.

"I—" he began, then stopped abruptly, shaking his head. "I'm not… it's not that simple."

Caleb tilted his head, his gaze calm but piercing, steady and unyielding. "Nothing about Lily is simple, Nate. You know that. But here's the thing—she's been carrying the weight of the past all by herself. She's been brave enough to come back, to face this town, to face you. And maybe… maybe you owe her a little faith."

Faith. The word burned in his chest. He had sworn he'd never trust again—not after the hurt, the betrayal, the years of silence that had settled like a shadow over his heart. And yet, seeing her—calm, composed, carrying herself with that quiet strength he remembered so well—he felt it flicker, tiny and infuriating, like a spark threatening to ignite.

"You think I can just… forgive her?" Nate muttered, more to himself than to Caleb, his voice tight, raw with bitterness that had festered for years. "After everything I've been told… after everything I've lost?"

"You weren't the only one hurt, Nate." Caleb leaned forward, elbows resting on his knees, his gaze unwavering. "But I don't think there was ever anything to forgive," he said slowly, letting each word settle like a stone in the pit of Nate's chest. "I wasn't there the night Derek told you what supposedly happened. I don't know why Lily accused you of sleeping with Cassie. I don't know all the pieces—and maybe I never will. But deep down, I feel… something isn't right about the story you were fed."

Nate's jaw tightened as his pulse throbbed in his temples. "Caleb… she left. That had to mean something. That was like an admission of guilt."

"Was it?" Caleb asked gently, tilting his head, eyes soft but searching. "Or… was it her way of asking if you thought she was worth fighting for? And you answered her by not going after her."

He let the words hang between them, weighty and deliberate. "You've spent years letting pride and hurt make your decisions for you. Maybe it's time to stop. Time to let what's real—what you actually know—guide you, not what you've been told, or what you think you've lost."

Caleb rose from the chair, looming over Nate with quiet authority, his presence commanding yet not unkind. "You know I'm here for you," he said steadily, voice measured, "but I will not avoid Lily. Not now. Not ever."

He paused, then added carefully, the edge of his certainty unmistakable, "And I was serious when I said—if you're not interested in Lily, I am. I'll give you a little time to work out what you want, but I *will* pursue her if you don't."

Nate gave a single, rigid nod, the motion tight and respectful, throat constricted. "Understood," he muttered, each syllable strained.

Caleb offered a small, knowing half-smile before stepping down the porch steps. "Night, Nate. See you tomorrow." He walked to his car, the engine purring to life before pulling away, leaving Nate alone in the fading light.

Nate's hands clenched the arms of the chair, knuckles white, chest tight, every breath heavy with the weight of what had just been said. The quiet after Caleb's departure was almost unbearable, filled with the echo of truths he hadn't wanted to face. Caleb's calm certainty cut through the fog of anger, suspicion, and stubborn pride that had been his constant companions for three long years.

And for the first time in years, doubt flickered—small, tentative, almost terrifying. Had he been wrong all this time? Could he have misjudged her, misread every glance, every word, every shared moment? The thought pierced him like a blade, reopening old scars while simultaneously offering a fragile, disorienting glimmer of something he hadn't allowed himself to feel in years: hope.

Because no matter how hard he had tried to bury it, no matter how many nights he had drowned himself in work, in anger, in resentment, he had never stopped loving Lily. Not for a single day. Not for a single heartbeat.

After Caleb left, Lily fed Mandy, bathed her, and tucked her into bed. Luckily, Mandy had started sleeping through the night at a very young age, and Lily silently hoped the change of environment wouldn't disrupt her carefully maintained routine. She lingered at the doorway for a long, quiet moment, brushing a stray curl from Mandy's forehead and planting a gentle kiss there. The little girl's soft, even breathing was a balm to Lily's frayed nerves, a small, perfect reminder of the life she had built amid heartbreak and loss.

By the time she returned to the living room, Edward had stirred from his nap. His eyes were half-lidded, heavy with sleep and the fragility his illness imposed, yet they brightened faintly at the sight of her.

"Where's Mandy?" he asked, voice soft and slightly hoarse, carrying the weight of his years.

"In bed," Lily replied, settling into the armchair across from him. "It's her bedtime. She was tired—went out like a light."

Edward's lips curved into a small, contented smile. "Good." He blinked slowly, then fixed her with a tender, searching gaze. "I'm so glad you're here."

"So am I, Dad," Lily said, her voice gentle but firm, carrying the relief and comfort of being home after so long. She leaned back in her chair, letting the quiet settle around them—a fragile peace she hadn't allowed herself in years.

For a long moment, neither spoke. They simply shared the living room's stillness: the soft tick of the clock, the faint rustle of curtains in the evening breeze, the unspoken bond between father and daughter reunited.

Edward finally broke the silence. "Have you seen Nate?"

Lily let out a weary sigh, shoulders sagging. "Yes, Dad. As soon as he laid eyes on me, he… he just fled."

Edward frowned, confusion knitting his brow. "I still don't understand what happened. You two were so in love. You'd just gotten engaged—a week before you left."

Lily's gaze dropped to her hands, memories flashing unbidden: betrayal, hurt, anger, the sharp sting of rejection she had carried for years. She spoke slowly, each word heavy. "I still love him, Dad. But… it's not going to make a difference."

Edward's eyes softened. "But… he loves you too, doesn't he?"

She shook her head slightly, a bitter edge to her voice. "Does he, Dad? He didn't come after me. He didn't try to explain why he did what he did. The moment I left… it was like I didn't exist. Maybe he never loved me as much as everyone believed."

A long, quiet sigh escaped her lips, the weight of years pressing down on her chest. "Even if he had… it wouldn't have made a difference. You can't come back from what he did—not without scars."

Edward reached out, placing a gentle hand over hers. "Lily… love isn't always fair, and sometimes it's not enough to fix the hurt. But that doesn't mean it was never real."

Lily met his eyes briefly, the familiar warmth of her father's wisdom grounding her amid the storm of her emotions. "Maybe," she whispered. "Maybe it was real… just not meant to last."

She studied her father carefully, noting how frail he had become—a shadow of the strong, steady man she remembered. Before she left Willow Creek, he had been full of life and determination, the town's sheriff with unwavering resolve. Now, his shoulders slumped, his movements slower, and the sharpness in his once-bright eyes had dimmed with fatigue. Over the past three years, Edward had visited her often, but this was the first time she had returned to witness him slowly fading before her eyes. She knew the days ahead would be difficult, emotionally and physically.

And the last thing she needed to spend energy on was an old boyfriend—a man who had once promised to love and cherish her, only to betray that trust. Over the years, Lily had wrestled with guilt and "what ifs." What if she had given herself fully to Nate? Perhaps then he wouldn't have been with Cassie. But thinking like that did nothing but twist the knife of regret and deepen the ache in her chest.

She let out another long, quiet sigh. "Come on, Dad. Time for bed."

Gently, she helped him up, guiding his unsteady steps toward his room. The familiarity of her childhood home offered some comfort—single-story, no stairs to navigate, quiet echoes of laughter and love from her youth whispering in the corners. She settled him in, tucking the blanket snugly around his frail frame and brushing back a loose strand of hair from his forehead. She lingered a moment, placing a hand lightly over his shoulder, silently vowing to make the most of every borrowed minute with him.

235

Chapter Six

Lily stepped into the shower, letting the warm water cascade over her, trying to wash away the heaviness of the day—the weight of old heartbreak, the ache of seeing her father diminished, and the lingering tension from the encounter at the café. She lingered under the spray longer than usual, each droplet massaging away the stiffness in her shoulders, though it could not reach the tight knot of longing and memory in her chest.

When she finally slid under the covers, exhaustion wrapped around her like a heavy, familiar cloak, both body and soul spent. And yet, as always, her thoughts drifted to Nate—the first and last thought of her day, persistent even now, despite everything. They had never made love; they had agreed to wait for their wedding night, honouring the promise of that special moment. But her mind inevitably returned to the night after he had proposed, the one time they had nearly given in.

Her father had been working late, leaving the house quiet and private. Lily had cooked dinner, and the air had smelled of garlic and rosemary, warm and inviting. Nate had been about to leave when he suddenly turned, sweeping her into his arms. His hold was firm, possessive yet tender, and before she could fully react, his mouth found hers. The kiss was anything but hesitant—deep, hungry, charged with all the restraint and longing they had carried for months.

Lily had gasped softly, melting into him, hands curling into his shirt as if anchoring herself. The world narrowed to the heat between them, the certainty of his arms, and the language of his kiss—a declaration of promise, desire, and love all at once.

Her arms slid around his neck, drawing him closer, and he trailed his lips along her jaw, down the curve of her neck. She shivered under his breath, her senses alight with every gentle caress, every surge of urgency held in check.

"God, Lily," he murmured against her skin. "I want you."

His mouth returned to hers, deeper now, fuller—every inch of restraint poured into a single, breathless moment. Lily met him without hesitation. She gave herself fully, the want between them humming, undeniable, fierce.

His hands tightened at her waist, pulling her impossibly close, until there was no space left between them. She felt his strength, the barely contained intensity he was restraining—for her, for them.

"Lily…" Her name left him like a sacred promise.

"I want you too, Nate," she breathed, the confession trembling out of her lips, fragile yet certain.

The sound he made was low, rough, a tremor of relief and desire, and he kissed her again—consuming, unrestrained—until the room seemed to spin. Then, smoothly, he lifted her, and her breath caught as her body responded instinctively, legs winding around him, drawn by instinct, by need, by love.

The house hushed around them, every step down the hall measured and reverent, the kiss unbroken, deliberate, sacred in its intensity. When he nudged the bedroom door open with his shoulder and closed it behind them, it felt like crossing a threshold into a world all their own.

He carried her the final few steps to the bed, and they sank together in a tangled, breathless embrace, laughter swallowed by kisses, urgency woven through every touch. Lily lay over him, hair cascading across their faces, mouths fused as if neither trusted the moment to be real.

His hands slid to her hips, anchoring her, and she shifted instinctively, moulding herself to him. A soft sound left her, answered by a deep groan of pleasure from him.

His lips left hers only to trace her cheek, her jaw, the sensitive skin beneath her ear, and she shivered, trembling at the tension that simmered between them—delicate, electric, almost unbearable.

"Lily," he whispered, voice rough and full of desire, yet tempered by tenderness.

She felt it—the pull, the tension, the edge of something irreversible. Her breath quickened, thoughts dissolving into sensation, into memory, into longing.

And then, suddenly, he stilled. Completely.

He closed his eyes, resting his forehead against hers, chest rising and falling hard beneath her hands. His grip eased, shifting from urgent, burning desire to restrained, careful love.

"I want you," he said quietly, honesty threading every word. "God, Lily… I want you so much it hurts."

Her heart hammered against her ribcage. "Nate…?"

He opened his eyes, and she saw more than desire there—she saw love, care, a fierce determination to honour her, to protect this fragile, perfect connection.

"I love you," he whispered softly.

"I don't want to rush you," he added, thumb brushing her hip in slow, grounding strokes. "Not here. Not like this. I want time. I want to cherish you—to give you everything this should be. No doubts. No fear."

Understanding dawned, warmth mingling with the ache, heat giving way to something steadier, deeper.

The moment didn't cool—it deepened.

"I won't go any further," he said, firm and tender all at once. "Not until we are married."

Lily rested her forehead against his, hands over his heart, feeling it race beneath her touch. The closeness steadied her even as it stirred everything inside, a bittersweet ache she had carried for years.

Dragging herself out of the memory, she curled tighter under the blankets. You need to stop this, she whispered silently. But a stubborn part of her heart refused to listen. The longing, the memory, the ache—they were indelible, refusing to be silenced, refusing to be denied.

The next morning, Lily woke to the soft babbling crackling through the baby monitor. Mandy was already awake—humming tunelessly, kicking her feet against the crib mattress, and happily chatting to her stuffed bunny as though the two of them were deep in conversation. The sound tugged an immediate smile across Lily's face. Pure, uncomplicated joy. Something she hadn't felt—at least not this freely—in far too long.

She rolled onto her side, listening for a moment longer, letting the cheerful noise ground her before the day could intrude. Then she climbed out of bed, dressed quickly, and gathered Mandy up for the morning routine. After changing and dressing her daughter, Lily carried her into the living room, Mandy's curls still soft and sleep-warm against her neck.

Edward was already awake, settled into his familiar armchair with a blanket tucked over his legs and a cup of tea cooling on the side table. His shoulders looked thinner today, his face drawn with fatigue that no amount of sleep ever seemed to fully ease. But the instant he spotted Mandy, his expression transformed—eyes brightening, mouth lifting into a smile so warm it almost erased the signs of illness.

"There's my girl," Edward said, his voice roughened by sleep and sickness, yet glowing with affection. "Come here, sweetheart."

Mandy squealed, her whole body wiggling with excitement as she reached for him, tiny hands opening and closing in eager anticipation. Lily lowered her carefully onto his lap, her own hands hovering close, instinctively protective until she was certain he had her settled and secure. His arms, though weaker than Lily remembered, still wrapped around the little girl with gentle confidence.

"You're the sunshine of this house," he murmured, pressing a soft kiss to the crown of Mandy's head.

Mandy responded by patting his cheek with her small palm—then immediately grabbing his nose with determined delight.

Edward burst out laughing. Not the thin, weary chuckle Lily had grown used to over the past months, but a full, rich laugh that filled the room and wrapped around her like a forgotten blanket. Her throat tightened. She hadn't heard that sound in far too long, and it hit her with a sudden rush of gratitude and grief all at once.

"You're trouble," he told Mandy, eyes twinkling.

And for just a moment—brief and precious—Lily saw him as he had once been. Strong. Steady. Unbreakable.

Mandy launched into an enthusiastic stream of toddler babble, arms waving with exaggerated importance as if she were delivering vital information. Edward listened with complete seriousness, nodding along as though she were confiding state secrets.

"Oh, I see," he replied solemnly. "Is that so?"

"Uh-huh!" Mandy declared, nodding so hard her baby curls bounced wildly.

Edward chuckled again, leaning back as she continued her animated monologue. Lily stood nearby with her arms loosely folded, watching the scene unfold. Her heart ached with a bittersweet mix of love and looming loss. This—this ordinary, beautiful moment—was exactly why she had come home. To give them these memories. To gather up what time remained and hold it close.

When Mandy eventually began to wriggle, clearly eager to explore, Lily moved in before she could squirm her way off Edward's lap.

"Dad, I'm going to run to the store and grab a few things," Lily said gently. "Will you be okay for a bit?"

Edward nodded, resting a tired but steady hand over hers. "We'll be just fine. Go on." He tilted his chin toward Mandy with a faint smile. "And don't worry—I promise not to teach her any bad habits."

Mandy gave him a mischievous grin, one hand already reaching out as if scouting for another nose to grab. Edward winked, the corners of his mouth lifting.

For a moment, Lily simply stood there, breathing it in—this fragile, perfect sliver of peace in a world that had offered her very little lately. Then she kissed Mandy's cheek, squeezed her father's hand, and quietly headed for the door, carrying the warmth of the moment with her.

The bell over the door of the Willow Creek General Store jingled as Lily stepped inside. The familiar scent of cedar chips, old candy, and laundry detergent wrapped around her like a memory she hadn't asked for. It should have been comforting. Instead, the tiny hairs along her arms prickled, warning her she was no longer invisible here.

Heads turned. Conversations stalled mid-sentence. And then the whispering began.

She kept her gaze forward, lifted a shopping basket from the stack by the door, and walked on as if she didn't notice the way Mrs. Donnelly nudged her friend or how two teenagers at the magazine rack exchanged a look clearly meant to be subtle—but wasn't.

As Lily reached for a box of cereal, she heard it—hushed but not nearly hushed enough.

"That's her. Lily Hart."

"Back after three years."

"Well, you know why she left."

"Poor Nate."

Her jaw tightened. She placed the cereal carefully into her basket and moved on, her movements deliberate, controlled.

But the voices followed her like shadows down the narrow aisles.

"I heard they had a huge fight."

"No, no," someone whispered with theatrical certainty. "She cheated and got herself pregnant."

"No, it wasn't her," another voice countered. "It was Nate who—"

Lily turned sharply into the next aisle, her pulse spiking. She focused on the rows of canned soup and paper towels, willing the shelves to swallow her whole. She hadn't realised how much this town still owned her story—how little time it had wasted rewriting it.

Mrs. Baxter stood at the end of the aisle, blocking her path with a cart piled high with groceries. Her smile was polite, practiced—but her eyes were sharp with curiosity.

"Lily, dear! Well, aren't you a sight," Mrs. Baxter said brightly. "Back home for good?"

"Just visiting for now," Lily replied, lifting the corners of her mouth into something that passed for a smile.

"Mm-hmm." Mrs. Baxter leaned closer, lowering her voice as though they were sharing a secret. "Here for your father, I assume. Terrible thing… cancer." She shook her head sadly—so dramatically it bordered on performance—before her gaze slid pointedly to Lily's bare left hand. "And I hear you have a little girl now."

"Yes. Mandy," Lily said, keeping her voice even, though it tightened around the name.

"Oh." Mrs. Baxter's eyes sharpened further. "And a husband…? No ring?" She clucked her tongue. "Well. Things don't always turn out the way we expect, do they?"

The sting landed fast and hot—humiliation, anger, grief—all tangled together. Lily forced her jaw to stay loose, her expression calm, even as her pulse thudded painfully in her throat.

"Have a nice day," she said, stepping neatly around the cart before Mrs. Baxter could trap her with another question.

She made it to the checkout without further interrogation, but the weight of every glance followed her—sideways looks, sympathetic smiles, whispered theories. Willow Creek had always thrived on stories. And Lily had just walked back into the middle of her own personal bonfire.

When the cashier finally handed her the bag, Lily released a breath she hadn't realised she'd been holding and pushed through the door into the fresh afternoon air.

Outside, she paused. Closed her eyes. Drew a long, steadying breath.

She had survived worse. She could survive this too.

Still, the sting lingered. Coming home wasn't just about her father's failing health… or giving Mandy time with her grandfather. It wasn't even about finding answers for herself. It was about facing the ruins of the life she once had—and the people who had stood around watching it burn.

People who still didn't know the truth.

Adjusting the grocery bag on her hip, Lily squared her shoulders and started toward home—toward the two people who mattered. Her father, fighting the hardest battle of his life. And her daughter, who could light up a room—and Edward's tired eyes—with a single giggle.

Whatever the town thought of her didn't matter.

Not compared to them.

Nate heard the gossip before he even finished paying for his lunch.

Willow Creek Regional Hospital wasn't large—around eighty beds, one ICU, a modest oncology unit, and the maternity and paediatrics wing he practically lived on—but it served every small town within a hundred-kilometre radius. Farmers, teachers, retirees, and young families from half the region passed through its bright blue double doors every day. And with that many people funnelling through a place this small, privacy didn't just vanish—it never really existed to begin with.

Especially not in the cafeteria.

He'd barely stepped inside when he caught the sound of two nurses whispering near the coffee machine, their voices pitched low but carrying anyway.

"Did you see her? Lily Hart—back in town. Mrs. Baxter said she came into her shop yesterday."

"Mm-hmm. And she's got a toddler now. Around two, I heard. No husband." A pause, then a cluck of the tongue. "Shame, really."

Nate froze mid-step.

A third nurse leaned in, lowering her voice—but not nearly enough. "Well, what did we expect? She left right after—"

"Shh!" one hissed. "Dr. Cahill is right there."

The silence that followed was sharp and uncomfortable, stretching just long enough to sting.

Jaw tight, Nate moved to the counter. He could feel the glances—quick, guilty, poorly disguised. The scrape of the card reader sounded absurdly loud over the pounding in his ears, each electronic beep landing like a strike.

This hospital handled surgeries, oncology consults, emergency cases, births.

And gossip, apparently.

He carried his tray to a corner table overlooking the courtyard, but he didn't see the flowers or the sunlight or the trickle of the fountain outside.

All he heard were the whispers echoing in his mind.

Lily Hart.

Back in town.

With a child.

His grip tightened around the coffee cup until his knuckles blanched white.

The hospital served half the region, but in that moment, it felt suffocatingly small—too full of voices that didn't know the truth. Voices that didn't know anything.

And he hated—truly hated—how much their words still sliced into him.

Because no matter how hard he tried, no matter how many years passed…

Lily's name still hurt.

Seeing her again had hit him harder than he'd prepared for—sharp and sudden, like someone had torn open wounds he'd convinced himself had scarred over. He hadn't slept more than a couple of hours, replaying her expression again and again. Shock. Hurt. Something else he couldn't quite name.

Guilt twisted deep in his gut.

You don't get to feel like this; he reminded himself grimly. You made your choices.

Across the cafeteria, two more nurses dropped into chairs nearby, unaware—or uncaring—that he was within earshot. Normally, he blocked out the background noise of the room. Today, every syllable cut through him like a scalpel.

"Did you hear?" the younger nurse—Courtney—whispered, not nearly quietly enough. "Lily Hart is back in town."

Nate's spine locked.

The older nurse, Brenda, clicked her tongue. "Half the town's buzzing. Poor girl couldn't even shop at Baxter's without being stared at."

Courtney leaned closer. "People say she ran off because she got caught cheating."

Nate's jaw clamped so hard it ached.

"That's not what I heard," Brenda countered. "My neighbour said Lily caught Nate cheating. With Cassandra Monroe, wasn't it?"

His stomach twisted violently, bile rising in his throat.

Courtney shrugged. "Either way, it must've been bad. No one disappears for three years over something small."

Brenda sighed. "They were the perfect couple… before the whole mess."

Heat crawled up Nate's neck, his pulse thundering in his ears.

Courtney added, "Someone said Lily had a baby. Alone."

Brenda nodded knowingly. "And the father's not in the picture. Probably why she came back."

Nate stood so abruptly his chair screeched across the floor.

Both nurses startled, eyes wide.

Brenda blinked. "Oh—Dr. Cahill. We… didn't see you there."

Nate stared at them, breathing hard, every muscle coiled tight as he fought the urge to explode. His voice, when it came, was low and razor-sharp.

"If you're going to talk about Lily—and about me—at least get your facts straight."

Courtney's face drained of colour.

Brenda lifted her chin, defensive but uneasy. "We didn't mean anything by it."

"Yes," Nate said coldly, steel sliding into his tone, "you did."

The tables around them fell silent. A doctor glanced over. Someone cleared their throat.

Nate leaned forward slightly, his words weighted with three years of regret—three years of silence and anger, much of it aimed squarely at himself.

"Lily doesn't deserve to be picked apart like she's some tabloid headline," he said. "You have no idea what she's been through. Her father is dying."

Courtney's gaze dropped. Brenda pressed her lips together.

"Well," Brenda muttered, "people are curious."

"Curiosity," Nate snapped, "isn't an excuse for cruelty."

He didn't wait for a response. He grabbed his untouched tray, dumped it into the bin with one harsh motion, and pushed out of the cafeteria. The doors swung shut behind him, the echo ringing down the hallway.

He paced the corridor, breath coming fast, adrenaline still burning hot through his veins. Gossip had always been part of Willow Creek. But hearing strangers twist Lily into a villain—hearing them paint her with the same brush he once had—

It was unbearable.

Because the truth was, he didn't even know the truth.

He knew what he had done. What he hadn't done. What he should have done.

But did he really know what Lily had done? What she hadn't?

And listening to people reduce her life—her pain—to nothing more than entertainment made something inside him fracture.

Caleb's voice echoed in his mind, calm and relentless.

Maybe it's time to stop letting pride and hurt make decisions for you.

Nate pressed his palms against the cold wall, bowing his head, breath shuddering out of him.

Maybe everyone else had the story wrong.

Maybe he had it wrong.

And maybe—just maybe—he wasn't the only one who'd spent the last three years hurting.

Chapter Seven

Lily woke to soft morning light spilling through the curtains, pale and gentle, as the quiet hum of the house settled around her like a held breath. Somewhere down the street a bird called, and the old floorboards creaked faintly as the house shifted with the day. Mandy had already wriggled into bed beside her, kicking her little legs beneath the covers and chattering happily to herself, blissfully unaware of the weight that hung in the air.

Lily smiled down at her daughter and brushed a stray curl from her forehead, her chest tightening with affection. Even if it was only for a week—maybe less—she had cherished these mornings. The small, ordinary moments of being home. Just her, her father, and her daughter, wrapped in the rhythm of familiar walls, worn furniture, and soft sunlight that made everything feel briefly whole again.

Edward was already awake.

He sat in his armchair near the window, a blanket draped over his frail shoulders, the morning paper forgotten on the side table beside a cooling cup of tea. His posture slumped with exhaustion, his once-broad frame diminished, and every movement carried the subtle tremor of a body worn down by late-stage prostate cancer. Yet when his eyes lifted to meet hers, there was still a flicker of warmth there—a trace of the man she remembered from her childhood, steady and reassuring.

"Good morning, kiddo," he rasped, his voice soft but steady despite the strain beneath it. "Sleep well?"

"As well as one can with a toddler for an alarm clock," Lily teased gently, smoothing Mandy's hair away from her eyes.

Edward managed a faint smile, the corner of his mouth lifting just enough to remind her of the father he had always been—the man who used to scoop her up and spin her until she laughed breathlessly.

Mandy squirmed, her small hands reaching eagerly for Edward's. "Grandpa, play!" she demanded, her words tumbling over one another as her giggles filled the room.

For a fleeting moment, the heaviness receded.

Lily carefully lowered her daughter onto Edward's lap, hovering close until she was sure he had her securely. Edward chuckled—a thin sound, but genuine—and the three of them settled into a quiet rhythm of bouncing knees, soft pats, and gentle coos. Mandy babbled as though narrating an important story, and Edward listened with solemn attention, responding as if every word mattered.

But the joy was fragile.

As Mandy eventually slid from his lap to chase a toy across the floor, Edward's energy visibly waned. A grimace flickered across his face when he shifted in the chair, the movement slow and deliberate. Lily's heart clenched painfully. She knew the signs now—too well. His body was struggling to keep pace with even the simplest routines.

"Lily," he said quietly, his voice cracking just enough to betray the effort behind it, "I'm so glad you and Mandy are here."

His hand rested on the arm of the chair, fingers trembling faintly, betraying the strength he no longer had.

Lily swallowed hard, her throat tightening as guilt and sorrow twisted together in her chest. She wished—no, she ached—for more time. Over the past week, she had watched the illness strip him piece by piece of his former strength: the stiffness in his shoulders when he reached for his teacup, the faint tremor in his hands as he tried to steady the mug, the careful shuffle of his feet across the room, and the weary sighs that slipped past his lips even as he forced a smile.

Each small movement carried the weight of a body fighting a battle it could not win.

"I should have come home sooner," she whispered, the words heavy with regret.

Edward shook his head slowly. "You had to sort out the house, Lily," he said gently. "I understand why you couldn't."

She reached out and squeezed his shoulder, forcing a small smile to mask the ache threatening to break through. "I just... I hate seeing you like this, Dad."

His eyes softened, glimmering with unshed tears he refused to let fall. "I know, kiddo. But you're here now. And that matters more than you realise."

Mandy crawled back into his lap, wrapping her tiny arms around his neck with fierce affection. Edward leaned forward to hug her back, using what strength he had, and Lily felt a sharp pang at the fleetingness of it all. These mornings—these moments—were precious. And time was slipping through her fingers faster than she wanted to admit.

Even as she helped her father rise for breakfast, the inevitability pressed in. The home they had always shared—the sanctuary of her childhood, the anchor of her youth—was no longer enough. Soon, Edward would need more care than she could give, and the knowledge settled in her chest like a quiet, unrelenting dread.

But for now, there was this morning.

Just them.

Just a father, his granddaughter, and the daughter who would not leave his side.

And Lily would hold them close for every fleeting second she was given.

The doorbell rang promptly at nine, its cheerful chime at odds with the quiet tension that lived beneath the surface of the house. Moments later, a male nurse arrived. Jason was in his forties, calm mandy unhurried, with a professional ease and gentle manner that immediately put both Lily and Edward at ease.

"Morning, Mr. Hart," Jason said warmly as he stepped inside, carrying a small canvas bag of supplies. "Time for your morning care."

Edward offered a weak nod, his expression resigned but trusting. Lily helped him to his feet and guided him toward the bathroom, her hand firm at his elbow. Jason moved efficiently and with practiced care—washing, shaving, and dressing Edward while Lily waited in the hall, listening to the quiet sounds of routine. Mandy sat on the rug nearby, humming to herself as she stacked blocks, completely at ease. To her, this was just another morning in their small, carefully contained world.

When Jason finished, Lily stepped forward, brushing back Edward's thinning hair and straightening his collar as he was eased back into his armchair.

"You're doing well," she murmured softly, her words meant as encouragement, though her chest tightened with every careful movement Jason made. The truth she tried not to dwell on pressed closer: Edward's independence was slipping away. Tasks that once required no thought now demanded planning, patience, and help. And soon—she knew it with a certainty that made her throat ache—home would no longer be enough.

By mid-morning, they were ready to leave for the hospital.

Edward leaned heavily on his walker, Lily steady at his side, while Mandy was secured safely into her stroller. The short drive to Willow Creek Regional Hospital felt longer than usual, every bump in the road and gentle turn of the wheel a reminder of how fragile her father had become. Lily drove carefully, hands tight on the steering wheel, her mind racing ahead to test results and quiet fears she refused to voice aloud.

The familiar blue doors of the hospital came into view—an anchor for Willow Creek and the surrounding towns alike. Inside, the air carried the sterile scent of disinfectant and the low murmur of voices. Jason helped Edward into a wheelchair, adjusting the footrests with practiced precision.

"I'll take him for his tests now," Jason said, his tone reassuring. "We'll meet you back at Dr. Winters' office in about thirty minutes."

Lily leaned down and pressed a gentle kiss to her father's cheek. "See you soon, Dad."

Edward managed a small, tired smile, his eyes lingering on hers as Jason wheeled him down the corridor.

Pushing Mandy through the bustling lobby, Lily took in the familiar scene—the focused staff moving with purpose, the tired but hopeful faces of patients and families, the quiet hum of a place where lives were measured in moments and margins. Her thoughts stayed anchored to her father: his fragility, his quiet courage, the preciousness of the time they were trying to stretch just a little longer.

Turning a corner near the elevators, she almost collided with someone.

She looked up—and froze.

Nate.

For a heartbeat, she expected him to glance away, to walk past her as if she were a stranger, as if the last three years—and everything before them—had never existed. But he stopped.

"Hello, Lily," he said quietly.

His voice was low, steady, threaded with familiarity and something else she couldn't quite name.

She blinked, startled by the sound of it, then gathered herself. "Hello, Nate."

The moment stretched, heavy with unspoken history. Their eyes met and lingered a heartbeat too long, and the old ache stirred in Lily's chest—sharp, unwelcome, achingly familiar. She forced a small, polite smile, willing her pulse to slow. "You're looking well," she said, her voice soft but careful, guarded.

She studied him without meaning to, taking in the man standing before her. Thirty now. Tall and broad-shouldered, with an athletic build that spoke of long hours on his feet and a job that demanded both stamina and focus. Dark hair fell slightly into piercing hazel eyes, and a shadow of stubble lined his jaw, giving him a rugged, just-out-of-bed edge—as if he'd forgotten to shave in the rush of the morning. Clean-cut, yet tempered by the relentless demands of hospital life, he carried an effortless air of competence and quiet authority.

God—he was more handsome than she remembered.

And despite everything—the hurt, the silence, the years apart—her heart recognised him instantly.

"So are you," Nate replied, his gaze steady, his voice low but weighted with meaning.

She saw the thought flicker in his eyes—quick as a flash, gone almost before it fully formed. Recognition. Not just of her, but of the woman she had become.

Twenty-three now. Petite, with dark blonde hair that framed her face softly instead of falling straight as it once had. Her blue eyes—always expressive—seemed deeper somehow, more observant, as if life had taught them how to see beyond the surface. There was an ease to her now, a quiet steadiness that hadn't been there before. Natural beauty, yes—but something gentler layered beneath it. Warmer. More present.

More beautiful than he ever remembered.

"You're here for your father?" Nate asked carefully, his tone measured, his expression schooled into calm. But she caught it—the effort it took to keep his concern from becoming something else.

"Yes," she replied, her voice steady despite the nervous flutter taking wing in her chest.

"I'm really sorry about Edward," he added. This time, there was no masking it. His eyes held hers with genuine sympathy, and for a brief heartbeat the weight of everything they had never resolved—the misunderstandings, the distance, the words left unsaid— settled quietly between them.

"Thanks," Lily murmured.

Before the silence could grow heavier, Mandy let out a soft, delighted squeal. "Mama!" she chirped, reaching up with both tiny fists, her whole body wiggling with enthusiasm.

Lily laughed softly and bent to her daughter's level. "Careful, sweetheart. You have to stay in the stroller for just a little while," she murmured, brushing a loose curl from Mandy's forehead before planting a quick kiss on her cheek.

Nate's gaze followed the movement without conscious thought. His jaw tightened slightly as he watched Mandy squirm and kick, so small, so alive, so utterly unguarded. An innocence that struck him straight in the chest. He noticed the same stubborn curl Lily had always tucked back behind her ear, the bright, open curiosity in Mandy's eyes—the very same look he remembered in Lily's all those years ago.

"And who is this little angel?" he asked quietly, lowering himself into a crouch so he was level with her.

Mandy's eyes widened, and a delighted grin spread across her face as if he'd said something fascinating. She reached for him with both hands, squealing again in pure, uncomplicated joy, as though instinct told her he was safe—even if she didn't know why.

Nate hesitated, his hand hovering uncertainly in the air. Then he let her pat his fingers with her tiny fist.

The contact was brief. Innocent.

And it sent a jolt straight through him—unexpected, disarming, and far more stirring than he was prepared for.

"This is Mandy," Lily said softly, her chest tightening as she watched the interaction unfold.

"She… she's beautiful," Nate said, his voice rougher than he intended. Emotion broke through the careful composure he wore like armour.

Lily offered a small, tight smile, hearing the admiration—and the undercurrent of something deeper—in his tone. "Thank you. She's… a handful," she added gently, "but she makes life brighter."

Mandy giggled and waved her hands at him again. Nate hesitated, then lifted his hand once more, allowing her to pat it as though sealing some silent agreement. The simple, fleeting connection made his chest ache in a way he hadn't expected—sharp and hollow all at once.

Lily's eyes softened as she watched them. Mandy's tiny giggles and unrestrained joy seemed to bridge the years between her and Nate, smoothing over sharp edges, if only for a moment. The tension eased, replaced by something quieter, gentler—anchored in the undeniable presence of her daughter.

Still crouched, Nate felt his heart twist with a mixture of admiration and something he hadn't allowed himself to feel in years.

Longing.

Seeing Lily with her child—so natural, so warm, so utterly herself—stirred a dull ache deep in his chest. He wanted to reach out. To hold them. To undo the past and make things right. But years of pride, guilt, and regret rooted his hands firmly at his sides.

"I should get going," Lily said softly, straightening and brushing a stray curl from her face. "We have an appointment with Caleb. Dad just went in for some tests."

They both rose.

"Oh. Okay," Nate replied, his voice steadier than he felt, even as disappointment tightened low in his chest.

She smiled at him then—gentle, sincere. "It was good to see you, Nate. I'm glad you're doing so well."

He met her gaze, and for the first time in years, he recognised the truth in her words. Caleb had been right. She meant it. The sincerity in her eyes, the quiet warmth there, hit him harder than he expected. Regret surged, sharp and undeniable, alongside the realisation of just how much he had missed—and how much he still wanted.

For a fleeting moment, he allowed himself to imagine what might have been. What could have been. If pride and miscommunication hadn't torn them apart.

Then he buried the thought beneath a thin veneer of control.

As Lily turned the stroller toward the elevator, Nate watched them walk away, his chest tight, his thoughts a storm of memories, regret, and the stubborn, inescapable pull of a love that had never truly faded.

Every step they took echoed through him—a reminder of everything he had lost.

And everything he still longed for.

When the elevator doors slid shut, the controlled calm Lily had been clinging to fractured all at once. A sudden rush of emotion surged through her chest, stealing the air from her lungs. Her breath hitched, a soft tremor running through her from shoulder to toe—and then the tears came. Quiet at first, then unstoppable.

She hadn't realised—hadn't allowed herself to realise—just how much she still loved him.

Not in the distant, faded way she'd told herself she did, not as a memory dulled by time. This was sharp and immediate, the kind of love that lived deep in her bones, stirred awake by the sound of his voice and the familiar gravity of his presence. Everything they had been—the promises, the laughter, the future they had once mapped out together—rose up and wrapped around her heart.

She pressed a hand to her chest, as if she could physically contain the ache there. Three years. Three years of distance and silence, of nights spent convincing herself she was over him. And yet the years between them suddenly felt cruelly thin, stolen by lies, by misunderstandings, by a betrayal that still throbbed like an old wound that never quite healed.

How she wished Cassie had never come between them.

How she wished things could have unfolded differently—without accusations, without doubt, without the moment where everything they'd built collapsed under the weight of suspicion.

Mandy shifted in her stroller, sensing the change before Lily could stop it. One tiny hand reached up, patting her arm with gentle insistence. Lily blinked hard, swiping at her cheeks and forcing a small, shaky smile for her daughter. Mandy gazed up at her, trusting and untroubled, and the sight both steadied and broke her all over again.

"I'm okay," Lily whispered, though she wasn't sure who she was trying to convince.

Inside, the longing and the pain twisted together, tight and raw, refusing to loosen their grip.

The elevator chimed softly as it reached their floor. Lily drew a careful breath and straightened her shoulders, lifting her chin as the doors slid open. She could not afford to unravel—not here, not now. She needed to be steady. Present.

But she knew the ache would linger. It would follow her long after this moment, long after she walked away, because a love this deep didn't simply disappear. It didn't fade just because time had passed or because she'd learned how to survive without it.

And yet, beneath the longing, a sharper truth pressed insistently against her heart.

She could never go back—not fully, not in the way she once had.

The memory of his betrayal was still there, jagged and unforgiving, etched too deeply to ignore. The thought of opening herself up again—of trusting him with her heart, her child, her fragile sense of peace—made her chest tighten with a bitter mix of yearning and resolve. Some wounds didn't bleed anymore, but they still shaped the way you moved through the world.

Her grip tightened on the stroller handle as she pushed forward into the bright, bustling hallway, the hum of hospital life rushing in around her. She would focus on Mandy. On her father. On the present she could control.

She would not let herself get lost in what might have been.

Not today.

And yet, even as she moved forward, a small, stubborn ache whispered the truth she could never quite silence—that some part of her would always carry the memory of what she had loved.

And what she had lost.

Chapter Eight

Dr. Caleb Winters was already waiting for them in the oncology wing, clipboard tucked under one arm, his familiar, warm smile offering a small but genuine sense of relief. "Good morning, Edward. Lily. And hello there, Mandy," he added, crouching slightly to Lily's daughter's level.

Mandy responded immediately, lifting one chubby hand and waving with solemn enthusiasm, as though she understood the importance of being properly polite.

Edward attempted a smile, but it faded almost as quickly as it appeared. Lily noticed the subtle tremor in his hands as he reached for the chair, the slow, deliberate blink of exhaustion that seemed to linger longer with each passing day. These small signs—so easy for others to miss—had become impossible for her to ignore.

"Let's go somewhere a little more private," Caleb said gently, his tone careful, already preparing them for what was coming. He gestured toward the door just off the oncology wing.

They settled into the small consultation room, the space quiet and neutral, designed to soften difficult conversations. Mandy wriggled restlessly on Lily's lap, tugging at her mother's hair, pointing at the anatomical charts on the wall, blissfully unaware of the gravity settling around them. Lily smoothed her curls and murmured soft reassurances, keeping her voice light for her daughter's sake, even as a heavy pressure built in her chest.

Caleb entered a moment later, tablet in hand, a slim folder tucked beneath his arm. His usual easy warmth was still there, but it was tempered by a seriousness that made Lily's stomach tighten instinctively.

"Hello Angel," he said gently, smiling at Mandy as she waved again. "And good morning to both of you." He pulled up a chair and set the tablet down carefully, deliberately, as though each movement mattered.

"Morning, Caleb," Lily replied quietly. Her gaze flicked to her father, whose head had lowered slightly, his hand resting over hers in a silent plea for steadiness.

Caleb drew in a measured breath before speaking. "Edward… Lily… I want to be completely honest with you about where things stand." His voice remained calm, compassionate, but unflinching. "The medications are still helping with symptom management, but the cancer has continued to progress. Your prostate cancer is now considered end-stage, and unfortunately, your body is beginning to lose the fight."

Edward's fingers twitched in Lily's grasp, but he didn't speak. His jaw tightened almost imperceptibly, the faint tremor there betraying the effort it took to remain composed.

"At this stage," Caleb continued, "our focus shifts fully to comfort and quality of life. You're managing at home right now, and you're doing remarkably well given the circumstances. But it's likely that you'll need increasing levels of support—daily care, medication management, and eventually hospice services."

Lily's throat constricted. She swallowed hard, her voice barely above a whisper. "So… he won't be able to stay at home much longer."

Caleb nodded gently. "Not without significant support. He'll eventually require either round-the-clock in-home care or a hospice facility. Right now, he's still alert, mobile, and engaged—but we need to plan for when daily tasks like bathing, dressing, and preparing meals become too difficult or unsafe."

Edward finally lifted his gaze, meeting Caleb's steadily. "I don't want to leave my home," he said, his voice rough but calm. "That house… it's where my life is. Lily and Mandy are there."

"I understand," Caleb replied softly. "And we'll do everything possible to keep you there as long as it's safe and comfortable. Jason has been doing excellent work, and we can increase his hours. But there may come a point when hospice care offers you more comfort and support than home alone can provide."

Lily reached across the table, clasping her father's hand tightly. "Dad… we'll do this together. Whatever it takes. You won't be alone—not for a single moment."

Edward's eyes glistened. "I just want as much time with you both as I can get."

Caleb tapped the tablet, bringing up a care plan. "We'll start by adjusting pain management and adding additional palliative support. A specialised nurse will monitor symptoms closely, and Jason's visits will increase as needed. The goal is to maximise comfort and give you meaningful time with your family—at home, if at all possible."

Mandy reached for Edward's hand, her tiny fingers curling around his with effortless trust. A faint, bittersweet smile crossed his face, pride and sorrow mingling in his eyes.

"See?" Lily whispered, pressing a kiss to the top of Mandy's head. "This is what matters."

Caleb gave a small nod, his expression warm but resolute. "Planning ahead doesn't make this easier—but it does make it kinder."

Edward exhaled slowly, the weight of reality settling over him, tempered by the reassurance of a plan and the presence of the people he loved most.

Caleb opened the door, signalling Jason to bring the wheelchair. Lily carefully settled Mandy back into her stroller, brushing her father's hand one last time before he was wheeled away.

"Thank you, Caleb," Lily said quietly.

He pulled her into a brief, supportive hug. "Stay strong. He needs you—but remember to lean on us, too."

"I will," she replied, her voice steady despite the ache tightening her chest.

As they left the consultation room, fear wrapped cold fingers around her heart—but beneath it burned a fierce, unyielding determination. Whatever time remained, she would fill it with love, presence, and dignity.

Jason helped Edward into the car with practiced ease. Lily squeezed his hand gently as Mandy drifted toward sleep in her car seat.

"We'll manage, Dad," Lily whispered, her voice soft but resolute. "Whatever comes next… we'll face it together."

Edward's fingers twitched faintly in response—a small, grateful acknowledgment.

As Lily pulled away from the hospital, she glanced once more at her father's lined face, then at her daughter in the rear-view mirror. Time was slipping through her fingers—but she would not waste a single second of what remained.

Not one.

Nate was halfway through a sandwich he had no appetite for when a shadow fell across the table. He looked up just as Cassie slid into the chair opposite him, uninvited and unapologetic, her lips already curled in a knowing smile.

"Did I just see Lily Hart in the hospital?" she asked, eyes glittering with interest.

"Possibly, Nurse Monroe," Nate replied coolly, not bothering to meet her gaze.

Cassie scoffed. "Really, Nate. Just call me Cassie."

He ignored that too, taking a deliberate sip of his coffee instead. It tasted burnt. "What do you want, Nurse?" he asked flatly.

Cassie leaned back, clearly enjoying herself. "Surely this means you'll finally need to ask me out." She tilted her head, voice dripping with confidence. "Do you really want Lily seeing you still pining after her?"

Nate let out a slow, exasperated breath, patience fraying. "No," he said bluntly. "Just stop. And if you don't have any work-related issues, leave me in peace. I'm on my break."

Her smile vanished. Cassie shoved her chair back with a sharp scrape, shot him one last venomous look, and stormed off—nearly colliding with Caleb as he entered the cafeteria.

"Whoa," Caleb muttered, steadying himself as Cassie swept past without so much as an apology.

He shook his head, then made his way over to Nate and slid into the chair across from him. "Hey," he said casually, though his eyes were sharp, observant—already reading the tension in Nate's posture.

"What did the witch want?" Caleb asked dryly.

Nate huffed under his breath, fingers tightening slightly around what remained of his sandwich. "The usual."

Caleb studied him for a moment before leaning back, arms resting on the table. "Word is, you defended Lily the other day."

Nate's jaw clenched. "Yeah. Well, everyone seems to think they know what happened. The truth is… I'm not even sure I do."

A small, satisfied sound escaped Caleb. "Finally. You're coming to your senses."

Nate frowned. "What's that supposed to mean?"

"It means," Caleb said evenly, leaning forward, "you've been running on assumptions, pride, and anger for three years. Maybe it's time you stopped. The only way you're ever going to know the truth is by actually talking to her."

Nate exhaled slowly, a dull ache twisting in his chest. Her face flashed in his mind— the surprise in her eyes, the way his heart had stuttered despite everything. "I did talk to her," he admitted quietly. "Ran into her in the corridor."

Caleb's brows lifted. "And?"

"It was… okay," Nate muttered, staring down at the table. His fingers tapped restlessly against the edge. The word felt inadequate, even to him. He couldn't explain how seeing her had shaken him to his core—how close he'd come to saying too much, or not enough.

Caleb shook his head. "I just came from Edward's appointment."

Nate's chest tightened. "How is he?"

Caleb's expression sobered. "Not good. He's fading… faster than I expected."

Guilt twisted sharply in Nate's gut. While he'd been nursing old wounds, Lily had come home to watch her father slip away—alone, with a child, and a town eager to tear her apart.

"That's going to be hard on Lily," he murmured, the words weighted with regret.

"Yeah," Caleb said quietly. "Especially with everyone talking about her." He paused, then added, "I heard about the scene at the general store."

Nate's jaw hardened. "She doesn't deserve any of it."

Caleb's gaze held his. "No. She doesn't."

And for the first time, Nate didn't argue.

Nate closed his eyes for a brief moment, drawing in a slow breath he didn't quite manage to steady. Anger, regret, longing—they collided inside him, a tangled mess he'd spent years trying to bury. He hated how deeply the gossip cut, how every whispered rumour made him feel like he should have been there—standing beside Lily, shielding her, defending her—instead of hiding behind wounded pride and stubborn silence.

And yet… seeing her with Mandy had unravelled him in a way he hadn't expected. Watching the tenderness in her movements, the instinctive way she soothed her daughter, had twisted a hollow ache deep in his chest. She'd built a life without him. A full one. And while a part of him had wanted her back for years, another part recoiled in fear at what that would mean—what it would demand of him, of his heart.

Caleb didn't rush him. He simply watched, steady and unflinching. "You can't change the past, Nate," he said quietly. "But maybe… you can start doing right by her now."

Nate's brow furrowed, frustration flashing through his eyes. "How are you so certain she never betrayed me?"

Caleb leaned back slightly, exhaling as though the admission carried weight even now. "Because I saw the way she loved you," he said, voice low but unwavering. "I was jealous—jealous of you, jealous of what you and Lily had. The two of you… it was obvious. I've never seen anyone love someone the way she loved you. And I envied that. I still do."

He paused, then met Nate's gaze fully. "No matter what anyone told you—no matter what Derek claimed—I couldn't believe she'd done what you accused her of. And I'll be honest with you… what shocked me most was that you didn't go after her. If she were mine, I wouldn't have hesitated. I would have fought for her. Every damn second."

The words landed hard. Nate swallowed, his throat tight, the truth of them cutting deeper than accusation ever could. Caleb's honesty stirred something long buried—raw regret, old pain, and the realisation of just how much he had lost… and how badly he still wanted to make it right.

"She accused me of sleeping with Cassie," Nate said at last, his voice rough, edged with the echo of old hurt. "I thought she was trying to deflect. I thought it was easier for her to blame me than admit what she'd done."

Caleb's eyes narrowed slightly. "Did you?"

"No." Nate looked up sharply, disbelief flickering across his face. "No. I would never have cheated on Lily. Never."

"Then why didn't you make her believe you?" Caleb asked quietly. "Why did you let silence do the talking?"

Nate looked down, shame settling heavily in his chest. "That night… everything was raw. We were both hurt, angry, saying things we couldn't take back. And when she left…" He exhaled slowly. "I didn't know if she wanted to fix it. I didn't know how to fix it. I thought I had time—time to explain, time to make it right."

Caleb didn't interrupt. He let the words hang between them, heavy with all the what-ifs Nate had carried for years.

"And now she's a mother," Nate continued, his voice tight. "She must not have wanted to fix things… if she got pregnant so soon after we split."

Caleb leaned forward, his tone calm but firm. "Be honest with yourself. If she became pregnant after you parted, can you really condemn her for that? You made it clear you didn't want to try. I'd understand your anger if it happened while you were together—but do you actually know that it did?"

Nate's jaw tightened. He wanted to argue, to cling to the last shreds of justification, but Caleb's words sliced through the noise of pride and resentment.

"You're letting assumptions speak louder than the truth," Caleb said quietly. "And that will never give you peace."

Nate dragged a hand through his hair, frustration and resolve warring inside him. "I have to talk to her," he said finally. "Really talk to her. No more silence. No more half-truths."

Caleb nodded, a faint, approving smile tugging at his mouth. "Yes. You do. And whatever happens, I'll be here for you. But I'll also be there for Lily. She needs support, Nate. She deserves that much."

Nate swallowed, the weight of those words settling deep. It had never been just about him—not really. And as the thought of facing Lily again took shape, his chest tightened with a familiar, aching blend of dread and longing.

Some truths, he realised, were worth the risk—no matter how much they scared him.

Derek Monroe stepped into the kitchen of the family home he still shared with his sister, Cassandra, after their parents had passed. The familiar scent of garlic and frying oil hit him instantly, mingling with the faint undertone of burnt toast from earlier. But it wasn't the smell that made the hairs on the back of his neck stand up—it was the charged energy in the air, sharp and electric, a warning that Cassie was already worked up.

She didn't even glance up from the dishes, her movements deliberate, almost mechanical, as if each scrub of the plate fanned the flames of her fury. "I can't believe that bitch is back," she spat, venom dripping from every syllable. "Just when I was finally winning him back."

"Who?" Derek asked, shrugging, feigning casual disinterest. He had long since learned to filter the drama that constantly oozed from his sister. He knew she thrived on manipulation, on control—and he'd survived by stepping aside when it suited him.

"Lily Hart," she said at last, finally lifting her gaze, eyes sharp as knives, burning with calculation.

Derek froze mid-step. Lily. Her name hit him harder than he expected. He'd liked her once—more than he probably should have—and the memory still clawed at him. He carried the weight of his own mistakes, the guilt of what he'd done to her, to Nate. The lies he'd agreed to spin for Cassie haunted him even now; he had known it was wrong the moment it left his lips.

"She turned up with a kid," Cassie continued, sly and deliberate. "So, Nate will probably think it's yours. It's the right age, the perfect story. You just go along with it—make it believable. That way he won't want anything to do with her."

"What… she has a kid?" Derek asked, disbelief sharpening every line of his face.

"Yeah. A little girl. About two. You can play the part, Derek. You'll make it look convincing," Cassie said, almost licking her words with relish. "Then Nate will stay away. He'll think it's your child, and Lily will have no choice but to keep her distance."

Derek shook his head, the mixture of anger, disbelief, and revulsion twisting inside him. "No. I am not part of this. I am done lying for you. Never again."

Cassie froze mid-motion, spatula in hand, turning to him with a glare sharp enough to cut glass. "Oh, come on, Derek. Don't tell me your conscience has suddenly grown a spine."

He gave her a flat look, disbelief radiating. "I only lied for you because you bailed me out of that gambling debt. I paid my dues. Lesson learned. It's over. I wish I had never touched that lie."

Cassie's lips pressed into a thin line, her face rigid with frustration. "Come on, Derek. You know I love Nate."

Derek clenched his jaw so hard it ached. He had already made enough mistakes. He wouldn't ruin more lives—especially not Lily's—because of her selfish obsession.

"You don't love Nate," he said slowly, deliberately, his voice low and sharp. "You don't care about him. You care about having him for yourself. You can't stand the idea of anyone else—anyone who might actually deserve him—being happy with him. You dated in college. That's it. He hasn't even glanced at you since, and Lily… Lily and he became the golden couple of this town."

Cassie's eyes flashed, indignation flaring, but even she couldn't fully escape the truth. She remembered all too clearly: the year-long relationship with Nate, her departure to travel, and her bitter return. By then, Lily and Nate were inseparable, adored by everyone, a perfect pair. And she had hated it.

She had befriended Lily under the guise of kindness, just to get close to Nate again. And when she discovered the proposal, she had stormed to his apartment, begging him to leave Lily and take her back. He had looked at her—calmly, firmly—and told her there was no way he could ever hurt Lily. He loved her.

Cassie had left that apartment angrier than she had ever been, a storm of wounded pride and frustration boiling inside her. That wasn't the end, of course. She had convinced Derek to lie to Nate about sleeping with Lily. Then, as if choreographed, she found Lily walking toward Nate's apartment and executed her performance flawlessly. She cried, played the victim, and painted herself as innocent, all while planting the seed of betrayal in Lily's mind. Shock, hurt, disbelief—Lily's face had been priceless. A small, cruel victory that Cassie savoured. By the next day, Lily was gone.

Now, with Lily back in town, that old frustration flared again—sharper, bitterer than ever. The sense of control she once enjoyed had slipped through her fingers, and she hated it. Every moment she imagined Lily reclaiming what Cassie had once tried to take, every interaction she could manipulate no longer seemed possible, stoked her fury.

Cassie let out a frustrated hiss, teeth gritted, but Derek ignored it. He moved past her to the stairs, mind racing. He had believed he could remain uninvolved, stay neutral, even out of harm's way. But with Lily Hart back in town, staying on the sidelines was no longer an option. Maybe it was finally time someone—maybe him—exposed the truth.

Chapter Nine

Cassie didn't care that Derek had refused to help. His moral grandstanding meant nothing to her. She had already decided to move forward with her plan, and once Cassie Monroe made up her mind, nothing—and no one—stood in her way. If Derek wouldn't play his part willingly, she would simply work around him. She always did.

She made her way down the corridor toward the maternity ward, her heels clicking softly against the polished linoleum, each step measured and deliberate. The hospital hummed with quiet purpose around her—nurses passing, doors opening and closing, the distant cry of a newborn—but Cassie barely registered it. Her focus was razor sharp.

There.

Near the nurses' station stood Beryl—clipboard tucked under her arm, eyes darting, ears always tuned for the slightest hint of scandal. The unofficial town crier of Willow Creek. If a story passed through Beryl's hands, it didn't just travel—it multiplied. By morning, the entire town would be buzzing.

Perfect.

Cassie smoothed her blouse, softened her expression, and approached with practiced ease.

"Hi, Beryl. Busy day?" she asked lightly, forcing a pleasant smile that never quite reached her eyes.

Beryl glanced up from the chart she was reviewing, her sharp gaze sweeping over Cassie in a single assessing look. "Always busy," she replied, lips curving with faint amusement. "But rewarding, all the same."

"That's good," Cassie said, nodding, then hesitated—just enough to plant curiosity. She tilted her head, her brow creasing as if weighed down by worry. "I just… I've had a bit of a shock today."

Beryl's interest sparked immediately. She arched an eyebrow. "Oh? You look worried, Cassie. What's going on?"

Cassie exhaled softly, as though reluctant to speak. "It's my brother."

"Derek?" Beryl asked at once, her attention sharpening.

Cassie nodded, lowering her voice. "Yes. He only just found out he's a father."

Beryl's eyes widened, the unmistakable gleam of gossip flaring to life. "Is that so? Well, that's quite the revelation. Who's the lucky girl?"

Cassie leaned in, lowering her voice to a conspiratorial whisper, careful to keep her face composed, almost sympathetic. "Lily Hart."

Beryl blinked, clearly taken aback. "Lily Hart?" She paused, thinking, then her gaze flicked toward the corridor. "You mean that little girl Lily brought with her… is she—"

Cassie nodded slowly, deliberately. "Yes. Derek's."

Beryl let out a quiet, intrigued hum, scribbling something onto her chart as though it were purely procedural. "Well," she said mildly, though her eyes sparkled, "that certainly explains a few things."

Cassie sighed again, this time with practiced concern. "He's reeling, honestly. Completely blindsided. Poor Derek doesn't know what to do or where he stands. It's a lot to process."

"Oh, I'm sure he'll figure it out," Beryl replied, her tone casual—far too casual to be genuine.

Cassie allowed herself a faint, tight smile, the kind that passed for polite sympathy. Inside, satisfaction unfurled, slow and delicious. She knew Beryl wouldn't keep this to herself—not for long. The seed had been planted. All it needed now was time.

As Cassie turned away, she could almost hear the story already spreading—soft whispers at first, then excited speculation, growing louder with every retelling. By morning, Willow Creek would have the narrative firmly in place.

Derek may have refused to play along, but that hardly mattered. The truth—or at least the version Cassie had so carefully crafted—would do the work for her. And Nate… oh, Nate would hear it. He always did.

The thought sent a thrill racing through her veins, anticipation sharpening her smile. The wheels were in motion now, and soon the town—and the people she most wanted to control—would be dancing to the story she had so expertly set loose.

The next morning, with her father still asleep, Lily bundled Mandy into the car and drove to Willow Creek General Store. She had a list in her hand, a clear purpose in her mind, and an unshakable determination not to let anything—or anyone—derail her. The drive was quiet, Mandy humming happily in her car seat, the engine's gentle hum blending with the soft morning light spilling through the windshield. Lily's thoughts were focused, sharp, and resolute. This was just a quick trip for groceries—a mundane errand—but in Willow Creek, even mundane errands carried the weight of the town's ever-watchful eyes.

The moment she stepped through the store's double doors, it felt as if the very air shifted. Conversations died mid-sentence, heads turned, and the usual hum of the store seemed to dim in her presence. Lily could feel the collective gaze like a physical pressure, heavy and unrelenting. She knew Willow Creek thrived on gossip, but this… this felt different. A cold shiver ran down her spine as she pushed the trolley toward the aisles, Mandy perched in the seat, obliviously kicking her tiny legs and chattering away, completely unbothered by the tension that seemed to hang like a fog around them.

She moved quickly, her eyes scanning the shelves, snatching items off with efficient motions, each step measured and deliberate. She ignored the stares, the whispers, the silent judgment that seemed to track her like shadows. Her grip on the trolley tightened, knuckles whitening, as she forced herself to remain calm and collected. This was a mission, nothing more. Nothing personal—she told herself—but inside, a low hum of anger and irritation built steadily.

But the inevitable confrontation came at the checkout.

Mrs. Baxter leaned over the counter, eyes bright with curiosity, a thin, knowing smile curling her lips. "Ah, so this is the little bundle of joy," she said, her tone cooing, sweet, and just faintly predatory as she looked down at Mandy.

"Yes," Lily replied curtly, forcing a tight smile that didn't reach her eyes. "This is Mandy."

Mrs. Baxter's smile broadened, and Lily could sense the calculating undercurrent beneath the politeness. "Derek must be over the moon to have such a beautiful daughter," she continued, her voice gentle, but her eyes gleaming with the thrill of imagined scandal.

Lily's head snapped up, disbelief anchoring her gaze on the older woman. "What?" she demanded, her voice sharp, controlled, but trembling with rising outrage.

"Oh, don't be so shocked, dear," Mrs. Baxter continued, tilting her head as if this were common knowledge. "The whole town knows. It's Derek's child."

The words hit Lily like a physical blow, twisting her stomach, sending a surge of heat up her chest, and making her ears ring with the pounding of her heart. Shock, disbelief, and fury collided inside her in a chaotic storm. She wanted to scream, to confront, to demand an explanation—but even as her blood boiled, she held herself in check. She would not dignify their assumptions with the truth. Mandy was not Derek's. She would not give them that satisfaction. Not one whisper, not one glance, would ever be fed by her confirmation.

Clutching the trolley handle tighter, her knuckles white, Lily forced herself through the motions of the transaction. Coins, notes, the swipe of the card—all mundane acts that now felt like a performance, each polite nod and forced smile a mask pressed over the rage and humiliation roiling inside her. She could feel eyes lingering, scanning, judging, and she refused to let them see even a flicker of what she felt.

When the register finally chimed its completion and the bag was packed, she practically stormed toward the door, Mandy chattering away, blissfully unaware of the tension that followed them like a shadow. She could feel the invisible fingers of gossip brushing against her back, the subtle burn of everyone's scrutiny.

Outside, she exhaled sharply, letting the crisp morning air hit her flushed face. She pressed a hand to her chest, feeling the rapid beat of her heart, trying to steady the storm of emotions whirling inside her. Shock, humiliation, and rage swirled together, a bitter, tangled mix she refused to unravel in front of anyone.

She would not dignify it with an explanation. She would not let anyone know the truth. But one thing was certain: she was angry, she was outraged, and she was leaving that store on fire with the knowledge that the town—and Derek, and Nate, and anyone else—had just been fed a lie, carefully controlled and untouchable.

And Mandy, perched innocently in her seat, had no idea. No idea that her mother's fury was for her protection, her secret, and the bitter, unspoken truth that no one—not even the entirety of Willow Creek—would ever uncover. Lily's jaw tightened as she pushed forward, a fierce resolve settling over her like armour. This lie, this deflection, was hers to wield—and it would protect her daughter at all costs.

Nate had barely stepped into Marigold's Café when the murmur of conversation shifted—subtle, almost imperceptible, but sharp enough to prick at his nerves. He didn't need to strain; the whispers were everywhere, rising and falling like ripples in a pond, brushing past him as he made his way to the counter, each syllable scraping at the edges of his thoughts.

"—Derek's, apparently."

"Two years old, someone said."

"Lily's been hiding it—"

"Poor Nate."

"Lily told Derek last night."

That last one landed with a pitying sigh that made his jaw tighten and a low hum of heat coil in his chest.

He froze mid-step, fingers curling at his sides. Derek? Lily's child? The words tangled inside his mind, impossible and yet undeniable, floating across the café, whispered between elderly women nursing their lattes, young mothers leaning over prams, and even two paramedics on break near the window. Every corner of the small room seemed saturated with it, the gossip slipping into every crevice, impossible to ignore.

He approached the counter cautiously, as though mere movement might steady the sudden rush of heat, anger, and disbelief coursing through him. Mary, the barista, looked up, her eyes widening, her smile flickering between friendly and awkward in a heartbeat.

"Oh—hey, Nate," she said too brightly, her tone teetering on nervous. Like someone stepping carefully across shards of broken glass.

"Morning," he replied, voice gravelly, tighter than he intended.

Mary hesitated, then, as if compelled by the unstoppable current of gossip in Willow Creek, she blurted, "I guess you've… heard?"

Nate's throat tightened. "Heard what, exactly?"

Mary winced, as though she could feel her own words crawling back inside her. "About Lily's little girl… Derek Monroe is the father. Apparently she went and told him yesterday."

For a split second, everything inside him froze—heartbeat, breath, even the restless frustration he'd carried for three long years. Time itself seemed suspended.

Then heat slammed into him all at once—disbelief, confusion, and something sharp and aching that he couldn't even name. Something that felt dangerously close to heartbreak.

He forced the words out, low and tight. "People say a lot of things."

"Yeah, but this… it's everywhere." Mary leaned in, voice dropping to a conspiratorial whisper. "Beryl told half her shift yesterday. And you know what that means."

He did. It meant the whole town had accepted it as truth. Repeated it as fact. Whispered it like gospel in every doorway and hallway.

Nate stepped back from the counter, suddenly unable to stand still. The café, usually a refuge of warm light and rich coffee aromas, now felt suffocating, too small, too close, too loud with the hum of rumours dressed as certainty. Derek? Lily? The pieces seemed to line up with impossible neatness—and that made his stomach twist harder, an ugly coil of jealousy, hurt, and suspicion.

If it was true…

If Mandy was Derek Monroe's child…

Then that was confirmation that Lily had cheated on him.

Just like Derek had said.

Just like Cassie had implied.

Just like he had tortured himself over for three years, replaying every moment, every glance, every word they'd shared.

His pulse hammered in his temples as he moved blindly toward an empty table, gripping the back of a chair so tightly his knuckles blanched white. His breath came unevenly, ragged, as though the room itself were squeezing him, pressing in from every direction. He stared at the floor, but the whispers followed, curling around his mind like smoke— Derek was Mandy's father. Lily had really betrayed him. He'd been a fool.

The thought crashed into him like a stone, sinking hard and deep into his gut, and for a long moment, he felt nothing but that stone, cold and immovable.

But beneath it—all beneath the jealousy, confusion, and the sting that felt far too much like betrayal—something else clawed its way up from the place he had kept buried, silent, for years.

Doubt.

Instinct.

Love that refused to die.

A quiet, stubborn voice whispered louder than the gossip, louder than the lies and assumptions:

This doesn't feel right.

None of it fit the Lily he knew. Not her heart. Not her loyalty. Not the way she had looked at him just days ago—with hurt, yes, but also with something real, something honest.

For the first time since she had walked back into his life, clarity cut through the noise like a sharp blade.

He needed answers.

Not whispers.

Not rumours.

Not other people's lies.

The truth.

From her lips. And no one else's.

Without a second thought, Nate turned on his heel and strode out of Marigold's Café. His pulse thundered in his ears as he crossed the parking lot, each step driving him forward, fuelled by a fierce, almost desperate determination. The hum of gossip, the fragments of lies he'd just heard, faded into the background, replaced by a single, urgent need: he had to know the truth.

Sliding into his SUV, he gripped the steering wheel with tight, white-knuckled hands. Every nerve in his body screamed that he was done wondering, done torturing himself with half-truths, maybe's, and three years' worth of poisoned assumptions. His chest ached, his jaw ached, and yet—every pounding heartbeat only sharpened his resolve.

He needed answers. Real ones. From the only person who could give them.

With a deep, shaky breath, he started the engine and drove straight to Edward Hart's house. Gravel spat under the tires as he pulled into the driveway. He barely registered stepping out of the SUV, barely remembered the walk across the porch. All that existed was the single question hammering in his mind, relentless and merciless:

Is Mandy Derek's child?

And God help him… he wasn't sure he was ready to hear the truth.

He knocked sharply.

"Come in," Edward's voice called, thin and weak through the door.

Nate stepped inside, his gaze immediately drawn to the frail figure in the armchair. A blanket rested across Edward's knees; the room dim and hushed. Seeing him like this hit harder than any warning Caleb could have given—different than hearing about his decline, this was tangible. It hurt.

"Nate," Edward rasped, a tired but genuine smile brushing his lips as he extended his hand. "Good to see you, son."

Nate grasped it, startled by how light, how fragile the older man felt beneath his fingers. "How are you holding up?" he asked, voice careful, respectful.

Edward exhaled softly, a breath heavy with weariness yet tinged with quiet contentment. "I'm happier now that Lily's home. Especially now that she has Mandy." His eyes flicked to Nate, warm, a shadow of pride lingering in them.

"Yeah," Nate said slowly, cautiously. "I met Mandy the other day. She's… she's a sweet little thing."

"She sure is," Edward agreed, gaze drifting toward a framed photograph on the mantle. "Miranda would have been so proud of Lily."

Nate blinked. Miranda—Edward's eldest daughter from a previous marriage, before he'd met Lily's mother. "Miranda? Your eldest daughter, right?"

"Yes." Edward's smile softened, edged with grief. "She was always the caretaker. Always looking out for everyone. She looked after Lily after… you two…" His tone was measured, never casting blame, only reflecting a quiet disappointment that life hadn't aligned as it should.

"I'm surprised Miranda isn't here too," Nate said gently. "To help Lily with you, I mean."

Edward's expression faltered, the shadow of loss passing over his face. "Oh, I'm sure she would be—if she were still here."

Nate's stomach tightened, a cold, hollow ache settling into his chest. "I… I'm sorry. I didn't realise. When did she pass?"

"Nearly two years ago," Edward said quietly, voice low, reverent. "Giving birth to Mandy."

Nate froze completely. The world shrank to a pinpoint.

"You're saying…" His voice cracked, a fragile, barely audible sound. "Miranda is Mandy's birth mother?"

Edward nodded, the weight of memory pressing down on him like a physical force. "Yes. Lily was with her when she went into labour. It went terribly wrong. They couldn't stop the bleeding."

Nate's breath hitched, caught in his throat, his chest tightening painfully.

Edward continued, voice trembling with grief and reverence intertwined. "Miranda named Mandy herself… then begged Lily to raise her. And Lily—God bless that girl— she kept her promise. She adopted Mandy the moment she legally could."

Chapter Ten

Silence descended.

Not gentle, not quiet—

but thick, crushing, suffocating. A silence that pressed into Nate's chest, filling every corner of the room with weight. The truth gathered like a storm around him, heavy, relentless, impossible to ignore. It left him raw, shaken, and acutely aware of just how completely he had misjudged everything.

The world seemed to tilt. His breath caught in his throat, vision narrowing, as three years of assumptions—three long, bitter years of anger, of jealousy, of heartbreak— collapsed under the undeniable weight of a reality he had never dared imagine.

Mandy wasn't Derek's.

Mandy wasn't anyone's scandal.

Mandy wasn't born from betrayal, or lies, or the nightmare he had tormented himself with for years.

She was Miranda's.

And Lily—sweet, loyal, heartbreakingly selfless Lily—had stepped in, had taken her sister's child into her heart and home, raising her with fierce love and quiet devotion, all while mourning her sister…

and mourning him.

A wave of nausea twisted in his gut. Shame scorched through him; hotter than any anger he'd ever felt.

He felt sick.

He felt hollow.

He felt like the biggest fool who had ever drawn breath.

All the anger he had carried—all the bitter shards he had clung to—crumbled into dust.

And yet, even in the wreckage of his assumptions, one thought sliced through the fog, sharp and terrifying:

Why had Derek told him he'd slept with Lily?

Nate's mind reeled.

None of it made sense.

Even if Mandy wasn't Lily's biological child… Derek's claim—that they'd been together—could still have been true. Could he have believed it? Could he have lied?

A cold, hollow dread coiled in his chest, growing, tightening, suffocating.

Had it all been a lie?

Had he destroyed everything—

had he thrown away the woman he loved—

because he believed a man who might have had every reason to lie?

Because he never found the courage to ask the questions that mattered?

Because he never chased the one woman he had loved with every fibre of his being?

He remembered that night vividly. The anger, the fear, the way his voice had trembled despite his attempt at control. He had accused her—flung the words at her like daggers—and she had flinched as though struck. Her eyes had widened in shock and hurt, her hands trembling slightly as she protested.

"No! Nate—no! That didn't happen!" she had cried, voice sharp with disbelief and pain.

And he hadn't listened.

He hadn't heard the truth in her voice. He hadn't told her that he believed her, hadn't denied the accusation like she had pleaded for him to. His pride, his hurt, had shut him down. It had built a wall between them, one he'd refused to scale, and he had left her standing there—betrayed by his own stubbornness, by his inability to trust, by his fear of being vulnerable.

The past he had clung to so tightly—the story he had repeated over and over until it felt like immutable truth—began to fracture.

It splintered, jagged and raw, under the weight of doubt, confusion, and the horrifying, agonising possibility that he had been wrong all along.

Horribly.

Devastatingly.

Unforgivably wrong.

"You look like you're going to pass out, Nate. What's wrong?" Edward asked, concern tightening his voice as he studied the younger man's taut posture and pale complexion.

Nate dragged a hand through his hair, teeth grinding as his pulse roared in his ears. "Edward… what do you know about Lily and my breakup?"

Edward's brows knit together, the faint lines around his eyes deepening with memory. "All I know is that the night before she left… she came home crying like I'd never seen her before. She was… broken, Nate. Completely broken. She told me you two weren't getting married anymore." His voice softened, heavy with recollection. "I asked her why. And she said… she said you had moved on."

"I moved on," Nate echoed, the words barely a whisper, fragile in the air, as if speaking them aloud made them impossible to believe.

Edward's eyes darkened with a quiet, sorrowful weight. "And the next morning, she told me she had to leave town—that she couldn't stay here and watch you with another woman. She said… it would destroy her."

Nate staggered back a step, as though Edward's words had punched the air straight out of his lungs. His chest tightened painfully, each breath scraping shallow and uneven.

"She thought I moved on?" he whispered, voice hoarse, stunned. "She thought I was with someone else?"

Memories crashed into him like shards of glass—Lily's tear-streaked face, the raw, unguarded hurt in her eyes as she accused him of sleeping with Cassie. He had thought she'd said it just to deflect, to throw his own accusations back at him, a reflex of anger and fear.

But what if… she had believed it?

Edward's face creased with confusion, deepening the lines etched by years of weariness and worry. "Nate… wasn't that the case? Lily said the other woman told her herself. Said you'd made your choice. That you two argued about it."

Nate's head jerked up, eyes sharp with disbelief, heart hammering wildly against his ribs. He couldn't remember half of what had been said that night—not clearly, not through the fog of shock and rage. Derek had come to his apartment, smug and certain, boasting that he was going to fight for Lily—that he and Lily had slept together—that she didn't want to marry him anymore.

"What?" Nate choked out, shaking his head violently. "Edward—no. I wasn't with anyone. I didn't…"

The words collapsed inside him. Both hands clawed through his hair, gripping until his scalp burned. A cold, bitter realisation sliced through him, a chill coiling like steel in his gut.

Then it hit him. Cassie. The night before Derek appeared, she had come to him, her voice dripping with false sweetness, begging him to take her back and erase Lily from his life. He had scoffed at her, refused her outright. But she must have told Lily that she and he had been together. And when Lily had confronted him, he… he hadn't even denied it. He hadn't defended himself. He hadn't thought to, caught as he was in his own pride and hurt. No wonder she had believed it. No wonder she had left him thinking he'd betrayed her.

"God… this is all such a mess," he muttered, voice cracking, raw with the weight of three years spent holding onto a story that wasn't true.

Edward blinked slowly, processing, trying to make sense of the tangled threads. "Then… she was wrong?"

"She was lied to," Nate said hoarsely, voice splintering under the weight of regret and fury. "Edward, I never moved on. I never even considered it. I was waiting for her—for us. And I thought she was the one who…"

His throat burned, closing painfully.

"I thought she had chosen someone else."

Edward's eyes widened, bewildered and aching. "Nate… she cried all night thinking she'd lost you."

"And I spent three years thinking she'd betrayed me," Nate whispered, horror settling in his stomach like lead. "Edward… this wasn't just a misunderstanding. Someone wanted us to fall apart. Deliberately."

Edward's confusion darkened, sharpened by the edge of suspicion. "But who? And why?"

Nate's jaw clenched, fury igniting like a storm behind his eyes, every muscle taut. His hands trembled slightly as he gripped the chair beside him for leverage, voice dropping low and lethal.

"I think I know exactly who," he said, each word heavy, controlled, and filled with deadly certainty.

Caleb pushed open the door of The Rusty Kettle—the only pub in Willow Creek worth grabbing lunch in—and immediately spotted Derek Monroe hunched over the bar. Not just drinking. Sinking. Shoulders slumped, head bowed, a near-empty glass dangling loosely from his fingers, as if the weight of his own shame was pressing him into the stool.

Caleb ordered a drink, then turned his gaze fully on him.

"Derek."

Derek lifted his head sluggishly, blinking as though Caleb had materialised from thin air. "Oh. It's you." His voice was thick, slurred around the edges, heavy with exhaustion and self-loathing. "Let me guess—you're here to ask how I feel about it too?"

Caleb frowned, eyes narrowing. "Feel about what?"

A bitter, humourless sound scraped out of Derek's throat—half laugh, half groan. "You haven't heard? Apparently…" He lifted his glass in a mock toast, shaking it slightly. "I'm a father."

Caleb froze. No. Not for a second did he believe it. Mandy wasn't Derek's. Lily wasn't like that.

He opened his mouth to say so—but Derek, already halfway drunk, barrelled on, louder this time, loud enough that heads turned across the room.

"It's not mine," Derek declared, voice rising, almost desperate. "It can't be mine. I never even slept with Lily."

A heavy silence rippled through the bar. Conversations stuttered to a stop. Caleb felt his temper spike, hot and sharp, coiling in his chest. "Then why," he ground out, teeth clenched, "did you tell Nate you did?"

Derek let out a harsh, ugly laugh—one devoid of humour, raw and bitter. "Why do you think?" He slammed his glass down; liquid splashed over the rim, a small echo of chaos. "My bloody sister begged me to lie."

For a heartbeat, Caleb didn't move. Then fury punched through him like a fist, so fast he saw red.

"You what?" Caleb's voice cracked like a whip across the pub, sharp enough to make three nearby tables flinch.

Derek winced, rubbing a hand down his face. "Save it, Caleb."

"No." Caleb stepped closer, jaw tight, every muscle coiled. "You lied to Nate? You let him think Lily cheated on him? For three years?"

The bar fell into a tense, suffocating silence. Even old Tom behind the counter froze mid-wipe, eyes flicking warily between the two men.

Derek swallowed, pale and drawn. "I… I was in debt," he admitted, voice tight, almost a whisper. "Cassie said she'd pay it off if I lied. She wouldn't stop. Said she needed Nate to walk away from Lily… said it was the only way."

Caleb's eyes narrowed, shock and fury mingling. "The only way for what? To feed her obsession?"

Derek looked hollowed out, guilt carved deep into every line of his face. "She said she loved him, Caleb. And she kept insisting—she had to get him back. You know what she's like. I thought…" His shoulders sagged, voice breaking. "…I thought I was helping my sister find happiness."

Caleb slammed a fist onto the bar, rattling empty glasses, making the air feel charged with electricity. "You destroyed two lives!" His voice shook with raw anger; every word punctuated with disbelief.

Derek's defences crumbled further, words slurred as shame and regret collided. "That's not all…" he muttered, leaning back, glass trembling in his hand. "…Cassie told Lily that Nate slept with her—the same night!"

Caleb stared, disbelief and horror warring across his face. That explained everything— the miscommunication, the pain, the years of silence.

"You and your bloody sister ruined their future," Caleb hissed, voice low and deadly. "And all this time—" He jabbed a finger at Derek, cutting through the pub like a blade. "You knew."

Derek flinched as if struck, staring down at the sticky wood of the bar, shame draining what little colour remained. Around them, whispers erupted, growing louder, spreading from table to table.

"Did he just admit he lied about sleeping with her?"

"Cassie Monroe—of course she's behind it!"

"I knew that rumour never added up…"

"Poor Lily… and Nate…"

Derek's voice wavered, muttering, "Great… now the whole town knows."

Caleb leaned in, fury barely contained. "Good. Maybe it's time the truth came out. Maybe people should hear the real story instead of the lies Cassie spun."

Derek's hands shook as he pushed his empty glass away, defeated. "I didn't mean for it to go this far…"

"You don't get to hide behind intentions," Caleb growled, voice low, sharp, dangerous. "You should've come clean years ago. You should've never opened your damn mouth in the first place."

Derek's voice fell to a small, bitter whisper. "I was going to… Because when Lily turned up with the baby, Cassie wanted me to tell everyone it was mine. But I refused. I—she must have started the rumour anyway."

Caleb's jaw tightened. "Refusing doesn't erase what you said before. Or the lies your sister twisted. You helped this happen. And now people are paying the price."

Derek closed his eyes, the weight of his choices pressing down like iron on his chest. The pub felt suffocating, the hum of conversation growing louder, whispers ricocheting off the walls like a storm.

"Lily never would've done that…"

"He believed her. Poor thing…"

"I knew Cassie had a mean streak, but this—"

The murmurs swelled, spreading through the room, a wildfire of curiosity and outrage. Derek could feel it pressing in on him, accusatory eyes and hushed speculation closing in—his shame now public.

He muttered, barely audible, "I'm going to talk to Nate…"

Caleb's gaze bore into him, steel and fire. "You're damn right you are. And then you're going to talk to Lily. And if you think this ends with a simple conversation…" His voice dropped to a low growl, heavy with warning. "…God help you."

Derek sank further into his chair, head in his hands, trapped beneath the weight of his own cowardice. Around them, the truth rippled outward, unstoppable—faster than any lie Cassie had ever spun.

This time, the truth wasn't waiting for anyone's permission. It carved its path through Willow Creek like wildfire.

And Cassie? She had no hand in it. No control. Her carefully constructed world was splintering, and Derek's confession had lit the match.

Derek exhaled, heavy, hollow, the realisation settling deep: there was no turning back. The lies had ended, and everything—his guilt, his shame, the lives of the people he had wronged—was about to collide with reality.

He pulled out his phone with trembling fingers and texted Nate:

"You need to come to The Rusty Kettle… NOW!"

Lily pushed open the kitchen door, the sound of the latch echoing through the quiet house. She had cried nearly the entire drive back from the general store, hot tears streaming down her face, leaving her cheeks streaked and raw. She couldn't believe the cruelty of Willow Creek—how easily people twisted stories, how quick they were to judge, to gossip, to try and shatter the fragile peace she had fought so hard to carve out for herself and Mandy.

She set the grocery bags down with a soft thud, their weight nothing compared to the heaviness pressing on her chest. Taking a deep, shuddering breath, she stepped into the living room, Mandy balanced on her hip—and froze.

Nate stood there, rigid, jaw tight, eyes dark with exhaustion and something raw that made her stomach twist. It was a look she hadn't seen in years, yet it struck her as painfully familiar. Her heart thudded violently, a jolt of shock, dread, and a fragile hope she wasn't ready to name. She glanced at her father—Edward had dozed off in his chair, oblivious to the tension crackling in the room.

"Lily…" His voice was low, hoarse, barely more than a whisper, heavy with all the words left unsaid over the past three years.

She lowered Mandy to the floor, where the toddler immediately began stacking blocks with her usual concentration. Lily's hands clenched at her sides. "Nate… what are you doing here?" Her voice cut sharper than she intended, brittle with tears, anger, and the fear of letting herself hope.

He took a careful step forward, gaze flicking to Mandy before returning to her. "I… I had to see you. I had to talk to you."

Her chest tightened. "Talk about what?"

He swallowed hard, running a hand through his hair, eyes dark, pleading. "Us. I need to know the truth, Lily. About… Derek. About everything I thought I knew."

Her throat closed, words catching in her chest. She wanted to scream, to rip open the years of pain and misunderstanding—but she couldn't. Not now. Not with Mandy at her feet, her father asleep, and the raw ache of recent cruelty still burning in her veins.

Instead, she let out a shuddering sigh, gripping the edge of an armchair for support. "Nate… you should have asked me years ago. Maybe none of this would have happened. Maybe I wouldn't be standing here, trying to keep my life together while the town spreads lies. I wasn't important enough for you to ask for the truth."

Nate's gaze dropped, shame and regret flickering across his face. "I know. I thought I knew the truth. I thought I understood. But… I was wrong. Horribly wrong."

Silence fell, thick and tense, broken only by Mandy's soft coos as she stacked one block on another. In that quiet, the possibility of forgiveness—or at least understanding—hovered between them, fragile and uncertain.

"You need to leave, Nate," Lily said finally, her voice stronger though it trembled, tempered with steel. "If you seriously believe I did the things you accused me of three years ago… you didn't know me at all. And even if you had, it wouldn't have changed anything. You… you slept with Cassie."

"No… no I didn't," Nate said, honesty plain on his face, eyes pleading. "I would never have—"

She studied him, searching, and for the first time in years, she believed him. "I actually believe you. But that doesn't change the fact that you still believed I slept with Derek."

"Lily…" He took a tentative step forward.

"No, Nate. Just go. You chose the three years of silence. You just let me go." Her voice hardened, brittle with raw emotion—too exposed after the general store, too drained from Edward's illness, too furious at the town—to allow this conversation to spiral now.

Nate froze, just inches away, hope and fear warring in his expression.

"Go, Nate… now." Her voice trembled, but beneath the fragility, there was steel.

He froze, pain and longing flickering across his face, chest rising and falling with the effort of holding himself together. For a long moment, he seemed poised between retreat and pleading before finally taking a hesitant step back.

The air between them was heavy with years of misunderstanding, heartbreak, and unspoken truths. For now, Lily needed space—needed peace—and he could see that.

Nate reluctantly turned toward the front door, each step weighted with the gravity of everything he had just learned. His mind replayed the truths, the lies, the cruelty of it all, the steadfast love and sacrifice of Lily. She wasn't Mandy's birth mother, yet she had raised her alone, keeping a promise to her dying sister. She had never slept with Derek, no matter what he had been told.

And Nate knew, with painful clarity, that it was going to take more than words—or apologies—to make right. Winning Lily back would require patience, proof, and the unwavering effort to show her he could be the man she deserved.

He paused at the threshold, glancing back one last time. Lily sat quietly, Mandy playing at her feet, the picture of resilience and strength he had failed to see for far too long.

His chest tightened. For the first time in years, he understood the depth of what he had lost—and the enormity of what he now needed to do to earn her trust.

With a quiet, resolute exhale, he stepped out into the sunlight, leaving the house—and Lily—for now.

Chapter Eleven

Nate's car crunched over the gravel driveway of The Rusty Kettle carpark. He hadn't wanted to come—didn't want to be anywhere near the place—but an urgent text from Caleb had dragged him here. His head was still reeling from the morning's revelations, the slow, sick realisation that everything he'd believed for three years had been wrong. Assumptions. Jealousy. Lies he'd trusted instead of the woman he loved.

Now hope and dread twisted together in his chest—hope that he might still fix what he'd broken, and dread at how much it might cost.

He walked toward the bar, boots crunching softly against the worn wooden porch, and froze slightly at the sight of the two men waiting. Caleb, calm but sharp-eyed, and Derek—pale, tense, shoulders slumped, carrying the physical weight of his own mistakes. Derek was the last person Nate wanted to see, and yet, here he was.

"Hey," Caleb said evenly as Nate stepped up to the bar, voice carrying quiet authority that left no room for evasion. "We need to talk."

Nate's jaw tightened. "I'm guessing this is about the rumours going around about Mandy."

"Partly," Caleb said, his gaze flicking to Derek. "But first… Derek needs to tell you something."

Derek hesitated, swallowing hard, his hands curling at his sides as if bracing for impact. "Nate… I owe you an apology. Everything I told you about Lily—that we… it's all lies. Cassie begged me to say it. She… she wanted you out of Lily's life, and I went along with it. I was stupid, weak… I didn't see the damage I was causing."

Nate's fists clenched at his sides, nails biting into his palms. Heat surged through him, a storm of fury and disbelief, and he grabbed Derek by the collar, forcing him to meet his gaze. "You have no idea the damage you caused. I already know you didn't sleep with her. And I know Mandy isn't your kid. Hell, she's not even Lily's by birth. You little shit."

All at once, every head in the bar turned. Nate—calm, measured Nate—was gone, replaced by the raw, unfiltered rage of a man who had been hurt, lied to, and misled for years.

He shoved Derek back, stepping away, chest heaving, breaths coming hard and sharp.

Caleb blinked in surprise. "Wait… what?"

Nate's gaze hardened, eyes burning with a mix of disbelief, anger, and dawning clarity. "Lily adopted her when her sister died in childbirth. Mandy's Miranda's daughter."

Caleb ran a hand through his hair, exhaling sharply, letting the weight of the revelation settle. Then, slowly, a proud, almost reverent smile spread across his face. "Bloody hell. That's Lily."

"Yeah," Nate said, jaw tight, voice low but raw with emotion. His gaze snapped back to Derek, full of heat and accusation. "And I… I'm a bloody fool. Believing you instead of standing by her when she needed me. I let lies and arrogance ruin what we had. I don't know if I'm ever going to be able to fix it."

Derek swallowed, eyes dropping to the floor, unable to meet Nate's intensity. "There's more… Cassie told—"

"I already know that too," Nate interrupted sharply, voice heavy with finality. "Lily told me. All bloody lies. Every last one."

"I'm really sorry, Nate," Derek muttered, voice low and thick with regret. He slid onto the bar stool, shoulders slumping, the weight of shame pressing down like iron.

Nate stood a moment longer, chest still heaving, letting the truth settle into the space between them. For the first time in years, the lies had been stripped bare, exposed, and the path forward—uncertain, fragile, and terrifying—was finally visible.

"I need a beer," Caleb muttered, breaking the heavy silence.

"Yeah… same," Nate replied, his voice rough, still tasting of tension and disbelief.

Caleb ordered two beers and slid one across the table to Nate before dropping into the booth opposite him. The pub's low hum faded as the weight of what had just been said settled between them.

"So… Miranda is Mandy's birth mother?" Caleb asked, voice calm but edged with curiosity.

Nate nodded, staring down at the amber liquid in front of him as if the truth had been poured into the bottle. "Yeah. I heard the rumour at Marigold's—about Derek being the father. I couldn't accept it, not without hearing it from Lily. She wasn't home, but Edward…" His voice faltered for a moment. He swallowed hard. "Edward told me what happened. The birth went wrong. Lily was with Miranda the entire time. She named Mandy, and… she knew she wasn't going to make it." His throat tightened, voice roughening with the memory. "They couldn't stop the bleeding. Miranda begged Lily to take care of her daughter."

Caleb exhaled slowly, shaking his head, letting the weight of it settle. "And Lily… being Lily, she kept her promise."

"Yeah," Nate whispered, the single word heavy with awe and lingering guilt. "She did."

"I knew she never betrayed you," Caleb said quietly, conviction cutting through the lingering tension.

Nate let out a bitter, rough laugh, humourless and self-directed. "Yeah… I know you did. I bloody wish I'd listened to you. I was just… blinded by my own hurt." He dragged a hand over his face, rubbing away the tightness in his jaw, then lifted his eyes to meet Caleb's. Pain sat there, raw, unfiltered, and unashamed. "Caleb… I don't know if I can fix this. She didn't even want to talk to me."

"You tried?" Caleb asked him gently, a steady anchor in the chaos of his emotions.

"Yeah—and she told me to go."

Caleb's voice was patient but firm. "You're still processing everything. So is she. Lily probably doesn't even know the full extent of the lies and manipulation yet."

Nate's jaw tightened again. "God… Cassie."

"I never liked that woman," Caleb muttered, a quiet edge of disdain in his tone.

"Yeah, I know," Nate huffed out, a humourless breath, heavy with both frustration and regret. "I need to listen to you more… I should've listened to you years ago."

Silence fell again—quiet, heavy, but not hopeless. The kind of silence that follows truth, that lingers over two men sitting in the wreckage of deception, finally seeing the whole picture in stark relief.

Nate set his beer down, hands finally steadying on the table, chest rising and falling in a long, uneven breath. The truth was out—every ugly, twisted piece of it—but the hardest part still loomed ahead.

Facing Lily.

Admitting everything.

And praying, with every raw beat of his heart, that he hadn't lost her forever.

Lily lowered herself onto the living room rug as Mandy toddled over with a handful of wooden blocks, babbling happily, blissfully unaware of the storm inside her mother. Lily forced a smile and helped her stack two, though her hands trembled and her chest felt tight. Her eyes still burned—from earlier tears, and from the sight of Nate standing there, wrecked and painfully honest.

She believed him.

God help her, she believed him.

Nate hadn't slept with Cassie.

The truth sent her spiralling backward—past the rumours at the general store, past today's humiliation, back to the moment Cassie Monroe had drifted into their lives again with her perfect smile and pointed questions. Cassie had been Nate's past, and Lily had trusted him when he told her so. You're my future.

She'd wanted to believe that.

Then Cassie had befriended her.

Shame curled low in Lily's stomach as memories flickered—Cassie everywhere. The café. The grocery store. The park. And worst of all, the movies. Cassie slipping into the empty seat beside Nate, smiling sweetly while Lily, young and terrified of seeming jealous, had swallowed her instincts and said nothing.

She wished she could go back and shake that girl.

Afterward, Nate had noticed immediately. He'd coaxed the truth from her, held her close, promised her she was the only one he wanted.

And she had believed him.

Now, sitting on the floor with Mandy in her lap, Lily's throat tightened. Cassie had lied. Manipulated. Orchestrated it all. And Lily had walked straight into the trap.

Mandy pressed another block into her hand, and Lily pulled her close, blinking back tears. "I should've trusted him," she whispered into her daughter's hair. "I should've trusted us."

Her heart ached—because trust wasn't something easily rebuilt.

But for the first time in three years, she wondered if Nate hadn't been the only villain in her story.

Maybe they'd both been victims of someone else's lies.

Nate woke from a restless sleep, the kind that never really lets you fall under. His eyes burned, his body ached, and his mind—God, his mind—kept replaying Lily's face from yesterday. The shock. The hurt. The way she'd held herself together with nothing but sheer willpower.

He dragged a hand over his face and stared at the ceiling. Dawn was only just starting to thin the darkness, pale light bleeding through the curtains. He hadn't slept more than a couple of hours; every time he closed his eyes, it was her he saw.

Lily.

How the hell was he supposed to fix this?

He pushed himself upright, elbows on his knees. The house was silent. Too silent. Normally he liked the quiet—it gave him space, clarity. But today it only sharpened the ache in his chest and the restlessness that had gnawed at him all night.

He needed to get her back.

He needed her back.

But wanting it and knowing how to make it happen were two very different things.

Nate exhaled slowly, trying to think. The truth was out now. She finally believed him— at least that he hadn't cheated. That alone was a miracle. But belief wasn't trust. And it sure as hell wasn't forgiveness.

Winning her back would take time. Time he wasn't sure she was willing to give him.

And that meant he had to find a way to be near her.

Not pushy. Not overwhelming. Just… present. Showing her who he truly was. Showing her what they'd lost—and what they could still have if she let him in.

But how?

He raked his fingers through his messy hair, watching the faint light creep across the floorboards. She wouldn't agree to long talks. She wouldn't sit for dinners or heartfelt confessions—she wasn't ready.

He needed something simpler. Something that didn't feel like pressure. Something that let them exist in the same space again, even for a little while.

Because the truth was brutal and crystal clear:

He didn't just want her back.

He didn't just miss her.

He needed time with her.

Time to prove he wasn't the man who'd broken her heart. Time to show that he saw her—really saw her—and that he would never let her feel invisible again.

Nate stood and paced slowly, the sun rising higher, warming the walls around him.

He didn't have a full plan yet. But he had determination, and a truth that had nearly torn him apart the night before:

He wasn't losing her again.

Not without fighting for her, step by step, hour by hour, moment by moment.

And that fight started with one thing—

finding a way to be near her again.

Lily hadn't slept well—if she'd slept at all. Her head throbbed, her eyes felt gritty, and every muscle in her body buzzed with exhaustion. All she wanted was one quiet Sunday. One service where people didn't whisper behind her back or stare at her with that awful mix of pity, speculation, and barely contained curiosity.

Just one break from the town rumour mill.

She pulled into the church parking lot and exhaled when she saw a handful of empty spaces. Maybe—just maybe—she could slip in without being cornered by well-meaning busybodies wearing saintly smiles.

"Here we go," she muttered, glancing in the rear-view mirror. Mandy sat kicking her little legs, humming to herself, and cuddling her stuffed rabbit, blissfully unaware of the storm around them.

Her father was already unbuckling his seat belt, slow but stubborn as always. Lily stepped out and rounded the car to help him—

Only to find Caleb already there, one hand braced on the door, the other offered to her father with steady patience.

"Morning, Edward," Caleb said warmly.

Her father smiled as he took the helping hand. "You're up early today."

"Trying to earn some points with the Big Man," Caleb quipped.

Lily blinked at him, caught off guard. "Caleb? What are you—?"

But before she could finish, movement at the other side of the car pulled her attention.

Nate.

He was already at Mandy's door, opening it gently—like it was a natural thing for him to do. Mandy lit up the moment her eyes landed on him.

"Up!" she squealed, little arms shooting toward him.

Lily's heart stuttered. Mandy practically launched herself into his arms the second he freed her from the car seat. He caught her easily, lifting her with a soft, low laugh that vibrated straight through Lily's chest.

"Hey, Angel," he murmured, pressing a kiss to the top of her head.

Mandy wrapped her arms around his neck, settling against him like she'd known him her whole life.

Lily swallowed hard.

Nate met her gaze over Mandy's shoulder.

Not hesitant. Not smug. Just… steady. Soft. As if seeing her mattered. As if he was grateful for even this fragile, complicated moment.

"Morning, Lily," he said quietly.

She opened her mouth, but nothing came out at first. Too many emotions pressed at her—bone-deep weariness, raw confusion, the echo of yesterday's truths, and the sharp, unwelcome pinch of hope she wasn't ready to face.

Behind her, her father and Caleb were already chatting. Mandy was babbling happily into Nate's neck. People began trickling into the parking lot, casting curious glances their way.

Lily straightened, trying to gather what was left of herself.

She rarely lost her temper.

But she was dangerously close to the end of her rope.

And yet… watching Nate hold Mandy—natural, protective, gentle—something eased inside her chest. Something she couldn't name. Something she wasn't sure she wanted to.

She forced herself to breathe.

"Morning," she finally managed, her voice softer than she intended.

Nate smiled, small but sincere. "Can I carry her in?"

Mandy didn't even wait for permission. She tightened her hold around his neck and rested her head on his shoulder as if she'd already decided.

Lily's lips parted in surprise. The sight of them together was… disarming. Calming. Terrifyingly comforting.

But she didn't have the strength to fight over something so simple.

"Yes," she said quietly. "Just—just stay close."

His eyes warmed. "That was the plan."

Chapter Twelve

Chapter Twelve

Mandy sat on Nate's lap through the entire service without making a single sound.

Lily kept glancing at her in disbelief. Mandy never sat still this long—normally she fidgeted, whispered, kicked her little heels against the pew, or dropped her toys every five minutes. But now?

She was curled quietly against Nate's chest, one tiny hand resting on his shirt as if she belonged there.

And Nate… he didn't take his eyes off Mandy. Every now and then he whispered something soft in her ear—too quiet for Lily to hear—and Mandy would smile sleepily; her cheek pressed against him.

Lily's heart twisted, equal parts wonder, confusion, and something she wasn't ready to name.

They sat in a neat row: her father on her right, Caleb beside him. And on her left—too close, too warm—Nate. The sanctuary felt smaller than usual, the rows tighter, the air heavier.

Halfway through the sermon, Lily tried to focus on the pastor's voice, on anything but the weight of Nate's presence at her side.

But then…

His hand moved.

Slowly. Gently.

And slid over hers.

Lily stiffened, breath catching. She looked down at their hands—his fingers long and warm, covering hers completely, like they had a hundred times before. The memory hit her like a punch.

Her first instinct was to pull away. To protect herself. To keep every wall exactly where it had been for years.

But she didn't move.

Not right away.

She didn't know if it was because Mandy was resting so peacefully on his lap, or because the revelation of the last twenty-four hours had shattered old certainties, or because Nate's thumb brushed the side of her hand with a tenderness she'd nearly forgotten he possessed.

She stared at their joined hands for several seconds, her heart pounding.

Nate didn't look at her.

He just held her hand like it was the most natural thing in the world—like he was anchoring them both in a moment neither quite knew how to navigate.

Finally, Lily exhaled, a tiny tremor leaving her chest.

She didn't pull away.

Nate hadn't expected this—hadn't expected any of it.

The moment Mandy reached for him in the parking lot, something in his chest cracked open. Now, sitting in the wooden pew with her curled on his lap, her warm little body resting trustingly against him… it undid him in ways he wasn't prepared for.

She didn't fidget. She didn't make a sound. She simply laid her head on his chest and played quietly with the buttons of his shirt until she fell still.

He tightened his arm around her, his throat burning.

God, she felt right there. Too right.

He risked a glance at Lily.

She looked exhausted—fragile in a way he'd never seen her. Shadows under her eyes, worry etched into every line of her face. And yet she kept her chin high, holding herself together for Mandy… and maybe for her father too. The weight she carried was staggering, and the fact that she'd carried it alone—because he hadn't been there— gnawed at him.

He wanted to help. He wanted to fix everything. He wanted—

He wanted her back.

But he didn't deserve that. Not yet. Maybe not ever.

The pastor's voice droned on, but Nate barely heard a word. All he could think about was Lily sitting beside him, close enough that her perfume—soft, familiar, devastating— kept drifting toward him each time she breathed.

Halfway through the sermon Mandy shifted in her sleep, her fingers curling around the fabric at his collar. He adjusted his arm automatically, steadying her, and his free hand— almost without conscious thought—brushed against Lily's.

His heart stopped.

He hesitated, his fingers hovering over hers. He shouldn't. He had no right. He'd lost the privilege to touch her years ago.

But he needed her to feel something from him. Something true. Something simple and honest with no lies between it.

So, he let his hand rest over hers.

Warm. Soft. So small beneath his.

He didn't look at her. Couldn't. Instead, he kept his eyes forward, listening to the fluttering panic in his own chest.

For a moment she went still—utterly still.

He waited for her to pull away. To jerk her hand back like his touch burned her. It would've hurt, but he would've understood. He deserved it.

But she didn't.

Seconds stretched out, slow and impossibly fragile.

She didn't move.

Hope punched the air from his lungs.

He let his thumb brush the edge of her hand—slow, soft, reverent. A silent apology. A promise he wasn't sure he had the right to make yet.

He could feel her pulse beneath her skin.

He could feel his own racing in response.

And for the first time in three long years, sitting in a crowded church with the woman he'd lost beside him and the little girl he already loved on his lap…

Nate let himself believe—just a little—that maybe he hadn't ruined everything beyond repair.

After the service, everyone rose, the soft shuffle of footsteps filling the church as people began filing toward the doors. Nate kept Mandy securely on his hip, her small hand clutching the collar of his shirt. Caleb moved to help her father, steadying him with a respectful hand beneath his elbow.

Lily forced a breath and followed them out, grateful for the cool air outside—even if it carried the weight of too many watching eyes.

She had just stepped onto the path when Derek appeared in front of her.

Nate, still beside her, stiffened instantly—his entire body going taut, protective in a way that made her pulse skip. Lily placed a light hand on Mandy's back, grounding herself.

Derek's expression was strained, guilt carved into every line of his face.

"Morning, Lily," he said quietly.

"Morning, Derek," she replied, her tone cautious.

He swallowed. "Could I talk to you for a moment?"

Lily hesitated only a fraction before nodding. "Yeah. Sure."

Nate's jaw flexed, but he didn't stop her. He simply shifted Mandy higher on his hip, eyes tracking every step Lily took as she let Derek guide her a few paces away from the crowd.

Once they were out of earshot, Derek let out a long, shaky sigh.

"I owe you an apology."

Lily crossed her arms, confusion knitting her brows. "What for?"

He wet his lips, face crumpling in shame.

"I told Nate… that we slept together three years ago."

The world seemed to lurch.

Lily's stomach dropped. Her breath caught.

"You what!"

Her voice rang sharper than she intended, slicing through the quiet courtyard.

Derek winced, but he didn't back down.

"I lied. I lied because Cassie asked me to. She pushed, she begged, she said it would… fix things for her. And I was stupid enough to go along with it."

Lily stared at him, the betrayal hitting her with a delayed, nauseating force. Her heart hammered painfully in her chest.

"Derek—do you have any idea what that lie did? What it cost me? What it cost us?"

Behind them, Nate had already turned fully in their direction—shoulders squared, eyes sharp and locked on Lily. Every line of his body said the same thing: one wrong move from Derek and he'd be there in a heartbeat.

Derek's voice wavered.

"I know. And I'm sorry. God, Lily… I'm so sorry."

The words hit her like a physical blow.

Lily's head swam, the edges of her vision blurring. Too much—too much grief, too much betrayal, too much truth unravelling all at once. Her breath caught, shallow and uneven, and the ground seemed to tilt beneath her feet.

"Lily?" Derek stepped forward, reaching to steady her. "Lily—are you okay?"

But before she could even form a word, Nate moved.

In one fluid motion he handed Mandy to Caleb—Mandy letting out a startled little squeak—and closed the distance just as Lily's knees buckled.

"Lily!" His voice was sharp with fear.

She collapsed forward, but Nate caught her effortlessly, one arm around her waist, the other cradling her head against his chest. She sagged into him, unconscious, her fingers slipping limply from Derek's grasp.

Caleb's eyes widened. "Nate—"

"I've got her," Nate snapped, protective instinct overriding everything else as he lifted her fully into his arms.

And the look he gave Derek over her pale, motionless form?

Cold.

Deadly.

A silent warning that needed no words.

Nate strode back into the church, each step measured but urgent. Heads turned, murmurs rippling through the pews as the congregation gasped at the sight. Edward followed closely, Caleb supporting him and Mandy perched on his hip, her small face scrunched in worry.

Nate gently laid Lily along one of the pews, her body trembling slightly. Mandy's tiny voice broke through the silence, crying out, "Mama! Mama!" Nate's gaze softened as he looked down at the little girl, then back to Lily.

The pastor rushed forward, a glass of water in hand. Nate's hand brushed a stray curl from Lily's face as he spoke softly, his voice low and steady, grounding her.

"Hey… it's okay. Just breathe. I've got you."

Her eyelids fluttered, and Nate kept talking in that calm, steady tone, refusing to let her drift back into unconsciousness. Each word, each gentle touch, acted as a tether to reality—and to the safety she'd thought she'd lost.

Slowly, she began to respond, her fingers twitching against his arm. Nate didn't loosen his hold; his presence was solid, unwavering, a protective anchor in the midst of the chaos.

"What… happened?" Lily murmured, her voice hoarse as she tried to sit up.

Nate eased her back against his chest, supporting her carefully. "Careful. You fainted. How do you feel?" His voice was soft but edged with concern, and his eyes scanned her face as if reading every nuance.

Mandy's small cries pierced the quiet, pulling Lily's attention. Her daughter's hands reached toward her, and Lily instinctively stretched out her arms. Caleb stepped forward and gently handed Mandy over, his own expression a mix of concern and relief.

"It's okay, sweetheart. Shh… Mama's right here," Lily murmured, cradling her daughter close. Mandy sniffled, then nestled against her chest, comforted by the familiar warmth and scent of her mother.

Nate's gaze lingered on them for a moment, tense but tender, before he moved slightly back, giving them space while still remaining close enough to act instantly if needed.

"You scared me," Nate admitted quietly, his voice low and rough with emotion. He stopped himself from moving closer, as if afraid of crossing a line he wasn't sure he was allowed to cross. "I thought—"

He broke off, swallowing hard.

Lily's chest tightened at his words. Fear and exhaustion still swirled inside her, but beneath them lay something deeper—raw, aching, and unresolved. She pressed Mandy closer, inhaling the faint, comforting scent of her daughter's hair, anchoring herself in the moment.

"I'm okay now," she whispered, her voice steadier than she felt. "Just… overwhelmed. I didn't expect…"

Her gaze flicked to Nate, and for a suspended heartbeat, the years between them—pain, misunderstandings, longing—hung heavy and unspoken in the air.

Edward stepped forward, worry etched into his face. "Lily, love… are you all right?"

She looked up at him and managed a small, weak smile. "I'm fine, Dad. Really."

Slowly, she shifted to stand. Nate was instantly there, his hand firm but gentle at her elbow, ready to steady her if she faltered. She noticed. And she didn't pull away.

Together, they made their way outside. The car park was still crowded—people lingering under the guise of politeness, curiosity barely disguised. Of course they were. In a town like Willow Creek, no one ever missed a moment like this.

Edward broke the silence. "Why don't you both come to lunch," he said to Nate and Caleb, his tone warm, almost hopeful. Then he turned to Lily. "That's all right, isn't it, sweetheart?"

Lily hesitated, her eyes moving first to Nate, then to Caleb. Something inside her resisted—but something else, quieter and braver, nudged her forward.

"Yes," she said at last. "Yes, please do."

Nate's breath eased out slowly, relief flickering across his face before he masked it. It wasn't forgiveness. It wasn't resolution.

But it was a beginning.

And for the first time in a long while, Lily didn't walk away from it.

Lily kept her hands busy.

Chopping vegetables. Rinsing them. Lining them up on the cutting board with more care than necessary. Anything to stop herself from thinking too hard about the sound of laughter drifting in from the living room.

Edward sat comfortably in his armchair, talking quietly with Caleb about hospital schedules and football scores, while Nate sat cross-legged on the floor beside Mandy. He was helping her stack her colourful wooden blocks, letting her knock them over with gleeful abandon before patiently rebuilding them again.

"No, Nate—down!" Mandy announced seriously, swiping the tower with both hands.

Nate laughed, warm and unguarded. "You're right. Down it goes."

The sound hit Lily harder than she expected.

She carried a glass of water into the living room, her father's medication resting in her palm. "Dad, it's time," she said gently.

Edward took the glass with a grateful nod, swallowing his pills without complaint. "Thank you, love."

But Lily barely registered it.

Her gaze snagged on the floor.

Mandy was sitting between Nate's legs now, her back resting comfortably against his chest as he guided her small hands to stack the blocks. She leaned into him without hesitation, completely at ease. Completely trusting.

Lily stopped short.

For a moment, the world narrowed to that simple, impossible sight—her daughter, safe and happy, laughing as Nate murmured encouragement in her ear. As if it were the most natural thing in the world. As if he belonged there.

Her chest tightened.

It frightened her—how easily Mandy leaned into him, how instinctive it looked, how right. Lily had spent three years building a life that felt stable, contained. Seeing Nate slip into it so effortlessly threatened to crack everything wide open.

She turned away before anyone could notice, retreating to the kitchen under the pretence of checking on lunch. The knife resumed its steady rhythm against the chopping board, but her hands trembled now, the blade striking just a little too hard.

She had just lifted the pot lid to stir when she sensed him behind her.

"Can I help," Nate asked quietly.

She stiffened, then forced a slow breath, keeping her back to him. "It's fine. I've got it."

He didn't move away.

"I'm sorry about your sister," he added softly.

Lily turned sharply. "How do you know about Miranda?"

"Your father told me," he said, meeting her gaze without flinching. "He told me Mandy was her daughter too." He hesitated, then added, "You're a good person, Lily. For adopting her."

"I love her as if she's my own," Lily said at once, her voice firm—protective.

A faint smile touched his mouth. "I can see that. She's a little angel."

Lily swallowed, turning back to the stove and stirring a little too forcefully. "She usually doesn't take to people that quickly."

"I know," Nate said after a beat. "I noticed."

Silence settled between them—thick, weighted, but not hostile. Charged with everything they hadn't yet said.

Finally, Lily turned to face him again. Up close, she saw the fatigue etched into his features, the strain around his eyes. He looked worn down—not the confident man she remembered, but not a stranger either.

"She likes you," Lily said quietly. Honestly.

Something softened in Nate's expression, a flicker of wonder breaking through the guilt. "I like her."

The words landed gently—and devastatingly.

Lily looked away first. "Lunch will be ready soon."

Nate nodded. "Can we talk after lunch?"

She hesitated, then gave a small nod. "Okay."

"Thank you," he said.

He lingered a second longer, then turned and walked back toward the living room.

Once he was gone, Lily braced both hands on the counter, her heart pounding.

Because it wasn't just fear tightening her chest now.

It was hope.

Chapter Thirteen

Lunch passed in a fragile kind of calm.

Edward talked quietly with Caleb about town news and old memories, his voice slower than usual, his appetite small but steady. Mandy sat on Nate's lap, content to poke at her food and babble happily, and Lily found herself watching the way Nate patiently wiped her hands, murmured encouragement, laughed softly when she dropped a spoon on the floor. He didn't rush her. Didn't distract her with noise or sugar. He simply… met her where she was.

It unsettled Lily more than she cared to admit.

When the plates were cleared and the last of the tea poured, Edward leaned back in his armchair, his eyes fluttering as the afternoon light streamed through the window. Within minutes, his breathing evened out, soft and deep.

As if on cue, Caleb stood and stretched. He stepped toward Lily, lowering his voice. "Thank you for lunch. It was good."

"You're welcome," she said quietly.

He kissed her gently on the cheek, brotherly and sincere. "Look after yourself, Lily. And if you need anything—anything at all—you call me. Day or night."

She nodded, touched. "I will. Thank you, Caleb."

He gave Nate a brief, meaningful look, then headed for the door, letting himself out with a soft click.

The house settled into silence.

Lily turned—and her breath caught.

Mandy was curled against Nate's chest, her head tucked beneath his chin, lashes resting against flushed cheeks. Her small hand fisted into his shirt, her body slack with sleep.

Lily softened instantly. "She needs her nap."

Nate nodded, already careful as he rose. "I've got her."

She followed him down the short hallway, watching as he pushed open Mandy's bedroom door with his shoulder. Sunlight spilled across the pastel walls, the familiar scent of baby lotion and clean cotton filling the air.

Nate lowered Mandy into her crib with infinite care, easing his hand from hers only when she was settled. She stirred, sighed, then stilled.

He leaned down and pressed a gentle kiss to her forehead.

Lily stepped forward and did the same, her lips lingering just a second longer.

They closed the door softly behind them, the click barely audible.

In the hallway, Lily hesitated, then gestured toward the back of the house. "Let's… go sit on the verandah."

Nate searched her face, then nodded. "Okay."

Together, they walked toward the back door—toward the conversation neither of them could avoid any longer.

They sat opposite each other at the small verandah table, the afternoon light filtering through the slats, cicadas humming softly in the distance. Lily folded her hands in her lap, then unfolded them again. She didn't trust herself to speak yet—one wrong word and the fragile calm between them might shatter.

Nate watched her for a long moment, his gaze steady, searching, as if memorising her all over again.

"I want you back, Lily."

The words landed softly—but with force.

Her head lifted in surprise, eyes widening. She hadn't expected that. Not so soon. Not so plainly.

"Nate…" she began, then faltered.

"I'm serious," he said, leaning forward slightly, elbows braced on the table. There was no bravado in him now. No charm. Just truth. "We belong together."

Lily swallowed. Her chest tightened, memories rising unbidden—laughter, plans, the life she'd once imagined so clearly. She looked away, out toward the yard. "I thought that once too," she said quietly. "And then everything fell apart."

His jaw tightened, regret etched deep into his face. "Because I believed lies. Because I didn't protect you when I should have." He shook his head. "But none of that changed how I feel."

She turned back to him, eyes glossy but steady. "It changed everything for me."

"I know," he said immediately. "And I'll spend the rest of my life owning that if you let me." His voice dropped, rough with emotion. "But I never stopped loving you, Lily. Not for a single day."

The silence that followed was thick and trembling, heavy with all the years between them—and all the love that stubbornly refused to die.

Lily's voice trembled, but she didn't look away from him. "But you didn't love me enough to trust me," she said quietly. "You didn't love me enough to come after me— to fight for me."

The words cut deep. Nate flinched as if she'd struck him, the impact visible—his shoulders sagging, his breath catching, regret carving hard lines into his face. He dropped his gaze to the table, his hands curling into tight fists as though he were holding himself together by sheer force of will.

"I asked my father so many times if you'd been looking for me," Lily said, her voice steady but threaded with years of hurt. "I asked if you'd come by. If you'd called. If you'd even asked where I was." Her throat tightened. "Not once. Not in almost three years did you ever wonder where I went."

She let that sink in before lifting her eyes to him again.

"And you tell me you love me."

The silence between them throbbed.

"Do you know why I left?" she continued, softer now, more dangerous for it. "I left because it would have destroyed me to stay. To watch you with Cassie. To live in the same town, breathe the same air, and pretend my heart wasn't breaking every single day." Her voice trembled despite her effort to control it. "I knew if I stayed, I wouldn't survive it."

She swallowed hard, pain flashing across her face.

"You were everything to me, Nate. My whole world. My future. My home." Her breath hitched. "And then—overnight—it was all gone. Just… gone in a day."

Nate stayed silent, shame radiating from him, because there was nothing—*nothing*—he could say that would make those words hurt any less.

She drew in a shaky breath, pressing on because she had to. Because this mattered.

"I didn't believe Cassie when she told me she slept with you. I came to you straight away to hear you deny it. But you just accused me of cheating. We both fell for their lies." Her voice softened, but the hurt remained. "So, what makes you think we it would be different this time?"

Nate looked up then, meeting her eyes fully. There was no defensiveness in him—only resolve.

"Because this time I know what I lost," he said. "And I know exactly who I need in my life." He shook his head slowly. "I was a coward back then, Lily. I let my pride and my hurt speak louder than my love. I won't make that mistake again."

She studied him, searching his face for cracks, for false hope.

"And how do I know that?" she whispered.

"You don't," Nate admitted. "Not yet." He leaned forward, voice steady, unflinching. "All I can give you is the truth. My actions. And time. I'll earn your trust back—inch by inch—if you'll let me try."

The breeze stirred between them, lifting a loose strand of Lily's hair and brushing it across her cheek. Her chest tightened, the ache familiar and sharp—caught between the hard-won safety she had built for herself and the man who had once been her whole world, who still seemed to hold her heart without even trying.

Lily's gaze drifted past him, unfocused, pulled under by memory.

She saw herself the day she left Willow Creek—hands clenched white around the steering wheel, tears blurring the road as mile after mile slipped past. Six long hours to Asheville, each one carved from heartbreak. She remembered pulling into Miranda's driveway and falling apart the moment she stepped out of the car. Miranda hadn't asked a single question. She'd simply wrapped her arms around Lily and held her while the sobs tore free, holding her until Lily cried herself empty and exhaustion finally claimed her.

It took a week before she managed to get out of bed.

She remembered the phone call to her father—her voice small, hopeful, terrified all at once. *Had Nate asked for her? Had he come by? Even once?*

No, love. I haven't seen him.

The words had shattered what little of her heart remained. That was the moment she understood she was truly on her own. That if she was going to survive, she had to build a new life from the wreckage. And she had. Brick by brick. Breath by breath.

The memory settled heavy and aching in her chest.

She looked back at Nate, her eyes bright with unshed tears, her voice barely above a whisper.

"I don't know if I can let you do that," she said honestly. "I don't know if I'm strong enough to risk breaking like that again."

Her hand instinctively curled toward the doorway, toward where Mandy slept.

"And now I have to think about her," Lily continued, resolve threading through the pain. "I couldn't put Mandy through that. I won't. It wouldn't be fair to her."

She held his gaze, vulnerable but unyielding.

"I can't afford to fall apart again."

Nate leaned forward, urgency and conviction written across every line of his face. "It will never happen again, Lily. Never," he said firmly. "I will never doubt you again. I swear it."

His voice softened, but the certainty didn't waver. "You're the best person I know. You always have been. You would never do anything to hurt anyone—least of all someone you love. I should've trusted that. I should've trusted you."

He swallowed, eyes shining, vulnerability and longing mingling in their depths. "I was wrong. And I'll spend the rest of my life proving that I won't make that mistake again— if you'll let me."

Lily's chest tightened, a fragile hope flickering amid the fear. "I want to believe you… I'm scared," she admitted, her voice barely above a whisper.

Nate stood, moving around the table with purpose. He took her hands, lifting her to her feet, the warmth of his palms grounding her. Slowly, he let the back of his knuckles brush lightly down her cheek, a tender, feather-light touch that sent a shiver through her.

Lily held her breath, heart hammering.

"You're so beautiful," Nate whispered, his voice husky, reverent.

"You can trust me, Lily. I will never hurt you again," he murmured, eyes locked on hers, steady and fierce.

He lifted her chin gently with his fingers, bringing their faces closer. His lips hovered, a whisper away from hers.

"I want to kiss you," he breathed.

Lily met his gaze, those familiar hazel eyes darkened with desire and something deeper—relief, hope, a promise she was almost afraid to believe. Her heart gave a traitorous leap.

Their lips met softly at first, a fragile brush of warmth and memory, tender and almost reverent. It felt like coming home to something she'd never stopped missing. Lily didn't pull away. Instead, her hands rose instinctively, sliding up his chest, feeling the solid strength beneath his shirt, grounding her even as her knees threatened to give way.

Nate's hands tightened around her waist, drawing her closer.

It wasn't tentative. It was certain. Purposeful. Like a choice he'd made long ago and was only now finally claiming. One hand slid up to cradle her face, fingers curving along her jaw with quiet reverence as his mouth deepened the kiss.

The world tilted.

Heat flared, sharp and intoxicating, years of restraint unravelling in a single, breath-stealing moment. Lily's thoughts scattered, leaving only sensation—his mouth, his hands, the way her body recognised his as if no time had passed at all.

Her breath hitched, and her palms pressed against his chest as if to steady herself. Instead, she leaned into him, drawn closer by instinct alone. Her fingers traced the line of his shoulders, the tension in his neck, before tangling in his hair, holding him there.

And when she kissed him back, it wasn't careful.

It was hungry. Needy. Honest.

A low sound rumbled from his chest as her response met his, and his other arm wrapped around her waist, pulling her flush against him, her body fitting against his with devastating familiarity. She gasped into his mouth when his tongue brushed hers, the soft, involuntary moan that escaped her lips answered by a rough groan from him.

"Lily..." he murmured against her mouth, his voice thick with need and something achingly close to devotion.

Her body answered before fear could resurface—arching into him, her grip tightening in his hair, her legs shifting closer as the kiss deepened, darkened. There was fire in the way he kissed her, yes—but beneath it was tenderness. Care. A quiet awe that made her feel cherished, not just desired.

One of his hands slid slowly down her back, settling at the small of it, possessive but gentle, anchoring her to him. He kissed her like he was memorising her—her mouth, the way she breathed, the faint tremor beneath his touch—as if he never wanted to forget again.

And she let him.

When they finally broke apart, it wasn't from doubt or hesitation. It was necessity. They needed air.

Lily's chest rose and fell in ragged breaths, her lips swollen, her eyes wide and shining with wonder and disbelief. Nate's hand remained at her back, fingers curling slightly, unwilling to let her go. He rested his forehead against hers, their breaths mingling, hearts pounding in unison.

"Please, Lily," he whispered, his voice breaking under the weight of everything he was asking. "Let me try."

Her answer came so softly it nearly disappeared into the space between them.

"Okay."

Relief hit him like a breath he hadn't realised he'd been holding. He bowed his head briefly, pressing his forehead to hers. "Thank you," he murmured. "You won't regret it. I promise."

Nate left not long after, though every instinct in him fought the decision. Every part of him wanted to stay—to hold her, to reassure her, to prove with his presence that he wasn't going anywhere. But he could see it in her eyes: the way the moment had shaken her, cracked something open she'd kept carefully sealed for years.

She needed time. She needed space.

And for once in his life, Nate understood that love wasn't about pushing or proving— it was about patience. About earning trust one careful step at a time.

He walked her to the door in silence, the house hushed around them. The late afternoon light slanted through the windows, painting soft gold across the floor. Mandy's door remained closed down the hall, the steady rhythm of her nap a quiet reminder of everything Lily carried on her shoulders.

Nate paused on the threshold, hands curling at his sides as he turned back to her. She stood a few steps away, arms folded loosely around herself—not defensive, just… bracing.

"I should go," he said quietly. "You've had a lot thrown at you. I don't want to be another weight."

Lily nodded, unable to trust her voice.

He hesitated, then took a single step closer—not touching her, but close enough that she could feel the warmth of him, the sincerity in his presence.

"Just remember," he said softly, eyes never leaving hers, "I love you. I always have. And I always will."

Her breath caught.

"I'm not asking you to decide anything right now," he continued, his voice steady even as emotion tightened it. "I know trust doesn't come back overnight. But I'm not going anywhere. I'll wait—for as long as it takes—for you to be ready."

Lily swallowed hard, her eyes shining. She nodded once, a small, fragile gesture that said more than words ever could.

Nate held her gaze for another moment, committing her face to memory like he might never see her again—then gently opened the door.

As he stepped out onto the porch, he glanced back. She was still standing there, watching him, her hand pressed lightly to her chest.

"Goodnight, Lily," he said.

"Goodnight, Nate."

The door closed softly behind him, the click of the latch sounding far too final in the quiet house.

Lily stood where she was, staring at the door long after his footsteps faded from the porch. The silence he left behind wasn't empty—it pressed in on her, heavy with everything that had been said… and everything that hadn't.

Had she done the right thing?

Her chest tightened as the question repeated itself, over and over. Letting him back in—even just a little—terrified her. She had survived once by walking away, by rebuilding herself piece by fragile piece. She wasn't sure she could survive another heartbreak.

Not like that.

Not again.

And this time, it wouldn't just be her who paid the price.

Her gaze drifted down the hallway to Mandy's room, the soft glow of the nightlight spilling beneath the door. Mandy. The centre of her world. Her heart. Her reason for being strong when she'd wanted to fall apart.

If Nate hurt her again—if he doubted her, abandoned her, or chose not to fight— Mandy would feel it too. Lily had built her daughter's life on stability, on safety, on promises she never intended to break.

Was love worth that risk? Was Nate worth the risk?

She pressed a hand to her chest, feeling the ache there, the place Nate still occupied no matter how hard she tried to deny it. Loving him had never been the problem. Trusting him had cost her everything once before.

Yet… the way he'd looked at Mandy. The way he'd held Lily, kissed her, promised without pressure. The truth finally uncovered. The lies laid bare.

Hope stirred, unwanted and dangerous.

"I don't know if I'm brave enough," she whispered to the quiet house.

From down the hall, Mandy shifted in her sleep and let out a soft sigh.

Lily closed her eyes, tears burning behind her lids.

The question remained—sharp and unanswered.

Was it worth the risk… *to let herself believe again?*

Chapter Fourteen

Nate stepped out onto the porch and pulled the door closed gently behind him, as if any louder sound might undo what had just happened. The night air was cool, clearing his head a little, though his chest still felt tight with emotion. He paused at the bottom of the steps, dragging in a steadying breath, then reached into his pocket and pulled out his phone.

He didn't hesitate.

"Caleb," he said the moment the call connected. "Can you meet me at the Rusty Kettle? I could really use a beer."

There was a brief pause on the other end, then a knowing chuckle. "On my way."

Fifteen minutes later, they were seated at the bar, the low hum of conversation and clink of glasses wrapping around them. Nate took a long pull from his beer, the cold bitterness grounding him in a way he desperately needed. Caleb watched him over the rim of his glass, patient as always, waiting.

"So," Caleb finally said, setting his drink down. "Lily's giving you a chance."

Nate let out a breath that was half laugh, half disbelief. "Yeah. She's scared—but she agreed to let me try." He shook his head, a faint smile breaking through. "Thank God."

Caleb nodded, unsurprised. "You understand why she is, though."

"Of course I do," Nate said without hesitation. His voice softened. "She's got Mandy to think of. Everything she does now is about protecting her."

Caleb's mouth curved into a small smile. "That little girl is easy to love. I noticed she clung to you most of the day."

Nate's smile grew, unguarded this time. "I know. She's an angel." He stared into his glass for a moment, emotion thickening his throat. "And Lily… she's incredible. The way she loves Mandy like she's her own. No hesitation. No resentment. Just pure, fierce love."

Caleb studied him carefully. "You sound different."

"I am different," Nate said quietly. "I have to be. I won't survive losing Lily again— and I won't be the reason Mandy gets hurt. I won't make the same mistakes twice."

Caleb lifted his beer. "Then don't."

Nate clinked his glass against Caleb's. "I won't."

The conversation had finally settled into something easy—quiet laughter, shared memories, the kind of relaxed rhythm Nate hadn't felt in years. The Rusty Kettle hummed around them, familiar and warm, the sting of the past dulled just enough by truth and beer and Caleb's steady presence.

Nate was halfway through telling Caleb about Mandy insisting on feeding her stuffed rabbit peas at lunch when a shadow fell across the bar.

"Nate… can we talk?"

The voice was tight. Fragile. Too rehearsed.

Nate looked up—and his jaw locked.

Cassie stood there, eyes red-rimmed, mascara smudged, her hands twisted together like she was the wronged one. Like she hadn't set half the town on fire and walked away smiling.

For a split second, Nate felt nothing. Then he felt everything.

"No," he said flatly. "You can't."

Her lower lip trembled. "Please, Nate. I have to explain."

A few heads turned. Glasses paused mid-air. The Rusty Kettle had always loved a spectacle, and this one crackled with tension.

Caleb turned slowly on his stool, his expression dark. "You've got some nerve even coming near him, you conniving witch."

Cassie snapped toward him. "Shut up, Caleb. This has nothing to do with you."

Caleb didn't blink. "It became my business the moment you deliberately hurt two people I care about."

Cassie ignored him, her gaze locking back onto Nate, desperation sharpening her voice. "Please, Nate. Just hear me out."

That did it.

Nate stood so abruptly his stool scraped loudly against the floor. The sound echoed through the pub, silencing the remaining chatter. He stared down at her, every ounce of restraint he'd been clinging to finally gone.

"No, Cassie," he said clearly, his voice cutting through the room. "You don't get that from me anymore."

People were openly watching now. Nate didn't care.

"You lied to Lily. You destroyed my relationship. I lost the woman I love for three years because of you." His voice hardened, each word deliberate. "So, listen carefully—because I'm only saying this once."

Cassie's face drained of colour.

"You are not to speak to me again unless it is at the hospital and strictly for work. If you come anywhere near Lily or me—anywhere—I will go to the sheriff and I will get a restraining order. You have caused enough damage to last me a lifetime. It stops now."

The pub was dead silent.

Cassie looked around, finally registering the stares—hard, judgmental—and the whispers already curling at the edges of the room like smoke. Heat flooded her cheeks, shame burning through the disbelief still rattling in her chest.

"But Nate, I love—"

"Love." Nate's voice exploded across the bar, sharp and unforgiving. "You don't know the meaning of the word. The only person you've ever loved is yourself."

"Nate, please—"

"Get out of my sight." His tone was ice-cold, stripped of even a trace of restraint. "I can't stand being in the same room as you. Hell would have to freeze over before I'd ever willingly spend another minute with you."

He leaned in just enough that she couldn't miss the absolute conviction in his eyes, the finality of it.

"Lily is worth a thousand of you."

Cassie's mouth opened, then closed. No defence came. No excuse. She looked shattered—humiliated beneath the weight of every watching eye.

Then she turned and fled, the silence parting around her as she escaped the room she could no longer survive.

The moment she was gone, the pub exhaled. Low murmurs resumed, heads bending together as the story reshaped itself once again—this time with the truth firmly in place.

Nate sat back down slowly, his hands shaking now that the adrenaline had nowhere to go.

Caleb slid a fresh beer toward him. "Well," he said quietly, "that was overdue."

Nate took a long drink, his chest finally easing. "I should've done that years ago."

"Yeah," Caleb said. "But you're doing it now."

Nate nodded, staring into his glass—thinking of Lily, of Mandy, of the fragile second chance waiting for him.

And this time, he wasn't going to let anyone take it away.

Lily made a conscious effort to keep her focus on her father, on the quiet comfort of being home with him. She helped him settle into his armchair, brought him a cup of tea, adjusted the blanket over his knees. These moments mattered now—every laugh, every shared silence, every ordinary thing that suddenly felt precious.

Edward looked content, Mandy perched happily on his lap, her small hands patting his chest as he murmured nonsense to make her giggle. The sight softened Lily's chest, even as it tugged at her heart.

Edward glanced up at her, eyes warm and knowing. "I'm glad you and Nate finally talked."

Lily hesitated, then nodded. "So am I."

He smiled faintly. "You both should have talked this out years ago. You belong together."

She exhaled slowly, leaning against the doorway. "Don't get your hopes up, Dad. It's not a done deal." She nodded toward Mandy. "I have her to think about now."

Edward adjusted Mandy on his knee, his expression gentle but firm. "That's exactly why you should be together," he said quietly. "Mandy needs a father, Lily. Two parents are better than one."

Lily's instinctive response rose fast and sure. "Dad, I turned out just fine with just you." Her voice softened. "Mum died when I was so little—I barely remember her. But I had you. And that was enough."

Edward's eyes grew distant for a moment, memories flickering there—loss, love, endurance. He reached up and squeezed her hand. "You did turn out just fine," he agreed. "But it wasn't easy. And I know how many nights I lay awake wishing I could give you more."

Mandy babbled, completely oblivious, patting Edward's chin and making him chuckle.

Edward looked back at Lily, his gaze steady. "Loving someone doesn't mean erasing the past. It means choosing a future—even when it scares you."

Lily swallowed, emotion tightening her throat. She looked at Mandy, at the way she laughed so freely, so safely.

"I'm not saying no," Lily said quietly. "I'm just… being careful."

Edward smiled, pride shining through the weariness. "That's my girl."

Nate kept his distance for two full days.

It was harder than he'd expected.

He told himself he was doing the right thing—giving Lily the space she'd asked for, the space she deserved. He filled his time with work, extra charts, longer rounds, anything to keep his mind occupied. But no matter what he did, Lily was there. In every quiet moment. In every pause between patients. In the way his chest still felt warm when he thought about her in his arms.

By Tuesday afternoon, restraint gave way to longing.

Now that she'd agreed to give them a chance—just a fragile, hopeful chance—he missed her more than he ever had in those three long years apart. The ache was sharper now because hope was sharper. Because he'd felt her again. The way she fit against him like she always had. The way she'd kissed him back—not carefully, not politely, but with the same fire and need he'd never forgotten.

He couldn't stop smiling.

It was subtle at first. A softened mouth. A distracted look. But it didn't go unnoticed.

"So," one of his patients said as he checked her chart, peering up at him over her glasses. "You're in a good mood today, Doctor Cahill."

Nate blinked, then chuckled under his breath. "Am I?"

"You are," she said knowingly. "Been humming too."

He shook his head, trying—and failing—to wipe the smile from his face. "Must be a good day."

"Mm-hmm," she replied. "Or a good woman."

That earned him a laugh, low and genuine. "Something like that."

Even as he finished his rounds, his thoughts kept drifting back to Lily. To the way her eyes had softened just before she'd whispered okay. To the way her hands had fisted in his shirt like she was afraid he'd disappear again if she let go.

He pressed his palm briefly to his chest, grounding himself.

He needed to see her.

Not to push. Not to rush. Just to be near her. To remind her—quietly, steadily—that he was still here. That he wasn't running this time.

By the time he grabbed his keys and headed for the door, the decision had already been made.

Tuesday afternoon or not.

Space or not.

He needed Lily.

The dining table was covered in colour.

Sheets of paper lay spread end to end—sketches of wide-eyed animals, soft pencil outlines waiting for watercolour, notes scribbled in the margins where words would soon live. Lily leaned over one illustration, brush poised, carefully adding warmth to the smile of a small bear she'd drawn curled beneath a starry sky.

It was a children's book. A new one.

Something gentle. Something safe.

Mandy sat on the living room floor nearby, fresh from her nap, stacking her blocks with serious concentration. Every so often one toppled and she'd giggle, delighted by the chaos, before starting again. The sound lifted Lily's heart even as it ached.

From the dining room, Lily could see her father in his armchair.

Edward slept lightly, his head tilted to one side, a blanket tucked over his legs. His chest rose and fell, slower than it used to, each breath shallow. Today was a bad day—she could feel it in the air, in the way his colour was a little paler, his energy gone before lunchtime.

Caleb's words echoed in her mind.

Good days and bad days.

She swallowed, setting her brush down carefully, afraid that even the soft clink might disturb him. Watching him like this—so still, so fragile—felt like a knife twisting slowly in her chest. This strong, steady man who had raised her alone, who had always been her anchor, now looked breakable in a way that terrified her.

Mandy toddled closer to Edward's chair, clutching a block, and Lily tensed instinctively—but Edward stirred, a faint smile touching his lips even in sleep.

That was the miracle of Mandy.

Since they'd arrived, she'd brought light into the house—into him. His eyes always brightened when she laughed, when she climbed onto his lap, when she pressed a sticky kiss to his cheek. She gave him purpose on the days when pain and exhaustion threatened to steal it away.

Lily watched her daughter for a long moment, then looked back at her father, tears pricking behind her eyes.

She wished—desperately—that there was more she could do.

More time she could give him.

More strength she could lend.

More moments she could somehow stretch and hold still.

But all she could do was be here.

Love him.

Care for him.

Make the days gentle where she could.

Mandy knocked over her tower again and laughed, loud and bright.

Edward stirred, eyes fluttering open, and for just a moment, the fatigue softened as he looked at her.

Lily pressed her fingers to her lips, holding back tears, and returned to her work—painting warmth, hope, and soft endings onto the page—while quietly praying she'd have just a little more time.

The knock at the front door came softly, almost tentative.

Lily barely looked up from her work. She was just finishing the last layer of watercolour on the small bear's fur, carefully blending honey and brown until it looked warm and alive. One more touch, one more breath.

"Come in," she called.

She dipped her brush again, adding a final highlight to the bear's eye when a familiar voice rang out from the living room.

"Nate! Nate!"

Lily's hand stilled.

She didn't need to look up to know what was happening.

Mandy's little arms flew into the air as Nate stepped inside, her face lighting up like he'd brought the sun in with him. Nate didn't hesitate for a second. He crossed the room in two long strides, scooped her up, and lifted her high above his head.

"There's my little angel," he said, laughing as he gently tossed her into the air and caught her again.

Mandy squealed in pure delight, her laughter ringing through the house—bright, uninhibited, contagious. She clutched his shirt, then demanded another lift with an enthusiastic, "Again!"

Lily finally looked up.

The sight hit her straight in the chest.

Nate held Mandy as if it were the most natural thing in the world, her small body fitting perfectly against his broad frame. He pressed a kiss into her curls, murmuring something soft that made her giggle again. Edward stirred in his chair, blinking awake, a faint smile tugging at his mouth as he watched them.

"Well," Edward said quietly, voice rough with sleep but warm with affection, "looks like someone's arrived."

Nate glanced over, lowering Mandy just enough to rest her on his hip. "Hey, Edward. Sorry if I woke you."

"Worth it," Edward replied, eyes lingering on Mandy. "She brings the house to life."

Mandy rested her head against Nate's shoulder, utterly content, one tiny hand fisted in his shirt. Lily's throat tightened at the way Nate adjusted his hold instinctively, protective without even thinking about it.

He finally looked toward her.

Their eyes met across the room.

Something unspoken passed between them—relief, longing, the fragile hope of something beginning again. His smile softened, losing its playful edge, becoming something just for her.

"Hi," he said gently.

Lily swallowed, setting her brush aside. "Hi."

The house felt different with him in it.

Fuller.

And that frightened her almost as much as it comforted her.

Nate walked toward the dining table; Mandy still perched comfortably on his hip. Her small fingers curled into his shirt as she rested against him, eyes already drifting with that drowsy, post-nap softness.

He slowed when he reached Lily, his gaze dropping to the spread of papers, sketches, and paint jars scattered across the table. Watercolours shimmered under the afternoon light—gentle lines, warm colours, characters that felt alive.

"Wow, Lily," he said quietly, genuine admiration in his voice. "These are really good."

She felt the praise land deeper than she expected. "Thanks," she replied, brushing a smudge of paint from her fingers, suddenly self-conscious.

Mandy wriggled slightly in his arms and leaned forward, pointing at the page Lily had just finished.

"Bear," she declared proudly.

Nate's smile widened, pure and delighted. "That's right," he said warmly, lowering his voice as if sharing a secret with her. "That's a bear."

Mandy beamed, clearly pleased with herself, then tapped the page again as if claiming it. Lily watched the two of them, something tender and aching blooming in her chest.

For a moment, the world narrowed to this—her work, her daughter, and Nate standing there like he'd always belonged in the middle of it all.

Chapter Fifteen

Nate lifted his gaze from the drawings and met Lily's eyes. There was something careful in his expression now, hope tempered by restraint.

"I hope you don't mind," he said quietly. "I… I had to see you."

Her breath caught, surprised by how honest that sounded. "No," she said softly. "I don't mind."

He shifted Mandy on his hip, nerves flickering beneath his calm. "I was hoping I could take you all out to dinner. Nothing fancy. Just… together."

Lily opened her mouth, instinct already rising to protect herself. I don't think so—

"That sounds good, Nate."

Edward's voice cut in, warm and decisive.

Both Nate and Lily turned toward him.

Edward was watching them with a small, knowing smile, Mandy's tiny hand resting trustingly against his chest now that Nate had set her down beside him. "We've been cooped up long enough," he continued. "It would do us all some good to get out of the house."

"Dad…" Lily hesitated, her worry surfacing. "Are you sure? Today's been… a lot."

"Nonsense," Edward said gently but firmly. "I'm tired, not made of glass. And I'd like to see my granddaughter out in the world." His eyes softened as he looked at Nate. "Besides, it's been a long time since we've been out for a meal."

Nate's expression shifted—gratitude, relief, and something like awe crossing his face. He looked back at Lily, waiting. Not pushing.

Lily studied them—her father, determined and hopeful; Mandy, content and oblivious; Nate, trying so hard not to ask for too much.

Finally, she nodded. "Alright," she said quietly. "Dinner sounds… nice."

Nate's smile was slow and careful, like he didn't want to scare the moment away.

The Riverside Grill sat just beyond the bend of the creek, its wide wooden deck stretching out over the slow-moving water. Fairy lights were already twinkling beneath the eaves, their soft glow reflecting off the surface of the creek like scattered stars. It was the kind of place people came to linger—not rush—where time seemed to slow in quiet agreement.

Nate parked close to the entrance, cutting the engine before turning to Lily.

"I thought this would be easier for your dad," he said gently. "Fewer steps."

Lily hesitated only a moment before nodding. "Thank you."

He got out first, already moving toward Edward's door before Lily could reach it. Edward waved him off with a tired smile but accepted the help anyway. Mandy, meanwhile, had her face pressed to the window, little finger pointing excitedly.

"Ducks," she announced.

Nate laughed softly as he lifted her into his arms. "I thought you might like that."

On the deck, the air smelled of grilled food and river water, warm and familiar. Nate guided them to a table right by the railing, angled so Edward could sit comfortably with a clear view of the creek. He pulled out Edward's chair first, then Lily's— unselfconscious, natural, like it had always been this way.

Lily noticed. Of course she did.

Mandy barely waited before twisting in Nate's lap, transfixed by the ducks drifting lazily below. She squealed every time one paddled too close, clapping her hands and leaning forward until Lily instinctively reached out.

"Careful," Lily said softly.

"I've got her," Nate replied, adjusting his hold, his arm secure around Mandy's middle.

And he did. Lily could see it—the ease, the instinct, the way Mandy settled against him like she trusted him completely. It unsettled her… and soothed her all at once.

Edward watched them with quiet satisfaction, his lined face relaxed. "Good choice, Nate," he said. "Your mother used to like this place."

Nate smiled. "I remember."

Menus arrived, and for a while the conversation stayed light. Edward teased Nate about ordering the same thing he always had. Lily laughed despite herself. Mandy was given a small bread roll, which she promptly tried to feed to a duck that was far too far away.

Between bites and sips of water, Lily caught Nate watching her—not openly, not intrusively. Just there. Present. As if committing the moment to memory.

When she met his gaze, he didn't look away.

"You okay?" he asked quietly.

She nodded. "Yeah. I am."

And for the first time since everything had cracked open again, she realised it was true.

This wasn't a date.

It wasn't a promise.

It was just dinner—by the water, with fairy lights overhead and ducks drifting past.

But it felt right.

They were halfway through their meals when Lily noticed the shadow fall across the table. She looked up to see Beryl—Marigold Café's long-time owner and Willow Creek's unofficial keeper of news—standing there with her handbag tucked neatly under her arm.

Her sharp eyes swept over them, then softened.

"Well now," Beryl said with a warm smile. "Look at you, Lily. It warms my heart to see you and Nate back together."

Lily nearly choked on her water.

"Oh—we're—" she started, ready to correct the assumption before it grew legs and ran through town—

"Exactly where they belong," Edward cut in cheerfully, leaning over to pat Mandy's hand as she sat in a highchair between Nate and Lily.

Nate stilled, just for a second, then relaxed, one hand still steadying Mandy. Lily shot her father a look, but he only smiled serenely, clearly pleased with himself.

Beryl nodded in satisfied agreement. "That's what I always said." Her gaze dropped to Mandy, and she reached out, gently pinching her cheek. "And you, sweetheart, being looked after so well."

Lily stiffened slightly as Beryl continued, her voice softening.

"And taking care of poor Miranda's daughter… you really are something special, Lily."

The words landed like a small shock. Lily's breath caught. She hadn't realised how far the truth had travelled—or how quickly.

Nate's eyes flicked to her, searching her face, ready to step in if she needed him to.

But Lily forced a small, steady smile.

"Thank you," she said quietly. "I'd be lost without her now."

Mandy chose that moment to lean into Lily, resting her head against her chest, utterly content.

Beryl smiled, satisfied, as if she'd just witnessed something deeply right. "Well," she said briskly, straightening. "Enjoy your dinner. It's good to see things settling where they should."

With that, she moved on, already greeting another table.

The moment she was out of earshot, Lily let out a slow breath.

"Well," Nate murmured lightly, though his eyes stayed on Lily, "that won't start any rumours."

Edward chuckled. "Too late for that, son."

Lily glanced at Nate, then at Mandy curled between them, and despite herself, she felt it again—that quiet, unsettling sense that the town wasn't the only one seeing them as something more.

And that maybe… it wasn't entirely wrong.

When they got home, Nate insisted on helping Edward to bed. He moved with easy patience, steady and respectful, listening as Edward gave Nate far more instructions than necessary, his voice steady but insistent, as if he needed the reassurance of being heard. Nate listened patiently, nodding, never once rushing him.

Mandy hovered in the hallway, refusing to be coaxed toward her bedroom. She stood barefoot on the cool floor, small hands clutching the doorframe, her gaze fixed on Edward's bedroom door as if sheer willpower might open it. It was as though she feared that if she looked away—even for a second—Nate might leave before saying goodnight to her.

Only when the door finally opened and Nate stepped back into the hall did Mandy visibly relax.

She let out a little breath, then toddled straight toward him, arms lifting without hesitation.

"Night-night."

Nate smiled, crouching to her level. She wrapped her little arms around his neck, hugging him fiercely. He returned it just as gently, pressing a kiss to her hair.

"Goodnight, Angel," he murmured.

Lily felt her chest tighten at the sight.

She carried Mandy to her room, laying her carefully in the cot. Mandy barely stirred, thumb finding her mouth, eyes fluttering closed before Lily had even finished tucking the blanket around her. Lily lingered for a moment, watching her breathe, then quietly closed the door.

The house settled into a soft, familiar silence.

They sat together in the living room, lamps casting a warm, amber glow while night pressed gently at the windows.

"Thank you for tonight," Lily said after a moment, her voice sincere. "I had a really good time."

Nate smiled, relaxed but attentive. "I'm glad. I did too." He hesitated, then added, "And Mandy… she's a delight."

Lily studied his face, searching for politeness, for obligation—and finding neither. "You mean that, don't you?"

"Of course I do," he said without hesitation. "She's part of your life. So, I want her to be part of mine."

The simplicity of it stole her breath.

"She doesn't usually take to people so quickly," Lily admitted. "But you… you've won her over."

Something almost awed softened his expression. "I'm glad. I feel pretty lucky."

Silence slipped between them again—but this time it wasn't heavy. It was warm. Expectant. Full of things Lily wasn't ready to say out loud but no longer willing to deny.

For the first time in a long while, more didn't feel terrifying.

It felt possible.

Nate wanted to pull her into his arms and lose himself in her—to forget restraint, to forget time. The want sat sharp and insistent in his chest, growing harder to ignore with every second he breathed the same air, felt the pull of her presence.

He stood abruptly, as if distance might save him from himself.

"I'd better go," he said, his voice rougher than he meant it to be. "Thank you for coming out tonight, Lily."

She blinked, caught off guard. "Oh… okay." She rose too, walking him to the door, even as disappointment tugged at her. She didn't want him to leave. Not when the memory of Sunday's kiss still lived on her lips—warm and vivid.

They stopped at the door.

Nate's hand closed around the handle. He turned to say goodbye—and froze.

Lily stood inches away, cheeks faintly flushed, lips parted as if she might say his name. The porch light caught her in soft gold, achingly familiar.

Something inside him gave.

With a low breath, he turned fully and gathered her into his arms, pulling her close before doubt could intervene. His mouth found hers in a kiss that was anything but hesitant—deep, hungry, charged with everything he'd been holding back.

Lily gasped softly, then melted into him, her hands curling into his shirt as if anchoring herself. The world narrowed to the heat between them, to the certainty of his arms, to the way his kiss spoke of longing and promise all at once.

Her arms slid around his neck, drawing him closer, as though letting go now might undo everything they had just reclaimed. Nate's lips left hers, lingering only long enough to make her ache before they traced along her jaw, unhurried, reverent, down the delicate curve of her neck. Lily shivered, a soft, helpless sound slipping from her as he breathed her in, as if committing her to memory all over again.

"God, Lily," he murmured against her skin, his voice rough with feeling. "I've missed this. Missed you."

His mouth returned to hers, the kiss deeper now, fuller—charged with longing and loss, with all the moments they'd been denied. Years of absence poured into a single, breathless instant. Lily met him without hesitation, rising into him, her hands tightening at his shoulders. She wasn't holding back anymore. The want between them hummed, electric and undeniable.

His hands firmed at her waist, drawing her closer until there was no space left between them, until she could feel the strength in him, the tension he was barely containing— for her sake as much as his own. It wrapped around her, steady and intoxicating.

"Lily…" Her name left his lips like a vow, heavy with meaning.

"I've missed you too, Nate," she breathed, the confession trembling free before she could stop it, honest and raw.

The sound he made in response was low and rough, vibrating against her as he kissed her again—consuming, unrestrained, as if the world beyond them had ceased to exist. Everything tilted, spun, narrowed to the feel of him, the warmth of his body, the truth beating between them.

Then, slowly—far too slowly—he pulled away.

She knew it cost him something. She could see it in his eyes, feel it in the way his hands lingered at her waist, reluctant to let her go. He wanted more—wanted to scoop her up, carry her to bed, show her how deeply he loved her, how fiercely he wanted her there, in his arms, in his life, in his heart.

"I'd better go…" he said quietly, restraint threading every word.

Lily nodded as they finally stepped apart, the air between them still charged. "Good night, Nate," she whispered.

He brushed a kiss to her cheek, tender and lingering. "Sleep well, sweetheart."

Then he turned and left, before temptation outweighed patience, before he did something she wasn't quite ready for yet.

Nate had been true to his word. He didn't pressure her—not once. He texted her often, sending little check-ins that made her heart flutter, called at least once a day with a calm, familiar voice, and came to dinner almost every other evening, sitting quietly beside her, letting her set the pace. Lily threw herself into her days, balancing time with her father and Mandy, sketching and storyboarding for her new children's book, and somehow managing to keep her heart steady against the pull she felt toward Nate. Each glance, each brush of his hand as he helped with Mandy, left her trembling with emotions she wasn't ready to fully name.

It had been ten days since that night—the kiss, the heat, the restraint—and with every passing hour, it was becoming harder to hold herself back. She wanted so badly to tell him she loved him, to let the walls around her heart crumble, but fear clenched tight. He had told her, over texts, over dinners, over quiet moments with Mandy at her feet, that he loved her. That he loved Mandy too. And still, she couldn't respond in kind—not yet. Not while the ghost of the past still whispered in her ear that he might hurt her again.

The house was quiet, filled with the soft, comforting sounds of everyday life—the clatter of Mandy's blocks as she built a wobbly tower, the scratch of Lily's pencil across her drawing pad. Lily glanced up, smiling at the sight of Mandy carefully stacking coloured blocks, when the calm shattered. A sudden, strangled gasp pierced the air. Her father's face was pale and slick with sweat, his hands clutching his stomach as he doubled over in pain.

"Dad?" Lily's voice broke as she leapt to his side, her heart hammering. Panic clawed at her chest as she caught him before he collapsed. "What—what's wrong?"

Edward groaned, every line of his body taut with agony. "Lily… my stomach… it's—" His words cut off in another harsh gasp as pain wracked him. Lily's mind raced. She had learned to watch for his weakness, for the signs that his prostate cancer was advancing, but this was sharper, more urgent than anything she'd seen before.

"Mandy, honey, stay there," Lily said softly, keeping her tone calm even as her hands trembled. She supported her father to the couch, helping him sit, pressing a damp cloth to his forehead. The room felt suddenly too small, the quiet shattered by the rapid beating of her own heart. She knew, instinctively, that this wasn't just another bad day—it was something more, something that demanded action, fast.

Her breath came fast, mingling with Edward's shallow gasps. "I'm calling an ambulance," she said, fumbling for her phone, the words tasting like fear and desperation on her tongue. "Stay with me, Dad. Just stay with me."

Mandy's small voice piped up, worried and confused, "Grandpa?" She toddled closer, looking from her mother to her grandfather, sensing the tension. Lily scooped her up quickly, brushing her hair back, trying to shield her from the panic rising in the room, even as her own chest felt ready to burst.

And in that moment, amidst the fear, the urgency, and the helplessness, Lily's mind spun—worrying, hoping, praying—that he would be okay. That they would make it through this, together.

Minutes stretched into what felt like hours, the quiet of the afternoon broken only by the distant wail of ambulance sirens growing closer, sharper, more urgent. Lily stayed at Edward's side, arms wrapped tightly around him, whispering soothing words she barely believed herself. When the paramedics arrived, they moved quickly, lifting him onto a stretcher with practiced efficiency, their calm professionalism doing little to ease the storm of panic in her chest.

The ride to the hospital was tense and fast. Lily and Mandy rode in the back with Edward, holding his hand and murmuring comfort while the paramedics monitored his vitals, adjusting equipment and calling out instructions. Mandy clung to Lily, wide-eyed and silent, sensing the gravity of the moment even if she didn't fully understand it. Lily kept her focus split—steadying her father, reassuring Mandy, and keeping herself from spiralling into fear.

Chapter Sixteen

Nate had just finished his last appointment for the day when Nurse Johnson came rushing toward him. "Doctor Cahill! Doctor Winters said you should go to emergency—Edward Hart has just been admitted!"

Nate's heart skipped, then pounded uncontrollably. Lily… Mandy… that was all he could think of. He didn't wait for another word. He bolted down the hallway, his shoes echoing against the tile, adrenaline surging through him with every step.

Bursting into the emergency department, he scanned the room and immediately spotted Lily, sitting rigid in the waiting area, Mandy clinging to her like a lifeline, her small face wide with fright.

"Lily!" Nate called softly, urgency and relief colliding in his voice. He pushed past the nurse and knelt beside her. "I'm here. He's going to be okay."

Lily's breath hitched, tears spilling over. "I… I didn't know what to do, Nate. I was so scared."

Nate took her hand, gripping it firmly. "I know. You did everything right. You got him here. You kept Mandy safe. That's all that matters right now."

He pulled up a chair beside her, draping an arm around her shoulders while his other hand rested lightly on Mandy's back, trying to ground them both in the midst of chaos.

Minutes later, Caleb emerged from the emergency bay, his expression serious but calm. Nate and Lily both rose instinctively, anticipation and dread written on their faces.

"He's stable now," Caleb began, placing a reassuring hand on Lily's shoulder. "But he had an acute urinary retention that caused a serious infection. It's painful, and it came on suddenly. They had to catheterize him and start antibiotics immediately."

Lily's hands flew to her mouth, eyes wide. "Is he going to be okay?"

Caleb nodded firmly. "Yes. The infection was caught in time, and the treatment is working. He'll need to rest here for a couple of days so they can monitor him, make sure the infection clears and that he's passing urine normally again. But he's stable, Lily. You don't have to worry—he's going to make it."

Relief hit Lily like a wave, and she exhaled shakily. Nate's hand tightened around hers, and she let herself lean into him, letting a fraction of the fear melt away. Mandy clung to her chest, oblivious to the seriousness but feeling the tension ease in her mother's arms.

Nate's jaw softened, eyes locked on Lily's. "See? He's going to be okay. And we're right here with him."

Lily nodded, swallowing past the lump in her throat, gratitude and lingering terror mixing into a fragile calm.

The hospital hallway smelled sharply of antiseptic and disinfectant, sterile and unyielding. Nate led Lily and Mandy through the sliding glass doors into Edward's room, where the steady beep of the monitor punctuated the quiet rustle of nurses moving in and out.

Edward lay propped up on pillows, a thin blanket drawn to his chest. His skin was pale, and his hair was a little more dishevelled than usual, the subtle lines around his eyes and mouth deepened by both pain and fatigue. Even so, when he saw them, a small, weary smile tugged at his lips.

"Lily… Nate," he rasped, voice weak but warm. "I'm glad you're here."

Lily hurried to his side, standing beside the bed, Mandy clinging to her shoulder. "Of course we're here, Dad. You had us worried half to death."

Edward's hand reached out, fingers trembling slightly as they rested over hers. "I'm okay… just a little scare. Nothing I can't handle. But… thank you for getting me here." His gaze softened as it flicked to Nate. "And you, Nate… thanks for looking after these two. I appreciate that more than I can say."

Nate stepped closer, placing a reassuring hand on Edward's shoulder. "We wouldn't be anywhere else. How are you feeling?"

Edward gave a weak chuckle, the sound hoarse. "Like I've wrestled with a wild bull… and lost. But I'll survive. This old body's stubborn."

Lily's eyes brimmed with tears, relief threatening to spill over. She squeezed her father's hand. "You scared me, Dad. I thought—"

"You thought the worst," Edward finished for her, his smile lopsided but sincere. "I won't lie; it was scary. But you got me here in time. That's what matters."

Edward's gaze lingered on them both, exhaustion and pride mingling. "You two belong together… I always thought so. Never understood why you split."

Nate's jaw softened. "That was my fault, Edward. But I will never make that mistake again."

"Good. She's a good woman," Edward said, looking at Lily tenderly.

"And standing here," she added tartly, unable to resist.

Mandy wiggled in Lily's arms, tugging gently at Edward's sleeve. "Grandpa," she whispered, small and serious, as if she understood the gravity of the moment.

Edward's tired eyes sparkled. "Hey, little firecracker," he rasped, his hand brushing over hers. "You've got your mama's spirit."

Lily leaned down, resting her forehead against his arm. "You've got to take it easy, Dad. No more scaring us like that."

Edward chuckled softly, a tremor in the sound. "I'll try… I'll try. But no promises."

Nate rested a hand on Lily's back, and she leaned slightly into him, their fingers brushing, grounding one another. For a fleeting moment, the hospital room felt warm and protective—a haven against the panic and uncertainty that had gripped them all earlier.

Edward's eyes softened further, drifting closed for a moment as he exhaled. "Being scared… it reminds me that I'm alive. And seeing you two together… that's worth everything."

Lily whispered, barely audible, "We're not going anywhere."

Nate's thumb brushed over the back of her hand, and he murmured, "Ever."

Edward smiled faintly, the lines around his eyes deepening. "Good… good. That's all I need."

The room fell into a quiet, comfortable rhythm—soft breaths, the gentle beep of the monitors, the small weight of Mandy nestled between them, and a fragile but unshakable sense of unity.

They sat and talked, helping the time pass, while Mandy started to get fidgety. Then she tugged at Nate's sleeve, her little voice uncertain. "Dadda… Grandpa okay?"

Lily froze for a heartbeat, startled by the word, and Nate's gaze shifted down to the tiny girl clinging to Lily.

"She just called me 'Dadda'," he said, voice filled with awe, a small, incredulous smile tugging at his lips.

Lily blinked at him, surprised, then nodded slowly, her lips curving into the faintest smile.

Nate gently took Mandy from Lily's arms and wrapped her tiny body in his. "He's getting the best care, sweetheart. You're safe. Mama's right here—and I'm here too."

Mandy's eyes widened, trust and relief shining through, and she nestled against him for a moment. Lily's chest tightened, a rush of gratitude and something warmer— something tender—spreading through her as she watched the two of them. In that moment, the chaos of the hospital, the fear for her father, and the weight of the world seemed just a little lighter.

Edward laughed softly, sleepily. "Well, looks like Mandy has it all worked out."

Lily's eyes met Nate's, but she couldn't say anything—not yet. Instead, she let herself simply breathe, savouring the fragile, fleeting calm that had settled over them.

They didn't stay much longer, gently tucking a drowsy Edward into bed and promising they'd be back the next day. As they stepped out into the corridor, Caleb caught sight of them. He smiled, taking in the image—Nate holding Mandy securely in one arm, his other hand wrapped around Lily's.

"Back where you both belong," Caleb said, warmth and quiet certainty in his voice. They both knew exactly what he meant.

Lily chose not to respond. Instead, she reached for Caleb's hand and gave it a grateful squeeze. "Thank you for looking after Dad."

"You know I'd do anything for you," Caleb replied softly, sincerity etched into his expression.

Nate led them out to his car. Lily climbed into the backseat with Mandy—no car seat—while Nate took the driver's seat. The drive home passed in a quiet calm, the kind that settles after fear has finally loosened its grip.

Once inside, Lily moved through the familiar routine—feeding Mandy, bathing her, and settling her into bed. Nate lingered in the doorway, then leaned in, pressing a soft, lingering kiss to Mandy's temple after Lily had finished, a silent promise in the gentle gesture.

When the bedroom door clicked closed behind them, the house fell quiet. Nate turned to Lily, his voice low, careful, as if the question mattered more than anything else.

"Lily… are we back together?"

She hesitated, honesty tightening her chest. "Honestly… I don't know what we are."

He stepped closer, lifting one hand to cup her face, his thumb brushing slowly over her cheek. "I love you, Lily," he said quietly, fiercely. "And I need you."

Her breath caught at his words. Love. Need. They struck too close to the fragile places she'd been guarding for years. She didn't pull away from his touch—but she didn't lean into it either. She stood suspended between longing and fear, her heart aching with everything she wanted and everything she was terrified to lose again.

"Nate…" Her voice wavered. She swallowed, forcing herself to meet his eyes. "I don't know. You broke me. I rebuilt my life piece by piece and I did it believing I was alone." Her throat tightened. "If I say we're back together, I need to know that when things get hard—when there are rumours, doubt, or someone whispers poison in your ear—you won't walk away again."

His thumb stroked her cheek, slow and reverent, as if memorising the softness of her skin. He understood the weight of what she was saying. His jaw tightened, emotion flickering raw and unguarded across his face.

"I don't blame you," he said quietly. "I wouldn't trust me either—not after what I did. I thought I was protecting myself, but all I did was abandon the woman I loved." His voice roughened. "I live with that every day."

She wrapped her arms around herself, shoulders curling inward. "I can't survive that kind of pain again, Nate. Mandy can't either. I have to be sure."

"I know," he said softly. "And I swear to you—I will never do that to you again. Ever."

Her voice dropped to a whisper. "I want to believe you."

He slid his hand to the nape of her neck, kneading gently, grounding her. Lily leaned instinctively into his touch, her resistance softening, melting beneath his quiet patience. His other hand settled at her waist—slow, deliberate—drawing her closer until there was no space left between them, until she could feel the steady strength of him anchoring her.

He kissed her then—soft and unhurried, barely there. Just a whisper of his lips against hers. Another followed, lingering at the corner of her mouth, teasing. Then one just beneath her ear, warm and intimate, his breath brushing her skin and sending a shiver straight through her.

When his lips returned to hers, deeper this time, a low sound slipped from her before she could stop it. She slid her hands up his chest, fingers fisting in his shirt, and kissed him back—no hesitation now, no fear—only the quiet, undeniable pull of a love that had never truly faded.

Something in Lily finally let go.

Her arms slid around his neck, pulling him flush against her, and she kissed him harder—sure, hungry, and full of everything she'd been holding back.

Nate kissed her with a passion he could no longer resist, all the control he'd been clinging to slipping the moment her lips softened beneath his. His mouth left hers only to trace the curve of her cheek, the line of her jaw, lingering at the sensitive skin beneath her ear where her breath hitched despite herself.

"Lily," he whispered, his voice rough now, threaded with emotion he wasn't even trying to hide.

She felt it—the pull between them, the taut, humming tension, the unmistakable sense that this moment was balancing on the edge of something irreversible. Her breathing quickened, thoughts blurring, dissolving into sensation and need.

"I want you," he said quietly, the honesty in his words almost painful. "God, Lily… I want you so much it hurts."

Her heart thundered in her chest. "Nate…?" The sound of his name trembled out of her, half question, half surrender.

He opened his eyes, and what she saw there stole the rest of her breath. It wasn't just desire. It was love. Care. A fierce, steady determination to do this right—to protect her even while wanting her.

"I love you," he said softly. "And I don't want to stop. But I don't want to rush you."

Her cheeks flushed, warmth spreading through her. "I want you too, Nate," she admitted, her voice barely more than a breath.

He groaned low in his throat and lifted her without effort, her legs wrapping instinctively around his waist as if her body had already decided. He carried her down the hall to her bedroom, shouldering the door open and nudging it closed again with his foot, the click sounding unnaturally loud in the quiet.

He set her on her feet at the side of the bed, hands firm but gentle at her waist, grounding her.

"Tell me if you don't want this?" Nate said, his gaze searching hers, serious beneath the heat.

She nodded, but her hands betrayed her words, moving frantically to unbutton his shirt. At the same time, his fingers found the zipper at the back of her dress, drawing it down slowly, deliberately, as if savouring every second.

His shirt slipped from his shoulders with her help, and then her palms were pressed to his broad, bare chest. He groaned at her touch, the sound vibrating beneath her hands.

When the zipper reached her waist, the dress loosened, sagging enough to reveal her bare breasts. His breath caught, his eyes darkening with awe. "You're so beautiful, Lily."

She felt suddenly shy, suddenly seen—but she didn't look away. She shimmed the dress down over her hips, letting it pool at her feet until she stood before him in nothing but her silk panties, heart racing.

Her fingers moved to his trousers, fumbling slightly as she worked them open and pushed them down his legs along with his underwear. His arousal was impossible to miss, and the knowledge that she was the reason for it sent a rush of heat through her.

They kissed again, deeper this time, their hands everywhere—exploring, holding, memorising. Without breaking the kiss, he lifted her once more and laid her back on the bed, following her down a heartbeat later, his weight warm and solid over her as the world narrowed to the two of them.

A strangled cry tore from her throat as he cupped her breast for the first time, his palm hot against her sensitised skin. He groaned low in his chest, flicking his thumb over her hardened peak—once, then again when she arched into him with a helpless whimper. Their mouths fused, the kiss deep and drugging, tongues tangling, breath mingling, until nothing existed beyond the blistering intensity of their connection.

His hands roamed over her body—learning her, mapping her. When he found the silken curve of her thigh, he stroked her with deliberate slowness, igniting a fresh rush of heat between her legs.

Then he tore his lips from hers, dragging them down her body in a scorching trail. His mouth closed over one taut nipple, his tongue flicking, teasing, before he sucked deeply, pulling a broken moan from her lips.

Her fingers tangled in his hair, clutching him close as her breath came in ragged, broken bursts. He kissed his way lower—slow, unhurried—tracing the smooth plane of her stomach, his lips and tongue reverent, worshipping every inch of her as if she were something sacred.

He hooked his fingers into the waistband of her panties and slid them down her legs with deliberate care, letting them fall away before tossing them aside with the rest of their discarded clothes, leaving her bare, exposed, and trembling beneath his gaze.

He pushed her thighs apart and reached between them. She gasped when his fingertip slid over her slick, satin heat—stroking, circling, coaxing more from her. Kneeling between her legs on the bed, he lowered his head.

"Lily…" he murmured her name like a prayer.

And then he tasted her.

Pleasure detonated inside her. It was so intense her hips shuddered beneath him. He held her steady, swirling his tongue through her wetness, drinking in every sound she made.

Then he was devouring her—tongue stroking, circling, teasing the tight bud of her pleasure until she writhed beneath him, sobbing his name. When he slid a long, masculine finger inside her, she nearly came undone. She was tight—so tight—her muscles gripping him. He withdrew slowly, then thrust in again, setting a torturous rhythm that dragged her higher, and higher, until she was teetering on the edge.

"Nate, please." Her voice was fractured, pleading.

He groaned against her, the vibration sending another jolt ripping through her. "God Lily, you're everything," he groaned, breath warm against her fevered skin.

Tremors slammed through her. Her back arched off the bed as she held her breath, eyes squeezed shut, lips parted in a silent gasp. His tongue stroked her—rough, relentless—then softened, twirling her with the delicate flick of its tip.

Her entire body tightened—arching once more—

—and she exploded with a scream of ecstasy.

Another strangled cry tore from her as wave after wave crashed over her. He held her through it, his mouth lingering, drawing out every last shudder until she collapsed beneath him, trembling and utterly wrecked.

Slowly, reverently, Nate kissed his way back up her body, tracing every dip, every curve, worshipping her with every touch. He hovered over her again, his body settling between her parted thighs, the heavy weight of his arousal pressing intimately against her softness.

Their eyes met, holding in the quiet intensity of the moment.

"I'll be careful," he murmured, voice low, heavy with promise. She could hear it, feel it—an anchor in the storm of firsts she was facing.

Heat flamed across her cheeks, and a fragile smile curved her lips. She slid her arms around his neck, tilting up to kiss him—slow, tentative at first, then melting into trust. Every inch of her said she belonged here, in this moment, with him.

He leaned in, letting the world shrink down to her. One long, deliberate stroke brought him inside her, brushing the edges of restraint. She was warm, impossibly tight, gripping him like her body had been waiting for his all along.

A soft whimper escaped her, and he froze, chest hovering above hers, letting her adjust, letting her feel safe. He brushed a kiss across her lips, gentle, grounding, and she responded in kind. Slowly, hesitantly, her tension began to ease under his touch.

When she softened, he moved again. Deliberate at first—slow, careful, attuned to her reactions. Gradually, he let the rhythm deepen, each stroke measured but insistent. Her breath caught. Her pulse thrummed against his chest. Every movement sent sparks through him, pleasure echoing back like a living thing.

Her nails scored his shoulders. Her hips clenched, pressing him closer, pulling him in ways that threatened control. Nate's jaw tightened. His eyes squeezed shut. Every muscle fought the instinct to lose himself, to sink fully into her.

Not yet. Not yet.

He slowed again, letting her set the pace, savoring the way she softened against him, letting every inch of him connect with every inch of her. Each thrust was a claim, a memory, a promise. She gasped, soft and desperate, winding him tighter with each shuddering breath.

And then—she broke.

A white-hot rush rolled through her, body clenching, trembling, pulling him forward. Her cry of his name pierced him, raw and beautiful.

"Nate…"

Every nerve screamed. He groaned low in her neck, surrendering the last threads of restraint. He moved with her, deep, slow, grounding, matching her body's rhythm, drinking in the way she clung to him.

Her warmth, her tightness, her trust—it consumed him. A guttural growl tore from his chest as he followed her over the edge, the world collapsing to heat, to moans, to the weight of her pressed against him.

When it was over, he stayed inside her, chest to chest, arms wrapped tight. The quiet aftershock settled around them, the kind of silence that hums in your bones.

And God… he never wanted to let her go.

Chapter Seventeen

He didn't move for a long time, simply savouring the feel of her beneath him—the warmth, the softness, the lingering echo of the pleasure they had just shared. Every breath felt heavy with awe, with disbelief, as if his body and heart were still trying to catch up to what had just happened.

Finally, carefully, he disengaged from her molten heat and rolled onto his back, drawing her with him so she lay curled against his side, her head resting over his chest. One arm wrapped around her instinctively, holding her close. He needed her there, needed the quiet reassurance of her weight and warmth.

"Nate…" she whispered softly, exhaustion threading through her voice as her lashes fluttered closed.

He bent his head and kissed the top of her hair, breathing her in. He couldn't speak. Couldn't move. He just lay there, staring up at the ceiling, stunned and reverent, his mind replaying the moments they'd shared, the connection that felt far deeper than anything physical.

He felt her shift slightly, her body relaxing fully against his, her breathing slowly evening out until it fell into a soft, steady rhythm. She was asleep.

The knowledge settled over him gently, almost reverently, filling his chest with something dangerously close to peace. Lily—strong, guarded, endlessly careful—had let go. She felt safe enough, trusted him enough; to surrender to sleep with her head over his heart, her warmth curled into him as though she belonged there.

Nate didn't move.

He barely breathed.

He stayed perfectly still, afraid that even the smallest shift might break the fragile spell of the moment. He wrapped his arm more securely around her, not to claim her, but to protect her—to be the solid thing beneath her rest. If staying awake all night was the price of this quiet, he would pay it gladly. He would stay awake as long as it took, just to keep her safe, just to be here when she woke.

His gaze drifted to the ceiling; his thoughts slow and heavy with awe.

He knew it now. With a certainty that settled deep in his bones.

Lily loved him.

She would never have given herself to him—body or heart—if she didn't. That kind of trust didn't come from confusion or weakness. It came from love, from a bond that had never truly broken, only bruised and buried under fear.

She wasn't ready to say the words yet. She was still too scared of what loving him again might cost.

But he could wait.

He would wait.

As long as it took.

Because holding her like this—warm, trusting, asleep against his heart—was proof enough that love had never truly left them. It had only been wounded, hidden beneath the lies, buried under fear and misunderstanding. And this time, Nate would protect it with everything he had, guard it fiercely, and cherish it without hesitation.

They came together again before the sun crested the horizon, the quiet intimacy of early morning wrapping around them like a promise. Lily was different now—bolder, more sure of herself, her confidence blooming as she reached for him first, unafraid of what she wanted. Nate felt it in every touch, every breath she shared with him, and it stole something deep and vital from his chest.

He didn't question it. He didn't slow her down.

He simply loved her—completely, overwhelmingly—focused only on her, on the way she smiled, the way she trusted him, the way being with her felt like coming home. If happiness was something he could give her, then he would spend the rest of his life doing exactly that.

Soft morning light filtered through the curtains, warm and pale, painting the room in gentle gold. Lily stirred slowly, awareness returning in layers—the steady rise and fall beneath her cheek, the solid warmth at her back, an arm curved securely around her waist.

Nate.

The realisation settled like a breath she hadn't known she was holding.

She shifted slightly, careful not to wake him, but his arm tightened instinctively, drawing her closer. His chin rested against the crown of her head, and she felt the faint brush of his lips in her hair—sleepy, unguarded affection.

"Mmm… morning," he murmured, voice rough with sleep.

Her heart fluttered. "Morning," she whispered back.

He pressed a slow kiss to her temple, then another to her cheek, his hand sliding up and down her arm in an absent, soothing motion. "You okay?"

She nodded, though a flicker of self-consciousness stirred. Being held like this—so open, so seen—still felt new. Vulnerable. She subtly tugged the sheet higher, hoping he wouldn't notice.

He noticed.

His hand stilled, then cupped her gently, thumb brushing her skin. "Hey," he said softly, tilting his head so she had to look at him. His eyes were warm, steady. "You don't have to hide from me."

She swallowed, forcing a small smile. "I'm not," she lied lightly.

His mouth curved, fond and knowing. "You are the most beautiful thing I've ever woken up next to," he said simply, like it was a fact, not flattery. "Last night was amazing."

Heat crept up her neck. She ducked her head, tucking her face against his chest. "Nate…"

"And hopelessly in love with you," he continued without hesitation, his arm tightening protectively.

She let herself breathe there, listening to his heartbeat, letting the moment exist without analysing it—until the door creaked open.

"Mama?"

Lily lifted her head just as Mandy padded into the room, curls mussed, clutching her stuffed rabbit. Her face lit up when she spotted them together.

"Mama! Dadda!" Mandy squealed, breaking into a run.

Before Lily could even react, Mandy launched herself onto the bed, climbing over the blankets with determined enthusiasm and wedging herself right between them.

"Oof," Nate laughed, shifting to make room as Mandy settled triumphantly on his chest.

"You happy?" he asked her, grinning.

Mandy nodded vigorously. "Mama dadda bed," she declared, beaming.

Lily laughed, the sound surprised out of her, bright and unguarded. Nate looked at her then, something soft and awed crossing his face.

"Best morning ever," he murmured.

Mandy leaned forward and pressed a sloppy kiss to Lily's cheek, then another to Nate's chin. "Together," she said proudly.

Lily felt something bloom in her chest—warm, terrifying, perfect. She wrapped an arm around Mandy and rested her head against Nate's shoulder, allowing herself, finally, to believe this moment was real.

For once, she didn't pull away from the happiness.

Maybe it was time to hold onto it.

After breakfast, the house buzzed with a quiet, domestic rhythm that still felt strangely new—and precious. Nate carried the plates to the sink while Lily wiped Mandy's sticky hands, their movements falling into an easy, unspoken coordination.

"I'll drive your car," Nate said, reaching for the keys. "Is that okay?"

Lily hesitated only a second before nodding. It felt natural. Too natural. And that both comforted and unsettled her.

Outside, Nate opened the back door of Lily's car and carefully lifted Mandy into her child seat. He took his time, checking the straps twice, adjusting them until they sat just right. Mandy watched him with solemn focus.

"There," he said finally, giving her nose a gentle tap. "All secure."

Then, almost thoughtfully, he added, "I need to get one of these installed in my car. So, I can drive you and Mama around."

Mandy's face lit up instantly. She giggled, the sound bright and delighted. "Mama," she echoed proudly, as if the word explained everything.

Lily's chest tightened. She turned away under the pretext of adjusting her bag, giving herself a moment to steady the rush of emotion his words had stirred.

The drive to the hospital was calm, Mandy chattering to herself in the back while Lily sat quietly next to him in the front. Nate listened, smiling in the rear-view mirror, the simple act of driving them together feeling momentous in a way he couldn't quite put into words.

At the hospital, the familiar scent of antiseptic greeted them as they walked down the corridor toward Edward's room. Lily's nerves fluttered despite herself, but the moment she saw her father, relief washed through her.

Edward was sitting up in bed, colour already returning to his face. He looked far more like himself—alert, eyes bright, a teasing smile tugging at his lips when he spotted them.

"Well, if it isn't my favourite people," he said warmly. His gaze dropped to Mandy. "And my littlest boss."

"Grandpa!" Mandy chirped.

Lily hurried to his side. "How are you feeling?"

"Better," Edward admitted. "Pain has eased off a lot. Still sore, but nothing like yesterday." He nodded toward the IV. "They've got me pumped full of antibiotics. Can't complain."

Caleb stepped in then, clipboard tucked under his arm, his expression relaxed but professional. "He's improving nicely," he said, addressing Lily and Nate. "The infection's responding well to treatment, but we're keeping him here a couple more days—just to be safe. With his history, we don't want to rush anything."

Lily exhaled slowly, tension draining from her shoulders. "A couple more days I can handle."

Edward reached for her hand. "See? Told you I'm not going anywhere yet."

Nate rested a hand at Lily's back, grounding her. "We'll come every day," he said simply.

Edward looked at him for a long moment, something thoughtful in his eyes, then nodded. "I know you will."

Mandy wriggled, reaching toward her grandfather. "Stay, Grandpa."

Edward laughed softly. "I'll stay right here, sweetheart."

As Lily watched them together—her father smiling, Mandy content, Nate steady at her side—she felt something settle deep inside her. The fear hadn't vanished, but it had loosened its grip.

For the first time in a long while, hope felt solid enough to hold.

Just as Caleb turned toward the door, Edward cleared his throat.

"Hey doc," he said, a hopeful note creeping into his voice, "tell me straight… will I be out before the town fair on Saturday?"

Caleb paused, glancing down at the chart, then back at Edward with a small, reassuring smile. "If everything continues progressing the way it is now, there shouldn't be a problem. A couple more days of IV antibiotics, then we'll reassess—but I'm optimistic."

Edward's face lit up. "Good. Wouldn't miss it for the world."

Lily blinked, the words town fair jolting her memory. Of course. The annual event she'd somehow managed to forget in the chaos of the past week. The whole town shut down for it—Main Street strung with lights and bunting, food stalls lining the sidewalks, the smell of fried dough and caramel apples drifting through the air. There were rides for the kids, local bands playing on the small outdoor stage, craft booths, pie competitions, and the much-loved raffle that half the town seemed to take far too seriously. It was the one day a year everyone showed up, no matter what grudges they carried or what secrets they kept.

Her gaze drifted briefly to Nate, and with it came a memory so vivid it stole the breath from her lungs. The town fair had always been their thing—long before heartbreak, before lies, before time pulled them apart. A memory she hadn't even realised she'd been avoiding.

She'd been eighteen then, standing near the old Ferris wheel with sticky fingers from fairy floss and laughter still bubbling in her chest. The air had been warm and golden, filled with music from the bandstand and the scent of popcorn and summer grass. She'd been wearing a simple sundress, nerves fluttering because adulthood still felt like something that belonged to other people.

And then she'd bumped into him.

Literally.

Her drink had sloshed, and his arm had shot out on instinct, steadying her before she could stumble. She'd looked up, ready with an embarrassed apology—and promptly forgotten every word she'd ever known.

Nate had smiled at her then. He'd been twenty-five, seven years older than Lily. Not the confident, guarded smile he wore now, but something open and easy, as though he hadn't yet learned how to shield his heart from the world. His eyes had crinkled at the corners as he laughed softly and said, "Guess the fair's already trying to knock you off your feet."

She'd blushed, mortified and flustered, and somehow that only made his grin widen. He'd offered to buy her another drink, insisting it was his fault, and she'd agreed—even though she knew she shouldn't talk to strangers. But he hadn't felt like one. Not even for a second.

They'd walked together beneath strings of coloured lights, sharing stories between rides, fingers brushing, smiles lingering just a heartbeat too long. When the Ferris wheel lifted them into the night sky, the town spread out below them in a scatter of glittering lights, he'd reached for her hand—hesitant, respectful—and asked if it was okay.

She'd said yes.

She hadn't been able to believe that a man like him—so calm, so self-assured, so undeniably grown—could be interested in an eighteen-year-old girl like her. But from that night on, they were inseparable. Even back then, deep in her bones, she'd believed they would be together forever.

Standing in the hospital room now, years later, Lily felt the echo of that girl—the one who had believed in beginnings, in love that felt simple and endless. Her chest tightened as she realised something she could no longer ignore.

It hadn't started beneath the lights of the fair by accident.

And maybe it had never truly ended either.

Caleb scribbled a quick note, then looked up at Nate. "You're on a rostered day off today, right?"

Nate nodded easily. "Yeah. I'll be in tomorrow."

Caleb smiled, clapping him lightly on the shoulder. "I figured. Good. I'll see you then."

With that, he gave Lily a reassuring nod and headed out, leaving the room quieter—but somehow warmer—than before.

Edward leaned back against the pillows, satisfaction written all over his face. "Looks like I'll make the fair after all."

Lily smiled, squeezing his hand, her thoughts already drifting ahead to Saturday… and the way everything seemed to be lining up whether she was ready or not.

Chapter Eighteen

After they left the hospital, Nate drove them straight to Marigold's Café.

The familiar bell above the door chimed as they stepped inside, the warm scent of coffee and fresh baking wrapping around them. Lily barely had time to take two steps before someone spotted Mandy in her arms.

"Well, if it isn't Miranda's little girl," Mrs. Hawthorne exclaimed from behind the counter, her face lighting up. "Look at those cheeks!"

Others turned, smiles spreading, chairs scraping back as people stood. There were no hushed murmurs this time, no sidelong glances or half-swallowed whispers behind Lily's back. Instead, there was warmth—genuine, open, almost reverent curiosity.

"Oh, she's beautiful."

"She's got Miranda's eyes."

"And Lily's heart," someone added gently.

Lily felt something loosen in her chest as hands waved, smiles greeted her, and Mandy soaked up the attention with delighted giggles. Nate stayed close, one hand resting at Lily's back, steady and protective without being possessive. When Mandy reached for him, he lifted her easily, and Lily caught more than one person smiling knowingly at the sight.

They ate lunch amid laughter and conversation, Mandy charming the entire café with sticky fingers and bright eyes. For the first time in a long while, Lily didn't feel like she was bracing herself against the town. She felt... accepted. Seen.

When they stepped back outside, Nate turned to her, his expression unreadable but soft. "I want you to see something."

She raised a brow. "What kind of something?"

He smiled. "A surprise."

She studied him for a moment, then nodded, curiosity flickering. He buckled Mandy into her car seat before sliding behind the wheel, and they drove in comfortable silence, the town giving way to quieter streets lined with trees and wide verandas.

When he finally pulled into a driveway, Lily's breath caught.

The house was beautiful—warm timber tones, wide windows that caught the afternoon light, a wraparound porch with white railings and a swing swaying gently in the breeze. A flowering garden framed the front path, roses and lavender spilling over neat borders. It felt solid and welcoming, the kind of place that held laughter in its walls.

"Oh, Nate..." she whispered before she could stop herself.

She loved it instantly—before she even stepped inside.

He shut off the engine but didn't move right away. "I put a deposit on this house," he said quietly. "A week before I proposed to you."

Her heart stuttered.

She turned to him slowly, the words sinking in, rearranging something deep inside her.

"This was going to be ours?"

He nodded. "It was supposed to be. I pictured you here—sketching on the porch, arguing with me about paint colours, filling the place with life." His voice roughened, emotion slipping through despite his control. "I'm hoping it still can be."

Lily's gaze drifted back to the house—to the porch swing swaying gently, the neat garden beds, the front door that felt as though it had been waiting for her all along. A home. Their home. The realisation pressed against her chest, warm and aching all at once.

Nate climbed out and unbuckled Mandy, then reached back for Lily's hand as she stepped out of the car. His fingers laced with hers, solid and sure.

"Come on," he said softly. "I've got another surprise."

Mandy clapped her hands, bouncing in his arms. "Surprise!"

Nate laughed under his breath and led them up the front steps. Inside, the house was just as beautiful—warm timber floors, high ceilings, sunlight spilling through wide windows. The living room opened into a soft, welcoming space with built-in shelves and a stone fireplace. Lily could already imagine books stacked everywhere, toys scattered across the rug, Mandy curled up with crayons while she sketched nearby.

The kitchen was bright and open, white cabinets and wooden benches, a long island that felt made for family meals and late-night conversations. Everything about the house felt intentional—lived-in already, as though it had been waiting for the right people to claim it.

Lily's chest tightened. "Nate… it's perfect."

He didn't answer. Instead, he carried Mandy down the hallway and stopped at one of the bedroom doors. Lily followed, her heart starting to race.

Nate glanced at her once, then opened the door.

The room beyond was unmistakably a child's room. Soft pastel walls, sunlight filtering through sheer curtains. A small white bed sat against one wall, dressed in floral bedding. Shelves held storybooks and stuffed animals, and in the centre of the far wall, wooden letters were mounted carefully and lovingly.

PRINCESS.

Lily's breath caught sharply. Her hand flew to her mouth as tears sprang instantly to her eyes, blurring the room before her.

Mandy wriggled in Nate's arms, pointing excitedly at the bed and the letters on the wall. "Mine," she declared happily, as if there had never been any doubt.

Nate swallowed, emotion thick in his throat. His voice came out quiet, careful. "I had it done a couple of weeks ago," he said. "I'm hoping one day you'll both be here… with me."

Mandy squirmed again, clearly ready to explore, and Nate laughed softly as he set her down. She toddled straight to the bed, climbing up with determined enthusiasm before flopping onto the pillows.

"Night night," she announced, curling onto her side.

Lily looked up at Nate, her eyes shimmering. "She's due for her nap."

"Mandy nap," Mandy echoed sleepily, already rubbing her eyes.

Nate glanced at Lily, a silent question in his gaze. When she nodded, something warm and grateful flickered across his face. He gently tucked Mandy beneath the covers, smoothing her hair and pressing a soft kiss to her forehead. She was asleep before the door even closed.

Nate took Lily's hand then, his grip gentle but sure, and led her down the hall. He pushed open the door to the main bedroom.

"This is our room," he said quietly.

Lily stepped inside and felt her chest tighten all over again. The room was calm and inviting—soft neutral tones, a wide bed dressed in crisp linen, sunlight spilling through tall windows. It felt intimate. Grounded. Like a place meant for shared mornings and whispered nights.

"It's beautiful, Nate," she breathed.

He stepped closer, lifting his hand to her face, skimming his knuckles along her cheek with aching tenderness. "Not as beautiful as you."

Her heart stuttered at the way he looked at her—like she already belonged there, like this room had been waiting for her as much as he had.

"I need you in my arms again," Nate murmured, the words barely more than breath, just as his lips brushed hers.

The kiss was slow, unhurried, full of everything they hadn't said. Lily melted into him, her hands curling into his shirt as if anchoring herself to the moment. Nate wrapped his arms around her, drawing her close, holding her as though he'd been afraid to let go for years—and now finally could.

They moved together without rush, shedding uncertainty with each soft touch, each whispered breath. It wasn't frantic or desperate; it was certain. Familiar. Two people finding their way back to something that had never truly been lost.

Nate laid her back against the bed, his kisses reverent, his presence steady and warm. Lily felt cherished, chosen, safe in a way that loosened something deep inside her chest.

She reached for him, fitting against him as though her body remembered what her heart had always known.

When they finally came together, it was with quiet intensity—no need for words, only the shared rhythm of breath and closeness. The world narrowed to warmth and connection, to the comfort of being held and the certainty of being wanted.

Afterward, Nate kept her wrapped in his arms, her head resting over his heart. Lily listened to its steady beat and felt her own finally slow, finally settle, as though her body had been holding its breath for years and was only now learning how to exhale.

Nate shifted slightly, careful not to disturb her, then tipped her chin up so she could see his face. His expression was open—unguarded in a way that made her chest ache.

"Lily," he said quietly, steady but full of feeling. "I know you're scared to say you love me. I get why." His thumb traced a slow, soothing line along her arm. "But I need you to know something."

She watched him, her heart thudding, afraid to interrupt.

"You're it for me," he continued, voice low and certain. "You always have been. I don't want a life that doesn't include you. I want you in my life… in my bed… in my home." He swallowed, emotion tightening his throat. "I want to wake up with you, come home to you, build something real—with you and Mandy. Every day. For the rest of my life."

Lily's eyes burned, tears gathering despite her effort to hold them back. She pressed her palm over his chest, feeling the truth of his words in the steady strength of his heartbeat beneath her hand.

"I'm not asking you to say anything you're not ready to say," Nate added softly. "I just need you to know where I stand. I'm not going anywhere. Not this time."

She leaned into him then, resting her forehead against his, breathing him in—familiar, steady, grounding. Her voice came out as a whisper, fragile but honest, as if saying the words aloud might shatter her courage.

"I'm still scared," she admitted softly. "I… I need a bit more time, Nate. To be sure."

His arms tightened around her immediately, protective and unyielding, as though he could shield her from every doubt and fear she carried. He bowed his head and pressed a kiss to her hair—slow, reverent, filled with everything he couldn't quite put into words.

"I won't rush you," he murmured against her temple. "I'll wait as long as you need. Days, months—whatever it takes." His hand smoothed up and down her back, steady and patient. "I'm not going anywhere, Lily. I'm right here."

She closed her eyes, letting the certainty in his voice sink in. For the first time in a long while, waiting didn't feel like fear.

It felt like trust.

Edward was finally released from the hospital on Friday afternoon, just in time for the town fair the following day. Caleb had promised to help Lily manage Edward in his wheelchair, escorting him through the festivities until Nate finished his shift, which wouldn't be until after noon.

By mid-morning, the fairgrounds were alive with laughter, music, and the rich, sugary scent of popcorn and funnel cakes drifting on the breeze. Mandy's eyes sparkled as she darted from one toddler ride to the next, shrieking with pure delight. Edward, smiling despite the lingering fatigue etched into his features, helped her win a small stuffed frog at the ring toss, laughing as she hugged it tightly to her chest. Caleb wheeled Edward along the winding paths while Lily guided Mandy in her stroller, the little girl pointing excitedly at rides, lights, and balloons, her joy infectious.

After a while, Edward asked Caleb to wheel him over to one of the exhibits. Lily stayed behind, settling in the shade of a broad oak tree with Mandy. Sunlight filtered through the branches above, dappling the grass in shifting patterns of gold and green. Worn out from the excitement, Mandy dropped her frog and gave a small, indignant squeal. Lily crouched, retrieving it and holding it out to her daughter with a fond smile.

And then she heard it—a voice like ice beneath the midday sun.

"Well, well, well... look who it is," it hissed. "The saint of Willow Creek. The wannabe mother. And wannabe Mrs. Cahill."

Lily froze for a heartbeat; her hand still extended with the frog. She looked up and saw Cassie standing there, arms crossed, lips curled with venom. The laughter and music of the fair dulled around them, as if the world itself had drawn back, leaving only the tension stretching tight between them.

Mandy, blissfully unaware, bounced lightly in her stroller, clutching her frog. Lily's heart began to race—but instead of shrinking back, she straightened, subtly positioning herself between her daughter and Cassie.

Cassie's gaze dropped to Mandy. "The girl looks tired. If you were a proper mother, you'd know that. Maybe someone should speak to social services about your fitness as a parent."

Lily stiffened, every instinct flaring. Around them, people slowed, curiosity sharpening as attention shifted their way.

Cassie's smile widened, cruel and assured, her eyes flicking briefly to the growing crowd—as though she welcomed witnesses. "You know, if you can't cope, you can always walk away. She's not even your daughter."

Lily's heart slammed against her ribs, but she didn't falter. She unbuckled Mandy and lifted her from the stroller, grounding herself in her daughter's warmth, the familiar weight anchoring her. Mandy's arms slid instinctively around her neck, trusting, secure.

Lily lifted her chin.

"That's enough, Cassie."

The calm in her voice cut sharper than any shout.

Cassie blinked, caught off guard.

"You don't get to question my fitness as a mother," Lily continued evenly, "especially not in public—and especially not after spending years lying to tear people's lives apart."

A ripple of murmurs moved through the crowd. Fairgoers paused mid-step, glances sharpening, whispers beginning to circulate.

Cassie's posture stiffened. "Lily, I think you're being emotional—"

"No," Lily said, unwavering. "I'm being clear."

She held Cassie's gaze, unflinching.

"You lied to me. You lied to Nate. You lied about my child. You even dragged your brother into your lies," she said, her voice steady despite the memories pressing tight against her chest. "You let me believe Nate chose you. You let him believe he'd been betrayed. And you did it while hiding behind your so-called love."

Lily kissed the top of Mandy's head, drawing strength from her daughter before facing Cassie again.

"That's not love. That's manipulation. That's control," she said quietly. "Nate never loved you. He loves me. He loves Mandy. And you are nothing more than a distant memory."

Cassie's lips parted. "Nate did love—"

"No," Lily cut in, her voice firm as stone. "He didn't. He's a one-woman man. And that woman is me. Always has been. Always will be."

The words settled into the air—final, immovable.

Then Lily delivered the blow Cassie hadn't anticipated. Not with anger, not with cruelty—but with absolute certainty.

"Nate and I will be getting married, and everyone in this town will be invited—even your brother, because at least he had the decency to own his lies. The only person who won't be there to witness my vows to the man I love, and who loves me... is you."

Silence crashed down.

Cassie's face drained of colour, the authority she'd worn so confidently dissolving beneath the weight of watchful eyes and whispered judgment.

Murmurs of approval rippled outward. A few people clapped softly. Others nodded, smiles forming—support unmistakable.

Mandy shifted in Lily's arms and reached toward someone behind her.

"Dadda," she said softly.

Lily turned—and there was Nate, with Caleb and her father beside him, all three watching with unmistakable pride. The word was small.

The impact was seismic.

Nate stepped forward without hesitation, taking Mandy from Lily and sliding his other arm around Lily's waist, solid and sure. Lily didn't flinch. She leaned into him, instinctive and right.

"This," Lily said quietly, her voice carrying despite its softness, "is my family. You stay away from my family."

Cassie had nothing left. She turned and walked away, shoulders rigid, the crowd parting around her—not in support, but scrutiny.

Lily exhaled, her knees trembling only now that it was over.

Nate bent toward her, his voice low and reverent. "That was incredible."

She looked up at him—really looked—and something settled deep in her chest. Not fear. Not doubt.

Certainty.

"I love you, Nate," she said softly. "I always have… and I always will."

His face broke into a bright, unguarded smile before he kissed her—right there, in front of the whole town—and neither of them cared who was watching.

Mandy clapped her hands happily.

"Mama! Dadda! Kiss!"

From the edges of the fair, laughter and gentle cheers rose, even carnival workers pausing to watch. Wrapped in that moment, Lily felt the warmth of the town around her—approval, respect, belonging—and for the first time in years, she knew without question that her life, her love, and her family were finally, fully hers.

Epilogue

Nate stood with Caleb in the small room just off the altar, the low murmur of the congregation filtering through the thick wooden door. Sunlight streamed through a narrow stained-glass window, casting soft ribbons of colour across the polished floor.

"You ready, Caleb?" Nate asked, adjusting his cuffs with a quiet, knowing smile. "Ready to join the club?"

Caleb huffed out a nervous laugh and glanced at his reflection. "I just hope Melanie and I are half as happy as you and Lily."

Nate's smile deepened, something reflective settling warmly in his chest. Three years. It felt like both a lifetime and the blink of an eye.

They'd married just three weeks after the town fair—the day Lily had finally found her voice and used it to shatter every lie that had once held power over them. Cassie had left Willow Creek not long after, her influence dissolving as quickly as it had poisoned things. No one had missed her.

Lily had walked down the aisle on Edward's arm, radiant in ivory lace, her eyes locked on Nate as though the rest of the world had ceased to exist. He'd known then—absolutely, irrevocably—that everything he had endured, every mistake, every loss, had led him right there.

Edward had lasted nearly a year after the wedding. Long enough to see his daughter settled. Loved. Safe. Long enough to hold his grandson—Marc—in his arms. He'd passed four weeks later, quietly and bravely, leaving behind a legacy of love and stubborn strength.

Only a couple of months into their marriage, Lily had come to Nate one evening, shy and glowing, her hands trembling as she told him they were having a baby. Joy had hit him so hard he'd had to sit down. Mandy had been ecstatic—already fiercely devoted to her baby brother before he'd even arrived.

Lily had been afraid. Nate had known that. The shadow of Miranda's death lingered, an unspoken fear neither of them could fully erase. But this time, the story had ended differently. Four hours of labour. One powerful, breath-stealing cry. Marcus Edward Cahill had been born strong and perfect, placed into Lily's arms while Nate wept openly, unashamed.

His family was his world.

Lily—his heart, his anchor, his forever.

Mandy—the firecracker who had chosen him first.

Marcus—the promise of everything still to come.

A knock sounded at the door.

"Time," someone called softly.

Caleb straightened, exhaling slowly. Nate clapped him on the shoulder. "You've got this."

As they stepped toward the altar, Nate felt it again—that quiet certainty he'd learned to trust. Love, once buried beneath lies and fear, had endured. It had grown stronger. Deeper. Unbreakable.

Lily sat in the pew, smoothing a hand absently over the dark fabric of her dress as the organ music swelled through the church. Five-year-old Mandy sat beside her, feet swinging slightly above the floor, her attention fixed on the front where Uncle Caleb stood beaming next to Nate. On Lily's lap, two-year-old Marc shifted and wriggled, warm and solid and utterly content, one chubby hand clutching her necklace.

She adjusted her hold on him, pressing a kiss into his curls, and felt her chest tighten with a familiar, overwhelming swell of gratitude.

Caleb was getting married. Nate's best friend. One of the constants in their lives. And Nate—her husband—stood tall and proud beside him, calm and sure in a way that still made her heart stutter after all this time.

Lily's gaze softened as she watched Nate laugh quietly at something Caleb whispered. God, she loved that man.

Three years ago, she had returned to Willow Creek convinced their story was over. Finished. She'd believed she was coming back only to survive—to rebuild a life for herself and Mandy in the quiet margins of a town that held too many memories. Loving Nate again had felt impossible then. Dangerous. Like touching something that had already burned her once.

Now, sitting here with their children in her arms, she couldn't imagine having ever believed that.

Happiness settled over her—not the dizzy, fragile kind she'd once chased, but something deeper. Steadier. Built on trust. On honesty. On choosing each other every single day. Nate loved her openly, fiercely, without hesitation. He showed her in a hundred small ways—coffee waiting when she woke, his hand always finding hers, the way he still looked at her like she was the centre of his world.

He had adopted Mandy the moment they were married. No fanfare. No hesitation. Just certainty. *She's my daughter,* he'd said simply, signing the papers with a steady hand and shining eyes. Lily had cried then—harder than she had on their wedding day.

Mandy leaned closer now, her small hand slipping into Lily's. "Mama," she whispered, eyes bright. "Uncle Caleb looks happy."

"Yes," Lily murmured, squeezing her fingers. "He really does."

Marc babbled softly and rested his head against her chest, already half asleep. Lily held him closer, breathing in the moment—the warmth of her children, the hum of the church, the sight of the man she loved standing exactly where he belonged.

Once, her life had been shaped by fear and lies.

Now, it was shaped by love.

Later, after the speeches had wound down and the clinking of glasses gave way to laughter and music, Mrs Baxter made her way across the reception room with Nate at her side. Lily was seated at a round table near the dance floor, Marc balanced on her knee, Mandy perched happily beside her with a half-finished cupcake.

Mrs Baxter smiled warmly, already reaching for Marc. "Lily, sweetheart, I've got these two angels. You go and dance with your husband."

Before Lily could protest, Nate was standing in front of her, his hand extended, eyes bright and unmistakably hopeful.

"You two behave yourselves for Mrs Baxter," he said solemnly, crouching to Mandy's level, "while I steal your mama for a dance."

Mandy grinned. "Okay, Daddy," she agreed, as if this were the most reasonable thing in the world.

Marc babbled in enthusiastic agreement, patting Nate's jacket with sticky fingers.

Lily laughed softly, her heart full, and slipped her hand into Nate's. He didn't waste a second—he pulled her to her feet and guided her onto the dance floor, one hand settling firmly at her waist, the other drawing her close until her body fit naturally against his.

The music was slow and familiar, the kind that invited closeness rather than show. Nate dipped his head, his lips brushing her ear as they began to sway.

"You look gorgeous tonight," he murmured. "That dress is incredible. I can't wait to take it off you later."

Lily laughed, warmth blooming across her cheeks, her fingers tightening lightly at the back of his jacket. "Nate... you're impossible."

He smiled against her skin, that familiar curve of his mouth making her heart stutter just as it always had. His voice dropped, playful and certain all at once. "You love me though."

His lips brushed hers—soft, unhurried, a kiss meant only for her—and she smiled into it before resting her forehead against his. "Yes," she said quietly. "I do. And actually... I have some news."

He felt the shift immediately. Nate pulled back just enough to look at her, his hand still warm and steady at her waist. "What kind of news?" he asked gently, though something in his eyes sharpened with instinct.

Lily swallowed, suddenly aware of the music, the lights, the people around them—and yet feeling as though they were the only two in the room. She took a breath, grounding herself in the familiar strength of his arms.

"I'm pregnant," she said softly.

The words landed between them like a heartbeat.

Nate stopped moving. The music continued around them—couples swaying, laughter rising and falling—but he heard none of it. He stared down at her, searching her face as if to be certain he'd heard correctly.

"Pregnant?" he repeated, his voice barely more than a breath.

Lily nodded, a small, tremulous smile forming. "Yes."

For a long moment, he said nothing. His hand tightened at her waist—not possessive, just anchoring, like he needed the contact to stay upright. Then his eyes filled, emotion breaking through so fast it stole her breath.

"Oh, Lily…" His voice cracked.

He pulled her into him, forehead pressed to hers, then kissed her—deeply this time, reverently, as though the world had shifted, and he needed her to feel just how much. When he pulled back, his eyes were bright, his smile disbelieving and joyful all at once.

"We're having a baby," he said, wonder threading every word.

Lily nodded again, tears burning now. "We are."

Nate laughed softly, a broken, beautiful sound, and rested his hand over her lower back as if he could already feel the future there. "God… I love you," he whispered. "I love you so much."

She leaned into him, heart full, surrounded by music and light and love—and knew, without a single doubt, that this was exactly where she was meant to be.

Beneath the lies, they had found the truth.

And it had been worth everything.

The End

Heart of the Outback

Alison Reid

A complete standalone romance
Previously published individually

Chapter One

The rain had stopped.

Melbourne's skies still brooded in shades of grey, but the silence that followed the storm felt like a mercy. A pause in the noise. A chance to breathe.

Jemma Prescott sat on the edge of a hard plastic chair in the fluorescent-lit police station waiting room, her hands wrapped tightly around a chipped mug of lukewarm tea she hadn't touched. Her fingers trembled—maybe from the cold, maybe from memory. It didn't matter. The shaking wouldn't stop either way.

"Miss Prescott?"

She looked up.

Senior Constable Mark Dwyer stood before her, his kind eyes a quiet balm in a world that had turned sharp. He was the one who'd draped the blanket over her shoulders earlier that morning, when they'd found her bleeding, barefoot and soaked on a neighbour's porch—shivering, silent, barely holding herself together. The same man who had cuffed Leo Evans without blinking, ignoring the curses, the snarls, the manipulations Leo used like second nature.

Jemma straightened, instinct forcing her spine taut. A flinch twitched in her shoulders, automatic and uninvited.

"He's being processed," Dwyer said gently, lowering himself to sit on the bench beside her—not too close. Just enough to feel human. "Charges will stick this time. We've got the photographs, the neighbour's statement... and your own." He offered a quiet nod. "You did the right thing."

She looked away. Her throat closed with a rush of heat—shame and relief fighting for space. This time. How many chances had she given Leo? How many times had she begged herself to believe his apologies? Told herself that maybe this outburst was her fault?

That maybe this was just what love looked like when you weren't good enough to deserve anything better.

Her voice, when it came, was soft. Fragile. "What happens now?"

Dwyer sighed, folding his hands loosely in front of him. "That's up to you. He'll be held in remand for a while—maybe longer. But when he gets out..." He didn't finish the sentence. He didn't need to.

She met his eyes fully for the first time. "I don't have anywhere to go."

"No family?"

She shook her head. "My parents died in a car accident when I was eighteen. I was still in uni."

"Friends?"

Another shake. Slower. More painful. "He… made sure I didn't keep any."

Dwyer didn't press. He nodded, absorbing it like he'd heard stories like hers before—too many times, probably.

"Honestly?" he said, voice quiet. "If I were you… I'd get as far away as you can. Start fresh. Somewhere he wouldn't even think to look."

She gave a hollow laugh. "Like where?"

His mouth quirked—not quite a smile. "I've got a cousin—used to work as a nanny for a cattleman out in western Queensland. Guy's looking for someone new. Remote property. Middle of nowhere. But safe. Peaceful."

Jemma blinked at him. "A nanny."

"You're qualified, aren't you?"

She nodded slowly. "Early childhood. I used to teach prep, before…" Before Leo. Before he intercepted her emails, called her during work hours, accused her of flirting with coworkers, tracked her phone, took her car keys.

Before he started locking her in the shed during storms, so no one could hear her cry.

Dwyer pulled a folded flyer from his jacket. "Callahan Station," he said, handing it over. "Windorah region. Needs a live-in caregiver for a little girl. Comes with a roof, meals, and space to breathe."

She took the flyer like it might disintegrate in her hands. Her eyes skimmed the words.

Seeking full-time caregiver for five-year-old child. Remote cattle station in Western Queensland. Experience with early childhood education essential. Accommodation and board provided. Must be comfortable with isolation. Discretion essential.

Her throat tightened.

She hadn't felt like a teacher in a long time. But that part of her wasn't gone—not really. Just buried. Like everything else Leo had tried to erase.

"But it's so far," she murmured.

Dwyer looked at her. "Sometimes far is good."

Outside, the rain started again—soft, then steady. A cold drumming on the windows.

Jemma flinched. The sound twisted in her brain, pulling her backward—to the tin-roofed shed, the soaked floor, the cold metal against her skin, and the sound of his voice behind the locked door.

She shut her eyes. Not anymore.

When she opened them, something had changed. Not strength—not yet. But the beginning of it. A crack of light in a long, dark tunnel.

"I'll look into it," she said quietly.

Dwyer raised a brow, surprised.

"I mean it," she added. "I'll apply. I just… I want to be somewhere I can't hear the rain so loud."

This time, he smiled. "Then the outback's the right place. Rain's rare out there. And so is trouble—most of the time."

Jemma stood. She smoothed her cardigan with shaking hands, her small frame barely filling the space of her own clothes. She looked younger than twenty-six, but her eyes— green and solemn—held the weight of someone much older.

"Thank you," she said, holding out her hand.

Dwyer shook it firmly. "You take care of yourself, Miss Prescott. And if anyone ever comes looking—"

"I won't let them in."

After leaving the police station, Jemma had returned to the house she once called home—a place that had become more prison than refuge.

The key still worked. The front door creaked open like it always had. Nothing had changed—and that was the problem.

The shadows were the same. The silence was the same. But now, she wasn't.

Leo was gone, in custody, but the walls still felt haunted by him.

She moved quickly, not letting herself pause. If she paused, she might start thinking— and thinking would undo her.

In the bedroom, she hesitated over a photo frame—her parents smiling, sunlit, frozen in a time before she ever learned how love could hurt. She slipped it into her bag. A reminder of who she used to be.

Everything he had given her, she left behind. Let the ghosts keep it.

She packed all her clothes, took every loose note and coin she could find, grabbed her car keys, and drove straight to the bank. She closed her account without explanation. It wasn't much—just enough for fuel, food, and maybe a week or two in a cheap motel. But for the first time in a long while, the money was hers. Her choice. Her escape.

The motel room reeked of bleach and stale air freshener, the kind meant to mask something worse. But to Jemma, it smelled like freedom.

She didn't bother to unpack. Just kicked off her shoes and curled into the scratchy comforter. Her ribs ached. She hadn't realised how shallowly she'd been breathing until the silence settled in, deep and still.

No footsteps. No shouting. No locked doors.

Just quiet.

She hadn't known how much she missed it.

The bed springs groaned beneath her slight weight. The mini fridge rattled in the corner like it was angry to still be alive. The curtains were thin, mustard-coloured, and hopelessly ugly—but they shut out the world. That was all she needed.

She sat still for a moment, letting the silence settle around her like a blanket. The space was cheap, bare, and impersonal. But it was hers.

And she was safe.

Finally—mercifully—safe.

She sat cross-legged on the edge of the bed with the cheap phone Dwyer had given her. "Start again," he'd said. "Clean slate."

She opened the browser and typed the words from the flyer:

Callahan Station – Windorah, Queensland – Help Wanted: Live-in Nanny

The first link took her to a plain listing. Bare bones. No fluff.

Seeking qualified, mature caregiver for five-year-old girl on remote cattle station in Western Queensland. Position is live-in. Must be comfortable with isolation, animals, and rural life. Experience and discretion essential.

Her thumb hovered over the screen.

She had the degree. The training. Her CV needed dusting off, but she could manage. And more than that—she had nothing else. No ties. No roots.

She copied the station name into the search bar:

Callahan Station Windorah

Images loaded slowly.

A rusted iron sign. Red dust stretching to the horizon. A large, weathered house with wide verandahs and a swing on the front porch. Windmills slicing the skyline. Paddocks fenced in forever. No traffic. No sirens. No neighbours.

No Leo.

Her heart slowed.

The photos didn't scare her. They didn't make her feel small or overwhelmed.

They made her feel free.

This was a place so wild it couldn't be caged. So wide it could swallow every scream she'd ever held in.

A place where the rain didn't drown out her voice.

She whispered, "Maybe this is it."

And for the first time in a very long time, hope didn't feel like a trap.

With trembling fingers—and a heart that was finally hers—she clicked Apply.

Chapter Two

The sun was already high over Callahan Station by the time Benjamin Callahan returned from the southern paddock, its glare painting everything in stark, bleached light. The dry air shimmered at the horizon, heat rising off the red earth in wavering waves. His Akubra sat low over his brow, casting long shadows across a face weathered by years of sun, wind, and the kind of grief that didn't soften with time—it calcified. Hardened into silence and habits and a kind of invisible armour no one dared question.

Dust clung to him like a second skin—coating the hem of his worn jeans, streaking the scuffed soles of his boots, settling in the sweat-soaked stubble roughening his jaw. His shirt clung to his back, damp at the collar, and his hands—broad, callused, capable— held the reins with a looseness born from decades in the saddle, in the sun, in the battle of man versus land.

He rode without hurry. Without words. The kind of man who didn't explain himself— and wouldn't, even if asked. People around Windorah said he was carved from the outback itself—all silence and steel and sunburned resolve. A hard man. A good one. Or he used to be, back before everything changed.

A ridge of sandy-blond hair curled beneath the edge of his collar, bleached at the tips by the relentless Queensland sun. It used to be even lighter—back when he smiled without thinking, when laughter came easy, when he didn't flinch at the sound of tyres on gravel or check every gate twice before bed. Before the world taught him how quickly something could be taken. Before it taught him that no one stays.

He swung down from the saddle with the fluid ease of a man born to the land. His boots hit the ground with a dull thud, and he murmured something low to his horse— a soft, private sound. A reassurance. A thank you. Something only the horse would understand.

Benjamin was good with animals. Always had been. With horses, dogs, sick calves, and spooked heifers. With fences and trough lines. With rifles, flood plans, and the brutal, never-ending dance of drought and rain.

But not with people.

Not anymore.

Especially not strangers.

And especially not women.

The last one had hollowed him out from the inside—and left wreckage in her wake. Since then, trust wasn't something he gave. Hell, he barely offered conversation. Just silence. Distance. Routine. It was safer that way—for him, and for Charlotte.

He kept a small staff. Not many, and only the kind who knew how to mind their own business.

Brad, the young station hand, was in his twenties—quiet, capable, the sort who could ride from dawn to dusk and not use up ten words. That suited Ben just fine.

Agnes, the housekeeper and cook, had been on the property longer than most of the buildings. Tough as rawhide and sharp as a stock-whip, she didn't suffer fools and baked bread like she was saving souls with it.

Then there was old Eric, the retired stockman who refused to actually retire. He drifted through the days like a ghost with a pocketknife, fixing things that didn't need fixing and muttering wisdom no one asked for.

They were the only ones he kept close.

But even then—never too close.

He'd learned that lesson the hard way.

And he'd bled for it—heart, pride, trust.

Wounds no one could see, but that still throbbed in the quiet.

He didn't offer trust anymore. He didn't offer much of anything. Just silence. Distance. Routine. It was safer that way. For him. For Charlotte.

Charlotte was waiting for him on the verandah steps; a battered picture book clutched in one hand and a smudge of Vegemite on her chin. Her knees were dirty, her hair wild from the wind, and her smile—so open, so bright—always caught him off guard.

"Daddy!"

The sound of her voice cracked something inside him. It always did. He didn't smile— not fully—but the tension eased from his shoulders as he crossed the dry yard to kneel beside her.

"Whatcha got there, possum?"

She held up the book. "The one with the wombat! He digs and digs and digs. Just like you."

Ben let out a breath that might've been a laugh. "Is that so?"

Charlotte nodded solemnly, her dark curls bouncing. She didn't look like him—not really. She had her mother's eyes. The same stormy grey that used to spark when Heidi wanted something. The kind of eyes that didn't ask—they demanded.

He pushed the thought away, brushing a curl from Charlotte's forehead.

"Go wash up, bub. Lunch in ten."

She scampered inside, barefoot and humming. Ben watched her go, something clenched in his chest. Guilt. Love. Fear. They were tangled now—woven so tightly he couldn't pull one from the other.

Heidi had been twenty-six when he met her—gorgeous, glamorous, and sharp as broken glass. A socialite from Brisbane with a designer wardrobe and a smile like lightning—bright, electric, dangerous. She knew what she wanted. And she knew how to get it.

He'd thought it was love.

It wasn't.

She got pregnant on purpose—he could see that now. She wanted the name. The land. The money. And he had plenty of all three. Callahan Station was one of the largest properties in the district. The Callahan name still meant something. Heidi had known that.

She told him the truth after the wedding once the ink had dried and the house was hers to redecorate.

"I never wanted kids," she'd said, brushing bronzer across her cheek like war paint. "Charlotte ruined everything. My body. My career. My life."

She said it coldly. Casually. Like she was commenting on the weather.

She said it in front of Charlotte.

Ben would never forget how his daughter flinched—just a toddler, but already able to feel the sting of a mother's rejection. Her small fingers had curled into the hem of his jeans like she knew, even then, who she could trust.

Heidi never softened. She grew bitter. Resentful. Motherhood hadn't made her gentle—it made her furious. And Benjamin, once warm and open, shut down one piece at a time, like a house preparing for a storm it couldn't outrun.

Then came the fight. One of many.

She was yelling when she left. He told her not to go. Told her not to drive.

She didn't listen.

She never came back.

Wrapped her car around a gum tree on a bend just outside Windorah. The town called it a tragedy. They said she was complicated. Said Ben was strong. Stoic. A good man grieving a beautiful wife.

But they didn't know the truth.

They didn't know he'd already started grieving long before the crash.

Because when the call came through, his first emotion hadn't been horror.

It had been relief.

And that, more than anything, was what haunted him.

Now, the rhythm of his days was quiet. Predictable. Wake before dawn. Saddle up. Ride the fence-lines. Fix what needed fixing. Feed the dogs. Check the water lines. Make sure Charlotte ate, slept, laughed. And try—God, he tried—not to let the silence win.

So, when the email came through that morning—from a Jemma Prescott, inquiring about the nanny position—his first instinct had been to delete it. No hesitation.

He didn't need a stranger on the property.

Especially not someone who might smile like Heidi had. Who might see the cracks in him and mistake them for invitation. Especially not someone who would leave. Because they always did.

But then he thought of Charlotte.

Of how she stared out the window at dusk, waiting for someone who wasn't coming home. Of how she whispered questions he didn't know how to answer. About heaven. About mothers. About whether love could disappear like fog in the morning sun.

She was lonely.

And he was losing the battle to be enough.

So, he typed a reply.

One month trial.

Start date: Monday.

Remote location. No drama. No lies.

Just space.

For her.

For them both.

By the time Ben stepped into the homestead kitchen, the scent of Agnes's beef stew wrapped around him like a blanket. Rich. Familiar. Comforting. Charlotte was already seated at the old timber table, legs swinging under her chair, a worn stuffed wombat tucked beneath one arm.

"Sit down, Ben. Lunch's ready," Agnes said, glancing over her shoulder. Her voice was brisk, but the warmth in her eyes gave her away.

He hung his hat on the peg, washed his hands at the basin, and took his usual seat.

Charlotte beamed at him, a smear of Vegemite still clinging to the corner of her mouth.

Ben cleared his throat, eyes on his plate. "I should let you know… a Miss Jemma Prescott will be arriving Monday. She's an early learning teacher. Coming on as Charlotte's nanny."

Charlotte gasped. "A real teacher? With books, games, glitter, and stuff?"

Ben nodded. "Yeah. Something like that."

Charlotte bounced in her seat. "Is she nice? What's her favourite colour? Does she like pancakes? Can I show her the baby lambs?"

Agnes chuckled. "Let the poor man eat, love. You'll have plenty of time to interrogate her when she gets here."

Ben caught the older woman's eye—grateful. For the food. The steadiness. The quiet loyalty. Agnes never pushed. But she saw more than he wished she did.

He stabbed at his stew. "It's just a trial run."

Agnes arched an eyebrow. "Mmm-hmm. We'll see."

Charlotte clapped her hands. "I'm gonna show her the drawing I did of Mummy in the clouds."

Ben's chest tightened. He nodded, voice low. "She'll like that, Lottie."

And for the first time in a long time, he allowed himself to hope. That maybe—just maybe—this stranger would bring something more than lessons and glitter.

Maybe she'd bring light. Or at least a little air into the silence.

Even if only for a while.

Chapter Three

Jemma Prescott tightened her grip on the steering wheel as the road stretched out ahead of her—endless and sun-bleached, cutting through the scrub like a faded ribbon. The land out here was raw, vast, and strangely beautiful. Red dirt rolled toward the horizon in every direction, broken only by the occasional skeletal tree, a windmill, or a lazy swirl of dust. She hadn't seen another car in over an hour.

The silence was deafening.

She glanced at her phone, resting face-up in the console. No reception, of course. She wasn't sure why she kept checking—it had dropped out two towns ago. Now it was just her and the road and the soft growl of the engine as she approached Windorah.

Her thoughts drifted—as they had for the last three days—back to the email.

One month trial.

Start date: Monday.

Remote location. No drama. No lies.

Just space.

For her.

For them both.

She could still remember how her breath had caught when she first read it. Not just because he'd replied—she hadn't truly expected him to—but because of the weight behind his words. No drama. No lies. There was a weariness there. A guardedness.

And something else.

Something that felt like a quiet ache.

Jemma knew about ache. She knew what it was to hold grief in your bones and fear in your chest. To want peace so badly you'd walk away from everything you thought you'd ever wanted just to find a sliver of it. She wasn't running—at least, she told herself she wasn't. But she wasn't standing still either.

"No lies," she murmured aloud, her voice soft in the cabin.

She wasn't a liar. Never had been. Her mum used to say she was "pathologically honest," even as a child. Couldn't fib her way out of a sticky-taped art project, let alone a proper mess. She didn't know what he was expecting her to hide—but whatever damage the last woman had done, it clearly ran deep. Jemma had no intention of treading in her footsteps.

She didn't know his daughter's name yet. The email had been clipped, spare. Just instructions, coordinates, a brief line about start time. But she'd picked up a few things anyway—a well-worn copy of Possum Magic, a simple alphabet puzzle, and a book about farm animals with sturdy cardboard pages and bright colours.

They weren't much. Just a start.

But sometimes, a start was all you needed.

The sign for Windorah appeared up ahead, rusted and leaning slightly. Her heart gave a nervous flutter. It wasn't much more than a speck on the map, a blip between nowhere and somewhere else. But it was the closest town to Callahan Station. Her new address. Her new beginning.

She pulled into the service station at the edge of town, climbing stiffly from the car and stretching her legs. The heat pressed in around her, thick and dry, wrapping itself around her shoulders like a heavy coat. Everything smelled of dust and diesel and distant eucalyptus.

Inside the roadhouse, the woman behind the counter gave her a quick once-over—city clothes, skin flushed from the heat, and not a trace of makeup. Not that she needed it. Jemma had the kind of natural beauty that didn't beg for attention but quietly held it— clean lines, clear eyes, and a softness that lingered even after hours on the road. Hands that hadn't dug post holes or wrangled a cranky goat, sure—but she looked like she belonged anyway. Somehow.

"You new in town?" the woman asked, not unkindly.

"Just passing through," Jemma replied with a small smile, then added, "Well, sort of. I'm heading to a property outside Windorah. Callahan Station?"

That earned her a second look. "You're working for Ben Callahan?"

"I am." She hesitated. "As a nanny."

The woman's eyebrows lifted slightly, but she just nodded. "You've got guts, love. He doesn't usually let people in."

Jemma tried to keep her smile steady. "I'm not looking to get in. Just to do my job."

The woman snorted softly, like she didn't quite believe that would be enough. But she rang up Jemma's bottle of water and muesli bar without another word.

Back in the car, Jemma sat for a moment with her hands on her thighs, gathering herself. The town disappeared in the rearview mirror quicker than she expected, and soon the road returned to dust and quiet. The GPS—when it finally loaded—estimated just under an hour until she reached the turnoff for Callahan Station.

She ran her fingers along the edge of the Possum Magic book resting on the passenger seat.

Who are you, little girl? she wondered silently.

What have you already lived through?

She didn't know what waited for her out there—not really. But she wasn't afraid of hard work. Or loneliness. Or silence.

She just hoped that whatever had shattered inside that little girl's father… there might still be enough left unbroken to let someone in.

Even if only for a while.

The turnoff came sooner than she expected—a weathered wooden sign half-swallowed by tall grass and dust; the words "Callahan Station" etched in peeling white paint. Jemma eased the car onto the dirt track, tyres crunching softly as she followed the narrow road deeper into the land.

She'd expected… nothing, really. A run-down farmhouse maybe. Something practical. Sparse. Functional.

Not this.

As she rounded the final bend, the homestead rose up before her—and her breath caught.

It was beautiful.

Not in the way city houses were. Not polished, symmetrical, or picture-perfect. But honest—sturdy and timeless, sitting proud and weather-worn beneath the vast blue bowl of the outback sky.

A long, wraparound verandah hugged the house like a protective arm, its posts draped in climbing bougainvillea blooming defiantly in the dry heat—wild sprays of fuchsia and crimson softening the strong lines of timber and tin. The roof shimmered silver in the sun, and a large gum tree cast a lazy patch of shade across one corner of the yard, where a pair of old rocking chairs sat side by side, faded but solid.

To the left, a windmill turned slow and steady in the breeze, creaking like an old man clearing his throat. Beyond it, a cluster of outbuildings stretched toward the horizon—sheds, stables, maybe a workshop—everything spaced out with deliberate simplicity.

And surrounding it all: silence.

No traffic. No voices. Just the low hum of cicadas and the occasional rustle of wind in the trees.

Jemma pulled up near the fence and climbed out, heart thudding for reasons she couldn't quite explain. She hadn't expected to feel anything—not yet. But standing there, under that enormous sky, staring at the house she would be living in, caring for a child she hadn't met, working for a man she didn't know—

It felt like something was about to begin.

And for the first time in a long time, Jemma didn't feel afraid.

She felt ready.

The station stretched before her, wide and golden under the outback sun, with the main homestead nestled behind a grove of old gum trees like a secret someone had decided to share. The house itself was unexpected—stately but not pretentious, wrapped in deep verandahs and painted in a soft, sun-faded white that gave it an almost dreamlike quality. The corrugated iron roof gleamed in the light, and beyond it, windmills turned lazily in the distance.

It was beautiful. More than she'd imagined.

She hadn't known what she was hoping for. But somehow, this—this quiet strength in timber and tin—felt like the answer to a question she hadn't dared ask.

Jemma stood beside her dust-coated car, one hand shielding her eyes, completely caught in the moment. She didn't hear the footfalls behind her, didn't register the soft scuff of boots on gravel until a voice spoke—low, easy.

"You must be the new nanny."

She spun around, startled.

A young man stood a few feet away, tall, and lanky, with sandy hair poking out from under a wide-brimmed hat. He had the kind of open face that belonged in a country town—tanned skin, kind eyes, and a lopsided grin that suggested he found the whole situation mildly amusing.

"Sorry, didn't mean to sneak up on you," he said, raising both hands slightly in a harmless gesture. "I'm Brad. I work here."

Jemma let out a breath and nodded, one hand still pressed lightly to her chest. "God, you scared me."

His grin widened. "You looked pretty caught up in it. Happens to most people the first time. She's a beauty, isn't she?" He nodded toward the homestead.

"She really is," Jemma said, her voice soft with wonder.

Brad gave her a once-over—quick, not rude, but appreciative. She caught it. Noted it. The way his gaze flicked to her eyes, then away again. The small, almost imperceptible hitch in his smile.

She wasn't surprised. She knew how she looked—fresh-faced, no makeup, long black hair pulled into a simple braid, skin flushed from the heat of the drive. She wasn't flashy, never had been, but she'd been told more than once she was easy on the eyes.

Still, something about the attention made her instinctively guarded.

"I'll let Ben know you're here," Brad said, shifting his weight. "He's probably in the shed. Won't be long."

She nodded. "Thanks."

Brad tipped his hat slightly before heading off across the yard with a slow, easy stride.

Moments later, the shed door swung open.

Jemma heard the heavy footsteps before she saw him. Then he stepped into view.

Benjamin Callahan.

She'd braced herself for gruff, maybe distant. But not this quiet intensity that seemed to reach across the space between them and press against her skin like heat. Not the way his presence settled into the air like a storm cloud that hadn't decided yet whether to break.

He was taller than she expected. Broad-shouldered, all sun-browned muscle and quiet power, with a jaw that looked like it had forgotten how to smile. His shirt clung to him in all the right places, sleeves rolled to the elbows, revealing forearms corded with strength. Dust clung to him like it belonged there—like it had been born on his skin.

And his face—handsome in a way that startled her. Rugged. Weathered. Arresting.

But it was his eyes that made her forget how to breathe. Blue, sharp, and assessing—like they saw too much, like they didn't miss a thing. They flicked over her in a glance that wasn't admiring, wasn't curious—it was… annoyed. Like he resented the fact she was young, or female, or maybe just standing there, full stop.

Jemma stiffened, shoulders pulling back instinctively.

Ben came to a stop in front of her, arms folded across his chest. "You're early," he said flatly.

"I—yes," she replied, blinking. "I left at dawn. I wasn't sure how long the drive would take."

He grunted. It wasn't approval or disapproval. Just… sound.

For a long second, he didn't speak. Just looked at her with that closed-off, unreadable expression. She got the sense that this man didn't offer pleasantries or explanations. That kindness, if it came at all, would be rare and hard-earned.

"You got everything you need?" he asked finally.

"I think so," she said. "Just a few bags. And some books—for the little girl. I—"

"You'll be staying in the cottage next to the main house," he cut in. "I'll show you. You'll be with Charlotte during the day. Routine's simple. Breakfast at six. Schooling in the mornings. Afternoons depend on the weather. Rules are the same for everyone—do your job, no drama, and stay out of things that aren't yours."

Jemma met his gaze, chin lifting slightly. "Understood."

His jaw worked like he wanted to say more but thought better of it. He gave a curt nod, then turned and strode toward the house, not checking to see if she followed.

Jemma stood there a moment longer, heart still thumping.

So that was Benjamin Callahan.

She exhaled slowly. He was colder than she'd expected. More guarded. And—God help her—more attractive than any man had a right to be.

Her stomach fluttered—not with nerves, exactly, but with the weight of the unknown. This man didn't want her here. Not really. But the little girl did. Hopefully. She had to. And Jemma? She'd come too far to back away now.

She squared her shoulders, picked up her bag, and followed.

Whatever came next—she was ready. Or at the very least, she'd pretend to be.

Chapter Four

Ben Callahan strode toward the house, boots thudding against the dry earth, jaw clenched tighter than it needed to be.

She was beautiful.

And he hated that it was the first thing he'd noticed.

Not her qualifications. Not her references. Not her tone or her so-called suitability for the job. No, what had slammed into him like a gut punch was the sight of her—petite and slim, skin flushed from the heat, long black hair pulled into a braid that fell like a ribbon of ink down her back. She looked like she belonged on a film set, not dusty boots on a cattle station.

He didn't know whether to offer her a contract or ask her what in God's name she was doing all the way out here. And those eyes. Striking, vivid green, set in a face that had no right looking that composed after a drive across the bloody outback.

Natural beauty. The kind that didn't need a damn thing to enhance it. No makeup, no pretence. Just her.

And that was the problem.

He'd hired a nanny, not a complication. Not someone who'd knock the air out of his lungs with a glance and make him feel like he was standing too close to something he shouldn't touch. It wasn't just attraction—it was the danger that came with it. The distraction. The memories of another woman who'd smiled sweetly and carved out every soft part of him with a scalpel.

He'd expected someone older. Maybe tired looking. The kind of woman who wore practical shoes and didn't care much for idle chatter. What he got instead was... her. All calm poise and soft confidence, standing in front of his homestead like it was hers to claim.

Ben let out a breath, hot and sharp, and scrubbed a hand down his face.

This was exactly why he didn't want strangers on his property. Especially not women. Especially not ones with eyes like that and a mouth that curved at the edges like it held more stories than she was willing to tell.

It wasn't fair. He knew that. She hadn't done anything wrong. Hell, she'd shown up early, had the decency to bring books for his daughter, and didn't flinch under pressure. But that only made it worse. Because she wasn't flighty or false. She wasn't some city girl looking for outback adventure. She was here to do the job.

And he was already reacting like a fool.

He'd seen it in Brad's face too—the barely concealed grin when he'd come to announce that the gorgeous new nanny had arrived. Jemma Prescott had walked onto the property for less than five minutes, and already the air felt different. Charged. Like something had shifted.

Ben didn't like shifts.

He liked order. Quiet. Predictability. He'd spent years building walls around this place, around himself. Jemma Prescott was a crack in the plaster—and the last time he'd let someone past his defences; it had nearly destroyed him.

His hands curled into fists.

This wasn't about her looks. It couldn't be. He wouldn't allow it to be. He had a daughter to raise, a station to run, and no time for distractions wrapped in green eyes and sun-kissed skin.

She's here to do a job, he reminded himself grimly. That's all.

But even as he reached the verandah steps and pushed open the screen door, the image of her standing beside her dust-covered car lingered.

Backlit by the late afternoon sun.

Eyes wide.

Lips parted in quiet awe.

Beautiful.

Damn it.

Ben shoved the thought away, locking it down tight, the same way he had every dangerous thing that had ever threatened his peace.

She'd learn the routine. Do her work. Keep to herself.

And he'd keep his distance.

He had to.

Because if he didn't…

Well.

That road only led to wreckage.

And he'd already walked it once.

Ben didn't say much as they walked across the yard, his long strides chewing up the distance between the shed and the back verandah. Jemma kept pace behind him, her bag slung over one shoulder, heart still doing an uneven dance in her chest.

At the door, he paused before pushing it open.

"Agnes," he called out.

A moment later, a woman appeared from the kitchen, wiping her hands on a faded tea towel. She looked to be in her sixties, wiry and upright with steel-grey hair swept into a no-nonsense bun. There was flour on her apron and a streak of it on her cheek, but her sharp eyes missed nothing.

"This her?" she asked, giving Jemma a once-over—not unkind, but thorough.

Ben nodded. "Jemma Prescott."

Agnes set the tea towel aside and stepped forward, offering her hand. "Well then, welcome to Callahan Station, love. I'm Agnes. I do the cooking, cleaning, and occasional nagging around here."

Jemma smiled as she shook her hand. "It's lovely to meet you."

Agnes's eyes softened. "Oh, and you've got a lovely smile, too. That'll help. Poor little Charlotte's had a rough trot. She'll need gentle hands."

"I'll do my best," Jemma said quietly.

"I reckon you will." Agnes patted her hand, then turned to Ben with a raised eyebrow. "You going to show her the cottage or just let her melt in that sun?"

Ben's jaw twitched. Agnes was right, of course. And if he wasn't careful, the new nanny would see straight through him—and he didn't like being read.

Ben grunted. "On our way."

Agnes gave him a playful swat on the arm with her towel before glancing back at Jemma. "Charlotte is in her room. Been quiet most of the morning. I didn't push—she has her moods."

Jemma nodded, feeling a mix of nerves and something warmer—relief, maybe. Agnes wasn't just kind; she was the kind of woman who felt like a safe place.

"If she doesn't come out soon, I'll bring her in," Ben said, his voice quieter now.

Agnes nodded. "Good. She'll be curious, even if she pretends not to be."

Jemma caught the flicker of something in Ben's expression—concern, tightly reined in. Then it was gone, replaced by his usual reserve.

"This way," he said, motioning for Jemma to follow.

As they stepped back into the heat, she glanced once over her shoulder and saw Agnes watching them with a look that was almost... hopeful.

And since arriving, Jemma felt the tiniest flicker of belonging.

The sun pressed down hard as they crossed the yard, but Jemma barely noticed. She was too aware of the man walking beside her—broad-shouldered, silent, exuding that same wary energy he'd greeted her with.

"This way," Ben said without looking back, cutting across a gravel path that wound past the edge of the main house.

Jemma followed, boots crunching softly behind his. The homestead's verandah gave way to open space, where a smaller building sat tucked beneath the dappled shade of a wide gum tree. The cottage was modest but charming—timber and tin, with a front porch just big enough for a chair and a pair of worn boots. A single window faced the path, white curtains stirring behind the glass.

"It's not fancy," Ben said, finally glancing her way. "But it's clean, got hot water, and the roof doesn't leak."

"It's perfect," Jemma replied honestly. "Thank you."

He didn't answer—just stepped onto the small porch and pushed open the door.

Cool air greeted her as she stepped inside, carrying the gentle scent of lavender and old timber. The space was quiet and shaded, the stillness wrapping around her like a balm.

The interior was simple but thoughtfully laid out. The main room held a small table with two chairs, a compact kitchenette tucked neatly into the corner, and two narrow doors along the back wall—one leading, she guessed, to a bedroom, the other to a bathroom.

It wasn't fancy. But it was calm, and clean, and hers—for now.

"It's stocked with basics," Ben said, stepping aside so she could enter fully. "If you need anything else, let Agnes know."

Jemma set her bag down near the bed and took a slow breath. After hours on the road, the silence of the cottage felt like a balm.

"It's lovely," she said again, softer this time.

Ben gave a noncommittal grunt. His arms were folded across his chest, his stance guarded.

"I won't be in your space," she added, sensing the tension radiating off him like heat from sunbaked tin. "I'm here for Charlotte. That's it."

His jaw worked for a second before he replied. "Just do your job. She's been through enough."

There was something behind his words—something sharp and tired and threaded with pain. Jemma nodded once.

"I understand."

Ben looked at her for a long moment. His eyes—blue and unreadable—lingered on her face, as if trying to decide whether or not to trust her.

"Dinner's at six," he said finally. "You're welcome to eat with us or not. Up to you."

"Thank you."

He turned to go, pausing at the door. "She might not come to you right away. Don't push."

"I won't."

A short nod. Then he stepped outside and pulled the door closed behind him with a quiet click.

Jemma stood there for a beat, her hand resting lightly on the back of the nearest chair. She let the door's soft click echo for a moment longer. This was it—the calm before whatever storm might come. And yet... she didn't feel afraid. Just anchored. Like maybe, if she was careful, this place might let her stay. The cottage was still, the kind of still that held its breath.

She looked around, took in the gentle worn edges of the place, the way the afternoon sun slanted through the curtains.

It wasn't much.

But it was hers.

And it was a beginning.

The water was lukewarm and the bathroom tiny, but after hours of red dust and stiff driving muscles, the quick wash felt like heaven. Jemma towelled her face, tied her damp hair into a low bun, and stepped back into the quiet of the cottage.

Outside, the sun had dipped lower in the sky, casting golden streaks of light through the window. The silence of the station stretched around her—soft, steady, peaceful. She lay down on the bed for just a minute, closing her eyes, letting her body relax fully for the first time in days.

When she opened them again, it was nearly five-thirty.

With a soft groan, she sat up and reached for her bag. She unpacked a few things—her book, a framed photo of her parents, the three children's books she'd brought for Charlotte—and arranged them on the bedside table. She smoothed the bedspread with her hand, grounding herself in the quiet hum of stillness, preparing herself for whatever came next.

Then—three gentle knocks at the door.

Jemma's heart gave a soft flutter. She stood and crossed to the door, pulling it open—

And froze.

A little girl stood there.

Five or six, by Jemma's guess, small and straight-backed in a pale blue cotton dress with dusty bare feet and curls the exact colour of her own. Her hair was half-pulled back with a crooked barrette, and her cheeks were pink with shyness and heat. But it was her eyes—wide, stormy grey, fringed with lashes that didn't seem real—that struck Jemma still.

She was beautiful.

And silent.

The little girl tilted her head, considering Jemma with a seriousness that made her seem older than she was. Then—

"You smell nice," she said softly.

Jemma blinked, startled, then let out a soft laugh. "Thank you," she replied, crouching to the girl's level. "That's the nicest thing anyone's said to me today."

Charlotte gave a tiny smile—shy, but curious. "Are you my new nanny?"

"I am," Jemma said gently. "My name's Jemma."

"I'm Charlotte."

Jemma smiled. "It's lovely to meet you, Charlotte."

The little girl stepped forward suddenly and reached for Jemma's hand without hesitation, her fingers small and warm.

"Dinner's soon," she said matter-of-factly. "I thought maybe you didn't know the way."

Jemma's chest tightened at the quiet confidence in that voice; the easy way Charlotte had reached for her—like she'd already decided this stranger was safe.

"That's very thoughtful of you," Jemma said, giving the girl's hand a gentle squeeze. "I'd love it if you showed me."

Charlotte nodded and turned without another word, still holding Jemma's hand as they walked back toward the house together, the dust rising softly around their feet.

For a moment, Jemma's throat tightened. She'd prepared herself for resistance, for silence or distance—but not this easy trust. It was a gift she hadn't expected.

And just like that, Jemma knew: this child—this quiet, guarded, lovely little soul—had already started to let her in.

Maybe… this was the beginning of something good.

Chapter Five

Agnes was setting the last of the cutlery on the table when the kitchen door creaked open. She glanced up, expecting to see Benjamin striding in, maybe Brad with dust in his boots.

What she didn't expect—what made her hand freeze mid-air—was Charlotte Callahan.

Holding someone's hand.

Smiling.

Wide and bright and utterly unguarded.

Agnes straightened, her lined face registering pure astonishment as her gaze flicked to the woman beside the child.

Jemma.

Fresh-faced and flushed from the walk over, her long black hair damp from her shower and caught in a low bun. Her green eyes—impossibly bright against her sun-kissed skin—were crinkled at the corners as she looked down at the little girl beside her, who was now half-hiding behind her leg.

Charlotte peered around Jemma's thigh; fingers still curled around the nanny's hand. "Agnes," she said shyly, "this is Jemma. She's staying with us."

Agnes blinked. Twice. Then looked at Benjamin.

He'd just stepped in from the verandah, sweat-darkened shirt sticking to his chest, his boots scuffing against the old wooden floor. He stopped in his tracks.

His brows drew together slowly, his expression unreadable.

He stared at his daughter—his guarded, cautious little girl who hadn't willingly touched a stranger in over a year—now standing beside the new nanny like they'd known each other forever.

He looked at Jemma next. Her soft smile. The way she tilted slightly to match Charlotte's energy. The quiet calm in her posture.

It rattled something in him. Something too close to wonder. Or worry.

"I went to get her," Charlotte added, still clutching Jemma's fingers. "I said I could walk her over. And she thanked me."

Jemma glanced down, her smile turning a little bashful. "She's quite the guide. She gave me a tour—told me which trees had the best climbing branches."

Agnes snorted under her breath, but it was affectionate. "She hasn't taken to anyone that quick since..." Her voice trailed off.

They all knew the ending of that sentence.

Benjamin folded his arms. "You told her where Jemma's cottage was?"

Agnes shot him a look. "Course I did. She's five, Ben. Not stupid."

Jemma's brows lifted slightly at his tone, but she said nothing.

Charlotte turned to her father then. "She brought me a book," she said, proud and serious. "It has a possum in it. I like her."

Benjamin swallowed, his throat tight. He forced a nod.

"Dinner's ready," Agnes announced, breaking the thick silence. "Let's sit down before everything goes cold."

Jemma gently let Charlotte's hand go as the little girl skipped to her usual spot at the table.

As she moved to take her own seat, she caught Benjamin watching her again. Still guarded. Still unreadable.

But there was something new in his eyes.

Not trust.

Something closer to distrust—sharp, watchful, like he was waiting for her to slip.

Jemma held his gaze for half a second longer than necessary before looking away.

Winning over Benjamin Callahan was going to be far more difficult than connecting with his daughter—that much was clear.

Not that she wanted to win him over.

But if they could at least manage civility, it would make things easier. For everyone.

Especially Charlotte.

And that was all that mattered.

Charlotte beamed. "I showed her the way."

"You did a fine job of it," Agnes replied, setting the jug on the table. "Sit wherever you like, love. We're not fussy."

Jemma thanked her softly and slid into the seat beside Charlotte, across from Ben. She could feel his gaze on her again, even as she reached for her napkin and tucked it into her lap.

Dinner was pleasant enough—thanks almost entirely to Charlotte.

The little girl chattered away between bites of roast pumpkin and mashed potato, asking questions that made Jemma smile even as they caught her off guard.

"What's your favourite dinosaur?"

"Do you know how to ride a horse?"

"Have you ever eaten a bug by accident?"

Each one came with such earnest curiosity that Jemma answered without hesitation, laughter bubbling up more than once.

Ben, meanwhile, said very little.

He ate quietly, methodically, his attention flicking from Charlotte to Jemma and back again, his expression unreadable. He didn't interrupt. Didn't scowl. But he didn't join in, either.

If Charlotte noticed, she didn't comment. She was too busy introducing Jemma to the rules of dinner at Callahan Station, "Agnes makes the best gravy but the worst peas" and outlining the important events of her week so far, which included finding a frog in the dog bowl and drawing a pony with three legs by mistake.

Agnes chuckled and added the occasional comment, her dry wit cutting through the quiet with perfect timing. "You'll learn quick, Jemma—Charlotte's the boss around here. The rest of us just do as we're told."

Jemma smiled. "I'm starting to realise that."

At one point, she glanced across the table and found Ben watching her again—elbows braced on the wood, fork held in one hand, unreadable eyes fixed on her face.

He didn't look away.

Neither did she.

A beat passed. Then another.

And finally, he spoke.

"She doesn't usually take to people that fast."

His tone was neutral, but there was something in it—an edge, a question hidden beneath the statement.

Jemma kept her voice steady. "She's a wonderful little girl."

"She is."

The silence that followed wasn't entirely uncomfortable, but it hummed with something unsaid. A test. A warning.

Jemma dropped her gaze back to her plate. She wasn't here to pass tests. And she wasn't here to fight.

When dinner ended, Charlotte offered to help clear the plates, proudly carrying two at a time to the sink while Agnes washed up. Jemma stood to help, but Agnes waved her off.

"First night," she said. "You just settle in."

Jemma nodded, grateful, and murmured a quiet goodnight to the girl who was still chatting about the stars outside.

As she turned toward the door, she caught Ben watching again. His arms were crossed now, leaning against the kitchen doorway.

Still silent. Still unreadable.

She gave him a nod. Polite. Measured.

He returned it after a beat—barely there.

But it was something.

And right now, something was more than she'd hoped for.

Ben leaned against the doorway, arms folded, muscles tight with something he couldn't name.

He told himself he was watching. Just keeping an eye on things. Making sure the new nanny wasn't all talk and charm. That she didn't crack under pressure or flinch at the first sign of hard work.

But the truth was—he hadn't taken his eyes off her all night.

Not once.

He watched the way she smiled at Charlotte. Warm. Unforced. The kind of smile that made his daughter sit up straighter, lean in closer. He watched the way she listened, really listened, like every strange little question mattered. And she answered each one with the same quiet patience, never talking down to her, never rushing.

He'd seen women fake interest in Charlotte before. Seen them offer brittle smiles or over-the-top enthusiasm. Jemma didn't do that. She didn't perform. She didn't push.

She just was.

And Charlotte had responded like she'd been waiting for her all along.

Ben didn't like how that made him feel.

Because it meant she wasn't just good at this—she was natural. She fit. And the thought of anyone fitting too well into his carefully guarded world made something bristle beneath his skin.

He watched her stand from the table, offer Agnes a soft thank you, then turn to say goodnight. Her gaze flicked to him—just for a second—and something passed between them. A nod. Nothing more.

But it stayed with him.

She didn't push him either. Didn't fill the air with pointless chatter or try to smooth the edges of his silence.

She just let it be.

And he wasn't used to that.

Most people, when faced with his quiet, tried to fill it. Explain it away. She didn't. She treated his silence the same way she treated Charlotte's—like it wasn't something to be fixed, just understood.

Ben watched her leave, the screen door creaking open, then shutting softly behind her. Charlotte trailed close behind, barefoot, and still talking.

He let out a breath, slow and heavy.

"She's something, isn't she?" Agnes said, not looking up from the sink.

Ben didn't answer right away.

Agnes glanced over her shoulder. "The girl. Jemma. You don't have to like her, but you've got eyes, don't you?"

He frowned. "She's only been here a few hours."

"Long enough for Charlotte to hold her hand." Agnes wiped her hands on a tea towel. "I haven't seen that girl smile like that ever. Even when her…" She trailed off, but Ben knew how that sentence ended.

Mother was her.

He rubbed a hand down his face, jaw tight.

Agnes softened her voice. "You're not wrong to be careful, love. But careful doesn't mean cruel. You don't have to freeze her out just to stay in control."

Ben didn't look at her. "I'm not freezing her out."

"No?" Agnes arched a brow. "You've said about ten words to her since she got here, and half of those sounded like warnings."

He didn't respond.

Because she wasn't wrong.

He didn't want to be like this. But letting someone in too fast had cost him before. And his gut—always sharp—was warning him now.

Jemma Prescott was calm, composed, and far too easy on the eyes.

She didn't flinch. Didn't rattle.

And that made her dangerous.

But then… Charlotte had taken her hand.

Without coaxing. Without fear.

That meant something.

Ben stared out the window, watching the last of the golden light settle over the yard.

Maybe Agnes was right.

Maybe this wasn't about trust.

Maybe it was about fear.

And if that was true, he had a bigger problem than one beautiful nanny with green eyes and a soft voice.

Chapter Six

Ben stood in the doorway to Charlotte's room, his large frame silhouetted by the warm glow of her bedside lamp.

His little girl was already tucked beneath the covers, her curls splayed across the pillow, one hand clutching the worn ear of a stuffed lamb she'd had since she could walk. Her eyes were heavy, fighting sleep, but when she saw him step in, her small face brightened just enough to tug something in his chest.

"You came," she said, voice soft and sweet.

"Wouldn't miss it." Ben crossed the room and sat on the edge of her bed, the old timber creaking faintly under his weight.

He reached for the sheet and pulled it a little higher under her chin, tucking it in around her shoulders the way she liked. She always wanted to feel cocooned. Safe.

Charlotte yawned, blinking up at him with those stormy grey eyes. "I showed her where the kitchen is."

Ben raised an eyebrow. "You did, did you?"

She nodded solemnly. "She didn't know the way."

He smiled—just a little—and brushed a hand gently over her curls. "That was kind of you."

"She smells nice," Charlotte said, her voice drifting with sleep. "Like flowers."

Ben's smile faltered for a second.

Then she added, "But not the fake kind. Not like how Mummy used to smell."

A quiet beat passed.

Ben swallowed the lump rising in his throat and managed a chuckle. "Is that so?"

Charlotte nodded, snuggling deeper beneath the covers. "Mmm-hmm. And she read the book with all the bees."

"The one with the silly voices?"

"She didn't skip any of the funny words," Charlotte murmured, clearly impressed. "Even the really weird ones."

Ben smoothed a wrinkle in her sheet, trying to ignore the way his heart tugged at her quiet joy. "Well. That's important."

"She's good at reading," Charlotte mumbled, her words starting to slur. "And she listened… even when I didn't say anything."

Ben stayed silent, thumb idly smoothing her sheet, as her lashes drifted lower.

He cleared his throat. "Do you… like her?"

Charlotte blinked slowly, then gave a tiny, sleepy shrug. "She's soft."

Ben's expression pinched, puzzled. "Soft?"

"Not soft like a pillow," Charlotte clarified, like it should be obvious. "Soft like… inside. Like when you don't have to be loud or fast because someone already understands."

He stared at her for a moment, the weight of her words settling deep.

"Do you want her to stay?" he asked quietly, hating how raw the question felt, even if he masked it well.

Charlotte's voice was barely above a whisper. "I hope she does."

Ben nodded once, throat tight. "Okay."

He leaned down and pressed a kiss to her forehead, breathing her in—sun, dust, and that faint lavender Agnes always snuck into the wash.

"Sleep now, button."

Charlotte smiled with her eyes closed. "Night, Daddy."

Ben stood slowly, casting one last glance at his daughter before switching off the lamp. The room slipped into shadow, the silence deep and still.

As he closed the door behind him and stepped back into the hall, one thing was suddenly, undeniably clear.

Jemma Prescott wasn't just a crack in the walls he'd built.

She was already inside.

And it was too late to stop it.

The house had settled into stillness.

With Charlotte tucked in and the dishes cleared, the silence felt heavier than usual. Familiar. But not comforting.

Ben stepped out onto the back verandah, the screen door clicking softly behind him. The night air was cooler now, tinged with eucalyptus and dust, and the vast outback sky stretched overhead, scattered with stars so bright they looked close enough to touch.

He lowered himself into the old rocking chair near the edge of the decking, its creak a low groan in the quiet. He leaned back, elbows resting on the armrests, and let out a slow breath.

It should've been like any other night.

But it wasn't.

His gaze drifted—almost against his will—toward the soft pool of light glowing from the cottage window. The door was open. And there she was.

Jemma Prescott stood on the tiny porch, barefoot, arms folded lightly over her chest, her long black hair loose now, tumbling over her shoulders like a dark river. She hadn't noticed him. Her face was turned skyward; eyes fixed on the stars like she was looking for answers only the heavens could give.

She wasn't moving. Just… standing there.

Still.

Present.

Ben frowned, rocking back slightly. There was something about the way she stood—calm, unguarded. As if the weight of her day had finally lifted, and she was just letting herself breathe.

She looked so damn peaceful.

And it unsettled him more than anything else had all day.

He should've been relieved that Charlotte liked her. That she'd eaten her dinner without fuss. That she'd let someone new read her a bedtime story without retreating into silence. That should've been enough.

But his eyes kept going back to Jemma. To the shape of her in the soft light. To the way she looked like she belonged there already, barefoot, and quiet and staring at the stars like she was having a private conversation with the sky.

He didn't like it.

Didn't like how she took up space without even trying or the fact that his daughter had already taken to her.

Didn't like the way something in his chest loosened—just a little—when she smiled.

This wasn't what he'd planned. He'd hired a nanny, not invited someone into the quiet corners of his life.

And yet…

Ben leaned forward, resting his forearms on his knees, still watching her. He told himself it was just caution. Just vigilance. A father keeping an eye on the stranger he'd let onto his land.

But deep down, a part of him—a part he hadn't listened to in years—knew better.

Because he wasn't watching her like a man guarding his peace.

He was watching her like a man who'd forgotten what peace looked like… and didn't know what the hell to do with it now that it was standing barefoot on his porch, gazing at the stars.

He scrubbed at the day-old stubble on his jaw, exhaling like he was trying to rid himself of thoughts he hadn't invited and leaned back with a sigh, eyes lifting to the same sky.

It was going to be a long damn week.

The stars in the outback sky were like nothing Jemma had ever seen.

They didn't just twinkle—they burned. Scattered across the darkness like diamonds flung by some wild, generous hand. She stood on the tiny porch of the cottage, arms folded loosely around her waist, the cool boards beneath her bare feet grounding her in a way she hadn't expected.

The air was quiet. No traffic. No voices. No tension curling in her spine like it used to.

Just the soft hum of insects, the occasional rustle of dry leaves, and the wide-open hush of the land itself.

She tilted her head back, letting the starlight wash over her face, and breathed.

For the first time in months—maybe longer—her lungs didn't feel tight. There was no pounding at the door. No footsteps in the hall. No voice rising in rage, no shadow looming where there should have been safety.

Leo couldn't touch her here.

She was free.

A tremor moved through her, but it wasn't fear. It was the kind of shiver that came with release—the slow, fragile unwinding of muscles that had been clenched too long.

She'd made it.

She didn't know how long she stood there, watching the sky, listening to the quiet. But in that silence, something inside her settled.

She thought of Charlotte—bright-eyed and curious, with her tangle of black curls and questions about bees and bedtime stories. Sweet girl. Wary, but not broken. Not yet. Jemma wanted to protect that—fiercely.

She liked Agnes, too. The no-nonsense warmth of her. The way she'd looked Jemma straight in the eye and welcomed her with a touch of humour and the comfort of flour-dusted hands.

But Benjamin Callahan… that was a different story.

She wasn't sure he disliked her—not exactly. It felt more like suspicion. Like he was bracing for something to go wrong. As if kindness, or even basic civility, cost him more than he was willing to pay.

That was fine. She wasn't here to win him over. They didn't have to be friends. But they did have to work together—for Charlotte's sake, if nothing else.

Still, the way his eyes had followed her at dinner hadn't gone unnoticed. Quiet, unreadable. Like he was trying to figure out what her angle was. Like he was building a wall every time she opened her mouth.

She could live with that.

It wasn't like she hadn't faced worse.

Jemma exhaled slowly, blinking up at the stars one last time. Then she turned and stepped back into the cottage, closing the door behind her with a soft click.

She didn't see the man sitting in the shadows on the verandah across the yard.

Didn't see how still he'd gone. Or how his grip on the armrest had loosened, like something inside him had quietly unclenched, quiet, and conflicted, as she disappeared from view.

Didn't know that, for the first time in a very long while, Benjamin Callahan wasn't thinking about the past—or the choices that had left him bitter, wary, and alone.

He was thinking about her.

And it unsettled him more than anything else had in years.

Chapter Seven

The cottage was still when Jemma woke, the hush of early morning broken only by the low hum of stirring cicadas. She dressed quickly—simple denim shorts, a fitted white T-shirt, and a lightweight grey jumper pulled over the top. The air raised goosebumps on her skin as she stepped outside, sharp, and cool against her legs, but the horizon already shimmered with the promise of heat.

She made her way up to the main house, the scent of eucalyptus heavy in the crisp morning air. The screen door creaked as she pushed it open, and Agnes glanced up from the stove with a small, welcoming smile.

"Mornin', love," she said, flipping a rasher of bacon in the pan. "Sleep all right?"

Jemma nodded. "Like a log. Morning, Agnes."

"Good. That bed in the cottage is better than it looks, eh?"

"Much better. Thank you again for setting it up so nicely."

Agnes waved a dismissive hand. "Please. Was just glad someone finally moved in. It's been empty too long." She reached for a plate and began piling it high. "Charlotte's still out like a light, by the way. Girl was wiped last night. Poor thing hasn't talked that much in months."

Jemma smiled as she slid into one of the kitchen chairs. "She's a joy. Sharp as a tack."

Agnes set a steaming plate in front of her—scrambled eggs, crispy bacon, sourdough toast—and then sat down with her own cup of tea. The kitchen filled with the soft clink of cutlery and the gentle sounds of birdsong drifting in through the open window.

They ate quietly, the kind of silence that was easy and companionable.

By the time they were done, the morning had warmed, and the sun was streaming through the panes above the sink. Jemma tugged her jumper over her head and laid it on the back of her chair. Her T-shirt hitched on the jumper as she pulled it over her head, lifting just enough to expose the edge of her side.

Agnes froze mid-sip.

Her eyes caught the darkened marks that bloomed beneath the hem of Jemma's shirt— old, yellowing bruises that traced her ribs and waist. Faint now, but unmistakable. She lowered her cup with care.

"Jemma."

The tone was different—gentle, but firm. Concern threaded through it like a wire.

Jemma looked up, startled. "Yes?"

Agnes's gaze was steady. Kind, but unflinching. "That bruising… on your side. What happened?"

Jemma blinked, the question landing with quiet weight.

For a second, she considered brushing it off. A fall. A knock. Something simple. But something about Agnes's expression—the way her lined face was furrowed with genuine concern, not curiosity—made her pause.

She took a slow breath. "It's nothing urgent. Just… not as old as it should be."

Agnes leaned forward, her voice low. "Did someone do that to you?"

Jemma didn't speak at first. Her hands were folded tightly in her lap now, the calm she wore like armour slipping ever so slightly.

She nodded. Once. Small.

Agnes exhaled, long and quiet. "Hell," she said softly. "I'm sorry, love."

Jemma gave a faint shake of her head. "It's not your fault."

"No," Agnes said gently. "But it's someone's."

The silence stretched again—thicker this time, tinged with something raw.

Jemma reached for her tea—more to keep her hands busy than anything else. "It's… behind me," she said quietly. "I got out. He's in jail."

Agnes's brow furrowed. "How long was it going on?"

"A couple of years," Jemma admitted, her voice steady but soft. "He was… controlling. Possessive. It took a long time, but I finally got away."

There was no bitterness in her tone. Just quiet truth. And maybe a trace of exhaustion.

Agnes didn't speak right away. Her eyes didn't leave Jemma's face.

When she did speak, her voice was low. Firm. "No one will hurt you here. You're safe now."

Jemma nodded, her jaw tightening. "Yes. I wouldn't have come if I wasn't."

Agnes gave a small nod of her own, her lined face softening. "Right. Well. Just know— if that safety ever starts to slip, you come to me. You don't wait. You understand?"

Jemma blinked. Once. Then again—this time against the sudden, stinging rush behind her eyes. "I understand," she whispered. "Thank you."

Agnes stood and reached out, giving her shoulder a light, steady squeeze. "You're not alone out here. We don't wear polished masks at Callahan Station. We look after our own."

Jemma exhaled slowly, letting go of a breath she hadn't even realised she was holding.

A long moment passed in quiet.

What neither of them knew—what neither of them could see—was the tall figure standing just down the hallway, frozen in place.

Ben had come in through the back door and stopped short when he'd heard voices. He hadn't meant to listen.

But now he couldn't move.

Someone had hurt her. Badly. Repeatedly. And something inside him burned at the thought.

His jaw clenched. His hands curled into fists at his sides.

He hated men like that.

And the worst part—the part that twisted in his gut—was how calm she'd sounded. Like she'd had to make peace with it just to survive.

Ben swallowed hard.

He hadn't trusted her. Hadn't even tried.

But now… he saw the truth beneath the polish. Not weaker. Not fragile. Just forged by fire.

Stronger than he'd given her credit for.

And far more than just the woman who showed up smiling at his daughter's side.

Ben stood in the hallway long after the women's voices had faded, the words echoing in his head like a slow drumbeat.

He's in jail.

Controlling. Possessive.

A couple of years.

He stared at the floorboards, jaw locked, something hot simmering in his chest. Anger—sharp and immediate—he knew that feeling well. But this was layered with something heavier. Guilt. Frustration. Maybe even shame.

He'd watched her warily from the moment she arrived, convinced she was too polished, too composed, too perfect. He'd assumed she was hiding something. He just hadn't expected it to be scars.

Not the kind that lived beneath skin.

Ben scrubbed a hand down his face, trying to ease the tension coiling in his shoulders. She hadn't flinched. Not when he barked a question. Not when he froze her out with silence. She hadn't buckled under his suspicion—she'd met it with calm. Measured. Steady.

Because she'd already been through worse.

A hell of a lot worse.

And suddenly, he felt like the bastard.

He'd been guarding his daughter, sure. Protecting Charlotte was his entire world. But he hadn't stopped to consider who Jemma might be protecting.

Herself.

Ben paced to the edge of the veranda, the early sun warming the boards beneath his boots. He stared out at the paddocks stretching wide and open across the land—his land. Normally, that view calmed him. Brought him back to centre.

But not this morning.

His chest felt tight. Uneasy.

He couldn't stop thinking about her. About the quiet way she'd smiled at Charlotte— steady, gentle, like she had all the time in the world. Like kindness wasn't a performance but a language she spoke fluently.

She hadn't asked for anything. Hadn't tried to impress or force her way in.

She'd just… been good.

And Charlotte, the same child who'd spent a year keeping everyone at arm's length, had taken her hand without hesitation.

Ben didn't understand women like that.

Or maybe he just hadn't let himself try.

He ran a hand over his face and gripped the railing, the wood worn smooth under his palms. The instinct to protect still burned hot inside him—coiled and ready, always. But this time, it wasn't just Charlotte he was thinking about.

It was Jemma, too.

That realisation hit like a jolt to the spine.

Because caring was dangerous. Caring meant risk. Risk of being wrong. Of letting someone too close. Of opening the door to things he'd fought damn hard to keep out.

Disappointment. Betrayal. Grief.

He'd built walls for a reason. High ones. Solid.

But now…

Pretending not to care?

That might've been the lie that cost him something real.

The kitchen was quiet now.

Only the ticking wall clock, the distant clatter of hooves from the stables, and the soft hum of cicadas filled the space. Agnes stood at the sink, rinsing breakfast plates with practiced ease—but her hands moved on habit alone. Her mind was elsewhere.

When Ben walked in, she didn't turn. She felt him behind her—the heavy pause in his footsteps, the weight of something unspoken hanging in the doorway.

He stood there a beat too long. Then:

"Agnes."

She glanced over her shoulder. His voice was low. Rougher than usual, like it had been dragged up from somewhere deep.

"Hmm?" she replied, drying her hands with a tea towel, her gaze landing on him.

"I heard you two talking." He didn't elaborate—he didn't need to.

Agnes nodded once. "Figured as much."

He crossed to the table, resting a hand on the back of a chair. "Didn't mean to eavesdrop. Came in through the back… then heard what she said."

His jaw flexed. "She didn't sound broken."

"No," Agnes said, firm. "She didn't."

He stared down at the woodgrain beneath his hand. "But someone did that to her."

Agnes moved to lean against the counter, tea towel still in her hands. "Someone did more than that. A damn good job of it."

His eyes snapped to hers. "What do you mean?"

She folded the cloth with slow precision before answering.

"I saw the bruises, Ben. Not little ones. Not old. Deep, stretching across her ribs and side. That wasn't from a knock or a clumsy fall."

His fingers curled tighter around the chair.

"She said it's behind her," he muttered.

"Maybe," Agnes allowed. "But something like that doesn't stay in the past just because you walk away from it."

Ben's mouth was set in a grim line. "She didn't even flinch. Not when I barked at her. Not when I questioned her in front of Charlotte."

"No," Agnes said quietly. "Because she's used to worse. That's the thing about women like her—they learn to stay quiet. Keep their chin up. Make calm look easy."

He didn't speak. Just let her words settle, thick and sharp in the still air.

"She's protecting herself," he said finally, his voice low.

Agnes nodded. "And Charlotte, too. She's here to work, sure. But she's also here to mend. Don't make it harder."

His gaze lifted to hers, and for a moment, there was something raw in it. Something unguarded.

"I wasn't trying to."

"I know." Her voice softened but didn't lose its edge. "But guarding your own wounds doesn't mean pressing on someone else's. You, of all people, should know that."

He gave a small, tight nod. No argument. No denial.

Agnes stepped forward and touched his arm, brief but steady.

"She probably didn't want anyone to know. She's not after pity. Just peace."

"I don't pity her," he said, voice like gravel.

"Good," Agnes said simply. "Then stop watching her like she's a snake ready to strike."

Ben didn't answer. He stood there for a beat, then turned to the doorway. Paused with one hand on the frame.

"She's stronger than I thought," he said.

Agnes gave a faint smile. "That's usually how it goes with women like her."

He left without another word.

Agnes turned back to the sink, the water now cool beneath her fingers, her thoughts still lingering on the girl with the green eyes and the quiet, steady heart.

Chapter Eight

The sun was already climbing high by the time Charlotte arrived at the cottage, backpack slung over one tiny shoulder and curls bouncing with each step. Jemma was waiting on the porch with two cold bottles of water and a wide smile.

"Ready for our first adventure?" she asked.

Charlotte nodded, eyes bright. "Yep! I brought my books, my pencils—and my rock collection."

Jemma grinned. "Excellent. I was hoping for a rock expert."

They started the day at the little table near the window, the light slanting across the surface in warm ribbons. Jemma kept the lesson gentle but structured—reading first, Charlotte perched on a cushion with her elbows propped on the table, sounding out words with proud determination. When she got one right, Jemma clapped softly, and Charlotte's whole face lit up.

"You're really good at this," Jemma said sincerely, tapping her pencil to the worksheet. "Do you like reading?"

Charlotte shrugged shyly. "Sometimes. If it's about animals or space stuff."

"Well then," Jemma said, reaching under the table, "you're in luck." She pulled out one of her old books she'd tucked away just for this—Big Book of Amazing Creatures. Charlotte gasped, her eyes going round.

"For me?"

"Yep," Jemma said with a wink. "It's all yours."

They pored over the pages together, pointing out narwhals and pangolins, koalas, and cassowaries. Charlotte's questions came fast, tumbling over one another, and Jemma answered each with enthusiasm—or curiosity when she didn't know the answer, which Charlotte seemed to like even more.

By midmorning, they took a break and headed outside. Jemma spread a picnic rug beneath a gum tree near the back fence, and Charlotte dumped her rock collection onto it like buried treasure.

"This one's my favourite," she said, holding up a smooth pink stone shaped like a tear.

"It's beautiful," Jemma said, holding it up to the light. "Looks like rose quartz."

Charlotte beamed. "I think it's magic."

"Well," Jemma said seriously, "I think we should write a story about it."

Charlotte lit up like the sun.

They spent the next hour inventing a tale about a lost princess who carried a rose quartz stone that could guide her home. Charlotte dictated, and Jemma scribbled down each line, exaggerating her serious author face to make Charlotte giggle.

Lunch came and went in the shade of the same gum tree—Agnes brought out sandwiches and apple slices, chatting for a bit before heading back inside. Ben hadn't returned from the paddocks, and Charlotte didn't seem to notice. She was too busy explaining how the princess's horse could talk, and the villain had been turned into a wombat.

After lunch, Jemma pulled out a tin of watercolour paints and a stack of thick paper.

"Time to illustrate our story," she said, setting up two jars of water.

Charlotte's face turned solemn with concentration as she dipped her brush and began to paint the princess's stone, careful and precise. Jemma painted beside her, letting the silence stretch between them like soft thread. It was a quiet, peaceful sort of bond—no need to fill every moment with words.

By the time Ben returned in the late afternoon—dusty, sun-warmed, and smelling faintly of hay—the veranda was scattered with pages of drying artwork, each one vivid with colour and the joyful chaos of a creative day.

Both girls were fast asleep on an old woollen blanket, tucked into one another like puzzle pieces. Jemma sat with her back against the wall, one hand resting lightly on a hand-painted storybook, the other gently threaded through Charlotte's curls. The little girl lay curled at her side, cheek pressed to Jemma's hip, tiny fingers still clutching the edge of the homemade book like it was a treasure she'd never let go.

Ben paused in the doorway, not wanting to wake them. But the sight stole his breath.

It hit him harder than he expected—this quiet, sun-drenched moment of peace. There was something in it… something soft and still and safe that wrapped around his ribs and squeezed.

Charlotte looked content. Truly content. Her little face calm, her body relaxed in a way he hadn't seen in months. She hadn't smiled like that in so long. Hadn't trusted enough to lean into someone—not even him.

And Jemma…

She held Charlotte like it was second nature. No stiffness, no awkwardness. Just quiet warmth. If someone didn't know better, they'd think she was Charlotte's mother. Their colouring was nearly identical—the same dark hair, the same sun-kissed skin, the same long lashes resting against flushed cheeks.

But it wasn't just the look of them. It was the feel. The ease. The unspoken bond forming right in front of him.

And somehow, without him noticing, Jemma had slipped past Charlotte's walls… and his.

Ben exhaled slowly, the sound barely audible. He leaned against the doorframe, arms crossed over his chest, something tight and unfamiliar blooming low in his throat.

He hadn't expected this.

He hadn't expected her.

And he sure as hell hadn't expected to feel anything this dangerous again.

Dinner was a lively affair—at least for one member of the table.

Charlotte talked nonstop, her little fork waving in the air with every new burst of excitement.

"And then we made a book—like a real book, Daddy! With pages and a cover and everything!"

Her eyes shone as she looked up at him, tomato sauce smudged near her mouth, her curls still slightly damp from the bath Jemma had given her earlier.

"Jemma wrote the words, and I drew the pictures. I did a princess with sparkles, and a dragon, and there's a rainbow horse! You have to see it!"

Ben smiled, setting down his cutlery. "Sounds like a masterpiece."

"It is!" Charlotte beamed. She wriggled in her seat, then reached under the table and produced a small, stapled booklet with colourful pages and crayon drawings that danced across each one. She handed it to him with both hands. "Here. It's for you."

Ben took it carefully, like it was made of glass. The cover was titled Charlotte's Magic Forest, written in Jemma's elegant handwriting. Inside, her words told a sweet little story about a brave girl and a shy dragon, paired with Charlotte's bold, joyful illustrations.

His chest pulled tight.

"This is incredible, sweetheart," he said, his voice a touch rougher than before. "Thank you."

Charlotte grinned and dove back into her plate, still chattering between bites about all the things they'd done—learning new letters, building a castle out of cereal boxes, baking scones that "sort of flopped, but only a little bit."

Across the table, Jemma sat quietly. She wasn't withdrawn—just... still. She smiled whenever Charlotte spoke, a soft, patient kind of smile that seemed to radiate warmth without demanding attention. She only answered when someone asked her something directly, and even then, her replies were gentle and brief.

Ben found himself watching her more than he meant to.

There was no trace of performance in her. No false modesty or effort to impress. Just calm. Kindness. Steadiness.

It was clear she'd done the lion's share of today's work—but she didn't try to take the spotlight. She let Charlotte shine, let her be the centre of attention, without ever once stepping in to redirect it.

And Charlotte... hadn't stopped glowing.

Ben looked back down at the little book in his hands, then up again—past the soft kitchen light, past the clink of cutlery and the familiar rhythm of family dinner—and let his gaze settle on Jemma once more.

Something about her presence in the room felt right. Like she belonged there.

Not because she was trying to.

But because she wasn't.

And that quiet certainty—that steadiness—was starting to chip away at the walls he'd spent years fortifying.

The soft glow of the bedside lamp cast a warm halo across Charlotte's room, brushing golden light over the little girl's curls as she nestled beneath the covers. The storybook lay on the nightstand beside her, its crayon-coloured pages proudly displayed like a treasure.

Jemma sat on the edge of the bed, smoothing the blanket over Charlotte's small form.

"You were very brave in your story today," she said softly, brushing a strand of hair from Charlotte's forehead. "You protected the dragon and made peace with the rainbow horse. That's not easy to do."

Charlotte giggled sleepily. "'Cause I'm magic," she whispered, her voice already thick with dreams.

Jemma smiled, then leaned in and pressed a gentle kiss to the girl's cheek. "You certainly are."

She rose quietly, careful not to disturb the stillness that had settled over the room.

Ben stood just inside the doorway. He hadn't meant to intrude—just meant to say goodnight—but what he saw rooted him to the spot.

The light kiss.

The tenderness in Jemma's expression.

The way Charlotte instinctively reached out, even in sleep, her fingers curling slightly where Jemma's hand had been.

Jemma turned—and caught sight of him.

She froze for a beat, then offered a small, startled smile as a blush bloomed high on her cheeks.

"Sorry," she murmured, brushing past him. "Didn't realise you were there."

Ben cleared his throat, stepping aside. "No need to be sorry. I was just coming to say goodnight."

She gave a quick nod and slipped past him, her steps already carrying her toward the front door.

Ben looked down at his daughter, now sleeping soundly, her cheek still pink where Jemma had kissed it. Something warm twisted in his chest.

He moved quickly, catching up with Jemma just as her hand reached for the doorknob of the cottage.

"Wait."

She turned, startled again—this time not from embarrassment, but surprise.

Ben stood a few feet away, one hand tucked into the pocket of his jeans, the other holding the storybook, his shoulders carrying the stiffness of someone unused to starting conversations like this.

"I just wanted to say thank you," he said. "For today. For the book. She—Charlotte— she hasn't lit up like that in a long time."

Jemma's eyes softened. "She's a remarkable little girl. I'm just glad I could help her enjoy herself."

He nodded, gaze dropping briefly to the space between them.

"She gave me this book like it was gold. She's proud of it. You gave her that."

"You gave me the time with her," Jemma replied gently. "So, thank you, too."

Ben met her eyes then, something quiet and unreadable in his own.

"I don't know what I expected when you showed up," he said. "But I didn't expect… this. Her being so at ease. You being so—good with her."

The blush returned, just a trace of pink in the porch light.

"I just tried to listen," Jemma said quietly. "That's all most kids need, really. Someone to listen."

He nodded slowly. A beat passed—comfortable but charged with something unspoken.

"Anyway," he said at last, stepping back. "I'll let you get some rest. Big day tomorrow."

Jemma gave a soft smile. "Good night, Ben."

"Good night."

She disappeared inside, and the door clicked gently shut behind her.

Ben stood on the veranda for a long moment, the night air cool against his skin. In his hand, he still held the little book.

He turned it over once, then tucked it under his arm and headed back toward the main house, the echo of Jemma's kiss to his daughter's cheek lingering longer than he expected.

Chapter Nine

Ben lay on his back, one arm slung across his forehead, staring up at the ceiling where the faint glow from the hallway bled under the door in a thin, golden line.

The house was still, wrapped in the hush of deep night—just the occasional creak of settling timber and the soft whisper of wind brushing against the eaves. He'd checked on Charlotte an hour ago; she was fast asleep, curled around her stuffed bunny, worn out from the day's adventures.

He should've been out cold himself by now. He'd been up before sunrise, worked hard enough to feel it in every bone and muscle. Most nights, that kind of fatigue would've knocked him straight out.

But tonight, sleep wouldn't come.

He couldn't stop thinking about her.

Jemma.

The way she'd kissed Charlotte's cheek like it was the most natural thing in the world. The way she'd smiled—soft, surprised, flushed—when she'd seen him watching.

It had hit something in him. Something buried deep and long ignored.

He rolled onto his side, exhaling roughly, eyes drifting toward the window where the moonlight threaded through the curtains.

It wasn't just that she was good with Charlotte—though she was. God, she was. Patient and calm, with a kind of quiet strength that didn't ask for praise but deserved every bit of it. His daughter hadn't just tolerated her—she'd trusted her. Opened up to her. Smiled like she hadn't in months.

But it wasn't just that.

It was everything else, too.

The way Jemma tucked her hair behind her ear when she was concentrating. The curve of her smile when she thought no one was looking. The way her eyes lit up when Charlotte said something clever. The way she listened—really listened—without judgment or agenda.

And the way she looked tonight in the porch light, cheeks still pink from that kiss, eyes soft and open, voice low and warm when she'd said 'Goodnight, Ben'.

He closed his eyes, jaw flexing.

What would it feel like to touch her cheek? To brush that dark hair back and lean in, just a little closer? To kiss her slow—no urgency, just the kind of aching softness that said I see you. I want you. You're safe.

His stomach twisted. He clenched his hand into the sheet beside him.

No.

No. This couldn't happen.

He'd made that mistake once—falling for softness, for beauty, for the lie of something lasting. He'd believed in promises, in change, in the idea that love could heal what was already broken.

Look where that got him.

Look where it got Charlotte.

This wasn't about him. It couldn't be. Jemma was here for his daughter—not for him. And he wouldn't drag her into the wreckage of his past just because he was lonely or tired or hadn't been touched by someone gentle in far too long.

He couldn't afford another mess. Not now. Not ever.

Ben let out a slow breath through his nose, turned onto his stomach, and buried his face in the pillow.

The smell of hay clung faintly to his skin. A trace of apple shampoo lingered in the hall. And beneath it all, that flicker of want he couldn't quite kill.

But he'd ignore it.

He had to.

Tomorrow was another day.

And he'd make damn sure to keep his distance.

The night was still, save for the rustle of leaves brushing against the cottage windows and the soft tick of the clock on the kitchen wall. Jemma stood at the sink, rinsing out the paint jars from the afternoon, her hands moving automatically while her thoughts drifted somewhere else entirely.

To him.

Ben Callahan.

She hadn't meant to think about him. Not like this.

But the way he'd looked at her tonight—after dinner, and then again on the porch—it had unsettled something in her. Something buried deep, something she'd locked up tight.

She'd seen kindness in his eyes. Real kindness. The kind that didn't ask for anything in return. And Charlotte… oh, that little girl had wrapped herself around Jemma's heart without even trying. Her giggles, her bright, curious eyes, her easy affection—it had been a long time since anyone had looked at Jemma like that, like they trusted her.

She dried her hands and moved to the small couch, sitting down with a slow exhale. Her whole body ached—not from exertion, but from the strange, steady unravelling that had been happening inside her all day.

Ben was different. He didn't crowd her, didn't probe. He watched carefully, spoke sparingly—but when he did speak, it meant something. He listened. He noticed things. He cared, even if he didn't always know how to show it.

And damn it, he was handsome. Broad shoulders, rough hands, that quiet, thoughtful way of moving through a room like he didn't want to disturb anyone. And his voice— low and steady—stayed with her long after he'd stopped speaking.

She let her head fall back against the cushion, staring at the low cottage ceiling.

What would it feel like, she wondered, to let him touch her? To feel his fingers, skim her cheek, to lean into the warmth of his chest, to let herself believe—for one second— that a man like Ben could be safe?

Her breath caught. She shut her eyes tight.

No.

Men didn't stay kind. They started out soft—gentle smiles, thoughtful gestures, words that felt like safety. But it never lasted. Sooner or later, they showed their teeth. Leo had. Sweet words had soured into insults. Gentle hands had turned violent. And even now, weeks later, her body still held the memory of fear. Her skin remembered the bruises, even after they faded. Her mind clung to every lie she told herself—It's not that bad. He doesn't mean it. He'll stop.

But he hadn't. And deep down, she knew—kindness was just the opening act. Sooner or later, the curtain dropped, and the monster stepped forward.

She pressed her palms flat against her thighs, grounding herself.

Ben was good to Charlotte. He'd been respectful to her. But that didn't mean she could trust him. She couldn't afford to.

Letting her guard down had cost her too much once already.

So, no matter how gentle his eyes were, or how warm his voice felt wrapped around her name, she wouldn't let herself go there. Not again.

Jemma rose from the couch, flicked off the lamp, and padded quietly to her bedroom.

She would keep her distance. She had to.

Even if part of her—quiet, aching, stubborn—didn't want to.

The smell of scrambled eggs and fresh bread filled the kitchen as sunlight streamed through the open windows. Agnes moved between the stove and the table with her usual briskness, setting down a plate of toast beside Charlotte, who was already halfway through her second helping of eggs.

"Slow down, darling," Jemma said gently with a smile. "You're not racing anyone."

Charlotte grinned, mouth full, and slowed only slightly.

Ben sat across the table, hair still damp from his shower, sleeves rolled to his forearms. He hadn't said much yet, but Jemma could feel his gaze now and then—brief, unreadable glances that landed softly and left her pulse a little unsteady.

She focused on cutting Charlotte's apple slices, trying to ignore the flutter low in her belly.

Then came the knock at the door.

Agnes turned, brow furrowing. "Now who—?"

Before she could finish, the screen door creaked open and in swept Mia Wilson, all perfume and lipstick, blonde waves bouncing like she owned the breeze. Her smile was wide, her stride confident, and trailing behind her—carrying a box of baked goods— was a tall man with an easy grin and a too-long look in his eyes the moment they landed on Jemma.

"Morning, Ben!" Mia called, her voice just a little too bright. "Thought we'd bring some treats out—Mum had extras from the bakery. Figured you could use a little something sweet."

Ben stood politely, hands sliding into his back pockets. "Thanks, Mia."

Mia's eyes flicked past him and landed on Jemma.

Her smile wavered.

"Oh," she said, blinking. "You have… company."

"Jemma," Ben said, gesturing calmly. "She's Charlotte's nanny."

Jemma offered a friendly, restrained smile. "Nice to meet you."

Mia's gaze swept over her, slowly. Assessing. Judging. "Hmm. From the city, I take it?"

"Melbourne," Jemma replied evenly.

Mia tilted her head. "That's a long way from home, isn't it?"

Jemma didn't rise to the bait. "It is."

At the stove, Agnes gave the eggs a bit more aggression than necessary as she stirred.

Mia's brother stepped forward then, sliding the box of cakes onto the counter but keeping his attention squarely on Jemma. "I'm Tyler," he said with a smile that made Jemma's skin crawl just a little. "You always this good with kids or just this one?"

Jemma gave a small, polite laugh and glanced back at Charlotte, who was watching the exchange with open curiosity.

"She's easy to love," Jemma said, brushing a curl from Charlotte's forehead.

Ben didn't miss the way Tyler was still looking at Jemma—like she was something shiny he wanted to claim before anyone else could. His jaw ticked.

"Appreciate the delivery," Ben said, voice clipped now. "We've just sat down to eat."

Mia blinked at the coolness in his tone. She turned her attention to Charlotte, crouching beside her chair with a saccharine smile.

"Hi there, sweetheart. Remember me?"

Charlotte shook her head, chewing a piece of toast.

"I brought you a cupcake," Mia added with false cheer.

Charlotte looked to Jemma first, a habit already forming.

Jemma nodded gently. "Say thank you, Charlotte."

"Thanks," she murmured, then promptly returned to her plate.

Mia rose, clearly thrown off.

"Well," she said, smoothing her hair. "We won't stay. Just thought we'd pop by. You know where to find me, Ben."

"Right," he said, not moving from his spot.

Agnes appeared at his side, arms crossed. "Don't let the icing melt," she said flatly to Tyler.

Mia blinked. "Oh. Yes. Of course. Bye then."

They stepped out just as quickly as they'd entered, the screen door snapping shut behind them.

Silence settled over the kitchen.

Then Agnes muttered, "That girl's been sniffing around here since she was sixteen. Still hasn't figured out he's not buying what she's selling."

Ben rubbed the back of his neck, looking vaguely embarrassed. "Don't start, Agnes."

Charlotte giggled. "That lady was weird."

Jemma bit back a smile and took a sip of her tea.

Ben caught her eye across the table, something half-apologetic, half-amused in his expression. But underneath it, a flicker of something darker still lingered—possessive, protective.

He hadn't liked the way Tyler looked at her.

And Jemma… well, she wasn't sure what she'd seen in Ben's eyes.

But it made her heart beat a little faster.

Chapter Ten

The next few days slipped into a kind of steady rhythm.

Charlotte's lessons kept Jemma busy—phonics, finger painting, scavenger hunts through the paddocks. She was thriving, her laughter ringing through the house like wind chimes in the breeze. And Ben… Ben kept his distance. The land demanded his attention, and he gave it willingly. Fencing, feeding, fixing—anything that kept his hands full and his mind off the woman sleeping in the cottage not too far away.

They only came together at dinner, when Charlotte launched into animated recaps of the day, her little hands flying as she described every storybook and spider discovery. Jemma smiled and listened. Ben listened and tried not to stare. Most nights, he failed.

It was the third afternoon after Mia and Tyler's last visit. The sky was soft with late sun as Jemma and Charlotte returned from a walk down to the creek. Agnes was already out front talking to someone—two someone's, Jemma realised, as they neared the house.

Mia stood by her white ute, dressed in a short floral dress and boots far too clean for someone supposedly dropping off supplies. Her smile was wide and purposeful. Beside her, Tyler leaned on the passenger side door, sunglasses hooked into the collar of his shirt.

Ben stepped out onto the veranda just as Jemma reached the fence. He paused, towel slung over one shoulder, clearly just back from the shed. The moment his eyes landed on Jemma, Mia stepped into his line of sight.

"Ben," she called sweetly, twirling a strand of her blonde hair. "Perfect timing. I was just about to come find you."

He blinked. "Everything alright?"

"Oh, everything's great," she said with a laugh that didn't quite reach her eyes. "I wanted to see if you'd go to the dance with me this Saturday. I mean—it wouldn't feel like a real town event if you weren't there."

Ben opened his mouth, clearly about to decline, when Tyler chimed in from beside the ute.

"I was actually just about to ask your nanny here the same thing."

Jemma glanced at him, startled.

"The dance," Tyler continued, grinning at her. "You should come. We could make a night of it—bit of music, few drinks. Fun, yeah?"

Ben stilled.

His gaze slid from Tyler to Jemma, then back to Mia, who was watching him with open expectation. Jemma, caught in the middle, wasn't sure where to look.

And then Ben said it—blurted it, really.

"She's going with me."

Mia turned slowly, her expression cracking at the edges.

"Excuse me?"

Ben's jaw flexed, but he didn't back down.

"I was going to ask her."

Jemma's eyes darted to his. Her breath hitched at the certainty she saw there—warm, steady, real.

Tyler let out a soft chuckle. "Well, damn. Didn't know I had competition."

"You don't," Ben said, too quickly.

Mia folded her arms. "So that's it, then? No to me, yes to the nanny?"

"Her name's Jemma," he said flatly. "And yeah."

Silence stretched. Tyler gave a low whistle and stepped back toward the ute.

Mia lingered another second, eyes hard on Jemma now. "Well. I guess you'll be the talk of the dance," she said, voice brittle. "Hope you like small-town gossip, sweetheart."

Jemma's spine straightened. "I'll manage."

Ben moved toward her then—just enough to close the space between them—and gently placed a hand on her lower back.

Mia saw it.

So did Tyler.

And neither of them liked it.

"Come on, Charlotte," Jemma said softly, breaking the tension. "Let's get inside."

The little girl skipped ahead, oblivious to the storm that had just passed through.

Ben lingered behind a beat, watching Mia and Tyler climb into their truck.

As the engine faded down the road, Agnes muttered from the porch, "Lord help us. Mia's going to set fire to something before Saturday."

Ben exhaled through his nose, then turned to the screen door where Jemma waited.

"Sorry about that," he said quietly.

Jemma looked at him for a long moment. "Are you?"

A smile tugged at his mouth. "Not even a little."

And for the first time in days, she smiled back.

The cottage was a cheerful mess—hairbrushes, folded dresses, and a half-toppled stack of hair clips scattered across the bed. Charlotte sat cross-legged in the middle of it all, clutching her stuffed bunny in one hand and pointing decisively with the other.

"Not that one," she said with a little wrinkle of her nose. "That one's too wrinkly."

Jemma laughed as she held up the plain navy dress in question. "Too wrinkly, huh?"

Charlotte nodded, very serious. "And it's not fun."

"Well, we can't have that," Jemma teased, turning back to the bed. "What about this one?"

She held up a soft, floaty blue dress with tiny white flowers printed along the hem. It was simple, but when she held it up to her frame, it swayed gently, catching the golden afternoon light.

Charlotte gasped. "That one! That's the princess dress!"

Jemma smiled and shook her head, amused. "A princess dress for the town dance. Alright then."

She slipped it on while Charlotte bounced excitedly on the bed, watching with wide eyes. When Jemma turned back to the mirror, adjusting the neckline and smoothing the skirt, Charlotte sighed like it was the most magical thing she'd ever seen.

"You look pretty," she said simply.

Jemma turned, touched by the honesty in her small voice. "Thank you, sweetheart. That means more than you know."

"Are you gonna dance with Daddy?" Charlotte asked, her voice hopeful.

Jemma paused at the mirror, pretending to fuss with her hair. "I don't know. Do you think he'd want to?"

Charlotte shrugged, swinging her legs. "He smiled when you helped me with my reading today. Like a big smile. Not his normal one."

Jemma smiled softly to herself. "Did he now?"

"Uh-huh," Charlotte said. "And you make him laugh. He doesn't laugh lots. But he does when you're around."

Jemma swallowed the sudden tightness in her throat and crouched beside the bed, brushing a lock of hair from Charlotte's forehead.

"You're a wise little thing, you know that?"

Charlotte giggled and nodded like it was obvious.

Jemma stood again and walked over to the pair of boots Agnes had dropped off earlier. The soft brown leather hugged her calves perfectly, worn in just enough to be comfortable, but still lovely. She pulled them on and turned slowly in front of the mirror.

Charlotte clapped. "You look like a cowgirl!"

Jemma chuckled. "A cowgirl in a princess dress. Think the folks at the dance can handle that?"

"Yes!" Charlotte hopped down and grabbed Jemma's hand. "You're the prettiest nanny ever."

Jemma pulled her into a hug, kissing her temple. "Thank you, lovebug."

Outside, the shadows stretched long across the paddocks, the sun dipping low behind the hills in a haze of amber and rose gold. The evening breeze carried the scent of eucalyptus and dust, warm and familiar. Jemma slipped on her jacket and reached for Charlotte's hand.

"Ready, missy?" she asked with a smile.

Charlotte nodded eagerly, her boots clomping along the cottage steps as they made their way toward the main house—toward Jemma's first country dance.

Inside, Ben stood in front of the bathroom mirror, jaw tight, trying to flatten a stubborn wave of hair that refused to stay down.

He wasn't nervous.

Not really.

But he'd changed shirts twice and cleaned his boots like it was Sunday service, not a local dance. Now here he was, fussing with his hair like some awkward teenager instead of a grown man with a thousand acres to run.

Nope. Definitely not nervous.

He just wanted to look… decent. Presentable. Respectable.

Especially tonight.

Especially with her going.

He was just… irritated. At himself. At the way, his shirt suddenly felt too snug across the shoulders. At the silence pressing in, making every thought echo louder than it should.

This wasn't a date. It wasn't anything.

Just a town dance. A bit of music, a few sugary cakes, a slow shuffle around the hall. Harmless. Ordinary.

Except it didn't feel ordinary.

Not this time.

Not with Jemma.

He hadn't planned to say it—that he'd be taking her. The words had just come out, fast and possessive, before he'd even registered what Mia was asking.

He didn't even care what Mia had been asking.

Not after Tyler turned to Jemma with that too-easy grin and asked if she'd like to go with him. Like she was some prize up for grabs. Like Ben didn't have to stand there and watch it happen.

He'd felt something lock tight in his chest.

And then the words had come out.

"I'll be taking her."

Like she was his.

He ran a hand down his face and swore under his breath.

He didn't regret it—not exactly. Because the truth was, he didn't want her going with Tyler. Didn't like the way the guy looked at her, didn't trust the smile or the casual charm.

But wanting to stop her from going with someone else… wasn't the same as wanting her for himself.

Was it?

The mirror didn't have any answers.

Ben turned away and grabbed his hat off the hook. His shoulders were stiff, his gut twisted, and the evening ahead felt like more than it had any right to.

He was ready.

But not really.

Because whatever this thing was building between him and Jemma—it wasn't simple anymore. It wasn't a line he could walk. It felt like a cliff.

And the scariest damn part?

He wasn't sure he wanted to stop the fall.

The sun had almost disappeared behind the hills, leaving the sky awash in burnt orange and soft lavender. The breeze had cooled, carrying the faint scent of dust, dry grass, and something faintly sweet from Agnes's kitchen.

Ben stood on the front verandah, hat in hand, one boot tapping restlessly against the timber boards. He wasn't pacing, not exactly. Just… shifting. Waiting.

And then he saw her.

She stepped out of the cottage, Charlotte's small hand tucked into hers, and for a second—just a second—Ben forgot how to breathe.

Jemma.

Her dark hair was down, long, and glossy, the ends curling just slightly at her waist. A soft blue dress—simple but pretty—fluttered around her knees, and those borrowed boots looked like they were made for her after all. But it wasn't the clothes, or the way the late sun kissed her skin.

It was the way she smiled at Charlotte's chatter, head tipped back in laughter.

So open. So real.

So damn beautiful it made something inside him clench.

He hadn't expected this. Hadn't expected her to look like that. Hadn't expected to feel like this.

His grip tightened on the brim of his hat.

She was walking toward him now, eyes finding his, that smile still lingering on her lips—and the air between them charged like a summer storm. Crackling. Bright. Dangerous.

She was still a few paces away when Charlotte let go of her hand and raced up the steps.

"Daddy, doesn't she look pretty?" she said proudly, twirling a little like she'd dressed Jemma herself.

Ben opened his mouth. Closed it. Nodded once.

Pretty didn't cover it.

"Yeah," he managed, voice low and rough. "She does."

Jemma came up the steps slowly, brushing her hands down the skirt of her dress like she wasn't sure where to look.

"Hi," she said softly.

Ben cleared his throat. "Hey."

For a heartbeat, they just stood there. Not speaking. Not needing to.

She was close now—close enough for him to see the flecks of gold in her green eyes, to catch the soft scent of something floral and warm.

And for the first time all day, he didn't feel ready.

Not even close.

Because this wasn't nothing. This wasn't routine.

It was her.

And that changed everything.

Chapter Eleven

With Charlotte safely tucked in under Agnes's watchful eye, Ben and Jemma drove out to the old community hall.

The building stood like a beacon at the end of the gravel drive, lit by strings of warm fairy lights twined with eucalyptus branches that fluttered gently in the evening breeze. Inside, the timber floors gleamed with polish, and music—old country ballads and boot-stomping classics—drifted through the open doors, mingling with laughter and the rich aroma of roast beef pies and caramelised onion tarts cooling on the long food table.

Ben parked beneath a spreading gum tree, its leaves whispering overhead, then came around to her side. He opened the door and offered his hand.

Jemma didn't need the help. But the way his fingers curled around hers, firm and steady, made her breath catch. His hand lingered at her waist as she stepped down, grounding her, steadying her more than she wanted to admit.

Inside, the warmth and sound of the hall enveloped them.

Heads turned.

Conversation hitched—just for a beat—as people registered the sight. Ben Callahan, the man who'd kept to himself since his wife's death, the man known for working from dawn till dark and rarely joining social events… had brought a woman. A beautiful one. And she was smiling up at him like she belonged beside him.

The silence didn't last long.

From the far end of the room, Agnes's cousin Pearl clapped her hands and called out, "Well, don't you two look like you've walked straight out of a magazine!"

Laughter followed. The spell broke.

A wave of warmth rolled through the room.

"Jemma! So glad you made it!"

"That dress is divine—look at the colour on you!"

"Oh, you're just as pretty as Charlotte says. And polite too, I can tell!"

One by one, the women of Windorah came to greet her—offering cheek kisses, compliments, and eager questions. They chatted about the weather, the new storybooks in the school library, and whether Ben had finally fixed that broken gate on the north paddock.

Jemma felt the tension in her shoulders slowly dissolve. These weren't sharp-eyed, suspicious women. They were kind, curious, generous. Not judging her. Not whispering about her. Just… welcoming her.

She glanced at Ben, who stood just behind her, his hand still lightly resting at the small of her back. Not possessive. Just present. She felt it like a promise.

When the band shifted to a slow, steady two-step, someone nudged Jemma playfully in the ribs. "Go on, Ben—don't leave her standing around. Let's see if you remember how to dance."

Ben looked at Jemma with that quiet intensity she was beginning to recognise—the kind of look that made it hard to breathe.

He extended his hand. "May I?"

She hesitated only a second before placing her fingers in his.

"I'm warning you," she said softly, "I haven't danced in years."

"Good," he murmured, pulling her gently into his arms. "We'll be terrible together."

She laughed—really laughed—and then they were moving, slow and easy, the floor beneath them creaking softly, the scent of eucalyptus thick in the air.

Ben's hand was warm at her waist. His eyes didn't leave hers. And for a moment, nothing else existed.

Jemma wasn't the nanny. She wasn't the girl with secrets or scars.

She was just a woman, dancing with a man who made her feel like she was the only one in the room.

And it made Jemma dizzy.

They didn't speak—didn't need to. He looked at her like he was trying to memorise her. And she let herself be looked at.

After the song, she pulled back gently, breathless. "I'm going to freshen up."

Ben nodded, reluctant to let go but respecting the space. "You alright?"

"Just warm," she said with a smile, squeezing his hand. "Too much cowboy charm in the room."

He chuckled, watching her disappear out the side door where the bathrooms were tucked behind the building, near the garden.

Ben had just turned back to rejoin a conversation with another landowner when he caught sight of Brad striding across the hall toward him, his expression tight, his movements brisk. Without preamble, Brad clapped a hand on his shoulder and leaned in.

"Can I talk to you for a sec? Alone."

Ben immediately tensed. Brad wasn't the kind of man to fuss over nothing.

"Yeah," Ben said, excusing himself from the group and stepping toward the corner with him.

Brad scanned the room, eyes sweeping the crowd before settling on the open doorway. "Where's Jemma?"

Ben frowned. "She just stepped outside. Needed a moment. Why?"

Brad exhaled through his nose, rubbing the back of his neck like he was trying to scrape the words out. His jaw worked, tense and tight. "It's Mia," he said finally.

Ben's spine went stiff. "What about her?"

"She's been going around to the blokes—quiet-like but pointed. Telling them Jemma's easy. That she's only up at your place because she's warming your bed. Saying you brought her here tonight to show off the new plaything."

For a split second, everything inside Ben went silent. No thoughts. No breath.

Then the blood roared in his ears like a bushfire tearing through dry grass.

He saw red.

The kind of red that made his hands curl into fists and his pulse pound behind his eyes.

His voice came out low, almost too calm. "Where is she?"

Brad grabbed his arm, his grip firm. "Ben—wait. I don't think she realises how serious this is getting. One of the fellows—Dave from the feed store—already tried asking Jemma to step outside for some air. Got a bit too handsy about it, too. I cut in before it got out of line, but—"

Ben's chest tightened. He didn't wait to hear the rest. His body moved before his mind could catch up.

Shouldering through the crowd with a force that had heads turning, eyes following. His boots hit the timber floor like thunder as he pushed through the open doors into the night.

The fairy lights outside flickered gently in the wind.

But there was nothing gentle about what he was feeling.

Not when the woman he'd brought into his home—into his life—was being humiliated.

Hunted.

And not when he had no idea what—or who—she was facing out there in the dark.

His boots pounded the gravel path as he strode around the side of the building, heart thundering like hooves against dry earth. The community hall faded behind him, replaced by shadows and rustling hedges. The low garden lights cast a dim amber glow, barely illuminating the narrow path that led to the bathrooms.

That's when he saw them.

Dean Foster.

The bastard had Jemma pinned against the corrugated tin wall. One hand braced beside her head, the other gripping her hip, pressing her back into the metal siding. His frame loomed over her, too close, too aggressive.

Jemma's face was streaked with tears, her arms braced against his chest, trying to push him off. Her voice cracked in panic.

"No—stop—please—"

Ben didn't think.

He exploded.

"Get your damn hands off her!"

Dean barely had time to flinch.

Ben's fist connected square with his jaw. The sound was sickening—a crunch of bone against bone. Dean staggered, then dropped like a felled bull, landing hard in the dirt.

Jemma crumpled too, sliding down the wall, her whole body shaking.

Ben was on his knees beside her in seconds, arms coming around her like a shield. His chest rose and fell like a bellows, but his voice was a low murmur as he gathered her close.

"Hey… hey, sweetheart. You're safe now. I've got you."

She buried her face in his shirt, sobbing so hard she could barely breathe. Her fingers fisted the fabric, clinging like she was afraid he'd vanish.

"I tried to tell him no," she choked. "He just wouldn't—he wouldn't let go—"

Ben's jaw clenched so tight it ached. "You don't have to explain. It's not your fault. Not one damn part of this is your fault."

He wrapped his arms tighter around her, his body shaking now too—but not from fear.

From rage.

Pure, blistering fury.

He looked over his shoulder toward the hall, voice like steel.

"Brad!"

Footsteps pounded up the path, and Brad appeared, breathless, eyes going wide when he saw Jemma trembling in Ben's arms and Dean groaning in the dirt.

Ben didn't even blink. "Take her to your car. Stay with her. Lock the doors. Don't let anyone near her. I'm going back inside."

Brad didn't hesitate. He crouched beside Jemma, voice low and steady, slipping off his jacket and wrapping it around her shoulders. She barely registered the gesture, too shaken to speak.

Ben stood slowly, breath heaving, his body coiled tight with rage. His knuckles were already split and bleeding, but he didn't feel it. All he felt was the fury churning in his chest, white-hot and righteous.

He turned toward the hall.

Toward her.

Mia.

He was done being polite.

With long, purposeful strides, Ben stalked back toward the old community building. Each step echoed like a war drum on the cracked stone path. He reached the doors and pushed them open hard, the hinges shrieking in protest.

He didn't pause.

Didn't smile.

Didn't soften.

He walked through the room like a thundercloud rolling in—dark, fierce, unstoppable. The air shifted. Conversations faltered mid-sentence. The band's rhythm stumbled and died away. Plates were lowered, glasses stilled mid-air.

Every head turned.

He didn't have to look long. Mia was at the drinks table, all done up in her best boots and a bright floral dress, laughing a little too loudly at something a local farmer had said. She was holding court, like she always did—smiling like she still ran the show.

Not tonight.

Ben's voice cracked through the hall like a stock whip.

"Mia."

She turned, blinking. "Ben?"

Her smile dimmed at the sight of him—at the blood on his knuckles, the fire in his eyes.

"You think this is funny?" he thundered. "Spreading filth about Jemma? Whispering to every man in the room that she's easy?"

A murmur spread like lightning across dry grass.

Mia faltered. "I didn't say that exactly—"

"You said enough," he snapped, voice cutting like broken glass. "Enough that one of them—Dean bloody Foster—cornered her outside. Had her crying, begging him to stop."

Gasps rippled through the crowd. Someone dropped a glass.

Ben barely noticed.

His eyes were locked on Mia.

"You're a jealous, vindictive woman," Ben said, his voice like gravel and thunder. "And I've let it slide for too damn long."

The room froze around him. Every word was a nail hammered in truth.

"But hear me now—and hear me well—you are no longer welcome at my home. Not for sugar. Not for fuel. Not for Sunday scones. Not for anything."

Mia's face went blotchy, eyes wide with disbelief, her smile long gone. She opened her mouth like she might still salvage it—but the weight of his fury silenced her.

"You're choosing her over your friends?" she choked, incredulous.

"I'm choosing my daughter's nanny—a good woman—and decency over poison," he spat. "And if you ever come near Jemma again, you'll regret it."

Silence.

Not just quiet—but breath-held, heart-stilled silence.

Even the children froze mid-giggle. No music, no chatter. Just the harsh breathing of one woman's disgrace, and one man's rage held barely in check.

Ben's eyes swept the room once, a storm behind his gaze. He wasn't looking for approval. He didn't need it.

Then he turned, his shoulders square, his stride deliberate, each step echoing off the timber floor like a verdict.

And as he disappeared through the doors, leaving a stunned room in his wake, something shifted.

For the first time, the community saw it plain:

This wasn't just Ben Callahan standing up for a guest in his home.

This was a man defending someone who mattered.

This wasn't just a line in the dust. It was a warning. And the whole town had heard it.

Chapter Twelve

The night air was cooler now. The fairy lights shimmered above the gravel path, swaying gently in the breeze—as if they, too, sensed the shift in the evening's mood.

Ben's boots crunched slowly across the stones toward Brad's parked car. He could see Jemma in the passenger seat, curled in on herself. Brad sat on the edge of the bonnet, arms folded, keeping quiet watch.

As Ben approached, Brad stood.

"She hasn't said much," he murmured. "Still shaken. But she's okay. I stayed like you asked."

Ben gave a tight nod. "Thanks, mate. I owe you."

Brad shrugged, clapping his shoulder. "No debt here. You did what any decent man should."

Ben opened the car door quietly.

Jemma looked up, her eyes red-rimmed, lashes still damp. She tried to sit a little straighter, swiping at her cheeks with trembling fingers.

"I'm fine," she whispered, voice paper-thin.

"You don't have to be," he said gently. "Not with me."

Her chin quivered, but she nodded.

Ben offered his hand. She took it.

She didn't need help—but like earlier that evening, she let him steady her. This time, her fingers lingered just a little longer.

"Thanks again, Brad," Ben said as he led her to his truck.

Brad gave a solemn nod, then turned away, granting them privacy.

Ben helped Jemma into the passenger seat, closed the door softly, and rounded to his side. The drive home was long and quiet. The tyres hummed over the dirt road, and the distant stars blinked down as if trying to listen in.

Jemma leaned her head against the window; arms wrapped around herself.

She didn't sob. Just quiet, shaky breaths.

Just those quiet, shaky breaths that told him the tears hadn't stopped—only slowed.

Ben didn't push.

Didn't speak.

He just drove.

And somewhere between the narrow bridge and the turnoff near the paddock fence, her breathing evened. Her shoulders slackened.

She was asleep.

The kind of sleep that came after fear—the kind the body demanded when the heart had been wrung dry.

Ben pulled into the homestead drive. The headlights swept over the yard, catching the edge of her cottage in soft gold.

He parked, cut the engine, and sat for a moment, watching her sleep.

So strong.

So damn brave.

Then, as gently as he could, he stepped out, walked around, and opened her door. She stirred slightly but didn't wake as he unbuckled her belt and slid his arms beneath her.

She fit against him like she was meant to be there.

He hadn't expected to care this much. But here he was, carrying her like something precious.

She sighed, her head falling to his shoulder.

Ben carried her through the garden gate and up the steps to her cottage. Inside, it smelled faintly of lavender and clean linen. He laid her down carefully, eased off her shoes, and pulled a blanket over her.

As he straightened, he hesitated—then leaned down and pressed a kiss to her forehead. Soft. Reverent.

Her breath caught, almost imperceptibly.

He didn't see her eyes flutter open just as he turned to leave.

Didn't see her fingers curl slightly around the blanket.

But she felt the kiss.

And for the first time in days, something inside her ached a little less.

Ben stepped through the back door of the main house, rolling his shoulders like he could shake off the weight of the night.

Agnes stood at the kitchen bench, her hair in curlers, the kettle just beginning to whistle.

She turned at the sound of him, arms folding. "Well," she said, her voice dry. "That didn't look like a peaceful end to the evening."

Ben let out a breath, rubbing a hand over his face. "No. It wasn't."

Agnes poured boiling water into a mug, dropped in a chamomile teabag, and held it out to him. "Talk."

Ben took the cup and sat heavily at the table.

"Mia ran her mouth. Started spreading filth about Jemma. Said she was sleeping with me for a roof over her head."

Agnes's mouth flattened into a hard line. "That woman's been jealous of every female under sixty who's so much as smiled at you."

Ben nodded grimly. "Some of the blokes believed it. One of them—Dean Foster—cornered Jemma outside. Put his hands on her. Wouldn't take no."

Agnes's hand flew to her chest. "Oh my God. Is she—?"

"She's safe now," Ben said, cutting gently through her panic. "I got there in time. But she was terrified. Still shaking when I found her."

Agnes sank slowly into the chair across from him, her eyes misting. "Poor girl."

"I decked Dean. Told Mia she's not welcome here again. Not for anything."

Agnes gave a single, satisfied nod. "'Bout bloody time."

They sat in silence, the soft ticking of the old wall clock and the kettle settling on the stove the only sounds between them.

Agnes's voice was quiet when she finally spoke. "She asleep now?"

Ben stared into his tea, as if searching for answers in the steam. "Yeah. Fell asleep in the truck. I carried her in… She didn't stir."

He didn't mention the kiss.

Didn't need to.

Agnes watched him for a beat, her expression unreadable. "She's been through enough already, Ben. The last thing she needs is more hurt."

"I know," he said softly. "She didn't deserve any of what happened tonight."

"Or what came before it."

Ben's jaw tightened. He nodded once.

Agnes tilted her head. "Do you care about her?"

He looked up, cautious. "Of course I do. She makes Charlotte happy."

Agnes raised an eyebrow. "Is that the only reason?"

Ben opened his mouth, then closed it again.

The silence that followed wasn't awkward—it was weighty. Full of things unspoken.

He wasn't ready to name what he felt.

Not yet.

Maybe not even to himself.

The door clicked softly behind him.

It wasn't loud—barely more than the creak of timber settling—but it was enough to stir her.

Jemma's lashes fluttered against her cheeks as the faint, familiar scent of dust and eucalyptus drifted in with the night air.

Warmth still lingered on her forehead—like a whispered memory.

A kiss.

Ben.

She blinked, the edges of the dim room sharpening slowly. She was in her bed. Her boots were gone. A soft blanket tucked around her.

He'd carried her. Tucked her in.

And kissed her goodnight.

Tears prickled, hot and unwelcome.

She rolled onto her side, burying her face in the pillow. Not crying—not really. Just… unravelling. Quietly. Privately.

She'd been enjoying the evening—until that man cornered her. Asking for a kiss she'd politely refused. But he wouldn't take no. When he pushed her against the wall, all she could think about was Leo.

How his abuse had started just like that.

She'd been terrified.

And Ben had seen it. Hadn't pushed. Hadn't pried. Just stood there—fierce, solid, unshakable. A shield between her and the past trying to claw its way back.

That kiss—soft, gentle—had felt like a promise she hadn't expected.

And somehow, that kindness undid her more than anything else.

She touched her fingers to her forehead, like she could hold on to that moment a little longer.

Then, with a slow breath, she closed her eyes.

And for the first time in a long while, let herself fall asleep.

Not because she was exhausted.

But because she felt safe.

The morning sun streamed in through the cottage window, soft and golden. It slipped across the timber floorboards, warming the edges of the bed and catching the curve of Jemma's shoulder as she stirred beneath the blanket.

She blinked slowly, for a moment unsure of where she was. Then it came back—like ripples settling after a storm. The party. The man. The fear.

And Ben.

Her hand drifted to her forehead, fingertips brushing the spot where he'd kissed her. The memory of it still lingered—quiet and steady—anchoring her.

But the panic was gone now. Distant. She could breathe again.

She sat up, the blanket pooling around her waist. Someone—Ben—had left a glass of water on her bedside table. She drank it gratefully, then pushed herself to her feet and padded across the room to get dressed.

By the time she reached the main house, the familiar smell of bacon and fresh bread was already wafting through the air.

In the kitchen, Agnes stood at the stove in a checked apron, flipping something in a pan. Her curlers were gone, replaced by a neat braid pinned at the back of her head. The radio played softly in the background—an old country ballad humming low.

Agnes looked up as Jemma stepped inside.

"Mornin', love." Her gaze swept over her gently. "You alright?"

Jemma hesitated for a beat. Then nodded.

"I think so," she said softly. "Bit foggy. But… better."

Agnes turned off the burner and wiped her hands on a tea towel, her sharp eyes never leaving Jemma's face. "You sure? You don't have to pretend with me."

Jemma offered a small, tired smile. "I'm not pretending. Not today."

Agnes studied her a moment longer, then gave a satisfied nod and pulled out a chair at the table. "Sit. You need feeding."

Jemma slid into the seat gratefully, the warmth of the kitchen already working its way into her bones.

"I heard what happened," Agnes said after a quiet moment, placing a plate in front of her. "Ben told me."

Jemma's fork paused halfway to her mouth. "I didn't want to cause a scene."

Agnes scoffed gently. "You didn't. Mia and that idiot Dean did. You, my dear, held yourself together better than most grown men would have."

Jemma looked down at her plate, swallowing against the sudden tightness in her throat. "I just… froze. It felt like everything was happening all over again."

Agnes reached across the table and laid a firm, warm hand over hers.

"No one blames you for that. Least of all Ben."

Jemma looked up, surprised by the certainty in her voice. "He didn't say much."

"He didn't have to." Agnes smiled, a little sly now. "He carried you in like you were made of glass and looked like he'd go back out there and rip Dean's head off if you so much as asked."

Just then, the kitchen door burst open, and Charlotte came bounding in, all tangled curls and morning energy.

"Morning!" she chirped brightly. "Did you dance with Daddy last night?"

Before Jemma could answer, Ben stepped into the doorway behind her, a faint smile tugging at the corner of his mouth.

"She sure did."

Jemma glanced up, startled—and a little flustered. Ben's eyes met hers, calm and steady. There was something warm in his gaze. Something unspoken.

Agnes arched an eyebrow, clearly amused, and turned back to the stove. "Well," she muttered under her breath, "isn't this getting interesting."

Chapter Thirteen

The days that followed settled into a strange, uneasy rhythm.

Ben kept his distance.

So did Jemma.

Not in any obvious way—there were still shared meals, still brief conversations over coffee or at the stables. But something had shifted. That soft moment in the truck, the kiss on her forehead, the way he'd carried her like she mattered… all of it lingered like a dream she wasn't sure she'd imagined.

At dinner, Charlotte filled the silence between them—chattering about her day, her pony, the baby calf that kept escaping the yard. Ben listened patiently, tossing in the occasional smile or nod. Jemma laughed where she could, smiled when she should. But her eyes rarely met his.

Ben didn't push.

And somehow, that hurt more than it should have.

Jemma didn't know why he'd pulled back. Maybe he regretted that moment between them. Maybe it had meant nothing—just comfort in a moment of fear. A kindness. Nothing more.

But she'd felt something shift that night. Something inside her had cracked open.

And it terrified her.

So, she stayed guarded. Polite. Careful.

Because even though the nightmares had quieted, the ache of what came before still lived in her bones.

And because falling for someone like Ben Callahan felt like walking a tightrope without a net.

Especially after what she'd overheard at the dance.

One of the women—Janine, or maybe Barb—had leaned in close after a shared laugh and said it like it was gospel:

"Ben's never looked at anyone since his wife passed. Still head over heels, that man. It'll take someone very special to change that."

The others had nodded sagely, some wistful, some resentful.

Jemma had smiled politely, said nothing.

But the words stuck.

Still head over heels.

What chance did she have?

She wasn't special.

Just broken in quiet places most people never saw.

Jemma rinsed the dishes, hands submerged in warm suds, the clink of plates a welcome distraction. Behind her, Ben leaned against the doorframe, drying his hands with a tea towel. Charlotte had already run off to the lounge, singing to the old Labrador curled up on the rug.

"You don't have to do that," Ben said softly.

Jemma shrugged, not looking up. "I don't mind."

Silence stretched between them—long, and full of all the things they weren't saying.

When he finally spoke again, his voice was gentler. "You sleeping okay?"

She paused; her fingers stilled on a glass. "Better. Thanks."

Another pause.

Then, "I'm glad."

She rinsed the last plate and set it on the rack. Dried her hands. Still didn't turn around.

"I should check on Charlotte," she murmured.

She didn't wait for a response—just slipped past him, careful not to brush his arm.

But as she walked down the hallway, she could feel his gaze on her back.

Steady. Searching.

And it made her wonder—just for a moment—if maybe he was keeping his distance not because he wasn't interested…

…but because he was scared too.

Ben stood on the back porch, one hand wrapped around a chipped mug of coffee, the other resting on the rail as the last sliver of sun dipped below the horizon. The paddocks stretched out before him—still and golden—twilight settling over the land like a blanket.

It should've been peaceful.

But his chest felt tight. Restless.

Inside, Charlotte's giggles drifted through the screen door as Jemma read one of her bedtime books, her voice soft and musical.

The same voice that had haunted his thoughts for days now.

He closed his eyes.

He'd meant to give her space.

God knows, she'd needed it.

After what that bastard Dean had pulled at the dance, Ben had wanted to hit something. Break something.

But more than that—he'd wanted to fix things for her.

Make it better.

Only… you can't fix what's already been broken.

Not the old wounds. Not the ghosts in her eyes.

So, he'd stayed back. Let her come to him.

If she wanted to talk, he was there. If she didn't, he kept quiet. It was the right thing.

But damn, it was getting hard.

Because ever since he'd carried her in from the truck—her breath soft against his neck, her head tucked into his shoulder like it belonged there—he hadn't been able to stop thinking about her.

The way she'd trusted him. Leaned into him.

Like—for just a heartbeat—he was her safe place.

And God help him; he wanted to be.

He wanted her in his arms again. Not because she was scared.

Because she wanted to be there.

But he didn't move. Didn't act on it.

Because he knew what damage could be done when a man wanted too much from a woman still healing.

He wasn't her ex.

He wasn't that bastard.

So, he waited.

Even when she avoided his gaze.

Even when she sat beside him at dinner but felt miles away.

He told himself she needed time.

Told himself pushing her would only make her run.

But pretending her absence didn't ache was getting harder by the day.

He exhaled sharply, raking a hand through his hair.

Maybe she didn't feel the same. Maybe she'd heard the gossip—that he was still hung up on Heidi, that no one would ever measure up. People in small towns talked.

And Jemma… she'd already been through too much to feel like a consolation prize.

But that wasn't the truth.

Heidi hadn't left behind a void.

She'd left behind a damn mess.

The only good thing that ever came from that marriage was Charlotte.

This wasn't about the past.

This was about Jemma.

And the way she made the world feel quieter. Softer.

Like maybe, after everything, there was still something good waiting on the other side of the wreckage.

He didn't want to keep his distance much longer.

Because every day he didn't reach for her was starting to feel like the bigger risk.

The afternoon sun streamed through the cottage windows, casting a warm glow across the floor where Charlotte sat cross-legged with her workbook. Jemma knelt beside her, offering gentle encouragement as the little girl carefully traced out letters, her tongue sticking out in concentration.

"That's it," Jemma said softly. "Beautiful 'B', just like we practiced."

Charlotte beamed. "I like writing with you."

Jemma smiled. "And I like teaching you."

Charlotte went quiet for a moment, then looked up at her with eyes too serious for five.

"I wish you were my mummy."

Jemma blinked, heart catching. "Oh, sweetheart…"

"I do," Charlotte said again, firmer this time. "I wish you were."

Jemma reached out, tucking a curl behind her ear. "I wish I had a beautiful girl like you. You're very special, you know that?"

Charlotte's smile faltered. Her gaze dropped.

"My mummy didn't like me."

Jemma froze. "Darling… of course she did. She was your mummy."

Charlotte shook her head. "No. She used to say I ruined her life."

Jemma's breath left her like a punch to the chest.

Charlotte's voice was flat—matter of fact. Like it was something she'd heard too often to question anymore.

"I didn't know what it meant when I was little," she added quietly. "But I do now."

Jemma reached for her dropped pencil, hands trembling.

What kind of woman says that to her child?

"Charlotte," she said softly, "you didn't ruin anything. Not ever."

"But she was always sad when I was around."

Jemma took her small hand in both of hers. "That sadness had nothing to do with you. Sometimes… people hurt inside so badly, they forget how to love properly. But that was never your fault. Do you hear me?"

Charlotte nodded slowly, eyes still downcast.

"You're kind, and clever, and beautiful, and so loved," Jemma whispered, brushing a hand through her hair. "And anyone would be lucky to be your mummy."

Charlotte looked up, blinking. "Even you?"

Jemma's voice cracked. "Especially me."

Then Charlotte leaned forward and wrapped her arms tightly around Jemma's neck.

Jemma held her close, eyes burning with tears.

In that moment, she wasn't afraid of love.

Not for this little girl.

Because Charlotte wasn't a risk.

She was a gift.

And something shifted in Jemma's heart—a quiet, fierce promise she didn't say aloud:

You'll never have to feel unloved again.

When Charlotte finally asked for her nap, Jemma helped her into bed, smoothing the blanket over her with a tenderness that surprised even herself. She stayed with her until her breathing softened and her lashes fluttered closed, then brushed a kiss across her forehead and slipped quietly from the room.

But her peace didn't last.

She couldn't stop thinking about what Charlotte had said.

She needed to tell Ben.

He had to know what his daughter was carrying inside her.

As she stepped outside, the air hit her like a wall—dense, heavy, and still. The kind of stillness that came just before a storm. Off in the distance, the sky had begun to darken. Ominous clouds rolled in low and fast, swallowing the horizon in layers of slate and charcoal. The wind picked up suddenly, dry, and sharp, rattling the trees and lifting the hem of her dress.

She swallowed hard, heart lurching. She hated storms. Hated the unpredictable crash of thunder, the flicker of lightning, the howling wind that reminded her too much of other nights—darker nights. Nights where Leo had dragged her by the arm and locked her in the garden shed for talking back. Left her there for hours with only the shadows and the cold and the sound of her own breath echoing against the walls.

Her steps faltered. For a heartbeat, the memory tried to drag her under.

But then she thought of Charlotte. Of the way her tiny arms had wrapped around her neck. Of the tremble in her voice when she'd said, "I wish you were my mummy."

No. Jemma straightened her spine.

She couldn't fall apart now. Not when that little girl needed someone to stand up for her.

Chapter Fourteen

She found Ben in the feed shed, the scent of hay and dust thick in the air. He was shirtless, hauling heavy bales like a man possessed—like he was trying to outrun something invisible. Sweat clung to his skin, making the muscles in his back and arms gleam with every movement. His jaw was tight, his focus razor-sharp.

He looked up when he heard her footsteps.

His expression shifted instantly—surprise, concern, and something deeper flickering behind his eyes.

"Is everything okay?" he asked, voice low and rough.

Jemma shook her head. "No."

She stepped further into the shed, the door creaking behind her as the wind picked up, scattering straw across the floor.

"Charlotte told me something," she said, voice steady despite the pounding of her heart. "Something I think you need to know."

Ben dropped the hay bale and crossed to her, his brows drawing together. "What is it? Is she hurt?"

"No," Jemma said quickly. "Not physically. But…" She drew a shaky breath. "She told me she wishes I were her mummy."

Ben froze, blinking.

"And then she said… her real mum didn't like her. That she used to say Charlotte ruined her life."

The colour drained from his face. He stared at her like she'd just ripped open a wound he hadn't dared touch.

"She remembered that?" he whispered.

"She understands it now," Jemma said gently. "What it meant."

Ben turned away sharply, dragging a hand through his damp hair. "I thought—" He swallowed. "I thought I'd protected her from the worst of it."

"She's not broken, Ben," Jemma said softly, stepping closer. "But she's hurting. And she needs to feel safe enough to talk about it. I just… needed you to know."

A flash of lightning split the sky beyond the open shed doors, followed by a low, rolling crack of thunder. Jemma flinched—just slightly—but enough for Ben to notice. Her hands curled into fists at her sides, knuckles pale.

"You okay?" he asked, voice gentling.

She nodded too quickly. "It's just the storm."

Ben took a careful step toward her. "You don't like storms?"

She hesitated, eyes flicking to the door. Before she could answer, thunder cracked again—sharper this time—and a sudden gust of wind slammed the shed doors shut with a deafening bang.

Jemma jumped, panic flooding her face. She turned to the doors, her breath catching. "I can't stay here."

She rushed over, tugging at the handles, but the wind had wedged them tight. They wouldn't budge.

"Make them open," she said, her voice cracking.

The fear in her voice gutted him.

And then the rain came. Sheets of it. Hammering the tin roof like a thousand stones. The sound was deafening—a relentless roar that filled the shed and swallowed everything else.

Jemma crouched to the ground, hands flying to her ears, her body curling in on itself. She was shaking. Violently. Her fear wasn't subtle—it screamed.

Ben's heart twisted.

"Hey," he said gently, crouching beside her. He placed a steady hand on her shoulder. "It's okay. You're not locked in. You're not alone."

She didn't look at him. Her eyes were wide, unseeing. Her chest rose and fell in short, panicked bursts—like she was trapped inside a memory that wouldn't let go.

"I need to get out," she whispered. "He locked me in the shed... during storms."

Ben went still.

Oh God.

This wasn't just fear. This was trauma.

It was in the way she flinched from sound, the way she curled into herself, the way her voice broke like glass when she spoke.

He crouched beside her again, slow, and careful. "You're not in that place anymore," he said, voice low and steady. "You're here. With me. And I would never—" He swallowed. "No one will ever lock you in again."

But she didn't hear him.

Her breathing stayed shallow, her gaze distant.

So, he did the only thing he could.

He cupped her face gently and kissed her.

Not out of passion. Not out of desire.

But as an anchor. A lifeline.

Soft. Steady. Real.

Her breath hitched against his mouth. For a moment, she was frozen—rigid with panic. Then her fingers curled into his bare skin, clutching him like she was trying to climb out of the dark.

When he pulled back, her eyes had cleared—just a little.

She was blinking. Present. Trembling. But here.

"Ben…" she breathed, broken and raw.

"I've got you," he whispered. "You're safe now."

And then—

She kissed him.

Not softly.

Not carefully.

But with everything she had.

Her mouth met his in a clash of heat and hunger, her fingers winding behind his neck, into his hair, pulling him down to her like she couldn't bear a breath of space between them. She kissed him like she needed it to survive—and he kissed her back like he'd been starving.

Ben staggered a step, caught off guard by the force of it, but then he caught her—hands gripping her waist, holding her steady as the world shrank to just the two of them.

Her hands roamed over his chest, skimming the sweat-slicked skin, learning the lines and planes of him. She moved like she needed to know every inch, like she wanted to burn the feel of him into memory.

He groaned into her mouth, deep and rough, as her lips parted and drew him in. The kiss turned fierce, frantic, his hands sliding up her back, then down to her thighs. He lifted her without breaking the kiss, pressing her against the wall of the shed, her legs wrapping instinctively around his waist.

She moaned softly, her body arching into his, her fingers digging into his shoulders like she couldn't get close enough.

The storm raged on, thunder cracking overhead, wind howling beyond the walls.

But they were already inside a different storm.

And neither one wanted to be anywhere else.

Ben's hands tightened on her thighs as he pressed her harder against the wall, his hips grinding into hers with a slow, deliberate roll that stole the breath from her lungs.

Jemma gasped into his mouth, her back arching instinctively. She could feel the strength in him—every muscle drawn tight, every movement controlled and aching with restraint. But there was nothing restrained about the way he kissed her now. Nothing careful. Nothing held back.

She felt him, solid and hot between her thighs, and the sensation sent a jolt through her so sharp she moaned again, desperate, and breathless. Her hands slid down his back, nails grazing his skin, and he hissed against her lips like the touch lit him on fire.

"Jesus, Jemma…" he groaned, forehead pressing to hers as he fought for air. "I—" He broke off, his breath ragged. "I don't remember the last time I touched someone and felt like this."

She cupped his face, her thumb brushing his jaw. "Then don't stop."

That was all it took.

He kissed her again, rougher this time, a growl low in his throat as he thrust his hips into hers—slow, grinding movements that made her head fall back with a whimper. His mouth moved to her neck, her collarbone, trailing heat along her skin while her fingers tangled in his hair, urging him closer, deeper.

Every touch sparked like lightning. Every kiss burned hotter than the last.

Jemma couldn't think. Could barely breathe. All she knew was Ben—his scent, his heat, the desperate way his body moved against hers like he was trying to crawl inside her soul. And God, she wanted him there. Needed him there.

She tugged at the waistband of his jeans, her fingers fumbling, urgent. His hands were already under her top, sliding along her ribs, reverent and hungry all at once.

"You feel like fire," he murmured against her throat, his voice wrecked. "Like I've been cold for years, and I just—"

He kissed her again before he could finish, his hips grinding into hers with aching precision. She felt the length of him pressed hard against her, and her body lit up like a match struck in the dark.

"Ben…" she breathed, her voice little more than a gasp. "Please."

His eyes met hers, green and stormy and full of something raw—something that looked like awe. He didn't just want her. He felt her. All of her.

And for the first time in years, she felt seen. Not as someone broken. Not as someone hiding.

As a woman. Wanted. Desired. Claimed.

He kissed her again—deep and consuming—his hands firm on her hips, her thighs wrapped around him, and the storm raged on around them. Thunder rolled. Rain slammed the roof. But inside the shed, nothing else mattered.

They were already lost in their own tempest.

And neither of them wanted to be found.

Jemma's fingers fumbled at the waistband of Ben's jeans, trembling with urgency as she worked the button free. Her breath came in shallow bursts, mingling with his. His forehead was pressed to hers, their eyes locked—dilated, dazed, lost in each other.

"God, Jemma…" he groaned, hips grinding into hers again, slower this time—teasing, torturous. "If you keep touching me like that…"

"I don't want to stop," she whispered, her lips brushing his. "I need to feel you."

He kissed her again—deep, open, hungry—and the sound he made when her hand slipped just beneath the waistband was low and guttural, a rough exhale that vibrated against her mouth.

She was just getting him free, her fingers curling around the edge of denim and heat, when—

BANG. BANG. BANG.

"Ben?" a voice called out, muffled but unmistakable. "You in there? The doors jammed again!"

They both froze.

Ben's body tensed against hers, jaw clenching like he'd been doused with cold water.

Jemma blinked, still breathless, her mind struggling to catch up as the real world shoved its way into their private storm.

"Brad," Ben muttered under his breath, his voice thick with frustration and something dangerously close to desperation.

Another sharp knock rattled the shed doors.

"Ben? Mate, you okay in there?"

Jemma slid her hands back, slowly, her cheeks flushed and her chest still rising and falling with each unsteady breath. She couldn't look at him yet. Couldn't speak.

Ben rested his forehead against hers for a beat longer, both of them suspended in the tight coil of a moment that had almost tipped too far.

Then he gently lowered her to the ground, hands steady at her waist, even as his pulse thundered beneath his skin.

"You good?" he asked softly, brushing a strand of hair from her cheek.

She nodded, still dazed. "Yeah… yeah, I'm good."

But she wasn't sure whether she meant it.

Ben turned toward the door, calling out, "Yeah, I'm here. The wind slammed it shut—it's stuck."

"I'll go 'round back and lift the latch," Brad shouted. "Hang on."

Ben looked back at her, jaw tight, voice low. "We're not done. Not even close."

Jemma's breath hitched.

Then the door groaned and creaked, and daylight slashed through the gap as Brad pushed it open with a grunt.

Ben took one last lingering look at her, eyes dark and unreadable, then stepped forward—pulling the door wide, slipping back into the world as though he hadn't just been seconds away from completely unravelling.

And Jemma…

She leaned against the wall, heart still pounding, body aching, lips swollen from his kisses, and her hand still tingling from where it had touched him.

They weren't done.

But now she was burning with the knowledge of just how much they'd started.

Chapter Fifteen

Ben barely tasted dinner.

Every time Jemma moved, every time she spoke, every time her eyes flicked toward him and then quickly away—he felt it.

The heat. The memory.

Her mouth on his. Her hands on his body. The way she'd clung to him like she'd never wanted to let go.

And the way he hadn't wanted her to.

He'd spent the entire meal with a fork in one hand and a death grip on his restraint with the other. Charlotte chatted away beside him, happily recounting her day between mouthfuls of spaghetti, completely oblivious to the charged silence pulsing between the adults.

Jemma sat across from him, too composed. Her shoulders were stiff, her cheeks a little too pink, her gaze fixed somewhere just to the left of his face.

He wanted to grab her. Haul her into his arms. Carry her to his bed and finish what they'd started in the shed.

But he couldn't.

His little girl needed him.

So, he listened to Charlotte talk about ponies and puddles and how the storm had made the chickens "all grumpy and feathery," and he smiled when he was supposed to, and nodded in the right places—but inside, he was coiled tight.

When the plates were cleared and Charlotte was halfway through her second helping of ice cream, Jemma stood up and smoothed her hands over her skirt.

"I think I'll turn in," she said lightly, though her voice wasn't quite steady. "It's been a big day."

Charlotte's spoon paused mid-air. "But—but I want you to read to me!"

Ben opened his mouth, but Jemma gently knelt beside Charlotte's chair and tucked a lock of hair behind her ear.

"I know, sweetheart. And I love reading to you," Jemma said gently, crouching beside Charlotte's chair. "But tonight, I need you to talk to your daddy about what you told me today."

Charlotte's spoon paused mid-air. Her big grey eyes grew serious. "About my mummy?"

Jemma nodded, brushing a soft hand over the little girl's arm. "Mmhmm. Your daddy needs to know how you feel. So, he can help you feel better. You did so well today, Lottie. I'm really proud of you."

Charlotte's lower lip wobbled for a moment, but then she gave a small, solemn nod. "Okay."

She leaned in and wrapped her arms tightly around Jemma's neck. "Night-night."

Jemma hugged her back just as fiercely, closing her eyes for a moment. When she stood, her gaze lifted briefly to Ben's—warm, proud… aching. Then she gave them both a soft smile, murmured a polite good night to Agnes, and slipped out the front door toward her cottage.

Ben watched her go, his heart thudding painfully in his chest.

The moment she disappeared around the corner; he exhaled hard and dragged a hand down his face.

He could still feel her. On his lips. In his arms. In every breath he took.

Then a small voice pulled him back.

"I'm sorry, Daddy," Charlotte whispered, her eyes round and uncertain. "I didn't mean to say anything bad about Mummy."

Ben's heart twisted. He turned to her slowly, kneeling beside her chair so they were eye level.

"Hey," he said softly, brushing a strand of hair from her cheek. "You didn't do anything wrong. Not one thing."

"But I said… she didn't like me," Charlotte said, her voice quivering. "And maybe that's mean."

Ben shook his head, his throat thick. "No, baby. It's not mean to tell the truth about how you feel. I'm glad you told Jemma. And I'm really glad you're telling me, too."

Charlotte's lip trembled again. "I don't want you to be sad."

"I'm already sad," Ben said, his voice cracking as he pulled her into his arms. "But I'm also really proud of you. You're so brave, Lottie. And I'm right here, okay? I've got you."

She curled into his chest, small and warm, and he held her like she was the most fragile, precious thing in the world.

Because she was.

And tonight, everything was changing. For the better. And all because of Jemma.

Charlotte clung to him for a long time that night. Longer than usual.

After her bedtime story, she didn't curl up under the blankets like she normally did. Instead, she stayed in his lap, small arms wrapped around his neck, her cheek pressed to his shoulder. Ben didn't rush her. He simply held her, rocking gently in the old armchair beside her bed while the wind whispered outside.

"Daddy," she said quietly, her voice muffled by his shirt. "Do you think I ruined things?"

Ben closed his eyes. His heart cracked wide open.

He pulled back just enough to look into her face. "No, sweetheart. No. You didn't ruin anything. You didn't ruin anyone's life."

Her eyes shimmered. "But she said I did. Mummy said it when she was mad."

Ben's throat tightened. He brushed her hair back, cupping her cheek gently. "Sometimes grown-ups say things they don't mean when they're hurting. But that doesn't make them true. You didn't ruin anything, Lottie. You made my life better. So much better."

She blinked at him, tears clinging to her lashes. "That's what Jemma said today."

Ben smiled softly, emotion thick in his chest. "See? And we both know Jemma's a very smart lady."

Charlotte gave a tiny nod, her lips curving into the smallest smile. Then she laid her head against his chest again, her breathing evening out.

Ben held her close, pressing a kiss to the top of her head.

She was healing.

And maybe, just maybe… so was he.

By the time Charlotte finally drifted off to sleep, it was late. The house had settled into a hush, the kind that only came after long days and longer emotions.

Ben eased the door shut behind him and stood in the hallway for a moment, debating. He wanted to go to Jemma—God, he needed to—but he didn't know if she wanted to see him. Not after the weight of today. Not after what nearly happened between them in the shed.

So instead, he turned toward the kitchen.

The light was still on. Agnes sat at the table with a cup of tea, glasses perched low on her nose as she paged through a crossword puzzle.

She looked up as he entered. "How is she?"

Ben sank into the chair across from her, running a hand through his hair. "She's better. I think it was a good thing she told Jemma. At least it's out in the open now."

Agnes nodded slowly, her gaze warm but tired. "I suppose. Jemma's really making a difference."

Ben's eyes softened, distant for a beat. "Yeah. She is."

Agnes studied him for a moment, then said carefully, "Brad mentioned you got stuck in the feed shed during the storm. Said Jemma was with you."

Ben stiffened slightly. "Yeah. It… wasn't good."

"What do you mean?" Agnes asked, her voice gentle but probing.

He hesitated, then sighed. "She was terrified when the storm hit. The doors slammed shut and—" He shook his head. "Her ex locked her in a shed during storms. Repeatedly. It wasn't just fear, Agnes. It was trauma. I could see it all over her."

Agnes sat back slowly, her expression clouding with quiet horror. "That poor girl…"

Ben nodded. "She didn't even tell me. Not at first. She just froze. I—" He broke off, his voice catching. "I didn't know what to do."

Agnes was quiet for a long moment. Then she reached over and gently patted his hand. "You were there. Sometimes, that's the only thing that matters."

He let out a quiet breath. "I suppose."

A small smile tugged at Agnes's lips, but her gaze remained warm, thoughtful. "Are you going to that charity gala on Saturday?"

"I have to," Ben said, no hesitation. "I'm one of the major donors."

Agnes gave him a knowing look over the rim of her tea. "Why don't you take Jemma? She could use a night out. A bit of sparkle might do her good. I'll stay with Charlotte."

Ben's eyes shifted to the window, where the soft golden light from Jemma's cottage still glowed against the dark. He stared at it like it held the answer to a question he hadn't dared ask, his jaw tight, then murmured, "You really think she'd want to go? I hate those bloody things."

Agnes chuckled under her breath. "Yes, and everyone can tell. But that's not the point. It's a chance to show her she's part of your world now—if you want her to be."

Ben's lips pressed into a line, thoughtful. Then, almost to himself, he murmured, "Yeah. I do."

He didn't say anything else. Just stood there a moment, staring out into the dark as if Jemma's light was holding him in place. Then he gave Agnes a soft goodnight and headed upstairs.

Sleep didn't come easily.

He lay in bed staring at the ceiling, the steady tick of the old clock on his bedside table counting out the seconds. His thoughts drifted to the charity gala—an annual event he'd supported for nearly a decade. A cause close to his heart. A night that usually passed in a blur of polite conversation, stiff suits, and empty small talk.

But this year, it could be different.

He didn't know if Jemma would want to go. Maybe she hated events like that—maybe she wouldn't feel comfortable, or maybe it would remind her too much of her old life. He didn't know. But the thought of spending an evening with her—just the two of them, away from the farm, away from the weight of everything they hadn't said—stuck with him.

They could breathe. Talk. See what this thing between them really was.

Because whatever it was… it had already started to matter more than he expected.

He turned over, running a hand through his hair, then let out a sigh and closed his eyes.

The soft glow of Jemma's light still lingered behind his eyelids.

And for the first time in a long while, the dark didn't feel like it was swallowing him whole.

Jemma lay in bed, the quilt pulled up to her chest, though the room wasn't cold.

She was staring at the ceiling, eyes wide open, listening for footsteps that never came.

Part of her—maybe the foolish, hopeful part—had expected to hear a quiet knock on her door. Or the soft creak of the floorboards outside. Something. Anything to tell her that Ben hadn't forgotten what had passed between them in that shed. That he hadn't changed his mind.

But the silence stretched on.

And with every minute that ticked by, something inside her twisted a little tighter.

She turned onto her side, hugging the pillow close, trying to convince herself that it was fine. That it made sense. Charlotte had needed him tonight. He was being a father—doing the right thing. Of course that came first.

But the ache in her chest didn't care about logic.

Because the truth was, part of her had needed him too.

She closed her eyes, remembering the feel of his hands, the sound of his voice, the way he'd kissed her like he couldn't breathe without her. That hadn't been casual. That hadn't been nothing.

So why did it feel like he was pulling away?

Maybe it had been too much too fast. Maybe he'd changed his mind. Maybe now that the storm had passed—literally and figuratively—he'd come to his senses and realised this was a mistake.

Maybe she was the mistake.

She turned again, blinking hard against the sting in her eyes. She wasn't going to cry. Not over this. Not over him.

Still… the emptiness beside her was undeniable.

And as she lay in the quiet of her cottage, the light from her bedside lamp soft and warm but doing nothing to ease the chill in her bones, Jemma whispered into the silence, barely audible even to herself.

"Guess it was just the storm."

She reached over, turned out the light, and let the darkness close in around her.

Chapter Sixteen

The kettle hissed softly as Agnes poured hot water into the teapot, her eyes drifting to the woman at the table.

Jemma sat silently, hands curled around her mug like it was the only thing anchoring her. She hadn't touched the slice of toast on her plate, and though her expression was calm, something in her stillness tugged at Agnes's instincts. She'd seen enough heartache in her years to know the signs.

Before Agnes could say anything, the front door creaked open, and the sound of Charlotte's chatter filled the kitchen.

Ben followed her in, one arm full of the little girl, her boots muddy from the yard.

"Morning," he said, his voice easy but careful.

"Hi!" Charlotte beamed, kicking her legs until Ben set her down. "The chickens are still grumpy!"

Agnes chuckled and handed her a banana. "Well, you would be too if the wind blew your house down every second night."

Ben's gaze shifted to the table.

Jemma didn't look up.

She murmured a soft "morning," then took a sip of her tea, her eyes fixed on the same spot in front of her like she hadn't heard Charlotte at all.

Ben felt it like a weight in his chest.

She was pulling back.

Not obviously. Not rudely. But enough that he noticed.

He sat down across from her, keeping his movements slow, unthreatening. Charlotte climbed up onto her stool beside him and began peeling her banana with the focus of a surgeon.

"Did you sleep okay?" Ben asked.

Jemma nodded. "Fine, thanks."

Another sip of tea. No eye contact.

Agnes glanced between them but said nothing, moving to refill the teapot.

Ben tried not to frown, but inside, something twisted. He didn't like this coldness—not after what they'd shared. Not after the way she'd clung to him in the storm, like he was the only safe place in the world.

He wondered if she was upset that he hadn't come to her last night.

And the truth was… he hoped she wasn't.

Because he hadn't stayed away reluctantly.

He hadn't gone to her because he hadn't wanted to.

Because the line between need and want had blurred too fast in that shed. Because what had started as raw, undeniable chemistry had nearly tipped into something deeper—something dangerous.

And that scared the hell out of him.

So, he'd stayed where he belonged. Close to his daughter. In his own bed.

Safe.

But now, watching Jemma sit across from him with her shoulders too still and her eyes too quiet, he wondered if he'd made a mistake.

He cleared his throat. "I was thinking of heading into town later. Pick up a few things. If you wanted to come…"

Jemma finally looked at him, just briefly. Her smile was faint. Polite.

"No, thanks. I've got a few things I need to do around the cottage."

Ben nodded slowly. "Right."

Silence settled again, heavy as dust.

Agnes broke it with a quiet sigh and reached for the butter. "Well, I hope someone wants toast, or we'll have enough to shingle the roof."

Charlotte giggled, but Ben didn't laugh.

His eyes were still on Jemma, who had gone back to staring at her tea.

And for the first time in days, he felt like a stranger in his own kitchen.

Jemma placed her mug down gently on the saucer, the quiet clink louder than it should have been in the heavy silence.

She could feel Ben watching her. Could feel Agnes's gentle worry, Charlotte's cheerful chatter trying to fill the space between them. But she couldn't stay. Not sitting here with the ache in her chest growing heavier by the minute.

"I should get started on the laundry," she said softly, pushing back her chair. "It's piling up."

Ben opened his mouth, maybe to say something—maybe to stop her—but she didn't give him the chance. She stood quickly, smoothing her hands over her skirt like that could flatten the storm rising inside her.

Agnes frowned slightly. "Love, you haven't eaten."

"I'm not really hungry," Jemma replied with a small, apologetic smile. "I've got a bit of a headache."

She leaned down and pressed a kiss to the top of Charlotte's head. "I'll see you later, sweetheart."

"Okay," Charlotte said through a mouthful of banana. "Don't forget my unicorn socks!"

"I won't," Jemma whispered, her smile trembling.

And then she was gone—moving through the hallway, slipping out the door into the morning light.

She didn't look back.

Once outside, she drew in a shaky breath, the crisp air stinging her eyes more than the wind should have.

This was for the best.

She had to remind herself of that.

She wasn't here for stolen glances or the false hope of something more. She was here for Charlotte—for the little girl who needed safety, love, and consistency.

Not for Ben.

Not for herself.

What had happened between them—it had been a moment. A beautiful, breathless moment born of shared pain and temporary closeness. But moments didn't last. And clearly, Ben had come to the same conclusion.

He hadn't come to her.

And she needed to stop wishing he had.

So, she squared her shoulders, blinking hard, and started toward the washing line.

Because that's what she was here for. To do the job she'd been hired to do.

And protect her heart before it cracked wide open.

Ben found her sitting on the cottage steps, her knees drawn up, a forgotten cup of tea cooling beside her. The early morning light caught in her hair, turning the black strands to soft ribbons of blue and silver. She didn't look up when he stepped onto the porch, but her posture stiffened slightly—as if she'd heard him coming long before he spoke.

"Hey," he said quietly.

"Hey." Her voice was calm, but not warm.

He hesitated, unsure if he should sit beside her or stay standing. She made the choice for him by continuing.

"I wanted to apologise," she said, her fingers tightening around the edge of her jumper. "For what happened in the feed shed."

Ben's brow furrowed. "You don't need to—"

"I do." Her voice was firmer now, though her eyes remained on the horizon. "It was inappropriate. I shouldn't have let it happen, and I hope it won't cause any problems between us."

There was a pause—long enough for him to hear the thud of his own pulse.

"Jemma," he said, but she finally looked at him, and the sadness in her eyes stopped him cold.

"I'm here for Charlotte," she said softly. "That's all. That's what this was always meant to be."

Ben stared at her, his throat tightening. She wasn't angry. She wasn't punishing him. She was shielding herself. He could see it now—the careful way she held herself, like she was bracing for the kind of rejection that didn't leave bruises but scars all the same.

Her chin lifted a little, like she was forcing herself to hold the line, even if it hurt.

And it did hurt. He could see that too.

She turned her gaze away again, blinking toward the paddocks, and he realised with a heavy, sinking clarity that this wasn't about pride.

It was about survival.

Ben stepped closer, the boards of the porch creaking softly beneath his boots. She didn't flinch, but she didn't meet his gaze either. Her shoulders were drawn in tight, like she was trying to fold herself smaller.

He crouched in front of her, slowly, giving her time to stop him if she needed to. Then, gently, he lifted his hand to her chin and tilted her face toward his.

Her eyes met his—cautious, guarded, shining with things she hadn't said.

"I'm trying not to stuff this up," he said quietly, his thumb brushing just beneath her jaw. "But I seem to be doing a very poor job."

She let out a breath that was almost a laugh, but it caught in her throat. "It was my fault. I—I lost it. Storms are… triggering for me. That's not your burden to carry."

Ben shook his head, his hand still resting lightly against her cheek. "It's not a burden," he said softly. "It's part of you. I'd rather know what hurts you than pretend it doesn't exist."

Her eyes flicked away, but only for a second. "I wasn't thinking clearly. I shouldn't have—"

"Jemma," he interrupted, firm but low. "I wanted to kiss you just as much as you wanted to. And I know you wanted to."

Her breath hitched. Her lips parted, like she might argue—but the words didn't come.

Ben leaned in just a fraction, not enough to crowd her, but enough to make sure she felt the truth in what he was saying.

"I felt it," he said. "In that shed. Before the storm. During. After. You weren't alone in it."

Her eyes shimmered, and her jaw tightened—like she was fighting herself more than him.

"I'm not asking for anything you're not ready to give," he added gently. "But don't pretend it didn't matter. Not to either of us."

She stared at him, caught between fear and longing, and for a moment, the quiet stretched so thin between them it could've snapped.

But it didn't.

Because even if she couldn't say it, she didn't look away.

And that, Ben thought, was something.

Maybe even everything.

He stood then, slow, and steady, his eyes still on hers. "Come away with me to Brisbane this weekend."

Jemma blinked, confusion rippling across her face. "What? Why?"

"I have to go to a charity gala on Saturday night," he explained. "I hate them, but I'm a major donor, so they expect me to show up in a suit and pretend I enjoy small talk over canapés. I was hoping you could make it more pleasant for me."

She opened her mouth, then closed it again. "I… I wouldn't have anything appropriate to wear."

"That's okay," he said simply. "We can go shopping on Saturday morning."

Her brows drew together, eyes narrowing slightly. "I can't let you do that. It's not right."

"Jemma," he said gently, "I'm asking you. Not out of obligation or charity. I want you there. And if you need a dress to be comfortable, it's the least I can do. You'll be doing me a big favour."

She looked down at her hands in her lap, fingers fidgeting with the hem of her sleeve.

He crouched again, voice softening. "It's just a weekend. A chance to breathe. No feed sheds. No thunderstorms. Just you and me, in a city full of distractions and no history hanging over our heads."

Her lashes flicked upward, uncertain but intrigued.

He smiled faintly. "Come with me, Jemma. Say yes."

"What about Charlotte? I should be—"

"Agnes has already volunteered," he cut in gently. "She offered before I even asked you. Said a weekend with her favourite girl and no grown-up drama sounded like heaven."

Jemma hesitated, her lips parting, the protest on the tip of her tongue. But then Ben leaned in just slightly, his voice soft and low.

"Please, Jemma."

And that was all it took.

She nodded.

It was small, tentative—barely more than a dip of her chin—but it was a yes.

Ben let out the breath he hadn't realised he was holding and gave her a smile that was warm, a little relieved, and just a touch hopeful.

"Okay then," he said quietly. "Brisbane it is."

She looked up at him through her lashes, still uncertain, still guarded—but not running. Not this time.

And that, Ben thought, was more than enough for now.

Chapter Seventeen

Charlotte bounced on her toes, clutching Jemma's hand like she was the one going on the trip.

"You've never been to Brisbane?" she asked, eyes wide with incredulity.

Jemma shook her head with a smile. "Not once."

"I've been lots of times with Daddy," Charlotte said proudly. "We always stay in a big hotel with tiny shampoos and pancakes in the morning."

Jemma laughed. "You're a lucky girl."

Charlotte grinned, her grey eyes shining. "So are you now."

That simple, innocent declaration caught Jemma off guard, softening something inside her. She gave Charlotte's hand a gentle squeeze. "I think I am."

Agnes came out onto the veranda, wiping her hands on her apron and squinting toward the clearing where the helicopter waited. Its blades spun lazily, still warming up. The morning sun cast long shadows over the paddocks, golden light glinting off the sleek machine.

"Alright, you two," Agnes called. "Time to get moving before Charlotte changes her mind and tries to stow away in your luggage."

Charlotte giggled. "I wouldn't fit in Jemma's bag. She packs boring clothes."

Jemma rolled her eyes. "Thanks for that."

Ben appeared beside them, his overnight bag slung over one shoulder, dressed in jeans and a crisp button-up that managed to look effortless and expensive all at once.

"Ready?" he asked, his gaze settling on Jemma.

She nodded, her nerves fluttering beneath the surface, but excitement winning out. "Ready."

They walked toward the helipad, Charlotte skipping a few steps ahead before turning to wrap her arms around Jemma's waist in a quick hug. "Don't forget to bring me something cool."

"I'll see what I can do," Jemma whispered, hugging her back tightly.

Agnes pulled Charlotte to her side, both of them waving as Ben helped Jemma into the helicopter. The noise grew louder as the blades picked up speed, whipping hair and dust into the air.

From inside, Jemma gave one last wave, her face lit with a rare, unguarded smile.

Ben, already buckled in beside her, watched her with quiet appreciation. He hadn't seen her this light in days—maybe ever.

"Excited?" he asked over the headset.

Jemma looked out at the landscape falling away beneath them and nodded, a laugh bubbling up as the ground disappeared below. "Terrified. And completely thrilled."

He smiled, the sound of her laughter still ringing in his ears. "Good. Firsts should feel like that."

They were bound for Charleville Airport, where a private jet would carry them the rest of the way to Brisbane. It was all new to her—the helicopter, the luxury, the idea of leaving the dust and memory-heavy quiet of the outback behind.

And Ben, watching her lean forward to peer out the window like a child seeing the world for the first time, felt something shift.

She was letting go. Just a little. And he was there to catch her joy as it unfolded.

For now, that was enough.

Jemma stepped onto the private jet and paused, eyes wide as she took in the plush cream leather seats, the polished wood accents, and the faint scent of something expensive in the air.

"This is…" She turned slowly; her voice hushed with wonder. "This is amazing."

Ben smiled as he watched her. There was no pretence in her reaction—no calculated charm or careful restraint. Just genuine surprise and delight.

He liked that more than he expected.

"You get used to it," he said lightly, dropping his bag onto a seat.

She shot him a look over her shoulder. "That's a shame."

Ben laughed, settling in beside her. "You keep looking at everything like that and I'll start seeing it differently, too."

Jemma ran her fingers lightly over the stitching on the armrest, her green eyes still scanning every detail as if committing it all to memory. "Feels like I should be wearing heels and diamonds, not sneakers and a cardigan."

"You wear both better than most," he said without thinking.

She glanced at him, surprised, but didn't look away.

The flight passed in a comfortable rhythm of light conversation, soft music, and quiet intervals where Jemma stared out the window like she still didn't quite believe this was real. And the whole time, Ben found himself wondering if this—her next to him, content and open—was what he'd been missing all along.

When they landed in Brisbane and the limousine pulled up beside the plane, Jemma's mouth dropped open again. "Of course," she murmured, more to herself than anyone. "Why walk when you can glide through the city in a palace on wheels?"

Ben chuckled but didn't argue. He just held the door open like a gentleman and enjoyed the way her eyebrows lifted every time the city offered another surprise.

But nothing topped her reaction when they stepped into the penthouse suite.

She froze in the entryway, her eyes widening at the grand foyer, the gleaming floors, the sweeping windows that revealed a glittering skyline.

"This is ridiculous," she said, turning to him, half accusing, half breathless.

Before he could reply, she spun in a full circle, laughing, then darted through the suite like a whirlwind of disbelief until she reached the terrace doors.

Ben followed, unhurried, drawn to her joy the way a man follows sunlight.

She stood at the edge of the balcony, hair tousled from the wind, hands braced on the glass railing as she looked out over the city.

"God," she whispered. "This doesn't even feel like real life."

He stepped up beside her, close but not touching, the warmth of his presence curling around her like the wind. "It is," he said quietly. "For the weekend, at least."

She glanced at him, her eyes alight—not just with the glittering skyline before them, but with something deeper. Something unspoken. "That's long enough," she murmured. "I'll never forget it."

Ben's gaze lingered on her profile, the curve of her cheek, the way the sun caught in her lashes like stars. He didn't answer right away. Just stood there, letting the moment settle between them.

"I believe you," he said finally, his voice low, honest.

Jemma looked away again, but her smile stayed, soft, still, and steady. A little quieter. A little sadder. But no longer guarded.

And Ben, watching her with the wind teasing her hair and wonder still flickering in her expression, felt something shift inside him.

Hope.

Not the loud kind. Not the reckless kind.

But the slow-burning kind that starts with moments like this—where silence says enough, and presence says more.

And for the first time in a long time, Ben Callahan let himself believe that maybe—just maybe—this weekend could be the beginning of something more.

Ben took her to the hotel's rooftop restaurant for lunch. The view was stunning—glass walls framing the sparkling skyline and a river that wound like silk through the heart of the city. Jemma wore her best sundress, a soft floral print that fluttered around her knees when the breeze caught it. She'd twisted her hair back loosely, slipped on a touch of gloss, and tried not to feel out of place among the sharply dressed diners and polished marble floors.

But the truth was, she didn't care.

She was having a wonderful time. And she hadn't smiled this much in what felt like forever.

Ben had been relaxed and attentive through the meal, his eyes lighting up each time she laughed at one of his dry remarks. He'd ordered sparkling water for them both, raised an eyebrow when she boldly asked for dessert, and didn't stop smiling when she devoured every bite of the lemon tart.

As they walked back through the grand foyer, Jemma caught her reflection in one of the mirrored columns. She didn't look like a nanny or a woman who'd barely scraped together the fare to leave her old life behind. She looked…happy.

And a little like the woman she might've been in another life—confident, unafraid, free.

Back in the elevator, Ben turned to her.

"There's someone coming by in an hour," he said. "A stylist. She's going to help you find a dress for the gala tonight."

Jemma blinked. "Wait—what?"

He nodded. "She'll bring a few options for you to try on. Something elegant. Comfortable."

Her expression faltered. "Are you sure? I mean… I feel bad. That you're paying for it."

Ben's smile softened. "Please don't worry about it, Jemma. I want you to feel comfortable tonight. That's all that matters."

She hesitated for a beat longer, then gave a shy, grateful smile. "Okay," she said softly.

Ben couldn't look away as the elevator chimed and the doors slid open. He didn't say anything at first, but his thoughts were louder than ever.

She hadn't asked for this.

Hadn't hinted. Hadn't schemed. Hadn't expected a single thing.

Heidi had always made it clear—expensive gifts were part of the deal. The more extravagant, the better. But Jemma… Jemma looked at a new dress like it was too much. Like it was more than she deserved.

And somehow, that only made Ben want to give her more.

Not because she expected it.

But because she didn't.

When the stylist arrived at the penthouse, Ben made himself scarce, offering a quick smile and a promise to "be out of the way." Jemma watched him go, her heart thudding just a little too hard. He was being thoughtful, respectful—but part of her wished he'd stayed, if only to steady her nerves.

The stylist, a warm and effortlessly chic woman named Vanessa, swept in with racks of gowns and the kind of energy that instantly put Jemma at ease.

"Well," Vanessa said with a grin as she hung up the last dress, "Mr. Callahan gave me very clear instructions."

Jemma raised a brow, amused. "Oh?"

Vanessa nodded. "He said—more than once, I might add— 'Give her anything she wants.'" She gave Jemma a conspiratorial wink. "You've clearly made quite the impression."

Jemma laughed softly, ducking her head. "He's kind. But he really didn't need to go to all this trouble."

"Honey, trouble is buying six dresses in five different sizes at midnight because someone changed her mind for the sixth time," Vanessa said with a wave of her hand. "This? This is a man who wants you to feel beautiful tonight. That's not trouble—that's intention."

Despite herself, Jemma flushed. She knew Ben was wealthy—of course she did. But this kind of luxury? It wasn't something she'd ever imagined being part of. She would never expect anything from him. Never ask. But she wanted to make him proud tonight. She didn't want to be the woman everyone wondered about. She didn't want him to feel embarrassed to have her on his arm.

She slipped into a soft, slate-blue gown with a fitted bodice and a gentle flare at the hem. It was simple, elegant, and when she stepped out of the dressing room, Vanessa gasped.

"Oh, that's the one."

"You think so?" Jemma turned in front of the mirror, the fabric catching the light like water.

Vanessa stepped closer and adjusted the strap slightly. "Absolutely. It's timeless, flattering, and you look like a dream."

Jemma smiled, both humbled and quietly thrilled.

As Vanessa packed away the other options, she added, "Now, don't worry—we're not done yet. Your hair and makeup stylist will be here soon to help you get ready for tonight."

Jemma's eyes widened. "Really?"

Vanessa nodded with a grin. "Yes, really. Courtesy of Mr. Callahan."

Jemma bit her lip, trying to keep her heart from fluttering too high in her chest. She wasn't used to being fussed over. She wasn't used to mattering like this.

But tonight, she would step into that gala beside Ben—and for once, she wanted to feel like she belonged.

Chapter Eighteen

Ben stood by the floor-to-ceiling windows in the penthouse living room, a tumbler of scotch untouched in his hand. The city lights of Brisbane glittered below, but his mind was far from the skyline. He kept glancing toward the hallway, wondering if Jemma was enjoying herself—if the dress she chose made her feel as beautiful as he already knew she was.

Then, he heard the soft click of heels on the polished floor.

He turned—and forgot how to breathe.

Jemma stood there in a slate-blue gown that hugged her waist and skimmed her hips before flaring just slightly at the hem. The neckline was modest but elegant, dipping just enough to reveal the graceful curve of her collarbone. The fabric shimmered subtly under the warm light, catching silver and dusk in every movement.

Her long black hair had been styled into soft waves, half pinned back to reveal the striking angles of her face. Her bright green eyes—already arresting—were somehow even more vivid, framed by delicate makeup that enhanced without overpowering. She wore no necklace, only a pair of simple drop earrings that caught the light when she moved.

But it wasn't just the dress, the hair, or the makeup.

It was her.

The way she stood there, unsure for a moment, like she didn't know the effect she was having on him. That soft, shy smile she gave as she met his eyes—uncertain, and yet full of trust.

Ben swallowed hard, stepping closer like he was approaching something sacred. 'Jemma… you're breathtaking.

Her smile widened, a blush warming her cheeks. "Thank you," she said softly. "I wasn't sure if it was too much…"

"It's perfect," he said immediately. "You're perfect."

Jemma ducked her head, but not before he caught the flicker of emotion in her eyes—surprise, maybe. Maybe something more.

Ben offered his arm, and she took it.

As they walked toward the door together, he couldn't shake the feeling that tonight—this night—was going to change everything.

The limousine slid to a stop in front of the grand hotel, its sandstone exterior glowing under golden lights. The moment Ben stepped out, the flash of cameras exploded around them—photographers calling his name, their lenses already turning toward the open door behind him.

Jemma hesitated, nerves fluttering in her stomach like butterflies caught in a storm.

Then Ben reached for her hand.

She took it, and he helped her out, steady and sure. The instant she stood beside him, the flashes intensified. She instinctively dipped her head, her grip tightening slightly on his hand.

Ben leaned down, his lips brushing her ear. His voice was low, calm, and just for her.

"Just breathe. You look gorgeous. Let them take their photos—you've already stolen the show."

She glanced up at him, smiled nervously, and took a steadying breath. With his hand in hers, the noise and the lights seemed to fade just a little.

Together, they walked the carpet and entered the hotel's grand lobby—cool, opulent, and humming with music and laughter from the ballroom beyond.

A waiter passed with a silver tray of champagne flutes. Ben smoothly plucked two, handing one to Jemma.

"For courage," he said with a wink.

She took it, her fingers brushing his. "Thank you."

Ben watched as she lifted the glass, the crystal catching the chandelier light, her green eyes sparkling over the rim. And in that moment, standing beside her in the heart of the city, he couldn't help but think she belonged here. Not because of the dress or the setting—but because she was luminous.

The ballroom shimmered with golden candlelight and the gentle clink of fine cutlery. The seated dinner was already underway when Jemma leaned over to speak with the older couple beside her—an elegant silver-haired woman and her distinguished husband. Within minutes, they were laughing softly at something Jemma had said, utterly charmed.

Ben watched her with quiet admiration. She was poised but warm, genuine without effort. Somehow, she made everyone feel like they mattered. Even here, in this high society setting she'd never experienced before, she carried herself with a natural grace that couldn't be taught.

Still, Ben wasn't blind.

He caught the lingering glances from two of the men seated across the table—their eyes drifting toward Jemma a little too often, their smiles a touch too appreciative. It stirred something primal and unwelcome in him. He wasn't used to feeling possessive, but tonight he felt it in every fibre of his being.

But Jemma?

She didn't seem to notice.

Her attention, when not kindly given to the couple beside her, always returned to Ben. Her eyes sought him out, her smile brightened for him, her laughter softened in a way that was just for him.

At one point, her hand slipped beneath the tablecloth and found his, fingers lacing with his in a gentle, unspoken reassurance.

Ben relaxed slightly. The noise of the gala faded into the background.

She was his for the night. Not because of the dress or the diamonds, but because she wanted to be.

And that made all the difference.

After the last course had been cleared and the band struck up a smooth, jazzy tune, guests began to drift toward the dance floor. The lighting softened, the atmosphere shifting into something more intimate, more romantic.

Ben stood as Jemma did, offering her his hand—but before he could say a word, one of the well-dressed men from their table stepped toward her with a confident smile.

"May I have this dance?" the man asked, extending a hand toward her.

Ben's jaw tightened.

But before he could intervene, Jemma gave a soft laugh—polite, but unmistakably clear. "That's very kind of you," she said, smiling up at the man. "But my date is the only man I plan to dance with tonight."

She turned back to Ben, slipping her hand into his without hesitation.

The man offered a gracious nod and stepped back, retreating into the crowd. Ben stared down at Jemma, speechless for a second.

Something in him shifted then—a fierce, protective pride mixed with awe. She'd chosen him. Not because she had to, but because she wanted to.

His heart flipped.

She looked up at him, the corners of her lips still curled in that sweet, self-assured smile. "I hope that's okay," she teased softly.

Ben didn't answer. He simply pulled her close, guiding her onto the dance floor, his chest aching with something warm and real.

"More than okay," he murmured against her temple. "You have no idea."

And as they began to move in time with the music, her body fitting perfectly against his, Ben knew something had shifted. This wasn't just a night out.

It was the start of something he hadn't even known he was missing.

They danced.

Jemma couldn't count how many songs had played. All she knew was the steady rhythm of Ben's heartbeat beneath her cheek, the feel of his strong arms around her, and the way the world seemed to disappear every time he looked down at her like she was the only thing that mattered.

She'd never felt safer—or more seen.

Ben, for his part, couldn't get enough of the way her head rested so naturally on his shoulder, like she belonged there. Her scent, the soft lilt of her laughter, the warmth of her hand in his—all of it was seeping into his bones, becoming something, he didn't want to ever let go of.

They left just before midnight, slipping out into the night while the party still hummed behind them.

As soon as they were inside the limousine, Jemma reached for his hand. Her fingers slid easily into his, and she turned to him with eyes still glowing from the evening.

"Thank you," she said softly. "For tonight. It was… it was wonderful."

Ben looked at her, at the sincerity on her face, the sparkle in her eyes, and felt something catch in his chest.

"No," he said quietly. "Thank you, Jemma."

And in that still moment, their hands entwined between them, something unspoken passed between them—fragile, new, but utterly real.

When they stepped into the penthouse, Jemma let out a soft sigh and immediately kicked off her heels, her bare feet padding across the polished floor.

"That's better," she said with a small laugh, rolling her ankles.

Ben chuckled as he closed the door behind them, loosening his tie and watching her with a mix of amusement and quiet affection. "Come on," he said, nodding toward the couch.

She crossed the room, the skirt of her gown swishing gently as she sank into the cushions with a contented sigh. He disappeared for a moment and returned without his jacket, carrying two glasses of wine. He handed her one and sat down beside her, close—but respectful. Always.

Their eyes met over the rim of their glasses. The mood was different now. Quieter. Deeper. The warmth that had been simmering between them all night settled into something slower, more certain. Something that buzzed beneath the surface like a current waiting to spark.

"Tonight was perfect," she murmured, her voice soft.

"It was," Ben agreed, his voice low and sincere. "You were perfect."

She glanced at him, that shy smile pulling at her lips again, but there was a new light in her eyes now—brighter. Braver.

They sipped their wine in silence for a while, letting the city hum beyond the windows and the softness of the moment stretch between them. When they finished, Jemma stood, took both glasses, and placed them carefully on the coffee table. Then she turned back to face him.

Ben watched her, his eyes following the gentle sweep of her dress, the loosened tendrils of her hair, the way her bare feet whispered against the floor. She looked like something out of a dream—and completely real all at once.

Without a word, she lifted the hem of her dress and slowly climbed into his lap, straddling him with quiet certainty.

Ben's hands rose instinctively to her waist, steadying her as her knees pressed into the cushions on either side of his thighs. Her fingers skimmed up his chest, over the line of his shoulders, and around the back of his neck. She threaded them into his hair, her touch featherlight but sure.

She leaned in, her lips brushing his ear as she whispered, "I've been wanting to do this all night."

His breath caught. "Jemma…"

He wasn't sure if it was a warning or a prayer.

But then she kissed him.

And the world narrowed to the soft press of her mouth against his, the heat blooming between them, the way she sighed into him like she was finally where she belonged. He pulled her closer, hands splaying against her back, anchoring her to him.

Everything else—the glittering city, the hum of the penthouse, the distance they'd both carried for so long—faded.

And for once, neither of them held back.

Chapter Nineteen

Ben's breath hitched as Jemma's lips brushed his, featherlight, like a question she was asking with her body.

His hands, large and calloused, gripped her waist—not to hold her back, but to anchor himself. It had been so long. Over two years since he'd touched a woman like this, since he'd let himself feel this kind of hunger. Not since before his wife died. The ache in his chest mingled with the heat pooling low in his belly, and for a moment, he was afraid of how much he wanted her.

Afraid of how much he felt.

Jemma shifted in his lap, her dress whispering as it slid higher on her thighs. Her hands moved in his hair, drawing him deeper, closer. Her kiss deepened, growing bolder, more insistent, and something inside him shattered. His control. His silence. His guilt.

He kissed her back.

With a groan that was half need, half surrender, Ben threaded his fingers into her hair and pulled her mouth to his. The kiss turned molten—hot, searching, ravenous. Their mouths moved together in perfect rhythm, lips parting, tongues tangling in a dance that was as much about claiming as it was about rediscovering.

She tasted like wine and woman and everything he hadn't let himself crave in years.

His hand slid up her back, feeling the warm, bare skin between the low dip of her dress. Her breath hitched, and she pressed herself more firmly against him, her hips shifting in a way that made his body jolt with want.

He tore his mouth from hers, his chest rising and falling like he'd just run a race. His forehead rested against hers, their breaths mingling.

"Jemma…" His voice was rough, broken around the edges. "I don't know how long I can resist you."

She cupped his face in both hands, her eyes searching his—soft, sure, and shimmering with something he hadn't seen in years.

"Then don't," she whispered.

She kissed him again—deeper this time, with a hunger that ignited every nerve in his body. Her mouth moved over his with deliberate sensuality, her lips teasing, tasting, claiming. She shifted closer, pressing herself to him, and he felt it—her softness against his hardness, the ache between them undeniable.

Ben groaned low in his throat, his hands gripping her hips as she moved in his lap. It wasn't just desire that pulsed between them—it was something deeper. A longing. A need to be seen, touched, wanted.

Jemma smiled against his lips, a slow, knowing smile, and then she pulled back just enough to look at him. Her green eyes glowed with confidence and care, her breath brushing his cheek as she whispered, "You feel incredible."

Then, without a word, she slid off his lap, her fingers skimming down his chest on the way. She knelt between his legs, her movements fluid, reverent. Ben's breath hitched as she reached for his belt, her fingers working it loose with practiced grace and a calm certainty that made his pulse thunder.

His hips shifted instinctively, lifting for her as she eased his trousers down over his thighs. She kept her eyes on him the entire time, her gaze steady, unhurried, and impossibly intimate. It wasn't just about what she was doing—it was the way she looked at him. Like he was safe. Like he was hers.

His arousal sprang free, and she paused, letting her fingers trail lightly along the edge of his waistband before resting them on his thighs. She didn't rush. She just looked at him—really looked—her expression softening with something like wonder.

"Jemma…" he rasped. He didn't know if he was asking her to stop, to keep going, or to save him from the storm building inside him.

Her hands moved to his hips, caressing him with the same tenderness she'd shown him all evening. "Shhh," she whispered, her voice low and soothing. "Just let me love you."

And in that quiet, electric moment, Ben stopped fighting it.

He let go.

Her hand wrapped around him slowly, carefully—as if memorising every inch of him with her fingers. He was thick, hard, and hot beneath her touch, and her breath caught at the feel of him. She'd only ever known one man before—Leo—and even with him, it had never felt like this. Ben was… more. In every way that mattered.

A flicker of uncertainty passed through her, but it was quickly overtaken by something stronger—desire, trust, and the quiet thrill of knowing this was her choice. She wanted to do this. To please him. To explore him. To show him what he meant to her in the most intimate way she could.

Ben was watching her, his chest rising and falling in shallow, uneven breaths, his eyes locked to hers. There was something raw in his expression—need, yes, but also restraint, tenderness. Like he couldn't believe this was happening. Like he didn't dare move for fear of breaking the spell.

She lowered her head, her lips parting as she leaned in. Her tongue flicked gently over the head of him, tasting him, testing her confidence. He groaned—a deep, broken sound that sent a shiver down her spine and made her feel powerful in the most unexpected way.

Encouraged, she slowly took him into her mouth, inch by inch, as much as she could, her hand stroking the rest in a slow rhythm. She wasn't perfect—she didn't know if she was doing it right—but she gave herself fully to the moment. To him. Her movements were unpractised but eager, her mouth warm, her touch gentle.

Ben's hands gripped the edge of the couch, knuckles white, his head tipping back with a low growl of pleasure.

"Jemma…" he rasped, his voice thick and hoarse. "God…"

It had been so long since anyone had touched him like this—with such intention, such care. It wasn't just her mouth on him—it was her heart in every movement, her tenderness in every breath. And it undid him in a way nothing else ever had.

He looked down again, watching the dark fall of her hair, the delicate curve of her shoulders, the pure concentration in her eyes. And he knew—he was already gone.

She continued, her hand and mouth working in perfect, aching rhythm—each movement slow but sure, guided by the soft sounds he made, the way his body tensed beneath her touch. The muscles in his thighs flexed, his breath turning ragged, his hand finally finding her hair, not to guide her, but simply to anchor himself to the moment—grounded by her, undone by her.

"Jemma…" he breathed, his voice fractured. "I'm not going to be able to hold on much longer."

She pulled back just enough to speak, her voice low, urgent. "Don't."

Just that one word. Certain. Unafraid.

It shattered him.

With a groan torn from somewhere deep in his chest, Ben let go, his body bowing forward as he came into her mouth. His hands clutched at her, not with force, but with reverence—like he needed her close, like he couldn't believe what she was giving him.

"God…" he gasped, his voice barely more than a whisper.

She stayed with him, gentle through the aftershocks, her hand softening, her mouth easing away slowly. When she finally looked up at him, there was a flush on her cheeks and something unguarded in her expression—shyness and pride, tenderness, and a quiet question in her eyes: Was I enough?

Ben reached for her, cupping her face in both hands as if she were something breakable, precious. His eyes searched hers, still dark with the intensity of what they'd just shared.

"You…" he said roughly, his thumb brushing her lower lip, "are extraordinary."

She smiled then—soft and sweet, a hint of mischief in her eyes, but more than that… trust. Pure and unguarded.

Ben couldn't resist. He pulled her gently back onto his lap, holding her close like she was something rare. "That was amazing," he murmured, his voice husky with lingering awe and heat.

Then he kissed her.

But not like before.

This kiss was deeper, slower—like he'd never kissed a woman before. Like her mouth was the first he'd ever tasted and might be the last. It wasn't just desire anymore—it was gratitude, care, connection. Every brush of his lips spoke of everything he hadn't said.

His hands slid to the hem of her gown, and he hesitated just long enough for her to nod. Then, slowly, he lifted the dress over her head and let it fall to the floor behind them.

She wore no bra.

He drew in a breath, stunned—not just by the sight of her, but by the way she held herself in that moment. Vulnerable and strong. Modest and unafraid.

"You're so beautiful," he whispered, his voice thick with emotion. "More than I imagined."

His hands moved slowly from her waist to her breasts, cupping her gently, like he was learning her shape by heart. Then he lowered his head and took one into his mouth, his lips and tongue worshipful, savouring every soft sigh she gave in return.

Jemma arched into him, her hands threading through his hair, her breath catching as heat bloomed across her skin. Every sensation felt new. Every kiss, every touch—it was all him, and it was everything.

And neither of them wanted to stop.

Ben took his time, exploring her with a kind of devotion that made Jemma's breath catch in her throat. He lavished both nipples with care, his tongue teasing, his mouth drawing gentle, precise circles that made her hips shift restlessly in his lap. Each flick, each warm pull, drew a soft gasp from her lips, and her fingers tangled in his hair, holding him close as her breath grew heavier with desire.

He pulled back just enough to meet her gaze, then gently laid her down along the length of the couch. His eyes roamed her body like a man seeing beauty for the first time—his hands following, sliding slowly over the curve of her hip, the smooth plane of her stomach, the softness of her thighs. When he reached the edge of her lace panties, he hooked his fingers in them and dragged them down her legs, slow and deliberate, never breaking eye contact.

Then his fingers returned—one slipping into her, testing the slick heat of her arousal. She gasped, her hips arching instinctively.

"Ben," she breathed, her voice a whisper of aching need.

His thumb found her centre, circling in smooth, patient strokes, and her body trembled beneath his touch. At the same time, his mouth returned to her breasts—sucking, tasting, as though he couldn't get enough of her. Her breath hitched again, her back arching, pleasure winding tighter inside her with every movement.

Then he began to kiss his way down her body, slowly, tenderly—along her ribs, the dip of her stomach, the inside of her thigh. Her skin responded to every brush of his lips, every pass of his breath. By the time he reached the heat of her, she was already trembling.

He parted her gently, and the moment his tongue slid between her folds, he stilled—mesmerised.

She was soft, warm, slick with need. Every flick of his tongue drew a new sound from her lips—a whimper, a moan, a whispered plea—and he savoured each one like a reward. He lost himself in her responses, in the way her fingers gripped the couch, in the way her legs tensed around his shoulders.

She was beautiful like this—open, unguarded, trusting him with every part of her.

And he planned to worship her until she came undone.

Ben worked her with a slow, focused rhythm, his tongue circling and stroking, drawing her closer and closer to the edge. He felt her thighs tighten around him, her breath coming in short, gasping bursts as her fingers buried in his hair, anchoring herself to him.

Every sound she made was soft and unfiltered—raw need wrapped in vulnerability—and it drove him to give her more, to push her higher.

"Ben… oh God…" she whispered, her voice trembling, hips shifting beneath his mouth. She was close—he could feel it in the way her body tensed, the way she pressed into him, seeking release.

He slipped a finger back inside her, curling just right as his tongue flicked faster, more deliberately, his other hand sliding up to cradle her breast.

Her back arched, a sharp cry escaping her lips as pleasure shattered through her like lightning.

She came in waves—tight, trembling pulses around his fingers, her thighs quaking, breath broken and desperate. He didn't stop, not until she was spent and boneless beneath him, her body sinking into the couch like she couldn't quite believe what had just happened.

He kissed her softly then, gently, easing her back from the edge, his lips trailing over her trembling stomach before moving up to her lips.

Her eyes fluttered open as he hovered over her, and the look she gave him—dazed, grateful, overwhelmed—nearly undid him.

"Ben…" she whispered, her voice barely there.

He leaned down and kissed her, slow and deep, as if trying to share her pleasure with his own breath.

"I've never felt anything like that," she murmured against his lips.

He smiled, brushing a strand of hair from her cheek. "You're incredible."

And as she curled into him, her body still humming from release, Ben held her like she was the most precious thing in the world—because in that moment, she was.

Jemma nestled against him, her cheek resting against the curve of his neck, her body still trembling slightly from the intensity of what had just passed between them. Her breath was warm on his skin, and he felt it—the honesty, the vulnerability—in the way she held him.

She whispered, barely audible, "I didn't know it could be like that."

Ben pulled back just enough to see her face, his brow furrowing slightly. "Like what?"

She met his eyes, hers soft and wide. "Like that. I've never… felt that before."

There was a beat of silence, the only sound the low hum of the city outside the windows.

He looked at her, a flicker of confusion in his eyes. "Your ex… Leo…?" he asked gently, not from jealousy, but with genuine curiosity and a quiet kind of disbelief.

She shook her head, her voice barely a breath. "No. Not once."

Ben's jaw tensed slightly, but not from pride. From something deeper—something aching. He reached up and cupped her face, brushing his thumb lightly along her cheekbone.

"Jesus, Jemma…" he murmured, his voice thick. "You deserved better than that."

She smiled faintly. "I didn't know what I was missing. Not until now."

He kissed her again, slowly, with devotion. It wasn't a kiss of hunger this time—it was one of recognition. Of understanding. Of something starting to grow between them that neither of them had fully expected.

Ben rested his forehead against hers, breathing her in.

"You make me want to take my time with you," he said quietly. "To give you everything you've never had. Everything you should have had."

Her fingers curled lightly around the nape of his neck. "Then don't stop," she whispered. "Please."

And just like that, the space between them disappeared again—no barriers, no past. Just skin, breath, and something that felt dangerously close to falling.

Chapter Twenty

Ben scooped her up from the couch, her bare skin soft and warm against his chest.

Jemma gasped, surprised, but curled into him, arms looping around his neck.

He didn't speak as he carried her through the dim hallway, his jaw tight, pulse thudding in his throat. This wasn't just heat anymore. This was need. Urgent. Consuming.

The bedroom door nudged open with his foot. Moonlight spilled in through the window, casting silver shadows across the room.

He set her down gently, letting her body slide slowly against his until her toes touched the floor.

Jemma looked up at him, lips swollen, cheeks flushed, hair tousled from his hands.

God help him—she'd never looked more beautiful.

But Ben stepped back a little, drawing in a breath. His hand came up to cradle her cheek, his voice low, rough with restraint.

"I didn't plan this," he said. "I wasn't expecting… any of this tonight. I don't have any condoms."

Her expression didn't falter. She didn't flinch or retreat.

Instead, she reached for his hand and pressed it against her chest—right over her racing heart.

"I have an IUD," she said quietly. "You don't need to worry."

His eyes searched hers, something fierce and tender flickering there.

"You're sure?" he asked. "Because if we go any further…"

"I want to," she said. No hesitation. Just truth. "I trust you, Ben."

A growl rumbled low in his chest, and then he was kissing her again—deep and claiming, all the pent-up desire spilling out at once.

Her clothes were already discarded, forgotten somewhere on the living room floor.

His shirt was yanked over his head and tossed aside; his trousers kicked away in a rush of tangled limbs and sharp breaths.

When he finally lowered her to the bed, the mattress dipped beneath her, and he paused—hovering over her, one hand braced beside her head, his blue eyes dark with need.

But he didn't move. Not yet.

His gaze swept over her like a caress—slow, reverent, hungry.

She was spread beneath him, moonlight gilding her skin in silver, her hair spilling across his pillow like spilled ink. Her chest rose and fell in rapid, shallow breaths.

But he held himself back.

"Ben," she whispered, her voice catching in her throat.

He closed his eyes for a beat.

"I'm trying to slow down," he murmured hoarsely. "But you… you make that damn near impossible."

Her hands came up to his chest, palms flat against the heat of his skin.

"You don't have to hold back," she said, barely more than a breath. "I want this. I want you."

That was all he needed.

With a groan of surrender, his mouth found hers again—hot, open, desperate.

He kissed her like a man starving, like he'd been waiting years instead of minutes to taste her like this again.

His body settled over hers, heavy and solid, and when he pressed against her, skin to skin, she arched into him with a soft cry.

Every inch of him trembled with restraint as he slid his hand down her side, fingers mapping the curve of her waist, her hip, then lower still.

She was already wet and aching for him, and the raw sound that tore from his throat made her shiver.

He braced himself, took a beat to look at her—really look.

One last pause. One final moment to make sure.

"You're sure?" he asked, his voice thick, barely holding together.

She nodded, her eyes blazing with heat and something deeper.

"I've never been more sure of anything."

And then he sank into her, slow and deep.

They both gasped—two halves finally fitting into place.

It was more than physical. It was a claiming. A promise. A beginning neither of them saw coming.

And as they moved together, every touch, every moan, every whispered name spoken into the dark told the same truth:

They weren't just making love.

They were falling.

Their bodies moved in rhythm, finding a pace that was both urgent and unbearably slow—like neither of them wanted it to end, yet couldn't bear to wait another second.

Ben buried his face in her neck, breathing her in like oxygen.

Her legs wrapped tighter around his hips, drawing him deeper, her fingers clawing at his back as pleasure coiled hot and fast inside her.

"Jemma," he groaned, her name a reverent ache against her skin. "God, you feel like… heaven."

She gasped his name in reply, her voice broken, desperate.

Pressure built to a fever pitch—tight, trembling, blinding.

"Please—," she whispered, one hand tangling in his hair. "Ben, I—"

"I've got you," he murmured, rocking deeper, harder. "Let go for me, sweetheart. I'm right there with you."

And then it shattered.

Her climax ripped through her like a wave, a cry torn from her throat as her whole body arched into his. He followed with a strangled groan, losing himself in her completely—every muscle drawn tight, every breath suspended in that white-hot, perfect moment.

For a beat, they didn't move.

Just stayed tangled together, breathless, trembling.

Then, with infinite care, Ben rolled onto his back—keeping her cradled against him, still intimately connected, not ready to let her go.

One of his hands splayed across her lower back, the other tangled gently in her hair.

Their foreheads rested together.

Their breathing slowed.

Neither spoke at first. The silence between them was tender, heavy with things unspoken—but not uncertain.

He brushed his thumb along the curve of her hip, still buried inside her, still wrapped in the heat of what they'd just shared.

Jemma blinked down at him, dazed and glowing. "That was…"

Ben gave a rough, quiet laugh. "Yeah. It was."

She kissed him—slow, sweet, lingering.

He kissed her back, not just because he could, but because he had to.

And somewhere in the quiet after, with her heart beating against his and her fingers curled over his chest…

He realised he never wanted this moment to end.

Never wanted her to go.

Ben spoke first, his voice low in the quiet room.

"You didn't deserve for Leo to treat you the way he did."

With her head resting on his shoulder, Jemma gave a small, tired hum. "Mmm, I know. I tried to get away from him so many times… but he always dragged me back."

His arms tightened around her instinctively. She felt the shift in his chest, the tension that coiled there.

"He controlled me," she said softly. "Financially, emotionally, physically. I thought I had no choice. I was scared, but I didn't know how to leave. Not really. And then… the last time when he was kicking me—I just couldn't take the pain anymore. I remember lying there, bleeding, begging him to just finish it. I asked him to kill me."

"Jemma…" His voice broke. Just that one word, laced with anguish.

"It's okay," she whispered. "I've come to terms with it. That night, I somehow made it to the neighbour's front door. They called the police. One of the officers—he was kind—told me not to go back. Told me to disappear. So… I did. And now I'm here."

He exhaled slowly, burying his face in her hair for a moment. "I'm glad you are."

There was silence for a beat, warm and weighted. Then she asked, her voice gentle and without accusation, "The women at the dance said you were still in love with your wife… are you?"

Ben looked up at the ceiling for a moment before answering. "No. I'm not. And I haven't been for a long time—long before she died. I'm not sure if I ever was."

He paused, his jaw tightening. "Heidi was… manipulative. After we got married, she told me she'd gotten pregnant on purpose. Like it was some game she'd won." He let out a humourless breath. "I still tried to make it work—for the baby's sake. I thought maybe it would get better."

He shifted slightly, his fingers moving in long strokes across Jemma's bare back as he looked down at her.

"But the further along she got with Charlotte, the more bitter she became. Like motherhood was some kind of prison sentence. She started saying that the baby had ruined her… even before Charlotte was born."

Jemma nodded slowly, her fingers drawing quiet circles over his chest. "I couldn't believe it either… when Charlotte told me she remembered her saying that. She was so little, but she remembered."

Ben's expression darkened with pain and regret. "I should've protected her sooner. I kept hoping if I kept the peace, things would shift. And I was scared—scared she'd take Charlotte and disappear. Heidi knew how to twist things, make people believe her side. And then when she died…" He swallowed hard. "I thought maybe that was my chance to finally be what Charlotte needed. Just me and her. But the damage had already been done."

Jemma pressed a kiss to his shoulder. "You are what she needs. You're enough, Ben. More than enough."

His eyes found hers, locking on with quiet intensity.

"The day Heidi died," he said slowly, "she'd asked me again to move to Brisbane. She hated it out there—the isolation, the dust, the quiet. She'd disappear for months at a time, off to the city while I stayed and ran the station. That day, I told her no. Told her that it was Charlotte's home. She flew into one of her rages, stormed out, slammed doors…"

He paused, the weight of memory pulling hard on his features.

"She got in the car, furious. I told her not to drive like that, begged her to wait. But she just screamed at me and left. Next thing I know, the police are at my door. She'd wrapped the car around a gum tree."

He exhaled, jaw working as he stared up at the ceiling.

"I've carried the guilt ever since. Because I didn't feel grief. I didn't feel loss. Just… relief. And that's not something a man's supposed to admit."

Jemma slid her hand up to cup his cheek, gently guiding his face back to hers.

"You survived something you couldn't fix," she said quietly. "That doesn't make you heartless. It makes you human."

His throat worked as he nodded, one arm pulling her in closer—like she was the only anchor he had left in the world.

She lifted her face and kissed him—slowly, sweetly, like a promise.

He kissed her back, his lips soft but deepening with each breath, each brush of mouths and mingled need.

As she shifted against him, she felt him still inside her… and growing.

A flush rose to her cheeks as she looked up at him, eyes dancing with mischief. "Again," she whispered, the word laced with both desire and joy.

Ben let out a low groan, half-amused, half-aching. His blue eyes searched hers, dark and intense. "I don't think I'll ever get enough of you."

Jemma's lips curled into a smile—tender, sultry, knowing.

She sat up, straddling him, her palms pressed to his chest, the heat between them sparking to life again. His breath hitched as she shifted her hips, guiding him back into her, slow and deliberate.

Her head fell back on a sigh as she began to move, unhurried, sensuous. The rhythm was hers this time—slow, deep, controlled. Her dark hair spilled over her shoulders, her skin glowing in the moonlight that filtered through the curtains.

Ben's hands slid up her thighs, settling at her waist, his fingers flexing as he met her movements, his gaze never leaving her face. It was reverent, almost awed—like he couldn't believe she was real.

"God, Jemma…" he whispered, voice thick with feeling.

She leaned forward, bracing her hands beside his head, her green eyes locking with his. "Feel good."

"Yes," he breathed, lifting his hips to meet her, their bodies moving as one.

In the quiet of the room, with hearts pounding and skin pressed close, they lost themselves in each other again—deeper this time. Not just in desire, but in something more. Something that felt like healing.

Something that felt like falling in love. For real, this time.

Chapter Twenty-One

Ben woke with the early light filtering through the thin curtains, soft and golden. The air was still, quiet—the kind of silence that only came after a storm had passed.

He blinked, disoriented for a second, until the warmth against his side brought it all back.

Jemma.

She was curled on her side, facing him, her long black hair tangled across the pillow and his chest. His arm was still draped over her waist; their bodies pressed together beneath the rumpled sheets.

She looked peaceful. Content. The faintest smile ghosted her lips, her lashes casting soft shadows on her cheeks.

Ben didn't move. Didn't dare.

He just watched her—watched the steady rise and fall of her breath, the gentle flutter of her lashes. A strange ache bloomed in his chest, not painful, but potent. He could've stayed there forever.

His thumb lightly traced a slow line along her hip, just to reassure himself she was real. That she was still there. Still his—for now.

She stirred, a small breath catching in her throat as her eyes slowly fluttered open.

For a moment, she blinked sleepily, adjusting to the light. Then her gaze found his, and she smiled.

"Morning," she murmured, voice husky from sleep.

"Hey," he said softly, his voice rough. "You sleep okay?"

She nodded, her fingers finding his on her hip. "I think I slept better than I have in years."

Ben's heart gave a little kick. He reached up and gently tucked a strand of hair behind her ear. "You looked peaceful."

Her smile deepened. "Were you watching me?"

"Maybe," he said, a faint grin tugging at his mouth. "You're not exactly easy to look away from."

She blushed, a warm pink rising in her cheeks as she buried her face in the pillow for a second, laughing softly. "That's not fair. I haven't even brushed my teeth."

Ben chuckled, shifting closer so their foreheads touched. "You're perfect. Morning breath and all."

She tilted her head, eyes narrowing in mock suspicion. "Are you always this charming in the morning?"

"Only when I wake up with you in my arms."

Her breath hitched a little, and for a moment, neither of them said anything. The weight of the night before lingered—sweet and quiet, full of unspoken promises.

Jemma reached up and gently stroked the stubble along his jaw. "You, okay?"

He nodded, his smile fading into something softer. "Yeah. I just… I don't want this to be a one-off, Jemma."

She searched his face for a beat, her expression unreadable—then she leaned in and pressed a kiss to his chest, just over his heart.

"It's not," she said quietly. "Not for me."

Ben closed his eyes, pulling her into him, arms tightening like he never wanted to let go.

And for the first time in what felt like forever… he let himself believe it.

A moment later, he shifted from her and slid out of bed, careful not to disturb the covers too much. Jemma blinked in confusion as he leaned down, scooping her into his arms like she weighed nothing.

She squealed, laughing. "Ben! What are you doing?"

"We need a shower," he said, his voice low, laced with mischief.

"Oh, do we now?" she grinned, wrapping her arms around his neck as he carried her to the ensuite.

The bathroom was cool and still in shadow, but Ben turned the tap and waited for the steam to rise before pulling the glass door open.

Once inside, the hot water poured over them, chasing away the last of the morning chill. Jemma tilted her face up into the stream, her eyes closed, a soft hum escaping her lips. Ben stood behind her, his hands gentle as they moved over her skin—washing her slowly, reverently. Her back. Her arms. Her hair.

But soon, his touch changed.

Slower. Firmer. Hungrier.

Jemma turned to face him, droplets streaming down her cheeks, her lashes damp and clinging. His gaze swept over her—wet hair, flushed cheeks, lips parted slightly as her breath caught.

She didn't say a word. She didn't need to.

Ben leaned in and kissed her—deep, wet, desperate. She rose up onto her toes, her arms wrapping around his shoulders, their bodies slick and hot as they pressed together.

And then he lifted her.

Jemma gasped, legs locking around his waist as her back met the cool tile. His hands braced her, strong and sure, as their mouths devoured each other in fevered, hungry kisses.

When he entered her, it was slow only for a second—just enough for their eyes to meet, for their foreheads to press together, for a gasp to leave both their mouths.

Then it was fast.

Urgent.

Like neither of them could wait another second. Like something raw and unspoken had finally broken loose inside them both.

Water cascaded around them, a curtain of heat and steam, as they moved in tandem—his grip tightening on her hips, her fingers digging into his shoulders. The slick glide of skin, the rhythmic slap of bodies, the deep groans, and breathless moans—all echoing off tile and glass.

It was wild and heated, but more than lust.

It was surrender.

His mouth found her throat, her jaw, her lips—never far for long.

And all the while, their eyes kept finding each other, like neither wanted to look away. Like this moment—this connection—was all that mattered.

When release finally came, it hit them both like a storm. Jemma cried out his name, her body clenching around his as pleasure tore through her. Ben followed with a deep, guttural sound, burying his face in her shoulder, his body trembling with the force of it.

For a long moment, they just stayed there—wrapped around each other, breathless and shaking, water pouring down over them like rain.

Then Jemma whispered, lips brushing his ear, "I could get used to this."

Ben laughed softly, pressing a kiss to her wet shoulder. "You'd better."

And somewhere in that steam-filled space, with her legs still around him and his heart beating like a drum against hers—

He knew she already had.

And so had he.

They dressed in a quiet rhythm, their movements gentle, smiles exchanged between soft glances and light brushes of fingers. There was an ease to it now—something unspoken yet comforting. As Jemma slipped on her sandals and Ben shrugged into his shirt, the sun poured through the windows, casting golden streaks across the room. It was time to go.

Back to the station.

Back home.

Outside, the day waited—like the rest of their lives hadn't quite started yet.

The limousine glided smoothly along the road toward the airstrip, the city fading behind them, replaced by stretches of sunburnt land and open sky. Inside, the atmosphere was quieter than it had been that morning. No more teasing laughter. No playful touches.

Jemma sat beside Ben; her hands folded neatly in her lap. She stared out the tinted window, watching the land roll by, her expression unreadable.

Ben sat back, one arm resting across the seat, the other curled loosely on his thigh. He glanced at her, trying to read her silence.

He didn't know if she loved him.

The thought sat heavy in his chest—heavier than he expected. The night they'd spent together had been more than just passion. He'd felt something in her touch; in the way she looked at him like he mattered. But maybe he'd been wrong. Maybe it hadn't meant the same to her.

And the truth was, he didn't even know what he wanted. Not exactly. His life had been so tightly controlled for so long, his emotions buried under years of damage. He hadn't expected someone like Jemma to show up—gentle, fierce, and somehow already tangled up in his world.

He wasn't used to wanting. Not like this. Not with his heart in it. Not when it could be taken away.

But he knew one thing.

He didn't want to lose her.

They arrived at the jet, and as they settled into their seats, Jemma finally spoke.

"Ben?"

He turned toward her.

"Until we work out what this is," she said, her voice careful, "I don't want to confuse Charlotte. I think… we should wait. At least until we know what we both want."

Ben stared at her, a flicker of something cold running through him. So, she wasn't sure either. Or maybe she was—and she just didn't feel the same.

Still, she was thinking about Charlotte. That mattered.

He looked down at his hands, then back at her. "Yeah," he said, keeping his voice steady. "That's fair."

She offered a small, apologetic smile, then turned her gaze back to the window.

Ben leaned his head back, closing his eyes.

He didn't have answers. Not about love, not about the future.

But he knew this ache in his chest—the fear of losing something before he'd even fully held it.

And for the first time, he realised how much Jemma meant to him.

Even if he wasn't ready to say it.

Even if she didn't feel the same.

He just hoped he hadn't already missed his chance.

The helicopter touched down softly on the sunbaked stretch beside the main house. Dust kicked up around the skids, whirling into the air before settling again. The familiar outline of the homestead, red earth, and gum trees felt like a balm after the intensity of the last few days.

Ben barely had time to unbuckle before a small blur came tearing across the yard.

"Daddy!"

Charlotte's voice rang out, high and joyful, and Ben stepped down just in time to catch her as she launched herself into his arms.

"Hello, Button," he said, hugging her tight, the ache in his chest easing the moment she touched him. "I missed you."

She planted a noisy kiss on his cheek, then pulled back with a grin. Her bright grey eyes sparkled as they turned toward Jemma.

Without hesitation, Charlotte leaned out, arms wide.

Jemma's breath caught. She reached for her instinctively, and Ben handed her over.

"Hi, little munchkin," Jemma whispered, hugging Charlotte close. "I missed you so much."

Charlotte giggled and wrapped her arms around Jemma's neck, resting her head there like it was the most natural thing in the world.

Agnes stood nearby, a quiet smile on her face as she watched the reunion unfold.

Ben looked at them—his daughter tucked safely in Jemma's arms, both of them smiling, comfortable, connected—and something deep inside him shifted.

This. Right here. This felt like home.

Chapter Twenty-Two

Life slipped back into its familiar rhythm with deceptive ease.

Dinner was just like any other night—laughter from Charlotte, quiet warmth from Agnes, the occasional glance between Jemma and Ben that didn't linger quite long enough. They sat at the table as if nothing had changed. No confessions whispered in the dark, no kisses that made her forget how to breathe, no touch that still burned on her skin.

Jemma smiled when expected, nodded along to the conversation, helped Charlotte with her vegetables. On the outside, she looked composed—graceful, even. But inside, her heart ached.

Because everything had changed.

She loved them. Both of them. This strange, unexpected, beautiful little family she'd somehow fallen into. She didn't know when it had happened—somewhere between Charlotte's sweet, trusting hugs and the way Ben looked at her when he thought she wasn't paying attention.

But now she did know. And it terrified her.

Because if Ben decided this thing between them wasn't going anywhere… if he quietly let it fade back into nothing more than shared silence and mutual respect, her heart would break. And she'd still smile. Still show up every day. Still read bedtime stories and brush her hair and help Charlotte with her lessons. Because she loved them too much to walk away.

Even if it hurt.

She glanced up once and caught Agnes watching her with quiet eyes, something knowing in the older woman's expression. But Agnes didn't say anything—and Jemma was grateful for that. Whatever this was between her and Ben, they'd have to figure it out in their own time.

After dinner, she helped clear the plates, then scooped Charlotte up and carried her to bed. The little girl snuggled into her side as she read a story, voice soft in the warm, lamplit room.

When Charlotte's eyes finally fluttered closed, Jemma kissed her forehead and rose quietly. She stepped into the hallway where Ben and Agnes were still lingering in the lounge.

"I'm going to head back to the cottage," she said, her voice gentle.

Ben looked up from where he sat, and something unreadable passed across his face.

"Goodnight," she added, glancing at them both.

"Night, Jemma," Agnes said, her voice kind, calm.

Ben only nodded, watching her as she turned and walked toward the door.

Outside, the night was cool and quiet. The sky stretched out above her, wide and dark, scattered with stars.

She made her way back to the cottage alone, every step echoing with the truth she hadn't spoken.

She loved him.

And she didn't know if he'd ever be able to love her back.

Ben watched her go.

The soft click of the door echoed louder than it should have in the quiet house. Jemma's footsteps faded down the path toward the cottage, and every instinct in him screamed to call her back. He didn't want her to leave. He wanted her to stay—right there, with him. To curl up beside him on the couch, or in his bed. To fall asleep with her head on his chest and wake up with her smile.

He wanted to make love to her again—slow, unhurried, like they had all the time in the world. But more than that, he wanted her beside him. In his space. In his life.

But he didn't move.

He sat in his armchair like a damn fool, staring at the door she'd just walked out of every muscle in his body tense with restraint.

The silence stretched.

Then Agnes spoke, her voice quiet but clear. "How long you gonna pretend you don't care for her?"

Ben's jaw tightened, but he didn't look at her. "I'm not pretending."

"No," Agnes said, standing from her chair and collecting the last of the teacups. "You're just being a coward."

That got his attention.

He turned to her, frowning, but she didn't back down. Didn't soften it. Just looked at him like she always had—like someone who knew him better than he knew himself.

"She's not going to wait around forever, Ben. You think you're protecting yourself, maybe even protecting Charlotte, but what you're really doing is pushing away the best thing that's happened to either of you in a long time."

Ben rubbed a hand over his face, sighing. "I just… I don't know what I'm doing. I don't want to hurt her. And I'm scared that if I let this go too far, I might."

Agnes tilted her head. "And you don't think walking away will hurt her more?"

He had no answer for that.

Because he knew it would.

Agnes gave him a long, searching look, then turned away. "You figure it out, Ben. But not too slowly. Love doesn't sit around waiting for permission."

She walked off toward the kitchen, leaving him alone with the truth she'd just laid bare.

He closed his eyes, and all he saw was Jemma—her green eyes, her laugh, the way she felt in his arms like she belonged there.

And for the first time in years, he wondered if maybe… maybe he was the one who needed to be brave.

The kitchen smelled of warm scones and freshly brewed tea, but the air held a quiet tension that no amount of homely comfort could ease.

Jemma sat at the breakfast table beside Charlotte, her smile gentle but distant as she buttered toast with mechanical precision. She hadn't slept much. She'd waited—hoping to hear footsteps on the gravel path, a knock at the door, something. But Ben never came.

And now she was telling herself that it was fine. That she didn't need him to come. That she was strong enough on her own.

Still, her eyes barely lifted when he walked into the room.

Ben paused in the doorway; hands shoved into his back pockets. His hair was damp from his early morning rounds; his shirt rolled at the sleeves. He looked like himself— solid, grounded—but something in him felt… off. Unsettled.

He scanned the room, found Jemma, and felt the shift instantly.

She didn't meet his gaze.

"Morning," he said, voice low, uncertain.

"Morning," she replied with a small nod, her tone polite. Not cold. Not warm. Just… careful.

Charlotte, oblivious to the undercurrents, chirped happily about today's lesson— something about painting native animals. She wiggled in her chair, already excited. Jemma nodded along, her hand absently brushing Charlotte's hair, but her thoughts were far away.

Ben sat down slowly across from them, picking up a mug and wrapping his hands around it like it could anchor him.

He hated this distance. He'd felt it settle in like a fog the moment he walked in—no, the moment he hadn't gone to her last night. He should have gone. He'd stood outside, hand halfway to the door, heart in his throat… but fear had gripped him.

Now he was watching the consequences unfold in real time.

Agnes placed a plate in front of him with a quiet clatter and gave him a look that spoke volumes—one part disappointment, one part warning.

She didn't say a word. Just shook her head at him and walked away.

Ben stared at the plate but didn't eat. Instead, he watched Jemma as she gently gathered Charlotte's painting supplies into a bag. Every movement was neat, precise. Detached.

She was slipping away from him. He could feel it. And it scared him more than anything else ever had.

He cleared his throat. "Jemma—"

She looked up, eyebrows raised.

He faltered. "Have a good lesson."

Her lips lifted slightly. "Thanks."

Then she and Charlotte stood. Jemma helped the little girl into her jacket, buttoned it with quiet focus, and reached for her own coat.

Ben stood too, instinctively.

"I'll be back around lunch," she said to Agnes. "Should be done before the heat picks up."

Agnes nodded from the sink.

Ben took a step forward. "Jemma—"

She turned, eyes steady but unreadable. "Yes?"

"I—" His mouth opened, then closed. The words lodged in his throat. "Nothing. Just… see you later."

She gave a small nod. Then she and Charlotte stepped out into the morning, their footsteps crunching softly over the gravel path.

Ben stood there for a long beat, silence pressing in around him.

Agnes didn't look up from the sink, but her voice was dry and knowing.

"Well, that went beautifully."

He exhaled sharply and rubbed the back of his neck.

"I'm an idiot."

Agnes snorted. "That's the first thing you've gotten right all morning."

The room smelled of sweat, cigarettes, and cheap disinfectant. The paint was peeling above the window, and the flickering fluorescent light buzzed like a mosquito in Leo's ear. But none of that mattered.

Leo Evans sat on the edge of the sagging mattress, hunched over his phone, fingers twitching as he scrolled through search results like a man starving for air.

He was out.

Free.

Finally.

They'd told him he was lucky to get bail. That the judge must've been in a generous mood. He didn't care why. All he knew was that he was out of that hellhole and Jemma wasn't here.

She should be.

She should've waited.

Instead, she disappeared—like a coward. Like she didn't owe him something after everything they'd been through.

He opened another tab and typed it in for the fiftieth time.

Jemma Prescott.

Melbourne. News. Socials. Old posts. Deleted accounts.

He heard nothing from her for months.

Then a new result popped up.

Children's Charity Gala – Photos from Saturday Night's Event

He tapped it before the page fully loaded, heart thudding, pupils wide.

And there she was.

Jemma.

Looking like a damn movie star in that slate-blue dress, her long black hair falling over one shoulder, a soft smile on her face.

His breath caught.

Then his jaw clenched.

She was standing next to some man. Tall. Broad. Sandy blonde hair. Smiling like he had every right to touch her waist like that.

Leo's lips curled back in a snarl.

"No," he muttered. "No, no, no…"

He zoomed in. The guy had his hand on her lower back. Possessive. Intimate. Like she was his.

A red mist descended.

She was not someone else's. She was his.

Leo's fingers tightened around the phone until his knuckles went white.

He stared at the photo until his vision blurred, rage boiling just beneath the surface. He swiped down to the caption.

Gala event held in Brisbane, Queensland — Reclusive cattle baron Benjamin Callahan, owner of one of Windorah's largest stations, turned heads as he arrived with a stunning mystery woman on his arm. The pair looked undeniably close, sparking whispers about the identity of the stunning raven-haired beauty who stole the spotlight — and possibly the bachelor's heart.

So that's where she'd run off to.

He laughed softly, eyes wild now. "You thought you could hide from me out there, Jem? You really thought that little outback hole was far enough?"

He stood up, pacing the tiny room like a caged animal.

"You're confused. You need reminding, that's all. You always needed someone to keep you grounded."

He grabbed his backpack from the corner and shoved his charger and wallet inside. He didn't have a car, didn't have a plan.

Didn't matter.

He'd find one. He always did.

Fuelled by obsession, adrenaline, and twisted conviction, Leo Evans slipped out the back door of the halfway house into the sun-drenched Melbourne streets, already picturing her face when she saw him again.

She'd come home with him.

She had to.

Chapter Twenty-Three

It was Monday afternoon, and Ben had finally made up his mind. He was going to tell Jemma the truth—how he felt about her. That he didn't want to lose her. That he needed her to stay... not just for Charlotte, not just for the station, but for him. For good.

The words were on the tip of his tongue, burning for release.

Then he saw it.

At first, it was nothing more than a faint smudge on the horizon—barely a whisper of grey against the endless blue sky. He almost dismissed it. But then the wind shifted.

The acrid stench of smoke hit him like a punch to the gut.

His heart dropped.

"Jesus," he muttered, reaching instinctively for his binoculars.

A curl of smoke rose from the western boundary, just past the scrubland. It was barely visible against the cloud-dark sky, but the wind was picking up—and that meant trouble.

"Call Mick," he snapped to one of the hands beside him. "Get the others up there now. It's fire."

He turned on his heel, already moving toward the ute.

A dry lightning storm had passed through the night before. He'd hoped they'd escaped any damage. He should've known better.

By the time they reached the site, the blaze had started to snake its way through the brittle grass, licking at the edge of a dry gully. Ben leapt from the vehicle before it had fully stopped, barking orders, adrenaline cutting through his exhaustion.

The air was hot and mean. Smoke clawed at his lungs. This was what the land did—it waited for a moment's neglect, then reminded you who was really in charge.

The crew moved like clockwork. They'd done this before. But that didn't make it easier.

Ben grabbed a hose from the fire tank and joined the line. His shirt clung to his back, sweat soaking through, but he barely noticed.

All he could think about was Jemma.

She'd looked so composed that morning. Too composed. That soft, polite voice. The way her eyes wouldn't meet his. She was slipping away from him, and he was standing here, letting it happen.

He'd meant to go to her last night. He'd almost done it—twice. But he hadn't. And now this fire had stolen his chance again.

Damn it all.

He gritted his teeth and sprayed the blackened earth in front of him. The smoke stung his eyes.

One more day, he told himself. I'll talk to her tomorrow. After this is dealt with. After the land's calm. Then I'll go to her. I'll say everything.

He had to.

But the fire didn't care about his timing. The land didn't wait.

Flames jumped from bush to bush as the wind shifted again, stronger now. One of the younger hands shouted, pointing to a patch of brush sparking to life to the east.

Ben cursed and ran toward it, hose swinging in his grip. The wind was playing tricks now, erratic, and cruel.

He thought of Jemma alone in the cottage, reading to Charlotte with that soft, steady voice, while he was out here chasing embers and guilt.

She needed to hear the truth.

She deserved to know she was loved.

But for now, all he could do was hold the line.

The sun dropped behind the ridge, and still they worked—cutting a firebreak, soaking the scorched soil. The flames were finally dying down, smothered by grit and determination. But inside Ben, the heat hadn't gone anywhere.

By the time the danger had passed, it was late Tuesday afternoon. The sun hung low, casting long shadows over the blackened edge of the paddocks, painting the scorched horizon in bruised gold and ash. The fire was contained. No stock had been lost. The land would recover—in time.

But as Ben drove back to the homestead, dust curling behind his ute, the relief didn't reach his chest. His muscles throbbed with exhaustion, his throat was raw from smoke and shouting, and still, none of it compared to the heaviness lodged deep in his chest.

Not the fire.

Not the fatigue.

But the quiet, relentless truth: another day had slipped through his fingers… and he still hadn't gone to her.

Every mile back, he thought of her. Every breath filled with soot carried her name.

He would talk to her.

Tomorrow.

He swore it.

Just one more day.

The night settled in, warm and heavy, thick with the scent of charred earth and eucalyptus. Somewhere in the distance, cattle lowed—unsettled, uneasy. The station was quiet but not calm.

Ben sat on the edge of the verandah, boots planted in the dirt, elbows resting on his knees. A half-drunk bottle of beer hung from his fingers, forgotten. Smoke clung to his clothes. Ash dusted his skin.

The fire was out.

The crew was bone tired.

The land was safe.

And still, there was no peace in him.

The past two days clung to him like sweat—muscles aching, skin sunburned, body weary in ways that went far deeper than fatigue. But it was the hollowness in his chest that hurt the most.

Because the fire was out there, yes.

But the real one—the one that mattered—was still burning inside him.

He'd caught a glimpse of Jemma earlier—just after dinner. She'd been in the kitchen helping Agnes with the dishes, laughing softly at something Charlotte said. It wasn't forced, not like the morning before. But it wasn't the same either.

There was a wall now. A carefulness. And it killed him.

He should've gone to her Sunday night. Should've knocked on her door, told her the truth while he still had the courage riding high in his blood.

But instead, he'd hesitated.

Waited.

And now?

Now he didn't even know if she'd still want to hear it.

The screen door creaked behind him. He didn't look up—just assumed it was Agnes making another lap of the house before bed.

But her voice caught him off guard.

"You planning to sit out here all night feeling sorry for yourself?"

Ben glanced over his shoulder. Agnes stood in the doorway with a cup of tea in one hand, her expression neutral but knowing.

"Not feeling sorry," he muttered.

"No?" She stepped outside, sat beside him. "Because from where I'm standing, it looks an awful lot like a man wallowing in his own mistakes."

He took a long pull from the beer. "It's been a hell of a week."

"I know," she said gently. "You saved the land. Kept the crew safe. Did everything you've always done. But you forgot someone."

He looked at her sideways. "Who?"

"Jemma," she said simply. "The girl who's been here every day. Loving that child like her own. Standing beside you, even when you barely let her in."

Ben didn't reply.

Agnes sipped her tea. "You keep telling yourself you'll talk to her tomorrow. That the timing has to be right. But life doesn't wait, Ben. It's never going to slow down enough for you to feel perfectly ready."

He stared out into the dark. The stars were faint tonight, hidden behind lingering smoke.

"I'm scared," he said finally. The words were quiet, honest.

Agnes didn't flinch. "Of what?"

"That I'll ruin it. That I'll let her in and lose her anyway. That Charlotte will lose her too. That I'll never be enough for a woman like her."

Agnes gave a soft snort. "Ben, she's not asking you to be perfect. She's just asking you to be real."

He rubbed his hands over his face, groaning softly. "I'll talk to her. Tomorrow. I swear."

Agnes nodded. "You do that. Before someone else does."

Ben froze at that. But she was already standing, heading inside.

The screen door creaked shut behind her.

Ben sat there long after she left, watching the horizon where fire had danced just a day ago.

Everything inside him still burned—but for once, it wasn't fear that sat at the centre of it.

It was love.

And tomorrow, he'd stop running from it.

A sharp knock shattered the stillness.

Jemma stirred, disoriented, the remnants of sleep clinging like fog to her mind. She blinked at the darkness; the cottage still steeped in pre-dawn hush. The clock beside her bed glowed 5:12.

Another knock. Firm. Insistent.

Ben. It had to be.

Her heart kicked, wild and hopeful. Maybe he'd finally come. Maybe this was it—words spoken at last, truth laid bare. She tugged on a hoodie over her sleep-rumpled T-shirt and shorts, pushed a hand through her tangled hair, and padded barefoot to the door.

The air was cool, edged with the scent of damp earth and charred eucalyptus. Her hand hesitated on the knob for just a moment—just long enough for another knock to sound, a little harder this time.

She opened it with a sleepy smile. "Ben?"

And froze.

Her breath caught.

Not Ben.

Leo.

He stood there on the front step like a ghost dragged out of her worst nightmare—eyes wild, hair longer, thinner than she remembered. But still him. Still that stare. That sick, twisted grin curling at the corner of his mouth.

"Hello, Jem," he said softly, voice low and laced with something far too familiar. "Miss me?"

Her stomach dropped. The world tilted sideways.

She took a single step back, fingers tightening on the edge of the door.

"What are you doing here?" she whispered, her voice barely holding steady.

Leo's eyes swept over her—bare legs, bare feet, the soft fabric of her shirt hugging her frame. His gaze lingered too long, hungry and possessive.

"I came to bring you home," he said. "We've got unfinished business, you and me."

She stared at him, frozen, the echo of old fear roaring up through her body. She hadn't seen him in months. Had prayed she never would again. But here he was—real and solid and standing on her doorstep in the middle of the outback before sunrise.

Her throat worked. "You shouldn't be here."

His grin widened, slow and chilling. "Neither should you. But here we are."

Jemma's blood ran cold.

She slammed the door hard, heart jackhammering in her chest, and shoved the bolt across just as Leo lunged. His body hit the wood with a solid thud, rattling the frame.

"Jemma!" he roared, his fist pounding again—violent, unrelenting.

She stumbled backward; breath caught in her throat and reached for her phone on the kitchen counter. No bars. No service.

Panic flared.

No one nearby.

No signal.

Just Ben. Probably somewhere out on the property.

Her thoughts scrambled as she backed into the bedroom, shoved the dresser across the door with all her strength, the legs screeching against the floorboards. Her hands were shaking, her skin clammy.

Outside, Leo's voice came again—calm now, too calm. The kind of calm that chilled her deeper than his shouting.

"How did you know I was here?" she yelled through the door, trying to keep her voice strong.

"I saw your picture," he said. "Some society gala. Another man's hands on you. Didn't look like you were grieving me, Jem."

She blinked. A photo. The fundraiser Ben had taken her to on the weekend—Ben in a suit beside her, hand on her back, smiling.

"How did you know I'd be in this cottage? Not the house?" she demanded.

"I took a chance," he said simply. "Your car was parked off to the side. Too easy."

"Go away!" Her voice cracked. "I'm not going anywhere with you!"

"I'm not leaving without you," he said, tone flat. "You belong with me, Jem. You always have."

She backed into the corner of the bedroom; her phone clutched in white-knuckled fingers. Heart pounding. Breath ragged.

Ben. Please. Please, Ben. Come now.

She dropped to the floor, hiding behind the bed, barely able to breathe as she whispered a frantic prayer.

Then glass shattered.

The side window.

"No—no!" she scrambled to her feet as Leo's body came crashing through the frame, boots landing heavily on the floor, blood on his sleeve from the broken glass.

She fought. Nails, fists, feet. Screamed. Kicked. But he was bigger—stronger—and twisted her arms behind her back like it was nothing.

"Shut up," he hissed, clamping a rough hand over her mouth.

Her scream was muffled, swallowed by his palm as he dragged her backward through the kitchen, her heels scraping uselessly across the floorboards.

Out the door.

Into the pre-dawn dark.

Toward the waiting car parked just out of sight behind the gum trees.

The scent of smoke still lingered in the air.

And Jemma was gone.

The sun was just beginning to rise, casting a pale glow over the paddocks as Ben turned the ute back toward the homestead. He'd been up since before first light, checking the fences and water troughs, making sure everything was in order after the fire scare. The land was quiet again, but his mind wasn't.

He hadn't slept much—not with the weight of yesterday sitting heavy in his chest. He was going to talk to Jemma today. He meant it this time.

As he crested the hill just past the stockyard, a flash of movement on the road caught his eye.

A dark sedan, unfamiliar, tearing down the edge of the property track like its driver had somewhere urgent to be. It fishtailed slightly in the gravel, then straightened and sped off down the dirt road toward the highway.

Ben slowed instinctively, watching the dust rise in its wake.

"Tourists," he muttered to himself. Or some city slicker who'd taken a wrong turn. Happens more often than you'd think.

He shook his head, let out a quiet breath, and turned his eyes back to the road. Probably nothing.

Still… something about it nagged at him.

But not enough—yet—to make him turn around.

He tapped the steering wheel with his fingers and kept driving. The sun was climbing higher, and he had other things on his mind. Like Jemma.

Today. He was going to talk to her—this morning, hopefully. After breakfast.

Chapter Twenty-Four

As Ben pulled into the homestead, the sky cracked open. Rain pelted the windshield in heavy, relentless sheets, drumming on the roof of the ute like a warning. He parked under the awning, water already running in rivulets across the gravel driveway.

He took a moment, gripping the wheel. His chest was tight, but it wasn't fear this time. It was resolve. He was done second-guessing himself, done letting moments slip past. Jemma was the one—the only one who'd ever made him feel like more than the sum of his scars.

Today, he'd tell her. No more delays. No more fire, no more fear. Just truth.

He jogged through the rain, boots splashing through puddles, and ducked inside the mudroom. Shrugging off his coat and dripping hat, he washed up quickly, scrubbing the grit and smoke from his hands and face. Then he stepped into the warmth of the kitchen, where the smell of toast and woodsmoke filled the air.

Charlotte sat at the table, swinging her legs, a half-eaten piece of Vegemite toast in her hand. Agnes stood beside her, sipping tea, watching the rain through the window with a frown.

But the chair Jemma always used was empty.

A sharp clap of thunder rattled the windowpanes.

Ben frowned. "Where's Jemma?"

Agnes turned, concern flickering across her face. "She hasn't come in yet."

Another rumble of thunder shook the walls. Lightning forked across the sky in a blinding flash.

"Maybe she's waiting for the storm to pass," Agnes offered, though her voice didn't sound convinced.

Ben shook his head. "No. She'd want to be here with us. You know she doesn't like storms."

Already moving, he grabbed his coat again, shrugging it on. "I'm going to check on her."

The phone rang, sharp and shrill in the quiet.

Ben paused, hand on the door, then turned and picked it up. "Hello?"

"Good morning. Senior Constable Mark Dwyer speaking. I'm looking for a Jemma Prescott," came a man's voice—polite, but with an edge of urgency.

Ben's brow furrowed. "She's not here at the moment. Can I give her a message?"

"Yes." The constable hesitated. "Could you please let her know that Leo Evans was released on bail Monday. He's missed two scheduled check-ins, and…" Another pause. "The last thing he asked about was Jemma. Just thought she should be aware."

Ben went cold, his blood turning to ice.

The phone slipped from his hand, hitting the floor with a dull thud.

"Ben?" Agnes stepped forward, alarmed. "What is it?"

But Ben didn't hear her.

He was already moving.

Out the door.

Into the rain.

Heart pounding, breath ragged.

He ran toward the cottage, legs pumping through the mud, one name repeating in his head like a drumbeat.

Jemma.

Please, God.

Let her be there.

Ben sprinted through the downpour, rain lashing his face, boots heavy with mud—but he didn't stop.

As he crested the small rise and the cottage came into view, his gut twisted.

The door was open.

Wide.

Rain lashed through the opening, pooling on the floorboards just inside.

No. No. No.

His chest seized with panic, his breath catching as dread wrapped icy fingers around his spine.

He bolted through the doorway, mud trailing behind him, his voice rough with fear.

"Jemma!"

No answer.

The cottage felt wrong. Too quiet. Not the peaceful kind of quiet—but the heavy, suffocating kind.

The kind that screamed danger.

He tore through the small space, eyes raking over every corner. Then he stopped cold.

The back window was shattered.

Shards of glass sparkled on the floor like ice. Rain dripped through the jagged frame, soaking the sill. The curtain billowed inward, ghostlike in the wind.

Ben's blood turned to ice.

"Jesus…" he whispered.

He stepped forward, his boots crunching over glass. His breath came shallow and fast, panic rolling through him like a freight train.

"Jemma…" he called again, voice hoarse with dread.

But the cottage was empty. She was gone.

And every instinct in him screamed one terrible truth—

She didn't leave on her own.

His gaze snapped to the drive.

Her car's still here.

"Fuck…" The word ripped from him.

If it wasn't her car being driven away earlier—

Then it wasn't her driving.

He turned and bolted back toward the homestead, feet pounding through the mud, rain stinging his face. Inside, he grabbed the phone, hands slick and shaking, and punched in the number.

It rang once.

"Sheriff McAllister."

"Sheriff, it's Ben Callahan. Something's wrong—Jemma's gone. Her cottage—door's wide open, back window is smashed. But her car's still here."

A tense beat.

"Then who took her?"

Ben's throat tightened. "I got a call from Melbourne PD this morning. Her ex, Leo Evans—he was released on bail. Missed two check-ins. Last thing he asked about was Jemma. And earlier—I saw a black sedan on the access road. Driving like hell toward town."

McAllister's voice sharpened. "We'll issue an alert. Units are on it. Stay put, Ben—we'll find her."

The wind howled outside, rain hammering the windows like fists.

Ben gripped the phone tighter.

"I'll wait," he said, voice low and tight. "Just… please hurry."

When Ben turned into the kitchen, the sight hit him like a punch to the chest.

Agnes sat at the table, cradling Charlotte in her arms. The little girl was sobbing, her face buried in Agnes's shoulder, her small frame trembling.

"Did a bad man take Jemma?" she hiccupped, her voice barely a whisper between gasps.

Ben crossed the room in two strides and gently lifted Charlotte from Agnes's arms, holding her close, his throat thick.

"She'll be okay, sweetheart," he said softly, pressing a kiss to the top of her head. "The police are looking for her right now. They're going to bring her home."

Charlotte sniffled, clinging to him, her tears soaking into his shirt.

Agnes stood, her expression pale and tight with worry. "It was her ex, wasn't it?" she asked, her voice low but firm.

Ben met her eyes and gave a small nod. His jaw clenched.

Agnes closed her eyes for a beat, her hand gripping the back of the chair. "Bastard."

Ben looked down at Charlotte again, brushing her damp curls away from her face. He forced his voice to stay steady, even as fear clawed at his chest.

"She's strong," he said. "And I'm not going to stop until I find her."

Jemma kicked at the back of the driver's seat with everything she had. Panic surged through her veins, but she refused to give in to it. Her wrists and ankles were bound with tight plastic zip ties, cutting into her skin. Her heart pounded in her chest, wild and terrified.

"Stop it!" Leo bellowed, the car swerving violently as he twisted around to glare at her.

The tyres screeched against the wet road, and for a moment, Jemma thought they'd slide straight off it.

"Let me go, Leo!" she shouted, her voice hoarse, desperate.

His eyes were wide, unhinged, darting between her and the road. "You think you can just disappear? Run off and play house with some cowboy in the middle of nowhere?"

Jemma struggled against the restraints, the plastic biting deeper into her skin. "You're sick. This isn't love. This is control."

"Shut up!" he snarled. "You ruined everything. You made me do this!"

The wind howled outside, the storm battering the windows as rain lashed across the windshield. Lightning flashed, illuminating Leo's wild expression, twisted with rage and something far more dangerous—obsession.

Jemma's voice dropped to a whisper, steady despite the fear in her chest. "They'll find me. Ben will find me. And you'll rot in prison."

Leo's grip tightened on the steering wheel, knuckles white. "No one's coming, Jemma. Not this time."

But deep in her gut, despite the terror, she held onto one thing—Ben would never stop looking.

The storm raged outside, wind howling like a living thing, rain lashing against the windows in violent sheets. Inside the kitchen, the air was thick with silence—broken only by the occasional crack of thunder and the ticking of the old clock on the wall.

Charlotte had cried herself to sleep hours ago. She lay curled on the sofa in the next room, wrapped in a blanket far too big for her small body, her thumb tucked into her mouth like when she was a baby.

Ben sat at the kitchen table, elbows braced on the scarred wood, head in his hands. His shirt was still damp; his boots caked with mud he hadn't bothered to clean. He hadn't moved in a long time.

Across from him, Agnes sat quietly, a mug of untouched tea cooling in her hands. She watched him with soft, sad eyes, waiting.

Finally, his voice broke through the storm and stillness—low, raw, cracking around the edges.

"This is the second woman in my care that I failed to protect," he said. "First Heidi, now Jemma. This is all my fault."

Agnes frowned gently. "How do you see that?"

Ben lifted his head slowly. His face was pale, jaw clenched, eyes hollow with guilt. "If I'd told her the truth two days ago… if I hadn't let fear stop me—she would've been with me. In the house. Safe."

Lightning flared through the window, casting a harsh light across his face.

Agnes shook her head slowly. "You think love is armour, Ben? That telling her how you feel would've protected her from a man like that?"

He didn't answer. Just looked away, jaw tightening.

"She's strong," Agnes said quietly. "And she loves that little girl like she's her own. That's what kept her here. Not your silence."

Ben swallowed hard. "I should've told her she wasn't alone. That she was mine."

Agnes reached across the table, her hand resting lightly over his. "Then tell her. When we get her back… you tell her everything."

Ben nodded once, but the storm in his eyes didn't ease. Not yet. Not until Jemma was back safe in his arms.

Chapter Twenty-Five

The floor of the car was cold against Jemma's cheek, the smell of wet carpet and stale tobacco thick in her nose. Her wrists burned from the plastic zip ties, the hard plastic biting deeper with every jolt of the car. Leo was driving like a madman—swerving, shouting, slamming his hand against the dash as the tyres skidded and shrieked against the rain-slick road.

"You think you're better than me?" he yelled, voice cracking under the weight of his fury. "You think you can just run off with that bloody cowboy and play house like none of this ever happened?"

Jemma didn't respond. She knew better than to feed his fire. Her body remained limp, submissive, but her eyes scanned the dark crevice under the front seat, searching.

A flash of silver caught her attention.

She blinked through a strand of damp hair. There, lodged against the seat rail—something small, metallic. She shifted subtly, inching forward, heart pounding. Leo wouldn't see her from this angle. He was too busy cursing at the windshield, swiping furiously at the fogged glass as he muttered threats under his breath.

Just a little closer.

Her fingers brushed metal—cold, thin, sharp. She swallowed hard. It was a razor blade. Rusted around the edges, dulled with time, but still sharp enough.

Her hands were zip-tied in front of her. Thank God.

Carefully, she palmed the blade and tucked it into her sleeve, forcing herself to stay calm, to breathe. One wrong move, one flash of silver in the wrong light, and he'd know.

Leo hit a pothole, and the car jolted violently. Jemma bit the inside of her cheek to keep from crying out. Her wrists twisted against the binds, raw and aching.

"You ruined everything," Leo snapped, voice barely above a growl. "I tried to be good for you. I changed for you."

She didn't answer. She focused on the tiny blade, manoeuvring it into her grip without making a sound. Her fingers shook, slick with sweat. Slowly, she began sawing at the plastic tie—one rough stroke at a time, the dull blade digging in, gouging the plastic.

Leo's rant continued, incoherent now. His grip on the wheel was white-knuckled. The car skidded around a bend, the tyres slipping for a breathless second before catching again. She could feel the madness rolling off him in waves. He was unravelling.

She pressed harder. The zip tie gave a little. Not much—but enough to feel it weakening.

Keep going, Jemma. Quiet. Calm. Invisible.

Leo thumped his palm against the horn as another car splashed past in the opposite direction. "They're all laughing at me. They think I'm weak!"

Jemma froze, the blade paused mid-slice.

Then he started muttering again, eyes wild, focused on some invisible enemy in the rain.

She moved again—back and forth, slow, relentless strokes. She could feel the tension in the tie start to slacken. A few more minutes. Just a few more.

Then she'd run.

And this time, she'd never look back.

The road had narrowed to little more than a muddy track, flanked by scrub and twisted gums, the storm clouds finally retreating to the far horizon. The car slowed, fishtailing in the slush, Leo squinting out the windshield like he expected something—or someone—to jump out of the trees.

Paranoia rolled off him like heat from a fire.

"Bloody cops… probably got a tracker on the damn car," he muttered, dragging a shaky hand through his hair. "Bet that cowboy's already sniffing after us."

Jemma didn't move. She lay curled on the floor behind the front seat, the half-cut zip tie biting into her wrist, her pulse thundering in her ears. The razor blade was still hidden in her palm, its dull edge now slick with sweat and blood.

Leo slammed the brakes.

"Gotta piss," he snarled, throwing the gear into park. He kicked open the door and stumbled out into the mud, boots squelching as he stalked toward the trees. He stopped just at the edge of the bush, pacing like a caged animal, muttering to himself, occasionally letting out a wordless roar of frustration into the wilderness.

This was it.

Jemma's heart lunged into her throat.

With trembling urgency, she began sawing again—harder this time. The tie gave suddenly, snapping with a soft snick. Her hands were free. She stifled a cry, immediately bending to the ones around her ankles.

Leo's voice was growing louder. Angry. Distracted. Good.

The tie around her ankles popped loose just as he disappeared behind a stand of trees.

No time to think.

She crawled toward the front seat, flinging open the glove box with shaking hands. Nothing useful. She grabbed the flashlight from the footwell, a half-empty bottle from the cup holder. Leo's coat lay crumpled on the passenger seat—she snatched it, heart hammering.

Then she slipped out the door.

Cold air slapped her bare legs as she bolted into the scrub, staying low. Rain-slick grass whipped her ankles, thorns tearing at her skin, but she didn't look back.

The bush swallowed her instantly—dense scrub, tall grass, scattered rocks. The mud sucked at her bare feet, but she didn't stop. Didn't look back. She ran like her life depended on it—because it did.

Behind her, a bird shrieked.

Leo's voice rang out. "No! No, no, no…"

Jemma dove into the undergrowth, crawling on her elbows, forcing herself through thorns and brambles until she found a hollow between two fallen logs. She pressed herself flat, barely daring to breathe.

Footsteps pounded in the distance. Closer. Then pausing.

A furious howl shattered the stillness.

"JEMMA!"

His voice echoed across the wilderness—raw, ragged, carried on the damp air like a war cry.

She didn't move.

Didn't blink.

Didn't breathe.

Seconds stretched. Then minutes.

And finally—he retreated. She heard the car door slam, an engine roar to life. Tyres spun in the mud.

Then… silence.

She waited a beat longer, trembling.

Only when she was sure—truly sure—she crawled out, soaked and shaking, clutching the flashlight and Leo's coat to her chest.

She was alone in the outback. No phone. No shelter. No shoes.

But she was free.

And that was enough.

For now.

Leo crashed back through the bush, branches slapping his face, rain-soaked and breathless, muttering curses under his breath.

He punched the side of the car with a savage grunt, then banged the door again and again, rattling the frame. His breath came in shallow gasps, his mind reeling.

How long had it been?

Ten minutes?

Twenty?

She couldn't have gotten far. Not barefoot. Not in this mud.

But if she found a station road—if she flagged someone down—

"Goddammit!" he roared, slamming his fists against the steering wheel so hard the horn blared.

He jumped in, gunning the engine. Mud sprayed in every direction as the tyres spun, fighting for traction.

"She's mine," he hissed, eyes wild. "She doesn't get to run. Not again."

He sped down the track, sliding dangerously around corners, eyes scanning every tree line, every flicker of movement. The storm had passed, but it had left chaos in its wake. Water streamed across the road in muddy torrents, low-lying dips already filling fast.

Ahead, a wide gully glistened with floodwater—swollen and fast-moving, carrying debris and foam. The riverbank on the far side had nearly disappeared beneath the surge.

Leo didn't care.

He punched the accelerator harder.

"I'll find you," he muttered. "Even if it kills me."

The car skidded to a halt at the edge of the flooded crossing, mud splashing high as Leo slammed on the brakes. The engine growled beneath the hood, steam hissing from under the bonnet where the earlier abuse had taken its toll.

Before him, the river roared.

What was usually a dry creek bed was now a surging torrent—wide, brown, and deadly. Water churned across the track in furious waves, swollen with storm runoff. Branches and debris raced past, carried along by the current like discarded toys.

Leo sat frozen, hands clenched on the wheel, jaw twitching. Rain dripped from his hair, his eyes wild behind the windshield.

"This is your fault!" he screamed suddenly, banging his fists on the dash.

"You did this to me, Jemma!"

His voice cracked, hysteria bubbling up beneath the rage.

"I only did what I had to. You made me do it. You made me!"

He stared into the water, breath heaving. A smarter man would've turned back. Waited. Lived.

But Leo Evans wasn't that man.

Gritting his teeth, he threw the car into gear and hit the accelerator.

The tyres screeched, then caught, launching the vehicle forward. Water surged around the wheels instantly, pounding against the undercarriage with bone-jarring force.

The car rocked sideways.

Still, he kept going—foot flat, eyes fixed on the far bank, veins pulsing in his neck.

Halfway through, the current caught him.

The vehicle jolted.

Drifted.

Then spun.

"NO—NO!" he screamed, wrestling the wheel. The engine roared, but the wheels lifted, weightless now.

The river didn't care.

It seized the car like a toy and dragged it downstream.

Leo clawed at the door, trying to open it, but the water pinned it shut. The interior began to flood—fast.

"No!" He punched the glass, panic overtaking fury.

Water rushed over the hood. The windshield spider-webbed under pressure. He thrashed, screaming her name again and again.

"JEMMA!"

But there was no answer.

Only the sound of the river, roaring louder than his cries.

And then—

Silence.

The current dragged the vehicle under.

Leo Evans disappeared into the flood, alone, nameless, consumed by the storm he thought he could outrun.

Chapter Twenty-Six

The storm had passed, leaving the land soaked and silent, the skies above washed to a dull grey. The rain had stopped, but the tension inside the homestead hadn't eased. Not in the slightest.

Ben paced the living room like a caged animal, boots still muddy, shirt clinging to his back. The clock on the wall ticked too loudly, each second dragging like a weight. The silence from the sheriff's office was deafening.

Agnes watched from the kitchen, arms folded tightly across her chest, a fresh pot of tea sitting untouched on the counter.

Charlotte was still asleep, curled beneath a blanket on the sofa. Every so often, she let out a soft whimper, and Ben's jaw would tighten just a little more.

"Dammit," he muttered, raking a hand through his hair. "Why haven't they called?"

Agnes stepped into the room. "Ben, you've done everything you can. The sheriff said they're looking—"

"It's not enough." His voice was sharp. "It's been hours."

Ben stormed into the kitchen, snatched the cordless off the wall, and punched in a number he hadn't used in years.

"Yeah, I need a chopper," he said the moment the line connected. "Immediately. I'll pay whatever it takes."

The voice on the other end hesitated. "Callahan, is that you? You all right, mate?"

"No," Ben snapped. "I don't care what it costs. I'll pay double. I just need it in the air within the hour.

His voice was like gravel, raw and resolute. "There's a black sedan, probably heading west on Ridgeway Road. I want eyes on it. And I want to find a woman. Jemma Prescott. She's been kidnapped."

The voice on the other end shifted instantly. "Understood. We'll notify the pilot. Do you have aerial maps, landmarks, tracking points?"

"I'll text you everything I've got. Get it off the ground. I'll meet you at the helipad."

He ended the call and stood still for a breath. Just one.

Then he moved.

Within the hour, the rhythmic thump of rotors echoed across the valley. The helicopter crested the ridge and descended into the open paddock behind the homestead, sending dust and grass swirling in every direction.

Ben met it at a run, ducking beneath the blades. The pilot—grizzled, sunburnt, and sharp-eyed—nodded as Ben approached.

"Where we headed?"

"South ridge," Ben shouted over the engine. "Then east, toward the floodplain. He won't be on the main roads—he's running scared."

The pilot lifted off seconds later, and Ben watched as the chopper swept across the sky, banking low over the tree line.

Back inside, Ben grabbed his keys and called the sheriff with his sat phone as he headed for the ute.

"McAllister. It's Callahan. I've got a helicopter in the air. They're starting a sweep from the south."

The sheriff sighed heavily. "Was just about to call you. One of our trackers found tyre prints near Mooney's Crossing. Fast-moving, fresh. Might be your guy."

Ben's heart kicked.

"Mooney's flooded."

"Exactly. That river's a bastard when it rises."

Ben's voice was ice. "If he tried to cross it—"

Just then, the radio on the dash crackled. The chopper pilot's voice broke through, static-laced but urgent.

"Ben, you there?"

"I'm here," he barked, already swinging the ute onto the main track.

"We've got something. Black sedan, half-submerged, about five clicks west of Mooney's. Looks abandoned. We're hovering over it now."

Ben's grip tightened on the wheel.

"Stay on it. I'm on my way."

He floored the accelerator.

The ute tore down the muddy track, throwing up sprays of red earth as Ben raced toward the river, a single thought pounding in his head:

Please God—let her not be in that car.

His ute fishtailed to a halt in the mud, tyres skidding just short of the flood-swollen river. He was out before the engine cut, sprinting toward the bank as the chopper circled overhead, its blades thumping a warning through the thick, humid air.

There it was.

The black sedan.

Half-submerged. Nose down in the rushing water, its back wheels jutting out like broken limbs. Trees leaned over it, their roots clutching at the wreckage as the current surged past.

Ben tied a rope to a tree and the other end to his waist. He didn't wait. He plunged into the river, boots slipping on the slick riverbed, water dragging at his legs. Each step was a struggle, but he kept going—heart hammering, breath ragged, dread swelling in his throat.

He reached the car, grabbed the door handle, and yanked.

Water spilled out, and a body slumped forward with a sickening lurch.

Leo.

Pale. Bloated. Eyes glassy and mouth frozen in a final, silent scream.

Ben flinched back, bile rising in his throat. For a moment, all he could do was stare.

Then his eyes scanned the interior—wild, desperate.

No Jemma.

His heart soared. She's not in there. She got out. She escaped.

He staggered back a step, water sloshing around him. "She got away," he breathed, half in disbelief. "She got—"

But then the thought slammed into him like a punch.

Unless…

Unless Leo killed her before the crash.

Unless he'd dumped her somewhere in the bush—buried her, left her, destroyed her in the very land Ben thought would keep her safe.

The hope in his chest curdled into dread.

He looked around wildly. The empty banks. The storm-torn landscape. No footprints. No sign of her. Nothing.

"She's not here," he whispered. "She's not in the car…"

His voice faltered.

"What if she's not anywhere?"

Ben turned back to the body, his jaw clenched, throat tight. The river roared around him, but the silence inside his chest was worse.

He staggered out of the water, panting, clothes soaked, mud clinging to him like guilt. He grabbed the radio from his ute, thumb shaking on the button.

"McAllister," he rasped. "Car's here. Leo's dead. But Jemma…" He swallowed hard. "She's not with him. I don't know if that means she got away—or if he… if he hurt her before the crash."

A beat of static. Then McAllister's voice: "We'll widen the perimeter. Trackers are en route."

Ben raised his eyes to the endless sprawl of outback scrubland.

"Then tell them to hurry," he said, voice cold and full of fire. "Because if she's out there, she's alone. And I'm not losing her."

The sun was merciless. A white-hot weight in the sky, burning through the stillness.

Jemma pushed through the low scrub, thorns and brittle branches clawing at her bare legs. Her pyjama shorts were torn at the hem, her oversized T-shirt soaked through with sweat and clinging to her skin. The hoodie hung heavy around her shoulders, streaked with dirt, snagged and fraying from the brambles.

The ground beneath her was baked and cracked, each barefoot step like shards of glass beneath her heels.

Still, she didn't stop.

Her heartbeat thudded in her ears, the only rhythm she had to march to. One hand clutched a half-crushed water bottle—empty. The other still held the small torch she'd grabbed from under the seat. Useless in the daylight, but something about its weight in her palm grounded her.

There was no path. No plan.

Just escape.

Just survival.

She tripped and caught herself on a jagged rock, skin splitting across her palm. She winced, bit back a cry, and kept moving. The scrub stretched endlessly, an unforgiving maze of red earth, wiry trees, and silence.

But she didn't stop.

Charlotte's face swam before her eyes. That sweet giggle, the way her tiny arms had wrapped around her neck, trusting her completely. And Ben—his quiet strength, the way he looked at her like she was more than the broken woman she tried to hide.

They were her anchor.

They'll come.

As the sun dipped low and shadows bled across the land, she stumbled upon a rocky overhang near a dry gully. She crawled beneath it, muscles quivering, hoodie pulled tight around her body as if it could shield her from the vastness of the wild.

She sat there, knees hugged to her chest, staring into the growing dark.

The air was cooling now, but her body still burned. Her lips were cracked, her throat raw, but she didn't make a sound.

Instead, she whispered—soft and fierce:

"Keep going. They'll come."

She closed her eyes.

Not giving in.

Not yet.

The night air was thick with tension as Ben pulled up to the makeshift coordination hub at the edge of the homestead—the old shearing shed now lit with floodlamps and buzzing with urgent voices. Dust clung to his boots, soaked up to his waist from the flooded crossing. He slammed the ute door and strode toward McAllister, who stood talking to two uniformed officers beside a whiteboard.

Ben's voice was hoarse. "She wasn't in the car."

McAllister turned, grim. "That's one small mercy."

"Leo obviously drowned." Ben swallowed hard, voice tightening. "But she's not in there. She must have got away."

A flicker of relief passed through the officer's eyes, quickly replaced by worry. "Then she's out there somewhere—alone."

Ben nodded. "Barefoot. No food. No shelter. And we don't know which direction she went."

McAllister cursed under his breath and barked orders to one of the constables to notify command. The helicopter that had touched down for refuelling was already spinning up again, blades whirring in the dark. Its spotlight cut across the paddocks like a sweeping eye.

Ben didn't wait. He moved to the centre of the shed where a handful of stockmen, neighbours, and station hands were starting to gather—boots muddy, faces tight with concern. Word had spread.

"We start at first light," McAllister announced. "Two choppers in the air by sunrise. We'll grid the terrain west of the river crossing."

Ben stepped forward, fists clenched. "I'm going with them."

McAllister hesitated. "You've been up for thirty-six hours. You're in no condition—"

"I don't care," Ben snapped. "You think I'm gonna sit here drinking bloody coffee while she's out there, scared and alone? No."

McAllister studied him a beat, then nodded. "Fine. You ride with the second team. But you stay on comms, and if you start fading, you pull out."

Ben's jaw worked, but he gave a stiff nod.

As the helicopter roared overhead, climbing into the sky once more, Ben looked out into the darkness stretching across the land—hostile, endless.

He stared into the dark, every shadow a threat. Every second, a mile between them.

"She's out there," he murmured. "And I'm going to bring her home."

Chapter Twenty-Seven

The bush was bathed in the soft, golden hush of dawn, but it brought little comfort. Every leaf shimmered with dew, every rock radiated with early heat, and Jemma could barely feel any of it.

Her legs trembled as she stumbled forward, dry grass crackling beneath her bare feet. Her lips were cracked; her skin, flushed with fever and sunburn. Sweat beaded on her brow, only to vanish almost instantly. She'd stopped crying hours ago—her body had no tears left to give.

The hoodie hung heavy on her frame, soaked through with a night's worth of shivering beneath a rocky overhang. Her pyjama shorts were torn, legs scratched and bleeding from bush scrub. The water bottle she'd grabbed was long empty. The flashlight dead weight in her pocket. The only thing that kept her going was the image of Charlotte's little face and the sound of Ben's voice in her head: You're safe now, Jem.

Only she wasn't. Not yet.

A low, distant rumble vibrated through the air. At first, she thought she was hallucinating again—another cruel trick of her mind—but then it grew louder. Steadier. Rhythmic.

A chopper.

Jemma's breath hitched in her throat.

She turned in a slow circle, eyes scanning the open sky. And there—over the ridgeline—she saw it: a helicopter slicing through the dawn light, sweeping over the treetops like a mechanical hawk.

"Hey!" Her voice cracked. "Hey, I'm here!"

She waved her arms, stumbling up a small rise, feet barely cooperating. She tripped on a root and fell to her knees. The helicopter started to pass.

"No," she whimpered. "Please…"

Her fingers fumbled at her sleeve, where she'd tucked the old razor blade. With shaking hands, she pulled it out and turned it toward the sun. The metal glinted. She angled it, tilted it, anything to catch the light and throw it back toward the sky.

She waved it like a beacon, heart hammering, hope down to its last fragile thread.

The helicopter hesitated.

It slowed.

Then—like a miracle—it veered sharply, banking back in her direction.

Jemma crumpled to the ground, her body wracked with dry, rasping sobs as the rotor wash swept over the scrub. Relief flooded her chest, too heavy to hold. She didn't even try to rise. Just laid there, trembling, whispering over and over:

"They found me. Thank God… they found me."

They'd been in the air for nearly an hour—nothing but endless bushland below. Ben's jaw was tight, eyes scanning every stretch of earth, every shadow beneath the trees.

Still nothing.

Then—

A flicker. A glint.

"There!" Ben sat forward, pointing through the glass. "What's that?"

The pilot narrowed his eyes. "I saw it too."

He banked hard, the chopper tilting as it veered toward the glint of light. The trees thinned. A patch of earth came into view—then he saw her.

"Oh God," Ben breathed. "That's her."

She was on the ground. Still. Too still.

The chopper hadn't even touched down before Ben jumped, boots hitting the dirt with a jarring thud. Dust exploded beneath him, the roar of the rotors deafening—but he didn't hear a thing.

All he saw was Jemma.

She lay crumpled at the edge of the clearing, a fragile figure barely distinguishable from the scrub and dirt. Her skin was burned, her lips cracked, her clothes torn and filthy. But she was breathing.

"Jemma!" he shouted, sprinting.

He dropped to his knees beside her, hands trembling as he touched her face. Dirt streaked her cheeks. Her lashes fluttered.

Then—

"Ben…"

His name. A whisper. A miracle.

He let out a shuddered breath and pulled her into his arms, clutching her tight. She felt weightless and feverish, all sharp angles and heat.

"Jesus, Jem," he whispered, voice cracking. "I thought I'd lost you."

She didn't answer—her eyes fluttered closed. Unconscious. But alive.

Ben stood, cradling her like something sacred, and carried her to the chopper.

He wasn't letting go. Not ever again.

He climbed into the helicopter with Jemma in his arms, the pilot reaching back to help steady them as the rotors thundered above. The moment Ben settled onto the bench seat, he tucked her close, shielding her from the downdraft and the chaos of the moment, whispering soft reassurances against her temple even though she couldn't hear them.

The door slammed shut, and the chopper lifted with a roar, banking sharply as the pilot called in their retrieval over the radio.

Ben barely heard him. His entire world had narrowed to the fragile woman curled in his lap—her skin hot to the touch, lips dry and cracked, her breathing shallow but steady.

"Hold on, Jem," he murmured, brushing sweat-matted hair from her brow. "Just hold on a little longer. You're safe now. I've got you."

She gave no response.

The headset crackled. "ETA fifteen minutes. Medics are standing by."

Ben nodded, though he wasn't wearing a headset. His gaze stayed fixed on Jemma's face, watching for the slightest change, the tiniest sign that she was still fighting.

As they flew over the floodplain, the sun hung low but steady in the sky, its golden light washing the land in a hazy warmth. The bush stretched out beneath them, no longer cloaked in shadow but still softened by the morning mist. The light wasn't harsh yet—just enough to gild the treetops and make the floodwaters shimmer like glass.

He pressed his forehead gently to hers, voice breaking. "You're coming home, Jem. I swear to God… you're coming home."

The helicopter banked again, descending toward the homestead, where the yard had filled with vehicles, emergency lights casting flashes against the shadows of early morning.

As soon as the skids touched down, the door flew open and paramedics surged forward, voices clipped and efficient. Ben stood, reluctant to let go, but forced himself to transfer her into waiting arms.

"She's dehydrated. Burning up," he said quickly. "Exhausted. Has been out there all night."

The medic nodded. "We've got her. You did good."

Ben followed them down, boots hitting the ground like thunder. He never took his eyes off Jemma as they loaded her onto a stretcher and wheeled her toward the waiting ambulance.

She was alive.

Barely—but alive.

And he wasn't going to leave her side for a second.

Ben followed the stretcher to the ambulance, heart pounding, boots crunching across the gravel. Paramedics moved fast—checking her vitals, fitting an oxygen mask over her face, hooking her up to monitors. One of them tried to block his path at the doors.

"Mate, we need room to work."

"I'm coming with her," Ben said, voice like iron. "Not negotiable."

The paramedic hesitated, then stepped aside with a nod. Ben climbed in, settling beside the stretcher, one hand gripping Jemma's as if it were the only thing tethering him to earth.

The doors slammed shut, the siren wailed, and they were moving—speeding toward the nearest hospital over rutted roads and through washed-out tracks.

Jemma stirred once, lips parting beneath the oxygen mask. Her eyes fluttered open, glassy, and unfocused.

"Ben…"

"I'm here, Jem." He leaned closer, his voice ragged but steady. "You're safe now. I've got you."

Tears burned his eyes, but he blinked them back. She needed strength, not breakdowns.

The paramedic adjusted the IV. "She's severely dehydrated. Fever's high. But she's fighting."

Ben nodded, jaw clenched. "She's strong."

Outside, the land blurred past, golden light rising over the bush. Inside the ambulance, the only thing that mattered was the slow, steady beeping of the monitor beside her—and the faint pressure of her fingers tightening around his.

She was here.

She was alive.

And he wasn't letting her go again. Not ever.

The ambulance screeched into the small rural hospital, tyres spitting gravel as it came to a stop. Nurses and orderlies were already waiting, the ER team prepped and alert. Ben jumped out as soon as the doors opened, refusing to let go of Jemma's hand until they wheeled her through the sliding glass doors.

A nurse stepped in front of him. "We need to take her now."

Ben's eyes burned. "I said I'm not leaving her—"

"You've brought her this far," the nurse said gently. "Let us do the rest. You'll see her soon, I promise."

He stood there, fists clenched, helpless as they disappeared down the hall with her. The moment the doors swung shut, the adrenaline drained from his body. He sagged against the nearest wall, chest heaving, jaw tight.

Agnes arrived minutes later with Charlotte in her arms, eyes red, face pale. She passed the little girl to Ben without a word.

"Daddy?" Charlotte's voice was small and unsure.

He crouched, pulling her into his arms. "She's going to be okay, sweetheart. Jem's safe now."

"Is she hurt?"

"A little. But the doctors are looking after her."

Charlotte pressed her face into his shoulder, and for the first time in what felt like forever, Ben allowed himself to breathe. Just a little.

Chapter Twenty-Eight

Hours had passed. A blur of coffee cups, medical updates, and pacing the waiting room floor. Finally, a nurse came to find him.

"She's stable. You can see her now."

Ben didn't wait. He practically ran down the corridor and stopped cold at the doorway.

Jemma lay in the hospital bed, pale and bruised but clean, a thin sheet tucked around her. Her hair had been washed, pulled into a loose braid over one shoulder. A nasal cannula fed her oxygen, and her IV beeped steadily.

She turned her head, eyes fluttering open.

"Hey," she rasped.

He crossed the room in three strides, sat on the edge of the bed, and gently cupped her face. "Jesus, Jem…"

"I'm okay," she whispered, voice raw.

"You scared the hell out of me." His voice broke. "I thought—"

"I know."

He leaned forward, resting his forehead against hers. "I should've found you sooner."

"You found me," she said simply. "That's all that matters."

A silence settled between them. Safe. Sacred.

Then her eyes shimmered, and she whispered, "I have to tell you. You don't have to say anything but… I love you."

Ben kissed her forehead, her cheeks, the corners of her mouth.

"I love you too. And you're not going anywhere," he said, voice fierce with love. "Not now. Not ever."

Ben didn't leave her side after that.

Through the long, slow hours of rehydration drips, blood tests, and quiet nurse check-ins, he sat in the chair beside her bed, holding her hand. Occasionally, Charlotte would curl up in his lap, thumb tucked in her mouth, content just to be near them both. Agnes came and went with fresh clothes and soft-spoken comfort, but the hospital room— hushed and softly lit—became their entire world.

Jemma slept more than she spoke, her body slowly reclaiming strength. When she did wake, it was only for sips of water, faint smiles, and whispered reassurances. Each day, her cheeks grew less hollow. Her eyes stayed open longer. The fever broke. Her colour returned.

So did her laughter—raspy at first, then fuller. Real.

Ben didn't push. He simply stayed.

At night, when the nurses offered to wheel in a cot, he refused. Instead, he sat with his boots off, her hand in his, head tipped back against the wall, unwilling to sleep until he'd counted every one of her breaths.

On the third day, she woke to find him reading Charlotte's Web aloud in a low voice, with Charlotte tucked under his arm.

"You're spoiling my daughter," she teased softly.

Ben looked up, startled—then smiled, slow and sure. "She's not the only one."

That night, she asked him to lie beside her—not for anything but warmth. Closeness.

His arms came around her gently, reverently, as if she might still break.

"I'm okay now," she whispered into his chest.

He kissed her hair. "I know. But I'm still holding on."

A week later, Jemma stepped out of the hospital and into the fading warmth of the afternoon. Her movements were slow—careful—but steady. Each step stronger than the last.

The gravel crunched beneath the car tyres as they turned up the winding drive. When the homestead came into view, she drew in a soft, shaky breath.

The wide eaves of the Callahan house stretched before her, sturdy and weather worn. The veranda glowed in the golden light, draped in shadow and sun. Beyond it, the bush shimmered with life—gum trees whispering in the breeze, cockatoos calling, the low hum of cicadas rising with the dusk.

Home.

Not just a place.

Not just shelter or safety.

This—this—was her real home.

She pressed her palm to the window glass as they drew closer, her heart full to the brim.

Not with fear. Not with pain.

With peace.

And love.

No shadows creeping at the edges. No secrets weighing her down.

Ben came around the vehicle and reached for her hand. She took it without hesitation, fingers curling into his.

Charlotte raced past them, laughing toward the front steps with Agnes calling after her, and Jemma laughed too—clear, bright, unguarded.

That sound made Ben close his eyes for a moment.

He'd missed it more than he'd realised.

They walked up the steps side by side. No fanfare. Just the quiet kind of return that felt like a beginning.

Inside, the kettle was already boiling. The dog barked from the paddock.

The world had kept turning.

But for Ben, everything had changed.

Jemma was home.

And for the first time in a long time, they were all safe.

That evening, the breeze was warm, and the wind chimes sang softly as Jemma stepped onto the front porch, a mug of chamomile tea cradled in her hands. The sky was a wash of navy and gold, stars blooming brighter with every passing minute.

Ben was already there, sitting on the timber swing, boot propped on the railing, a bottle of beer resting between his hands. He looked up as she stepped out, eyes soft—tired in the way of a man finally at peace.

"She finally asleep?" he asked.

Jemma nodded, settling beside him. "Out like a light. Agnes swears it's the lavender bath soak, but I think she's just happy."

"She's not the only one." Ben smiled. "She loves you, you know."

Jemma turned, her striking green eyes catching the starlight. "I love her right back."

They sat in comfortable silence, the kind that didn't need filling.

The creak of the swing. The rustle of trees. A night bird calling from somewhere in the dark.

Jemma leaned her head on his shoulder. "I never thought I'd feel this... steady again."

Ben reached for her free hand, fingers threading through hers.

"I didn't either," he said softly. "But then you walked into our lives, and everything changed."

She turned, brow arched slightly. "I was a total mess."

"So was I." He gave a faint, wry smile. "But it wasn't the mess that mattered. It was you. You made this house feel like home again. You gave Charlotte her spark back. You gave me a reason to believe in more."

Her eyes shimmered. She didn't speak—just watched him, breath caught somewhere between a sob and a sigh.

Ben reached into his jeans pocket and pulled something out—no box, no fanfare. Just a bold glint of green and silver in his calloused palm.

Jemma's breath caught.

The ring was stunning. An oval-cut emerald, deep and vivid as wet leaves, flanked by two smaller diamonds that sparkled in the starlight. It was elegant. Striking. Unapologetically real.

Just like her.

"I've been carrying this around for weeks," Ben said quietly, eyes never leaving hers. "Waiting for the right time."

She said nothing. Just stared, wide-eyed and wonderstruck.

"There's no perfect moment, Jem. No grand plan. Just this: I love you. I want you here. With me. With Charlotte. Always."

He offered the ring across the space between them, steady and sure.

"Marry me."

Jemma blinked. Once. Twice. Her hand trembled as she reached for his, brushing her fingers against the cool metal.

"You're serious?" she whispered.

"Deadly," he said, smiling now. "But only if you say yes."

A breathless laugh slipped through her lips—part sob, part joy.

"You idiot," she whispered. "Of course I'll marry you."

Ben slid the ring onto her finger. It fit perfectly.

She stared at it for a long moment, as though she couldn't quite believe it was real.

Then she looked up—and there was nothing hesitant in her smile now. Only wonder. And love.

He cupped her face in both hands and kissed her—slow and reverent, like the world had finally landed where it belonged.

They stayed that way a little while longer, wrapped in each other, the stars above bearing witness.

No fireworks. No grand declarations.

Just quiet joy, and the kind of love that lasts.

Epilogue

Two Years Later…

As the car turned up the long gravel drive to the Callahan homestead, Jemma glanced out the window, her heart full. The afternoon sun cast a golden haze over the familiar landscape—the tall gums swaying gently, the fence line rolling out like an old memory.

She thought of the first time she'd arrived here, uncertain, and afraid, with nothing but a suitcase and a guarded heart. She never could have imagined how much this place would come to mean to her. Not just safety. Not just shelter.

Home.

She turned her head to look at the man beside her—ruggedly handsome in the fading light, one hand on the wheel, the other resting over hers on her knee—and was overwhelmed by love. Nearly two years of marriage, and the feeling still caught her off guard sometimes.

They hadn't waited long. Just two weeks after Ben had proposed, they'd stood barefoot beneath the gum trees at the edge of the paddock and said their vows with nothing but wide skies, wind in the trees, and their closest friends gathered around. She'd worn a flowing white dress, her hair down, her heart wide open. He'd promised her everything—but all she wanted was him and Charlotte.

The whole town had come, it seemed. Even Mia had shown up with tearful eyes and a heartfelt apology, and Jemma, full of forgiveness and joy, had embraced her. Charlotte had looked like a dream in a white lace dress with wildflowers in her curls, taking her role as flower girl very seriously. But it was Ben's face—raw, tender, alight with devotion—that Jemma would never forget.

The car came to a stop out front, and Jemma opened her door.

"Mummy! Finally, you're home!"

Charlotte's voice rang out like sunshine as she flew down the steps of the verandah, throwing herself into Jemma's arms. Nearly eight now, she was all legs and laughter and fierce, loyal love. Jemma scooped her up with a grin.

"Hello, sweetheart. Did you miss me?"

"Yes! I love you, Mummy."

"I love you too, baby girl."

Ben stepped out of the driver's side and stood for a moment, taking it all in—his wife, radiant with joy, their daughter wrapped around her neck, the homestead glowing in the dusk. He would never, ever get tired of this.

Then Ben opened the back door and carefully unhooked the capsule carrying the newest Callahan. Their son—Nathan Liam—was barely two days old, still pink and soft and impossibly small, with a full head of dark hair and his mother's mouth. He gave a sleepy grunt of protest at the disturbance, his tiny features scrunching before he settled again with a sigh.

Jemma's pregnancy had been a revelation to Ben.

She'd embraced every moment—every flutter, every shift—with quiet joy and unwavering devotion. As her body grew round with their child, she wore it like something sacred, never once treating it as a burden. She glowed—not just in the way people say pregnant women glow, but with a light that came from within. A calm certainty. A deep love.

Ben had been in awe of her.

In the stillness of night, he would lie beside her with a hand resting over the curve of her belly, marvelling at the miracle growing inside her—and at the woman who carried it with such grace. Watching her made something shift in him. The old guilt he'd buried for years slowly loosened its hold, replaced by something softer, something healing.

Hope.

Ben glanced up to find Jemma at his side, Charlotte still in her arms.

"Is that him?" Charlotte whispered, peering in.

"That's your baby brother," Jemma said, smiling.

Charlotte leaned closer, eyes wide with wonder. "He's so cute."

Jemma laughed. "Remember that when he's older and starts annoying you."

"He won't annoy me," she declared proudly. "He is my brother."

Ben chuckled. "He sure is."

They turned toward the verandah, where Agnes stood waiting with open arms and misty eyes.

"Come on, you lot," she called, beaming. "Let me hold that precious little thing."

Ben reached for Jemma's hand as they climbed the steps together, Charlotte skipping ahead.

The door swung open. The scent of home—lavender, fresh bread, the faintest trace of eucalyptus—rose to meet them.

Inside was warmth. Inside was love.

And as dusk settled over the paddocks and the stars began to rise, Jemma knew without a single doubt:

This was everything she'd ever wanted.

When the last light faded behind the hills, Jemma leaned into Ben's side, her son in her arms, her daughter's laughter echoing through the house—and knew, deep in her soul, that she was exactly where she belonged.

Home wasn't just a place.

It was them.

And it was forever.

The End

Before You Go…

If you fell for these characters and want more love stories filled with emotion, passion, and second chances, my newsletter is where I share them first.

You'll receive:

- Early access to new releases

- Exclusive reader-only content and extras

Join my reader list here: https://alisonreidauthor.com

I'd love to welcome you.

Alison Reid

Thank you for reading Hearts & Secrets!

If you enjoyed this collection of irresistible heroes and heroines, keep an eye out for more upcoming romance collections by Alison Reid, including:

Accidental Heirs - *A Billionaire Legacy Romance Collection*

Alpha Kings - *A Billionaire Alpha Male Romance Collection*

Cautious Hearts - *A Trust-After-Heartbreak Romance Collection*

Dark & Dangerous - *Brooding Heroes Romance Collection*

Final Surrender - *Alpha Heroes Yielding to Love Collection*

Forbidden Hearts - *A Forbidden Love Romance Collection*

Forever Mine - *A Longing-for-Love Romance Collection*

Guarded Hearts - *A Surrender to Love Romance Collection*

Hearts in Peril - *A Suspenseful Romance Collection*

Hidden Truths - *A Secret Identity Romance Collection*

Lies & Hearts - *A Lies, Secrets & Betrayal Romance Collection*

Love After Regret - *A Second-Chance Redemption Romance Collection*

Misjudged Hearts - *A Love After Judgement Romance Collection*

Torn Between Hearts - *A Love Triangle Romance Collection*

All of Alison Reid's books feature standalone stories, swoon-worthy heroes, and guaranteed happily-ever-afters.

Books by Alison Reid

A Billionaire for Christmas

A Heart in Florence

After The Storm

Always You

Before I Fell

Before the Thaw

Beneath the Lies

Billionaire Bodyguard

Billionaire Rancher

Blueprints of the Heart

Branlow

Collide

Echoes of Deception

Falling for the Billionaire

Forever Yours

Heart of the Outback

Hearts on the Line

Hidden Gem

Kept Promises

Mended Hearts

Mistaken Hearts

New Year's Eve Kiss

Quiet Danger

Reckless Hearts

Reflections of Deception

Second Glance

Shadows of the Past

Shattered Dreams

Shattered Hope, Stolen Kisses

Still Yours

The Billionaire's Accidental Legacy

The Billionaire's Bargain

The Billionaire's Mistake

The Billionaire's Regret

The Billionaire's Return

The Billionaire's Secret Baby

The Billionaire's Unexpected Heir

The Blood Debt

The Playboy's Surrender

The Wrong Sister

Trust in Time

Undercover Billionaire

Until you Loved Me

Vows of Vengeance

Wife in Name Only

Find all my books on Amazon:

https://www.amazon.com/author/alisonreid1970

About the Author

Alison Reid writes contemporary and small-town romance filled with heart, passion, and second-chance love stories. Her novels feature strong heroines, irresistible heroes, and the happily-ever-afters readers adore.

Before turning her love of storytelling into a publishing career, Alison spent thirty-five years working as an engineer—proof that happily-ever-afters can be built as carefully as any blueprint. She began writing as a hobby during the COVID lockdowns and quickly discovered a passion she couldn't ignore.

Alison is happily married, has two grown children, and shares her home with two beautiful dogs who are convinced they deserve to be her main characters. When she's not writing, she enjoys reading, spending time with her family, and imagining new love stories. She hopes her books give readers a few hours of escape, joy, and swoon-worthy romance they won't soon forget.